To Meme & Popee,
Because of you two dear souls,
I have grown into the Woman
who dared to step into the light,
to bring Humanity into the
Aquarian Age. Thank you for
being wise enough to keep me
in the womb long enough to
get me safely across the portal
of time. I love you both dearly.
Deborah Haight

The Hierophant

BOOK ONE

The Return of Memory

Deborah Haight

The Hierophant – Book One: The Return of Memory

Copyright © 2020 by Deborah Haight

Manufactured in the United States of America.

Cover Design: Tomas Contarino
ISBN: 978-1-7351413-1-2 Print book
ISBN: 978-1-7351413-0-5 ebook

Published by:
Three Streams Resources, LLC.
3048 Yankee Clipper Dr.
Las Vegas, NV 89117

info@thehierophantseries.love
www.thehierophantseries.love

Dedication

First and foremost, I would like to thank my husband and partner of 35 years, Brian. His presence in my life at an early age was a catalyst for my growth in ways that I never saw coming. I thank you for your support and I love you dearly.

To our children, Alexander, Hillary, Sierra, and Sage: You have lived a balance life of magic and normalcy, as much as I could provide. I thank you for understanding when I was not available during the many retreat times that was required of me to bring this book to life. You were my first Creations...this book is as much for you as it is for the readers.

To Trinity: Who held me in a bubble of belief and love, without which I could not have mustered the courage to write this. Our love for one another builds bridges!

To Bill: Thank you for demonstrating a way to walk this Earth as a Peaceful Warrior. You are and will always be The Great Earth Gnome!

To Stephanie South: You taught me by example, the importance of discipline to achieve my goals. You steadfastly mirrored to me all of the qualities that were required for me to dig deep and pull this manuscript out of the ethers. I love you to the moon and back.

To Votan/Jose Arguelles: Though you have passed into the realms of the ancestors, I thank you because you believed in me before I knew who ME was.

The work that Jose Arguelles and Stephanie South have given to the world is the inspiration for much of this ongoing story. It is a living testament to who we all are as the people of OMA, and I am so grateful to have been blessed to be a part of their life story.

To Peter and Jackie: My love and gratitude to you both for your unwavering loyalty and friendship. You both have been some of my greatest teachers.

To Deb and Steve: My gratitude for our friendship and ease of communion when we are blessed with the opportunities to be together. Love you both dearly.

To Jim, Jenni, Jen, Bob, Arabella, Nikita, Cornflower, April, Jim and Elaine Butler, Randall, Wayne and Alma: Each of you have contributed to my growth as a human being, and I thank you and love you all dearly.

To my parents, who raised me in the ways of service and opened me to the path I walk today, I sincerely thank you and I am happy to present this book to you...finally!

For my Grandchildren: It is with all the joy in my heart to have become your Gnoma! Each one of you are magical creations of God. I hope that you read this book one day and it brings your highest potential into alignment for you.

To all of my friends, neighbors and acquaintances that I have not mentioned by name, know that each of you has played a part in my life story, and I would not be the same person without having known you.

Finally, to the reader that picked up this book, prepare for something to unlock within you! Enjoy the journey...

Table of Contents

Part One

The Remembrance

Chapter 1

The Falling of a Tree

It was a cold autumn evening in Aberdeen, Scotland, where Bridgit Phare lay in the bed at her favorite Scottish Inn, writing in her journal of the memories she had of her grandparents on her mother's side. The Carr's were more than just her grandparents; they were who raised her after a freak storm took the lives of her parents during the Lyrid meteor showers on a fateful day, April 21, 1990.

Recently, Bridgit had suffered the loss of both of her Grandparents to illness within a six-month window of one another. As Bridgit wrote, she wiped her eyes, feeling lonely and a bit scared as she contemplated the fact that she was the only one left in her lineage. This thought hit her deep in her heart, and for some unknown reason, Bridgit knew that her life was about to change, now that she had no attachments to family. She knew it was time to begin what she came to earth to do, "but what was that again?" she wrote in her journal.

She placed her journal down and picked up a different one, the one with her lengthy notes on her studies of trees. In particular, world trees. Those ancient trees which stand for centuries as Time's special witness.

Bridgit had collected stories from around the world of these sacred trees, as she had studied about them from childhood while helping out on her grandparent's tree farm in Louisiana. She now had the time and resources to dive into her studies, as she was an Arborist by profession.

She got up from her cozy bed to look out the window as the evening progressed into the night. A storm was brewing. The trees surrounding the Inn were swaying, yet no rain seemed to be forecast. Bridgit yawned, grabbed her toothbrush and headed down the hall to the shared washroom to brush her teeth and wash her face. She came back into her room, contemplating a specific world tree, which lived, anchored, on an adjacent property near the Inn.

Tuuru, named by the community who loved her, was a brown oak with roots that spanned a large perimeter while its branches provided shade. Bridgit had truly and utterly fallen in love with Tuuru. The great tree reminded her of her parents and grandparents. It felt familiar to her like the trees of her childhood. This tree, she contemplated, was the Grandmother tree of them all.

Bridgit climbed back into bed and laid her head on her pillow. A tear dropped from her eye, and then another. The comfort of the tree was her only visceral reminder of her family. She contemplated how odd it was to feel such a familiarity to it, being that its location was in another country, the country of her ancestors.

She reached for her journal once more, and grabbed her pen, wiping away a salty tear that escaped from the corner of her eye. "What is this memory at the edge of my mind?" she wrote in her journal. She stared at the ceiling, trying to recall a memory, any memory of her parents.

Bridgit fell asleep and dreamt immediately of her parents and grandparents and the tree farm in Louisiana. In the dream, she walked the perimeter of the family's tree farm and found herself in the exact location where her parents died. She looked up and saw a tree crashing down in front of her and feeling absolute terror, not for her safety, but the safety of the tree. She recognized the tree in her dream as the World Tree, Tuuru. Bridgit was lucid in the dream, knowing that she was dreaming, but it felt all too real.

She made herself wake up from the dream as the winds whipped on the outside of her window. Bridgit jumped out of bed and threw on her boots and raincoat then ran down the hall and into the woods.

She arrived at the edge of the woods before Tuuru hit the ground. Bridgit felt a dark presence then experienced a prickling sensation on her skin as if tiny arrows were hitting her body. Electrical pulsations zapped her with every step she took advancing towards Tuuru.

All she could see was a bright light and a whirling sound, then an explosion of some kind, as the rain and winds continued to bellow. It was all too much for Bridgit to process. She felt that she was somehow still within the dream. Suddenly, Bridgit felt the presence of a protective force around her. She moved on. Her only concern was for Tuuru. She was oblivious to the interactions happening behind her of a Druid battling a sinister force for her life.

In a fateful moment, the Druid pointed his wand towards the tree, chanting a mantra, just as it was falling from the force of the dark beings attack. At that moment, everything went dark, and Bridgit fell towards Tuuru. Then suddenly, a green light emanated from Tuuru, enveloping Bridgit within the tree's energy field. Everything faded back to darkness.

The great World Tree, Tuuru, the very one that Bridgit had traveled to Scotland to commune with, had uprooted completely and crashed to her death in the early morning darkness. Bridgit was nowhere to be found as the morning sun appeared.

And the wheel turns...

Chapter 2

Bridgit's Meeting with Shamalaine

As Bridgit awoke with hazy sight, she reached for her head, feeling a tremendous throbbing sensation, accompanied by nausea, coming in waves. Bridgit tried to open her eyes as someone touched her with a pat on her arm to console her. She could hear him say, "Be still." The warmth of his hand sedated her as she once more faded into an unconscious state.

The being, a Guardian of the doorways, stood watch over Bridgit. He kept his hand upon her, monitoring her energy as he sent a healing wave into her body. A telepathic message entered his mind from the ancient one of the Clan of Phare, known as Shamalaine.

Shamalaine spoke, "Who do we have entering through our most precious Tuuru?"

Eldorman, a very distinguished elf, reported to Shamalaine, "It is a human, and she is hurt." He continued his efforts to heal the wound.

Shamalaine monitored Eldorman's thoughts as he held the focus of healing energy over the human.

Moments later, Bridgit began to move her head, regaining consciousness. She reached up to touch her head, wiping her hair away from her forehead, and securing it behind her ear.

Eldorman's heart beat faster as he saw the perfect pointed features of the human's ear. "A hybrid!" he exclaimed in his mind to Shamalaine.

Shamalaine heard his thoughts. She replied, "Is she who we have been waiting for?"

He reported that, indeed, it was most probably Kaialena. Eldorman attempted to nudge the human to her feet.

All the while, Bridgit's eyes were adjusting to the wavy, transparent nature of her reality. Her eyes continued to flutter due to the brightness of the light. "Where am I?"

Eldorman responded, "You have hit your head; I am sorry to say." The elegant cadence of his voice and his stately body with pointed features, including his ears, gave him away immediately. He bowed and said, "I am Eldorman. And you would be?"

Bridgit took his hand as he lifted her to her feet. She smiled at her helper as if she recognized him. Then the memory of what had happened resurfaced. She whipped around, still shaky, to see the tree standing tall and majestic. Bridgit turned away from Eldorman at a loss for words. Tears ran down her cheeks. She was now on the ground at the base of Tuuru, feeling for the damage.

"I don't understand!? She fell!" Bridgit wiped her face and examined the world tree. She was happy to know that Tuuru was okay and that there were no signs of damage to her trunk, but the other fact that remained was that perhaps she, herself, was not at all okay. Bridgit was talking to herself out loud, making a note of each branch and root as an Arborist would.

Eldorman observed the human and asked once more, "You are???"

Ignoring the question, Bridgit shook her head, amazed at the perfection of the ancient tree and remarked out loud, "She is even more pristine than I remember her from yesterday! I don't understand?!"

As she turned back to Eldorman, she could see that he was anticipating her answer to his repeated question. She responded, "Bridgit. My name is Bridgit Phare."

"Indeed, Miss." Eldorman's eyes sparkled with joy, but he did not give away his excitement.

She extended her hand outward to shake Eldorman's hand, and at that moment, she noticed his hand, as he reached for hers. His fingers were long, and his skin was strangely iridescent. A mix between shiny and dull, she thought. She took a mental note of his body as she processed that he was not human. Eldorman was amused as he understood that he had just been cataloged.

She watched as he leaned towards her hand to kiss it, like a prince from a fairy tale. "Fairy tale! That's it!" she thought. But then in the next moment, she laughed internally at the silly notion.

Bridgit latched onto the lowest branch of the tree once more to make a connection to the energy that she had grown so fond of, an unconscious move to feel something that she knew was real. Tuuru was an ancient world tree who moments ago had seemingly fallen. Feeling the strength from the tree, Bridgit centered herself. She knew there was a reasonable explanation for this. The only thing familiar to her was Tuuru. She needed to know where she was and now.

In her regained clarity, Bridgit observed her surroundings and understood that the scenery was different. Much different. "What is going on?" she voiced out loud her query.

Eldorman bowed his head and said, "This way Miss. All will be revealed shortly. Do come along."

As he walked away, Bridgit noticed his form. She would categorize it as being wispy as if he walked too fast for his body, and part of it was left behind. It caught up to him soon enough, like a cloud merging with another cloud. Eldorman wore clothes that suggested he was a gentry from another era. They, too, were wispy and free-flowing.

As Bridgit followed him, she looked down to observe her own body, thinking that perhaps she was having an out of body experience. She was still in her nightgown, with her raincoat and boots her only protection from the weather that was seemingly, only moments ago, raining, with the wind whipping the entire area.

Contemplating all of the recent events as she followed Eldorman, a feeling came over her. She felt as if she had lost everything, yet from the looks of it, Tuuru was still standing. In her mind, she was trying to scientifically examine all of the evidence before she would allow herself to lose her composure completely. Nothing looked familiar as she walked away from Tuuru.

"Is this a Dream? An Out of Body Experience? Reaction to my mouthwash? What is going on?!" She somehow managed to laugh out loud at the absurd thoughts rolling around her mind as she followed Eldorman. She knew that it should be night time, but wherever she was now was more like late afternoon, close to dusk, with the ground perfectly dry, and she was following a non-human, seemingly Elven man, to parts unknown.

As Eldorman continued to walk steps ahead of Bridgit, another elemental trailed behind. An elf named Avery had been watching from a distance.

Eldorman stopped momentarily to listen to his inner dialogue, and as he did, Bridgit asked him a question as politely as possible, "Where are we going? You haven't answered my questions."

Eldorman snapped out of his inner thought, swooping down to catch a brilliant yellow flower falling to the ground at that very moment. Knowing that nature is fully informed, he knew he was given an opportunity here. I must present her properly, he thought.

He swirled around on his toes in a gentlemanly manner and leaned down to a slight curtsey. He motioned towards Bridgit's ear and asked, "May I?"

Bridget looked down shyly, surprised by his kindness and allowed him to gift her with the yellow flower that matched her now brilliant yellow flowing gown that had suddenly appeared on her body without her realizing.

The dress was a lemon chiffon material, with a hood that draped onto her back. Her feet were adorned with a simple sandal of woven reeds, with small yellow flower buds accenting the string that laced around her toes and ankle. She was comforted to be wearing clothes. In particular, clothes that gave her the appearance of fitting in, she thought, to wherever she was. She let out another chuckle, the kind of nervous laugh when one knows not what to say. She did know one thing. This gentle being was no threat, and her curiosity about where she was began to outweigh her concern temporarily.

Eldorman lifted her hair over her ear to give way for the flower to perch upon it, and as he did, he examined her pointed ear more closely. Bridgit could see that he noticed her point and immediately stepped back and gazed downward with a bashful look. She said, "I know. They're pointed. Weird, huh?"

Her cheeks were now flushed as he patted her on the shoulder to nudge her forward and said, "On the contrary, we have just found something in common, and that is a good thing." He winked at her then moved in front of her to lead the way, making sure he kept his pace a little further ahead on the path.

The path was clean, with no leaves upon the ground. The land was pristine with flowering trees, birds singing in the meadow nearby, and the sounds of water trickling from a stream close to the path. Bridgit was lulled into a peace she had not felt in a very long time.

She was mesmerized by the environment, which was completely different than the land near the Inn. She snapped out of her peacefulness when she thought of Tuuru once more.

Bridgit grew concerned again. Her internal dialog was like a mathematician trying to solve a problem. She was freaking out in her mind but trying to play it cool. She went back over the last things that she could recall before she found herself in a dimension that was not her own.

Bridgit thought, "I packed my day pack for my fieldwork, I read my notes on Tuuru, I brushed my teeth, wrote in my journal and then went to bed. It would make sense that this is a dream, but.." Bridgit was hoping that she was lucid dreaming and that she would wake up soon, but something felt entirely different from the other dreams that she had had of this kind.

Turning back inwardly, Eldorman telepathed to Shamalaine that he had everything under control and that he and the human would soon be arriving.

Shamalaine, the Elder of the Clan, awaited her arrival with mixed emotions. Her appearance portended a fulfillment of a prophecy, and it was the beginning of a new era. Her daughter had come home. Shamalaine knew that it also foreshadowed a dark time.

Avery, a capricious little elf, darted quickly behind Bridgit to get a look at this stranger, the human, who somehow entered the realm of the Fae. He darted to and from trees and bushes while observing her. Just as Avery made his next attempt to get closer to her, Bridgit swung around and somehow caught him by the arm.

Astounded that a human had caught him, and shamed as the slowest elf in history, he melted in her arms, red-faced and embarrassed for his mentor, Eldorman, to see his horrifying capture. He wiggled out of her grasp as Bridgit scrutinized him.

"Who are you? And why are you darting back and forth around me like a pesky mosquito?" Bridgit asked, trying to act as if she belonged in his world. She was agitated and needed answers.

"I am sorry, Miss. My name is Avery." He adjusted his vest and wiggled his trousers up to try to gain some dignity. "I have never seen a human before. That's all. I do apologize for being pesky???"

Avery did not understand the word she used to describe his actions, but it was clear to him by the way the human was distressed that it was not a good thing. Smiling, he used his charm to get closer to Bridgit. He twirled around, creating a colorful vortex of energy around his body. The colors sparkled then faded. He could see that Bridgit enjoyed his fanfare.

The elf studied her, then asked, "Do you mind?" he pointed to her ears as if he wanted to see them.

"What? My ears?" she laughed and leaned down towards the 3-foot-tall elf, pulling her hair back to the other side of her neck so that he could see the pointed ear upon which a beautiful yellow flower adorned it.

Avery let out a gasp as soon as he saw it. He was internally excited beyond measure to have witnessed the sight of this human in the fairy realm.

After Bridgit was examined twice now, by two elves, she asked once more, "I think that I deserve to have a simple answer to my question. Where are we?"

Eldorman turned to give her a sincere answer. He stood tall, with his hands held in front of him, and said, "Indeed ma'am, you do deserve a simple answer, but a simple answer I do not have. It is complex, in the very least, to say that you are no longer where you were."

He shooed away a dragonfly that had come to see the human and then continued, "I shall deliver you to those who can give you the answer you seek, that I assure you. Come along. It is not far." He shifted once more so swiftly that his form once again was left behind. The billowy elf made haste to get them to their destination. This time, his red hair went up in a flaming cloud, then streaked behind him for a short distance before it settled back upon his head.

Avery followed from behind as they continued walking the path. To ease the situation, he pulled out his small stringed instrument hanging from his belt loop. He began to pluck at the string to bring it into tune. A sweet melody came forth from the instrument, and much to Bridgit's delight, the melody sounded familiar. As he played, she began to hum along to the tune, of which she had no memory of the song's origin, she just knew it in her heart. They walked for some time enjoying the music. Bridgit was biding her time.

Avery was quite pleased with the blending of her voice, his instrument, and the sounds of the crickets and insects flying overhead as dusk became nightfall. It was at that moment, as they were swept up in the sounds being heard in the twilight, that they came upon an old stone archway where the Clan of Phare stood waiting for the trio. One of the Elders listened to the voice of the one who had been prophesied to return. Shamalaine stepped forward.

Bridgit was startled out of the song when she saw the group of robed beings, much taller than she, and certainly taller than her companions. Eldorman stopped ten feet from the Clan. He made the initial maneuver to greet the Clansmen first, telling Avery to stay back with Bridgit. Bridgit fixed her hood upon her head to remain somewhat hidden from them since she was a human, and clearly, they were not. Her heart raced.

Eldorman addressed the Clan, "Shamalaine, let me present to you, Kaialena. She goes by the name of Bridgit Phare in her world, as I am sure you already know. She is bewildered, and is in distress over our beloved Tuuru."

He looked at Shamalaine with a pain in his eyes, "You do know what happened? To Tuuru?" Eldorman searched in Shamalaine's eyes, hoping that he did not have to be the bearer of bad news.

"Yes. We know. Tuuru uplifted in the third dimension, to save her." She wiped a tear, cleared her throat, and motioned for him to bring her to the Clan.

Eldorman walked halfway back and motioned for the two to come forward. Avery gave a little heave-ho to Bridgit's backside when she hesitated slightly.

As Bridgit came closer, the clanswoman asked her to remove her hood. Just as the moonlight came into full light, it shone brightly on Bridgit's face and her pointed ears, and at that moment the Clan all knew who she was...though Bridgit could not see them clearly, as they stood in the shadows with the brightness of the moon prohibiting her from seeing their faces.

Shamalaine greeted Bridgit with kind words. "Precious one, you have journeyed far from home. Let me offer you some tea, and perhaps we can attend to your wound. Afterward, I would be honored to show you around and answer any questions that you might have." She looked over the slight marking on Bridgit's forehead and nodded to Eldorman, taking note of his excellent healing capabilities.

"Agreed?" Shamalaine searched within Bridgit's eyes for a sign.

"Yes. Thank you. That would be lovely." Bridgit felt a feeling both unfamiliar to her, and yet she noted that it was familiar all at once. In the sense of the origin of the word. Somehow, seeing Shamalaine, or rather, feeling Shamalaine's energy, felt familiar to her.

Bridgit was escorted through the arched gateway into the realms of the Clan. They made their way into a Great Hall. The room was a massive round stone enclave with dining tables made of thick slabs of wood and a large stone fireplace with embers popping back and forth within it. Bridgit could see tiny little beings playing within the fire.

Shamalaine stood waiting while Bridgit took note of the details of the room. Several hallways exited the main room in multiple directions. Bridgit was curious about the place, the people, the little fire beings, and the feeling of home she felt, which made no sense to her mind. She just knew that she found it comforting.

The design of the enclave was that of a wheel with the Great Hall being the central hub, with the hallways as it's spokes. It was clear from the sloped, darkened passages and fire lit alcoves that they were going deep into the Earth. The enclave had been cleverly built and cloaked with a force field of protection. Had they been merely passing by, they would not have even noticed the archway entrance.

Bridgit warmed herself by the fire as she took it all in, still waiting patiently for answers. Tea was poured in ceramic cups, which had leaves etched into the sides. After Bridgit was handed her tea and had a few sips of the drink, the clanswoman lifted her hood and pulled her hair out from under her cloak. Bridgit found herself staring at the magnificent creature, of what type she could not tell.

The leader of the Clan of Phare was a beautiful woman with long auburn hair, green starry eyes, and ears of light with the most distinct point along with a slight bend to them. Her tanned skin tone had a similar iridescent effect as Eldorman's, like an inner glow that shone through her skin. Her features were cat-like, with a delicate nose and mouth which looked more feline than human. Bridgit's mouth hung open, and her eyes wide with curiosity as the clanswoman spoke.

"I am sorry that I did not formally introduce myself to you. My name is Shamalaine, and I am the leader of the Clan of Phare." She lifted her hand to point to the room, where other clans people were preparing food and setting the table for an evening meal.

Bridgit nearly choked on her sip of tea when hearing those words. She set her teacup down, shocked, and asked, "Clan of Phare?!"

"Yes, dear. You have many loved ones here, who remember you and have loved you from afar."

Bridgit stood dumbfounded and a bit week at the knee, speechless in the moment.

Shamalaine's delicate fingers fidgeted with her robe, feeling a bit nervous herself, then motioned for Bridgit to sit and listen to her as she went on to share about how her people came from a distant planet, Avyon, in Lyra. She spoke of the Orion wars and how her people migrated to Sirius A and B, as well as other star systems during a great rebellion, leading them finally to their present location.

Bridgit was quite taken with Shamalaine, holding her tongue as she listened to her present the history of the Clan of Phare with a regal quality about her, but still, she had one burning question. Where were they? Her mind was fighting the fact that she was in her bed at the Inn only hours ago, and now she had somehow relocated physically to parts unknown.

The feeling of the hearth felt very familiar to her, but she had no basis of understanding why she felt calm in the presence of non-human beings who call themselves the Clan of Phare, the same surname of her lineage.

Shamalaine monitored Bridgit's thoughts as she continued to tell her the many duties that the Clan holds and how they came to live in a "pocket" of Earth so many ages ago. Shamalaine wanted to spark Bridgit's memories of her time there, rather than just blurt out who they were to one another.

"Bridgit, our peoples are the guardians of planetary systems. We play many roles under that title. Some of us are what is known to be Keepers of the Flame, and others are Keepers of Time. Still, some are known as the Bridge Builders, and some are Life Bearers that hold the codes of creation. There is only one in our lineage per epoch, that is the carrier of all of these qualities." Shamalaine looked Bridgit straight in the eyes and let out a faint purr.

Bridgit got the uneasy feeling that Shamalaine was testing her for some reason. She thought, "I'm listening," feeling like she was back in college, put on the spot by her professor. Then it hit her. She silently wondered, "Could Shamalaine being referring to me as that person?" Her right hand unconsciously went to her chest. She felt a flicker of heat in her chest rising slowly.

Avery was standing nearby with a scroll, taking notes of everything spoken as well as the nuances that he was picking up. He was a dutiful scribe. Bridgit was glad to see that there would be documentation. Her logical mind kicked in again.

Shamalaine took note of Bridgit's distraction. She motioned for

Bridgit to walk with her, dismissing the others. Avery lingered a bit, listening for a few last words, and then he was escorted away.

The two women walked down a corridor off of the Great Hall and entered a room, exuding a golden hue. The room had a very high ceiling, and it had the feeling of being out of doors. Bridgit immediately noticed the forget-me-not flowers planted in a garden area near a beautiful wooden carved door. The flowers were beginning to climb up the wall, and Bridgit was unsure how they grew in this place, but it seemed to be growing fine without sunlight. In her mind, she wondered if it was the golden glow in the room that enabled the flowers to grow.

Shamalaine was pleased that Bridgit was taking such interest in the flowers as she had once been the very one to plant the seeds from which they grew.

"Bridgit, come over here. Please, sit in this chair." Shamalaine pointed to the seat.

Bridgit gently walked away from the flowers, and without questioning Shamalaine, she sat in the Chair of Remembrance. The chair's use was for rapid cellular memory, but to Bridgit, it was just a chair. As Shamalaine continued her stories of the Clan of Phare, she monitored Bridgit's emotions.

Bridgit's body began to activate on a cellular level. Pockets of memories held within her DNA effervescently popped up to the surface of her conscious mind. Bridgit's facial expressions and body language shifted.

Shamalaine continued to monitor Bridgit as she began to speak about an entirely new topic to Bridgit, the issue of multidimensionality.

Shamalaine said, "I want you to close your eyes and just imagine what it might have been like to live here, in this enclave, as a member of our family."

Bridgit fidgeted with the thought, feeling a strange sensation welling up within her. She wrinkled her nose a bit, which alerted Shamalaine to her discomfort on the idea.

Shamalaine said, "This is just an exercise to help you understand where you have found yourself, so if you would appease my request. Simply relax and allow yourself to feel what it would be like to have lived here as a young woman, the daughter of two members of this Clan. Imagine that you studied the Orion wars and worked diligently to understand the dynamics of world-building, and working with the elemental kingdoms."

Bridgit peaked at Shamalaine, keeping one eye closed, then asked, "Elementals?"

Shamalaine continued, "Yes, dear. Elementals. Those precious beings that are unseen in the world of man, but in our realm, walk among us. You have met two already. As an example, Eldorman and Avery are elves, who are a part of the elemental caste. Others would be fairies and gnomes. These beings help us hold focus upon a creation. I, too, have Elemental DNA." After a few moments, Shamalaine asked if she understood so far.

Bridgit closed her eye once more and agreed with the explanation, and allowed Shamalaine to continue. Her body was receiving impulses from the chair, and as Shamalaine spoke, she kept her focus on this other life that Shamalaine wanted her to experience. Bridgit began to relax, watching the tale Shamalaine spun, which was activating within her mind's eye.

Shamalaine then said, "Imagine as you grew into your role within the Clan, the time came for your mission to be activated. This meant leaving your Clan and all that you knew, and all of your relations, to incarnate into a lower realm, a world of chaos and confusion. A world of Maya."

Shamalaine shifted her robe and continued, "The activation of your Earthly mission came at an inconvenient time for you, but you were well trained and knew your place. You temporarily dissolved your physical body and placed your frequency within a crystal here in this

17

realm, and leaped into a new life in the 3rd dimension for an extraordinary mission with the understanding that you would return one day to your true family of origin." Shamalaine monitored the looks of anguish on Bridgit's face as she listened to Shamalaine speak.

Within moments, her mind's eye opened to receive vision after vision of her true self in times long gone. Bridgit sat in the chair no more than ten minutes, trying her best not to lose consciousness when suddenly she gasped for air, with tears in her eyes. She let out a guttural whaling sound of pain and sorrow. The emotions that accompanied the visions were genuine and real. These were her emotions and her memories flooding her body. She remembered this place.

Bridgit jumped from the chair and into her mother's arms. "Mother!!!"

Bridgit sobbed, with her head buried in her mother's embrace. Shamalaine held her daughter and began to purr with her, transmuting her pain and sorrow and assisting her in coming to terms with the knowledge that she had just regained.

Bridgit looked at Shamalaine differently now. She asked, "How could I have forgotten you? How could I have been in your presence and not know that you are my mother? How did I lose myself so entirely that I could not recall my people the moment I came here?"

Smiling, Shamalaine said, "Kaialena is your true name, given to you by your father. Dear one, do not be hard on yourself. There are mechanisms in place when we make our jump into the lower dimensions. These mechanisms are for our own wellbeing."

Reaching for a box on a nearby table, she turned to Bridgit and gestured for her to lift her hair so that she could place upon her neck something that was her daughter's birthright, a shell necklace given to her by one of her past teachers.

"Allow me to tell you more about who you are since you were not in the chair long enough to have your memories fully restored. They will come more gradually so as not to overwhelm you by these revelations."

They walked over to the wooden door with engravings upon it. Shamalaine showed Bridgit the detailed carvings, which began to morph while Shamalaine continued to remind Bridgit of the history of their people.

"When our people fled Lyra, we went to many star systems, and our race became blended, much like it is in your human world." Shamalaine continued to purr from time to time. Bridgit found the sound and vibration deeply soothing.

A map of the star systems emerged from the grain in the door as Shamalaine spoke. "The Clan of Phare means family of divine light," Shamalaine said with a smile as she pointed to where Lyra's position was in the galaxy.

"Our DNA is a mixture of Lion-Feline attributes as well as attributes from the Elemental race." Bridgit had more tears coming as she recalled the many races that pulsed through her veins. She automatically lifted her hand to feel the pointed tip of her right ear.

Pointing to a specific area on the map, Shamalaine said, "We have been here, in this frequency band of Terra Firma, Earth as you know it, for a very long time now."

Bridgit looked deeply at her mother, and with a pang of sadness, she asked, "Tell me, when I left this place to take on the life that I am living now, what happened to my body in this realm? Will I ever be that person, Kaialena, again, or am I to be like this from now on?"

Shamalaine said, "That is an excellent question, and the answer is entirely up to you. When I said that you placed your frequency within a crystal, what I mean is that your essence is here, a sort of duplicate copy of your DNA, held within a crystal that holds all of the essential elements to re-apparate your body should you choose to do so. You may also simply reabsorb those elements of yourself into the body that you have now. The vibrational field here is higher, so you would physically begin to change in this body to reflect a finer vibrational body, but that is all too much to think about at this moment. Just know that you have been here, living amongst us, and a piece of you is ever-present within our Lair."

Looking at her daughter with pride, she said, "You will remember those days more fully as your memories reawaken."

Shamalaine continued by saying, "Your father will be so happy to know of your return."

Bridgit wanted to ask about her father just as there was a noise that interrupted her train of thought. Her heart was pounding, and tears now welled up in her eyes, then the torrents of saline flowed.

All of these revelations were overwhelming to Bridgit. The tears were a mixture of joy, gratitude, and overwhelm. At the same time, she still had a lingering feeling of being out of place. She was about to ask more questions when, at that moment, Avery wandered into the room, having been hovering near the doorway the whole time, to see if he could be of service in any way, and to get it all down for his report. He had been tasked to watch over Bridgit, as Eldorman was needed elsewhere after delivering Bridgit to the Clan.

Shamalaine motioned for Avery to enter. He walked over to Bridgit, pulling a red cloth from his bag and ever so sheepishly presented it to her in the hopes that she would regain her composure and rid herself of the line of goo running down her face.

Bridgit did just that. She handed it back to him quickly with gratitude, and with that, he now had a mess to handle. Wiping his hands on his pants and picking up his writing pen once more, Avery noted that this human was not just another human elemental hybrid, but that she was THE Human EL that they had been waiting for.

And the wheel turns...

Chapter 3

Breacher the Dragon Rider

The stirring of the dragons did not go unnoticed by Breacher as he synched the straps of his arm armor. Surveying the mists that shrouded the mountainside, he had the light of the setting sun to give him enough forewarning should an intruder come anywhere close to his camp. Preparing the dragons for flight had been his daily task since the new Hieros dragons were born.

Breacher sat down on a rock outcropping overlooking a valley. His mind was preoccupied with thoughts of his beloved. Ever since he was a child, he and Kaialena were soul linked. He smiled as he recalled the games that they would play as children as they were training for their roles within the Clan. His training eventually took him onto a different path than Kaialena's.

Breacher was now a commander and a peacekeeper spending his days on a unique assignment training dragons on Terra Firma, the realms of the Fae on Earth.

The assignment to train the Hieros dragons was an honor bestowed to him by the Council of Trustees for Peace. Breacher did not take this task lightly, for he was chosen as a son from the Melchizedek lineage for his ability to breach time and space, and this unique gift was a requirement for the mission.

When asked to use his talents to bring about the descent of the dragons that could assist him in preparing an entirely new grid around planet Earth and upgrade the frequency of the planet to serve a higher cause, he knew that his time of action had come.

He thought in his mind, as he kept watch, "Earth will need to make her ascension into her rightful place soon, but first, the dragons must be ready."

He turned to look at the dragons and then the sunset once more. And then it happened. An overwhelming feeling of sadness crept into his heart, and one lone tear fell down his cheek, in remembrance of her. It had been so long since he held Kaialena in his arms. He was beginning to fear that he would forget the sparkle in her eye, the smell that was uniquely hers, and the feeling of utter joy to be in her presence.

Breacher did his best to keep these feelings contained deep within him, knowing that Kaialena did not willfully leave him. Someday they would reunite, but in the meantime, he must focus on his mission at hand.

The dragons caught his attention. They could feel his energy shift. Breacher knew better than to dwell on what had happened in the past, as his feelings directly affected the group of dragons that were spiritually and emotionally tethered to his soul. The dragons puffed up, snorting and thumping their tails on the ground, anxious for flight.

He jumped up and whistled towards them. "Come on! Let's see how far we can go tonight!" Breacher climbed onto one of the dragons, and they flew over the valley into the night's sky.

And the wheel turns...

Chapter 4

Memories of a Life Forgotten

Bridgit's senses were adjusting to the sounds and smell of the home of the Clan of Phare as Shamalaine continued the process of reawakening her memories the next morning.

Shamalaine asked, "How did you sleep?" as she reached out to touch her beloved daughter.

Bridgit shyly responded, "I slept deeply, once I finally was able to go to sleep. I'm sorry, this is all a bit much for me. To be honest, I am overwhelmed and a little scared. I love being here and remembering my place here, but I also belong in the 3D world, and I am concerned that people might be looking for me."

Bridgit put her head down, chin to her chest. She said quietly, "And Tuuru... I can't stop thinking of her."

Shamalaine began to purr as she too could feel Bridgit's division in her heart. She addressed her primary concerns first, "Time is different here. All is well, and we will get you back home before anyone knows that you are missing. For now, I hope that you can put your fears aside and enjoy this precious time that we have together, and as for Tuuru, she is still living in this realm and another. Her memory on the 3D Earth will live on, I assure you, and her spirit will be with you always. She is ever near you." With those words said, she took Bridgit by the arm and gently guided her across the room.

They now stood at the carved wooden door. Shamalaine spoke a few moments in their native Lyran tongue, then she looked deeply into Bridgit's eyes and said, "We have so much to talk about, and it might be easier if I show you."

They stood by the door as it creaked open, and light poured forth from the other side. Shamalaine gave Bridgit access into a holographic world that felt seamlessly real to Bridgit as she entered into it. The hologram generated a familiar environment. The return of her memory began the moment she walked through it.

Bridgit found her way to where she had once lived in another time and place. She was still processing in her mind the fact that she had lived in this other world, as she walked in the garden. The flowers distracted her as they were in full bloom. All of her favorite flowers and fruits were ready for their gifting to her. She walked by them and could feel their healing energy enter her body without so much as a taste of the fruit or the smell of a flower. It was instantaneous. She felt her energy rising, and as she looked at her arms, a diamond-like sparkle shone from her skin.

The energies permeated her entire being. As she closed her eyes and stood in awe of the gifts from nature, she let her mind turn off, and her heart open. She remembered her connection to the plant kingdom, which she realized was why she incarnated into a family of tree lovers. Moments passed as she opened her eyes once more, wholly filled, and at peace.

Looking around, she noticed a shiny object near the garden wall on the pathway leading to the forest. She could hear the faintest sound of harp music playing, which struck a chord within her.

Walking over to inspect the glittering object, she noticed it moving away from her as she began to walk at a faster pace to keep up. The object of her interest took flight and buzzed right by her head and then zipped out of sight. Soon after, it came back for another flyby, flitting directly in front of Bridgit's eyes.

It was a tiny fairy with shimmering bronzed colored wings holding a miniature harp. Bridgit had an immediate recognition of her beloved friend, who helped her maintain the flower garden by playing melodious music to keep perfect resonance for the plants and flowers. As she reached up to touch her, the scene faded, and Bridgit was once more standing in the doorway with Shamalaine. The sound of the door closed with the fragrance of the garden immediately ceasing, which pulled at Bridgit's heart. Yet another part of her life taken from her, she thought.

As a tear began to well up in her eye, Bridgit asked, "What happened to her... my fairy friend?"

Shamalaine sweetly spoke words of comfort. "I am pleased that you remember your friend from the garden. She has evolved into a well-respected Deva. Arrea is now one of the Builders of Form, under the hierarchy of the Elohim. She and many others are in service to the higher Builders, all working together to bring consecrated thoughts into form."

Bridgit was so pleased to hear of her new position and curious to know more about Arrea's role as a Builder. She also thought deeply upon the words spoken about consecrated thoughts. It rang a bell, but her mind was still fuzzy.

Shamalaine moved across the room to a table where there were two copper goblets filled with a beverage. She explained, "Consecrated thoughts are when one dedicates one's thoughts to a specific purpose. In the case of Arrea, she brings the highest vibration possible into her flower creations as a dedication to all around her. Those who have access to her creations will imbue themselves with the energy of her creation, and as they go about their daily lives, they take that high vibration with them into their thoughts, and the cycle of creation is uplifted."

Shamalaine held her hands over the two goblets momentarily to imbue the drinks with an intention.

Bridgit watched her mother imbuing the goblets. She noted how Shamalaine moved with elegance and measured grace. Shamalaine came back to her side and handed Bridgit a goblet. As Bridgit sipped the drink, the beverage slipped down the back of her throat with a familiar feel. As she drank more, the essence of the beverage appeared to open her senses more fully.

"Bridgit, there is more for you to see and remember," said Shamalaine as they walked back to the carved wooden door. This time the carving had morphed once more with a forest scene emerging from the grain. With her hands, Shamalaine tapped on the door in a melodic sequence, and the door opened wide. Bridgit was taken once more within a hologram of another place and time that was familiar to her. She entered into the hologram and made her way through the trees, being ever so careful with each step that she took, not to disturb new life. Mushrooms, moss, ferns, and tiny flowers growing in the undergrowth were present everywhere she looked.

Taking a deep breath in, she picked up the smells of the dark soil, rich in nutrients as the life force was now pulsing through every fiber of her being. She could feel the energy of the woods moving up her body from her feet to the top of her head, giving her the feeling of being a tree.

She moved her arms out from her body, visualizing them as branches of a tree. She was informed at that moment, of the importance of trees as carriers of the vital life force that every planet must have to stay in perfect balance with the cosmos. Her love for trees grew even more profound. Her real life, or what she knew as her real life, was merging with the life she once knew.

Her memories of the sentient beings, the trees, were coming back to her now. She understood now why she had always been so attracted to trees as a child.

She remembered the importance of the World Trees and how they were the bridge between the heavenly and earthly realms. She knew that trees filtered carbon dioxide, purifying the air, but they were so much more than that. Bridgit thought of the many cultures that used roots, bark, and leaves for healing. It saddened her heart at that moment thinking of Tuuru and her cosmic and spiritual importance to the planet on which many souls lived, and it broke her heart to know how much Tuuru gave up helping her to return home.

As Bridgit stood in the forest, a branch snapped. She was sure that it was coming from her right, and it jolted her back from her thoughts. She moved towards a melodic sound, walking between several trees in search of the player. She mentally asked if there was someone in the forest and, if so, to come out. Her heart began to race. Visions began to appear on her mental screen as she closed her eyes to feel it. The sound was that of a tune that her friend, Tabor, would play for her during her days when she planted the original species of plants and trees on many a planet.

Tabor's music was so melodic that it would induce her into the highest form of pure love until she flowed with life-giving light codes of love encased in the waters of life, her tears. She held her hands to her heart to feel for her shell necklace remembering how she would capture her tears with the shell in those moments and gift them to nature as it was always meant to be.

As the music began to fade, she opened her eyes to see Tabor's hooved bottom merging back into the shadow of the distant trees, and the vision ended with Bridgit once more on the other side of the closed door.

Breathing deeply to regain her balance, she looked at her mother and said, "That was Tabor, wasn't it?"

Shamalaine had the very same life-giving tears in her eyes as they both held so much love and gratitude for not only Tabor's gift but in remembrance of Tuuru's gift of uprooting from the human realm to assist Bridgit in her return home. They held one another for more than a few minutes, and in a synchronized manner, began their ritual of collecting their tears to be given back to the plant kingdom. They both carried shells in the form of jewelry. Bridgit having a necklace and Shamalaine's shell was atop a ring.

"I know that this is overwhelming for you, but there is more, and we must continue the memory recall. Time is of the essence."

And the wheel turns...

Chapter 5

The Council of Trustees for Peace

The Council of Trustees for Peace meeting was commencing. A voice came over a speaker announcing that everyone was to find their stations in preparation to receive the reports from the speakers representing each quadrant. Bewain would be speaking on behalf of the Lyran-Sirian Council. He, being the commanding officer in the Lyran Brigade, a small group of leaders that created and maintained the Seven Points of Peace Treaty that was utilized within the Council and all Intergalactic communications.

Bewain's powerful lion features gave him the appearance of having a dignified manner. His hair had streaks of silver tufts on both sides of his temples, intermixed with the dark burnt orange mane that trailed down to the middle of his back. He stood out as a true guardian and gave the impression that he was a born king. It was clear that he was a sovereign being in his full power and authority.

Bewain's name was called to present. As he made his way down the crowded row of seats, he passed a plethora of beings ranging in size and shape. Lizard beings, great Mantis beings, small dwarf-like beings with long tails, and finally, the shimmering translucent beings were part of the entourage. The shimmering beings put off the scent of an unknown flower essence, which created an audible frequency, like a celestial chime. The council members represented at the meeting were from contingencies all over the galaxies.

Bewain cleared his throat as he pulled what looked like a pen from his jacket pocket. He turned on a pointer by clicking the end of the object as he pointed to a screen where a hologram popped up, and he began his presentation. He spoke for some time on sovereignty and planetary hospitality, then ended his presentation with the Seven Points of Peace.

A graphic came up on the screen of a square with numbers one through four at each intersecting line. Within the square was placed a triangle with the numbers five, six, and seven at each intersecting point as well. He spoke the words of the seven qualities within the seven points of peace. "They are Trust, Cooperation, Compassion, Service, Protection, Love, and Generosity."

Bewain expounded upon the Seven Points of Peace and in particular, the fifth point as it related to the 3rd dimension life forms on Earth. He passionately explained why he was determined to keep peaceful solutions on the table to protect the people living within the 3rd dimension of Earth, as Earth was the precious jewel of the galaxy.

He left everyone in the arena with the feeling of deep understanding that the Divine Presence was the voice through which the message was being delivered that day. He gave clear guidance that if one practiced the Seven Points of Peace, lived as spiritual principles, that one would come into alignment with the indwelling presence within them. His presentation reminded everyone who attended that day of their duties as a Galactic Citizen. Bewain gave thanks to the audience as he walked away from the podium, concluding his presentation. All of the attendants rose from their seats with heads bowed as they gently gave a heartfelt round of applause.

The arena was filled with whispers as he made his way down the aisle once more. Before reaching his row, a group of Angelic's who had been taking notes bowed to him and then motioned for him to exit the arena with them. Bewain could tell that they had some important news to share with him, and he did as they requested.

And the wheel turns...

Chapter 6

More Memories Return to Bridgit

Back at the doorway, Bridgit took note of the new images on the door that were coming through the grain in the wood once more. Symbols were surfacing. Bridgit's memory was slowly returning, with her intuition heightened. Shamalaine asked Bridgit to examine the symbols and see if she could recall what they represented.

Bridgit walked closer to the door and intuited the meanings of the various symbols that all had a theme. As she gained more insights from her past coming back to her, she began to share with Shamalaine her thoughts.

"Each of these glyphs is triadic in nature, and all represent water in its different forms." She pointed to the first glyph and said, "This one is the trident, the symbol of Neptune. It represents the force of three".

She continued, "Look at all of these symbols."

Bridgit pointed to what they all had in common. "All of these symbols are in triads or groups of three. The three spirals within the triangle and here, this one with three triangles within one another, looks like waves to me, like interdimensional doorways."

She ran her finger over the edge of each carved line and said, "Here is yet another aspect of water. The drops of water in the form of tears within tears is the life-giving tears glyph?" Bridgit looked to Shamalaine for acknowledgment.

Shamalaine was quite pleased with Bridgit's intuitive examination of the glyphs. She walked to the door and motioned for Bridgit to watch as Shamalaine performed a water mudra with her hands, which energetically opened the door. The energy of this action swiftly enveloped Bridgit into darkness.

Gasping for air, Bridgit was pulled through the door and emerged from the water, spitting out water from her mouth as she trod.

Shamalaine had sent her once more into a hologram within the wooden doorway, and now she had to find her bearings within it, or she would tire quickly. She looked around as she bobbled in the frothy ocean waves, and then realized where she was. She had once been assigned here to give the life essence of the aquatic plant life. Bridgit now recalled her memories of the elementals who assisted her in that task.

As she looked above, she took in the beauty of the pink sky with the yellow-tinged clouds and felt the soft breeze against her cheek, which was one of her favorite things about the ocean. She recalled the feeling of being weightless, with the breeze blowing her wherever it wanted her to go. She silently greeted the intelligence of the wind in a reverent way, as if it was a Grandmother being. She floated on her back for a while until she could figure out what Shamalaine had in store for her.

Splashes of water lapped upon a large rock outcropping nearby. Bridgit could make out the faint sounds of a conch blown in the distance. It sparked a vague remembrance, but who could it be, she wondered.

She dived down into the water, holding her breath. As she got closer,

Bridgit's head emerged from the sea to discover that there, on the other side of the rock outcropping, was her elemental friend from long ago, holding a conch to her mouth. It was the mermaid known as Mersea.

Bridgit watched in silence, not wanting to disturb her while Mersea worked with the ancestral conch of her people. When Mersea blew on the conch, waves of aqua green water danced nearby. The conch summoned the very atomic structure of the water to do her bidding. She was an elemental of water itself, chosen by the directors of the water element, the beloved Neptune and Lunara.

Mesmerized by the sounds, Bridgit listened and observed her friend in action. The water ebbed and flowed as she focused on the trickling sounds coming from the nearby falls. Mersea blew the conch in a precise beat, inviting the water to come up to her belly as she lay flat upon the rock.

Bridgit felt the waves speaking to the creatures of the oceans. The whales and dolphins came in close. She could hear them sending Mersea their greetings in the form of sonic sounds, again with a particular beat that seemed to communicate with Mersea like a code.

Bridgit was about to make her way closer just as the sounds faded, and with that, the scene. She was once again at the doorway when Shamalaine said, "Breathe!"

Bridgit gasped as her entire body was wet from the swim.

It occurred to Bridgit that there must be a reason for Shamalaine to be focusing on these memories of her elemental relations. Bridgit was enjoying the visit, and yet, she knew that her being there was not by accident, and at this point, she wanted more answers.

Shamalaine had mentioned that time was of the essence. Bridgit knew that this dream would soon be over. A part of her wanted desperately to go back to her familiar world, but each memory that Shamalaine tapped within her gave her pause to reevaluate where she felt most at home. She looked at her mother and asked, "What is happening?"

Shamalaine responded as she handed Bridgit the goblet once more, urging her to drink more of the liquid. "You must have noticed that Mersea blew the conch with precision?"

Bridgit swallowed the milky substance and nodded yes with her eyes wide to emphasize that fact. "But, I mean, why am I here... with you?"

Shamalaine continued, "Oh my dear, we will get to that soon enough. For now, let us stay focused on the return of your memory in a gentle manner. If I give you too much too soon, it may be difficult for your mind to comprehend. Delicate doses are best." Shamalaine searched Bridgit's eyes for understanding, but what she saw was a general blankness.

"I want to continue with the tutorial if you would be so kind?" Shamalaine pointed for Bridgit to take a seat once more, which she did, biding her time. Bridgit wiped her wet hair from her forehead and breathed in deeply as she settled into the chair once more.

She said, "Ready," and managed a smile towards her mother.

Shamalaine gladly continued, "Nature is very well organized and is created from precise patterns, wouldn't you agree?", looking at Bridgit for a response.

"Yes... That is an accurate statement." Bridgit responded, curious to hear where Shamalaine would take the conversation next.

Shamalaine went on, "As we move into the higher frequencies, we step up the beats, so to speak, to ever higher frequencial levels of awareness." She looked to see if Bridgit understood where she is going with this.

Bridgit said, "I understand the concept of the higher frequencies as a time signature if that is what you are meaning?" Bridgit recalled her vague knowledge of time and space at that moment.

Shamalaine responded, "That is precisely what I am getting at."

Shamalaine smiled, feeling very proud to of her heir, and yet she had a sudden communication that needed tending too, so she shifted her demeanor suddenly.

"We will talk more about this as time allows, but I wanted you to see just how Mersea could communicate with the water creatures through rhythmic sounds. Let us take a break for the time being. We do not want to overwhelm your senses any more than what we have already. I will answer your questions soon enough." Shamalaine smile at Bridgit and gently touched her cheek. She stared into her daughter's eyes and said, "How I have missed you."

Bridgit was now thoroughly confused with so many emotions. Shamalaine left her in the golden-hued room alone to contemplate all that she had experienced as she excused herself to attend to another matter at hand.

And the wheel turns...

Chapter 7

Bewain Returns Home

Shamalaine escorted Bridgit into the Great Hall after the very long session with her daughter earlier in the morning. "Let's get you fed, shall we?", squeezing her close to her body in a walking hug. In the Great Hall, many of the wise ones of the clan were seated at a long table in quiet meditation, awaiting the return of Bridgit's father, Bewain.

Shamalaine motioned for someone to provide Bridgit a plate of food. Avery was peeking through the doorway, salivating at the food being prepared for Bridgit. At that moment, Bewain, stood beside Avery, clearing his throat.

Avery looked down at his feet, and next to them, he discovered another pair of feet, but much more significant, with tufts of hair coming out of the edges of the shoes. Avery realized that logically, there must be a substantial size being standing next to him, one that was surely as hairy as its feet would suggest.

Bewain could sense the little elf processing this information while he waited in the doorway. As Avery braved a glance upwards, Bewain put his gentle, yet firm, hand on Avery's back just as Avery began to sway backwards towards the floor.

Bewain asked, "Are you the brave elf that brought my beloved daughter home?" reassuring Avery that he was safe from harm.

Avery puffed up his chest while stabilizing himself and squeaked out a reply, "Yes sir. Master Bewain, I presume?"

Bewain smiled and corrected him, "Commander, if you would," indicating Bewain's status to Avery.

Avery's eyes got bigger and said, "Yes, of course, Commander, Sir!" standing at attention.

Bewain began to laugh with a roar at the seriousness of the little guy. Hearing the loud laughter, Bridgit looked up to see a very stately, lion-maned gentleman lifting Avery into his arms with great affection and wondered who this man was until he spoke loudly to Avery.

"WELL...where is she? Where is my daughter?" Bewain looked around until his eyes landed upon her.

Bridgit saw Avery point in her direction, and at the moment that her eyes meet with Bewain's, it was instant recognition of a father and daughter.

Bewain's twinkle in his eye gleamed brightly, and the silly grin on his face welcomed her from across the room. Bewain gently released Avery to the floor and guided him to a spot at the table. He rubbed Avery's head as a gesture of gratitude for a job well done, never looking away from his beloved daughter, the Life Bearer. He slowly made his way around the table and down to the end where his daughter had been sitting. The wise ones began to speak an ancient prayer of gratitude for the reunion that was now complete.

Bridgit moved away from her seat to present herself to her father.

Avery, not one for all the fanfare, lifted a silver plate to use as a mirror to fix the fluff that was now his hair, as a wise one smiled at him. He gestured that he wanted to be presentable for dinner, but inwardly he was coming to terms with his hair being out of sorts, which was not becoming for an elf of his stature, he thought.

Bridgit began flashing as if she was still in the Chair of Remembrance. Memories flashed quickly, codes unlocking of her time learning the ways of peace from her father, the diplomat.

Bewain was now standing in front of her, seeing that she was transfixed in a vision. As Bridgit became present once more, he stood with his shell, holding it to her cheek, ready to catch the tears. Her tears flowed as she reached out to touch his arm. She made the connection physically because he seemed like a distant memory, like the holograms that Shamalaine presented to her.

He placed the tear-filled shell on the table in front of her, and then he put his hands out for her to come into the warm embrace of her father. They held one another for quite some time, all the while, Shamalaine watched the precious gift of her daughter's reunion with her father. Shamalaine then walked up to where they stood, and the three energies combined into a blissful signature. The power of the triad was palpable in the room.

And the wheel turns...

Chapter 8

The Reality of Bridgit's Return to the The Clan of Phare

Bewain and Shamalaine spoke softly in their sleep chambers that night. Shamalaine asked, "With all of the excitement of Kaialena's return, I did not have time to ask how your council meeting went?"

Bewain folded his vest and sat in the chair near where Shamalaine sat on the edge of the bed. He looked at her, not sure where to begin. She could sense it and said, "Go on. Out with it."

Bewain smiled slightly and said, "After my presentation at the Council of Trustees, the Angelics asked to seek my aide in a matter. We met after the meeting had concluded, and I am still pondering what to do about the information."

Rubbing his shoulders while listening, Shamalaine prompted him to continue as she kneaded a knot on his upper back.

"The Angelics brought news of the latest antics of the Dark One and his followers. It seems that the Dark One has his eyes on Earth, and he will fight to the bitter end for what he feels is his birthright." Looking up at Shamalaine, he took her hand, swinging her in front of him, and eased her onto his lap.

Bewain stared at her for a moment and softly said, "We will need to call on Breacher for assistance with Kaialena."

Shamalaine got up from Bewain's lap. She looked down at her hands. Her feline features always reminded her of her origins and all that had transpired in the past. She knew that things could potentially get very complicated now. She was in deep thought.

Clearing his throat, Bewain said, "As you know, with Kaialena's return, it indicates that the time is at hand to make our move." Looking into his beloved's eyes as she turned to look at him, her understanding look relayed it all.

She said, "I knew the moment she returned it would be the beginning of the next phase of humanity's evolution, for she is the Life Bearer of our lineage. She was sent on special assignment into the human world for a reason. I also know that she will be in grave danger with this War Lord fighting for all of our worlds, but to call upon Breacher at this time? I think his time would best be spent training the dragons."

"Who better to protect her than Breacher?" Bewain asked.

He looked intently into his beloved's eyes as a champion for his daughter. "I am sure he will have plenty of time to get the dragons ready."

Shamalaine responded in kind. "Bewain, I always appreciate your council as my husband and as a diplomat. While you were away, I, too, gained some clarity on the matter. I do not want harm to come to our daughter, but as the Leader of the Clan of Phare, my duty comes first. Kaialena will continue her memory review with me in the morning. I will give her instructions on where she needs to go to find her way back to the human world. I am already looking into her security needs."

Bewain tried one last effort on Breacher's behalf, "Shamalaine, this is why I feel that Breacher would be the best person to take her back. With his particular skill set, she would be back in the human realm by nightfall."

Shamalaine breathed in deeply, and with a voice of authority and the full force of the divine feminine that she embodied, Shamalaine spoke. "No, Bewain. We have time enough to get Kaialena back to the human realm with her few memories intact, and without the heartache involved should she recall her feelings for Breacher. I fear that if Kaialena comes into contact with Breacher now, she may not be willing to go back on her own accord, and it would cause her pain."

Bewain opened his mouth to try once more, but Shamalaine said sternly, "The heart knows more than our mind, never forget this. If she is with him for any length of time, she will remember him." With that settled, Shamalaine shifted the focus of the conversation.

Looking into Bewain's eyes, Shamalaine asked, "Could we possibly hope for a new world where we all live in peace?"

Making light of the subject, Bewain held Shamalaine, knowing full well that she was on a timetable, and everything must go according to the protocols set forth from the council. Now all they had to do was assist their beloved daughter in remembering her gifts, for she was one of the carriers of the life codes that will establish a whole new realm. Kaialena would need to quickly recall the plan if she was going to find the others, he thought.

Shamalaine came out of her deep thoughts with a final statement on the subject. "I am assembling the Builders for a council meeting. They should be involved now. I will handle this part; you keep the peace talks going. Our time is at hand, my love."

Smiling at her beloved husband, Shamalaine said, "Get some rest. We will think clearer in the morning." They settled into the comfort of their lair as they held one another.

The next morning Shamalaine entered the golden-hued room, and with an invocation, she opened the portal through the wooden door to meet with the team of Builders of Form to make sure they were all prepared for their missions. Shamalaine would take council with the Ancient of Days to understand how she needed to proceed with her daughter's progress, as memories were a delicate thing.

And the wheel turns...

Chapter 9

Breacher Dreams of His Bride

Breacher woke with a jolt, coming out of a dream that he had had over and over again. The one where he and Kaialena were enjoying their newly married life, spending time in the garden when an envoy of Bewain's came to their home to inform Kaialena that she had been called into active duty as the role of Life Bearer of the Clan of Phare.

Just as they were beginning talks of having a family of their own, she was called away. The dream ends there, as that was the last time he saw her.

Breacher wiped the sweat from his brow and reached for the shell near his bed, the one that Kaialena gave him on their wedding day. He held it just under his eye and blinked several times and filled the shell with his tears. He walked over near the window and looked at the enchanted orchid that she placed there on their wedding night. He remembered how she loved to watch it catch the moonlight as they lay in bed together. He gently poured his life-giving tears on the base of the plant and set the shell back down on the nightstand for he knew that his dream would return again and again until he was reunited with his beloved Kaialena.

The next morning he left the house at first light to make sure that all of the veil perimeters were still intact over the Clan of Phare's lands. As he was walking near the land of the Phare, he heard a stringed instrument playing and came upon a small elf with his eyes closed. This one was unfamiliar to him, but judging by his attire, Breacher guessed that he must be from the Elven Clan that resides near the great tree, Tuuru.

As Breacher stepped closer, Avery opened his eyes and took notice of him. Avery continued to play the song all the way through. Breacher stood in reverence until it was complete.

Avery turned to Breacher and made introductions. "Good morning. I am Avery. I brought the human here, to the Great Hall yesterday."

Avery was very proud to be the one to keep watch over Bridgit, though in truth, he knew that Eldorman was truly responsible for bringing the human to her clan. He put his harp down to bow to the gentleman. "Good Morning."

Breacher looked confused and asked, "Human?"

Avery said, "Oh, I am sorry, I thought that the news traveled fast here. Let me start over. I feel I have erred and must give clarity for truth's sake."

Avery started the whole discourse by straightening up his vest and then went on to tell Breacher how Tuuru, the tree, had brought the human woman into the Elven realm. He clarified that Eldorman was actually the elf who attended to the human's injury and brought her to the Clan of Phare. He went on speaking, enjoying his own story when he turned to find that Breacher had disappeared without a trace.

And the wheel turns...

Chapter 10

Breacher's Reunion with Kaialena

The Great Hall was bustling with food being laid out on the table. Bewain was standing by the grand fireplace, staring intently, which was his usual way of formulating a plan when he felt a quick breeze. Standing next to him was Breacher.

Breacher bowed out of courtesy and said, "Commander."

Bewain looked at him and responded similarly, "Commander Breacher!" Bewain was not surprised to see him, though he knew Shamalaine would not be pleased to know of his visit.

He then said, "Glad to see you, son. Let's walk, shall we?"

Bewain placed his massive hand on Breacher's shoulder and twirled him so fast that Bewain had to steady him. "I got you," he let out a nervous laugh as he led him towards the study.

"I have some strategy to go over with you." Bewain patted him as they walked out of the Great Hall. Breacher had a sense that Bewain was hiding something from him.

As Bewain led him to the hallway towards the study, Shamalaine came through the doorway and stopped quite suddenly. Bridgit was following closely behind her and bumped right into her mother's backside.

"Sorry!" she said, as she waited for Shamalaine to move out of the doorway into the Great Hall.

Shamalaine's eyes were wide and looked a bit confused as she looked directly at her husband for an explanation. Her eyes and demeanor told Bewain that he had some explaining to do.

Bewain shook his head and looked down, not sure how to explain Breacher's presence as he only had just arrived.

At that moment, Bridgit darted out from behind Shamalaine and made a beeline to the long table in the room. She was famished and thought she could sneak in a bite of some grapes as Shamalaine and Bewain spoke. She noted that they did not seem to need as much nourishment or at least in the same intervals as she did. Stuffing her mouth with several grapes, she turned around to find standing next to Bewain, a nicely presented dark-headed man who was somewhat younger than her father.

With her hand behind her, she tried to feel for a cloth, then swirled around towards the table to cover her mouth as she chewed the grapes and swallowed. Wiping her mouth, she turned around once more, red-faced, then walked towards Breacher. Bridgit apologized for moving past her mother to feast when there were guests to greet.

She wiped her hands on her dress, then said, "I did not see you there. Please forgive my rudeness. My name is Bridgit...well..., um..., I suppose I should say Kaialena?" Bridgit looked to Shamalaine for clarity. Bridgit was still confused with the multidimensional aspects of who she was. She momentarily was in thought, trying to make sense of how to present herself now. She was still looking in Shamalaine's direction, though she extended her hand towards Breacher.

Speechless, Breacher stared at her presented hand for a few seconds, stunned at who was standing in front of him.

Bridgit then looked his way again, noticing his facial expression and finding him familiar. She said, "I am sorry, have we meet? I am still in the process of regaining my memories." She retrieved her hand from Breacher's grip and continued, "It has been a while since I have been here."

Breacher still could find no words. He retook Bridgit's hand as he knelt towards her, and like a prince finding his princess, he kissed her hand then released it. As Breacher was about to speak, Bewain jumped in.

"I'm sorry, how rude of me! Commander Breacher, this our daughter Kaialena, also known as Bridgit in the third dimension." Bewain looked at Breacher with a look that suggested that he go with it. Breacher understood not to let Bridgit in on who he was to her.

Breacher stood up, and with a bow, he said to her, "Madame."

Breacher's heart was racing, and his mind was spinning, but he knew he had to play it cool. He stood formally, with a straight back, and looked towards Shamalaine and said, "I am here on important business. I wonder if you wouldn't mind if I took up a few minutes of the Commander's time?"

Shamalaine nodded her approval.

Breacher and Bewain were off to the study swiftly. As Bewain passed Shamalaine, she leaned into him and whispered, "Be sure to see him out when you are through," and then she smiled towards Bridgit and suggested that they get to their breakfast because there was much to learn, and time was of the essence.

And the wheel turns...

Chapter 11

Breacher's Brooding

It was getting late into the evening. Breacher stood looking out the window in his small cottage with Kaialena on his mind. Everything in the home reminded him of her. More tears began to flow, too much for the one small shell to hold, as these tears would fall in torrents to the floor as he wept for his beloved.

He heard a knock at his door, but he could barely bring himself out of his pain to bother answering it. The rap at the door grew louder and persistent. He eventually opened it to find Shamalaine at his door. She held a brightly lit torch, as it was now pitch-black outside and overcast with no moonlight in the sky. He moved to the side to let her in, not saying a word.

She laid the torch in the fire pit several feet from the front door then entered the home. She turned to face him while lowering her hood as he motioned for her to sit. She looked at him with the love of a Mother, and as she sat down, she patted the spot next to her as if to say, come, sit...it will be okay.

Breacher sat down but could not bear to look at Shamalaine. It was because of her that he was not holding his beloved that night. Shamalaine could sense all of these feelings as an empath. She knew how much Breacher and Kaialena loved one another, so what she had to say would not be easy for either of them.

"I am sorry for your pain Breacher, I truly am. I hope to share with you what I have seen and what the potential outcomes are for the perilous times that we are living through. Once I have shared with you what lays before us and what each of our roles will be in the divine plan, I hope that you can see that it would be too risky for you and Kaialena to come together at this time. Are you ready to hear the plan?" She rubbed his back as a mother would as she tried to make eye contact with him.

Breacher wiped his face and just stared at his feet and said, "I will listen to what you have to say, but I cannot promise that I will stay away from her. She is my wife!"

Shamalaine nodded and said, "That she is, and that is why you must hear what I have to say."

Shamalaine began her story. "When there is difficulty maintaining the boundaries between the frequency bands of a planet, it is an indication that the transformation, or ascension of a planet, is taking place. A spinning action begins to occur, bringing with it great light. This light throws off the dross of the lower vibrations, and things become unsettled." Shamalaine lifts her hands upward to indicate the ascension.

She continued, "During these tumultuous times, our defense systems break, and all life is at risk from moving higher along the spiral, due to the planned fear and chaos agenda that is running rampant upon the many dimensions of Earth."

Shamalaine cleared her throat to bring Breacher back to center as his thoughts continued to go back to Kaialena. Breacher sat upright and motioned for her to continue and said, "I am listening. I am visualizing what you are saying."

She smiled and continued, "There is always a flow of devolution and evolution happening at the same time. Those who are devolving are the ones who are chosen to enter the 3D world on their own accord to bring light into the darkness. Most of those dear beings had already made their way into the higher realms and have been and continue to be of great service to the Creator. Kaialena is one of those great souls who was chosen to return to the world of 3D form to be of service to the God Source." She looked at him to see his reaction.

Breacher was experiencing a vision and was seeing the truth of what Shamalaine was saying. "I knew when we married that she would not be with me for long."

Breacher looked down at his feet again and said, "She told me that she was a Life Bearer then and that there would come a time when she would be called into service to create a new world for us all to live in."

He paused then turned to Shamalaine and said, "I know all of this, and yet I just miss her."

Shamalaine patted him on his back and allowed him to feel the emotion. After a short pause, she continued her story. "As I was saying, there are those that devolve into the 3D Earth to bring the light, and then there are those that were born into it for learning how to clear the patterns of imperfection. The 3D world is the perfect place for learning. The good news is that the Creator has seen the good works of the 3D world, and the light within most of the humans has tipped the balance. There are, of course, the small number of imposters that have caused great havoc upon humanity and this precious planet. A decree has come directly from Creator that this will no longer be allowed, as it is now damaging not only the humans and the planet, but also the actions of these malevolent beings could eventually affect the entire Galaxy."

Shamalaine sent the visual picture to Breacher of the earth changes and how it could cause a rift in the cosmic ocean. She spoke once more. "Breacher, as you can see, all existence will be affected if we do not create a higher vibrational frequency band for all beings of this planet to come together in peace. It is a great honor for Kaialena to be of service to the Creator in this way. She has been preparing for this for some time. She will not be alone."

Breacher nodded, agreeing that Kaialena had trained for this time.

She continued. "There are twelve other Life Bearers that she will bring together in the 3D realm. There will also be a team of Elementals assisting in this plan. These particular elementals are under the banner of the Elohim, as the Builders of Form, who are trained in the manifestation of worlds. They have great mental faculties, which are a requirement to build a whole new planetary system. Worlds within worlds. Now, of course, they will need the assistance of the Angelics whose role is to bring the Blueprint or the Divine Design from the Creator, and then finally, they will have the help of the Guardians." She looked at him as he heard the last bit.

Breacher turned to her with a renewed hope. He repeated her words, "the Guardians?"

"Yes. Bewain has had you working with the new breed of dragons for this very reason. They will be of great assistance in weaving the new energy grids for the new world, and of course, you will possibly be called as a Guardian to assist her when the time is right."

He was overjoyed hearing those words for two reasons. The fact that he could be with Kaialena was more than he could have hoped for, but to have been chosen to be a part of this divine mission was a tremendous honor. He looked at Shamalaine and said, "I don't know what to say?"

Shamalaine said, "Breacher, we have loved you like our own son, and we couldn't be more proud of you and Kaialena."

Shamalaine began to rise and mentioned one last thing. "Can you understand the importance of keeping who you are to Kaialena a secret for now? Her heart would be torn if she remembered you as her husband. She needs to focus completely on finding the other Life Bearers at this time, and soon enough, she will need the Guardians and the dragons on her team. She does not have much time for this."

Shamalaine looked away, and Breacher caught the feeling of concern from her.

"What do you mean? How much time does she have? What are you not telling me?" Breacher grabbed Shamalaine's wrist to keep her from leaving.

She turned and said, "There is a window of opportunity for Kaialena to find the other twelve Life Bearers and enter the jump points on time. The frequency bands have been distorted by the malevolent ones, so this will prove difficult for all the Life Bearers to make it through the jump points. The malevolent ones will stop at nothing to keep all of the 3D Worlder's under their control."

As she prepared to leave, she turned once more to Breacher and said, "The souls who live within the third dimension will be making the ascension while in form. This has never been done before. It is an amazing time to be a part of the Divine plan."

Breacher still had so many questions.

Shamalaine put her hood up and said, "I will answer your questions soon, but for now, I must go." With that, Shamalaine was out the door and into the evening as quickly as he could appear and disappear.

And the wheel turns...

Chapter 12

Meeting of the Two Commanders

The next morning Bewain called Breacher to his study for more counseling on the matter. Breacher breezed by Bewain as he was reading the latest council report near the fireplace. The paper flew out of his hand as Breacher made his swift entrance and fell to the floor.

Quickly, Breacher picked up the report and scanned a few words.

"Artificial intelligence? Anomaly?" Breacher question Bewain as he handed the page back to him.

Bewain lifted the page from his hand and said, "I will brief you later on that."

Turning, he made his way to the chairs sitting by the fireplace. "Come sit by the fire."

Bewain had positioned the chairs perfectly in front of the beautiful stone fireplace with carvings on the mantle of the Lyran star system. It was a reminder of the war that drove them from their homeland.

"I wanted to see how you were feeling today, after your talk with Shamalaine. We must include you in the plan, as you are both the husband of Kaialena, but as Shamalaine has shared, you are a Guardian as well." Smiling, he poured the two a cup of hot tea from the table sitting next to his chair and passed Breacher his cup.

Breacher said, "I could hardly sleep last night. I have so much on my mind, but to say that I am pleased with my mission, is an understatement for two obvious reasons."

Bewain chuckled, "Yes, we thought you would be happy to learn that if all goes according to plan, you will possibly be able to be with Kaialena soon. Your life review indicated that you would be a great match for this particular mission at hand."

Breacher sipped his tea and asked, "So what anomaly is happening? What is the artificial intelligence issue?"

Bewain placed his cup on the table and pulled the report out. "The council has been monitoring fluctuations in the various planes within the realms of Gaia, our beloved Earth. They are also gathering more intel on the Dark One. The council has found an anomaly with vast surges of negative energy."

Breacher was dumbfounded at this news. "How is this possible?"

Bewain began to explain what had happened at the beginning of Gaia's creation. He spoke to Breacher of what he knew.

"Something happened at the onset of Gaia's creation, like a pure thought, being interrupted by a malevolent force during the manifestation period of her creation, which caused a tremendous harmonic disturbance. It acted as a virus would." He referenced this disturbance as being an anomaly.

He continued, "A plan was put into place to quarantine Gaia until the light forces could learn how to clear it. It was then that the hologram was put into place around Gaia. Unfortunately, the anomaly has intelligence and is fed by heinous thoughts and actions. It seems that the Dark One has figured this out and has been feeding the anomaly by creating negative energy within Gaia's many dimensions. He has learned how to manipulate the hologram also. The Dark One wants to keep the dimensional veils separated."

Breacher took it all in and then asked, "Well, don't we want the dimensions separated? I have been trained to repair rifts in the veil to keep the dimensional veils separate. What are you saying?"

Bewain shook his head while drinking his tea and then continued. "At this point, the Blueprint Angels have received the plans for the repair of the "flaw," which is already underway. The clearing of the anomaly will soon be complete. Once the new creation is complete, we can clear the hologram, and the merging of our light and dark aspects will begin. The Dark One will be left without a source of power since the higher aspects are only light. He will try to keep Gaia and all of her inhabitants from reconnecting to their higher aspects, the part of themselves that loves unconditionally. You see, when Gaia was affected by the anomaly, so was every living being. It was then that we experienced duality. When we all merge back into our original Divine Creation, then all is love and light. Pure and simple."

Bewain stared upward as if he received a new thought, and continued, "When the merging begins, everything will be absorbed into the light. All duality, good vs. bad, light and dark, will be no more. Only the Divine will be present within us all. The Dark One will merge into the light as well, and this is what he is trying to keep from happening. He is afraid. Afraid of losing control, and as he sees it, the end of his reign of terror. But, until this event occurs, he will wreak havoc upon the earth planes and do everything he can to keep the chosen Life Bearers from getting to the jump points, and this will prove difficult for them to make it to their designated places, but not impossible. Luckily, our intel suggests that he does not know who the Life Bearers are at this time."

Bewain put the report back on the table and looked at Breacher. "Kaialena and the other Life Bearers are responsible for the overlay of the new manifested creation. The Infinite Creator has given the divine dispensation that the new manifest creation of a higher, purer plane of existence is to be created. The Life Bearers, along with the Builders of Form and the Blueprint Angels, will be following the blueprint of this new creation. They must not be disturbed while in this creation period; for obvious reasons, least we have the same issue all over again. This is where the Guardians come in."

Breacher shook his head in acknowledgment at the depth of his mission. "Why didn't you tell me about the repairing of the veil? I could have been helpful in that, as you know?"

Bewain said, "There is more for you to do, and thankfully we have several others skilled at that. No, I need you here with the dragons. Tomorrow is Kaialena's last day of review. She will be sufficiently activated. Regulus has called for her. We will prepare for her to be sent back."

Bewain had a sinking feeling and looked deeply into Breacher's eyes as a way to fully align with Breacher's thoughts and emotions. He asked, "Do you understand that if you were to present yourself to Kaialena as her husband, it could complicate matters and possibly cause an even greater ripple in the plan?"

Breacher nodded his understanding.

Bewain continued. "The chosen ones are always the ones that carry a heavier load, but along the path, they find that as they come fully into the light of their being, the burden lessens. Let her remember you in her own time. She will do her job to activate the light codes to seed the new creation, and she will need you by her side when she has prepared the way. For now, we need to gather the Guardians to watch over all of the Life Bearers."

Bewain sat his teacup down on the table after his last sip then stood up. He reminded Breacher, "The dragons must be ready soon. Only a Melchezidek trained Guardian, trained in the energetics of time and space, could accomplish the requirements for training this new breed of dragons."

"I understand my role with the dragons, sir. They will be prepared for

57

the service. I just wish I could be the one watching over Kaialena now. Who did you appoint to get her back to the 3D world?"

"Butler... temporarily, of course," Bewain said with a smile.

Knowing Butler was watching over Kaialena put Breacher's concerns at ease. "Thank you, sir." Breacher said as he finished his last sip of tea and placed the cup on the table beside Bewain.

And the wheel turns...

Chapter 13

Breacher Prepares the Dragon Lair

Breacher's hair blew in the wind as he soared through the air on his courageous friend, Leto, a Violet Dragon. Leto was the first of the dragons from the hatchlings that was born. Breacher gave Leto his undivided attention during the early days, as it was just the two of them for some time before the rest of the dragons decided to hatch.

They flew high over the trees and water. Breacher was more focused than ever to prepare the dragons for service. He recalled how Bewain shared the plan for the new breed of dragons, which would be different from any other known dragon.

Bewain knew that Breacher's time spent with the ancients would prove to be valuable in the dragon's training. In his early days, Breacher trained as a Dragon Rider, and now he had an opportunity to train the dragons and riders for an epic mission.

Some time ago, Breacher was inspired to create the perfect hatching environment for the dragons. The environment of the eggs had to contain all of the elements, balanced in such a way that the very elements themselves would be a part of these dragon's DNA.

Breacher's care and devotion were required for this breed to come into existence. He knew that it had to be within a womb-like cave where they would not be disturbed. Within this cave, he set up a long stone trough. He lined the base of it with lava rocks, then used a special oil on the stones and ignited them on fire.

Now that he had the earth and fire elements in place, Breacher created a hologram around the trough that would provide a self-contained atmosphere.

He placed the dragon eggs upon the lava rocks and waited. The atmosphere around the trough sealed. It was a perfectly balanced ecosystem, but this womb space would take time to hatch the eggs.

At times, the atmosphere would precipitate upon the eggs, and at other times the fires would ignite once more, warming the rocks that held the eggs. The steam from the water purified the air, and in this way, air, water, earth, and fire became the perfect environment for the dragon eggs to hatch and hatch they eventually did.

Each of the dragons was a different color of the rainbow, and all were wise from the beginning. Breacher was their father for all intents and purposes. He fed them, he trained them, and he loved them dearly. Each day the dragons grew bigger. Their first flight was one he would remember clearly as the dragons looked like a moving rainbow in the sky.

Breacher telepathically communicated with each of them, and they developed a close bond quickly. He took them out on missions to repair the energetic breaks in the frequency bands, strengthening the hologram. This activity would be a valuable lesson as they were going to need to be experts at weaving energy into a whole new grid system soon. Leto began his descent to the dragon's lair, as Breacher came out of his daydream of the early days. He was now ready to prepare them for their final lesson.

And the wheel turns...

Chapter 14

Bridgit's Last Day As Kaialena

The next morning Shamalaine and Bewain shared a morning meal with the clan, with their daughter by their side. It was a bittersweet moment, as they knew it would come to an end soon. They cherished every moment with her.

Bridgit's long hair swooped to one side, giving sight of her right ear, which poked out of the little bit of hair left there to hide her apparent inheritance.

Shamalaine stood from her seat and motioned for Bridgit to join her in the golden-hued room with the engraved wooden door. Bridgit bowed to the elders who were sitting near her as she removed herself from their company. One of the elders slyly handed her a snack for later, which reminded her of a granola bar in the 3D world. She smiled and nodded her head in gratitude and quickly hid it in the pocket of her dress, then followed her mother silently into the golden room.

They walked over to the door to inspect the engravings. "It is time to remember more of the Builders," Shamalaine said as they stood watching an ancient text in cuneiform appear upon the door.

"How many are there?" Bridgit genuinely wanted to know, but Shamalaine was already in her teaching mode, and it looked to Bridgit that her question annoyed her.

"There are seven in total for this particular teaching." Shamalaine urged Bridgit to focus on what was about to occur. As Shamalaine spoke, ancient words of light appeared on the door. The words were Gordavin-Gnome-EL. The energy in the room became vibrant. Bridgit felt a golden vortex of energy pull her towards the doorway and into a hollow place deep within the center of a mountain.

As soon as she landed, she recognized this place from long ago when she would meet with the Masters. Moving through the corridor of the cavern, she made her way towards the sound of voices. The cavern walls began to look more like polished granite and marble.

Above the doors were crystal mosaics, similar to stained glass, but these mosaics were grown this way. As she approached the nearest door, it began to open, and within the room was a large contingent of earth dwellers and Galactics at a council table. There were also humans in their pajamas standing to one side of the room with another group of galactic envoys. It was clear to Bridgit that this was a present moment situation and not a vision of her past.

A stately gnome walked over to Bridgit. She looked at his beautiful brown eyes, which twinkled like stardust as she remembered this one well.

"Gordavin!" She could not keep from hugging him in her excitement to see him. The two had worked together many times and had become quite fond of one another. He showed her to a seat at the strategy table, and as she walked with him, she continued to scan the room to see who was present.

Some beings she recalled, in her vivified state, but many she did not. Introductions were made as a formality, as they all knew who she was, but given the circumstances of Bridgit's return, adjustments were being made to refresh her memory.

At the table were the other twelve Life Bearers in their dream bodies, who were each introduced to her. They had all been in training together at some point over the eons of time, serving the divine plan. Because the Life Bearers were in their dream bodies, they were all told that once Bridgit returned to the 3D world, she would have to find them on her own.

Bridgit understood from the conversation that the others would not look like they do in their "light" forms, which would make it a bit more complicated of a task in finding the Life Bearers, mainly because she would not know their names or where they live. The reasoning for this, she was told, was to keep with cosmic protocol and divine will of the 3D humans involved. She was told that though the higher aspects of the Life Bearers were entirely on board, their 3D aspects would not remember the covenant made. Bridgit would have to find them and remind them of the mission.

Gordavin took a seat at one end of the table as the representative of the element Earth. His role was to oversee aspects of mineral growth, imbue healing properties within the minerals, as well as monitor the intelligence from the crystal kingdom. He was also a liaison to the Galactic Federation, the Intergalactic Federation, and the Andromeda Council. It was the Andromeda Council present today, giving instructions to the Life Bearers while in their dream bodies, as they could not risk attempting to contact them in their human forms at this time.

The Ascended Master Saint Germain walked into the room. The violet color that emanated around his body filled the room, and everyone bowed to him with respect as he walked to the far end of the table near Gordavin.

"Blessings to each of you present." Lifting his hands to his heart, he closed his eyes in silent prayer. As he moved his hands away from his chest, he held a spark of the Violet Flame.

"I would like each of you to come forward, one at a time, to receive the blessing of the All-Consuming Violet Flame." Each being present took turns in front of St. Germain as he gave a special blessing and lit the individual's own internal Violet Flame.

"This flame is a gift from the Creator. It is to be used to clear the dross or negative energies connected to your being." After each being present in the room received this gift, St. Germain ceremoniously cleared the entire room with the Violet Flame. The vibrational force of this clearing caused a slight tremor in the mountain as it went deep into the heart of Gaia. He called forth the elemental forces of the flame to traverse all time and space with this frequency and clear all of the dross that every man, woman, and child had ever created.

For Bridgit, it was a great honor to be in the presence of an Ascended Master, and especially the Master of the 7th Ray. When he was complete with the violet flame invocation, they all took their seats for the Strategic Presentation.

In the center of the table was a large inlaid world globe, which had articulated closures that looked much like two eyelids opening and closing. As the lids opened, it was an eye. But as the lids blinked once more, it turned into a world globe. "A multi-purpose, intelligent mapping system," St. Germain shared as the globe was activated.

"The Strategists have worked to prepare the coordinates. We will use this system to measure precisely the jump points, through which each Life Bearer will enter." He pointed to the various lit up spots around the world, and then the strategic meeting began.

Each of the Life Bearers received their coded information. "Entering the void will prove difficult given the situation with the malevolent ones, but we have provided each of you a steady flow of assistance that will be nearby. We will be monitoring your path and providing as much nudging as we can, and we are very confident that each one of you present today has it within you to feel, hear or know when the time is right and where you will need to be." St. Germain allowed a representative from the Ashtar Command to speak.

Telepathically, Gorloj transmitted his thoughts to the group. "It is an honor to be here today with you all. I have been sent by Ashtar and Ashtera, to give you encouragement and acknowledgment in your efforts thus far. We want you to know that each of you has worked with the Command in your dream state for some time and before and during your incarnation on the 3D plane of planet Earth."

He pointed to the globe on the table and continued, "These jump points will be coded into your system to be a strong beacon when the time is right. You all will be guided along the way, and there should be no fear as to how you will find one another. The divine plan is mysterious, and it is always flawless."

Each of the individuals looked at the world globe as even more lighted areas magnified.

He finished his presentation by saying, "Bridgit will be downloaded with the information required to bring you all together in the 3D world. It will be up to her to find you should you miss your opportunities to convene together at the appointed hour." Everyone looked at Bridgit for assurance that she had this under control. She assured them that she would do her best to find them.

The twelve Life Bearers began to fade as the allotted time for the meeting came to a close. Before Bridgit was taken back through the wood door, Gordavin approached her, bending down on one knee to give her the respect of someone of her authority. She lowered her head in honor of the celebrated earth gnome that she had come to love.

"I am honored, my lady, to be a part of your seeding team once more. We have worked well in the past in many a multiverse and all to great success, I would say." Gordavin stood, then pulled up his pants over his belly in a proud moment.

"Yes, I agree. I, too, am pleased to see you on this team with me as one of the Builders of Form, as this will prove to be our most challenging seeding of worlds." Bridgit hinted.

Gordavin shook his head in acknowledgment of the truth in her words. "Before you go, I do want to mention that there is one slight glitch in the plan, and I have been tasked to rectify it," he said.

"What is the glitch?" Bridgit asked, concerned.

"Well, as you know, the Builders of Form are chosen based on many criteria. Each of the seven builders works with a particular ray of energy, life force, as we will call it. I work with the fifth ray in particular. We have all but one Builder chosen for the teams. Those Builders are working with rays two-seven. We have yet to pick the Builder of the first ray." Gordavin was noticeably bothered by this turn of events.

"Gordavin, explain to me what characteristics of a first ray builder would be?" Bridgit's methodical mind tended towards solving problems naturally, so she felt she could be of help in this issue.

Gordavin put his hands in his pocket and stuck out his belly as he positioned his feet firmly with a wide stance. "Well, they generally have a strong will and a particular way of doing things. They are well organized and have a dominant personality, you know, to get things done, one must be persistent."

He laughed and rubbed his beard while waving his other hand in a circular motion as he attempted to be discrete in his description of what Bridgit recognized as the typical "A" personality type.

He went on to say, "They may be considered annoying at times, but they get their job done." He winked at her as she formulated her response.

Bridgit said, "I think I know of just the elemental that would be perfect for this mission!"

Looking intently at Gordavin, she went on to say, "He is a born leader of his elven clan and has been assisting me while I have been in the home of my parents."

"What is his name?" Gordavin's eyebrow raised with a little curiosity and a little bit of concern.

66

"His name is Avery, and he is a very particular little elf, but I have grown accustomed to him and think he would be an excellent addition to our team." She said, smiling.

"Ah, Elmwood's offshoot. Let me check his records. There is a protocol for this sort of thing, you know. One must be able to hold focus for long periods and stay on task, you know."

Bridgit laughed, "I don't think he will have any trouble staying on task, and he is always focused. Perhaps you could mentor him?" she nudged his shoulder.

She leaned in to hug him and whispered, "You can do it. You have so much wisdom to share."

At that moment, Bridgit could hear Gordavin's response as she was pulled back through the wooden doorway, "I will see what I can dooooooo...", his voice echoed then trailed off.

As Bridgit made her reentry through the doorway, she noticed a new glyph immediately coming into form. There was no time for rest or conversation as the next meeting was clearly about to take place. Bridgit grabbed the bar from her dress and took a bite from it while examining thirteen dots forming a glyph that resembled the letter Y or possibly an antenna, she thought. She was visibly tired. Shamalaine delayed the lesson temporarily and offered her daughter a cold beverage as Bridgit ate her oat bar to build her energy up one more time.

    And the wheel turns... ⊕

Chapter 15

The Blueprint Master's Graduation

In a large amphitheater filled with the presence of the Heavenly Hosts, sat well over one thousand participants in the Divine Creators Blueprint Master program. Each of the participants prepared for the application of seeding new worlds. In this room sat the Angels at the top of their class, and only nine of them could be chosen for the mission of seeding a new frequency within the realms of Earth.

Those not chosen would have their gifts used on other planes of existence as there were always worlds within worlds to be seeded, but they all hoped to be chosen for the coveted New Earth project. These particular Blueprint Angels were on the path to becoming Archangels, and seeding new worlds where they were able to work with human Life Bearers would tip the scale for their eventual jump to Archangel.

"Each system of worlds is built on frequencies or energetic signatures that resonate with the highest potential in form, which is love." The Archangel Gabriel spoke these words at the beginning of his address to the class.

"On behalf of the Keeper of the Scrolls, I, Gabriel, am honored to make the following Scroll presentations. When you hear your name, please come up to the stage." He prepared the scrolls next to the podium and continued the presentation.

"Malachi, of the sixth ring, please come to the stage," Gabriel spoke his request of the first graduating candidate. The silver-haired Malachi was seated with the others from the sixth ring and made his way to the stage. He floated up towards the podium, wearing an ornate gold graduation gown. The gown had a V-shaped neckline with elaborate diamond studs along the hem. On the right side of the gown, upon the chest area was a Violet Flame insignia.

As Gabriel congratulated Malachi on a job well done, Malachi faced the audience. As the cheers roared, the Violet Flame insignia burst into a real flame and activated the scroll given to him. At that moment, Malachi absorbed the blueprint within his very essence for all to see.

His work would be to assist the Life Bearers working on the whole systems of the new world. A biosphere engineer would be the best words to describe his talents. Fireworks began to explode above Malachi's head, and great jubilation was heard in the auditorium. Malachi humbly bowed to Archangel Gabriel and then to the audience. He took a seat upon a golden chair.

Gabriel called the next candidate to the stage. "Jermaine, of the tenth ring, please come to the stage."

Jermaine made his way down the long corridor from where the other tenth ring angels sat. He wore a similar graduation gown as Malachi, indicating his equal level of attainment within the Angelic Hierarchy. Jermaine arrived at the stage to receive the scroll from Gabriel and bowed in reverence to him.

His height was substantial, compared to the others, and therefore a larger chair had been prepared for him. As Jermaine stood on the stage, he held the scroll in his hands. The flame on his robe began to brighten at that moment, just as Malachi's did. With his eyes closed, he absorbed the energetic upgrade to receive the download.

Numerical codes began transmitting above his head in a green matrix. New theories and equations were transmitted and absorbed by Jermaine, and the crowd was applauding as they saw the codes downloading into him.

Much like Malachi, Jermaine was a Noosphere engineer. His angelic talents were in the realms of the cosmic mind. Jermaine bowed to the crowd and turned back to Gabriel to humbly accept his new position on the team.

Gabriel bowed to him, and Jermaine made his way to the second golden chair next to Malachi.

Gabriel called forth the third name on the list of nine. "Hiiyup, from the second Order of the Star, please come to the stage."

Hiiyup was the first female Angel who received a scroll. Her long dark hair flowed midway down her back with violet-colored embers that lit up her locks. Wearing the same golden robe with the Violet Flame insignia, she flowed effortlessly to the podium to receive the scroll from Gabriel.

As the scroll touched her hand, Hiiyup, read the contents with every atom of her being, then she began to glow. Hiiyup's specialty as a Blueprint Master was with the minerals of a planetary system. Her ability to imbue intelligence within gems and minerals made her a candidate for the coveted role of a Blueprint Master.

She went into a full-on flare of the Violet Flame, and as she opened her eyes, she now had diamond star-shaped pupils, which would stay with her from this point on. Her hair was now in a blaze of Violet Fire. It danced around her sparkling hair in waves. This, too, would be her new look as she transformed into the third Blueprint Master. She bowed to Archangel Gabriel and found her seat next to Jermaine.

Abdonna was the next Angel called. Gabriel spoke, "Abdonna, from the seventh Order of the Star, come to the stage."

Abdonna was moving up the ranks to Blueprint Master quickly. She had been chosen for this honor for her work in the Pegasian Star System, where she worked to assist animals in their evolution, and mainly the Pegasus being her primary interest.

Abdonna's pitch-black hair was wild with streaks of white, and as she received her scroll, like Hiiyup, the energy transmission caused her eyes to transform.

She burst into flames of multi-colors, and as the sparks began to smolder, she stood to present herself with two black stars around her eyes that took up most of her face as the points reached down towards her cheeks. Above her head, a saying floated within the smoldering smoke. It read, "She knows now what the stars mean, so, shall she wait for one to fall or shall she try to catch one."

The audience was captivated by the meaning of the words as they watched the words get reabsorbed into the scroll that Abdonna held upward in her hand.

Abdonna's work would continue to be seeding new species of animals in a star system on the brink of extinction. Everyone could feel the dire straits of the mission of the Blueprint Masters being commissioned to the third planet from the sun in the Milky Way Galaxy. A task that all were very aware of being a vital one for the entire galaxy and one that would affect the Andromeda Galaxy as well.

Gabriel thanked Abdonna for her service and asked her to take a seat in the golden chair next to Hiiyup. He then turned to the podium to call forth the next Blueprint Master.

"Graeceous, of the first ring, please come to the stage to receive your scroll."

Graeceous was an angel who worked with the ley lines of world systems. He maintained the energetic grids that held the frequencies of a planet. A humble being, he floated up to the podium in a humble manner.

The audience was exuberant that he had been chosen for this mission. He arrived at the stage and bowed to Gabriel.

He gratefully accepted the scroll in his hand, and as he felt the energy of the scroll, he saw the work he would be doing updating the planetary grid system. He also saw dragons and guardians, who would be the protectors of these grids, and a relationship between the two would be vital.

Graeceous bowed to Gabriel and said to him, "It is an honor to be chosen for this mission." His robe began to catch fire. The Violet Flame entirely consumed him. The crowd watched as they could see new colors being born. Around his head emanated a rainbow of light which blended with his feathery blond hair, and as the flames smoldered, he would carry the new rainbow colors within his hair. It was a glorious sight to see. The energy continued to build as Graeceous made his way to his golden chair.

Gabriel let the cheering subside before he called the next scroll candidate. He could see in the eyes of all of the observers in the auditorium and a brilliance in their auras. It pleased him greatly.

He then announced, "Starseed, of the fourth Order of the Star, would you please come forth to accept your scroll?"

Like the other two female angels before her, she floated down the long corridor, making her way to the podium. Her presence could be detected by merely listening to her as she moved. Starseed's appearance was unique in that her hair was shaved almost entirely, except for the golden hair spun on top of her head in a swirling vortex, and within that vortex was a tiny galaxy. Balanced within this galaxy, were small planets that could be seen whirling around. One could hear the soft pitches and tones in various octaves, like a cosmic signature of her very essence, a celestial perfume. Her beauty was flawless, the perfect picture of a blueprint followed to the measure.

Starseed bowed to Gabriel as she accepted her scroll. Closing her eyes, she held the scroll to her heart flame and absorbed the details of her mission. Her assignment would be to hold resonance with the Builders of Form and Life Bearers to create the perfect pitch of the new world, the new frequency that would keep the world in balance.

Pleased with her mission, she began to transform into a higher octave of herself. As she opened her eyes, she had a six-pointed star around each of her eyes, which balanced out the pink diamond shapes that now were upon her cheeks. Starseed maneuvered to her golden chair as the audience could detect a new celestial sound, the music of the spheres harmonizing as she took her seat.

Gabriel looked at the six Blueprint Masters seated next to him on the stage. He still always marveled at the brilliance of the Divine Plan in action. He gave thanks to the Creator for his part in it.

Gabriel spoke, "It is a special privilege to announce that we have Twin Flame angels to receive their scrolls together. Platter and Platina, two of the Keepers of the Platinum Ray, please join us on stage to receive your scrolls."

He waved his arm to his side to indicate the others on the stage, and he listened as the auditorium murmured in awe of these two Twin Flame Angels of the Platinum Ray being called into service to seed a new world. The Platinum frequency usually reserved for higher dimensions indicated the degree to which this new world would be different.

Platter and Platina exhibited giftedness in energy transmissions, being experts in plasma infusion techniques for healing and protection, which had been well received in other planetary systems. Gabriel watched as the twin flame angels approached wearing dark silver colored spandex jumpsuits. Their sleek, long, silver hair was kept in a ponytail with a platinum metal clasp with leaf features displayed on them.

The twins stood before Gabriel and bowed when receiving their scrolls. Plasma orbs rotated above their heads as they breathed in new codes and frequencies of light. The twins acknowledged the fact that both of them would be bridging the energy of the Platinum Ray in new ways into the Time Matrix with other Time Masters on the seeding team. This new assignment would be a challenge and a gift.

Platter held his scroll in his right hand as his twin flame, Platina, held hers in her left hand. They raised them upward and, in the same moment, were engulfed in a Platinum Violet fire. When the blending of energies completed, the twin Blueprint Masters gratefully walked to the golden chairs to join the others.

Gabriel prepared the last of the scrolls to be presented. Looking at the audience, he spoke. "TurAgus, of the fifth ring, please come up to receive your scroll. The last Angel stood, and it was clear that from his appearance, he was an angel of order and balance. His hair and clothing were black and white, a walking yin and yang symbol.

This unique being carried himself in perfect balance, with one white shoe and one black shoe, with the left side of his hair white and the right side of his hair black. He kept his shiny hair in a bowl cut that curved under in a slight curl at the bottom. Even the color of TurAgus's feathers was black and white. This angel brought balance in all his activities.

TurAgus now stood in front of Gabriel to receive the scroll. Holding the scroll to his heart flame, TurAgus was informed of the task at hand to seed the nutrients in the planet and mineral kingdoms with new cellular information, which would assist the life forms in this new world to advance quickly into higher forms of light. It would require a perfect balance of the elements, as well as that of male and female energies present in nature. This balance would weave the innate nature of Father-Mother God into the air and the water.

TurAgus was in complete rapture as he felt a surge within his being. He was in such appreciation that he folded his wings around himself and morphed into the scroll, leaving a less physical form standing as he explored the scroll in depth. Moments later, he came back into form, holding two vials of life force dangling from a cord, which he then placed around his neck. One was a silver vial, and the other was in an onyx colored vial. It was the life force of the male and female aspects of the Creator, which now hung from TurAgus's neck. Gabriel and TurAgus bowed to one another, and TurAgus took his seat next to the others.

Gabriel blew his horn to conclude the Scroll presentations and indicated that everyone was welcome to share in the celebration afterward to congratulate the Blueprint Masters. He mentioned that these angels were chosen out of thousands of applicants.

He ended his talk, saying, "There is so much untapped potential sitting here upon this stage, and what they do in the field will be blazing a trail for others to follow." With that, he dismissed the Blueprint Masters from the stage, and the well-wishers began to approach them with congratulatory sentiments, and they all joined in the fellowship.

And the wheel turns...

Chapter 16

Meeting of the Final Two Builders of Form

Standing in the golden-hued room, Shamalaine was discussing with Bridgit the words spoken by Gordavin in the planning session about the jump points. She went on to talk about the presence of the Ascended Master St. Germain and the Life Bearers who were present in their light bodies.

Shamalaine looked at Bridgit and said, "The time has come to gather the Life Bearers in the third dimensional realm. You will need to find them as swiftly as possible."

Bridgit was tasked to find the Life Bearers, and as she heard the words come from Shamalaine's mouth, she felt a reverberating sound within her body, like an anchor hitting the bottom of the ocean floor. Her mind was still reeling from the fact that she lives in the 3D world as Bridgit, an Arborist. Just an ordinary girl, she thought, and now she found herself in another realm being told of her destiny as a Life Bearer and that she is tasked to find the other Life Bearers soon.

In her mind, she was calculating how long it would take her to find them when she came out of her contemplation with a strange sound.

The wooden door began to emit a sound that moved Bridgit's energy to her third eye. She could hear the singing of an Indian song coming from a female voice. The chanting wrapped around her body and lifted her into the air. She levitated there for a while, and then the energy pulled her into the doorway.

Shamalaine held space for her, allowing for Bridgit's memory of the sixth Builder of Form to return.

On the other side of the door, Bridgit found herself in an ancient garden near an Indian temple. Realizing that she had not been in this landscape before, to her recollection, she was eager to explore the surroundings. She could hear the faint singing of the Devi Prayer coming from nearby.

Bridgit, transfixed by the way the frequency delivered the song to her heart and her third eye, could barely stand as the energies began to rise. She knew she must sit because any movement was not an option at this point.

Finding a spot near a lotus pond where an ancient tree stood, Bridgit went even deeper into the frequency of sounds within the prayer as she slid to the ground next to the tree. She felt the uncoiling of her energy rise from her root, along her spine, pulsing from one side of her spine to the other, as a spiral of energy flowed up her chakra channel to her head. As it reached her mind's eye, the force of this libidinal energy caused her to fall back against the tree behind her.

Floating down from the top of the tree was the source of the song that brought Bridgit into the state of rapture. Bridgit could feel the presence of the Divine Mother, being delivered to her through the energy of the song. Finally, as her energy stabilized, the tiny Goddess, sitting on top of a lotus, floated in front of Bridgit's head and presented herself as the next Builder of Form.

She gently nodded her head as she presented herself, "I am Padmavati, the sixth Builder of Form for the New World."

Her appearance took Bridgit by surprise. This tiny Builder of Form was no more than eight inches in height and was ethereal. Her dark black hair had strands of Indigo mixed throughout her head, and she wore a tiny crown with two white lotus petals positioned over her forehead with a dark blue jewel at the center just over her third eye.

Bridgit spoke once she felt she could hold her body up. "Thank you, Padmavati, for the gift that you have given me. Your song pierced my soul and activated my sight in a way that I have not felt before."

Padmavati smiled, and with her hands together, she bowed to Bridgit and said, "The path of the Rainbow Bridge is now open. I am at your service."

She bowed once more to Bridgit and then pulled out a small bansuri flute that hung from her flowing skirt and began to play.

Codes of light infiltrated Bridgit's mind's eye, codes that would unlock her mind, heart, and soul. As the sixth Builder of Form played, the sounds wove a unique tapestry within the ether, a gift, blending nature and music, the music of the spheres.

Bridgit could barely move as she was unwrapping this gift in her heart. She heard a chime from a distance, which brought her out of her inner world. She could feel the familiar pull on her energy from the doorway. She could not speak due to the tremendous energies that she was experiencing. In her mind, she telepathically sent a message to Padmavati that she would see her again soon. A second chime sounded. Bridgit was pulled back through the doorway, back into the golden-hued room, and into the arms of Shamalaine.

Shamalaine said, "Come, sit here," as she brought Bridgit back to the Chair of Remembrance. She gave Bridgit the liquid that would stabilize her energy. Bridgit could barely hold the cup to drink as Shamalaine assisted her. Shamalaine toned a musical sound, as she put her hand on her daughter's forehead to balance the energies.

Shamalaine continued to work on Bridgit's energy around the third eye, and suddenly, with a swift movement of her hand upward, Bridgit felt heat moving up to her crown chakra. The energy expanded within her head as she took deep breaths.

The chair began to accelerate once more, with Bridgit going inward again as if she was under a psychedelic spell. She could feel the presence of a higher frequency, not in form, but still very much real.

As she continued being absorbed in this energy, she felt like she was floating in the sun. The brightness took over the room. She began to acclimate to this ever-living force of intelligence and codes. She breathed deeply once more, filling her being with the incoming light, and as she did, the energy in the room came back into focus. She opened her eyes, hoping to still be in the physical.

Shamalaine monitored Bridgit's process and brought her attention to the wooden door once more. There, emblazoned upon the door, was an orange and yellow sun, turning clockwise, then counter-clockwise, growing and then shrinking as it turned in both directions. She watched as the sun began to rotate faster. Two tubular-shaped rainbows started to form, one on each side of the sun.

Shamalaine helped Bridgit up, and the two of them walked over to the door to inspect the image displayed. The rainbows then extended from the door, as her energetic pathway to the next Builder of Form. Bridgit looked at her mother, then turned to look at the door once more, not sure that she had the energy within her to make this last journey.

The violet color stood out more prominently now and filled her with a renewal of spirit. She absorbed it into her entire being, then she breathed deeply and took a step upon it. Bridgit was whisked away through the door once more on a violet-colored magic carpet.

Upon her arrival, she stood in the space of no time. It was dark. She could hear the sounds that resembled a whale, from deep within the ocean, but this was more of a celestial sound, she thought. Still trying to get her bearings, it was clear that she was on a different planet, but where she had no idea.

She looked at her feet to see if she was even in a physical reality. She noted that her feet were on a solid terrestrial sphere. She could not see much else, as it was extremely dark. Her intuition was that she was on holy ground. It felt sacred, like that of a temple. She used her newly opened third eye to try to sense where she was, as she began scanning the landscape. Directly to her left, no more than twenty feet, she could sense what felt like an entrance to a temple.

"Come to me," she heard in her inner ear. "Do not be afraid. I see you in the night," the voice continued.

Bridgit was unsure of herself and what she was hearing. Then the voice was heard again.

"I will shine the light. Come." At that moment, Bridgit stood her ground. The darkness lifted. There to her left, as she sensed it, was indeed a temple that looked like the Grecian temples of the past, with columns at each corner and a vast stairway that ran the length of the temple.

Bridgit was somewhat unsure how to proceed, wondering what was within the temple. Then she heard, "I have opened the door for you. Enter the door of freedoms light."

From the moment that she stepped inside the temple, she felt the energy of the Violet Flame engulf her from her feet to the top of her head. Everything that she once held deeply within her, hiding from the light, was now coming up to be released within the all-consuming violet flame of transmutation.

"Enter Life Bearer." She looked to the center of the room for the voice. She moved towards the middle of the room to find a square-shaped pool of Violet-Platinum colored liquid, with stairs on all four sides of the pool.

"What is this place?" Bridgit wondered in her mind.

A voice answered her. "This is a temple consecrated to the Violet Fire used to transmute all negative energies."

Bridgit slowly walked down the steps of the pool. She instinctually knew to immerse herself in the pool completely.

She heard the voice again. It began to make decrees on Bridgit's behalf to demonstrate the use of the violet fire. "I AM A BEING OF VIO-LET FIRE... I AM A BEING OF VIOLET FIRE." Over and over again, the voice chanted the decree until the shift was palpable.

Bridgit took a breath, and again, she dunked herself completely and stayed submerged as long as she could, allowing for the purification of her being to anchor fully.

She came up for air, and as she stood in the center of the pool, contemplating what was being sharing, a flicker of light caught her attention. On the walls were mounted flaming torches. On the far wall, to the right of the pool, shadows of the flame danced with wild abandon. The sounds of the flickering flames and the movement they made upon the wall captivated Bridgit's attention.

Bridgit noticed the shadow from the flame bounce off of the wall with great stealth and was no longer a shadow, but a living embodi-ment of the Violet Flame standing before her. The being, dressed in a dark purple ninjutsu attire, took off the hood that veiled his face and bowed to her. "I am Phyre, a Keeper of the Violet Flame, and the seventh Builder of Form. I am at your service."

She looked at his hair at that moment as it began to blaze with the most fantastic Violet flames with nuances of a Platinum overtone of color and frequency. She bowed to him and announced who she was, and they smiled, knowing that he had been expecting her. He reached within his flaming hair and pulled out a small lava stone. He placed it in her hand and said, "This holds your very own flame. I have been holding it for you, as Kaialena instructed me to do."

She looked at him with both gratitude and confusion.

Bridgit held the stone to her heart. As she did, it jumped from her hand and absorbed into her chest. She looked at Phyre as he spoke, "As a Keeper of the Flame, you are asked to burn the flame within you always, using it daily to not only keep yourself clean of all debris but those around you. This is a gift that has been given to humanity at a time of grave peril. Use it for the ALL from this day forward. The gift of the Violet Flame is to be the saving grace that opens the door when fear you face."

They bowed to one another in recognition of the sacredness of the moment. The swirling sound of energy began as they looked into one another's eyes. She said, "Phyre, thank you for this gift. I am honored to have you on the team with the Builders of Form. It is time for me to go back now, but we will see one another soon."

Bridgit put her hand to her heart in reverence, feeling the flame within her, and was taken back through the door so quickly, it felt to her like a rubber band snapping after being fully stretched.

Bridgit emerged through the wooden doorway, not spent, but revitalized. She walked into the embrace of her beloved mother, the one that had been her champion, confidant, and greatest teacher in days past. Bridgit said, "I am ready."

She looked into her mother's eyes, thinking how much she admired her for the work that she has done on behalf of the ALL. She felt deeply blessed to be born into this lineage and, in particular, to be her daughter.

And the wheel turns...

Chapter 17

The Appointing of the Final Builder of Form

The journey to the banyan tree could potentially have many challenges. Bewain was designing a plan to have Bridgit escorted to the Cave of Doorways.

The cave location was situated near the boundaries of the overlap zone, where the human realm and the elemental kingdom, at times, merged. This area was the zone of "bleed-through" that Shamalaine referred too earlier. Because of the energetics of this region, other things were concerning her.

The cave would provide a safe passage to get Bridgit closer to another world tree that existed in multiple realms like Tuuru, but the journey was considered to be dangerous. Anything could happen while traveling to access this cave, and all involved would have to be very cautious.

While Bewain focused on the mission at hand, Shamalaine called for Avery to give him the news that he was called to stand before the Elohim, but hearing this news put Avery into a tailspin.

"What do you mean, your excellence? Why would they call for me? I haven't done anything wrong!" He began to search his mind for any clue to help him come to terms with this highly unusual turn of events.

Shamalaine just watched him fret for a few moments, enjoying the entertaining expressions on his face as he tried to figure it out. She decided to ease his mind and let him in on the secret.

"Calm down, Avery. You're not in trouble. On the contrary, you are being asked to present your credentials to the council for consideration as a Builder of Form for the New Earth." Holding her hands in front of her, Shamalaine watched Avery's delayed reaction as he processed the information.

Avery took every word in that Shamalaine said, "Council... my credentials", he wrote each word in his journal, like a good scribe.

Speaking out loud, to help him process, he continued, "For consideration as a Builder of Form for the New Earth." As he wrote the words, New Earth, his writing went off the page, and his hand smeared the words, due to the jerk reaction he had, as he finally understood what Shamalaine was presenting to him.

Eyes wide open and a heart that picked up its pace, Avery looked up at a smiling Shamalaine, who was waiting to see what he might do. Avery took his cap off and kneeled at her feet with his head bowed down. He spoke, "Your Grace, I don't know what to say. For the first time I am truly speechless."

Amused, Shamalaine said, "Come now, Avery, surely a momentous occasion as this would warrant a few words." She made her way to a chair and twirled her dress in front of her as she sat. Waving her hand to him, she motioned for him to join her. Avery walked to where she sat, and with his head bowed and staring at the cap in his hand to focus, he spoke.

"I have dreamed of being on a team of Builders of World-Systems ever since I can remember, but I fear that I do not have the qualifications

84

in the years of experience to be able to make a successful candidate. I am sorry to disappoint you your excellence", Avery said sadly.

Shamalaine appreciated his gestures and his concern and said, "Avery, look at me." She reached over and pulled his chin upwards so that she could look him in the eye.

"It came to Bridgit's attention that the committee for the seeding of the New Earth was having trouble finding a Builder who displayed certain characteristics that would be needed for the team to be complete. When hearing this, Bridgit asked the team leader what qualifications were required. It became clear to her that you were the obvious candidate for the position. Given her status and her experience, they took her recommendation to heart, but you will need to present your qualifications yourself, with confidence, I might add."

She winked at him as Avery stood straight and cleared his voice and said, "Yes, your Excellency."

Dumbfounded by what he was hearing, Avery got a little choked up hearing the news that he had been handpicked by the team leader of the Life Bearers.

"You must gather your things and prepare for this meeting to take place in two days. Do you think two days is sufficient?" Shamalaine asked.

"Ah," he exaggerated his comment to give him time to think. He then said, "Two days is more than fair." Avery again bowed his head in reverence to Shamalaine for the opportunity that she was providing him.

Looking at him, Shamalaine had an intuition come to her. With a bit of a giggle, Shamalaine asked, "You already have your petition prepared, don't you?" while looking for a reaction from the little guy standing before her.

A long "ahh" sound came out of his mouth. Avery grinned as he looked up at Shamalaine. Twisting the string of his pouch with one hand and pointing his left foot forward while making swirls on the ground, he said with a sheepish smile, "I have had my petition ready for many a moon, your Excellency. Just in case the opportunity ever came up, but I assure you that in my wildest dreams, I could not have presumed that it would come so soon."

Not surprised at all, Shamalaine asked, "And is it completely up to date?"

Clearing his throat, he responded. "As of last night." They both started to chuckle at the realization that he was exceptionally qualified for the job in the way of efficiency.

Shamalaine nodded her head with utter amazement at this elf's attention to every detail.

She said, "Gordavin will come for you, but in the meantime, why don't you get started filling in today's information?" She winked at him, then took her leave. As he watched her leave his presence, he pulled out his scroll and quill to do just what she said and then realized that there wasn't anything else to add, and at that moment, he understood just precisely why she found him humorous.

And the wheel turns... ⊕

Chapter 18

The Guardians

Standing by the fireplace in the study of the Great Hall, Bewain entrusted Eldorman with gathering a team of qualified kinfolk to journey with Bridgit to the Cave of Doorways, which included the Guardian Butler.

Bewain said, "Safety in numbers, right ole boy?" He patted Eldorman's shoulder as they concluded their meeting in his study. Eldorman was kind in his reassurance to Bewain that the team would have sufficient protection, and that Avery would tag along to give him more time with Kaialena before her return to the human world as Bridgit.

Bewain was glad to hear that Avery would accompany Kaialena on the journey, as he knew that it would be a boost to Avery to have some final words with the Life Bearer in preparation for his upcoming meeting the Elohim. Once Eldorman left the room, Bewain pulled out his pipe and held it in his hand, tamping down the herb concoction within it while in his mind giving considerable thought to the whole scenario. Fate would have to be on their side.

He knew it would be a dangerous journey as factions within the realms were not all at peace, something that Bewain monitored and continued to work towards every day of his life, and the reason for the cloaking of the Clan of Phare's lair.

The next day the Guardian, Butler, arrived. He was known to have a massive heart within the elemental realms, as his love for all of creation preceded him. Butler was by far the most unique of individuals, and notably, an exceptional Guardian. His skill at wielding a hammer was known far and wide, but what was most interesting about Butler was his Zen-like nature and his particular care of the animals. He was a faithful Guardian of all life forms.

Butler was described by many as having the strength of a bear. When push came to shove, he would not hesitate to protect the preciousness of life, and given that the Life Bearer, Kaialena, was a most valuable part of the divine plan as Bridgit in the 3D world, Bewain was grateful to have two well-qualified Guardians to watch over her.

And the wheel turns...

Chapter 19

Breacher Breaches the Human Realm

Breacher made his way to the human realm and was standing in Bridgit's bedroom at the Inn, looking for something specific. Shamalaine had requested Breacher's assistance because of his useful bilocation skills. She told Breacher that Kaialena would need a few things once she returned to the human realm as Bridgit.

Breacher looked around Bridgit's room to get a feel for the human aspect of his beloved. He noted all of the pictures taped to the mirror above her chest of drawers were mainly of trees. Interestingly, she had drawn a few space ships as well.

As Breacher looked at the hodge-podge of pictures from a human perspective, one would possibly feel that the spacecraft was out of sync with her nature-oriented images. Breacher understood all of the images that Bridgit had so carefully chosen to place around her room were remembrances of other places in time that she somehow recalled. He took it as a good sign that even in her human form, she had an affinity for things similar to her interests in her other life.

Another example of her memory bleed through was an orchid placed on the table next to her bed. Around the orchid was a set of seashells in an intricate pattern as an energetic grid. Breacher examined the pattern and grinned. She had somehow recalled from her life with him how to assist plants with specific geometric designs, especially when water was scarce.

Bridgit left a water bottle sitting on the writing desk, which he grabbed and reverently administered to the plant. Placing the water bottle back on her writing desk, next to her purse, he noticed something that Bridgit had scribbled on the sides of her pictures, like a frame. On the framing of each picture were always the words, WHERE IS HE?

One picture that touched his heart had a water stain. It was her tears that had stained the print, and he guessed that in this world, Bridgit did not use a shell when she cried. What was equally clear to him is her love for someone that she seemed to be haunting her heart. He hoped that it was he that she was thinking of.

He grabbed what he had come for and took the tear-stained picture to have near to his heart. He moved his hand in a motion that seemed to move the molecules in the room and swiftly moved through the fabric of space and time and walked through a doorway. He was gone.

And the wheel turns...

Chapter 20

The Journey to the Cave of Doorways

Trekking through the dark woods with Butler at the front of the ensemble, the troop walked in silence. As they approached a clearing, they could hear sounds nearby.

Butler motioned with his eyes to be vigilant and watch for anything. As he pulled back on a branch to widen his view, he chuckled out loud, motioning for the others to come closer. They all gathered at the edge of the woods as they watched a parade of mushroom beings and other whimsical elementals display their regalia as they made their way to the fair.

The mushroom beings were decorated in fancy clothing with ruffled collars as they rode on top of small woodland rabbits with saddles that allowed the mushroom people to stand tall, keeping their plume intact.

The leader of the mushroom brigade carried a staff and stood at attention as if he was a commander in a private army. His curly gray hair ruffled out from under his tall hat, and wisps of his gray eyebrow hair shot out over his eyes, pointing wildly in multiple directions. His intense stare and staunch demeanor confirmed his leadership. His mushroom body was decorated with swirls of creamy brown and gray colors. He wore a jacket made of a silky brown material that matched the colored swirls on his plume.

Butler made sure to go ahead to see where the mushroom elementals were heading. The leader halted the troops to speak with Butler. The commander spoke of a festival nearby and mentioned to Butler that there would be plenty of food, and his group was welcome to make camp there for the night and enjoy a festive evening.

Butler, thinking it a great idea to camp with a larger group for protection, accepted the commander's offer and went back to the group, who were waiting at the edge of the forest.

Butler approached the group and said, "We have been invited by the mushroom beings to join them at this evening's festivities. It is not a far walk from here, but I think we should take a short break now, to refresh ourselves with some water, and then we can meet up with the others before nightfall."

Bridgit said, "Butler, I am happy to take a break for just a little while." She smiled at him as he curtseyed in a playful manner that made them all laugh with joyful anticipation of the kind of entertainment they might look forward to later in the evening.

Bridgit rubbed her head in a moment of weakness. Eldorman was keeping a keen eye on her, given the fact that it was only a few days since she had come through Tuuru, with a head injury.

Eldorman asked Bridgit, "Are you okay, my lady?", looking at her forehead.

"Oh, yes. I just feel a little light-headed. Perhaps some water will help me hydrate. I am sure I will be fine", trying to reassure him.

"Let me serve you some water." Eldorman pulled the flask from his side belt loop. Attached to the flask was a water stone hanging on a cord. Knowing that water stone would balance her, he offered it to Bridgit. Thankful, Bridgit placed it on her neck, holding the cord, so that the stone stayed in place.

She could immediately feel her energy balance, and the discomfort eased. Astonished, she thanked Eldorman and said, "It is much better already. Shall we go on now?" Looking at the others to see if they had sufficiently rested.

They walked the distance in silent contemplation of the following day, the day where they would arrive at the Cave of Doorways if all went well. Each was contemplating the stories that they had heard of the hidden chambers and the many doorways, wondering how they would navigate the pathways correctly to get Bridgit to her destination, the exit from their realm and back into the human world. The task was to help her safely find the passage that would lead her to the World Tree.

"We are near the campsite," Butler announced, as he glanced back at the worried looks of his companions.

Eldorman said, "Let's try to enjoy ourselves this evening. Keep a good watch, but try to mingle with the Mushroom folk and participate in their festivities." He winked at the whole lot of them with a cheerful smile, and that seemed to uplift the weary travelers.

The group enjoyed the fellowship of the mushroom beings and filled their bellies with deliciously light, creamy foods grown from the fertile lands. The music played softly, late into the evening as they all settled in to prepare for sleep. The group was grateful for the company and the abundance that flowed freely in the land.

Bridgit was contemplating all that she had rediscovered in her homeland as the thoughts of going back to the 3D human world was becoming overwhelming. How was she going to find the other Life Bearers, she wondered.

That evening Bridgit's sleep came quickly, as she was utterly exhausted over the last few day's events. Traveling by foot to the Cave of Doorways had taken its toll on her. While in twilight sleep, lucidly aware, codes and symbols began to flow in her mind's eye. Glyphs and numbers in sequences presented upon her mental screen. The codes kept repeating as her mind began to decipher the meaning of the codes that would unlock the dimensional doorways.

She could see the doors opening one by one, and what was behind them was frightening. Tricks of the mind, mechanized spiders and all sorts of other horrid things behind each door she opened. Then suddenly, the energy shifted. Bridgit could see symbols of trees, shapes, colors, and numbers. The possibilities for the activation of the doorway were endless. Stressed within the dream, she jolted out of sleep.

Opening her eyes, she saw hovering over her a vision of Phyre, the seventh Builder of Form that she met in the Violet Flame Temple. She could hear him decree once more. "The gift of the Violet Flame is to be the saving grace that opens the door when fear you face." She breathed in so deeply that the vision entered her being. The Violet Fire consumed her body, mind, and spirit and prepared her to enter the Cave of Doorways.

The next day, Bridgit and the others said goodbye to the mushroom clan, who so kindly fed and entertained them the evening before. They gathered their things and moved onward towards the Cave of Doorways.

As she walked, Bridgit kept having flashes of her dreams. The codes popping upon her mental screen took her into a higher mental plane, one where she could pick the lock, activating the codes and visualize her safe return to the 3rd-dimensional world of the human beings of Earth.

At the same time, Butler was on full guard, as was Eldorman. After walking for some time, Bridgit came out of her thoughts as they neared the area not far from the Cave of Doorways. The group could see the rock outcropping in the distance as they came down a sloped area, with a riverbed running between them and the cave.

Butler's hair on his forearm stood on end, a sign to him that they were not alone, and that danger was lurking. He turned to get a full 360-degree view of the terrain and saw a glimpse of a strange red cloud formation. As he watched it, he could see an ominous creature within it. Butler turned to the others and yelled, "RUN!!!"

Everyone began running swiftly down the rugged slope. The cloud formation was moving in closer now, as a pack of hyenas were in sight and closing in on the group. The ground was difficult to navigate, with the rock and fissures between the group and the Cave of Doorways.

Bridgit was running for her life as the hyenas were gaining on them. She yelled out to Eldorman, who was behind her to her left, "Who sent these hyenas?"

Eldorman yelled for her to duck under the branches of the trees ahead so that they could get a better look at the shape forming within the cloud. Butler stayed further behind, trying to lead the hyenas away from Bridgit and Eldorman, but a few of the hyenas separated from the pack.

Bridgit and Eldorman watched the cloud morph into a face of an evil bird-headed man, and as they watched, his eye began to grow larger, and soon, they could only see his eye, as if it was looking into a magnifying glass, searching for his prey. As he spotted Bridgit, the eye began to glow. Pulses of red light began shooting out from the eye, onto the ground, causing the Earth to shake, like lightning striking the ground. They had to get to the Cave of Doorways.

Just then, Butler caught up to them and yelled for Bridgit to follow him. He said, "This isn't good!!! That being... that is the Dark One of Aln! Come on!" Butler directed them to follow him down the riverbed as the earth floor shook once more.

Bridgit looked back to the others and yelled, "This Way!", always concerned for others over her own well-being.

Tears ran down her face as memories flowed. She realized who she was up against. The Dark One of Aln was the cause of the Clan leaving their home planet, and now he was trying to take over all of Earth.

This time, she thought, she will not let Earth be taken in the same way. We have to make it to the Cave of Doorways, she thought.

Bridgit and the others could hear the yelping of the hyenas approaching. She thought that the best way to maneuver would be through the water, knowing that the hyenas would most likely choose to cross at the lower water crossing and backtrack. She hoped that it would give them the time they needed to get to the entrance of the cave.

Butler said, "There!" pointing to a small raft that could get them over to the other side of the water a bit quicker. "Jump on," motioning to the smaller elves and Bridgit. Butler helped them all get onto the raft and pushed off swiftly into the deeper water just moments before the hyenas arrived.

A mist had formed across the valley upon the arrival of the Dark One of Aln. It was almost now impossible to see the other side of the riverbed at this point. Eldorman, sat in the front of the raft, in case of a frontal attack, and was completely ready to protect the Life Bearer at all costs. He began to chant an incantation that cleared the path in front of them.

He looked backward at Butler and yelled out, "We won't have much time once we get to the other side. I will need you to stay positioned at the edge of the water to intercept the hyenas. Remember, they are under the spell of the Dark One. Use force only when necessary."

Looking at the others, he continued, "We will take Bridgit to the doorway while Butler distracts the animals." Butler was in full agreement and pushed with all of his strength to get them to the other side of the narrow riverbed. The hyenas took the low water crossing as Bridgit suspected, and they were already in pursuit once more.

The group hit the other side of the river's edge and began to quickly unload from the raft, all the while hearing the hyena approaching closer. They spotted the cave approximately one hundred feet from the shoreline up a gentle incline. The cave was located on the side of a cliff wall.

The Dark One of Aln was relentless in his pursuit to reach Bridgit, to keep her from getting to the Cave of Doorways. Rain began to down-pour, making the ground muddy and slick in spots, giving the hyenas the advantage now.

Eldorman continued his chanting as did the other elementals, invoking the cooperation of nature and the elements that they have mastery over. Avery worked with the trees to provide an umbrella of branches above their heads as Eldorman hardened the ground that they walked upon. They soon reached the face of the cave.

Standing at the mouth of the cave, Bridgit was shocked to see that it literally looked like a stone face, carved into the side of the cliff, with a massive boulder in front of the mouth or entrance of the cave.

Butler caught up with them within fifteen feet and warned them of the hyenas' approach. Avery and the other elves joined forces with Butler to create a barrier between the Life Bearer and the hyenas. Eldorman stayed with Bridgit holding a calming and protective force field while Bridgit attempted to activate the entrance of the cave.

Butler, Avery, and the others fought off the ferocious hyenas, one by one. They used every weapon they had, something that they had never had to use before, but this was no ordinary fight. Bridgit concentrated on her task. Butler swung his hammer as the sounds of arrows from the elves whizzed past the trees near them. Yelping hyenas were heard as the elementals continued to hold their ground.

Eldorman stood in front of the wall and examined the nose just above them. Bridgit concentrated on the stone area around the mouth of the cave, not having a clue how to open the doorway of the cave.

"Anything?" she asked Eldorman.

He took a stance in front of the cave and brought forth his inner knowing. He communed with the intelligence of the minerals and asked for the assistance required to pass. He began to speak in a mixture of Elvish dialect and a light language of long ago, the language of the galactic people of Lyra. Light flashed in front of them, covering the large round rock that had been keeping them from entering. The stone began to vibrate as Eldorman continued to focus his intent on moving it, but it would not move.

Bridgit noticed that along the edge of the stone were carvings that she could not see until Eldorman brought the energetic light to it. She replayed the codes on her mental screen from her dream the night before and recalled a pattern that she played out in her mind's eye. The symbols in her dream were there within the design etched in the stone, so she began to touch each symbol that she recalled.

Avery began yelling, "Anytime now!!!!" while magically moving in and out of the trees keeping the hyenas from reaching them. The forest floor was littered with the helpless hyenas that were controlled by the Dark One, and more were coming up the other side of the river's edge. Butler was growing more and more concerned about Bridgit's safety.

Bridgit hit the last symbol that she recognized and heard a clicking sound, and there was movement. Suddenly the massive stone rolled to the side of the mouth. Bridgit called to the elves, "Hurry!"

Butler motioned for the elves to go on, and he would follow up behind them. They all swiftly moved towards the opening of the cave, entering just as the new pack of hyenas was upon them. Butler continued to fight them off, one at a time.

Bridgit yelled to him to hurry, but the rock began to roll once more. "Butler!!!!!," she screamed. Bridgit dropped to her knees as the others tried to find a way to keep the doorway open, but their strength was no match for the large rock that rolled back into place, locking them in and Butler out.

Eldorman lit a torch hanging on the wall of the cave with the wave of his hand, another gift of the element's cooperation. He could see the droplets of tears racing down Bridgit's face as he lifted her from the cave floor.

Eldorman comforted her by saying, "It will take a lot more than a pack of hyenas to take down ole Butler, besides they were after you. They will dissipate now that you made it inside the Cave. Butler will be fine."

He winked at Bridgit, and she caught a glimmer of hope in his eyes from the reflection of light within the cave. "He has survived a lot worse than a pack of hyenas and lived to tell about it. Let's move on", gesturing for her to look around.

Hanging from the ceiling of the cave was a very long rib cage, large enough to line a long corridor. The group gathered in close and were on alert for any danger that might present itself. They walked in silence, looking for any sign of the Doorways. Soon enough, they came to the end of the corridor, where they found six small round chambers with doors.

Eldorman looked at Bridgit with some concern and said, "Madame, this is your journey home... be wise which door you choose."

Pointing towards the doors, he said, "All but one will lead to your worst fears."

She replied with a determined look, "I had a feeling it would not be easy based on my dreams last night." She remembered the Violet Fire and invoked it silently.

Looking around, she began to murmur as she paced the floor in front of each door. They each had a number etched into the wood ranging from one to six. The numbers were in the very center of a square, which seemed odd to Bridgit since the room was round, and most things in nature are round rather than square. And why six, she thought?

She looked at Eldorman pensively, requesting the torch. She walked next to Avery, who was trembling, still shaken from their ordeal. Bridgit felt for him, knowing that she was the reason for him being in this mess. They were both standing at the center of the room, looking at the six doors, with the flame from the torch the only illuminating light in the cave.

Avery began to pace back and forth. His fidgeting was out of control. He attempted to maneuver his sword to the other side of his body, but his hands trembled, accidentally causing him to drop his sword at Bridgit's feet. The others went crazy with agitation as if Avery was mauling Bridgit with his sword after they had just gotten her to safety. Everyone was on edge.

Bridgit did not react to the fact that he had dropped the sword near her feet as the others did. She had heard something when the sword fell. A clanking on metal.

The others calmed down as Avery cried out loud, "Sorry, sorry, I am just out of my element here. I should not be here. I do apologize." He bent down to pick up the sword as Bridgit moved her foot to remove the dirt by the sword. Eldorman took the torch from Bridgit so that she could examine more closely what was beneath them.

As she and Avery cleared the rest of the dirt, the others stood behind them in anticipation. She began to see the codes pop up on her mental screen as she had before, while Avery kept clearing the area. Avery pointed to the center of what looked to be another door. He said, "Here!" pointing to a carving.

She felt the etching of a circle inside another circle and a number, and laughingly said, "Could this be lucky number seven?"

She had seen the number seven in her dreams. She pulled her hair away from her face as she leaned in closer and cleared the last bit of dirt, which was, in fact, a seventh door with the number seven within two circles. Bridgit tried to push the number seven, but it did nothing. She pushed the inner circle, which was two feet in diameter and again nothing. She tried the outer ring, which was about four feet in diameter and still, nothing. She stood up with some frustration and tried to bring back her vision of the codes from the dream. "Seven... what could that mean?"

Avery commented as he took note that there were seven of them present in the room. "Perhaps the seventh door is an energetic lock that requires all of us to push it?"

Bridgit pondered that for a moment and noticed that the seventh door had circles around it rather than a square. The circles were quite large, with the outer ring almost as wide as the door itself. She shared her thoughts with the group.

Avery said, "In nature, things grow in a spiral, or circular if you will. He went on explaining for some time about the Fibonacci sequence. Annoying the group, Avery extrapolated on the possibilities of how they could activate the door, giving Bridgit a flash.

"Thank you, Avery, I think you have got it! We simply need to organize ourselves around the outer circle according to size, and I will stand in the inner circle." Smiling at her brave little elven friend and sure of the plan, they arranged themselves as Bridgit suggested.

As soon as all the elves were in position, Bridgit stepped into the center of the inner circle. She leaned down to place her hand on the number seven. A series of clicks started, and the floor beneath them began to shake. They all jumped out of the way as an articulated door folded upon itself to reveal a spiral stairway beneath them. They all looked at each other with joy and excitement. Bridgit then said, "Let's go!"

They looked at her with great sadness as she realized then that they could go no further. There was no time for goodbyes as they heard the clicking starting up again. "Go!" they all yelled, nudging her to get moving.

"I will return, I promise! Thank you all so much and please thank Butler for me!" The sounds of her voice began to trail off as she descended the spiral staircase, and the doorway clicked shut once more.

At the bottom of the stairway, a hallway led out of the cave to a beautiful tree. A gatekeeper stood, awaiting Bridgit's arrival.

The tree was glowing with a vibrant energy field of gold and green, Bridgit noted, as she recalled the golden-hued room where she was first presented with her life plan, then she felt that familiar pull as the gatekeeper said an incantation. She was pulled forward, directly into the tree. The vortex rearranged her molecules at that moment, and she was gone.

And the wheel turns...

Chapter 21

The Return of the Faithful

Shamalaine and Bewain waited for a report back at the Great Hall. They were both engrossed in thought when the motley elven crew presented themselves. Avery, Eldorman, and the three others stood in the doorway disheveled, with Butler taking up the rear.

Shamalaine invited them in as she rushed to their aide. She poured them all a refreshing beverage and waited for them to relieve their parched bodies.

"What happened? Did she make it?" Shamalaine drilled them with question after question scanning their eyes for answers before any of them could respond. She was unable to tune into Bridgit, which could mean that she was between the realms, but the mother in her needed confirmation.

Butler spoke for the group of Elves, "Yes, my lady, she made it," winking at her with a twinkle in his eye.

Everyone could see the relief in Shamalaine and Bewain's eyes and their demeanor. Shamalaine observed each one of the elementals and Guardians in her presence with such love and admiration.

Bewain walked up to Butler, placing his hand on Butler's shoulder, then extended his other hand to him with gratitude. They shook hands, and then Butler playfully gave Bewain a bear hug, and all began to laugh at the sight.

Bewain said, "Tell us all about your adventures as we feast tonight. We owe you all a debt of gratitude!" He pointed to the table set with fruits, cakes, and creamy dishes that smelled divine. The cold mead sat waiting for them as well, something that Butler was very appreciative to have after a weary journey.

The Elves ditched their etiquette and began to sample the food and drink, as Avery tried to stay calm and not rush his way to the table, having lingered behind a bit longer. Just as he went to take a seat, one of the other Elves would sit down in the spot again and again until there was only one seat left.

As Avery readjusted his vest and took a deep breath before finding his seat, a gentle breeze blew by his neck, rustling his hair out of place. Turning to look where the breeze came from and then turning back to his seat, he found Breacher there smiling at him, commenting on his disheveled hair in the process.

Breacher could see that this little elf was at the end of his rope, and before they saw him lose it entirely, Breacher offered him his seat and handed him a cup of mead. Patting his back, he said, "Avery lighten up, we are glad you are back."

Avery nodded and sat at the end of the table opposite Bewain.

Bewain raised his glass to toast their homecoming and successful mission. Looking at all of the Elves at the table, he said, "Please... eat! We would like to hear your stories as to how you managed to get our beloved daughter through the Cave of Doorways."

More members of the Clan of Phare began to enter the hall and gathered around the others to hear the stories, which would be told in the kingdom in times to come. Sounds of drums, flutes, and a harp filled the room in a delicate balance, not to overpower the conversation, but to add an exclamation to the excitement that was building. The feast began, and the celebration ensued.

Afterward, when the food was mere crumbs and everyone's plates were empty, the room silenced in honor of the Elves and Guardians as they continued to share with the Clan the adventures with the mushroom beings and the codes and symbols within Bridgit's dreams. They left the Dark Lord of Aln attack for last.

Butler recounted the attack of the bird-headed Dark Lord and his use of the hyenas. He wiped his eyes as it truly broke his heart when he recounted how he had to protect Bridgit, no matter the costs. "I never expected that I would have to bring harm to an animal, but they were under the Dark One's power and not themselves. They just could not be tamed."

Bewain jumped in, giving praise to the whole team, allowing Butler a moment to compose himself. "Avery, why don't you continue the story? Tell us what happened inside the Cave of Doorways. How did you gain access anyway?"

Avery had been in his own world at that moment contemplating why Shamalaine had chosen him to go on this journey when Breacher would have been the obvious choice. Bewain jostled Avery to attention by clearing his throat.

Avery positioned himself so that the whole crowd could hear him speak of Eldorman and Bridgit, working together to activate the doorway of the cave. He recounted the heart wrenching and bold act of Butler staying behind fighting off the hyenas to save them all, and how the cave was lined with the ribs of an enormous creature, the likes of which no one would ever want to meet up with in life. Avery was a talented storyteller, weaving in all the nuances of the story. He would often make slight fun of himself, to quash any opportunity for the others to do so at his expense.

He went on to share about how they all worked together as a team to bring Bridgit to her journey's end, the seventh doorway. He hesitated slightly, trying to determine the most delicate way to share the story when Eldorman interjected and took the story from there.

Eldorman, in a very delicate manner, recounted the story in such a way that left out the small detail of Avery almost cutting Bridgit's foot off with his sword. He gave the account of a massive thud that echoed in the room, which is how they located the seventh door. He also shared how it was Avery's idea that the six of them surround Bridgit as she touched the number seven. Winking at Avery, with a noble gesture, Avery relaxed, knowing that the Elves were genuinely protecting him, as a friend.

"Well, excellent Avery," Shamalaine chimed in. "I am sure that this was a great experience for you, and one that you can build upon, seeing as the committee has selected you as the First Ray Builder of Form."

Yells of cheers and congratulatory handshakes filled the room. Avery experienced both joy and a slight tinge of anxiety hearing the news.

Shamalaine stood up to speak to the crowd. "I feel I must share with you my reason for sending our beloved daughter through the Cave of Doorways." She moved her dress out of the way as she maneuvered through the room. The Elves and others in the Clan were wide-eyed, eager to hear Shamalaine's story.

She began, "Kaialena has been regaining a few of her memories from her time here with the Clan of Phare, but we must understand that too much of this life bleeding into her other life as Bridgit could cause her great pain in her heart." She looked at Breacher before continuing.

She explained that it would have been just as easy for her to have had Breacher bilocate Kaialena to her home, but she said, pausing, as she chose her words carefully, "What some of you do not know is that Breacher is Kaialena's husband."

She could hear Avery gasp and took note as Eldorman reached over to assist his companion in regaining his composure by gently lifting his jaw upwards to close his mouth.

Shamalaine continued, "Some of you here, at this table tonight, might know that not soon after Kaialena was called forth as a Life Bearer, that her sister, Tulina, was also called into the lower realms in service. She, too, is a Life Bearer and has specialties of her own that will prove useful. Tulina doesn't remember her life here, that we know of, but she has deepened her connection to the stars and recognizes kindred feelings when she thinks of the Lyran star system. Her current geographic location at this moment is in a country called India. I have done my best to send her thought suggestions to be at a specific Banyan tree. That Banyan is the world tree that Bridgit will emerge from."

She looked at Breacher and pointed towards him, "I even sent Breacher on a special assignment to retrieve some of Kaialena's... I mean Bridgit's belongs, that will help her travel back to the place called Scotland, where she first encountered our beloved Tuuru."

She looked at everyone sitting there, some having the same dropped jaw as Avery had earlier.

She smiled and continued, "I think I have successfully reached Tulina, but what happens from this point is in the hands of the Life Bearers now. With the two of them together, they will have the support and comfort one needs to complete such a vast mission."

The room was silent as everyone pieced together all of the stories of the evening. It was so quiet that the sounds of the flickering flames crackling in the fireplace amplified in the room. It was clear to all who were present that they were part of a multi-faceted plan and that each person present was a part of it.

Shamalaine continued to speak further that the time had come when the dimensions were blending into one another, causing chaotic nodes and affecting each of the realities in ways that had never before been affected in this manner. A new world was the plan. One in which the realms unified into a higher frequency of love and light. It would be unprecedented; Humans, Elementals, Angels, Dragons, Guardians, and Galactics, living, working and playing together as co-creators of a whole new world, and it all hinged on the cooperative endeavors of them all.

Shamalaine looked at the crowd and then into Breacher's eyes and said, "We know that the sacrifice is worth it, and we know just how difficult it is."

With that said, Breacher moved through the air and was gone. Soon enough, the crowd dissipated as it had been quite the night of celebration and revelation.

And the wheel turns...

Part Two

The Gathering

Chapter 22

The Other Side of the Tree

Stella sat in the hotel lobby, waiting for her father to return from his business meetings on the first full day of their trip to India. She was on break from her master's program back in the States, where she studied Music Theory and Psychology, two programs that she felt went reasonably well together. She was fascinated by what made a person tick and how music could affect the mood of an individual. She could understand a person's state of mind by merely checking out the music that they listened to on their phone.

Tired of waiting for her father and ready for an adventure, she left a note for her Dad with the hotel concierge that read:

"Dad, the cat in me needs to explore. Not hungry. Don't wait up. Meow - Stella." She ended the note by drawing a tiny paw print next to her name with a XOXOXO by a heart.

Stella ran upstairs to the room to grab her phone and harp. She backed a few things into her purring kitty backpack that her Dad gave her on her ninth birthday, some seventeen years ago. She loved that old beat-up thing and always made a point to use it when she and her Dad took trips together.

Stella ran outside the hotel, flagging down a cab to take her to the park situated just on the edge of town. She loved everything about the city as she watched out the window of the cab. Upon arrival at her destination, Stella asked the cab driver if he would return to pick her up at an appointed time. He agreed and drove away. Stella beamed with excitement to discover the ancient tree that she saw when they first arrived in town. She exited the cab and took a deep breath.

She walked calmly and then began to run towards the Banyan. The magnificent tree celebrated as one of the most ancient trees in the entire region came into sight. Stella stopped for a moment contemplating the oddity of a small white fence around a large area near the tree.

A brick courtyard near the tree had small colorful lanterns hanging from the extensive branch system, giving the tree light within the undergrowth at night. The lanterns looked like lotus flowers with the lamp in the center of the flower. At night, the lotus lanterns looked like an optical illusion as if they magically floated under the branches of the trees, adding just enough sparkle to make for a beautiful scene, one that brought visions of fairies and magical creatures to mind.

Stella pushed her cat-rimmed glasses up her nose so that she could take in the scenery and feel the vibe. She grabbed her long black hair, putting it into a ponytail. It was time to get serious, Stella thought. She now had her backpack in one hand and her harp in the other as she tapped into the energy of the earth, asking for just the right spot to plant herself.

She walked up to the base of the tree that looked away from the courtyard and felt that the spot had more natural scenery and fewer distractions. She laid her crumpled up shawl on the ground, pulled out her music paper in case inspiration struck, then set up her harp to lean on the tree.

She grabbed her cell phone to record whatever was about to come through. Many times, she had spontaneous compositions that she could not capture, so this time she wanted to be prepared for it. She turned on her phone recorder and called in her ancestors, not prepared for what would happen next, though she was as prepared as anyone could have been.

Ever since she could remember, she had visions of starry worlds and, in particular, a planet with beings that looked like felines. These beings were always in her dreams. They felt so familiar to her that she began to call forth their energies in her prayers. Her study of music and sound seemed to activate an alien part of her that she enjoyed exploring. She adopted the characteristics of the feline unconsciously at first and then more consciously by the use of makeup to create cat-like features on her eyes with a black liner that streaked outward towards her brow. She also felt that her cat rimmed glasses gave her superpower eyesight because she began to be more visual when she started wearing them.

She snapped out of her thoughts of felines and refocused her attention on the Banyan tree. Stella just knew that she needed to be at that tree, at that moment, in that place. What was going to happen, she did not know. She merely thought that she would experience the energy of the tree, and perhaps it would invoke new sounds and new music within her.

She maneuvered her shawl in preparation. She could feel something was about to happen, so she sat quietly on the ground next to the Banyan tree in anticipation. As she waited, she readjusted herself by moving closer to the tree for back support. Leaning backward on her hands to pull her body up closer to the tree, she hit something that hid in the shrubbery. She turned to see what it was and discovered a water bottle and a woman's purse hidden there.

"Oh, Great!" she thought out loud. She just knew that someone was going to come looking for their things, most likely when she was in the middle of a transmission. She blurted out loud again, "Well, I might as well play the harp and wait for her."

Stella sat, strumming the strings of her harp as she relaxed once more. Then a thought hit her. Thinking back to the first song that she played on her harp, she began strumming the tune.

When Stella was younger, she heard an internal musical loop, over and over again in her mind. It was magical and soft, like the sounds of a harp. It is what spurred Stella to pick up a harp in her youth. As she stroked the strings of the harp, a tear came to her eye, which she quickly wiped away, smearing the black eyeliner.

She continued to play her harp once more. Strumming this particular tune always gave her comfort, like the feeling she felt when she was with her mother. It also made her sad at the same time because it was her mother's favorite song. Stella would play it for her mother during her rounds of chemotherapy for breast cancer.

It had been thirteen years since her mother's passing, but it felt like it was yesterday. Her sadness began to well up. Stella played harder and faster to keep the dam from breaking. At that moment, she felt a vibration from the ground. The earth began to shake, as did the tree.

With pools of tears welled up in her eyes, she thought that she saw something strange. She wiped her eyes to verify what was happening. Stella's eye makeup was now a complete mess with black eyeliner streaked across her face from eye to ear. As the vibration stopped, she looked up to see a woman standing there with a bizarre look on her face, a look of confusion.

Bridgit looked at Stella somewhat frightened, as she observed this young woman with eye makeup streaked across her face. The ladies just stared at each other for moments on end until Stella realized that the woman was most likely there for her purse and water bottle, though how she just appeared out of nowhere would need to be addressed. In her mind, Stella was fighting back the obvious, the fact that she just appeared out of the tree.

"Is this yours?" Stella held the water bottle upward towards the woman as Bridgit looked at it with disbelief.

Hesitating while trying to rationalize everything happening, she said, "Yes. Yes, it is. Thank you. Where did you find it?" She took the bottle into her hands and looking at Stella with an appreciative glance.

Stella said, "Well, this must be yours also. I found them laying up against the tree under the shrubbery." Pushing her cat rimmed glasses up her nose once more and wiping her face with the back of her hand to look a bit more presentable, Stella offered the purse to Bridgit.

Bridgit reached for the purse and inspected it. Stella said, "Don't worry, I didn't open it."

Bridgit was distracted by what was happening and opened the purse to verify the contents were indeed hers. She lifted a tissue out of the packet that was there and handed it to Stella, saying, "Here, ah, you have a bit of eye makeup just there," pointing to the side of her face.

Bridgit smiled as she watched Stella begin laughing uncontrollably at how she must look right now. They both got a sweet relief from the laughter.

Bridgit looked further into the purse while Stella cleaned her face. At the bottom of her bag was one of her most favorite possessions, a shell that she used to create the grids around her orchid plant.

Now Bridgit had even more appreciation for it after remembering how she used shells in her other life.

Bridgit became lost in thought as to how her purse and water bottle showed up there, and for that matter, she was not even sure where she was.

Stella finished cleaning up her face. Her bulging brown eyes looked up at Bridgit from behind her silly glasses, which made Bridgit giggle just a bit. Bridgit had a feeling of Déjà vu that the girl in front of her had a familiar and comforting presence.

Stella asked frankly, "So are you going to tell me how you did that little trick?" eyeing the tree next to them.

Bridgit acted coy, hoping she wouldn't have noticed that she used the tree as a doorway. Shifting herself towards the tree and glancing at it and then back to Stella, she said, "What trick? What do you mean?"

Stella let out a nasal chortle and said, "I may not see well, but I am not blind!", as she plucked the strings of her harp for emphasis.

Bridgit responded by trying to change the subject, "My name is Bridgit. What's yours?"

Stella dramatically presented herself as if she was a movie star, "I am Stella Maris." Giving Bridgit a slight curtsey while still sitting down. It was the name that Stella always envisioned using when she became an accomplished musician.

"Nice to meet you, Stella Maris." Bridgit exaggerated the Maris part to give the name its appropriate flare.

Stella then returned the greeting by exaggerating the name Bridgit, "Why thank you, Briiiddddgit." Winking at her in jest while waiting for Bridgit's real story.

There was an awkward silence when Stella said, "Come on, I saw you come out of the tree. Your purse and water bottle were hidden at the base of the tree, and from what I can tell, they must have been there for a few days with the film of dirt that was on them. What gives?" Stella looked deep into Bridgit's eyes.

Bridgit said, "The tree? Really? Do you think I came out of the tree?" She looked at Stella as if she was taking crazy pills.

Stella blurted out, "Look, I have an idea. I bet your story is a bit of a long one, and I am getting hungry. You want to get something to eat?" Stella quizzed Bridgit.

"You look famished, come on!" trying to persuade Bridgit to trust her.

Bridgit opened her purse and said, "Let me look to see what I have for cash."

Examining the currency, she said, "I seem to have American money and a few pounds. For some reason, I don't seem to have my credit card with me." Bridgit wondered if this was all part of Shamalaine's plan. She knew that she was in a predicament and that she would have to rely on the generosity of a stranger now.

"Hmm..." Stella made a mental note to ask about the currencies later. "That's okay. Where are you staying?" Stella inquired.

Bridgit wrinkled her nose as it was yet another question that she did not know how to answer. She said, "I... haven't got a hotel just yet."

Stella blurted, "I knew it! Something is going on here!" She looked at her dusty water bottle and purse and said, "Bridgit... for some reason, I was guided to come here today. I think that reason was you. It seems that you are in a bind, and I really want to help you. You can exchange your money at my hotel."

Getting up to gather her things, not waiting for a response, she turned to Bridgit and asked, "Where do you live?"

"I live in America, but I have been studying trees and have a place... somewhere else..." Bridgit stopped, not knowing how to explain her circumstances.

Stella urged Bridgit, "Let's just go to my hotel. I came here with my Dad on a business trip. We are from America also."

Looking up at the lanterns now beginning to glow, she said, "Dad is probably still in meetings, so that means we will have the suite to ourselves. We can order room service." Winking at her in a comforting way, again causing Bridgit to have that familiar Déjà vu feeling.

"Bridgit, I know that you came through that tree, and you're not going to lose me. I will understand, trust me. Once you know my crazy ways, coming through a tree won't seem like such an odd thing." She patted Bridgit's shoulder and escorted her towards the fence, where she entered the area earlier.

The cab pulled up just as Stella had requested previously. Stella pointed to the taxi, "Look, our ride is here."

Bridgit was too spent to argue. She was hungry, tired, and in need of a shower and a place to sleep for the night.

"Okay, let's go. Lead the way." She winked, again, wondering if this was divine intervention and hoping that it was. In the cab, she remained inward as Stella blew her nose and stuffed the tissue into a strange pink backpack with a kitty on it. Bridgit was in no place to judge, though she did ponder the size of it, as Stella had it stuffed with papers and pictures in various zippered pockets.

Stella smiled at Bridgit while holding onto her harp with utter devotion. Bridgit knew there was a story there, one that would have to wait as they were already arriving at the hotel. The two ladies climbed up the steps of the hotel and entered the lobby.

Stella pointed to the counter where a sign read Currency Exchange and said, "A nice perk for an international hotel." She winked at her, proud of her father's choice in hotels as if it was an omen for just this moment.

Stella noted that the hours of business were 9 am to 6 pm, so she looked at her and said, "We just missed it! Oh well, you can stay with me. My room has two beds. You can get the money exchanged in the morning."

Bridgit felt drained from her journey, trying to come to terms with everything that had happened in the last few hours and did not have the will power to argue. She gratefully accepted the offer.

Before they went upstairs, a hotel concierge saw Stella and called out for her. "Miss Phare! The young women both stopped and turned to him, responding, "YES?" in a questioning tone.

Bridgit was confused. In her mind, she was trying to process how this gentleman knew her name and why Stella answered.

The gentleman spoke, "Ah... no, ma'am, I was speaking to Miss Stella", bowing gently with respect, he pointed to Stella.

Stella looked at Bridgit with excitement. She felt every hair on her body raise, knowing that something extraordinary was happening. From the first moment she saw Bridgit walk out of the Banyan tree until now, she knew that magic was afoot. Could Bridgit really have the same last name? Stella thought.

Stella was preoccupied, trying to unravel this mystery when she heard the male voice once more, "Miss Stella??"

Stella turned and answered the hotel concierge, walking towards him, leaving Bridgit a few paces behind. Stella conferred with the gentleman and then came back over to where Bridgit was waiting. "That's odd."

Bridgit couldn't imagine what could be odder than what the two had already experienced together in the short hour that they had met. She asked, "What is it?"

Stella lifted the note from her father that the concierge had just delivered to her.

"My Dad had to rush off to another meeting in a nearby town, and since it will be late when he gets finished, he has decided to stay the night there and return in time for dinner tomorrow night." Stella was emotionally looking at the note, with a look of sorrow that made Bridgit feel very uncomfortable as if there was an underlying reason for Stella needing some company that night.

Bridgit tried to get Stella to look at her and asked, "Are you okay?"

Stella crumpled the note into her backpack and swiped at her face quickly. She took a deep breath and looked at Bridgit, blinking her eyes a few times and forcing a smile. "Yeah, I'm fine. It's just that tomorrow is the anniversary of my mom's passing. My Dad and I try to be together each year on this day, no matter where we are or what we have going on. That is why I am in India. He has a big project that needed his attention here, so he brought me along to see the sites." She smiled a half-smile, one side of her cheek raising and the other clearly not having it.

As they walked to the elevator, she continued. "It was a last-minute thing that came up for Dad, and we decided to make an adventure out of it. He seems to be working a lot, so it is up to me to pull him out of it and remind him of all the fun times we had with mom. I am an only child, so we just have each other now."

A tear began to form in her eye as she took another deep breath and said to herself, "Suck it up, Stella!" motioning for Bridgit to join her in the elevator.

Trying to change the mood, Stella said, "Well, this means that we will have the place to ourselves! Let's order some food, and then you can tell me your story since you already know mine! And don't think the name thing has flown out of my mind either!" She winked at her with determination, like a reporter after a big story.

Stella was a pro at breaking intense moments with humor, something Bridgit did not have in her bag of tricks. They both went silent again and stared at the elevator lights as Bridgit wondered what floor they were going to get off on. Finally, they reached the last level of the building, and they exited the elevator in deep thought.

Stella unlocked the suite, and Bridgit stood there in the doorway with her eyes wide, looking at the large room that had to include a quarter of the top floor. Sheepishly, Stella said, "Yeah, it's the penthouse."

Bridgit walked into the suite with hesitation as Stella pulled her arm to help her in so that she could close the door. "Don't let the flies in!" Stella joked to lighten the mood.

"We need some wine because clearly, we have had a Bi-polar day! Many moods make for a great country song, but since I'm not into country music, I drink now and then!" Laughing, Stella pulled the wine bottle towards her and lifted two wine glasses by the stems and motioned for Bridgit to relax. She poured Bridgit a glass of merlot.

They both drank their wine in silence for a few moments.

They sat in thought while staring at the French doors that led out to a balcony. It was a beautiful night view of the city, and with the wine, the two women were able to relax a bit.

Stella looked at Bridgit for a few moments. Bridgit could feel her stare and turned to Stella.

"You hungry? Stella popped the question so suddenly, and somewhat louder than the situation called for, that her body shook, and a bit of her wine flew from her glass.

Laughing at her awkwardness, she went over to the nearby counter and wiped the stem of the glass down with a napkin and said, "I am going to order some room service. You should take your stuff into my room and get a shower."

Bridgit looked down at her body and noticed smudges of dirt on her pants and said, "That would be nice." She walked to the dining table and sat her wine glass down. She scanned the room for her things as Stella pointed out where she had placed them. Bridgit picked up her purse and went into the bedroom.

Stella yelled out, "It looks like we are about the same size, so go ahead and grab something from the drawer to put on. Just put your clothes on the chair outside the bathroom door, and I will call for the concierge to have them cleaned for you. They can have them back here in the morning, fresh as new!"

Bridgit agreed that her clothes could use a washing. She went into Stella's room and placed her purse on the bed next to where Stella laid her harp.

From the other room, Stella yelled out, "Indian, okay?" and just started laughing hysterically. That was probably the first moment that Bridgit laughed as she yelled back sarcastically, "When in Rome!"

Stella picked up the phone and began to order a lavish dinner that

120

could feed ten from the sound of it.

Bridgit rummaged through the clothes in Stella's dresser drawers but was distracted by a picture frame of Stella and a woman who was obviously her mother. She lifted it to see it better, thinking the resemblance was uncanny.

Stella entered the room as Bridgit set down the frame. They looked at each other with calmness. Stella cleared her throat and said, "Now that the food is on its way, how about that shower? Housekeeping will be up here any minute." Stella motioned for Bridgit to scoot into the bathroom.

"Do I smell that bad?" Bridgit exclaimed.

Laughingly, Stella waved her hand by her nose as if she reeked. Bridgit went into the bathroom as Stella went to the dresser to pick out some clothes. Bridgit opened the bathroom door in a crack, playfully throwing her clothes across the room at her.

Stella felt as if there was something so familiar about Bridgit, assuming that this must be what it felt like to have a sister. They had an immediate bond that was unexplainable.

Stella gathered up Bridgit's clothes and placed them into the laundry bag. After setting the bag out in the hallway for pick up, she went back into the bedroom. Stella laid out a pair of sweats and her favorite purring kitty T-shirt on the bed next to Bridgit's purse. Her eye's widened, and at that moment, she picked up Bridgit's bag to look inside. A wallet, passport, some tissue, a shell, and some crumpled papers were the only contents inside.

Opening the passport, Stella turned the pages noting the last country stamped. "Hmm, Scotland aye?", feeling like she was playing out a scene from a Sherlock Holmes novel.

"This is getting very interesting." Stella murmured under her breath as she flipped the pages to the one with the photo. On the last page was a photo of Bridgit with her full name under the picture, which read,

Bridgit Gay Phare.

This dazed Stella. It was true! She really did have the same last name. Her mind went wild with questions. Why have they not been talking about this already? Her mind was on overload when she heard the shower turn off. She quickly shut the passport and placed it back into the purse and ran out of the room.

Bridgit wiped the fog off the mirror in the bathroom and breathed in deeply. She talked to herself in her head while watching her facial expressions in the mirror. She thought, "Get it together! Think, think, think! What is going on here? Who is this girl? Are we related? We have to be! This is all too weird!"

She rubbed her head and looked back into the mirror, trying to find any sign of her previous head injury, but there was nothing there.

Again, thinking to herself, "How am I going to explain all of this? I don't even know what the hell is happening!!!"

She let out a heavy sigh as she began to blot her hair in the towel, then wrapped it up onto her head. She could hear Stella talking to someone in the other room. She peeked out the bathroom door wearing a large towel around her body.

"Dinner is here!" Stella yelled from the other room.

Bridgit went over to the bed and put on the sweats that Stella had laid out for her. She then unwrapped her hair from the towel and quickly threw on the t-shirt.

Bridgit walked over to look in the mirror attached to the dresser. She just laughed at the ridiculousness of her in a purring kitty t-shirt. She grabbed the towel again to finish drying her hair. She leaned down and began to flop her head up and down to help air-dry her hair until the count of ten, something her mother taught her when she was a young child. With her head going back and forth towards the floor and ceiling, she turned slightly and caught sight of her purse lying there on the bed.

She walked over to pick it up and sat down on the bed. She had not had time to carefully examine the contents since her arrival in the 3D world. She pulled the white shell out of the purse first and whispered, "How did this get into my purse? Or for that matter, how did any of it get there?"

She then pulled the crumpled-up pieces of paper from her purse and unfolded the smaller one first. In the handwriting of a poet were the words:

"Everything you need to get home should be here. At your service, Breacher."

There was a small, perfectly drawn tree icon next to Breacher's name. In Bridgit's mind, she traced her memories, and with excitement, yelled out loud, "Commander Breacher!"

She immediately wondered how all of this was possible. How did Breacher put this note in her purse in the 3D world?

Stella yelled out loud, "You coming? Dinner is getting cold!"

Bridgit yelled back, "In a minute!"

Thinking more on the purse, she remembered leaving it in her room back in Scotland. Her mind was overwhelmed with what had occurred, as memories of herself as Kaialena came back, and the plan that was presented to her to find the Life Bearers was ever-present in her thoughts. "Am I crazy?" she wondered. "Yep. That's it. I am crazy!"

She then pulled the other piece of paper out of her purse, and in tiny print was Avery's account of what happened while she was in the elemental realm. At the end of the report, Avery left her a personal note.

"Miss Bridgit, I wish you well on your journey in the human realm. Please don't dally, for we have to stay on task if we are going to make a WHOLE NEW WORLD. PS: Thank you for the recommendation. I will be joining the team as the First Ray Builder of Form. While you are away, I will prepare and will be at the designated jump point when the time is right. At Your Service, Avery."

He, too, had drawn a small acorn by his name with such precision a squirrel would mistake it for being real.

A knock on the door brought Bridgit back to the present. "You okay?" Stella asked from the other side of the door. She didn't wait for a reply before she peeked her head in, "Are you ready to eat? I'm starving!"

Bridgit smiled and nodded in agreement. She put the papers back into her purse and joined Stella in the living room. Stella had all of the food set out on the dining table, and the curtains fully opened so that they could enjoy the view while they ate. She poured them each another glass of wine as they sat down to embrace the nourishment that the food offered their weary bodies.

Dishing up the food, Stella served Bridgit and then fixed her plate. Bridgit delved in, making sounds that indicated the food was pure heaven. Stella was pleased that she approved of the food. They ate ferociously, not stopping to speak, and barely taking a breath.

Stella wanted to get the food out of the way because there were questions, many questions that needed answers, and she intended to get straight to it.

Once they both had appeased their appetites, Stella jumped in. "Okay, Bridgit, let's do this.", spoken as a proposition about to be given.

"You tell me a bit about you, and I will tell you a bit about me, and that way you won't feel so overwhelmed."

Smiling, she said, "You go first! What is your full name?" knowing full well what it was, but she didn't want to give it away that she had peeked in Bridgit's handbag.

Wiping her mouth, Bridgit drew in a long breath and conceded to Stella's request, after all, she was feeding and clothing her, and for that, she was genuinely grateful.

"Well," pausing for words, "My name is Bridgit." Again she paused, then slowly said the word "Phare," spelling it out to be precise.

Looking at Stella, she grabbed her glass in the hopes of washing the words down with large gulps of wine. She thought perhaps being inebriated was exactly what she needed to get through this day.

"Huh. That's how we spell it! So, you think we are related?" Stella asked calmly, really trying to keep her "over the moon" excitement under control. She could sense that Bridgit could bolt like a cat in the night at any moment, and she couldn't risk that no matter how excited she was.

"Is that it?" Laughing, Bridgit set down her pacifying wine glass. "Is that all you have to say after we have just met under the weirdest of circumstances?" She exaggerated the entire event by pulling at the kitty t-shirt to make her point. "And you told me that your name was Stella Maris! What's up with that?"

They looked at each other and just burst out laughing. Bridgit flung her hand outward toward Stella and shouted, "Your turn!"

Stella retorted, "Yeah, sure! Put it on me to decipher it all!"

After she had a small sip of wine she added, "Stella Maris is my stage name. I wanted to present myself as a musician, so you wouldn't think it was weird of me to be playing the harp in a park by a tree!" She laughed loudly, as did Bridgit, and then she repositioned herself.

"Fine, yes, I think we must be related because weird things only happen to people like us. It has to be a lineage thing!"

Bridgit stiffened up a bit, cocking her head sideways with a furrowed brow, and said, "What do you mean, people like us? We just met!"

Stella explained, "Well... I am what I call quasi psychic. I can tap into certain knowledge, shall we say." She used her fingers as quotation

125

marks at this point in the conversation.

"Quasi psychic? What is that?" Bridgit giggled and looked at Stella with a raised eye as if she was a professor asking her student to defend a thesis.

Stella replied, in a serious manner, " Under the proper circumstances, you know, when I really focus, I can tap into the universal mind, or the psi bank, as it is scientifically called."

She pushed her glasses higher on her nose and continued, "I had an inner knowing to be at that particular tree today, and voila...there you were!"

She waited with anticipation as to how Bridgit responded to this, hoping it would lead them quickly into the whole thing about the tree and the fact that Bridgit just popped out of it only hours earlier.

Not getting an immediate response, she went on. "I am not a full-on psychic, but I am getting there. I mainly get downloads when I am playing music, and sometimes I have this inspiration of how to play music in a way that taps into the heart for healing energy to flow through."

Bridgit, seeing Stella's harp in her mind's eye, realized that the harp was much more than just an instrument, but a healing modality for her to get through the loss of her mother. Bridgit motioned for Stella to continue when she saw Stella pause.

"Well, it seems to run in the family, on the Phare side of the family that is." Looking at Bridgit to see her response, continuing as if she was carefully reeling in a big fish on her hook.

"Great, Great, Great Grandfather Phare was from Scotland. The name was changed from Phare to Faire just before our ancestors came over from Scotland by way of England, but our particular lineage would never stand for it, so we continue to spell it PHARE. That is why I feel that the odds of us being related are pretty good."

126

She sipped her drink and then, as a final thought, said, "My Dad says we come from the Fairies!" Stella grabbed her fork, stabbing the last samosa, and shoveled it into her mouth to give her time to judge Bridgit's reaction to all of this.

Stella's phone rang just then, so she got up and walked over to where her phone was sitting on the desk near the doorway of the suite. She picked it up to read the caller id. She swallowed the last bite of food and cleared her voice, "It's Dad, just a minute," wanting to make sure they continue the conversation.

"Hi, Dad. Yes, I got your note. Are you doing okay? Oh, no. It's okay. I will be fine by myself tonight, and I have plenty to do tomorrow."

Looking at Bridgit with a Cheshire cat smile, she continued, "It will give me some time to get some work done on my music. You're planning on making it back here in time for dinner tomorrow, aren't you? Oh good. Goodnight Dad. Love you too, and Dad, may you be guided and guarded until we meet again." She made kissing sounds and listened as he repeated the same mantra to her, then she hung up the phone.

Coming back over to her chair at the table, she said, "We always say that to each other. We are all that we have. Well, until now." She looked at Bridgit as if she had found a long-lost big sister.

"So, back to the story!" Stella blurted out in an uneasy transition.

"My family can trace our heritage as far back as Scotland, as I said earlier. Is that where your line goes back as well?" trying to pull more out of Bridgit.

Bridgit said, "Yes, actually it is. Maybe we are related." Bridgit felt a strong sense that there was indeed a deep connection forming between the two of them, a connection that was both new and eerily ancient as well.

Bridgit continued, "I was actually in Scotland recently, for two reasons. One was for work; I am an Arborist."

Stella's eyes widened as she said, "Are you freaking serious?!" almost spraying her last sip of wine into Bridgit's face.

Laughing at Stella's response to her ordinary job, Bridgit went on. "I took some time off to go abroad so that I could research trees for a book that I want to write and at the same time I thought it would be great to do a bit of research on my family lineage, which admittedly, I didn't get far on, I am afraid."

Letting this information sink into Stella's blown mind, Bridgit continued to blow it even more by adding, "My love of trees has now taken on a whole new meaning, wouldn't you think?"

Grinning, Bridgit just left the conversation hanging there for Stella to make her move. She sipped her wine slowly, eager to hear Stella's thoughts. Bridgit wondered if Stella would focus on the fact that she is an arborist, the fact they shared a surname or the more significant conundrum of using a tree as a portal to the 3D world.

Stella took it all in quickly. Loudly, and with grand flare, she threw up her hand in utter amazement, having three deliciously equal and competing topics that all needed explanations.

Stella retorted, "Let's get back to the tree!"

Bridgit grinned with a pause, sipping her wine and contemplated what to say.

Getting comfy in her chair, Stella sat on her foot to get elevated in her seat, then looked at the clock on the wall and said, "Okay, it's time to fess up, and we have all night!"

She continued, "Tell me, how DID you come through that tree? And don't give me a song and dance story about it being magic or a figment of my imagination!" Stella contorted her hands as if she was using a magic wand.

The rest of the night, Bridgit shared how she had been studying a magnificent tree in Scotland when a tornadic dark force attacked her and how she found herself in the elemental realm among the elves and the Clan of Phare. It was three in the morning when Bridgit completed the wildest story that either of them had ever heard. She went into the bedroom and came back out with her purse. She sat at the table with Stella sitting there in shock and showed her the two crumbled notes that were in her purse.

Handing them to Stella, she said, "If you don't believe me, here is the proof." Bridgit realized at that moment that she was genuinely desperate for Stella to believe her. If she didn't, then where would that leave her?

Stella took the note from Bridgit's trembling hand, noticing the energy of Bridgit's auric field changing, and she knew that Bridgit was not making this story up, and she knew that Bridgit needed her to believe in her no matter what.

Stella opened the small note to see the words from Breacher. Looking up at Bridgit, Stella loudly said, "Oh, Wow!!!"

Laying it down, she took the other note. Seeing how detailed the little note was, she looked up and said, "I am going to need some more wine!" They both laughed hysterically, giving such a relief to Bridgit.

Stella got up to get the wine and swirled around, feeling all of the energy from the other side of the veil, and knowing that Bridgit was exhausted, she said, "Actually, I think we need some sleep. There is so much more to talk about, but we can save that for the morning."

The ladies got up and made their way into the bedroom. Stella walked over to her bed, picking up the harp and said, "Interesting that Dad got called away tonight."

She plucked a few strings for emphasis and set the harp down on the chair by the door. They fell fast asleep that night, exhausted and happy.

And the wheel turns...

Chapter 23

Breacher Trains the Dragons

Breacher stood at the precipice of a cliff overlooking the realm of the Clan of Phare. From the highest vantage point in the early morning, just as the light of day began to greet him, he sent out his prayer of love and forgiveness.

He filled himself with the silver light present between dark and light, a technique that he learned at an early age. It was to invite the light of the heavenly parents into his heart each day. In this way, he always remembered who he was, a son of the ancient of days.

He breathed deeply, tuning himself like a fine instrument to what he would be playing that day. He looked at the training of his dragons as if he were conducting an orchestra; it had to be done with excellence and precision.

He turned around and beheld the raw material in which he had to work, a variety of dragons feeding and stirring about after their night's slumber. He saw in them a perfect rainbow, each being a shade or frequency that, when combined, would make an epic rainbow of light.

But the dragons would be even more than that. They would be the creators of a living structure that holds the New Earth in place, which is one of the activities of the Rainbow Bridge. The vibrations of each color that the dragons represent were crucial in the building of the bridge. Breacher contemplated it all as he held the vision for the Rainbow Bridge to be made manifest, and this was just the first step in many.

As a mobile lighthouse, his plan for them was to weave their particular streams of light together, creating an etheric structured dome to hold the light of the creator. This would allow the plants, animals, and people of all realms to acclimate to the new energy in waves.

Another thought kept Breacher in constant focus on the divine plan; his relationship with Kaialena. Breacher knew that each day brought him closer to his beloved, and this was an incentive of the heart.

He shook his head, coming out of the daydream. He looked again at his precious dragons as if they were his children. He had trained them in many ways like a father would teach his children, and now it was time to put that training to good use.

Breacher was to assist the dragons by honing their skills of navigating the magnetic lines of the planet. The dragons also would need to learn how to weave energy, repairing blockages in nature, or an actual tear in the fabric of the dimensions. It was easy to tell where these places were located due to the chaotic energy building up in the areas of concern.

Breacher was up for the task as a Dragon Rider. He whistled to bring the dragons to the edge of the cliff, then jumped onto Leto. He and all of the other dragons catapulted into the sky as a rainbow in flight.

And the wheel turns...

Chapter 24

The Emissary

Back at the hotel room in India, Bridgit and Stella were having morning tea trying to wake up when Bridgit noticed a note slide under the door of the hotel room. She motioned to Stella to bring it to her attention. Stella walked to the door and opened it to see if she could get a glimpse of who left the note. She picked it up and tried to open it with one hand while trying not to spill her tea in the other.

Bridgit laughed and said, "May I?" to help the not quite awake Stella keep from having tea on her pajama top.

Stella blurted, "Please!" in an exasperated voice as if she was offended that anyone would disturb them at this hour.

The note read, "Meet me at the tree in an hour."

Bridgit looked at Stella with a questioning look as Stella shrugged and said, "Dad must be getting back sooner than he thought, and he knows I love that tree."

The girls had hoped to chat more about the conversations from the night before but quickly readied themselves for a day out. They took a cab to the tree area and noticed that Stella's father had not yet arrived. They sat next to the tree from which Bridgit had emerged, not even 24 hours earlier. They noted how it was only yesterday but that it felt like days since they had first met. They shared much of their stories, and to Stella, it truly felt like they were already family.

As Stella was showing Bridgit photos from her phone, they both experienced the sound of humming, or more correctly, a buzzing sound. The veil began to dissolve around them, and suddenly a woman wearing a beautiful black and gold satin wrap emerged from the tree and introduced herself as an emissary of the one known as Regulus.

Bridgit's ears perked up when she heard the name. Regulus was the one who called her into service as a Life Bearer. Was it he that they were to meet today? Bridgit wondered.

The emissary requested the girls join her and assured them that it would not take much of their earth time and that they would be back before anyone would miss them. Stella looked to Bridgit for a cue, seeing as it was Bridgit that had already been through the tree.

Bridgit could see Stella's apprehension and said, "Stella, you don't have to come with me, but I would really like it if you would. I need someone to come with me on this crazy adventure! If you're up for it?"

Bridgit made a face that lightened the moment, and Stella jumped to her feet, looking at the emissary and said, "Is Regulus the one who has been coming to me in my dreams?"

The emissary nodded, yes, pleased that he had gotten through to her as well.

Stella asked, "Then what are we waiting for?!"

They stepped forward, following the emissary into the opened portal of the tree. On the other side of the veil, they climbed into a small craft which held a crew of four. Bridgit and Stella were guided to a seat within the bridge of the craft. They watched as the ship went into hyper-drive. They were amazed that they were in deep outer space within no more than 10 to 15 minutes.

Stella whispered to Bridgit, "Is this a normal part of your daily life?" Her nose was wrinkled as if she was uncomfortable with the prospect of Bridgit's answer, hoping that the answer would be no.

Bridgit answered her quietly, "I don't recall ever being on a spacecraft before... but that doesn't mean that it hasn't happened." Based on the past week, being away from her normal life, she was not at all sure what was real or normal at this point.

Soon they were docking at what looked like a large round satellite. The craft entered the docking bay and landed near the entry port. Before they left the craft, the emissary showed them into a room with a small wardrobe closet.

She explained, "A digital library of clothes and hairstyles can be found on the wall there." The emissary pointed to the flat screen on the wall within the closet. On the inner wall was a long, rectangular digital display that doubled as a mirror.

The emissary encouraged Bridgit to enter the small wardrobe. Bridgit smiled and walked in, stepping up on a round platform and examined the flat digital device to select her look. The emissary noted that it was essential that they both looked their best.

Both Stella and Bridgit were not sure why, but they were girls who didn't mind dressing up, so they just followed along.

Bridgit selected a style of dress and hair design and then pushed the button. Suddenly a chiming sound began playing, like elevator music, as they watched the fabric holographically imprinting onto Bridgit's body to the exact fit.

A beautiful, flowing, rose, and cream-colored gown with a tight bodice was now upon her body with golden bracelets placed high on her arms. Her hair flowed with wavy ringlets, accentuated with a rose gold crown encrusted with jewels set high upon her head. The girl's marveled as the platform turned and allowed them to see the beautiful train of the gown, which had tiny diamonds sewn into chiffon fabric in a V shape.

Bridgit was the ideal image of the divine feminine. She smiled as she stepped down off of the platform and motioned for Stella to take her place.

Stella made her way onto the platform and perused the looks as if it was the latest fashion magazine. She looked back at the emissary and said, "I am more of a Grecian Mermaid kind of gal," as she winked at both of the ladies waiting for her transformation.

She turned and pushed the button of her selected look. They were mesmerized as the sounds of the ocean tides played, and a gorgeous pale blue gown was woven upon Stella's body while a sea-foam green cord wrapped around her breast and waist in the flattering style of the Grecian Goddesses. Her eyes glittered with teal tones upon her eyelids accented by white foamy waves of cream just below her eyebrows.

Her dark black hair was now wrapped in shimmering jewels that hung from various strands of hair as a Mother of Pearl crown appeared on her head, which dipped down onto the center of her forehead with a brilliant pearl drop dangling at her third eye.

Her neck was bejeweled with a starfish necklace hanging from a delicate chain. Stella had never thought that she could be this beautiful in all of her life. She had a tear well up, and the emissary smiled, pleased that the ladies were at their most enchanting while being presented to the Masters, who were waiting for their arrival.

The emissary said, "These adornments are merely accentuating your inner beauty." She smiled and gestured that it was time to take their leave.

As the two women prepared to leave the craft, the emissary handed Stella her harp, and remarked, "This harp will be more than a harp from this point on," giving Stella a nod of assurance.

They were escorted from the craft by one of the male crew members as the emissary followed from behind. The male assisted Stella by carrying her harp as they entered into a Grand Amphitheater.

When the women saw the room and all of the people and beings, who really couldn't be labeled as people, they were not sure what was going on. Looking at one another, Stella and Bridgit were feeling out of place.

The emissary came up from behind as the women stopped to stare at the crowd and said, "The two of you have an audience," gesturing that the entire place filled with beings of light was for them. She pointed towards a table on the stage where many Masters were waiting for them to approach.

As the women began to walk towards the center of the amphitheater, they were taken to two platforms and asked to stand upon them. Stella took the hand of her escort and placed one foot on the platform and then the other, wobbling just a bit and then took her harp from her assistant.

Bridgit lifted her gown and walked upon the other platform with such elegance and grace that the whole crowd began to cheer. The amphitheater was in a complete uproar over the two beauties. Suddenly the platforms started to rise high in the air for the women to be presented for all to see.

The announcement introduced them as the Sister's Phare, Life Bearers of multiple realms. The girls looked at each with surprise. Stella was holding her harp and had the urge to strum it at that moment. When she did, the sounds reverberated throughout the amphitheater and came back to her like a boomerang.

The frequencies, as a collective from the room, hit the chords on the harp, creating a higher resonance, an overtone, as the harp transformed in her hand. The harp was now slightly larger with an extra string, and as she strummed it once more, the frequency of peace echoed in the theater, silencing the crowd.

Everyone stood with his or her heads bowed in silence. The women were lowered from the platform and taken to where the masters were waiting.

The Council of Twelve sat at the table, emitting a warm and loving glow as they were introduced. Both of the girls recognized one Master over all of the rest. It was the Royal Lion, Regulus.

Bridgit was seated opposite him at the table and Stella next to her. A field of light enveloped them inside an energy field where it was just the two of them with the Masters.

The girls each received instructions for their mission that they were to perform on behalf of the light and all of humanity. The group, as a whole, spoke to Stella first.

"Stella, you have been ordained with the gift of harmonic midwifery. Frequency is the key that unlocks the heart. Harmonic resonance is vital to living in bliss and is a key to the birth of the new human."

Stella absorbed into the words as she listened to the Master speak again. "Percussions stir the heart, melody allows for a steady flow, and your voice creates the doorway for the creator to flow through you. Use your voice and your music in all ways." Each of the Master's blessed her and her harp at that moment. They then turned to Bridgit.

"Bridgit, you will monitor the levels of activity through the various dimensions and dissolve the blockages within the membranes of past life memory so that others will begin to recall their part in the up-leveling of consciousness. Those under your radiation will be drastically accelerated. To assist you, you will be joined by the Builders of Form and the Blueprint Masters. We are in the flux of the New Creation now, and the Life Bearers will go forward into the veil, and like a beautiful dance, twirl the energy from the heavens into a graceful tapestry which, will become the new living sequence and order for all beings. You will not be alone, for there are many beings called to take their rightful place."

Bridgit was anointed in the same way as Stella, blessed by the Masters.

A Master spoke once more as he placed an oil upon the women's foreheads, "The seal of your fate is open. The vibrations of wellness and peace come to you, Life Bearers, as you hold the light for others. You two, sisters of the light, are of the Clan of Phare, lighthouses for the souls of man. It should come to pass that you will both find the other lighthouses, and between the thirteen, you will receive and implement the creation codes for the New Earth."

As the Master completed the blessings, the energy field faded, and the amphitheater was hushed as the Master's once more blessed the two sisters from the Clan of Phare for all to see. The women had tears in their eyes, and their hearts were wide open. The urgency was apparent, and they had to return and find the others.

And the wheel turns...

Chapter 25

Back on the Other Side

"Stella... Stella... Wake up!" Stella's father was nudging her. A bit annoyed that the two girls were asleep in public next to the tree, he asked, "Stella, are you alright?"

Stella was groggy as she began to come back and could see Bridgit sitting up against the tree sound asleep.

"Dad, what time is it?" Stella grabbed his arm to stand.

"It is 6:30. When you were not at the hotel I came by here to look for you. We were supposed to meet for dinner thirty minutes ago. Remember?" Todd looked into her eyes to see if he could make out what was going on with her.

"Who is this?" he pointed to her companion. "Did you stay up late with a new friend?" recalling the empty wine bottle and two glasses in his suite when he returned from his trip.

"Yeah, Dad, we did." She pointed towards Bridgit, "This is my friend

Bridgit. Help me wake her up." As Stella moved towards Bridgit, she accidentally kicked her harp lying on the ground next to her foot. As she bent down to pick up the harp, she noticed the difference in her harp immediately. Yep, she thought in her mind, "We're screwed!"

"Bridgit... wake up! Can you hear me?"

Stella's voice seemed so far away, but Bridgit could faintly hear her. She felt the cold touch of Stella's fingers tickling her under her chin. "Wakey, Wakey! Dad is here!" saying it in a way to let Bridgit know to be quick about it.

Stella nudged Bridgit's torso to try to help her get to her feet, concerned that she was not waking. Stella's father looked at her with a stern look as if to say, "We will talk about this later."

He bent down and said, "Come on, young lady. It is time to go."

As Todd got a better look at Bridgit, he stared with wonder. It did not go unnoticed by Stella. Bridgit opened her eyes to see a man intensely staring at her. She turned white as she stared back at Stella's father, startled. She thought she saw a ghost.

Stella said, "Guys, what's going on?"

Bridgit tried to move. Todd grabbed her arms to help her up. They looked at each other deeply, then Stella said, "Dad let me introduce you to Bridgit ... Phare.", she elongated the word Phare for emphasis.

Smiling at her, he asked, "Phare, did you say?"

Stella nodded, yes.

"It is no wonder you look familiar to me. You are the spitting image of my Grandmother, Kaitlyn Phare. Do you recall that name in your lineage?" he asked.

Bridgit was discombobulated, and Todd was confused as to what was happening. He could not understand how the two girls met and why they were asleep at the tree and how did his daughter come to find a woman that shares their surname.

Bridgit was at a loss for words, but even if she had any, she surely couldn't make her mouth move well enough to say them.

Stella took the cue and said, "Dad, come on... let her have a moment to wake up before you ask her twenty questions."

He looked at Stella with amazement and then back to Bridgit and said, "Forgive me. Where are my manners? I am Todd, Todd Phare. It seems that you two have some explaining to do, but let's move on from here and find a quiet place where we can eat, and you two can tell me everything."

The girls nodded as Stella spoke for both of them, "Sounds like a great plan, Dad. Thanks."

Stella nudged Bridgit as they walked to the car, both woozy from their anointing's. She held out the harp for Bridgit to see so that she would know that what just happened was real. Bridgit looked at Stella with big eyes that relayed the question, how are we going to tell your Dad everything that just happened?

Stella picked up the vibe and just shook her head "Nooooooo." They all walked silently to the cab.

In Todd's mind, he thought how odd that this young lady would show up now, on the anniversary of his wife's passing. He was happy that it was this night, the one night that he and Stella embraced, in remembrance of his beloved, and now with the addition of a potentially long, lost family member, it could ease their sadness just a little.

They all jumped into a cab and were taken to a quiet restaurant down the street from the hotel. After the waiter brought them tea, they all settled into the comfort of a horseshoe-shaped booth, Stella sitting in the middle, with Bridgit and Todd facing one another.

Todd began to pose questions to the girls about what happened at the tree. Stella and Bridgit both seemed to him very distant and almost comatose since bringing them out of the tree area.

"Stella, are you okay?" He peered deep into her eyes and shook her shoulder slightly as if to jar her back into her body.

"Yes, I'm okay. I am just still a bit sleepy. I am sure that you want to know how I came upon Bridgit here." Throwing her gaze over to Bridgit, Stella winked at her to make small talk.

"Todd, thank you so much for this meal. I can use some food right now. Something to ground me a bit." Bridgit began to fidget.

"It is my pleasure." He looked at Stella and made a nervous hum. "Well, I still am at a loss for why you two grown women were asleep at the tree?" He seemed a bit flabbergasted at the idea.

Stella made an identical hum sound like her father, as she made a quick comeback. "Let me see if I can explain... I am sure I have a reasonable explanation!" She made a joke trying to ease the situation, but her father was not amused.

She then relayed what happened the day prior. "Yesterday, I went to the banyan tree to play my harp and connect with the Earth... and with Mom. I was playing my harp when Bridgit arrived to retrieve her belongings. They were in the bushes near where I was sitting. We struck up a conversation, and we realized that we had the same last name! Strange, huh?!"

She glanced at her dad, and he nodded his head and asked her to continue. She shared, "Bridgit had just arrived in town to study the banyan tree as part of a book that she is working on, but somehow she lost her credit card and did not have anywhere to stay. She was going to hang out in the park until she could have a replacement card sent to her, but that would take days!!!"

She looked at Bridgit, whose eyes were as huge as Todd's at this point. Bridgit was amazed at how fast Stella was on her feet, to have come up with that elaborate tale.

Stella said, "I couldn't just leave her there to fend for herself, now could I?"

Todd replied, "Absolutely not. So why were you two asleep at the tree? Todd ate some bread as he focused on Stella's story.

"Well, Bridgit and I wanted to go back to the banyan tree as she wanted to share some details on how the banyans grow. She suggested that I bring my harp, which I was happy to do. Once we arrived, and she had given me a lesson on the trees of this area, she requested that I play my favorite song. At one point, Bridgit began to do a spontaneous and totally beautiful visualization, like a meditation, to accompany me."

Bridgit started choking on her water when Stella described the part about her leading Stella in a meditation.

Stella smiled and continued, "We just wove so much magic that it took us into a profound state. I guess we simply fell asleep after that, which has totally never happened to me before."

Stella hated to lie to her father, but she did not have a better plan. She grabbed some bread as Todd watched as the two girls began to devour everything on the table that was edible.

Bridgit felt the need to add a bit more to help Stella out. "I have suddenly found myself in the strangest of circumstances and do appreciate your patience. I have never been so swept up in the kind of energy that we just experienced, so I do apologize. I hope that I have not given you a poor opinion of myself. I am not prone to bad judgment or sleeping around."

Bridgit shook her head, laughing and clarified her statement. "Ah, you know what I mean, sleeping outside under trees with strangers."

Bridgit wiped her mouth and then let out a huge laugh and just said, "Todd, I am obviously not capable of choosing my words correctly right now."

Todd chuckled, then they all started laughing.

Bridgit made one more attempt. "When I came upon Stella at the banyan tree yesterday, I was mesmerized by the music that she was playing. It brought me to tears seeing Stella so completely vulnerable with tears in her eyes as she played. I had to pause and hear it all the way through. It moved me deeply. I guess I needed a good cry too." She reached over to Stella and touched her arm with a comforting affection.

"It was the song that I would play for Mom. Then I played a new song, one that I had just started working on." Stella chimed in.

Todd looked adoringly at Stella, understanding the need to play her mother's favorite song. He understood that her music was her therapy.

Bridgit continued, "When I discovered that I had lost my credit card, I was in a bind. Stella came up with the plan to have me accompany her to the hotel so that I could exchange my currency in the hope of getting a hotel room. We didn't make it in time to do that, and that is when your daughter generously offered to let me stay with her for the night." She smiled as she reached for her teacup.

"We decided to go back to the tree today, and as Stella played the harp, I felt guided to do a visualization, and after that, I honestly do not know what happened. The next thing I knew, we were being awakened by you, though it does feel like something amazing happened during all of this."

Bridgit looked at Stella. Both of the girls were counting the moments when they could discuss with one another what had just happened to them.

"Well, I think this is all extraordinary! Especially the fact that you could potentially be a long-lost relative from the US and to stumble upon one another at the Banyan tree, in another country? Remarkable! It all sounds quite absurd, but stranger things have happened." He chuckled and looked at Stella once more.

Stella's eyes were wide open, and Todd could see her eyebrows arched over the top of her glasses as she nodded her head in agreement and repeated his words in an even more emphatic way, "Stranger things HAVE happened!"

The meal was served, and the girls continued to gorge themselves on each dish that arrived. Todd could not get over how much food the two women could put away.

"So, tell me, Bridgit, what do you know of your ancestry? Perhaps we can solve the mystery of our possible connection?" Todd was fully prepared to hear Bridgit present her lineage.

"Well, that will be a bit difficult for me because I lost my parents, Thomas and Prudence Phare, when I was six years old." She managed a slight smile and then continued as Todd looked at her with compassion for her loss.

"I went to live with my Mother's parents, the Carr's, in Louisiana. Grand Dad, Brian, was an arborist and operated a tree farm. He taught me most everything I know about trees." She winked at Stella, as a way of mentally saying that she didn't know that one could travel through them.

"Oh, so you are an arborist as well?" Todd engaged her to explore the subject further.

"Yes, I am. I went to college in California at UC Davis. I received an Environmental Sciences degree and then directly out of school I naturally gravitated back to the trees, as they have always been an obsession of mine. Right after my final year of college, when I was working a new job with the forest service, I, unfortunately, had to handle the closing of my Grandparents business after they both passed that year. I really couldn't maintain the business while working a new job, nor could I do much of anything quite frankly. It was just too stressful. So while I was back in Louisiana, I went through my Grandparents estate, and put the sentimental family things, you know, the keepsakes, into storage so that I can go through it another time."

She looked down at her hands and softly looked back up at Todd, her eyes opening up again slowly as if she wanted to hold her Grandparents in her mental image and bring them with her into that moment.

Todd could feel her need for a moment of silence, and when he thought she was complete with the memory, he continued quizzing her.

"So, you have no parents and no Grandparents? What of your Dad's side of the family? The Phare's?"

"Well, from what I understand, my Grandpa died in the early 80s, and my Grandmother passed away not long after that. So obviously, there was no one else to take me when my parents passed."

"Bridgit, we too have lost Stella's mother, but I am wondering if you feel to share about how your parents both passed. Was it together?" He was trying to be as gentle as possible, but he felt it was a crucial part of healing, to talk about their loved ones.

"Hmm, that fateful day. The day my life changed forever." She cleared her throat and pulled her hair back behind her ear, and formulated where to begin as she leaned into the table to speak quietly on the subject.

"My parents were avid stargazers and never missed a chance to catch a meteor shower. We had been at my Grandparents farm in Louisiana and on the night of April 21st, 1990, they drove down the road from the farm, into an open field, so that they could get a good view of the Lyrid meteor showers. The area was rural and a perfect place to have a front-row seat to the Cosmos."

She paused for a moment, with a smile on her face, and then continued as she could tell that Todd was intrigued to hear more.

"A wind storm began to kick up out of nowhere, and they had to jump into the car. A neighbor had driven by and saw them fleeing the storm towards the farm as he was headed in the opposite direction to his own home. Anyway, they tried to get back to the farm but as they were just a mile or so away from the property a huge tree uprooted and fell on top of the car. They perished together that night."

Stella had tears in her eyes and reached over to hold Bridgit's hand, as Todd reached for her other one. The three of them realized that they had so much more in common than a surname.

Bridgit said, "The irony is that it was a tree that took them." Her voice trailed off as the three sat there holding the memory. Todd shifted the conversation to his travels to help ease Bridgit out of an uncomfortable moment.

After the meal, the three of them went back to the hotel, where they insisted that Bridgit stay with them again in the Penthouse. The next day, Todd assisted Bridgit in making her plans back to Scotland. He also insisted that she come for a visit once she was back in the States.

And the wheel turns...

Chapter 26

Bridgit's Return to Scotland

Days later, Bridgit awoke from a dream in the room that she kept at an Inn, in Scotland, where the whole saga began. She looked around the room and thought about everything. She had gotten in from the airport late the night before from India, to regroup and collect her things.

She had never imagined her interests in trees would have taken her into other realms and other countries, via the other realms. It seemed like a year had passed, but it had only been a week since she was pulled into this saga.

The night before she arrived back at the Inn, as she walked into the front entrance, the caretakers were having a warm cup of milk before bedtime. They jumped up, happy to see her back in Scotland, and asked how she got along in India. Bridgit, exhausted from the trip, was startled at their knowledge of her whereabouts. They reminded her of the note that she had left for them, explaining that she had to take a quick trip to Mumbai to take the place of a colleague who was supposed to be presenting at a conference but had a family emergency.

They then went on to ask her about the conference. Bridgit just made up something because she had not thought through what she would tell people. The Innkeeper then pulled the note off of a stack of post and showed it to Bridgit as they spoke.

Bridgit immediately noticed the small tree that was drawn on the note with great precision. Clearly, the drawing was Breacher's.

She responded to the note, "Oh yes, I was so crazed when I left here, and I wasn't sure if I put the reason for the trip. The conference was great. Thanks for asking." Bridgit winked at the Innkeeper with a smile, trying to act casual.

Looking at the time on the wall clock, she said, "I hope you don't mind, but I think I will go on up to the room now. Perhaps we can catch up in the morning?" They all wished one another a good night with the blow of an air kiss, then Bridgit trotted up the stairs with her purse over her shoulder.

Bridgit entered her room, immediately noticing her credit card on the dresser. She set her bags down on the floor and plopped on the edge of the bed, letting everything sink in as if she was laying out a thousand piece puzzle in her mind, sorting all of the edge pieces to frame the happenings of the week, in search of clues that she may have missed.

In her mind, she began to see all of the happenings as a spiritual catharsis, having both an emotional aspect and a cognitive one as well. She knew her life was not ever going to be the same again.

In her psych class in college, she remembered how an emotional breakdown was known as emotional-somatic discharge, and on the other side of the coin was the cognitive aspect where the unconscious becomes conscious. She felt like that part had been achieved. Laughing to herself of her own warped analysis, she got up to get dressed, thinking about the emotional aspects of Catharsis. She could feel it coming.

In the early morning, Bridgit slipped on her boots, grabbed her jacket, and headed out the door before tea. She just couldn't deal with the questions that the Innkeepers would have for her in their attempt at polite conversation.

Her thoughts went to Stella at that moment. She had feelings of sentiment and longing for her companion. Bridgit did not realize how much comfort Stella had brought her until now.

Todd, Stella's father, whose kindness overwhelmed her, as did his generosity, was also someone warm in her heart. He had paid for her airfare and put her on the plane from India back to Scotland. He even hugged her goodbye and insisted on her calling when she came back to the United States. Oddly, he felt like the father that she did not have.

A smile covered her entire face as she strolled towards the hedges at the end of the walkway. Laughing to herself, she felt that Todd was unrelenting in his quest to determine their familial connection. She mentally made a note in her mind to visit the Registry office later that day to gather the genealogical information.

Bridgit pulled her jacket closer to her neck as the wind began to pick up. She was taking her last walk down to the tree where her life changed for the second time, to somehow honor Tuuru for her service.

Bridgit continued replaying in her mind everything that had happened, like rewinding an old film. The cast of characters so dear to her heart now played out on the screen: Shamalaine, Bewain, and members of the Clan of Phare.

She smiled when remembering Eldorman's face when she first awoke to find that she wasn't in the 3D world anymore. She laughed out loud about it now. She took in a deep breath of fresh air, noticing the leaves falling and the smell of fertile soil under her feet. She realized that the 3D Earth was much like the 4th dimension in this way.

She then saw in her mind's eye the sweet, yet pesky, elemental, Avery. His presence was also heartwarming in a familial way.

150

She continued down memory lane as she walked. Bridgit thought of the Guardian, Butler, and all the Builders of Form that were introduced to her. She smiled as she recalled them in their natural habitats, and then it happened. She saw Breacher suddenly pop onto her mental screen. She recalled the day she met him in the Great Hall, with her mouth stuffed full of grapes. She remembered connecting with his eyes and then suddenly, like the films in days gone by, the screen froze, and all that was there were his eyes. The face...that face, she thought.

Memories came flooding back to her as the movie changed. It was she, as Kaialena now, with Breacher, standing in a lover's embrace. Then another memory came, going even further back in time.

She stopped at that moment, losing her breath. The membrane that had held her memories at bay had dissolved completely as she made her way to the nearby tree. She leaned against it to brace herself as she felt herself going down.

Her heart was beating fast, and a tear rolled down her cheek as she saw in her mind's eye the memories of her life with Breacher, her husband. Flashes of their wedding day replayed over and over. She then saw the shell and how they used it in sacred rituals or when emotions were strong.

"The Shell!", she cried out in anguish. Her hand covered her mouth now, realizing why Breacher had put the shell in her purse.

She fell to the ground sobbing. "It's him! All of this time! All of this time... it was him!!!"

She wiped the torrents of saline flowing from her face. Her hands grabbed the earth for traction, soil now deep in her nail beds as she stumbled to her feet. She ran as fast as she could to get to Tuuru. As she came around the bend, in the woods, she came to a sudden stop. There on the forest floor laid one of the most sacred treasures of multiple dimensions, Tuuru, the World Tree, uprooted.

Bridgit yelled out in a guttural, sorrowful manner and nearly fainted. She managed to fall on her old friend, and this time she tried in vain,

151

once more, to gain access to her home.

"Let me in!!!" She yelled, grieving for her love, and at the same time grieving for everyone that she had lost in her lifetime as Bridgit.

She yelled again, "Let me in!! I choose him!"

She pleaded, "PLEASE!!! Let me in", as her body shook violently with such force as she sobbed.

"I choose him," she said in a whisper as her voice trailed off to a barely audible sound. There was nothing but silence. Bridgit lay on top of Tuuru until nightfall, waiting with a glimmer of hope.

As she waited, she processed the knowing that Shamalaine and Bewain knew who Breacher was to her but did not tell her. She also knew that Breacher was able to go between the realms with his bilocation skills, so she questioned why he had not come for her.

Her life was officially a mess in two realms, and it emotionally drained her. She went back to her room, falling on the bed, and went into a deep sleep. She slept for hours, lucid dreaming of all the characters that had shown up in her life.

Gordavin was in her dream. Bridgit dreamt of herself as Kaialena, who was crying in the dream. Gordavin was comforting her as she shared with him how she felt betrayed by Shamalaine and Bewain. Gordavin brought Kaialena's attention to her homeland and beyond, reminding her of her galactic heritage and the mission that she had agreed to fulfill.

Gordavin told Kaialena that her mission was beyond the love of one and that truly, it had to do with the love of all. He told her to look deep into her heart, and she would remember her part in the planning of this multidimensional mission.

He said, "You knew that your love for Breacher would bridge the worlds, and it would be what would compel both of you to complete your missions as the two aspects of our beloved Gaia come together. It would take your love of not only each other but of your clan and Gaia herself to gather up the chosen ones who will take their places at the appointed time to usher in the new world."

Kaialena watched as Gordavin presented the visual on a movie screen. She saw it all playing out and understood what he shared was true.

As Bridgit stirred in her bed, she could hear Gordavin's voice trailing off as he said, "He will meet you again, and it won't be long now." His voice faded as the dream evaporated in thin air, and the sounds of chirping birds in the early light of the new day sounded.

She threw the blankets off her weary body and walked over to her window, not sure how to go on. She wiped the fog off the window and looked at the grass outside, densely layered in dew. Her breathing fogged the window once more.

She looked around the room, ready to put it all behind her. It was too painful. She walked over to the dresser and began to collect the tree drawings that were all over the room. She walked over to the mirror, where she had placed her favorite picture between the mirror and its frame.

"That's funny," she said out loud as she realized that the picture wasn't there. She got on her hands and knees looking for it, hoping that it had simply fallen behind the dresser. The picture was the one of Tuuru, with a border that said, Where is he?

Frustrated, she pulled out all the dresser drawers, and then looked in all of the stacks of papers sitting on top of it and nothing. She sat on the bed to think, wondering where she could have put it.

Then she had a thought, "Breacher!" she yelled. "Could he have taken it?" she thought out loud. She smiled, thinking of him and she knew that had to be it. She also knew that he would have taken it because it was proof that she was searching for him. She hoped that he could tell from her drawings that she missed him and loved him deeply even though at the time, she did not remember who it was that she was in such agony over.

She realized that had Shamalaine and Bewain told her of her husband, she would not be standing there at that moment, and she knew it was the right thing to do. She took a deep breath to let it all go. The dream with Gordavin had been very helpful and comforting to her, so she whispered a prayer of gratitude, addressed to him, in the hopes that he would feel her appreciation for his words of wisdom in the Dreamtime.

She grabbed her wrap and went downstairs for tea and toast to plan the rest of her day. For some reason, knowing that Breacher had the picture comforted her and she knew that it would all be okay. After her morning tea, she intended to find the other pieces of her life's puzzle, the ancestry of the Clan of Phare, and how she and Stella were possibly linked in the 3D world.

On the other side of the veil, Breacher sat in his room, staring at the tree drawing of Tuuru that he found in Bridgit's room. Looking at the border of the picture, he placed his finger on the words, Where is he?

He was able to connect with her emotion, her pain. A tear rolled down his face, hitting the picture on the exact opposite side from where there was already a tear stain, which created a beautiful effect in the watercolor print. He blotted his tear with his shirt and held it to his heart as he whispered, "I am here."

And the wheel turns... ◉

Chapter 27

Bridgit's Heritage

The next day Bridgit thanked her host for a lovely lunch, the first real meal she had eaten in days. The innkeeper forced it upon her in a motherly way that could not be resisted. She felt nurtured by it and full.

Bridgit had escaped the Inn earlier that morning to search for clues of her heritage at the General Registrar's office. She had scoured through the materials as quickly as possible, with the intent to make copies of the documents and then delve into her ancestry more fully when she returned to the US. She was confident that she found a starting point, the crest of the Clan of Phare, and that she and Stella would find out how they were related.

Placing the material on the table in her room, Bridgit opened the window to catch the warm afternoon breeze. This time of year, in early spring, was chilly in the morning, a few hours of warmth in the afternoon, and then back to cold evenings. Bridgit didn't want to miss her chance to breathe in the warm, clean air on her last day in Scotland.

Once she opened the window, she felt a gentle breeze on her face and inhaled the air, relaxing her body as she contemplated her time there in Scotland. A buzzing sound brought her out of the reminiscing as she fixed her attention on a solitary bee that found its way into the room.

A gust of wind blew through the window at that moment, lifting her hair in the breeze, just as the bee flew by her ear. Bridgit knew that she would need to be calm, as she could feel the bee was now tangled in her hair. She went over to the mirror to watch as she leaned forward over the dresser and pulled the strands of her hair apart from the bottom, trying to open up the space between the strands of hair that had entangled the bee.

The hair loosened with a little shake of the strands, but it was just enough motion to agitate the bee as it flew out away from her head. She breathed deeply and ran her hand through her hair, moving it away from her forehead as she looked for the bee in the room.

She backed up towards the bed, still looking at the area near the mirror, not sure where the bee went. Then suddenly, the bee came at her with great agility, flying right into her face. She knew better, but she began flailing her arms until she felt the strike. It zeroed in on her forehead, and like a power drill, the bee stung her with a mighty force. Shocked, she fell backward and landed on the bed.

Stunned and dazed, she lay there for a moment. When she tried to sit up, she realized that she felt her blood pumping faster than she had ever felt it, and her vision began to fade. Her mind escaped the physical as she was now floating in an inner world, dark and quiet. She let go as her spirit explored the in-between world, only being aware of one thing, a silver cord.

Bridgit was stunned by what she was experiencing. She had no awareness of the physical, but wherever she was, it was clearly not physically on Earth. She had her cognitive abilities and knew that she was having an out of body experience from the silver cord being with her as she floated in space. She looked around and wondered where she was.

A voice responded to her internal thoughts. "You are at the edge of the hologram." Bridgit began to see a hexagonal grid coming into focus, that was wrapped around the outer reaches of Earth. She hovered between the Earth and the hologram for some time, trying to understand what was happening.

She then heard a voice say to her, "Breathe. Fill yourself with the plasma around you. Breathe in and out from your head, not your nose. See the plasma enter your crown and out the back of your head at the base of your neck, in a rhythmic breath, as it makes a circle of energy feeding your crown." The voice was sporadic and ancient and somehow calming as it reminded Bridgit of Tuuru.

Still floating, Bridgit breathed in through her crown and out the back of her head and repeated it eight times as she was suspended in the space above the Earth. She noticed a shift in her perception. She saw an opening on the edge of the hologram as if suddenly the entire atmosphere around the planet was now two-dimensional, and she could see a flat edge around the hologram.

With her intention, she propelled herself to this area where she found an opening at the flat lines of the hexagon-shaped hologram. She willed herself to the opening and entered it. She was now in an unknown space outside the matrix of the hologram.

After some time adjusting to her new environment, Bridgit found herself inside what appeared to be a Beehive within the cosmos.

The voice spoke, "Very good child, we have been waiting for you."

It was still pitch black within the hive, but she was not afraid. She recalled the moment when she was introduced to Phyre and knew to readjust her perception of her environment.

She focused for a few moments until the flickering of a flame began. It was enough to offer her the guidance needed to make her way within the outer core of the hive.

The voice spoke once more. "We hoped that once you arrived, you would remember where to go. Please forgive us. Follow the light into the inner sanctum."

The walls began to glow, and Bridgit could see that they were made of an amber-colored substance. She followed the light down the hallway into the main cavernous space where the Bee Masters awaited her.

They asked her to joined them at the table where the Master's had been waiting. At the other end of the table was a beautiful woman with golden hair spun high on her head like a beehive. She was the leader and what Bridgit could only assume to be the Bee Mistress.

Once Bridgit sat at the appointed seat, an attendant came to her with a white conical headdress that had golden rods that came out from the side and then up at a right angle, like an antenna. As soon as it was placed upon her head, she began to see clearly.

Bridgit recalled this place from eons past and saw herself as part of a hive sisterhood called the Melissae. She remembered the power that surged through this very hive, a force that was able to propel one into the realms long forgotten. The Bee Masters were silent as she explored her own memories of a life long ago, early in the life of mother Gaia.

"We have held the Bee mysteries as long as the count of days. You have been brought here to recall your training in the activation of portals, which is one of the blessings of Bee medicine."

Bridgit remained still and took in the information that the Bee Mistress was sharing, feeling happy to be with her sisters of the hive, the progenitors of Goddess Mysteries.

The Bee Mistress continued her instruction. She helped Bridgit recall how to use the sound of the bees to create a vibrational shift, an opening, and said, "We have waited for you, dear Melissae, for the time has come to open the portal."

Bridgit had a deep sense of knowing this was true, but she still had the need for clarity as to exactly why they wanted her help and where she was exactly.

The Bee Mistress intuited her thoughts and responded. "You have come back to yet another part of your past, another aspect of your being. You have learned thus far that an aspect of your being resided in the 4th dimension as Kaialena, would you agree?"

Bridgit had an expectation now welling up in her as she knew that she was about to be given another part of her spirit back or at least the memory of her soul's journey. "Yes, it is true that I have dwelt within an octave of the 4th dimension as the one known as Kaialena", she responded.

The Bee Mistress continued, "You have lived for eons of time and have had numerous lives within many realms and densities. With each of these lives that you lived, you have gathered knowledge and gifts that you are being called upon to remember, to gather and to utilize for the enlightenment of the ages. This time is the culmination of all of your lifetimes, this is the time of your bridging the worlds."

She walked towards Bridgit and placed her thin, cold finger upon Bridgit's forehead, in the very spot of the sting and energized her pineal gland in the center of her brain. Bridgit felt a tingling sensation, both in her body lying on the bed and as the dimensional double Bridgit that was within the hive.

The Bee Mistress addressed her once more, "We are well hidden in a star cluster known to your world as Praesepe. We have concentrated our feminine energy within this hive for a moment in time upon Gaia when the membrane around the earth dissolves, and a new world emerges."

She held her hands in front of her, with fingers folded upon the other and said, "It is time to pierce the veil between the worlds, to allow the pulse of the Divine Feminine to resurrect all life in preparation for the new creation. This will be your task as it will prepare you for future encounters as a Gate Keeper. The Bee Cluster gateway must now be opened and anchored on the Earth in a most sacred land of Galactic heritage, the place known as Tintagel. The bees will be your guide."

Bridgit had felt into everything the Bee Mistress shared. She felt it deep in her core that she was exactly where she needed to be at this moment in all of her life existences. She silently laughed at the thought of keeping up with so many aspects of her soul, though this task seemed reasonably easy compared to creating a new Earth.

"I am ready," Bridgit replied.

The Bee Mistress began, "Close your eyes and go within, Melissae. You must view the hive as the womb of the Divine Feminine. See the veil that is between Gaia and the womb of the Divine. She is the virgin awaiting her lover's touch."

In the in-between realms, Bridgit sat at the table listening to the Bee Mistress but was also floating within the Beehive cluster, in the constellation of Cancer. She viewed the hive and then detected what looked like a hexagonal-shaped portal just on the edge of it. She then heard the Bee Mistress say to focus on the sound of the bees.

Bridgit could hear the buzzing as it built up energy around her. In her mind's eye, Bridgit could see the actual veil within the hexagon portal. Just off in the distance, she saw a phallic-shaped energy floating towards the veil. She observed it as the bee's sound vibrated the gate, while the phallic energy came into contact with the veil, piercing the hymen of the portal. Male and Female energies merged, activating the Bee Hive for service.

The Mistress stated, "The portal is open for the pulse to enter. The manger is now activated."

Bridgit noticed that the buzzing of the bees lessened until it was a low hum.

The Bee Mistress then said, "Very good, Melissae. Now, view your physical body from here. I want you to erect an antenna from the crown of your head up to the hexagon portal."

Bridgit easily could see this happening without much effort at all. The antenna itself was effortless to extend, and as it made its way through the heavens, it stopped just short of the portal.

"Now imagine that your antennae can be molded to fit any doorway. Shape it into the form of the hexagon. Once you do this, connect your hexagon to the hexagon portal magnetically and wait until it clicks into place." They all waited until Bridgit accomplished bringing her antenna upward and clicked into the hexagon portal.

"That is very good, Melissae. Now with your intention, bring your antenna, with the portal connected, to the place upon Gaia where the Great Bear, Arthur was conceived. There you will find a cave with a throne prepared and a crown placed upon it."

With intention, Bridgit willed her antenna and the portal to energetically connect to the landscape within the region of Cornwall, in the UK. She remotely viewed a cave that looked familiar. Yes, she recognized it as Merlyn's Cave. As she moved through the cave, she imagined planting her feet directly in front of a throne, precisely as the Bee Mistress had presented.

She could see a royal crown sitting upon the throne, waiting for the rightful owner. She felt the portal clicking into the geomantic landscape and knew that it was accomplished.

The Bee Mistress spoke, "You have accomplished much at this moment, and great energies will come from this effort. You are to retain this gift of activation as a facet of your work during the great transformation. You will know without a shadow of a doubt when the Divine Feminine pulses through this portal as all upon Gaia will be transformed."

The Bee Mistress moved closer to Bridgit, "We thank you for your service to all of the realms. You are cherished in the hearts of the Fates. Peace is willed for you, and love is not an expectation but a known force that moves everything in the direction of home."

With those words, the attendant removed the headdress from Bridgit's head and gave Bridgit a sip of the divine nectar of the Gods. The humming of the bees sped up once more, and Bridgit was snapped back into her body that lay on the bed at the Inn. She opened her eyes and was elated by the experience of the Bee Masters and more curious

161

than ever to know more about why the portal needed to anchor at Tintagel, and what did Arthur have to do with anything?

And the wheel turns...

Chapter 28

Bridgit's Return to America

Stella peaked out the window of her home to see a familiar face stepping out of a car in the driveway. She ran to the door, opened it, and screamed with joy to see Bridgit once more. It had been three weeks since Stella had arrived home in Calabasas, California, from the trip to India, and she found that she couldn't concentrate on much of anything since the tree incident.

By now, she and her Dad, Todd, had discussed the rare events that had occurred the moment Bridgit entered their lives, and it made them both wonder what they could expect when she came for a visit. So many things happened in just a few days of knowing Bridgit that they were sure her visit would most likely be otherworldly.

As Bridgit entered the Phare home, the ladies hugged as sisters would. Stella brought Bridgit into the foyer of the sprawling house. It was clear to Bridgit that Todd was a success at making a living. Their home, filled with antiques from his travels, was mixed with Stella's musical influences in such a beautiful manner that to Bridgit, it was comforting as she took in the tour of the home.

The house had an open floor plan with a large kitchen in the back, left side of the first floor. Stella's piano and harp were centrally located in the enormous conservatory area between the kitchen and living room, making the house the perfect home for entertaining.

Stella led Bridgit up the wide staircase to the guestroom. She hoped that Bridgit could stay forever, but they both knew that they had some things to do, like creating new worlds, and all sorts of wild things to figure out that she would never have imagined contemplating had she not been at that tree at the very moment when their lives collided.

"Here it is, your home away from home." Stella grinned as she opened the door. Bridgit walked into the room and saw beauty everywhere. Stella had bought an orchid, which she placed in a decorative glass container with seashells placed nearby. The symbolism touched Bridgit deeply.

Two large paintings of trees hung over the queen-size bed, and a writing table held ample art supplies in the drawer in case she was inspired to draw. A Tiffany stained glass lamp sat on the writing desk giving off an amber hue.

Bridgit had a small tear in her eye as she realized that all of the things that Bridgit had shared with Stella, from her time with the Clan of Phare, had been absorbed and recorded in Stella's mind.

Stella noticed Bridgit's tears about to fall. She ran over to the side table, pulled the drawer open, and grabbed a tiny flat shell and handed it to Bridgit, immolating the idea of capturing her tears. They laughed gently and hugged one another, then Bridgit inspected the shell in her hand and for a moment was lost in thought. Her mind went back to Breacher.

"Let's not get all mushy right off the bat!" Stella said, trying to lighten the mood with a quick shift of energy that only she could bring, though she was unaware of the real reason why Bridgit was in tears.

"I will get your bags in a bit. Let's go down to the kitchen for some coffee. We have some catching up to do before Dad gets home. He is stopping on his way home to grab some food", she turned around, and her body language suggested to Bridgit that she was going to love what Stella had planned.

Stella said, "We thought that in honor of your visit, it was only appropriate that we have Indian food!" She started chuckling and grabbed Bridgit's arm to lead her to the kitchen for girl time.

Bridgit chimed in, "When in Rome!" and they both realized that they had a thing, a shtick all their own.

Walking into the kitchen, Stella escorted Bridgit to the barstool at the center island. The stool was like a miniature version of a Queen Anne chair and more comfortable than most standard-sized chairs that Bridgit had ever experienced.

Bridgit took it all in and chuckled at her life, thinking how bizarre it had become, almost overnight, with new friends that truly felt like family. That is when Bridgit remembered something that she had brought along to share.

"I tell you what, while you are making the coffee, I am going to run out to the car to grab my satchel. I have some things to show you. A bit of genealogy! I haven't had much time to look at it, but today is the perfect time for it." Bridgit winked and turned quickly and was out the door so fast it crossed Stella's mind that perhaps Breacher had taught her how to bi-locate.

Giggling with that thought in mind, she pulled the kitchen drawer open to get a wooden spoon out, the one her Mom gave her. She wanted to bring her mother's energy into the room, as the kitchen was always where the center of all the action was growing up. She poured the water into the coffee maker, measured the grounds, and placed the long carved wooden spoon out to show Bridgit.

Stella looked up at the pictures in the kitchen and suddenly realized that most of the images in the kitchen had a spoon or spoons in them. She began laughing out loud, surprised at her lack of awareness at this detail. At that moment, Stella's mental screen lit up, and an image of her mother spoon-feeding her came up. The tears came flowing.

Bridgit returned to the kitchen to find Stella with her eye makeup all over her face, and just like the first day they meet, they just stared at each other, not quite sure what to say or do for one another. This was the sort of thing they should have been trained for, something that their mothers would have taught them how to handle.

"You okay?" Bridgit asked, maintaining her distance.

"Oh, Plop!" was the response from Stella, seeing her reflection in the glass of the oven door.

"Plop?" mortified by the response, Bridgit could not translate this one.

Stella laughed out loud, "Yes! PLOP!!! My new word! It's a polite way of saying, "OH, SH...!" Stella didn't finish saying the word, but Bridgit got it.

Stella said, "I promised Dad that I would try to stop my vulgar swearing." She placed her hand over her mouth like she did not know what he could be referring too, as she grinned and grabbed a tissue to wipe her nose and yet again, her eye makeup.

"What is it about our union, that seems to make my makeup fly off my face in a sticky mess?" Stella smiled to hide the pain, half teasing Bridgit, and half serious.

Bridgit retorted, "Don't blame me! One minute, your making coffee, and the next, you're PLOPPING all over the place! I wasn't even in the room!" Bridgit laughed at the insanity, and now, her own use of the word Plop!

She then refocused on Stella and asked, "Seriously, though, what's going on? Did I do something?"

Stella said, "Oh Geez, no! I am just a sentimental dork! That's all."

166

Picking up the spoon, she wiped the residue of ground coffee off with a towel and handed it to Bridgit and showed her the chain carved within the handle and the symbol of an anchor etched inside the heart-shaped bowl of the spoon.

"My Mom passed this spoon on to me. It is called a Lovespoon. She said that each Lovespoon has a specific symbol, and this one has a chain and an anchor inside a heart. The chain symbolizes the hopes that a loved one has for another, the hope that they would be able to be together forever. I am not sure what the exact meaning of the anchor inside the heart represents, but you get the picture. Often, they were given as a betrothal to a man's true love; at least that is what my Mom told me."

She wiped her eyes again, leaving a trail of mascara on the side of her hand. "It is actually a Phare family heirloom. This spoon was a gift from Grandmother Phare, who gave it to my parents as a wedding gift. Dad might know more about it. I like to use it to make my coffee. Just as a measuring spoon for the grounds. When I use it, it feels like I am putting a little bit of my Mom's love for me into the start of my day."

Bridgit touched her heart with her hand and patted her chest, silently showing Stella that she deeply felt what she was saying. Stella gave an irreverent smile as she made the motion of a magic wand. She was immolating stirring her coffee and then continued, "When you were outside, I was thinking about the spoon, and when I looked up I realized something that I had never realized in all of the years that we have lived here."

Bridgit waited as Stella wiped her eye once more with the towel. Using the spoon as a pointer, she pointed to all the pictures on the wall in the kitchen. "The pictures! They all have spoons in them! A couple of them are even bent!"

Laughing at the absurdity of this realization now, she said, "As I realized that the pictures had spoons in them and that my mother gave me this spoon, I heard the words in my head, we are spoon-feeding you. I saw my Mom feeding me with it. You know, when I was a kid.

But the words, we are SPOON-FEEDING you... what do you think that means?"

Her eyes were wide, with a bizarre look on her face. "I know, I'm crazy, right?!"

She looked up as Bridgit was digesting her words, all the while examining the eclectic hodge-podge of pictures that really did not go together as a collection, but somehow, they were a perfect match.

Bridgit said, "Spoon-feeding, huh? I don't think you're crazy. Odd, perhaps, but not crazy!" they nudged each other and laughed.

Stella showed her the bent spoon pictures in the corner. "These here, the bent spoon ones, what do think they mean? I mean, after our time in India, I am reevaluating every detail of my life!"

Bridgit felt a deep pang within her belly to pay attention to the meaning of the spoons. She whirled around and knew it was her turn to shift the mood.

"Well, I for one will take what I can get, if that means a spoonful at a time, so be it. Let's not get too far into the meaning of the spoons when there is coffee to be had!!!" Bridgit lifted the cup that Stella had set out, waiting for it to be filled. "How about that coffee?" winking at Stella.

Bridgit grabbed her journal to jot down the spoon references while Stella walked over to the island to pour the coffee. The smell of the dark roast was enough to wake up an army by smell alone. Bridgit inquired, "Do you have cream? I normally drink coffee with my cream if you know what I mean."

While grabbing the cream from the refrigerator, Stella felt comforted by Bridgit's presence and realized that Bridgit is the only person aside from her Dad that she has talked about her mother. It felt good not to be judged for how she was feeling. She felt that she could be her authentic self around Bridgit.

Bridgit pulled out the stack of papers that she acquired in Scotland and laid them out on the island.

Stella handed her the coffee and said, "Did I tell you how glad I am that you are here?" She just smiled at her then came around the island and gave her another hug, this time a bit longer than the first. Then Stella barked an order, like a mother, "Now drink up, don't let it get cold!"

Bridgit grabbed the cream and sugar and fixed it so that she would not have a literal heart attack with the first sip. It looked good, now to taste it, she thought. Just as she took her first sip, Stella heard the garage door open.

"Oh, PLOP! Dad's home already! We've hardly had any girl time either!"

Bridgit about spit her first sip of coffee out when Stella yelled plop again.

Bridgit replied calmly, "We are going to have to come up with a better word for you, sweet one." They both start cackling when Todd walked into the kitchen with his arms full of Indian take out.

"Hello there!!! I see you girls haven't missed a beat." Smiling, he placed the food on the table as Stella helped to grab a few of the bags from his hands.

Bridgit smiled at Todd, still amazed at how much he reminded her of her Father, at least what she could remember of him. She chimed in, "Todd, your home is beautiful! I am so happy to be here. Thanks again for inviting me."

Todd walked to the kitchen sink to wash off the sauce that leaked out of the bag. Shutting off the water, he reached for a sponge to clean up his mess and then grabbed a hand towel.

He said, "Well, we are certainly happy that you could take the time to come see us."

It was clear to Bridgit that he knew his way around the kitchen by the way he wiped down the sink to keep the water spots at bay. He smiled and looked towards Stella and realized that she had red eyes.

"What is all of this, pumpkin?" As he looked into her eyes, the redness was a clear give away that she had been crying.

"Oh, Dad, you know me, a sentimental fool." She smiled to keep it light for fear of going into the whole thing all over again.

"What is it, Stella?" wanting the truth, he looked at Bridgit for an answer.

Bridgit chimed in, "Oh, um, we were talking about spoons! You have quite the collection of spoon pictures on the wall, and Stella had not taken much notice of them before. Especially these two, the bent spoons here."

She brought him over to the spoon wall and showed him the two pictures. Stella chimed in while getting the plates out that she was showing Bridgit the Lovespoon, and then she noticed the spoons in all the pictures.

Todd commented, "Well, your mother loved these pictures. Every trip we took, she was always looking for just the right spoon picture. It seemed to be something that spoke to her."

Bridgit pointed back to the bent spoons like an art critic and said, "But what do you think she liked about these?"

He grinned, "Well, she actually took a course on spoon bending. She always said that we were powerful beyond belief and that we could use our minds to affect things outside of us."

Laughingly, he picked up several spoons to set the table and said, "I had to buy a whole new set of flatware, she bent all the ones we had!"

Stella couldn't believe what she was hearing. He looked at her and said, "Be happy that the spoon your holding is wooden! Every other spoon in the house was fair game. I will tell you about that spoons origin after we eat. Dig in!"

Stella didn't recall this about her mother. It made her wonder what else she did not know.

Todd motioned for the girls to join him at the table. He continued, "It was Evie's insights that helped me get to where I am today. She helped me harness my ability to focus. I miss that." No one knew what else to say, so they just piled their plates and left it alone. It was another awkward Phare family moment.

During dinner, they made small talk about Bridgit's trip and how it felt to be back in America. After dinner, they cleaned up the dishes and relocated to the living room to discuss the origins of the Lovespoon and to dive into the family tree.

Bridgit brought her papers from the kitchen and laid them out on the large coffee table, choosing to sit on the floor next to the table. Stella threw Bridgit a pillow to sit on as she laid out two more for herself and her Father. She then lit a few candles and put some instrumental music on while Bridgit organized the papers.

In the meantime, Todd went back into the kitchen to grab the Lovespoon. "What I wanted to share about this spoon if memory serves me correctly is that I recall that Grandmother Kaitlyn shared that my great, great grandfather carved it, but I can't remember his name off the top of my head. I do remember my Grandmother sent us a write up on the spoon that was in the gift box. I am so grateful for her sending it too, because she passed away about two years after Evie and I were married, and this is our connection to the past."

Todd stood looking at the spoon and then had a determined expression.

"I am sure that I have the write up here somewhere; nevertheless, I can recall that my great, great, grandfather was a seaman and spent many a day away from his love, who did become his wife. I remember her name oddly enough. It struck me as strangely familiar, and somehow it always stuck in my memory. Her name was Barabell Akira. Strange name, isn't it?"

He paused to look at the girls, seeing Bridgit writing his words in her journal. He continued, "I will look for that paper tonight. I might know where it is," Todd reassured the girls.

Both Stella and Bridgit were thrilled to hear the story of the family heirloom and encouraged him to find it. Stella offered to help him look for it later.

Bridgit got up to get a glass of water, carrying the papers with her. She sat them down on the island in the kitchen and pointed at the cabinets to locate a cup.

Stella yelled out to indicate to the left of the refrigerator while following her into the kitchen. Bridgit helped herself to the water from the refrigerator door as Stella began to peruse the stack of papers that Bridgit laid on the island. She looked up and watched Bridgit move about the kitchen, discovering the opened package of biscotti and pinching off a small piece to nibble on, entirely in her own world at that moment.

Once Bridgit swallowed the bite, she began to explain that she had had very little time to look through all of the documents given the circumstances that happened to her while in Scotland. She had not shared with them the journey outside of the veil but just indicated that she had a lot of loose ends that needed to be tied up.

Stella noticed a paper poking out of the stack with a colorful shield and asked, "Whatcha got there?" pointing to what looked like a family crest with her fingers twitching like a little girl wanting her dolly back.

Bridgit grinned at Stella's youthful expression and nodded for her to pull it out. Bridgit walked to her side, wiping the crumbs from her mouth and placed her hands on the document while Stella held it in her hands as well.

"Well, this is probably the most significant thing that I found. The crest of the Clan of Phare." Bridgit stated as she looked at Stella with a smile.

Todd walked over to Stella's side to take a look. All three noses pointed towards their family's past.

Stella read from the paper attached to the shield as Todd and Bridgit listened. She began the tale of the Clan of Phare with the acknowledgment of the name itself. "The word Phare has many meanings. The obvious meaning is that of someone being fair, or handsome even. Phare can also be derived from the word fairy." They looked at one another with big eyes. "I never even once thought of that!" Stella blurted.

Stella looked back to the page for more insights and continued to read from the pages of the text. "It goes on to say that the Clan of Phare settled in many places around the 16th and 17th centuries."

Looking the text over a bit more, she said, "They seemed to have scattered throughout England, Ireland, and Scotland but the earliest place that the name was found is in Cumberland, where it is stated that the Clan was well equipped with manors and estates in the Northern County. It goes on to say that a group of the Clan of Phare splintered off and relocated to Cornwall in Southern England, the famous land of Arthurian legends."

Stella began to coo and looked at Bridgit and Todd and said, "This is getting juicy now!"

Again, the three of them looked at each other as goosebumps formed on Bridgit's forearm. She stood there in a very pensive state, not cooing as Stella did with this news, but more inward and then said, "I had no idea that our ancestors lived in Cornwall. I am not sure I can take many more surprises, but my gut is telling me that that is what we are in for. Just based on what I have experienced recently and the fact that my hair is standing on end, which is usually a dead giveaway."

Bridgit was momentarily brought back to the Beehive in her mind and the fact that she had anchored a portal at the place of Arthur's birth. She still was not quite ready to share that part of her journey with Stella and Todd, as it felt like it just was too much to deal with at the moment.

She turned and walked over to the door that leads to the back yard, off of the kitchen, and stared out the window for a moment. The energy of the room shifted. It felt as if they all needed a moment or two to sift through this information in their minds. Stella and Todd were not sure why Bridgit was having such a reaction to the data but allowed her space to process it.

Todd said, "I tell you what, I am pretty sure I know where Evie kept the paper that went along with the Lovespoon. If you two will excuse me a moment, I am going to run upstairs and see if I can find it. In the meantime, Stella, this would be a great time to put on some coffee. Would you be a dear and take care of that, please?" He patted Stella's shoulder as he moved past her to make his escape.

"Sure, Dad. I will pull out the biscotti to go with it. I think caffeine is what is needed, stat!" She moved around the kitchen island and began to pour out the coffee from earlier and put fresh water in the coffee maker. Bridgit settled back at the island chair on the other side of the kitchen bar.

Stella warned, "I'm going to make some noise!" as the coffee grinder buzzed for ten seconds or more, letting off the rich aroma of Italian Roast, Stella's favorite after-dinner choice.

Bridgit stared at the family crest. The most obvious thing that she noticed was the anchor on the red shield.

"Hmm, do you know if the Phare family were seafarers, other than the Grandfather that carved the spoon?" She made quotation marks with her fingers when she said the farers part to lighten the mood. It worked.

Stella laughed. "Honestly, I don't know."

174

Looking at Bridgit's disappointed face, she said, "I know. It is sad that we don't know much about our heritage other than the few do-dads that we have from the family. That is about it." She whirled her Lovespoon like a wand and pointed to the pictures on the wall once more, indicating that that's all she wrote.

Stella then set the spoon down and pulled out the cups, cream, and sugar, along with the chocolate biscotti that she purchased from the bakery down the road.

"If I had a Grandmother alive, I am sure she would have taught me how to bake... but I don't, so you will have to settle for these yummy little gems."

The biscotti were decadent, filled with nuts and chunks of chocolate inside and a thin chocolate layer on the outside, having been dipped to cover one side of the bar.

Stella said, "I have some Butterscotch ones too, but I was going to save those for tomorrow morning's treat. Do you have a preference?"

Bridgit said, "Chocolate is fine!" eager to receive her plate.

Todd came back down, having changed into a pair of jogging pants and a "Keep Calm" t-shirt. It was his way of bringing happiness to the evening.

"Found it!" He smiled as he made his way into the kitchen. He was so happy to have another Phare female in the house. He could feel their home coming back to life just with the sheer presence of Bridgit being there, even if the mood turned solemn on occasion.

They fixed their coffee and settled back in for more investigative work. This time, Todd would provide some background.

Todd pulled the paper out of an envelope, which had Kaitlyn Phare's handwriting on it.

He read the note out loud.

"Dearest Todd and Evelyn,
Enclosed is a unique heirloom of the Phare family. This Lovespoon was carved by Airleas Athdar Phare, Todd's Great, Great, Grandfather. Over the years, the love note attached to this spoon weathered, so I have written the words below:

Dearest Barabell,
Your love anchors my soul and is the chain that binds us as one heart. I bestow this token of my esteem to you with the purest of intentions that we wed as soon as I have your Father's blessing. By the time you receive this, I will already be out to sea. The waiting will be more than I can bear. To wait for you, even one more day may be the end of me. I love you, my dearest Barabell Akira. Without you, the Lighthouse of my soul would extinguish.

Yours for Eternity, Airleas"

Todd then read Kaitlyn's explanation of the Lovespoon.

"The wood was taken from a great oak after it had fallen, and the carving includes a chain that makes up the handle of the spoon, indicating his desire to be forever connected with his love. You will notice that Airleas carved the bowl of the spoon into the shape of a heart, and within it, he carved the symbol of the anchor. The anchor had more than the obvious meaning, as is stated in his love letter. Barabell's middle name was Akira. Akira means anchor. Interestingly enough, the Phare Family has an anchor within its family crest."

Bridgit looked at Todd, "Wow!"

She grabbed the paper once more to look at the anchor and said, "On the paper that shows the Phare family crest, it says that the anchor is a symbol of salvation and hope. She literally was his salvation! I can feel his longing for her was more than love, as he said in his letter, he dared not think of life without her. He needed her, desperately." Bridgit's voice trailed off as she looked down at the picture of the anchor now resting on her lap. Her voice cracked as she said the last few words.

176

"You okay?" Stella put her hand on Bridgit's shoulder. Bridgit was quiet.

"I will be right back!" Stella went to the stereo and put some different music on.

Bridgit gave her a half-smile. "Thank you. There is more that I need to tell you."

Bridgit paused for a moment and continued, "More memories have returned, but at this moment, I just can't talk about them yet." She made an effort to smile, but her mouth moved slightly, in a painful way, and both Todd and Stella knew it was related to a love lost.

At that moment, the background music was playing A Time for Us, from Romeo and Juliet. Stella looked at her Dad, as he motioned with his head to go change it. Stella jumped up and changed the music to instrumental selections then came back to Bridgit.

Stella touched Bridgit's arm and said, "We've got you. We are pretty intuitive and could tell something wasn't quite right. I am so sorry, Bridgit. The loss that you have endured is beyond my comprehension, but we are here for you."

Stella smiled at her and then looked at her Dad in gratitude that he was with her in her need to provide Bridgit comfort.

Todd shifted the energy quickly and referred to the paper from his Grandmother Kaitlyn. "It has been so long since I have seen this. I have an idea. Let's look online to see if we can find out more about the good ol' Phare family. The night is still young. You girls game?" He was trying to liven up the place, and it seemed to work.

"Sure," the girls both chimed in at the same time.

"Great. I will just set up a new account on the genealogy website, and we will see what we can find. Let me grab my laptop." Todd launched himself into the study and back again in less than a minute.

He and the girls set up the computer around the kitchen island, and he quickly created an account. Todd entered his date of birth, name, and various other tidbits that he could remember, and immediately his name popped up. He had a little flashing sign that indicated when the information was available, so the chase was on. In less than fifteen minutes, he had his family tree started.

"Let's see now, my Dad's name was August Todd Phare." He spoke out loud to keep the girls in the loop.

Bridgit turned to him and looked at him funny.

"Did you say August?" quizzing him for clarity.

"Yes, his name was August. Does that sound familiar to you?"

"I suppose they wouldn't have called him Atti, would they?" Bridgit was hoping that Atti would be a nickname for August, but it was just too far of a stretch.

Bridgit went on, "As I shared with you, back in India, I lived with my maternal grandparents growing up, the Carr's. I had very little information on my Dad's side of the family other than a few small black and white photos, but I was looking at them again recently. One was of Dad and Mom when they first got married, and the other was of my Dad's Father and his two brothers, which would have been my Grandpa Phare. The picture had a written note on the back that said, Atti, with brothers. Sadly, I don't know what Grandpa's given name was. The only thing I know is that Grandpa Phare had two brothers, and one of the three in that photo was named Atti."

"Interesting," Todd replied. "Well, let's dive a bit deeper here."

Before Todd continued the search, he made one more point. "The Phare's were a tattered group. I remember Grandmother Kaitlyn being sad when we asked about her other sons."

Todd shook his head as if a shiver came over him and then said, "Anyway, our family moved from Air Force base to Air Force base, so I did not know my Grandparents very well or any cousins for that matter. It came as a surprise when Grandmother Kaitlyn chose to pass the Lovespoon on to Evie and me."

Todd cleared his throat then shared with Bridgit that his Dad had died suddenly also. "He was an Air Force pilot killed in a tragic plane crash. While flying, he experienced engine failure, and he didn't survive.

Todd was thinking about Kaitlyn as he said, "It broke her heart, besides the fact that one of her sons went missing and the other, older son, was killed in a tragic accident ten years earlier. This family has seen its share of tragedy."

He turned back to the computer screen and positioned the cursor to the search bar within the program and wrote the name Kaitlyn May Phare and pushed the search button.

"Well, here it is. Kaitlyn May Phare, born in 1919, died in 1981. It shows she was married to Thomas Dand Phare, who was born in 1918. It doesn't show the date of his death. Let's see if we can see their children." He clicked on the flashing icon that showed the clues, and there was his Father's information along with the two other sons.

Todd said, "Well, it looks like I found it. Kaitlyn had three sons. Her first son was James Atwood Phare, born in 1938 and died in 1980. Her second son was named August Todd Phare and was born in 1940 and died in 1990. There he is. That is my Dad." Todd paused for a moment staring at the screen then continued.

"And finally, her third son Christopher Lennon Phare was born in 1943, but it doesn't indicate a year of death, so perhaps he is still out there?" He shrugged, trying to be optimistic. He looked at the girls who were very attentive to what he was feeling.

Bridgit asked, "Is your mother still living?"

Todd shook his head. "No, she passed away when Stella was three. Stella has no memory of her, which is another tragedy. Catherine was a great woman." He smiled at Stella, then turned back to the computer.

Bridgit said, "I am sorry to hear that."

Todd had moved on and was back to his focused search. Bridgit made a request of Todd. "Can you do me a favor? Can you see if James had a family? You said his name was James Atwood, right?"

"Yes. I will see what I can find here." He clicked on the icon for James.

While he was searching, Bridgit looked at Stella and said, "The picture that I was talking about, do you think that Atti could have been short for Atwood?"

Stella felt the hairs now standing on her arms and put her arm out for Bridgit to see her bodily response. She crossed her fingers and hoped that her Dad had the answer.

Todd was focused on the computer and was not listening to their conversation. He chimed in, "Okay, here we go. It looks like James Atwood Phare had one child, a son named Thomas Oliphant Phare. Born..."

At that moment, he and Bridgit both said at the same time, "Born 1957, died 1990." Todd looked at Bridgit, realizing that Kaitlyn lost both a son and a grandson in the same year in tragic accidents.

Tears rolled down Bridgit's face. Stella grabbed her and held her as they all realized that they genuinely had been brought together by some strange fate; they were indeed blood relatives. In a very bizarre spiritual event that they had no control over, destiny was steering the wheel, and their ancestors were coming back through the veils of time to remind them of who they are. They could only imagine that time would tell what it was all about.

They stayed up late that night exploring as much as they could, and when the girls went to bed, they felt emotionally spent but incredibly happy. The news was both exhilarating and exhausting to their souls. Todd stayed up late into the evening, still looking for more to discover.

In the morning, they all reconvened in the kitchen for some breakfast. Todd made scrambled eggs to give the girls the protein to sustain them. He also set out various scones, jam, biscotti, and coffee.

Bridgit slept deeply that night as if she suddenly belonged somewhere. She could finally lay her head down, knowing that she was not alone on this planet. It had been some ten years since her Grandparents on the Carr side had passed.

The clanking of silverware got Bridgit's attention, and she was hungry.

Todd said, "Bridgit, if you are up for it, I have a few more things to share." He looked deeply into her eyes, like he did the day before with Stella, looking to see her true feelings. Then he took a sip of coffee to quickly fuel before the next round.

"Sure, go for it." She truly was prepared.

"Well, I went all the way back to Airleas and Barabell. I am fascinated by their names. Barabell's maiden name was Killigrew. Barabell Akira Killigrew, how is that for a name?!"

Todd was like a nerd making a discovery. He went on to say, "I found out that Barabell means Stranger." Contemplating them with enthusiasm, he said, "I kept saying her name was so strange that it stuck with me, and it turns out to mean stranger!" he just laughed out loud with joy.

"I thought it odd, but my gut just said to look further into their names. So I dug a little deeper and found out that Barabell married Airleas Athdar Phare, my Great, Great Grandfather whose name Airleas means Oath. This guy... he is the fella that made the Lovespoon."

He turned to them and said, "I think he was named well, wouldn't you agree?" he looked at the girls who were shaking their heads, both having just taken bites from their butterscotch biscotti.

181

The moans of delight coming from Bridgit made Stella bust out laughing.

"See!!! I told you they were yummy!"

"The food and the conversation. I am in heaven!" Bridgit delighted in the joy of the morning's conversation and company as she wiggled in her chair and crossed both legs, with her feet under her thighs for warmth.

"Dad, what does Athdar mean?" Stella nudged him to continue.

"Athdar means, from the oak tree ford. So, he was very well named indeed, if you recall that he used the oak to make the very spoon you have right there." He had a silly grin, knowing he was reaching for some meaning and was pretty happy with that one.

Bridgit chimed in, now that she had swallowed. "I am still mesmerized by Barabell. STRANGER... ANCHOR..., that has to have some underlying clue. What does Killigrew mean?"

Todd did a quick search online to discover that it was a place name originating from Cheligrevus Manor, near St. Erme in Cornwall.

"There is Cornwall again!" Bridgit exclaimed. "Sorry for the interruption Todd, go on."

Todd said, "It says here that Killigrew is a variant of the surname Kilgore." After he shared the information, he went back to Barabell's page. There was a story attached to another person's tree, and he wanted to see if it would give some more information.

"Well, there is more. Another long-lost relative has connected a story to Barabell in which it relays that Barabell was the mother of three daughters and four sons. One of those sons was my Great Grandfather, named Darach Dand Phare. I think its pronounced like Derek, at least that is how I am going to pronounce it." He laughed and then got a bit more stoic.

"The story relays that Barabell and her three daughters were on board a ship headed for Cornwall when a sudden storm came upon them, and all 4 of them died in a shipwreck off the coast of Cornwall in April of the year 1900. The story says that it was a freak storm, completely unexpected and that 65 people lost their lives that day."

Bridgit and Stella were just stunned at the news. "How sad! Does this family ever catch a break?" Stella yelled out in an emotional outburst.

Bridgit looked solemn and replied, "It doesn't. I figured that out a long time ago. That is why I do not plan on having children. I couldn't bear it if I brought a child into the world, and life circumstances repeated itself. That pattern stops here."

She looked up at Stella, who had tears streaming down her face and said, "Well, at least with me."

Stella excused herself. The emotion overwhelmed her as she thought of her mother. She could barely get a word out. Bridgit and Todd were left in the kitchen feeling like the ghost of Christmas past visited them, but this was not Christmas, and it felt all too real. For whatever reason, they were drawn together at this time. A great mission was put upon the girls to remember who they are, to honor the pact they made, even if they didn't remember what that was, and Todd seemed strangely okay with it all.

Bridgit was starting to get the feeling that there was a lot more to Todd then he was letting on. Who was he in all of this, she wondered? What was he really doing in India, she thought? She just knew that if she and Stella, two of the three Phare family members present were being tapped for a monumental job, like bridging Heaven and Earth, then why is he getting off the hook? She was just too tired to figure it all out, so she excused herself, thanking him for all of his efforts and went to check on Stella.

And the wheel turns...

Chapter 29

On the Other Side of the Veil

Breacher had kept himself busy with the training of the dragons. He also took a trip with Bewain to speak with the Lyran-Sirian Council, to get an update on the efforts of the Light Liberation Movement, a group of both physical and non-physical beings who are freedom fighters on behalf of all the realms of Earth. The two Commanders, being part of the LLM, were reminded of the plan of the opposition, which consisted of hijacking humanity and all life forms for another 26,000-year cycle.

The Council spoke of how clever the opposition had been. So clever that most of the people of Earth had yet to realize the fact that they were slaves. The Council reiterated how the Dark forces took the people's sovereignty by trickery, and worse of all, they took their ability to remember who they are; they took everything. Bewain and Breacher listened, already aware of the situation, yet it still stung to hear it verbalized.

The Council spoke of a shift, a window of opportunity when there would be a perfect alignment of the dimensions. A doorway, which would be the light forces chance to break through the barriers around the Earth and shine a light on all of humanity through a pulse or wave of love that would essentially jar the technologies that the opposition had been using to keep humanity asleep.

They continued to speak of the need for this energy to be filtered through certain allies, the Life Bearers, and to some degree, the dragons and their riders. They noted other starseeds that had incarnated into the density of 3D Earth at this time as well, who could be transducers of this energy because, without these allied forces on the ground, the Council would not be able to anchor the light from within the 3D plane.

Bewain had been one of the critical allies who created the original Treaty for Planetary Peace, and it was his lineage of Freedom Fighters who had suggested the rescue strategy for Earth and her inhabitants, as the hijacking of Earth was now affecting the Galaxy.

This plan was a long time in the making, and it was to be that the best of the best had to be positioned in the various dimensions, shining the light and holding the frequencies of love, which was the highest form of light from the Divine source. They would be lighthouses amid a storm.

Breacher had the skills required to implement an essential facet of the plan. He was tasked with working with a team that would perform the creation of an entirely new grid system around the planet, from which would sustain the love pulse once it entered the atmosphere and keep the Earth from being destroyed.

For his part of the plan, the Council told him that he was to visit the Divine Mother of the Milky Way Galaxy to receive her blessings. It would be the Divine Parents who would sanction the new dragon lines, to be woven like a net around the Earth, which would create a garment of light.

Breacher received personal instructions from the Council then took his leave. Bewain stayed on to make further arrangements with the Council members to bring the Guardians into the 3D earth plane. It was time to prepare.

And the wheel turns...

Chapter 30

Distant Tollan

It was time for Breacher to meet his fate. He went into a deep state of meditation and activated his Kuxan Suum, an inter-dimensional doorway connected to his eternal cord and soared through the Galaxy, staying spiritually and physically anchored to his physical body. His bilocation skills worked within the lower frequencies, but where he was going, it required that he travel out of his body. His cord assured him of finding his way back to his realm.

He arrived at the heavenly realms of Tollan, the abode of the Celestial Parents, who were by all accounts the Celestial Sun and Moon. It was dark in the heavens. The moon and the stars were out as Breacher made his way to the heavenly abode.

Standing at the edge of a floating island, the Divine Mother awaited his arrival. She sent out her beloved guardian, the Blue Magnetic Dragon, to greet him.

Breacher floated nearby as the dragon stealthily came upon him and suggested that he ride her wave. Breacher climbed upon the female dragon as she swirled swiftly in the cosmic ocean and flew back to the celestial retreat.

Upon approach, Breacher recognized Tollan immediately. He recalled everything from the tower, to the Heavenly courtyard where the ancient Grandmothers sat by a fire, watching over the star systems.

The Grandmothers were Weavers. It was the Weavers who created the patterns of the net or grids within planetary bodies, as well as the human bodies. This ability was why he would need counsel with the Divine Mother and the Weavers, for it was they who worked closely with the Dragons, the carriers of the waves.

Breacher met with the Divine Mother within the Tower of No Time.

The Divine Mother spoke, "I am known as Regina of the Waves, the Celestial Mother of this Galaxy. I am pleased that you have remembered your presence here from a time long ago."

She placed her hand on his shoulder, leading him towards the window of time. A visual popped up on the window, like a computer screen, more ethereal, rather than having a fixed form. The energy informed him through his senses.

"It is time to cast a new net for a new surge of energy to be born from the heart of Tollan that will reset the fabric of Time and Space. It will take the efforts of the many forces of light to achieve this. Are you ready to take up the mantle of Tollan, my son?"

Breacher got down on one knee and bent his head, like a knight of the Round Table. He pledged his life force for the cause of the New Heaven and the New Earth. He remembered this all somehow, flashes of memories began flooding back to a time when he trained at the very island in the sky that he was now visiting.

As his memory flashed, Breacher had not realized that the Mother had her hand on the top of his head. As she released her hand, he looked up at her, his Mother. Regina of the Waves was the Divine Mother of his soul, and she was calling him home, for within his

DNA were the codes of a Warrior of Light, someone who carried the spark of the original divine essence and knew how to guard it. It was he and the Dragon Riders who would build the new grid of love and light around the planet Earth.

Breacher and the Divine Mother stood in the tower overlooking the Grandmothers by the fire. Suddenly he could see a vision of Gate-keepers superimposed over the Grandmothers, where the fire was burning but was now a large Sri Yantra. Four males sat at the Gateway in the positions of North, South, East, and West. They moved quickly, opening and shutting the gateways of time. It all felt so familiar to him.

"The Gatekeepers of Time work with the Divine Father. Like the Grandmothers, the Gatekeepers continually open and close the gateways, modulating the galactic energies. Very soon, there will be a cosmic alignment when the doorways stay open. At that moment, a great wave of love will pulse through all dimensions at once. This pulse will bring back the balance of all things into the Oneness. The dragon lines will be woven into a new net holding the frequencies of the Songs of Heaven."

She continued, "The dragons will be of great benefit to us now. The dragon eggs that you have in your keep came from the two Celestial Dragons, the Blue Magnetic Dragon, and the Red Electric Dragon. They are the celestial parents of the new breed of dragons that have been your task to train. They are to be known as Hieros Dragons."

She turned to him and said, "The dragons are the carriers of the waves of the Sun. The wave is a frequency that is delivered or birthed through the Heavenly Song of Creation. Keep the song alive from this day forward, and you will have done a great planetary service."

She looked him in the eye and placed her hands upon his shoulders and said, "Keeping the song alive is what is known as taking up the Mantle of Tollan."

She smiled, profoundly penetrating his heart with her love. Breacher felt the spark within his heart flame ignite into a burning desire to achieve this task beyond any other he had ever been given. He knew this was what he was trained for, this was his purpose for being, and he also knew, at that moment, that his time with Kaialena would not be forthcoming.

Truly understanding her path and his, he was determined to guard the Galaxy, set the new plan-net grid with the help of the dragons, and other planetary brethren. This task was monumental in that it was aiding Mother Earth to transcend her current state into one of pure crystalline energy in the exact moment of the alignment of the gateways.

She motioned for him to follow her out to the courtyard where the Grandmothers sat in silent contemplation. The Grandmother Weavers of Light rose to greet them as they came towards the fire. As he looked upon the ancients, they were not aged at all, but beautiful Goddesses with stars in their eyes.

He looked at the one coming closer to him. She had long black and silver hair that stood on end but in multiple waves, like a turbulent ocean. Her starry eyes sparkled.

When she opened her mouth, various pitches, like sine waves, poured forth. Breacher somehow could translate the waves into words. He heard her say, "Precious one of adoring light, we thank you for your devotion."

The Weavers bowed to him as another opened her mouth with a song, "We gift you this day with a song from our hearts to take with you as a promise of love everlasting."

They all stood in a circle and wove a fairytale into a song of divine love that is never lost, just stretched to the boundaries of time and space. The kind of love that knows no bounds and finds a way back to itself. The force of love that can bridge worlds and move mountains. He knew that kind of love well.

Another Weaver spoke these words, "Dragons and their riders are woven from the same star. You must find the proper candidates.

Look wide and far, for our beloved Hieros dragons will know their hearts. The Dragon Riders can be found on the Pegasian Star. Trial by elements, these brave one's face, you will know them by their love and grace. The Riders all have in common one thing, service to the plan to save the Human race."

He had tears in his eyes as she placed a golden six-pointed star upon his chest, like an etheric tattoo that provided him a passageway back to them but in his physical body.

The Divine Mother watched as Breacher received his activation and said, "Bring the riders to us once they have been found, and we will gift them with their starry remembrance as we have for you. Once all bear the starry emblem of the unifying principle, the MER KA BA, they can begin the casting of the net. It is of some urgency as we do not know the exact hour of the Divine Pulse. Be prudent with all that you do, swiftness in this matter is vital."

Breacher nodded in full agreement. He thanked them all from the deepest place within his heart as the darkness started to turn into light.

Before he left, the Divine Mother called for the Blue Magnetic Dragon once more to see him safely through the dimensions. She said one last thing.

"Bridgit, your precious Kaialena, is the Bridge. She will remember what is hers to do. She has already remembered you."

The dragon swirled Breacher off into the Cosmos as the Sun was rising. He turned around for one more glance at Tollan as the heavenly abode was turning. To his surprise and delight, Tollan was a dual Celestial abode that seemed to rotate from lunar activity to solar. The Divine Father, the Solar aspect of Deity, was now standing at the edge of the Celestial Tollan with his Red Electric Dragon greeting the new day.

Breacher's heart was full of the Heart Songs that the Weavers sang to him, and the knowledge that Bridgit, his beloved Kaialena, remembered him. He was taken to the edge of his realm and was soon back in his body, with his whole heart restored.

And the wheel turns...

Chapter 31

Breacher and Shamalaine Reconcile

Shamalaine was in the golden hue room tending to the forget-me-nots when Breacher appeared with the swiftness of wind. She felt his breeze and smiled. She stood up to turn to greet him as he launched himself into her arms.

"Breacher, what is this about?" Acting as if she had no clue in all the worlds where he had just been. They laughed and held each other for a tender moment.

"I wanted to thank you for all that you have done." Breacher looked sincere when he said, "I want you to know that I am fully on board with what is mine to do." He spoke from his heart to the leader of the Clan of Phare. They walked out of the room and towards Bewain's study to have a full update on Breacher's travels.

She said, "You sound like someone who has taken up the Mantle of Tollan," just as they entered Bewain's study.

Bewain looked up from his work and asked, "Commander, to what do we owe the pleasure? And what mantle might you be referring to, Shamalaine?"

Shamalaine explained, "He has had a starry remembrance of Tollan."

"I see," said Bewain.

He stood up from his desk and greeted his son in law. Bewain extended his hand, and the two commanders shook hands, then a full hug ensued. "I couldn't be happier for you, Breacher. To remember one's true origins is a deep and personal thing. There is a powerful shift that happens when one recalls their origins completely."

With a hearty laugh of absolute pleasure, they moved around the fireplace to prepare for a long afternoon. Bewain brought Breacher up to date on the strategies that he had just put into place along with the Council, while Breacher was visiting the Celestial Tollan.

Shamalaine left Bewain and Breacher in the study to catch up on the plan. All seemed to be going well, but Shamalaine was not at all settled.

And the wheel turns...

Chapter 32

A Message From a Druid

Bridgit stood at her kitchen window, watching the birds feeding their little ones as she rinsed a glass. Her mood had been one of deep introspection after her visit with Stella and Todd. Especially after she eventually opened up about her memories of Breacher. It had been two months since she and Stella were together, but it felt like yesterday. The memories of the lovespoon and the anchor still flashed in her mind. They were a gentle reminder during her busy days, a reminder of the other realm, and the ancestors and loved ones lost in this one.

As she stood in a gaze, the mail slipped through the front door mailbox shutter and landed on the entry rug. She heard the clatter of the mail slot, bringing her back to this reality once more. She walked over to the door and picked up the mail, which was mostly an assortment of catalogs and market flyers, except for one letter with an unusual postmark.

She wiped her hands on the side of her jeans and moved her hair to one side as she sat on the sofa near the window. The light from outside filtered through, and as she sat in the sunlight, she inspected the postmark. It was from Aberdeen, Scotland, addressed to Mistress Phare.

"Well, here we go," Bridgit said out loud. Someone thought enough of her to call her by her proper name, she thought, as she laughed at the very idea.

The letter was handwritten on beautiful flaxen paper with an eight-spoke wheel emblem in the top right-hand corner. On the left side of the page was a Celtic stylized version of the Yggdrasil, the Tree of Life. It was just below the Yggdrasil that the heading of the letter began. Bridgit read the letter out loud as if she had an audience.

"Dear Mistress Phare,

It has come to the attention of the Order of Bards, Ovates, and Druids that you have been keenly interested in our native trees, and in particular, a grand brown oak, as the case may be. We were most saddened to hear of the falling of the great Dryad, Tuuru, whose most precious life, we hear, was given for your very own."

Bridgit gasped as she read those words, and her reaction was to look out the window to see if someone was watching her. How could anyone know about how the tree fell? She began filtering through the layers of memories to see if she had any clue as to who could have known this outside of Stella and perhaps Todd.

The letter went on to read:

"It is our duty and privilege to invite you to a discreet Druid cere-mony as we honor the life and essence of the most ancient wise one, Tuuru. We understand that this must come as a surprise to receive this notice, but eyes are everywhere in nature. We can assure you that your presence would be most graciously appreciated, given the circum-stances that surrounded Tuuru's fall.

We will pay homage to Tuuru on the last day of the Quercus Moon (Oak Moon), this coming seventh of July. Should you be willing to be our guest, we shall make all of the required arrangements for your travel and lodging. The ceremony will be at the location of the tree, so naturally, we would accommodate you at the Inn, which you have grown accustomed.

We would also like to extend the invitation to your beloved relation that is most astute at playing the harp. We hear it has just the right "pitch" required to celebrate Tuuru's return to source during her last rites by fire. This ceremony will seal the bonds between you and Tuuru, as those who guard the lands witness this bond in deep respect and gratitude.

Please reply via the email attached to this letter, with your thoughts. We can assure you that we will be able to provide some insight into what might be a gaping hole in your present life situation. We only ask that you join us here in the land of your ancestors to discover what has been foretold and now coming to pass."

May you find peace within the silence of the grove,
Druid David (Ovate)
On behalf of Elder Druid Christopher

After contemplating the letter and the attached contact card, Bridgit was somehow relieved to know that others knew about her situation and that she could get some clues as to how to find the other Life Bearers. Time was ticking, and she knew that she had to go back, back to the land of her ancestors, Barabell and Airleas.

She pulled her phone from her purse and dialed Stella's number.

"Hello!!!!" Stella blurted out loud in a musical tone, hoping that it would brighten Bridgit's day.

"AHHHH... hello." Bridgit replied. The tone in her voice gave Stella the feeling that something was going on.

"What's going on, Bridgit? You sound to stoic for a young woman of your beauty and brilliance." Chuckling a bit to ease the feeling.

"Well... I have a proposition for you. Do you have a minute so that I can bring you up to date? It might take a few." Bridgit hinted.

Stella teased, "Oh yeah... I am REAL BUSY. Just cleaned the furry critters out from my big toenails... you gotta keep up with that, or they just move on in!" Being silly as usual, she then slipped into serious Stella mode.

Hearing the silence of Bridgit processing her humor, she said, "I'm sorry. Yes, of course, I have time to talk. Always..."

Bridgit began, "I received a letter in the mail today with a Scottish postmark. It was from a man from the Order of Bards, Ovates, and Druids."

"PL... please go," Stella caught herself about to say the PLOP word.

Bridgit continued, "The letter is an invitation for the two of us to go to Scotland, where I was staying at the Inn, and be the guests at a fire ceremony for Tuuru. The gentleman, David is his name, indicated that he would be able to shed light on our life situation and that it was important for us to come. I think he is right, Stella; I think we need to go. It would be all expenses paid too. As soon as we accept, David will make the arrangements for us."

"Let me have a moment or two. This is a crazy offer!" Stella remarked.

After a few moments, Stella asked, "What did you feel when you first read the letter...your initial reaction?"

Bridgit chuckled with embarrassment and said, "I honestly felt like I was being watched, and I literally looked out the window for surveillance vehicles! Is that crazy or what?!"

After she heard Stella make a sound of contemplation, Bridgit said, "The funny thing is, is that after I read the entire letter, I had this immediate knowing that I need to go back and honor Tuuru. I hope that you will consider going with me this time."

"Bridgit, if you feel like we need to be there, then I am in. Plus, it would be nice to spend some time sightseeing. Could we plan extra time to explore and maybe even look up more of our ancestry?" Stella asked as if she was a kid begging for ice cream.

"I was thinking the same thing. I want to take five to six weeks if you can swing it. If you can't stay for all of that time, we can work it out, but I had planned on getting more accomplished the last time I was there, and well, you know things did not turn out how I had planned."

"I think five to six weeks is plenty of time to do what we need to do. I won't have any classes then, because I graduate at the end of the month!"

"That is great, Stella. That is so exciting, and if I may add, perfect timing. Congrats!"

Remembering one other thing, Bridgit said, "Oh, by the way, David asked that you bring your harp. They know about your harps transformation from the sound of it."

"REALLY?!" Stella got a buzz down the top of her head to the bottom of her feet at that moment. "Whoa, I just felt that. Did you feel that?"

"Feel what?" Bridgit was puzzled. No telling what Stella was feeling, but curiosity always wins out. Bridgit waited to hear what had happened.

Still, she waited in silence until she couldn't stand it any longer and asked once more, "WHAT? What did you feel?"

Stella was silent as she was receiving a vision. "Hold on. Give me a minute."

Bridgit could tell this was incoming, so she patiently waited for Stella to catch whatever was being thrown down from the heavenly realms into her basket.

Stella started to come out of it enough to speak. "I am seeing us walking in a forest at dusk with tall beings that look like Elves but are in disguise as humans. We are all in hooded capes, and we are now

199

singing around a large tree in a language that is not from here. It feels like a portal is opening, and we can see the other side of the veil. Yes. That's it. You and I and many others standing around a tree and the tree has this blue light that is emanating from it."

Stella went silent once more. Then moments later, she said, "Oh wow! A being just came out of a tree. It is a dryad. You know, the spirit of the oak tree. We are all singing, just standing still, as the dryad walks off, and now the landscape has changed. We are all still with her, and the songs are vibrating so much that I can barely stay in my body. Oh! I see, she is choosing another tree to embody!"

Bridgit interrupts at that moment, "Stella, is this Tuuru? Could it be the spirit of the great tree Tuuru?"

Stella stayed with the vision and didn't answer the question as she was now more in-depth in her examination of the events playing out on her mental screen. "Tuuru will live again, through another, not the same as before, but she will be near."

"Now I see a woman in a long green dress turn away from the tree, and she is looking at us. She is beautiful with feline features. She has the most exquisite pointy ears that are more light than physical. She smiled and turned away. She is gone."

Crying, Bridgit said, "That was my mother, Shamalaine. You described her perfectly. You were really there." She let out a huge gust of air from her belly, unaware that she had been holding her breath the whole time.

"Thank you, Stella. I am so glad that we have each other. Thank you for coming with me! Not just on the trip but here, to this world. I don't think that I could do it on my own."

Stella felt her love and said, "I got your back, besides, we have not been alone. We just haven't been able to see them until now." Stella inwardly thought that Shamalaine felt very familiar, like a visitor from her dreams.

200

She let go of the feelings that she had of Shamalaine because she couldn't bear it any longer. Not wanting to say any more to Bridgit about the connection she felt with Shamalaine, she just dropped it.

Bridgit replied, "Well said, Stella. Thank you for that reminder. I do have people that have my back. I am just not used to asking for it."

She changed the subject quickly. "Please talk to Todd about this trip soon, because I will need to contact David to let him know we are coming. In the meantime, make sure to tie up loose ends on all of your school things."

Stella replied confidently, "Go ahead and email him that we are coming. Dad and I had already been talking about a trip for my graduation present, so this is perfect. Who knows, if he has some time, maybe he can fly over for a week or so?"

"Oh, that would be lovely. Ok, I will respond now and let you know when I have the details on the trip. WE ARE GOING TO SCOTLAND!!!! I have goosebumps all over my arms!" Bridgit finally broke loose and became excited now that Stella was on board.

Stella laughingly said, "HELLO! When the Ladies Phare get a call, we answer it!" the girls both laughed as Bridgit visualized Stella writing a big Z in the air ending it with a snap, like a hip chick in a mood.

"Talk to you later!" Bridgit, still laughing, hung up the phone and pulled her laptop from the kitchen counter. She opened her mail program and wrote an affirmative response.

And the wheel turns...

Chapter 33

Home of the Scottish Ancestors

The time had come for the Ladies Phare to make their journey abroad. Stella received a Master's degree in Psychology with an emphasis in Music Theory and was now ready to put her talents to work.

Bridgit felt the need to remove all things in her life that pulled her from her mission. Stella agreed to do the same. All the loose ends were tied up, and they were both fully ready to be globetrotters or do whatever Life Bearers do. They lived on trust now, because what they came to do had not been done before, at least not in a very long time.

They boarded their flight to Aberdeen, having no idea what to expect when they arrived. The flight was long. They had plenty of time to go back over the parts of the plan that made sense, which was very little. As the plane made the final descent into the Aberdeen International Airport, Stella began to perk up as she gazed out the window, seeing this part of the world for the very first time.

The ladies un-boarded the plane and walked towards the Baggage Reclaim Hall, where they had agreed to meet David, the Druid.

Stella and Bridgit immediately spotted David sitting on the top part of a row of connected seats, with his feet in a chair and holding a sign that read Ladies Phare.

It was as if they had spotted a leprechaun, but much bigger. He was a very tall, slender man with auburn hair that had wisps of gray hidden within the curls around the edge of his hairline. His long thin nose had a square tip on the end, and his sweet smile complemented his rosy cheeks perfectly.

Grinning, David jumped off the chair and stood tall at 6' 5", give or take an inch. Receiving the clue by the ladies' facial expressions, he knew that it was the women that he had been waiting for.

As the ladies approached, he leaned forward in a bow, "Ladies. I am David, at your service."

Stella's eyes were wide with joy seeing this elf of a man in real life; she could barely contain herself. She extended her hand to greet him, and he turned her hand to kiss it instead. Bridgit moved her bags out of the way and extended her hand as he put his hand out to greet her as well.

"Lady Bridgit, I presume?" David spoke in a Celtic knight kind of way.

"Yes. I am Bridgit, and this is my cousin, Stella. Stella Phare." She realized how strange it was to say cousin, but this was true. They were blood relatives, they concluded. Stella looked at her with a silly grin, happy to hear those words as well.

"Well, it's good to be meeting ya lass, and you too." David nodded to both of them and said, "While we wait for your bags, would ya fancy a cuppa?" Looking into their eyes, eager to serve.

"Sure, we would love one. Coffee please. We probably will need it to wake up after the long flight," Bridgit replied. David bounded down the corridor to the nearby coffee bar to grab beverages for the ride to the Inn.

Stella watched as he walked away and looked at Bridgit with a puzzled look on her face. "What did he just say? Fancy a cuppa?"

Laughing at the look on Stella's face, Bridgit explained. "He is getting us some coffee, but usually a cuppa means tea."

Bridgit said, "Don't worry, you will get used to the lingo soon enough."

Stella saw him standing in the line to get their cuppa's and decided to help so she could get the proper assortment of sugar and creamers. Stella was particular about her coffee, and it would give her time to assess the new guy.

He watched her coming towards him. On her approach, she apologized for not responding. "I have never been to Scotland before. I am a bit slow to pick up the dialect." She rolled her eyes in a look of embarrassment.

David returned the look, "I do apologize, Miss Stella. I... will... keep.... that ...in...mind...." He said the words slowly, carefully choosing how he structured his sentence. Stella let out a chortle when she realized that the Druid was hilarious.

The server asked for his order. He stood at the counter for a few seconds, glanced at Stella, then said, "Ah... three Americano's, please." He grinned at her from ear to ear.

Stella lost it. "I think I am going to enjoy hanging with you, David!" He smiled and nodded in a goofy manner as they collected their Americanos and accouterments.

By the time they came back to the baggage area, Bridgit had the bags in front of her and could see that Stella and David had managed to understand one another.

Bridgit said, "Everything good?" looking at her two cohorts.

David replied with a cheeky grin, "Smashing."

They each took a bag and followed David to the car. "Your chariot awaits. Isn't that what you American's say? Your chariot?" He made a gallant bow and motioned them towards the back-end of the vehicle.

Stella was starting to feel the vibe of sassiness come upon her, "Oh yes, we have grown accustomed to our chariots. So, what do you call this?" Poking fun at the white miniature chariot model before them.

"Touché. Well, um..., it is more like a shopping trolley really. It is called a Leaf." He grinned, proud to be driving it, and went on to explain that it ran on electricity. He showed them the other key reason why he chose this model.

Stella handed him the container that housed her precious harp. David's expression was priceless. "Is this it?" He tapped on the case with delight. "Is this your sacred instrument?"

Stella said, "Yep. That is my girl. Do you play an instrument?" She just knew he must be a music geek too, by the way, he gently put the case in the back carriage.

"Oh...I have been known to tickle the ivory from time to time." He wiggled his fingers as if he was a grand pianist. Stella was very amused at the bizarre personality shining through this genuinely unique man.

David continued to place their travel bags in the hatchback, then brought them to the front of the car to show them her face. She, the Leaf, had angled headlights and a front bumper that sort of looked like a mouth. The ladies could see that he clearly had a thing for her.

"She is adorable. What is her name?" Stella asked.

"Pearl. Like the sparkling white gem from the ocean. She is a beauty." He gestured for the ladies to climb in.

"We have a wee bit of a ride to the Inn. If you'd like, I will explain my background as a Druid, or Ovate as the case may be, and I can share a bit of my occupation as well."

They all climbed awkwardly into the little "Gem" of a chariot, while Stella and Bridgit commented how appropriate it was to be picked up by a Druid in his Leaf car, named Pearl.

Stella and Bridgit had so many questions for David, but patience was not their strong suit. He drove away from the airport, feeling happy to be in their company but wholly outnumbered.

And the wheel turns...

Chapter 34

The Ride Back to the Inn

In the car, David shared that he was an Associate Professor in Astrophysics and that he lives in Edinburgh but was spending time in Aberdeen over the summer for his extracurricular activities. He grinned at the ladies as he said that and continued to share about his studies of neutrinos and antineutrinos, rather than go into druidry and the reason they were being called to Scotland.

David explained that his work is focused on neutrinos, which he gave a simple explanation of in case they were not up on the latest and greatest Astronomy headlines. David noted that neutrinos were subatomic particles born from stars, among other things.

The ladies enjoyed their cuppa and the diverse conversation, as the information presented took some concentration to follow, but David presented it well, and surprisingly, Bridgit and Stella picked up what he was saying.

He proudly included that he was also into Sacred Geometry. David began a whole discourse on how everything in creation follows a sequence. This sequence was why he was closely following the work of another Astrophysicist who had discovered that there was a star in the Lyra constellation that was blinking in a manner that suggested it had a rhythmic pattern. He was so animated as he talked about the potential implications.

As the conversation unfolded, Bridgit was able to share that she was an Arborist and that her study of trees was the reason that she had been in Scotland, when Tuuru fell.

As the conversation led to Tuuru, David began to shift his demeanor to a much more serious one. He said, "Bridgit, I will share with you what I can today, and you will have to bear with me as many things are playing out right now, and I seem to have parts of a story to share, but I am still missing some pieces."

He looked at her briefly, trying to keep his attention on the road. Bridgit saw the genuine feeling in his face and asked that he continue.

"I have known all my life that I am different than other people. I see everything around me as patterns, pieces of a large puzzle that I sort through and place. I am very good at it, and my joy knows no bounds. I genuinely love this planet and everything and everyone in it. When the puzzle is complete, we are all one, and those of us who remember who we are must show the others how to put their life into order, in a sequential manner, balanced, like nature." He caught a glimpse of Stella's facial expressions from the rearview mirror, and Bridgit's face had the same look.

"What I am trying to say is that we, the three of us, carry the same codes of creation. We are all Life Bearers, and we must find the others."

"OH, MY GODDESS! Get out of here!" Stella slapped David's shoulder from the back seat and started squealing with excitement.

"You waited all of this time to say that!!??" Stella could not contain herself.

Bridgit waited for Stella to calm down and smiled at David. She said, "I am so relieved that we have found one another. Well, technically, you found us. You know what I mean."

She smiled and said, "I see we are almost to the Inn, and this conversation needs to continue. Are you staying at the Inn as well?"

"Yes, I have taken a room at the Inn as well, so that we can make preparations for the ceremony. We can talk more about how I came to find you perhaps tomorrow evening after the ceremony is complete; it is an interesting story." His eyes got big, and he gave them the feeling like it was such a juicy story that it warranted an excellent delivery, not one that could be rushed that evening.

He went on to say, "I have someone I need to meet with in the morning, and the preparations begin shortly afterward. The ceremony is from 4-6 pm tomorrow." David concluded his conversation as they pulled into the driveway of the Inn.

It was late in the evening. Bridgit and Stella were both worn out. Everyone agreed to get some rest and allow the information to unfold organically. They grabbed their keys from the front desk, as was the usual routine for late arrivals.

Stella went to her room while Bridgit entered the room that she had so many memories in. She lay on her bed for a few moments to rest her body, mind, and soul after hearing about David's background. Bridgit was disappointed that David did not go into detail about Tuuru, as Tuuru was the reason they had traveled to Scotland in the first place. Now that David claimed to be a Life Bearer, Bridgit knew that tomorrow would be a magical day of remembrance of Tuuru, and hopefully, she would get the information that she had been waiting for from David.

Still lying on the bed, Bridgit willed herself to get up to brush her teeth. She managed to pull herself up, grabbed her toothbrush from her bag, and opened her door to the hallway. Just as she was near the bathroom, David waltzed out of his room, and the two passed one another in the hall.

He casually asked Bridgit, "Do you know if the Innkeeper might have a telescope here?" Oddly, the two felt such familiarity with one another, that the casual conversation felt curiously comfortable.

"Yes, they do, but do you want it tonight?" Bridgit looked at him with disbelief, thinking he was going to go out at this late hour to look at the stars.

"Oh, No! Not tonight. Heavens, no! I am staying over again tomorrow night. It will be the perfect night to catch that blinking star that I mentioned earlier." He used his long fingers to simulate blinking by wiggling his fingers quickly in a playful manner.

"Maybe we can have that chat while we look for the Lyra Constellation? I have been waiting for a long time to have a chance to get out of the city and see the stars out here where it is pitch black at night."

"Okay, great. I have a lot to share about Lyra too." Bridgit winked at him as they said goodnight. He walked away, and then they both stopped and turned to look at one another in disbelief that this was happening. With smiles on their faces, they said good night.

The next day came sooner than they had hoped as they only had 6 hours of sleep before they heard the breakfast bell. Bridgit was looking forward to seeing the Innkeepers again and having some of their delicious ginger scones with tea.

Everyone filtered into the dining room, along with others who had come for the ceremony. David introduced Stella and Bridgit to several of the other Druids that were there to prepare for the ceremony on behalf of Tuuru.

They all seemed like ordinary people to Stella, as she observed them having tea and scones. One of the Druids asked her if she was the one with the harp. "That is correct. I brought her." She smiled and then looked over to Bridgit, who knew exactly what she was thinking.

"Stella, we need to get going on that errand, remember?" Bridgit pulled Stella away, excusing themselves from the others as they made their way back up the stairs to call for a cab to take them to get a rental car. They had many things that they needed to figure out, and the day was already filling up.

Once the cab arrived, they gathered their things for an afternoon out. They had the cab driver drop them off at the hire car office in town.

Bridgit had already driven a car in Scotland, so the procedure was effortless, and they had the keys to a rental in no time.

The first stop was to get Stella some coffee, stat. They arrived at a coffee shop and settle at a table near the window. The server took their order, and the two cousins began to unravel what they knew so far.

Bridgit started with the fact that David knew that the two of them were Life Bearers, as was he. He also apparently knew about Stella's harp and its specific frequencies, which they didn't get a chance to ask him how he knew about the harp.

Stella then chimed in that though he seemed to be a super nice man, it made her feel a little violated that he had this type of information on them. She wondered if he was a government type person and if they had just blindly come to Scotland without any forethought.

"Have we been naïve?" Stella asked. It was the first time Bridgit saw fear come out in Stella. She was usually the carefree one, she thought.

"No, Stella, we are fine. David has a lot to handle this morning for the ceremony. I met him in the hall last night, and he said that later this evening, we can have time to talk while we do some star gazing on the deck outside. He plans to stay an extra night so that we can talk about everything. Don't worry. It is all happening as it should." Suggesting the mission that they were given is activating and for Stella to not buckle at this point.

Stella was listening and nodding to Bridgit while looking out the window at two magpies that had jumped on top of the rental car. She then looked back at Bridgit and asked, "What do you mean it's happening?"

"Can't you feel it? We are in Scotland, summoned here by a Druid. We were surrounded by a slew of them this morning, and at least two of them know about your harp! I think we are about to discover more about our mission during this trip. We need to be ready for anything." She took a sip of her coffee as Stella nodded in agreement, drank her coffee, and pointed to the window.

"Look at that. There are magpies on top of the car! Is that normal?" They both laughed at the question of something being normal. They had not had an ordinary moment together from the instant they meet. They watched in amazement for a few minutes, then Bridgit poured over their itinerary for the day.

The next item on their list was their genealogy research. "We will start at the Aberdeen City Hall for some clues on where the Phare's lived and maybe look for the cemetery where some of them might have been laid to rest. You ready to get going?" Bridgit stood up, drinking the last sip of her coffee and urged Stella to do the same.

"Sure, let's do it. I think I am awake. Pinch me! Maybe I am just dreaming that there are birds on top of our car!" Stella pointed once more to show Bridgit that the two magpies had multiplied.

Stella grabbed the biscuits that they had with their coffee and took them with her outside as a diversion. As they walked towards the car, the birds started to caw and flapped their wings. Stella broke up the biscuits into seven pieces and threw them to the side of the vehicle so that they could make their getaway without harming them.

David had just come out of a building across the street from the coffee shop and watched as Stella lured the birds away with the pieces of biscuit. The seven magpies ate the gifted treat and flew behind the car as Bridgit pulled away.

David knew that it was a sign, and these women were attracting all sorts of attention. That was why he paid a visit to the person who asked David to bring them there. Elder Christopher was delighted to hear that the Ladies Phare had arrived. He gave David his final instructions in preparation for the ceremony and more. David's visit to the Elder Druid was to gather the final pieces of the puzzle for himself and the ladies. It all was so very mysterious, even for him.

David jumped into his little chariot, Pearl, following behind the ladies briefly and then made the turn off that looped back towards the countryside Inn where Tuuru lay waiting for her closure.

And the wheel turns...

Chapter 35

The Ceremony for Tuuru

Bridgit and Stella returned to the Inn with a dozen or more magpies landing on the trees around the house.

Stella jumped out of the car and grabbed her things from the back seat of the vehicle. Bridgit pulled her folder from the back seat that held the data from the Aberdeen City Hall and sheepishly put it over her head for cover, in case a magpie flew overhead.

They noticed several more cars in the drive and went inside to put their things away. They spoke a few moments to the Innkeeper, who told them that they would be ready to walk down to the ceremony in twenty minutes.

The ladies went up to their rooms to put away their things and prepare for the ceremony. Bridgit was feeling overwhelmed. She knew Tuuru had fallen because of her, and she wondered if the others all knew the reason why. She felt vulnerable and saddened by the events in her life as she began to remember more.

The time had come to meet the other's downstairs, where they would all walk in a procession to where Tuuru lay. It was a very solemn walk. The druids were all dressed in their hooded robes as they chanted.

Stella carried her harp and played a tune that resonated with the chants. The unique frequencies from her harp would create the space for the dimensions to open.

Bridgit found her place near Tuuru. The chants continued for a few moments and then suddenly ceased as the elder Druid came forward from within the tree line of the woods. The druids chanted a different tune as the elder Druid stood next to the Ladies Phare. David cast a vibrational circle around Bridgit, Stella, the elder Druid, and Tuuru, who was lying prone on the ground. He held his arms up to silence everyone and began the ceremony.

The Elder Druid turned to the group and said, "We are here to give the life force of the great tree Tuuru back to nature. We desire to see Tuuru transformed through this rite of passage. Where there is an ending, there is a beginning." He lifted his hand and traced a circle in the air.

The Elder Druid instructed Bridgit to stand on the other side of the tree, to the left of him. Stella would be to his right, making a triangle around the tree. He began to lift his staff and spoke in words of an ancient tongue.

Bridgit could see David just on the perimeter of the circle, and somehow, he looked entirely different to her. More powerful, she thought. He held the space for the triad to open the portal through sound. At that moment, the elder Druid instructed Stella to play her harp as she felt guided.

As soon as Stella began, the energy shifted. It was palpable. Bridgit felt intense heat in her forehead and crown. Stella began to sway forward and backward as the Druids made the circle tighter. David came around to Stella's backside, prepared to catch her should she fall, which allowed Bridgit to relax, knowing that Stella was supported.

215

Bridgit 's vision shifted as if the physical world around her had disappeared, and she was in an overlap of time and space. She could see the other side of the veil, just like Stella had envisioned months ago.

Standing on the other side of the veil, were Shamalaine, Bewain, Gordavin, Eldorman, and Avery in a deep meditative state. Shamalaine began to raise her hands in the air and commanded the spirit of Tuuru to expel her energy from the physical in all three dimensions altogether.

The others were in a circle around her, now chanting a specific sound, waiting for the release. It was then that Bridgit spoke out loud for all to hear.

"With the stroke of the harp, we send you back, dear one." Motioning to Stella to sound the tone from the harp. Stella could barely move but managed to strike the chord that spiraled around them in a wave.

The Elder Druid spoke, "We thank you for the blessing that you have been in all the realms. Our love for you has grown from a twig to the highest tree. We consider it an honor to have experienced you in this realm, and we give you back your essence now so that you may grow once more."

Suddenly the stroke of the harp reverberated. Stella was playing the harp strings as she had never done before. The frequency coming from the harp vibrated into the other side of the veil. At that moment, the dryad burst forth into the arms of Shamalaine in a flash of light. Bridgit began sobbing, as did Stella and the Elder Druid, for all three of them saw the same thing occur. Tuuru was free.

Shamalaine filled the dryad with crystalline energy from her staff, and the precious Tuuru walked away to find another spot to grow as a world tree for the New Earth.

"The great Tuuru will live on," said Shamalaine as she turned around towards Avery and the others in the land of Phare.

She stated, "The power of the Phare Triad has activated. Let us all rejoice in the knowing that Tuuru's offering has not been in vain. We are blessed this day." Shamalaine's ears shimmered as the vision began to fade.

Bridgit looked at the elder Druid and noticed tears running down his face as well, and she nodded to him to indicate that she was released. He closed the circle and walked back into the woods in silence. David then took over the ceremony at that point. It was the time of harvesting her precious limbs for their sacred tools. There would be a fire to conclude the service once the harvesting was complete.

The Magpies had gathered in the nearby trees. This time, at least thirty had collected. It was amazing how silent they had become during the ceremony and how they now were cawing louder and with greater zeal.

The druids played flutes, as the drumming began. A few of the Ovates started to work with the wood of the fallen tree. Bridgit and Stella, exhausted from the ordeal, were ushered out of the area and taken back to the Inn to rest. It would take the druids several hours into the evening to harvest the limbs and dismantle the body of the great Tuuru.

As the ladies were resting in the living room of the Inn, the Innkeeper came in with tea. Bridgit inquired about a telescope for the evening's star watching, to take her mind off of Tuuru. It felt as if she had lost her Grandmother and her heart wanted desperately to find a way out of the pain. Stella observed all of this and knew that Bridgit blamed herself.

Stella offered to assist Bridgit with the task of getting the telescope from the backroom to take Bridgit's mind off of the day's events. The two of them walked out onto the side deck of the Inn, clumsily setting up the telescope for the night's evening of discovery.

There were now double the number of magpies landing on the railing of the deck and squawking to get attention, with more circling overhead. Bridgit looked at Stella like it was her fault.

Stella said, "WHAT?? This is not my fault!" exasperated at the sheer ridiculousness of the situation.

Bridgit just shook her head and said, "Well, let me just say, Miss bird whisperer, I have never seen this many magpies in the entire time that I have been in Scotland, so they must have liked your biscuits this morning!" The two girls were enjoying the playful squabble, although they were more than slightly annoyed with the birds. They went back inside to wait them out and get some rest.

Bridgit had one question before they went upstairs. "Stella, when we were in the ceremony, did you see the beings on the other side of the veil?"

"Yes, I did. I wanted to talk to you about it, but I didn't want to say anything while you were mourning Tuuru." Stella said with both hesitation and delight that Bridgit bought it up first.

"The beings... they were the ones that I saw in the vision. I saw a feline woman and a male with hair that resembled a lion's mane". She stood at the bottom step of the stairway, holding onto the railing and looked at her feet to concentrate.

"Hmm, I also saw a tall, slender elven male and a shorter, younger, looking elf as well. There was one more, ah", her voice trailed off, trying to remember. She looked up at Bridgit, who was on the stairs ahead of her.

"Did you see a short male gnome?" Bridgit expectantly asked.

Stella nodded with joy at seeing this being. "YES! He was adorable!"

"That was Gordavin." Bridgit's smile returned as she went on, "Let's go into my room. I will tell you who they all are." Bridgit turned to continue up the steps when Stella grabbed her arm. Bridgit turned back to see what more Stella had to say.

Softly, Stella said, "I am sorry."

Bridgit said, "For what?"

"He wasn't there, was he?" looking deep into Bridgit's eyes.

"No, he must be elsewhere. Come on, let's go up and share what we experienced. I'm okay." She patted Stella's hand, which was still holding her arm, and the two girls retreated into Bridgit's room to digest the day's events, complete with magpies outside their window.

And the wheel turns... ⊕

Chapter 36

Breacher's Visit to Alpheratz Base

On the other side of the veil, Breacher was on a journey outside of Earth's atmosphere. He traveled to Alpheratz, a star within the Andromeda Constellation, in search of the riders as the Weavers had suggested.

The Weaver's had given him a hint about their duties beyond the weaving of the celestial garments. Breacher learned that the Weavers unified the solar and lunar energies of the Divine parents and that there would be a great alignment happening soon, which the Dragon Riders would be utilized as aligners in the lower densities and assist bridging the heavens with Earth. It was made clear to Breacher that the Dragon Riders were an essential facet in the Divine plan.

Breacher contemplated all of this as he sat on a ship on the way to a region within the Pegasian star system where the riders were training.

One of the trainers was an old friend, Commander Benoit, who was a breeder of the most exceptional Pegasian creatures. Breacher had a sense that if he worked with Benoit, surely, he would find the most experienced riders.

On the final approach to Alpheratz, one of the brightest stars within the Great Square of Pegasus, Breacher was viewing the Andromeda Constellation from a screen in the deck room. He stood in awe of the spectacular sight.

A voice came over the intercom to announce the preparation for the approach. Upon entering the atmosphere of Alpheratz, the craft began to shake, and Breacher heard a whizzing sound. The technology of the ship was such that it could move through matter, which was what the whizzing sound indicated.

Finally, the craft slowed down enough that Breacher was able to observe from the viewing screen the ship was moving through the physical strata of Alpheratz, into a hollow area through which one could access the center of the star. Within the interior of the star, Alpheratz had a beautiful inner world, much like what could be found in Earth's dimensional bandwidth of the third and fourth dimensions.

As Breacher began unloading the dragons, he was captivated by the beauty within the surrounding countryside. It was a mixture of meadows and mountainous with ancient volcanic areas as well. The interior of Alpheratz looked much like Earth, but the sky had pink and golden hues, but instead of the grassy areas, Alpheratz had moss and fungi as ground cover.

After taking in the beauty, Breacher unloaded the dragons and allowed them to graze on the moss and drink from the pools of water nearby. He picked fruit that resembled a plum, but it was green and speckled with purple and white flecks within the flesh of the fruit. He packed the fruit in his satchel for a treat for the dragons later in the day.

Breacher let out a whistle, and the dragons gathered around him. He grabbed the reigns of the violet-colored dragon, Leto, then jumped upon the dragon's back. All seven dragons were now in flight, low to the ground so that he could see the landscape at a closer vantage point.

The dragons flew in a V-shape pattern allowing Breacher to guide them in the front. Everywhere Breacher looked, there were variants to the landscape. He flew a little higher to acclimate to the region, then dipped back down to the lowlands. He knew that the training camp was in a lowland area surrounded by a volcanic caldera. Breacher had also heard that during the colder season, there was icy terrain as well, which was why this was the perfect area for training riders.

As Breacher got closer to the volcanic region, he spotted an area with man-made structures and flew in that direction. As he approached, he could hear the sounds coming from the training camp and could see the riders being trained in combat, something every rider must excel in.

Breacher found an area outside the camp to land the dragons and secure them. He did not want the riders to see them just yet. He instructed the dragons to stay hidden and rest while he was away. He gave them the fruit to steady their energy and then took off on foot.

Breacher walked to the camp and stood at the entrance for some time, watching the riders train. He walked over to where an attendant was brushing one of the Pegasus and introduced himself.

"May I?" he inquired, motioning that he wished to brush the Pegasus.

The attendant was quite amenable to him spending time with the animal and handed him the brush and demonstrated how the Pegasus liked its hair brushed.

Breacher was mesmerized by the magical presence of the animal. With the brush in his left hand, he gently stroked its wings.

He placed his right hand on the side of its body, patting the magnificent beast to make an energetic connection. As he stood there communing with the animal, he closed his eyes, sensing the emotions of the creature. It was clear to Breacher that its joy was a service it rendered to the rider.

He opened his eyes when he heard the sounds of boots crunching the rocky surface. He handed the attendant the brush and thanked him for the pleasure of sharing a moment with the magnificent Pegasus and turned to move on. There, coming towards him, was the man that he had come to see.

"Commander Benoit, it is great to see you, old friend." Breacher placed his left hand upon Benoit's shoulder and extended his right hand outward. Benoit's dark complexion shimmered in the sunlight. His steady hand firmly squeezed Breacher's.

Benoit wore his uniform with pride. Each word spoken, measured, each step he took, calculated.

Breacher took a good look at Benoit, whose tall combat boots strapped up to his shins with his pants tucked inside. Breacher was pleased to be in the company of this fine man.

"What a pleasant surprise to see you here." Benoit's voice modulated in a deep velvety tone.

He, too, placed his left hand upon Breacher's shoulder and extended his right hand in kind. "How time flies! Tell me, old friend, what do I owe the pleasure of your visit?"

The sound of clashing and maneuvers played out in the background, becoming more intense as they attempted to speak. The riders were tested on physical strength and mental prowess in the current exercise, Benoit shared.

Breacher leaned forward and, in a lower decibel, asked if they might find somewhere to speak that was out of the way from the loud noise. The training camp was in full session, from which the elite cadets would be chosen for active duty.

The Pegasus riders were highly regarded all over the various quadrants for their unique abilities. Their training also included the precognitive arts. It was this kind of training that Breacher received when he learned the skills of bilocation and telekinesis, moving matter with his mind. This training camp reminded him of his training days.

Once Commander Benoit heard Breacher's request, he knew that discretion was required and escorted Breacher into his small quarter's off of the training field where they could have a refreshment and a quiet conversation. It was here that Breacher shared with Benoit the need to find six riders.

"Six riders!" Benoit chuckled at the nerve of Breacher strolling into his training compound to request such a thing. "You always were gutsy, Breacher. I will give you that. Why don't we start at the beginning so that I have all of the intel before I make any gesture one way or another?"

"Fine." Grinning, Breacher sat down and suggested that Benoit do the same. The look on Breacher's face indicated that it was a long story. Before Benoit sat down, he poured them both a drink.

"Proceed, kind sir," Benoit winked at Breacher, feeling amused and prepared to hear a fantastical story.

"Benoit, I can't tell you how glad that I am to know that it is you that is here training the cadets. I don't know what you know of the Weavers of Tollan...", he paused as Commander Benoit sat up and paid more attention to the reference of the Weavers, indicating that he might have a clue.

Breacher continued, feeling hopeful for a positive response from Benoit. "I have just returned from ah, a mission, in which I was tasked with the job of finding six strong riders."

Breacher leaned forward to take a sip of his beverage and looked into Benoit's eyes to gauge his response, then continued. "I cannot tell you the pertinent details of the mission, but I will tell you this... It is most assuredly the most important mission that I have ever been tasked, and it all hinges on finding these six riders." He placed his cup down upon the table and was in thought as to how to proceed.

"Breacher, you and I have been friends for a very long time. We trained together for the better part of our childhood. I have honed my precognitive skills during the time that we have been apart." He

224

motioned for him to join him by the window so that he could get a good view of the cadets outside in the training arena.

"I have been prepared for a visit of this nature for some time but had no idea that it would be you who came with this request." It was a proud moment for Benoit.

He turned to look Breacher in the eyes and continued, "I have had many dreams indicating the need to prepare a certain type of rider for an event, that is admittedly fuzzy. It is the same recurring dream, and every time that I dreamt of it, the same feeling comes over me. I know that this event is monumental and that it will come to pass."

Benoit pointed out the window and continued, "The cadets that you see here are the finest from all of the local quadrants, and they all have training in various perceptions." He stood tall, pleased with himself for having the precognition to act on his knowledge.

He said, "As you can see, we will have more than enough cadets for your choosing." They both watched the riders training from the window of the room.

Benoit walked over to his digitized pad and activated it. He launched the screen with information about an upcoming tactical exercise. A game that will test the skills of the rider, which will target those who possess qualifications beyond the standard Pegasian rider training. This game is to be an event that showcases their critical thinking skills and their perception skills in new ways.

Benoit showed Breacher a map of the testing area based on the dreams that he had received. He discussed all of the various levels of play introduced to the riders. He turned to Breacher with almost a panic in his voice and asked, "Please tell me that you have them with you?"

Breacher looked at him with confusion. "Them?"

"The DRAGONS." He spoke the word dragons with reverence.

"How did you know that I wanted the riders for dragons? I haven't seen you in years?" Breacher responded curiously.

"What I have pieced together from the dream is that the entire web of creation is disintegrating, and a group of Dragon Riders weave a new frequency around a planet. I think it is Earth. These riders have advanced skills, knowing how to weave the new energy around the blue jewel." He momentarily paused while he envisioned it once more, then he continued as Breacher listened carefully.

"I remember in the dream seeing a group of Grandmothers sending waves of energy through the galactic ocean and the dragons and riders took that energy and broadcast it into the filaments of the grid work."

Benoit snapped out of a vision as he was retrieving the dream. "When you mentioned the Weaver's, I knew why you were here. So, where are the dragons?" He smiled at his friend with curiosity and a bit of smugness.

Breacher smiled and said, "Thank you, dear friend, for the clarity of mind and the vision that you hold. The dragons are outside the arena area. They are resting now. They could use a bit of nourishment and also somewhere to keep them out of the way for now. I am not ready for the others to see them just yet."

"It is an honor to serve once more alongside you, Commander Breacher." Benoit placed his tablet down and shook his hand. "I will make the arrangements as you wish. Shall we go meet some cadets?"

And the wheel turns...

Chapter 37

A Bridge of Magpies

Bridgit and Stella were discussing the ceremony for Tuuru when David knocked on their door.

"Come in," they both yelled out.

"Ah, excuse me." David put his head down out of respect.

"It is quite alright, David, come in. Grab a chair." Bridgit pointed to the one in the corner. Stella jumped up and arranged it for him at the edge of the bed.

"I saw the telescope set up out there, and I wanted to thank you for setting it up. I could have done the set up myself. You lasses really shouldn't have put yourselves out." His eyes had such compassion for the two girls, and he did not want to be the cause of any other misfortune.

"David, come now. We weren't put out. We are looking forward to stargazing tonight." Bridgit assured him.

"That is if those magpies will leave us alone!" Stella laughed as she pointed towards the outdoors.

"Ah... the magpies, yes..." He trailed the "S" sound of the word a bit as a way to segway into the magpie situation.

"It has been my experience that when massive amounts of magpies show up, it is a prelude to the veils parting or, in other words, a bridge to the other side. I am sure that it could be an omen for the opening of the portal for Tuuru's release, but somehow, I think it is more. They are still out there and gathering in number!"

"Really?" stunned by his remarks, Stella was dumbfounded.

"Why do you think they have been following us? Stella asked.

As he pointed his fingers in Bridgit's direction, he lifted his eyebrow her way and said, "Well, I can only speculate that there is some unfinished business to attend to."

"Hmm. I can't think of anything outstanding at this moment. We are still in the "gathering of the troops" phase, so I don't think it is time for me to go back if that is what you are thinking?" Bridgit looked puzzled, assuming that David was meaning that it was something having to do with their mission.

"Well, we will know soon enough," David spoke with some authority as he sat upright in his chair. "Until then, perhaps we can discuss a bit more about how we have been brought together."

The girls transfixed on him and settled themselves into a comfortable position on the bed as if they were preparing for a long movie.

Looking at them, he said, "Well... what can you tell me?" clapping his hands together in a goofy manner as a way to turn the floor over to them.

"Ah... what do you mean? We thought you were going to give us some insights as to how you found us and your role in what is happening."

Bridgit spoke while she looked at Stella and then back to David. Stella nodded with disbelief.

David then retorted, "Oh, I see. Okay, well, here is what I know to date for my part in all of this." He rolled his hands in the air towards them, clearing his voice, and then repositioned himself to think back to the beginning.

"As you know, I am a practicing Druid. We, Druids, have a special bond with nature and the old ways. Many druids throughout history were known to be keepers of the veil. We see symbols in nature and honor the natural path. I am also an Astrophysicist, learned in star folklore, and without going into a lecture, I can tell you that the magpie's arrival, to me, portends a veil event."

"Ah-ha," Bridgit reacted to his words. "Go on."

David then recalled a fable that he thought was most appropriate to share. "Have either of you ever heard of the tale of Vega and Altair? It seems most appropriate to share it if you haven't heard it before?"

"No, I haven't." Responded Bridgit, a bit annoyed with another delay. Stella nodded her head to indicate no as well, transfixed on what he could relay about the massive magpie infiltration that was upon them.

"Well, from what I can recall, this particular piece of folklore interested me because it falls on the last day of the Quercus Moon, or the Oak moon, and what is today?" He grinned with large beaming blue eyes and sparkling whitish teeth.

The girls looked confused. Stella said, "July 7th?"

"Yes! Today is July 7th in the Gregorian count, but it is also the last day of the Quercus Moon, and in Japanese culture, it is related to Tanabata. The dates for Tanabata celebrations vary, but with these magpies showing up, it feels like something is afoot!" David began to wiggle in his chair with excitement as the ladies had a puzzled look on their face.

Stella asked, "David, you are going to have to fill in the holes for us here. What is Tanabata?"

"It is basically Japan's version of Valentine's Day!" He chuckled as he knew they were most likely going to start throwing things his way if he didn't make his point.

"I recall learning about the Summer Triangle when I attended the academy. It has some of the most tantalizing star histories in today's folklore!" He smiled at the girls, proud of his star knowledge.

He continued, "The fable of Tanabata connects to the Summer Triangle: Vega in Lyra, Altair in Aquila and Deneb in Cygnus. Aquila means cow herder, and Vega is the star that marks the position of the Winter Solstice. But in folklore, Vega is a Weaver who weaves the celestial garments of the Gods and who fell in love with the lowly cow herder, Aquila. One day Vega left her post as a Weaver to be with Aquila. It concerned the Divine Mother when she heard that Vega had left her post."

David was so animated as he told the story that he began to move about the room and pointed towards the stars.

"What happened to them?" asked Stella, relishing the dish on the star-crossed lovers.

"Well, the Divine Mother had told Vega that her celestial position was irreplaceable and that she could never leave her post. To make sure that it never happened again, the Divine Mother took things into her own hands and put the Milky Way between the lovers. Now there was no way for them to be together."

He then sat on the chair once more and leaned into them and said, "Except that our Father God is merciful. He saw how much pain it caused the lovers. He decreed that every year, for one night only, a bridge of... Are you ready for this?" He asked.

"YES!" the girls both were about to push him off his chair.

230

He jumped off the seat and pointed towards the window and said, "For one night only, a bridge of MAGPIES would be built between Altair and Vega, and the lovers would be given one night each year on the 7th day of the 7th moon for a lover's reunion!"

"Magpies, ladies!" David went to the window, pointing to the birds and said, "Wow, there are even more out there!"

He whizzed around and said, "Today is the 7th day of the 7th moon in the Gregorian count and the last day of the Oak moon in the Druid count. It is the day that the two lovers reunite in the heavens. We should be able to see the Triangle in the night sky tonight!" He beamed.

The two ladies smiled and thanked him for the story as they contemplated it all, but Bridgit was still thinking of more pressing matters than the magpies, like how David knew to contact them, and what was his connection to the whole mission?

Bridgit spoke, "David, thank you for the delightful information about the magpies. I truly will not look upon magpies the same way ever again. Can we please touch on some other subjects, perhaps?"

"I will do my best to answer your questions, Bridgit. Shoot." David calmed down and centered himself.

"Maybe you can start at the beginning, like how you knew that I was involved with Tuuru's fate."

"Sure. That I can do." He began his understanding of the events that had transpired.

"We had been monitoring a dark force around the time of the incident, an energy if you want to call it that. It created a sort of microburst weather event, which is what hit the beloved World Tree, Tuuru. Elder Druid Christopher sensed a dark presence and was walking between the veils monitoring the situation when he saw you, Bridgit, running towards Tuuru." He let the information sink in.

Bridgit's eyes widened and said, "I did not see anyone out there that night! The storm came upon me so fast, as I was trying to get to Tuuru. I say storm for lack of a better word; it was more like an energy vortex." Bridgit looked at David for confirmation.

David shook his head in total agreement and continued. "Well, what you don't know is this. Elder Druid Christopher blazed through the veil and fought off the dark force that was surely planning on taking your life. At that moment, a powerful energy hit the entire area, like an electromagnetic pulse, and it knocked you both to the ground.

Elder Christopher spoke an incantation to Tuuru to open her field for you just as it hit, and you, thankfully, were pulled through the veil. He, on the other hand, was hit in the leg and has been recovering from the hit ever since."

"Oh, no! Is he alright?" Bridgit and Stella were both equally concerned for him.

"Was he the Elder that did the ceremony today... was that him? I noticed him limping slightly." Bridgit inquired.

"Yes, that was Elder Druid Christopher. He is better now, as you saw earlier, and is anxious to meet up with you again. Just for you to know, he only gives me insight on what I need to know at the moment, so I don't have much else to share with you other than the fact that it has been Elder Druid Christopher, who has been monitoring you both for some time. Again, he assures me that it will all come out soon and to be patient." David rested his hands on his knees and looked at the ladies apologetically.

Stella blurted, "This makes no sense to me... like, why am I involved in this? And how did you know about my harp?"

"Again, I am only given what I need to pass on to you on his behalf. The best I can gather is that you are a key player in the mission at hand and that your harp is significant. Now, what can you two tell me? Surely you have something that will shed some light on why the dark force was coming at you Bridgit, and Stella, what IS the deal

232

about your harp anyway?"

The ladies looked at each other at that moment, and Bridgit took on the task of giving David the low down on what had happened to them in the short time that she and Stella had known one another. They decided to take the conversation outside to sit on the deck to prepare for the evening's show, the blinky star within the Summer Triangle.

Bridgit shared the story about what had happened to her after she was brought into Tuuru's energy field, from her perspective. She shared how she met her elemental family known as the Clan of Phare and how she came to realize that she had entered the 4th density and that this was where she had previously been residing until her incarnation into the third density world of Earth.

"Your story is fantastic!" David kept repeating the same thing, every time Bridgit shared more.

She then told David her mission. "I am to gather the Life Bearers, to assist in the resurrecting of the Earth, and it's peoples, through the creation of a new energy or density that will help them achieve a light body in the physical. Once this is achieved, we will all live together in peace and harmony within a new creation on Earth."

She shared how the Blueprint Masters held the blueprint of creation from God. She continued by saying that the Life Bearers were the ones carrying the activating energy of the codes for the new creation like a key to a lock. Finally, she shared that the Builders of Form added the mental concentration for the manifestation of the creation.

Bridgit told him that they needed to find the other Life Bearers so that they could work together with the Angels and Elementals, as three lifestreams, in a cooperative endeavor, as it once used to be. She said that humans implemented the plan of creation. "We are the bridge between the realms and are a key part of the whole plan."

As Stella listened, she was distracted by something that Bridgit mentioned. The Blueprint masters. It triggered a memory of a dream that she had the night before with angelic beings. She needed to keep this

233

memory fresh, so she wrote the word angel on the edge of her thumb with a pen that she grabbed from her jacket pocket. She then continued listening to Bridgit's explanation.

Bridgit told David that there were many other galactic players with missions of their own, but thankfully she did not need to concern herself with that because she knew that it was Breacher's area to implement, as well as the Clan of Phare and the Galactics.

She then told him of her family in the 4th density and how she had left her beloved behind. David, being an empathic person, could feel her heart torn inside. Stella was a little shocked to hear Bridgit share so openly with David when it took her a while to open up to her on the subject of Breacher. She let it go, preferring to see it as a good sign.

Stella pointed at the first star to show up and then remarked that the Magpies were quiet, given that there were now approximately one hundred of them roosting on tree branches at the edge of the woods near the deck of the Inn. As they continued talking about the fantastic way in which Bridgit and Stella found each other, the birds began to flap their wings.

Bridgit let Stella continue the story of their incredible journey in India while she investigated the noise at the edge of the woods.

Bridgit said, "I will be right back." She walked down the steps of the deck and towards the woods. The birds began to quiet down on her approach.

Bridgit stopped in her tracks when she saw a flash, then a distorted energy wave opening a portal. To her surprise, out walked Breacher. Bridgit thought her heart would stop and hoped that it was not an illusion. She watched as he approached her. He took her hand in his and held it to his heart. He had the most brilliant smile, and his eye sparkled. They stared at one another for a moment longer before he pulled her into his embrace and kissed her. "Do you remember me now?" he gave her a mischievous look.

Tears were running down Bridgit's face, and she could barely breathe.

He truly did take her breath away. She began to shake a little as he wrapped her in his arms, all the while, she quizzed him in disbelief. "How can you be here?"

She pulled outward from his embrace and stared into his eyes, trying to remember every feature and speck within them.

At that moment, Breacher could see through her human disguise, and all he saw was his beloved Kaialena. Once he peered into her heart and felt her love for him, he was secure in their love for one another and was able to respond. He placed his hand upon her cheek and lovingly whispered so only she could hear his voice.

"I have come from very far away to see you, my love. Shamalaine summoned me to her and said that there was not much time to explain but that I had an extraordinary opportunity to be with you. She felt that she owed us this as a gift, the gift of our reunion for just one night."

He paused and rephrased the words, "Well, night is an exaggeration. We don't have much time at all, and there is so much to say and do," his voice trailed off to a murmur.

He leaned in to smell her neck. His scent was overpowering. Bridgit was weak in the knees and almost collapsed. His presence was more than she could bear. She needed to hold it together.

"I have much to share with you, my Beloved." Breacher kissed her on the forehead, and as he pulled back to look at her beauty, Stella's face popped into view.

"Oh... you must be Breacher?!" putting her hand out to shake his and smiling from ear to ear.

"Well, this settles it!" Stella said with surety.

Bridgit, a bit annoyed at the intrusion, said, "Settles what?"

"That even fourth density guys are hot!" Stella just busted out laughing and then apologized, unconvincingly.

Breacher chuckled and turned a teensy bit red while holding out his arms to Stella too.

"Tulina, it is good to see you again!" He pulled her close and hugged her, as if she was a child, then he rubbed her head like a pet. Bridgit moved to one side to allow for what seemed to be a family reunion.

Stella stood still in shock and then said, "Ah, actually, my name is Stella."

"Oh, yes, of course. It is just that I am not used to seeing you in this form." Breacher stepped back to gaze upon her.

"We've met?" looking confused, Stella quizzed Breacher.

"Yes, of course, we have met." Breacher was kind but also in a hurry to find somewhere private to be with Bridgit.

The birds began to make a scene as the druids were coming back from the ceremony near the walkway.

Bridgit looked at Stella and said, "Please give David my apologies and tell him that something has come up. I am going to sneak Breacher into my room." She winked at Stella and pulled Breacher towards her to steal him away for the evening.

Stella stood there in that spot for several moments, processing what just happened. Of course, if something weird is going to happen, it is always when she is hanging out with Bridgit, she thought.

Stella contemplated the fact that Breacher said that they had met. In her mind, she was thinking, "What the heck? Why is it that every time I think I understand who I am or this situation, something else flattens me, and I have to rethink everything?!"

At this point, Stella had just about all the weirdness she could handle and went back to the lesser of the weirdos to enjoy the stargazing with the Druid. She just laughed at the absurdity of the whole situation as she had done many times and just said to herself under her breath, as she sat next to David, "Truth IS stranger than fiction."

David said, "Excuse me, what were you saying?" as he had his head towards the telescope lens the entire time while the scene with Breacher played out.

"Bridgit had to excuse herself and asked that I apologize for her. She wanted to see the blinky star, but something super important came up. She might be back a bit later...hopefully."

David waved his hand in her general direction without as much as looking her way. He said, "Oh, that is quite alright. Though I was hoping that we could all share a bit more."

Stella said, "Well, tell me what you are looking at. We will go from there."

David began to yammer on about the forces of nature and how everything is connected. Stella grabbed the blanket in the seat next to her and hunkered down.

Back inside the Inn, Bridgit pulled Breacher into her room and shut the door behind him. She pressed her lips onto his and planned on keeping them there. He held her tight, kissing her passionately. Then, as all good kisses like this end, they came up for air, both touching one another's face to see if they were dreaming.

"I can't believe that you are here; I am so sorry for everything!" Bridgit began to make her explanations for why she did not recognize him when she was in the elemental realm.

"Shhh, don't apologize. I do not blame you for your memory lapse. I was shocked to see you that day in the Great Hall and wanted nothing more than to take you into my arms, but I was counseled not to introduce myself as your husband." He massaged her face and removed her tears, intuitively looking for a shell to capture them.

Kissing her forehead, he said, "Listen, I cannot stay long, and there is so much to tell you." Breacher looked deep into Bridgit's eye then guided her to the bed to sit.

"How long do you have? Will we have the night together?" Bridgit was already missing him while he was next to her. She could feel her heart breaking in anticipation of his leaving.

"Kaialena, I regret that I won't be able to stay much more than an hour of earth time here. I have much to do and have been to many fantastical places. Everything is accelerating now. Shamalaine wanted us to have this time together to give us something to hold on too. She felt your sorrow as you regained more of your memories. For me, it gladdened my heart to know that you remembered that I was the one that you love." He held her in an embrace once more.

He then pulled her tree drawing out of his pocket and unfolded it. They both held the drawing in their hands, and the energy between them was palpable.

Bridgit felt the time was too precious to waste. "Please. Tell me what you have been doing." She pulled his hand to bring him towards the bed and held it in hers, while he shared that he had traveled to Tollan to see the Divine Mother. He told Bridgit about the Weavers and how he was to prepare the dragons to receive their riders.

Listening intently, she turned to put the picture down on the table as he placed his hand upon her back to keep the physical connection with her. His hand began to massage her back as he used to do for her while they prepared for bed at night. Feeling his warm touch on her back sent chills up her spine and activated all of her senses.

As he was relaying the fact that he had to return to the Andromeda constellation to watch the riders compete in the skills test, he did not realize that Bridgit had unbuttoned her blouse. She turned around and pulled the hair tie out of her hair, letting her long locks flow in front of her chest. Breacher stammered, not remembering what he was saying.

She smiled and said, "You always were a talker, but if we only have one hour, then there is something else that I would like to say."

She placed her finger on his lip and said, "Stop talking."

The two had their lover's reunion and forever forged their bond as husband and wife in two realms. They held one another close until Breacher could feel the pull of the vortex.

"My love, I must go now. I will be away for a while, and I don't know when we will be able to be together, but Bewain assured me that I would be with you as a Guardian during the time that you make it to the jump points. Use extreme caution from this point on." He kissed her forehead and jumped up. He dressed quickly and glanced her way.

Before he walked out of the door, he said, "Do not hold anger in your heart towards Shamalaine and Bewain. This mission is bigger than any of our own needs, and they truly did not intend to cause you pain. Trust me. I have had to let that go. We chose this... remember that. We chose this because we knew our love could build bridges, and this beautiful jewel of a planet needs our love now." He bowed to her at that moment, kissed her lips once more, and was out the door.

Breacher passed Stella in the hallway and once again patted her head as he whisked by. "Take good care of her for me!" he yelled.

Stella just chuckled and kept walking and yelled, "Sure thang Romeo!" Noticing his pants were barely gathered, and he had only one button holding his shirt closed. The bottom of his shirt flapped as he walked quickly down the hallway.

Bridgit heard Stella in the hall and dressed quickly. She opened her door as Stella was coming back out of the restroom. Peeking out the door, she motioned for Stella to go to her room.

Stella's eyes were huge, and she had a big grin on her face. Seeing Bridgit let down her hair was a treat. As she entered Bridgit's room, she was about to open her mouth to tease Bridgit when Bridgit said, "Shut it!"

Stella zipped her mouth shut with hand motions and threw out the proverbial key, but she kept the grin going a bit longer.

Bridgit tidied the bed and sat down as Stella grabbed the chair in the corner. Bridgit was reeling from her escapade with Breacher, having mixed feelings.

Stella relaxed her smile and said, "You okay? He just swooped in and swooped out, didn't he?"

Bridgit just breathed in deeply and ran her hand down her throat, as if to keep from sobbing. "Yeah. I'm good. I'll take what I can get." She looked at her hands and then back up at Stella.

"That man," she shook her head slowly and said, "I do not know how I lived this life without him by my side. He is incredible and so loyal." She had fallen even deeper in love with him.

Stella piped in, "It doesn't hurt that he is an ABSOLUTE hottie!" the word hottie was carried out for several seconds as Stella shook her head and said, "Damn, where can I get me one them?" The two laughed, and then it got quiet again.

"We had less than an hour together, and yet it has renewed me in ways that I could not have imagined were needed or required." A tear rolled down her cheek as she wiped it away swiftly and jumped up.

She turned to Stella and continued, "Breacher has been sent on a mission by the Divine Mother herself. He is on the hunt for Dragon Riders with the skills required to weave a new frequency around the planet."

"Well, how did he get here? That sounds kind of far!" Stella quizzed.

"There was a moment in the heavens that opened up, which allowed us to have a quick rendezvous. Pardon the phrase." Bridgit chuckled lightly. The kind of chuckle that could quickly turn into a sobbing breakdown.

Stella intuitively listened. "I suppose the Tanabata fable that David was babbling about had some merit?" Bridgit sat back down, contemplating her words as Stella leaped to the window.

"Holy Plopamatic! They are flippin' gone!!!" Stella was over the moon that the birds had left and not a moment too soon. She held out her fingers to show the measurement of an inch and said, "I was this close to telling you that I am out of here. I am not much for horror movies, and those birds were making me feel like we were about to be the stars of a new film!"

Bridgit rolled her eyes at Stella's dramatic flair.

Stella sat back down and said, "So what else did Breacher say? And why did he feel the need to pet my head like I was a dog or something?"

"Hmm... he called you Tulina. Honestly, that name sounds familiar, but I can't place why at this moment. He seemed to know you, though." Bridgit smiled while thinking of his face, his body, and how good it felt to be with him.

"Hey! Snap out of it! You can do that wooing thing later. Focus!" Stella broke through Bridgit's fantasy.

"Anyway," Bridgit continued, "He said that Shamalaine arranged for him to meet me as an apology for keeping us apart. She knows that I have remembered him, and she and Bewain have not held him from me because they are horrible people, they just tried to do what was best for me during my remembrance phase. Which I can understand."

Bridgit fluffed the pillow and scooted up to lean on the headboard of the bed and said, "We need to find the other Life Bearers. If we can only get David to open up a bit more about what he knows."

With that, the girls went back outside on the deck to try to learn more about David, the Druid.

And the wheel turns...

Chapter 38

The Return of the Elder Druid Christopher

Bridgit and Stella wrapped up in blankets on the deck while waiting for David to return with some cocoa to keep the girls not only warm but also alert to the cosmic pulses happening all around them. They were getting a bit worn out from the happenings that day, and David was stalling.

"Bear with me, ladies. Here are your drinks. I am going to grab a jacket and some gloves. Drink up and stay put, and I will be back in a flash!" David bounded off, while the ladies giggled and drank their cocoa.

Stella raised her cup and noticed the smudged writing on the edge of her thumb, "Angels."

"Bridgit, earlier today, I was triggered by something you said, and it made me recall a dream I had last night. It had beings in the dream that I can only assume are angels. It's kind of weird because I have never dreamt of angels before, have you?"

Bridgit replied, "Can't say that I have. What was the dream about?"

Stella moaned, "Mmm. Not sure. It was more like me seeing into the veil and having glimpses of them. I could see groups of these being in various rays of light overshadowing us while we were planting something. And when I say planting, I don't really think it was a plant, but you know, kind of like seeding thoughts or codes."

Bridgit sat up and listened intently. "Keep going. How many of us were in the dream? Try and recall it."

Stella had her eyes closed and began to describe a scene where they were in an ethereal world where many groups were working together. David bounced back onto the deck and sat down next to Stella, eavesdropping as she continued to describe the team.

"There was a female energy with what looked like the cosmos in her hair. She had starry eyes...."

"OHHHHHH!!!!! The Star born!" David exclaimed.

Stella jumped, startled by his energy and excitement.

"Oh... so sorry to startle you, lassie. But what you were describing is an angelic order that I have dreamt about ever since I was old enough to think. I was about two years old." He had a cheeky grin and motioned for her to continue.

"So, these beings, are they the Blueprint Masters?" She looked at Bridgit to make some sense out of it.

As Bridgit was contemplating Stella's question, another set of footprints could be heard coming up the side steps of the deck. The footsteps were staggered, and with every other step, a slight thud could be heard, consistent with someone with a cane.

Bridgit turned her head to see that Elder Druid Christopher had come to join the star watching. David stood and let out a sigh of relief to see him.

243

Christopher smiled and patted him on the back, "You didn't let out any of my secrets yet, did you, son?"

David bowed slightly and said, "Not yet, Elder, but I was starting to think that you weren't going to show. These ladies are thirsty and not just for cocoa!"

They all laughed as Stella removed some things off of a chair and offered the Elder Druid a warm blanket and a comfy spot to sit. Bridgit sat there mesmerized by his presence, with the hairs on her forearm standing straight up.

Bridgit held her hand out to Elder Christopher, and as he reached out to accept her hand, she looked into his eyes, with tears in her own.

She said, "There are no words to tell you how much I appreciate what you did for me." She launched herself into a sudden embrace with Christopher. He held her for as long as she wanted to be there.

He said, "We have much to share, and it was not only my honor to protect you, but it was my duty." She pulled back, wiping her face, and looked into his sparkling eyes.

"Why don't we sit and get caught up, shall we?" Christopher suggested.

"Would anyone be offended if I pull out my pipe?" Christopher quizzed as he took the seat that Stella offered and joined in. Bridgit grabbed a blanket and prepared herself for another part of the plan to unfold.

Everyone motioned for him to be their guest and watched as he packed his pipe with tobacco that had a ship prominently displayed on the packaging. He leaned forward to make room in his pocket for the pouch and searched for his lighter. He leaned back in his chair, lighting the pipe and blowing a few puffs of smoke upward into the night air.

The aroma was pleasing to Bridgit and brought back memories of her father sitting on the porch, watching stars, and puffing on his pipe.

Elder Christopher turned to Bridgit, winking at her, and said, "Backy helps me think clearly, and it relaxes my old bones."

Bridgit smiled and took in a deeper breath, feeling comforted by his presence and the aroma.

"I wanted to thank the two of you for coming to the ceremony today. It was quite successful." He winked at both of them as he relit the pipe. The two girls were able to see his eyes clearly from the flame of his lighter. Stella had a tinge of energy run up her back, which generally occurred when something important was about to happen. She paid close attention.

Exhaling, Christopher began his explanations. "Bridgit, I would like to hear from you, if you feel comfortable, that is, about your own experience with Tuuru, and secondly, what you experienced during the ceremony to release her spirit."

He sat back in his chair and waited for Bridgit's response. David propped his feet up on a side table and crossed his arms to get ready for an exciting story, all the while keeping one eye on the night sky.

Bridgit responded, "Well, let's see... to begin, I am an arborist, and I am, or WAS... studying trees from all over the world, and in particular, grandparent trees or World Trees; trees that have been around for hundreds of years. Tuuru was one that called to me after seeing a documentary about world trees a few years back. I planned on staying in Scotland a bit longer the last time that I was here because I also wanted to find out more about my heritage."

"Well, we will get to that in a bit. Let's stay focused on Tuuru at this moment if you please." He gestured for her to continue.

Bridgit was a bit intrigued by that last statement but continued about Tuuru.

"I was in my room at the Inn the night Tuuru fell. I had fallen asleep,

245

barely. It was the kind of sleep where I was in between sleep and wakefulness. I felt an intense calling from her. Tuuru, I mean. It was a windy night, and as I lay there trying to sleep, I kept feeling like she was calling out to me. This is not something that I would say had ever happened before, so I got up, and I grabbed my boots and jacket, and took a flashlight with me. I walked down by the hedge. At this point, the wind began to howl. It picked up rather quickly, and I had this feeling of dread in the pit of my stomach. I just felt like a dark presence was behind me, so when I turned around, I could make out a swirling energy coming towards me like a tornado. I ran as fast as I could for protection under Tuuru, still hearing her calling to me, and then it hit." Bridgit held back tears again.

She looked up at the Elder and said, "Thank you."

He stiffened up a bit, in a stoic manner, rubbing his leg and said, "Yes, well, I couldn't let that thing take out one of my own." He sniffled and reached for his handkerchief to wipes his eyes.

Bridgit responded, "One of your own?"

Christopher deflected that question in a way and asked, "Were you able to get very far in your search for your ancestral connections to Scotland?"

"Well, under the circumstances, ah... no!" She laughed at the question. "Stella and I are planning on doing more of that while we are here." She looked at the Elder for clues as to why he asked.

"Well, let me save you some time, my dears. I can tell you everything that you need to know." He smiled and lit up the pipe once more, and this time, a massive plume of smoke rose in the sky, and David jumped up with excitement. He looked into the telescope to verify his suspicions.

"There it is!!! The blinking anomaly in the Lyra constellation!" David behaved like a two-year-old at the zoo.

"Ah! Excellent David! Say hello to the home planet!" Christopher

246

got up and laid his pipe down to adjust his jacket. "It is getting late, and what I have to share will take some time. Would you two ladies do me the honor of meeting tomorrow in town at the Union Terrace Gardens?"

He did not wait for a response and asked David, "Could you manage to show them the way, say 10 am?" He grabbed his pipe while David agreed without looking back at him. Christopher then looked at the girls and, at that moment, was so pleased to see these two precious beings. It was hard for him to keep from choking up, so he cleared his throat and began to turn away.

Both Stella and Bridgit had lumps in their throats. One of them managed to squeak out an affirmative response as Christopher made his way down the deck stairs with a pipe in one hand and his cane in the other.

He yelled out, "Fine. I promise you will have your answers tomorrow!"

Bridgit just looked at David, who was still leaning over his beloved, the telescope. Stella and Bridgit got up and said goodnight to David. As they began to walk away, David shouted, "Trust me when I say that tomorrow will be a GOOD day! Get some rest. Meet me down in the living room after breakfast, and we will drive into the city. Union Terrace Gardens is in Aberdeen!"

"Ok, David. Enjoy your ogling! Stella responded with a teasing gesture.

Once the girls were back upstairs, Stella joined Bridgit briefly in her room once more.

"What do you make of that?" Stella asked Bridgit for her commentary.

"Well, when Christopher first sat down and lit his pipe, I had an image of my Dad smoking his pipe. The pipe tobacco smelt the same..."

"Not that!!!!" Stella was crazed at this point.

"What do you think of the fact that the Elder Christopher said to say hello to the home planet, Lyra... Hello! Were you listening??? Now he is going to tell you everything about your ancestry!? Who is this guy? A long lost relative???" When Stella blurted that part out, they both looked at each other and said, "CHRISTOPHER... LENNON... PHARE!!!"

"Did you ever hear David say what Christopher's last name was?" Stella quizzed.

"No. And for that matter, did you hear him say that he couldn't let that dark thing take out one of his own? I didn't want to interrupt him, but I was so curious about what he meant by that." Bridgit contemplated it all.

Stella sat on the chair and said, " I can go grab David and make him spill the beans if you want me too."

"No. He is clueless and a little busy." Bridgit laughed, not wanting to make fun of him, but he gave them a lot of material to work with.

She continued, "Let's get some rest, and in the morning, let Christopher tell us who he is in all of this. If he is who we think he is, then this keeps getting more interesting. We need to get on with it. We need to find the other Life Bearers. I am starting to feel like we are behind in the search. Breacher is doing what he needs to do; I don't want to disappoint him."

Bridgit grabbed the pillow that he had laid upon and smelled it. It was only a few hours prior that he lay in her arms, and now another piece of the puzzle was presented.

"Tanabata kicked my arss today! Let's go to bed!" Stella blurted out as she let out a yawn.

Bridgit led Stella to the door, hugged her goodnight, and went to sleep that evening with renewed hope and yet a bit of anxiety in her belly.

And the wheel turns...

Chapter 39

Shamalaine and the Dreamer

Stella's dream time continued from the night before. Shamalaine entered Stella's dreamscape that night with the gentleness of a mother. In the dream, Shamalaine and Evie were in the kitchen at Stella's house in California, talking in-depth about the Lovespoon. Shamalaine mentioned that the spoon had three links in the chain, within the handle of the spoon, to indicate three lifestream's that were part of a spiritual path. The three links in the chain would represent the Father, the Son, and the Holy Spirit, but as Shamalaine described, the chain had a dual meaning. The lifestreams, as she shared in the dream, were to indicate the Humans, Elementals, and Angels.

Shamalaine handed Stella the Lovespoon and had her touch the angelic link. It pulled her into the angelic world where the Blueprint Masters were preparing for the mission at hand. They gave Stella a code- ACG.

The code was written in puffs of smoke, which then immediately pulled her to the Elder Christopher. In this part of the dream, Elder Christopher pulled from his pipe and blew the smoke upward while he prepared Stella tea at his home. As he served her a cup, she noticed the Phare Family Crest over his fireplace. "Uncle, why do we have to be so secretive about who we are?" she asked Christopher.

He responded within the dream, "For your safety, my dear. Your mission is far more important than either you or your sister realize. There have been many in this family who have attempted to do what you are asked to do. They did not survive the mission." They sipped their tea, then Stella was brought back to her kitchen.

In the next segment of the dream, Evie had her birth certificate out on the kitchen island, and on the document, it read Baby Girl Truce. Stella woke up, startled in the early hours of the morning, and grabbed her journal. She wrote : Baby Girl Truce and Uncle Christopher.

She then blurted out loud, "He called us sisters and what is Shamalaine trying to tell me? Baby Girl, Truce!"

She had completely forgotten that her mother had a surname of Truce since she was adopted at birth by the Binti Family. She scribbled on her note, trying to get more information out the lingering dream.

Stella closed her eyes and remembered the angels and the connection to the Lovespoon. She wrote the strange code down and the words of Shamalaine.

Stella got out of bed and walked down the hall to use the restroom. She noticed Bridgit's light on and lightly knocked on her door.

Bridgit opened the door and brought Stella over to the window. With the lights off, the two girls stared at the last visible signs of Lyra before dawn broke. They held onto each other as Stella recounted her dream to Bridgit.

Neither one of them was getting much sleep since their arrival in Scotland, and they knew it would likely be their new routine. Breakfast wouldn't come fast enough for Stella's. She wanted answers even if she had to pull it out of David.

Bridgit just asked one thing, "Be gentle?"

She phrased her words as a question rather than a statement, not sure if Stella had it in her to use honey to get what she wanted at this point.

Stella laughed and said, "I've got this!"

At breakfast, the Ladies Phare grabbed a danish and coffee to go and were waiting patiently for David to finish his meal and grab his things. Once he came out of the dining room and saw the ladies waiting, he moved into high gear.

"A good breakfast is an essential start of the day!" he winked as he rotated around and bounded up the stairs in three steps to the top landing and grabbed his things. Just as he was halfway down the stairs, he stopped with his finger pointing upward, shook his head and said, "Right... Teeth!"

They watched as he swirled around and took one giant leap upwards and back down the hall to the shared washroom. Upon his return, Stella took note that he had forgotten to brush his hair, but his pearly whites were close enough to white, and the girls just wanted to get the show on the road.

He opened the front door of the Inn, holding it open for the ladies. After unlocking Pearl, he lifted the hatchback and placed his bag there. Stella climbed into the back, removing his work satchel out of the seat to make room. When she lifted the satchel, David's ID badge from the University fell onto the floor. As Stella reached down to grab the badge, David shut the hatch and yelled that he would be right back. He ran back into the Inn to grab another danish for the road.

Stella examined David's badge, at first making fun of his hair and quipping that he could use a lady friend, and then all of a sudden, she said, "Holy Mother of Pearl! Look!" She slapped Bridgit's shoulder from the back seat and shoved the ID badge in Bridgit's direction.

Bridgit took the badge as Stella pointed to David's given name. She did not know of its significance and asked, "What is it?"

"David Medwyn Truce! TRUCE!!!!!" Stella was yelling Truce in a high pitch sound so loud that David could hear her as he came around to the driver's side of the car and jumped in.

"YES?"

David thought that Stella was enraged at his delay in getting off to Aberdeen until she shoved his work ID into his chest and said, "Who are you?!"

David had the pastry in his mouth, looking at her strangely, not sure what she was getting at. After starting the car, he grabbed the pastry with his left hand and received his ID badge from Stella with the other.

"What do you mean? Who am I? It says who I am right here." David pointed at his picture with his title and looked at her like she was taking crazy pills.

Bridgit chimed in to keep Stella from going into a full-on frenzy. "David, I think what Stella is getting at is your last name, Truce. Your badge fell out of your bag, and we noticed that your last name is the same last name as Stella's mother's birth name. Any clues on this one?" She was trying to keep things calm.

David just turned around with the sincerest look in his eyes and just stared at Stella without saying a thing. It was a heart-wrenching stare. One that broke Stella's ire and gave her cause for concern. He began to cry. He tried to find somewhere to place his pastry and wipe his mouth, fidgeting as a way to deal with the ball of emotions within himself and from Stella.

Stella and Bridgit were not prepared for this sweet goofball of a guy to break down into a messy emotional wreck, but that is what happened. They gave him a few moments, then Bridgit realized that she needed to take control of the situation.

"David, let's switch spots." She took his pastry and his badge, handing them to Stella.

She said, "I am going to drive Pearl into Aberdeen. You and Stella need to talk. Maybe you can push my seat up and sit in the back with Stella, and we can get on the way?"

David was shaken and agreed to Bridgit's request. He moved around to the back as Bridgit ran around to the other side quickly, and they were off to Aberdeen in moments.

Stella said, "David, I am sorry. I don't really understand why you are so emotional. I mean, if I hurt your feelings, then I am sorry, but we have been trying to get some answers out of you, and I really just need some now!" She began to feel riled up again.

"Stella, I don't know what to say to you! Well, I guess I will start with this. I was adopted out as a boy. I do not know anything about my family. I was in foster homes, and the only thing that was on my birth certificate was Baby Boy Truce. So, my heart breaks a little each time I allow myself to wonder who I really am, because honestly, Stella, I DON'T KNOW!"

The force of his words was so strong that it jolted Stella when hearing them. David looked out the window, then apologized for being testy with her and assured them both that he is as much in the dark on all of this as they were. At that moment, all three of them realized that they were all pawns in a vast game, and they did not even know how to play the game. No rule book was left behind, and just enough synchronic information was given to keep it all going.

Stella then said, "David, I want to apologize...sincerely. I guess it is a sore subject with me because I lost my mother years ago, and I have to piece together my life based on little clues. Our family is tattered, and there are very few of us left, but suddenly it feels like we are gaining new family members." With that last word, she touched his leg gently, and he faced her once more.

"Family? Do you think that there is a chance that we could be related?" It lit him up from the inside, just the thought of it.

Stella could see a glow coming into his face, and his coloring came back to his cheeks. "It's possible! Come on... weirder things HAVE happened!" They all started laughing and began to chat more freely.

To lighten the mood, Stella relayed her dream of how the Angels gave her codes and then how she was in Elder Christopher's home and noticed the family crest over the fireplace.

David quipped in that the Elder did have a crest over his fireplace! Stella made a note of that in her journal and continued to share how her mother came into the dream and had her birth certificate out on the kitchen island and how the words Baby Girl Truce were prominent on the birth certificate.

Stella said, "So clearly, due to the dream last night and seeing your last name, I think the odds of you being related to my mother's side of the family is a pretty good chance."

David was still in a bit of a shock and wanted his pastry back. Bridgit passed a bottle of water to David, providing whatever comfort she could to a man she barely knew, while Stella unfolded his pastry from the napkin and handed it to him.

Bridgit just smiled as she looked back into the rearview mirror, watching the two get on so well. She trusted that Stella and David would bond on the drive to Aberdeen, so she concentrated on questions to ask Christopher.

After ten minutes of driving, a strange animal suddenly ran out in front of the car. Bridgit swerved to keep from hitting it.

Stella was screaming, "Watch out!!!!" Bridgit quickly regained control of the vehicle.

David held onto the handles overhead to keep from knocking heads with Stella. He was as white as his car when Bridgit looked in the rearview mirror to see if they were okay.

"Did you see that!?" Stella asked David, realizing by his face that he did.

"I can't believe it! I think it was a Cu' Sith!" David kept his eye out to see if he could get another glimpse of the animal, but no sooner did it cross their path, then it was gone.

Bridgit pulled the car over to catch her breath. She turned around and looked at David and said, "What is a Cu' Sith?" But no response came. David's eyes were dilated, and he was silent.

Looking at Stella, she asked, "You did see that it wasn't a normal animal, right? It was a greenish-grey colored phantom dog!"

Both Stella and David were nodding, yes, but no words came out. "David, what is a Cu... whatever you just said?"

David snapped out of his mental retreat and said, "A Cu' Sith. I have heard tales of such a creature, but never did I ever think for one moment that they could be true... just rubbish, something to entertain the wee ones."

"Well, what are they?" asked Stella.

"They're Beasts!!! That's what they are! Something conjured up and let loose, I suppose." David started turning in his seat, looking for energy waves, portals that might have opened to allow this thing to come through.

"This is bad, ladies... this is very bad." David shook his head as he monitored the landscape.

"Bridgit, I would drive, but I don't think it is a good idea to get out of the vehicle at the moment. Do you mind carrying on?" He motioned for her to high tail it out of there.

Bridgit got them back on the road, and all of them spent the next 10 minutes of the drive in somber thought. David went very internal.

And the wheel turns...

Chapter 40

Breacher Returns to Alpheratz

The whizzing sound woke Breacher as the craft began its final descent back at the training camp in Alpheratz, in the Andromeda Constellation. He heard the commander over the intercom say, "Delta Pegasi, final approach, Alpheratz. For those disembarking, head to Level Yellow docking bay. Commander Breacher, please come to the Captain's quarters before disembarking."

Breacher grabbed his jacket and stuffed paperwork that he had received from Commander Bewain into the front inner pocket of the coat and walked out of the resting bay. Breacher was not sure why he was called to the Captain's quarters, but he was anxious to get back to the camp and begin the arduous task of finding the riders.

He made his way down the corridor, following the colored arrows on the floor leading to the bridge and Captain's quarters. Military personnel was on the floor, standing near the entrance to the door that Breacher needed access.

Breacher confidently walked up to the personal and introduced himself. After inspection, the militiaman let Breacher move into the interior of the space that was the Captain's quarters.

"You must be Commander Breacher?" A man of high rank sat at a desk reviewing papers, then stood as Breacher approached.

"Yes, sir." Breacher sounded off.

"Commander Breacher, I wanted to introduce myself and see if I can be of any further assistance to you? When I heard of your journey to the Alpheratz Base, I was intrigued." He motioned for Breacher to take a seat, but Breacher declined.

"I am in a hurry, so I prefer to stand. I am not sure I understand what your interest is?" Breacher had an uneasy feeling in his sacral center, the place within his being that gave him unwavering truth.

The Captain cleared his throat, "Well, word gets around when new folks come into these territories. Given you are headed to the training camp, I assume you are meeting with Commander Benoit. Is that correct?"

He stood up and walked towards the window as the camp came into view. As he turned around, he continued, "It just so happens that my daughter is in training there, and she is quite extraordinary. Kali is her name. Best rider you will find."

Breacher cleared his throat and thanked him for giving him the heads up about his daughter. At that moment, the Militiamen came into the room to inform the Captain of their arrival at the camp. The small craft landed on the landing pad, just outside of the camp walls.

Breacher was distracted by the amount of militant protection the Captain had, feeling unclear as to why there was a need for such protection until he saw the emblem on the Captain's jacket as he swirled the coat around his body to prepare for an excursion to the training camp himself.

The emblem on his jacket answered all of his questions — the winged serpent. Breacher, was now on edge as he realized that the Captain was a Draco sympathizer.

And the wheel turns...

Chapter 41

The Phare Family Triangle

Bridgit parked the car, Pearl, on the street, near Union Terrace Gardens, and jumped out immediately to get the creepy feeling out of her body. Stella had been silent in the back seat, and as she got out, she just looked at Bridgit and said with absolute amazement, "I think the Druid left his body!" She pointed for Bridgit to take a look. Sitting in the back seat, David was staring straight ahead; eyes open, but no one was home.

Bridgit rolled the windows down as the two girls decided to sit on the knoll next to the street, near the car, and wait for David to return. Bridgit checked her watch to make sure that they still had time before meeting up with Elder Christopher.

Stella nudged Bridgit and pointed to the car, "What do you think is going on?"

"I imagine he is checking out the situation. Just be patient." Bridgit was concerned, but she knew that David was a well-trained Druid and that he was on it.

Stella looked at Bridgit and said, "You did well. How did you stay so calm? I'm still creeped out about whatever it was that jumped out in front of us", Stella quizzed Bridgit.

"I don't know. I just had a feeling to stay calm as if a protective force was with me, within me. You know what I mean?" She smiled at Stella and continued, "We have had a few warnings to be careful, and now we have some unwanted attention. We need to start being more observant from this point on."

David started wiggling the backseat door handle, slowly opening the door. Stella noted that he seemed to be having what looked like his first fight with his love, Pearl.

He managed to pull his long legs out of the backseat, one at a time and stood up slowly. Once he shut the car door, he leaned back upon it to give him the stability to stay vertical.

"Ladies, what time is it?" He began to look around, a bit disoriented.

"It is right at 10 am." Stella walked up to him and pulled his arm towards her and said, "Come on, brother from another mother. We need to get you moving. What part of the park are we supposed to meet Elder Christopher anyway?"

Bridgit grabbed his other arm, and the girls walked with David, arm in arm, to find Christopher.

The sun was already coming up strong as they walked towards the central part of the gardens where there were some benches to sit.

David pointed and said, "This is the spot that the Elder likes to visit and watch the birds."

They decided to wait for Christopher there. Soon enough, the threesome could make out his silhouette walking towards them. David recognized him by his limp.

The sun was shining on Christopher's back, making it hard for the three to see his face until he was much closer. Christopher was sauntering, carrying a large bag across his shoulders. As he approached, the ladies stood up to greet him, but David was too weak to do so.

"How is he?" Christopher took off his hat and waved it in David's face as he leaned in to get a look at him, not surprised in the least that he was in this shape. David batted at the hat and smirked, "I will be okay."

Christopher's astute nature surprised Stella. She reviewed the happenings and knew that he had not been informed of the strange event that had just occurred thirty minutes past, but he seemed to be aware of it none the less.

As if Christopher was reading Stella's thoughts, he said, "No need for any explanations. He will be fine. It is part of his training." He winked at the ladies as he sat next to David and placed his bag on the ground.

"Lad, you did well." He patted David on his knee and looked at the girls, who were both completely clueless.

Confused, Stella inquired, "What did he do?"

"Well, take a seat, ladies, and I'll tell you." He motioned for them to sit close so that he did not have to raise his voice. Stella and Bridgit sat near his feet on the grassy area near the bench to hear his explanation. Obviously, Christopher already knew about the monster from what they could tell.

"After the monster ran out in front of your vehicle, David went into a trance state and was able to contact me about the situation, telepathically." He winked at the girls with a proud grin and continued.

"We assessed that a gateway had been artificially opened, which allowed this monster loose in the countryside. We both called it back into the hole whence it came and were able to shut the portal. I won't go into the boring details, but this is the kind of thing that David has been training for, and as you can see, it took some of his energy to do it."

Christopher patted David's shoulder and said, "We will work on that lad." He had a proud, fatherly look on his face that showed the girls how much he cared for David.

Then he turned serious and looked at the two Phare ladies. "I want you to know that you were protected, but you should also know that this is serious. That monster was a scout, and it was looking for you two. We now have to be extremely careful about our next steps moving forward. Under the circumstances, let us head over to my home for our visit, but before we go, I do want to show you my favorite tree in the garden."

He smiled and helped David to his feet. "You just need to hug a tree, my man, let's go say hi to Crisdean."

"Crisdean?" Bridgit repeated the name and followed. She looked around to verify that they were not being followed, as she still felt a pang in her gut that they were being watched. Stella was right at her side and kept pace with Bridgit to keep from getting snatched.

David was starting to feel his energy return as he caught sight of Crisdean, the old Elm tree that Elder Christopher had chosen as his ally.

Christopher walked up to the old-growth Elm and patted it on the trunk. "How are you, my old friend?"

David also stepped up to greet it. He placed his arms around the trunk to hug it and receive an energetic boost.

All the while, Bridgit was examining its structure, checking for signs of disease.

Elder Christopher saw that Stella was distracted and asked that she relax. "Stella, I have the veil of protection around us. You can relax, we won't stay long. I want you to introduce yourself to Crisdean, my ally." He had a twinkle in his eye as he winked at her, and she relaxed so effortlessly in his presence once she was assured of their safety.

Stella leaned up against the tree and asked, "Tell us about his name,

Crisdean. What does it mean?" She felt herself melding into the tree as she slid down to the ground. She did her best to anchor her field, as the intense flow of energy surging through the tree flowed into her body.

Christopher laughed at the sight of Stella merging with the tree and Bridgit assessing its strengths and weaknesses like a nurse taking vital signs on a patient.

"Crisdean is a powerful force to be reckoned with, and as I came to know him, he told me of his name. It is not a coincidence that his name means Christopher, as is my own name."

He paused and watched Stella closely. She had the top of her head touching the base of the tree as she was looking up into the branches. "Stella, your crown, at the top of your head, is the very same as the top of the tree branches. Both you and the tree receive input, pulses of light, from above."

He pointed to the heavens and continued, "As the energy moves down into the trunk of the tree, the energy gets transduced and then flows into the Earth, energizing the ley lines of the Earth with potent energy. The life force flows within the trees and is transformed in many ways."

Stella began to get up and wobbled for a moment, completely feeling the rush of energy coming through her crown at the top of her head and pulsing down her body into the Earth.

"Likewise, the energy can come upwards from the ground, up and out the limbs of the trees to send earth energies skyward." He walked over to David and saw that he seemed to be back in his body.

"Very good. Soon you will pick your own tree ally, my lad." David was beyond grateful to have the assistance from the tree ally, knowing that the interplay between tree and human is a gift.

Bridgit concluded that the tree was a magnificent specimen and had virtually no issues aside from the need for proper watering. She gave her respects to the ancient ally and stepped back for one more look from a few feet away. "I thank you, Crisdean, for the anchoring of the ancient energy that holds worlds together." She bowed with her hand to her heart and stepped backward.

Christopher did his blessing with his tree, and they all walked towards where the little white chariot, Pearl, was parked.

"Time for more involved things!" Christopher led the way with a jig in his step, and the others found that he was able to maneuver quite quickly once he had his energizing connection with his tree ally. Bridgit had the feeling that the tree offered Christopher something akin to the elixir of life.

After they walked for several minutes, they all jumped into the Leaf. David drove them to the home of the Elder Christopher. Stella kept thinking of the scene in her dream where Christopher served her tea, and where she saw the Phare family crest on the wall. She looked forward to seeing just how a druid lived.

They made small talk along the way as each was scouting possible dangers along the path.

And the wheel turns...

266

Chapter 42

In a Realm Far Away

In the elemental realm of the fourth dimension, the clouds were crashing in the turbulent air. Darkness took over as it was a night filled with terror. The Bird Lord of Aln went on a rampage, taking flight in the night sky and striking anything that moved. He was the demented Lord from a warring tribe in the Orion Constellation, who felt that this planet and all of its dimensions was his personal playground.

Shamalaine and Bewain shored up the defenses at the Great Hall of the Clan of Phare and sent out patrols to monitor the situation. Keeping peace in the realms between the third and fifth dimension was vital to the plan, and the fourth dimensional bandwidth was right in the middle. The elemental realms of the Clan of Phare were well hidden, but they couldn't take any chances of the Bird Lord finding their lair.

The Bird Lord was furious when the Cu' Sith scout was sent back into the underworld from which it was summoned, and a cloak was placed around his targets, the Life Bearers. These two women and the others stood between him and his hold on all the realms.

Avery ran into the Great Hall, frightened and out of breath. "The Bird Lord was seen near the transformation falls, and the creatures are being transfigured into grotesque monsters!" He cried out to anyone who could hear him.

Shamalaine grabbed her cloak and maneuvered. She and Bewain flew out the door into the night. Avery fell to his knees out of breath and stared at the fire, breathing deeply. He was transfixed by a violet-colored spark within the flames. Suddenly, out popped Phyre, the seventh member of the Builders of Form. "Come with me! We don't have much time!" Phyre pulled Avery into the fire.

Avery and Phyre rode within a rainbow-colored wormhole, a field within a field. The swooshing sounds whirled around them then spit them out of the portal and onto the ground near the cave of doorways. The other five Builders of Form joined them there and created an energy field over the entire area. They stood in concentration as they began to build a new construct that would lessen the power of the Bird Lord and seal him out of this particular envelope of space.

Shamalaine and Bewain were running towards the group of Elementals in the darkness. She was holding her staff, as she shot liquid light upwards to hit the bird with positive doses of love energy.

The new energy bubble was set and launched as Bewain grabbed Shamalaine and threw her into it for protection. She was now in the bubble of energy, through which nothing but love could penetrate.

She and the Elementals stood inside the bubble and expanded it upwards as the Bird Lord came back for another chance to make a hit on the leader of the Clan of Phare.

Bewain pounced upon a rock outcropping and timed his attack. As the Bird Lord came back around, Bewain leaped into the air, hitting the Bird Lord with his massive paw. At the same time, he let out a deafening roar.

As Bewain landed on his feet, he watched the Bird Lord fall to the ground, screeching in pain from the energetic shattering vibration of Bewain's roar. Then Bewain made his final move. He jumped from rock to rock, running as fast as he could towards the Bird Lord with such a fierce look of attack that Shamalaine watched in horror not knowing what her husband was capable of doing, or what the consequences of his action would be.

The Bird Lord of Aln screeched once more and disappeared with a flash of light just as Bewain was about to attack. Bewain stood there waiting for a reappearance, but it was clear that the demon was gone, hurt in the attack.

Bewain rejoined Shamalaine and the Builders as they all reconvened at the Great Hall. Reports were coming in of the damage that had been done, and the Alliance was contacted. It was clear that the presence of the Bird Lord meant that the time was fast approaching for the Life Bearers to make it to the jump points. It was also clear that they would need better protection. Shamalaine and Bewain decided it was time to contact the team of Guardians.

And the wheel turns...

Chapter 43

The Home of Elder Druid Christopher

David drove Pearl straight away to Elder Christopher's home in Old Aberdeen. He passed the Botanical Gardens a few blocks away from where he turned off onto a drive that went through a small grove of trees.

The girls watched in amazement as the driveway was lined with trees on both sides, which opened up to a beautiful green lawn with a two-story cottage with large stone walls and a beautiful maroon toned composite roof that curved under the eaves of the house like something out of a fairy tale. There were two chimney stacks, each on opposite sides of the home and a small white metal table with two chairs placed on the side lawn under a vine trellis, where Christopher took his morning tea in the summer.

As they drove around to the back of the home, there was a portico through which one could park during inclement weather. The back door led into a mudroom and, from there, straight into the kitchen.

Christopher instructed everyone to enter the mudroom and to place their shoes within a basket next to the back door. They followed behind Christopher, as he grabbed his lounge sweater and waved his hand, gesturing for them to follow him into the kitchen. "Come on in!"

The kitchen and dining area was a large L shaped space that took up a good portion of the bottom floor. The wide central island held papers and mailings, spice jars, a variety of teas, and a fruit basket. The kitchen counter was tidy, save for the kitchen towel that had been thrown over a few dishes that had been left to dry.

Christopher grabbed a kettle to put water on for tea and began to pull out items to prepare some finger sandwiches. On the other side of the room was a large fireplace that took up the whole back wall. The stone and mortar were a work of art. Hanging above the fireplace were a couple of stag heads situated in an arch over the many plaques and a central piece, the Family Crest.

David went to the restroom while Bridgit insisted on gathering the teacups for the tea, setting them on the island. Stella asked if she could help, and Christopher instructed her to grab some biscuits from the cupboard. He laid out a plate for her to put them on and several more dishes for each of them to use.

Stella grabbed the biscuits and plates and made her way to the table. She placed the four plates down and laid out the cookies on a serving dish in the middle of the table. She walked over to get the honey and spoons, setting them on the table as well. Once she completed her task, she walked around the room, looking at various books that were lying around, trinkets on the shelves, and then she made her way to the fireplace.

She was taken aback by the stags staring at her intently and moved more towards the center of the fireplace to see the plaques, and there it was, the family crest, just like she had seen in her dream. She stepped up on the stone ledge of the fireplace to get a better look at the name of the Crest.

The Ancient Arms of Phare had a red shield with a golden anchor front and center with the mantle laid over the armor. She was about to interrupt Bridgit and Christopher's chit chat when David bounced back into the room, exclaiming that he was famished. He glided into one of the seats and reached for several biscuits at once.

Christopher motioned for both the ladies to take a seat as he carried the tray of teacups and tea to the table. Stella bided her time until it was appropriate to ask, but she didn't have to wait long as Christopher was tickled that she had found it and allowed her to open the conversation with questions. Bridgit followed behind Christopher with a plate of sandwiches and passed them to David.

"I see that you were admiring the stags." He jokingly said to Stella as he handed her the cup of tea.

"Did you see anything that you found interesting?" His eyes twinkled under his bushy white eyebrows. He prepared his tea in anticipation of her discovery.

"As a matter of fact, I did!" Stella pointed to the Crest and insisted that Bridgit take a look. Bridgit accepted her teacup and set it down to go take a look at the Crest. She stood in front of the fireplace and, just like Stella, launched herself up higher by standing on the edge of the fireplace. As she held herself up with one hand on the fireplace, she turned around and motioned for Christopher to explain.

"Well, my dears, welcome to our home. This home is the ancestral home of the Phare family. It has been in the family for four generations." He chuckled to allow the girls to fully grasp what he just said.

Stunned, Stella asked, "So you are Christopher Lennon Phare?!" She said it both as an exclamation and a question in her voice.

"Impressive Stella! I am indeed. Both of you are my Grandnieces." Christopher announced with a great chuckle.

David dropped his biscuit in his tea when Christopher revealed the truth of who he was. David had only known him as Elder Christopher, never being given his mentor's surname for privacy reasons. To find out that Christopher was the Great Uncle of these two ladies was quite the surprise.

"This home was the homestead of Airleas and Barabell Phare. Barabell being the original Life Bearer of the Clan of Phare, and might I add, who bears a striking resemblance to you, Miss Stella."

Stella and Bridgit were stunned at the facts that were being presented. Having read about their ancestors recently and then to have another long lost Phare family member pop up was beyond their wildest dreams.

"Christopher, let me get this straight. You are the brother of both of our Grandfathers?" A tear was welling up in Bridgit's eye at that moment.

"Yes. Your Grandfather James was my older brother", he said to Bridgit, then turning to Stella.

He continued, "And your Grandfather, August, was the middle brother. I was the youngest in the line and left home quite suddenly, I do admit, but for a good reason." He took a sip of tea and a bite of his biscuit.

David fished his biscuit out of his teacup and poured himself another cup, then helped himself to several sandwiches, being both famished and fascinated.

"If you allow me, I will give you a synopsis of what has happened with the lineage of the Phare family, and hopefully, it will shed some light on how we have all gathered here in the land of our ancestors."

The girls and David happily agreed to hear the story, one in which Christopher promised would be worth their while.

"I was born in the United States in 1943, the youngest son of Thomas Dand Phare and Kaitlyn May Phare." He turned to look at Bridgit this time and said, "And you, young lady, are the spitting image of my dear mother." He nodded his head, pleased to be in the company of these two lovely ladies.

Bridgit smiled and looked at Stella while placing her teacup on the saucer. Stella was in complete heaven, hearing this news and seeing that her dreams and visions have been leading her correctly down this very path.

Christopher continued, "We lived a low key life in a coastal town of California in the '40s and '50s. One day when I was thirteen years old, I fell ill with a high fever and deliria. At that time, I lost consciousness and had an out of body experience where somehow, I slipped out of this world and found myself back in my home of origin, within the fourth density."

Stella and Bridgit looked at each other, and then Bridgit asked, "Was your home of origin the same as my home of origin?"

"You mean, did I go home to the Clan of Phare?" He paused and answered for them, "Yes. I went back to the home of the Clan within the fourth density and was given healing. At the same time, I was given the mission that is unfolding before our eyes."

"Who did you meet there? What was the mission?" Stella blurted.

Bridgit asked for him to continue as she listened intently.

"I was being cared for by many of the elders in the clan, and then, of course, I was being counseled by the most gracious leader of the Clan herself, the beloved Shamalaine."

Both of the girls were quiet, each feeling tenderness in their hearts.

Christopher looked at Stella and said, "You have not yet been given the truth of who you are Stella. Bridgit has had her time, like I have, where she was able to go back home for her mission download, but what I want to tell you, dear Stella is that in the fourth density, you are the younger daughter of the leader of the Clan of Phare, Shamalaine and the Commander Bewain."

Stella started to cry as she knew it was true but did not dare bring it up. Bridgit had a tear in her eye, as the joy of Stella being her fourth density sister felt more real than anything she had known.

Christopher turned to Bridgit and continued, "When you, as Kaialena, left the fourth density to incarnate in this lifeform as Bridgit, your parents Shamalaine and Bewain actually incarnated first to bring you through the portal of the third density world. They could only stay in the third dimensional realm for six years as they had another that needed to come forth, their beloved daughter Tulina." He looked at Stella at that moment.

"Tulina! That is my fourth density name? Breacher called me that!" Stunned once more, she pulled her hair back into a ponytail as her neck began to heat up.

Bridgit was reeling from this news as well, mainly the part that Shamalaine and Bewain incarnated into this world to birth her as Prudence and Tom Phare, and that would explain why they died in a meteor shower. She said those words out loud. "METEOR SHOWER!"

"Yes. Your parents had to leave quickly and together, and that was the best way they could do it; during the meteor showers when a portal could be easily accessed. By the way, many of the Phare family men have left the earth at an early age, but this was because they are all in training as Guardians and Commanders in the Alliance. We will talk more about that later."

He continued, "So back to my illness. During my time with the Clan, I received my mission, and when I returned to my body, the doctors found that I had suddenly recovered. I told no one what had happened to me, only that I felt much better. A few years would go by, and when I turned seventeen years old, I hitched a ride on a mariner's boat, jumping from boat to boat until I made it to the Scottish coast. There, I was met by an Elder Druid who took me in and brought me up on the druid path. I trained in the art of walking between the worlds. I am a Gatekeeper as well as a Life Bearer."

All four of the people sitting at the table were Life Bearers, three of which were related to the Clan of Phare. David sat listening to the story in amazement, and then Christopher directed the conversation to him.

"David was also, like me, brought into the Druid path at a fairly young age and raised away from his true family. His birth mother was not wed and gave him up for adoption. Her name was Cecilia Truce." David had his head down with a slight pout on his face. He was overwhelmed with emotion and thanked the ladies for agreeing to come on this journey.

"We are all learning so much!" David loudly exclaimed. He jumped up to throw some wood in the fireplace and went about building a fire to give himself some time to think and get the subject off of him.

Christopher continued speaking about him anyway. Stella wanted to ask if she and David were related, but David's emotions were high, and she wasn't sure he could handle any more questions on the subject.

Christopher continued, "He is in his final preparations to advance to the level of Druid as he is currently at the Ovate stage of his initiation. His lineage is as ancient as the days and is a close relation to you, Stella."

He pointed to her with his last bite of sandwich flopping between his fingers. "The Truce family lineage is where your third density mother and his third density mother come. All I know so far is that both of your mother's lineages are a direct descendant of Isis."

David and Stella looked at each other and said at the same time, "That is so cool!" Stella contemplated this information further. David returned to the table after getting the fire started, a bit more chipper with the news of his maternal family line being connected to the Goddess of all Goddesses.

Stella finally hopped in, given David's chipperness, "Does this mean that we are cousins, like Bridgit and I are cousins?"

"Well, I have yet to find the family connection, but it is most likely the case, as the Truce family name is not a common one, wouldn't you agree?"

Stella mulled it over and then changed the subject back to Christopher, "Why did you not communicated with your family to let them know that you were okay? I imagine that must have been hard on your parents."

"Well, I had my training, my mission. I couldn't let anything keep me from preparing. I have been preparing for this day ever since. During this time, I have done quite well with some investments that were left to me through our Scottish Phare ancestors. I have been able to put aside a large endowment that will be needed for the next part of the mission."

Bridgit chimed in, "And just what is the next part of the mission?"

"We find the other Life Bearers and get to the jump points. It is imperative that we find the others now. Without a moment to spare."

They all stared at one another and sipped their tea, contemplating the web that had been woven, predestined for them. All of them had chills and felt both excitement and trepidation.

Bridgit leaned over and placed her hand upon Christopher's aged hand and said, "Thank you, dear man, for all that you have done. It is a true honor to meet you at last." She smiled and blew a kiss in his direction. The moment was captured in Christopher's heart as a moment in time that he had waited for most of his life.

And the wheel turns...

Chapter 44

Quadrivium Trials at Alpheratz Training Camp

Breacher and Benoit made the final arrangements for the skills test. They placed within the tactical terrain energetic and physical keys that would advance the riders to the next level within a vast grid-work consisting of all of the elements.

This type of strategic terrain was called a Quadrivium. A circular landscape that, layer by layer, would allow the riders to enter a field of light at the very center of the terrain via four distinct pathways.

The Alpheratz base, located at the edge of a sizeable arid terrain, was hidden within the caves nearby were volcanic openings led into a deeper territory, where fire and ice were both prominent land features.

Benoit handed Breacher the map of the Quadrivium grid to demonstrate to him the four paths from which the riders would take. The outer grid of the testing range was an Orange/Red Lava zone. Benoit explained that the riders would first enter into this zone to reach the next level, the Blue/White Ice zone. Once through the first two zones, the riders would then enter the Green/Brown Rock zone.

From there, they would have to be vigilant to find the light within the Air/Ether core of the grid.

Benoit explained that during each level of the skills test, the riders would be using all of their precognitive abilities. Their agility would be tested, and their intuition would be of utmost importance. Breacher was pleased with the level of detail that Benoit had placed on the test environment.

Breacher added a few things to the list of items that he would grade the rider's on. These included their interaction with others, the speed in which they moved through the grid, and how they accessed the keys. Those candidates that exhibited all of these qualities would be considered for the dragon rider team. Yet, the riders were all under the impression that they were training for the prestigious Pegasi games.

Though the Pegasi games were formidable and many riders performing in the Quadrivium trials would be considered for that honor, none of them knew that a handful of riders were to be hand-picked for an even bigger task.

It was now time for the riders to enter the fields. Over 60 riders were participating. These riders were from all over the various star quadrants in both the Milky Way and Andromeda galaxies. A few of them were there as representatives of their star lineage, who had the best training that could be provided, and then there were those that were unassuming in their demeanor, but equally powerful riders.

Breacher observed each candidate as they entered the field. He stood on a stage in front of the crowd of riders prepared to give the instructions as Benoit introduced him to the riders.

"Riders, you have been given a particular set of coordinates within the gridwork to start your trials. You will be tested on skill, precognitive ability, and overall agility and speed. Once you enter the first level of testing, you will be looking for coded keys that will give you a clue you need to move onto the next testing phase. These keys will not look like keys, so use all of your abilities to find them. Once you have garnered the information from the key, then use its knowledge to move forward to the next level. You must interact within each level or risk being disqualified. That means for those of you who can teleport or bilocate, you cannot simply move to the inner core." Breacher heard boo sounds, and some laughter in the crowd as the riders realized the restrictions.

Breacher continued, "I caution you all, there will be surprises along your path."

He paused for a moment to look at the riders in attendance this day, "You are the best of the best. May you have the intelligence and the heart to find your way out of this matrix. See you at the finish line. I will be waiting for those who have proven themselves worthy."

Commander Benoit gave a prayer, and the drums began. The riders were confused when they called their Pegasus, but none came. Benoit spoke again, "This skills test is for you alone; one that will test your mental, physical and spiritual capacity. Move now to your coordinates swiftly." The drumming continued as the riders ran to the mapped-out area of the caverns nearby.

As the riders came to the first level, the Orange/Red zone, immediately, it was clear that they were all in trouble. Having no Pegasus to ride, they stood on the outer rim of a lava flow and were instructed to make it across the lava flow to the blue area. There was a way to do it that would take hours to climb, to cross safely, and they all knew that they were being timed and tested for their ingenuity. Everyone spread out, looking for the key.

A tall, slender rider with short, light brown hair made the first move. He simply sat down. The riders that were near him just laughed and ran off, looking to find the key or a hidden hovercraft or some other means to cross the lava, but the lanky rider sat, with his legs crossed and went into meditation.

Soon he began to feel a shift in the energy within the space, and with his mind's eye, he scanned the cavern for the key. What he found was something glowing approximately 30 feet away tucked under a rock.

He walked over to this area and turned the stone over. Under the rock, he found a glowing disk with a symbol that had an X mark on top of several circles, which resembled a bull's eye. He recognized it as the Quadrivium symbol. One of the quadrants had a colored dot to indicate where to go. The rider returned the rock to the original position and moved on to the area shown on the symbol.

There were multiple entrances within this first level, and the lanky rider could see a female heading in the same direction. He took long strides to arrive at the spot around the time that she did, and they both stood staring at each other, wondering how to proceed. Finally, the female rider, dressed in a gray jumpsuit and a leather jacket adorned with service pins, decided not to waste time and presented an offer.

"Would you like to work together to complete the task or is working with a female beneath you?" She was gentle at first and then rammed the last few words down his throat so fast that he jumped backward, nearly slipping into the lava.

The female grabbed his arm and brought him back from the edge just before his foot touched the fiery flow, and with a giggle, she said, "Wow. I guess you need some help!"

His body was tingling as he stood in her energy field. The lanky blue-eyed rider introduced himself. His feathery hair came over his forehead, covering one eye at times, and his fitted shirt wrapped his torso so tightly that his abdominal muscles rippling through the material.

He responded to her remark. "Thank you! Yes, you can say that. My name is Arbor." He smiled at her, hoping she wouldn't joke about his being named for a tree. Being tree-like was one of his traits, having a long, sturdy trunk and even longer arms. Feeling and seeing auras was another less obvious trait that always came in handy in situations like these.

"I would be honored to work with you if you will have me." He placed his hand over his heart and bowed to her, as a subject would to someone of royalty. He recognized her once he was close enough to make out the emblem tattooed on the inside of her wrist. He saw it when she grabbed him, and now, she stared at him with horror.

"Stop! Don't do that!" The female covered her wrist with the leather straps of the jacket sleeve and looked at Arbor.

"Listen, I am sorry for being rude. I didn't realize that you were from around here." She looked away to see if anyone else could hear what they were saying. No one else was around as she turned to introduce herself.

"I am Praeta, the third daughter of the Pegasian dynastic ruler, Lord Praestid." She said quietly.

"So, you are the Princess Praeta," Arbor repeated her name in an average decibel, presenting the facts as he knew them. He attempted to bow again, but Praeta grabbed him before he could make the gesture.

"Shhh! Don't say it that loud!" She moved him closer to her to strike a deal for his silence.

"Listen, you seem like an nice guy. Can you keep who I am a secret for now?" She pleaded with him, not realizing that he had no intention of using this information against her.

Arbor stepped back and looked around and spoke, "Princess Praeta, I am a loyal subject of Pegasus. I will do whatever it is that you ask of me. I do think it would be wise that we continue the search, as we are wasting valuable time. Are you still interested in working together?" He gave her a devilish smile to indicate that an adventure awaited them. His smile diffused her instantly. He could read her aura and see that she had relaxed.

"Yes. That would be great." She pulled her hair to the side of her neck and looked upward to see his charming smile looking at her. Then his eyebrow raised, his head cocked to one side as he stared with a look on his face that had him both concerned and curious. Her aura had shifted into a soft pinkish hue, one that would indicate amorous energy.

"Shall we get moving? He coughed and strutted onward, two steps ahead of Praeta as she yelled to him, "Wait for me!"

Arbor turned to her and held his arm out to give her the lead. She smiled and walked in front of him, holding her head high and then stopped suddenly, causing Arbor to nearly bump into her. She tuned into the environment, feeling a movement, and said, "Watch out!"

Suddenly a red, fire breathing dragon flew by them, almost hitting them with its tail. It landed twenty feet from where they stood and turned to face them. Praeta took a deep breath in and centered herself. Arbor walked ahead of her as a shield, as he instinctually knew that the dragon did not mean them any harm but thought it best to be protective of the princess just the same. He pulled out a small flute that he carried with him to tame his Pegasus and began to play it.

Praeta then did something unbeknownst to Arbor. She bilocated to the other side of the dragon and jumped upon its back. She began to caress the red dragon as Arbor continued to play.

With her mind's eye, she sent a visual to the dragon to move towards Arbor. The dragon received the thought and swiftly launched forward towards Arbor. The dragon began to lift in the air with Praeta reaching down for Arbor as it launched off the ground.

"Let's go!" Praeta announced. Arbor grabbed Praeta's arm and mounted the back of the red dragon as the dragon flew them over the lava flow.

Praeta could feel Arbor's heart pounding as he held onto her tightly. She melted at that moment, trying to hide the fact that she could stay held in his arms forever. She felt a familiarity with him. She had always sensed that she would meet someone tall and enchanting, but as a princess, there just were not many opportunities to mingle.

As she contemplated the strange sensations she was feeling, being so close to Arbor, he again felt her amorous energies building. This time, he could not bear to dispel them. Something about her felt familiar as if he had met her in a dream. He held her closer to his body, reaching over her to hold the ridges of the dragons head.

The two discovered the layout of the area from the higher vantage point. They noticed the blue zone coming up to the left. This thing between them would have to wait.

Praeta once more sent a visual image to the red dragon to bring them to the Blue/White zone. She motioned to Arbor that they were headed to the Blue/White zone and pointed out a few others making their way below by rocks that they were manipulating to rise. They could see other riders jumping from stone to stone to make it to the next level.

The red dragon dove downward in the Blue/White zone of ice. The two riders jumped off quickly as the dragon slid during the landing and took back off into the air without stopping. Praeta and Arbor were the first to reach the Blue/White zone.

And the wheel turns...

Chapter 45

The House of Phare

Christopher and David started tending to the fire building as the ladies cleaned the dishes from lunch. They then made themselves comfortable in the living room where the fire was crackling. Even though it was the hottest month of the year, the temperature still warranted a cozy fire to offset the chill in the air.

Stella sat on the sofa looking out towards the window contemplating the fact that Barabell had lived here. She whispered her thoughts, "Her husband and children, they all lived here."

Then a thought hit her. She blurted out loud, "Does Scotland hold the key to the New Earth frequencies?"

Bridgit sat next to her, grabbing a blanket nearby to lay upon her knees and waited to hear Christopher's response, but it was David who chimed in.

"Scotland is a place of timelessness, where the ancient and the new live together, side by side, in perfect complement. It is a place of our ancestors, who left many stones for us to turn." He said in a particularly Scottish brogue.

"Everything in our environment points to a mystery, from the cairns, the megaliths, and to the sacred chapels, where the ley lines cross, to the Fairy Hill of the Caledonians."

He stomped his foot on the ground and said, "Right here. In this very place lived your ancestors. Tis truly a magical place, where the veil is thin enough to see through it at times."

Stella slowly batted her eyes at David, stunned once more. David then turned and pointed to the things in the room.

"This room is full of secrets waiting to be unveiled. But what I know," David paused for a moment out of frustration, "What I know is that within the sacred landscape of this beautiful island is clues to the inner realms. There are reasons why the stone circles were built. There are reasons why the monoliths are located where they are. For those with eyes to see, it is clear the land of our ancestors is exactly where we need to be to repair the grid work, to reset the planet to a higher vibrational frequency."

With a rhetorical question, he continued, "How does one do that?" He turned to them with such vigor and waited. No one spoke.

"The stones! The water! The earth itself!" He wiggled in his seat to look straight at the ladies and said, "We can shift the frequency by attuning to the ley lines and making the necessary amendments where the flow seems to be blocked." He stalled when he saw the look in women's eyes.

David looked at Christopher to see if he could continue with a deeper explanation, but Christopher indicated with a nod that his answer was sufficient for the time being.

David apologized for his enthusiasm. "I'm sorry. I could go on and on about this subject. It is probably a good thing that I am presenting this information at a conference next week. I shan't bore you with any more of the details."

He sat down on the fireplace ledge as the Ladies Phare processed the information and, more importantly, the energy within the room. The silence in the room was more from the shock of David's enthusiasm when he spoke on the subject than anything else.

Christopher had a thought as he stood to get more tea, "While I know that you ladies want to do more research on your lineage and given that I have just filled in the many blanks that you had, I have a proposition for you."

He looked at David, pointing to him and asked, "When do you need to be at the conference?"

David looked puzzled, "This coming Monday."

Christopher responded, "Good. What would you say about spending some time showing the lassies the Stone Circle Trail?"

"Yes! That would be splendid." He smiled with approval and grateful to share what he knows.

Christopher continued, "I think it is best to continue the deeper mysteries of the stones when the ladies can actually feel the energy of them, wouldn't you agree, David?" He winked at David with encouragement.

David nodded in full agreement.

Bridgit nodded in agreement as well and said, "That sounds like a great idea!"

"David, what kind of conference are you presenting at that you could be talking about this kind of thing. It isn't exactly neutrino stuff, is it!?" Stella inquired.

"It is a Geomancy Conference. Another hobby of mine, more in line with Druidry and nature. I guess you could say it is my other passion.

Perhaps you ladies would accompany me? I could get you in for free." He squealed with such excitement of having some groupies that the ladies agreed to hear more.

Bridgit asked, "What are the topics?"

"There will be a variety of presentations related to Geomancy, such as Vastu Shastra, Feng Shui, and natural geomantic landscaping. Real cutting edge stuff", he explained enthusiastically.

"Well, that sounds intriguing. Anyone presenting anything on the subject of trees?" Bridgit inquired.

"Absolutely! There is a chap presenting on tree magic as it is related to the Celtic Lunar Calendar." He smiled her way and noticed her response.

"Oh. I see." Bridgit was hoping to hear him say that some brave soul would be talking about trees as portals into other realms, but he didn't. "It sounds interesting. So, anyone can sign up?"

She looked at Stella for approval, and Stella chimed in, "Yeah, ah, what do we need to do to sign up for the workshop?" She smiled, knowing that Bridgit wanted to support David in his efforts, but secretly she was genuinely interested in hearing more about geomantic landscapes.

"It is as simple as filling out a form, which I can pull up on my computer. Let me go retrieve it."

He jumped forward across the room as Stella replied, "Thanks Davy, ole chap!" in a ridiculous Scottish brogue that had everyone laughing.

David stopped momentarily to appreciate Stella's attempt to fit in. "Barry! I shall get you the details, and we can get you lasses signed up straight away!" He dashed to his car to find his laptop as Stella and Bridgit laughed at his enthusiasm.

Stella commented, "Barry???"

She shook her head and continued, "I look forward to the day that I am more acquainted with the Scottish dialect, and he was doing so well, too!" admitting that he had been Americanizing the conversation for their convenience.

Making his way to the kitchen, Christopher turned and quipped, "Barry is another way of saying fantastic." He winked at Stella then went into the kitchen.

Bridgit and Stella commented to one another that things kept getting stranger and more lively than ever. They had monolith's to discover and geomantic training to do on top of finding the other Life Bearers.

Christopher sensed their joy and apprehension and remarked, "It will be fine. You might just find what you are looking for."

And the wheel turns...

Chapter 46

Level Two of the Quadrivium

The riders were all at various levels within the Quadrivium grid. Many had given up, not having the skills alone to get through the terrain without their Pegasus. Those who could maneuver through to the next stage, into the Blue/White zone, had used their developed precognitive abilities to make it to the next level. Two were fortunate to come across a dragon who helped with their progressing into the Blue zone. This connection was what Breacher had hoped for. Dragons choosing their riders was the goal.

The Warrioress, Jinnby, stood at the center of the Blue/White zone taking in the landscape. She, too, had found a hidden key giving precise coordinates to the Blue zone. She used her telekinetic skills to maneuver rocks as a pathway for her and a companion to cross over the lava to make it to the Blue zone.

Her companion, Alderson, was behind her, holding her bow made of willow as she knelt in prayer, giving thanks to her relations, the stones. She stood up, put on her cape, then took the bow from Alderson and placed it over her shoulder. She then went into a prayer stance, hands over her heart.

"Thank you for your power of protection while we traversed the fiery river. I must ask of your protection once more as we scale these walls of ice." She pointed upward as they viewed the height of the wall of glass-like ice sheets.

"As your people live amongst the water element, and I, the rock, I will step back now and give you the lead in this realm of ice." She flowed backward, gracefully, every move a choreographed one as she moved her bow to her back and awaited his suggestion.

He held his hands to his heart and said, "I will carry you where you cannot walk yourself."

He shifted his stance and removed his wand. The wand of his people was that of the alder tree, from which he received his name. The wand had a rune upon it that represented the element water. He wielded it like a sword at first, swishing it about and maneuvering his feet to a timed rhythm.

Alderson swirled it around his body as he began to turn. He aimed the alder wand upwards while twirling until a vortex of energy surrounded Jinnby. She turned, fully encapsulated in his protective field, and ran towards the ice wall with the speed of a cheetah, leaping into the air, grabbing each ice ledge, one at a time, in a zig-zag pattern. All the while, Alderson's full attention was on assisting the Warrioress to the top of the ice wall. A pillow of energy surrounded her like a net for a high-wire acrobat.

Once she made her ascent, she returned the kindness by lowering woven ropes that she had wrapped around her waist. She tied them together and threw them over. Alderson was small in stature, light-weight, and muscular. It took him no time to traverse the vertical sheet of ice. The rope was merely a gesture of support, should he miss a ledge.

With the two of them at the top of the ice wall, they began to look for the clues. Alderson once again used his alder wand for divination. Not able to pick up any clues himself, Jinnby offered to be of assistance and motioned for him to use the wand on her. He simply touched Jinnby's forehead, and she spiraled deeply inward. All that could be heard was her heartbeat. The silence was calming and terrifying, all at once. Something was wrong.

Jinnby began to sway, her head first, then her body, falling forward. Alderson grabbed her and held her close as he gently led her to the ground. A premonition overtook her. She saw the planet in which she was born, within the Tigris Galaxy, crashing into another world. Then she saw nothing but a bright light in her mind's eye.

Jinnby sputtered and gasped and held onto Alderson's arm for protection and support as her entire being felt the gravity of the situation. She looked up into his eyes and spoke in her native tongue. The words were more like pitches of sound as she tried to explain that her home planet was in trouble. Her premonitions almost always came true.

He held her arms for support as she tried to get to her feet. Alderson could see others were advancing up the ice wall now, and they needed to complete the task of the Quadrivium first. Though Jinnby was taller than Alderson, he provided his back for her to ride. He took on the burden of finding the key himself as Jinnby was not mentally present.

He used his wand on his own third eye once more, with determination, and saw a ley line of energy leading to the source of the current. He soon came upon a disc with three circles and an X with a dot that informed him where to go. With Jinnby limp upon his back, he followed the path laid out on the disc, and soon he came to a series of ice steps that led downward into an area of the ice plateau that resembled a labyrinth.

Within the center of the labyrinth was a separate, spiraled stairway that Alderson quickly made his way. Once he arrived with Jinnby, he could see an energetic doorway with symbols upon it that looked like mathematical equations made out of musical notes all scrambled together as if it was a song.

He blurted out a tone nervously, but it resembled a sound like something scratching metal. Jinnby opened her eyes while he gushed with embarrassment, and she noticed the doorway lighting up momentarily. She opened her mouth and spoke in the language of light and then roared like a lion. The door opened before their eyes. She rested her head on his shoulder, still weak with despair.

The other riders had made it to the edge of the labyrinth upon the plateau. Some of them could see that the duo had made it down to the center of the maze and watched as they disappeared. The doorway had closed behind them as a few of the other riders were nearing the door.

Through the doorway, Alderson and Jinnby entered the unknown. Alderson put Jinnby down as he took a few steps inside. They could not see anything in any direction, just darkness.

Jinnby was coming out of the mind fog and indicated that she felt well enough to move about on her own. She began to take a few steps, then slipped, falling down a slide made of ice.

Alderson could hear her in need and moved forward only to slip and fall down the ice slide as well. His heartbeat pounded as he slid to an unknown fate.

They could see a light as they plummeted downward on the ice slide, enough to know that they were about to be dropped into a pool of water. The ice slide began to crack in the light as the temperature started to change, and the weight of two of them proved to be too heavy. They were spat outward and fell below as the ice slide began to break, shards falling upon them in the process.

A shard of ice hit Alderson in the head just before he hit the water, knocking him out cold. Jinnby had managed to flip and enter the water headfirst. She dove deep enough that the broken-up ice slide did not harm her.

Suddenly, she saw something swim by her quickly, as she pushed her way upwards to get air. Popping her head out of the water and gasping for air, she began treading water, looking around the pool.

She couldn't see Alderson but found his alder wand floating upon the water.

She swam over to retrieve it when a gush of water came upward from the center of the pool and out flew a blue dragon with Alderson hanging from its feet. The dragon flew over to the green area and dropped him on the ground and flew away.

Jinnby swam as fast as she could and jumped out of the water onto the sand leading to the Green zone. She quickly jumped rock after rock and then leaped upward to the area where Alderson lay on his stomach.

Jinnby rolled him over to check his breathing and began to push water from his lungs. Nothing happened. She touched her heart to reach inward to find her center and asked for help from her ancestors. She heard the words, "It is only his ancestors that can help him now."

That's it, she thought. She pulled Alderson's wand out and traced a circle around his body and looking at the alder wands runes. She traced the water rune in the air above him. She used her ability to move the energy of the water rune into his body.

Jinnby stood above him, praying to his lineage to bring forth his life force. She heard him sputter and jerk. Leaning down, she rolled him to his side to release the water leaving his body. He coughed the water out and looked up to see standing next to Jinnby, an apparition of his beloved mother, who was beginning to fade.

He heard, "Love always heals." He looked at Jinnby, who had a tear in her eye, her body soaked, and they embraced one another.

Jinnby helped Alderson to his feet as he questioned her on what had happened. She told him that it was not she who saved him but a blue dragon. Amazed at the turn of events, they gave thanks for the gift of the dragon and continued with the task of making it through the Green zone, both feeling better suited to being on land once more.

And the wheel turns...

Chapter 47

Avery's Secret

Avery climbed up high into the mountainous region of the outer zone of the lands of Phare. He was called there by the Watchers, who dwell within the caves of no time.

Avery had been on special assignment unbeknownst to all, but he and the Watchers.

As he summited the last peak, he looked down on the lands where he had been serving a dual purpose. He gave thanks to the Eternal Being, the Holy Creator. He had pledged his energy stream to make a difference as an elemental and as something more. He stood looking out upon the land that he and many others were instrumental in creating with the instruction of the Divine Blueprint of the Holy Creator. He, being an instrument of God.

Avery turned around and faced the cavern. He wiped his brow and pulled the waistline of his pants up, and tightened his belt. Shifting his pouch that hung from the belt, he pulled out his report and walked towards the opening of the cave.

Inside the cave, the warmth of a summer day filled the space. At the height of the mountain, the heat felt good. He perused the etchings on the walls as he meandered through the first corridor leading into the inner chamber.

Once he made his way down the corridor and into the large room, he paused at the doorway to be announced. Chimes began to play a melodic sound while the three Watchers turned from their duties observing planetary situations. One of them motioned for Avery to come to him.

"Avery, it is indeed a blessed moment in the eternal now to have you join us here," the male Watcher said as he turned to greet him. This particular Watcher had an intricate spiral design of galaxies imprinted upon his elongated skull, which Avery assumed represented the planetary bodies that the Watcher was responsible for.

The Watcher wore a violet-colored robe with star symbols upon it, embellished with crystalline beading. His hands were equally embellished with jeweled rings and upon his neck laid a simple chain of platinum with keys dangling from it.

He motioned for Avery to come closer. "We have been monitoring your progress, not only your elemental form but also as your other 4th density humanoid in the Pleiades."

Avery bowed and thanked them for the attention that they were giving to his lifestream. He offered to give his report to the Watchers, detailing his abilities to hold focus on all his duties as a Builder of Form, all the while staying connected to his other 4th density aspect, The Sage.

He shared that once he manifested his energy into the incarnation of a male humanoid, he had learned a lot about emotions. He could see and feel how temperamental humanoids could be with just the slightest change of energy to their emotional field from an outside source.

He explained what he had learned on how emotions of one being could unbalance another and cause a downward spiral that resulted in

296

a disharmonic vibration for both people.

He reported how troublesome this was to experience but how it enlightened him on how the human being came to fall from the higher frequencies as they began to interact within duality.

Avery paused there for a moment, ashamed of his earlier apprehensions of not trusting humans in the lower frequencies of Earth. He explained that this experience opened his heart and vision on how the Divine Creator planned for each of his castes of lifestream's to see and feel from another's point of view. He added that this was how he was finding his way to compassion for all beings of God's creation.

His words touched the Watchers, and they were pleased that this little being of God's creation was pouring forth his precious light to assist Earth in raising her light quotient by agreeing to be more than he ever thought he could be. "Thought" being the keyword they reminded him.

"Because you have allowed yourself to think higher thoughts, which have indeed manifested, we offered you the opportunity to be of greater service to the Divine Plan. As you took on the assignment of a multidimensional incarnation, simultaneously, as both elemental and humanoid, we have seen that your elemental aspect has grown in depth and capability. We have a surprise for you, Avery."

Pulling up Avery's other 4D aspect on the screen, they continued. "We have seen into The Sage's future, and we think you should perhaps see this, if for nothing other than to prepare you for this next level of attainment on behalf of the blue jewel and all life upon her."

The Watcher brought him over to a screen where they pulled up a scene of a young man known as The Sage, Avery's humanoid form. This other incarnation known as The Sage, Avery was well aware of and had been kept a secret from those in the Clan of Phare, as Avery had every intention of being a bridge himself for the galactic energies to enter the planet.

As an Elemental being, he knew that he could use his power of mental focus to align the pulses of energy that would need to be woven into a new net for anchoring the vibration of peace.

The Watchers had come to Avery in his dream time while he was in the tutelage of Eldorman and spoke to him of his mental abilities being needed in other realms. They encouraged him to think of ways to be of service, and it was he that brought up the idea for him to manifest another body. It was not unheard of for fourth density beings to incarnate in other dimensions for brief missions, but he was suggesting that he use his power of focused intention to not only maintain his essence in the elemental realms of the Clan of Phare but to also split his awareness in another body within the same fourth density, just elsewhere.

His particular talents would be needed, and there was no time to choose one incarnation or the other. So, the test was put upon him to bring forth another form, one in the form of a male humanoid who would be able to hold a frequency of light that could unite the realms.

Avery peeked into the screen upon which he sheepishly watched his humanoid aspect doing something so incredible that he stood in the spot just staring. The humanoid, known as The Sage among his people, was shown flying high in the heavens, upon the back of a dragon! Avery's eyes got wide, and he froze, barely able to speak.

The Watchers brought Avery to the round table where they could continue to monitor the past, present, and future, all the while instructing Avery on this vital task.

"Dear child, you have accomplished much in the way of sending forth your life force to manifest a humanoid existence all the while keeping a strong focus on your elemental life force. This is why you have been chosen as the first ray Builder of Form. We realize that seeing the future of this humanoid aspect of yourself is overwhelming, given that he is mounted upon a dragon, an animal that you have in the past not been successful at befriending."

Avery had been asked to shift more than he was comfortable with, many times in this incarnation alone, and now he was not only secretive about his true abilities with all of the beings that he holds dear, he was being asked to be more.

"Great teachers of the Watch, I have gained much in my expansion of self, which has sparked the life of a humanoid rider. I have given him much of my vital life force and will continue to do so, for I believe in the mission at hand. There needs to be a rider with the ability to hold the currents of the dragon, and though I have not as yet been successful in this form, I am resolved in the fact that the aspect of me, The Sage, can and will be successful with the team that Breacher is forming; That is if he is chosen." Avery looked down at his feet, noticing a stone on the floor, resembling a heart. He leaned down to pick it up and held it. He tossed it a bit and smiled.

The Watchers said, "Like that stone, Avery, you have the heart, as does your counterpart, The Sage, to be great at all you do, for it is through the heart that one naturally adds to their light quotient. This future record that you are seeing is a probable future."

Avery looked at the Watchers with gratitude and thanked them for the opportunity to advance in this way. Avery desired to be of service to all realms, leading him into the role of a Watcher in later days, as this is what he was ultimately training to be. He bowed his head to send The Sage his focused energy. The Sage needed to hold the vibration of love in everything that he did, in all of his encounters.

And the wheel turns...

Chapter 48

The Final Round of the Quadrivium

The skills test was coming to an end, with many riders failing to make it past the first two zones. The air was thick as the riders made their way into the Green/Brown Rock zone, the third area of the Quadrivium grid.

A tall male stood on a grassy knoll, having just jumped from the ice cliffs into the cold pool of water 75 feet below. As he stood dripping, he squeezed the excess water from his long brown hair that had been held in place by a leather binding. He removed the binding and the headband from his forehead to reveal a white spot above his right ear.

He continued to dry off from the exhilarating jump, pleased with his ability to move within the elements. He pulled his hair back up to re-tie his locks behind his head. His slightly pointed ears were the only thing that resembled his true elven nature. He always pulled his hair around his ears and fixed his headband so that he could conceal his ears.

The Sage had been riding Pegasus for most of his adolescence. He had excelled in his abilities as a rider and as a manifestor, allowing him the opportunity to compete in what he thought was acceptance in the Pegasi Games.

His name, The Sage, came from his being born with the white spot of the Sages, a mark of wisdom and peace. A group of men and women raised The Sage in a peaceful realm within the fourth density of the Pleiadian moon, Taygeta. On Taygeta, children are given descriptive names once the child is understood. Rarely would one be born with the white spot of an ancient one, and thus he was known as The Sage.

He knew that he had to leave his home world to gain experience as a rider, so here he stood, prepared to do what it took to make it to the Pegasi Games.

As he stood in contemplation, he heard an inner voice say, "Behind you!" The Sage turned to see a snow-white leopard coming towards him. The animal was fierce.

The Sage drew from the wisdom of his people in situations like these. He was taught to match frequency with an opponent, and once he was at the same vibration, then he could bring his opponent's energy up to match his own frequency, which was that of love and peace.

The Sage hung his arms downward and began to move like the leopard, in a stalking manner, bringing his vibration to that of a hungry beast. He got on all fours, his muscular body rippled and expanded with every breath he took.

The leopard slowed down its approach and felt the vibration of his meal. The Sage then stood tall and continued to interact with the leopard until both of their energy fields shifted, and after a while, matched the frequency of peace.

The leopard laid down and licked his lips, no longer able to gather a meal from this being. The Sage pulled out a cloth from the pouch that hung from his belt. He took out a protein roll, like a loaf of bread, but chewy, made from nuts and fibers. He threw it to the beautiful animal and began to climb the rocks upward to find a vantage point.

He could see a silhouette moving through the trees ahead. He saw flashes of a magenta-colored robe weaving in and out of the tree line. Then suddenly, a heavenly vision appeared out of the trees; a beautiful Goddess emerged. His heart pounded as he felt his energy lift.

Her energy was pure and heightened his own. He quickly began to run down the side of the mountain. He felt an immediate need to meet this woman who he felt sure he had met before in some other time or place. His foot barely touched the ground as he lightly coasted the terrain to make it towards the beauty in magenta.

The Sage had lost his wits entirely as he was no longer pursuing the path towards finding the key. All he could think of was getting to the vision, the beauty in the trees.

She, the ninth Kumara in her lineage to become a rider, held her breath as she felt the vibration of someone coming. She pulled her cloak over her head as it encapsulated her in invisibility. The Sage ran to where she stood to pause in the silence of the woods. He listened for her, but he heard nothing. He had lost her scent. He began to wonder if she was an apparition of the mind.

The Sage sat on a rock near the tree line contemplating his next move, finding the key, and moving on to the next level. The Kumara watched from behind her cloak as The Sage closed his eyes and went inward. He knew that he must channel his energy to locate the key within the Green/Brown Rock zone.

He heard others running by, looking for signs of the key. What he saw first was something moving again in the tree line. He noticed a vast energy field and something running through the trees coming towards him. The leaves on the trees began to shake, and the ground shook as well. He witnessed the woman in magenta running towards him with a green dragon coming up behind her.

The Sage stood upon the rock and moved his energy into his core and prepared to rope the dragon with the lasso that he wore crisscrossed upon his chest. The Kumara ran behind him, with no words spoken between them. The green dragon came towards them, and then suddenly, a yellow dragon came out of nowhere, flying over them at close range.

The Kumara twirled her robe around, turning it inside out. A reflective surface shone into the eyes of the green dragon, halting it in its path. Then as the yellow dragon came back for another pass, The Sage used his lasso and threw it just as it passed, knowing that the green dragon was subdued for the time being by the woman with the cloak.

The yellow dragon flew in a zigzag pattern, trying to lose its rider until The Sage stroked its neck. It felt the touch of the rider and melded minds with him. The dragon could feel the pure heart of its rider and eased its flight, coming full circle and returning the rider to where the green dragon and woman were.

As he came over the tree line, the female was no longer there, nor was the green dragon. His heart pulsed quickly, as his dragon lifted upwards again. They flew in the air, surveying the area of the Green-Brown Rock zone.

Near the brown caves at the edge of the zone, The Sage spotted the green dragon flying the female rider to an area that contained a pulsing, energetic signature. Upon approach, The Kumara jumped off of the green dragon, running as fast as she could to a cave.

She entered the cave in darkness, following the vibration. The only light within the cave was a slight light emitting from her silver solar shoes. As she walked along the cave wall, she used her left hand to feel her way by touch. She came to an area within the cave that felt like a niche in the wall. As she felt around in the dark, a sudden flash of light occurred.

She could see a crystal skull within the niche. She went to touch it but immediately yanked her hand away as the skull had a morpho-cryptic intelligence around it, a security system that sent a loud screaming vibration outward. Startled, she could see the crystal skull morph into a frightening object.

She calmed down and then felt for it again, knowing that this was the key to the exit of the Quadrivium grid. The Kumara placed her hands within the niche again, and once more, the crystal skull emitted an image of a screaming head on the attack, but this time she placed her hand in a halting position, sending a higher frequency and yelled out in a stern voice, "NO! I AM THE MOTHER!"

The system deactivated, and The Kumara retrieved the small blue crystal skull, which was no more than four inches wide. She had recovered what she was looking for, something that she had seen in visions within her meditations many times before. She knew this skull, the blue skull called Aluca, the skull of peace.

She held it to her body and moved back towards the entrance. The Sage saw The Kumara come out of the cave, holding something and watched as she mounted the green dragon.

Both dragons now flew in the air, over the thick clouds, and soared with the two riders. The Sage was mesmerized as he watched The Kumara ride the green dragon so effortlessly. He, too, was getting the hang of riding the yellow dragon, as if his being and the dragon were connected. He directed the yellow dragon with his mind to keep pace with the other dragon. He did not want to lose sight of the woman in magenta again.

Soon both dragons hit a wall of ether at the edge of the final zone, causing the dragons to spiral down to the ground. The riders were trained to dismount in these situations at the last possible moment as the dragons rolled and slid into the side of the rocky terrain. It was clear that they would not be entering the tube of light that was their exit on the back of the dragons until they used the key.

The dragons were dazed but not injured and flew off after they got back on their feet. The Sage and The Kumara were now face to face. She was real, and he was not going to lose her again. He complimented her riding, and she timidly thanked him and quickly found somewhere to sit in silent contemplation.

The Sage could sense her coolness towards him and went into hero mode. It was then that he turned around and walked off. The Kumara was pleased that he understood her need for solitude to tune into the situation. He, too, required isolation to make contact with his higher mind to learn more about the situation.

The first visionary input in his mind's eye was a blue light merging with a stone. He then saw others in his vision standing around the light, in a circle, invoking peace and calling for the light to activate the exit point. He understood what to do, and at the same moment, he heard movement.

The Sage jumped up and ran towards The Kumara, as The Kumara was running towards The Sage. When they came face to face once more, they smiled at one another and energetically communicated in silence. They telepathically linked their minds while in mediation, and both had seen the same thing. They knew they needed to get to the edge of the tube of light together.

They jumped rocks and weaved through the great cedar trees, moving towards the light at the center of the Quadrivium. Praeta and Arbor were found standing near the light in deep contemplation, the first riders to make it there, but they too were not able to enter the ether tube as it was coded and not activated.

As The Kumara and The Sage came upon them, the riders all bowed to one another in recognition of each of their efforts to get to this area of the grid. The Kumara began to tell them what she felt needed to happen, based on her vision. She shared that they would have to wait for the last two riders before the light code could be activated.

She began to tell Praeta and Arbor about finding the peace skull, Aluca, just as the last two riders made their way towards the light tube. Jinnby and Alderson were breathing heavy, but exhilarated, having found their way to the area via an underground tunnel that came out just below where the light tube anchored.

Now with six riders present, The Kumara set the blue crystal skull at the edge of the light and had each rider hold hands and sing a song of gratitude and peace. The song of peace vibrated the energy shield holding the light tube, and as they sang from their heart, a rose color beamed from each of their chests, connecting to the tube of light. Aluca, the blue skull, activated and unlocked the light tube. The six riders were pulled into a vortex.

Breacher and Benoit were sitting by a fire back at the edge of camp where seven dragons were now all gathered. They were monitoring the skills test and were waiting for the riders to exit the tube of light.

Suddenly, one by one, the riders walked out of a mist near where Breacher sat, the fire between them. The six riders stood looking to see if they were the first one through the tube of light.

Breacher said, "You are the only ones to make it through all of the zones, and you worked together in teams to make it through the grid. I am impressed with every one of you."

Breacher got up and moved from the fire. Behind the fire, lay the dragons from the Quadrivium.

The riders were happy to see the dragons again, outside the grid, but there were confused expressions on their faces at the same time. Breacher began a discourse on the mission at hand, offering them a place to sit by the fire.

He began by telling them that he had put them through the test to see if there might be a handful of strong riders that could train with him for one of the greatest missions on Earth in the history of the planet.

The riders sat in the circle around the fire as Commander Breacher and Commander Benoit told the story of the need for great Dragon Riders. The kind of rider whose hearts and minds are pure and loyal and whose skills were highly evolved.

These Dragon Riders would be holding the planet in a safety net while others were creating a new world within a world. Their job was to work together to keep Mother Earth safe during her most spectacular planetary transition into the higher octaves as they create the new Ley line structures to hold the unique vibration of the New Earth.

"Commander, it will be a privilege to ride with you." The Sage stood up and held his hand in a fist over his heart. He knew this was his destiny and was elated at the surprise of being chosen. It made everything that he had ever been through, all the trail's and tribulations, worth it. He always knew that he had an extraordinary mission, and here was the invitation to his life's destiny.

Praeta followed suit and placed her hands over her heart and bowed to Breacher. A tear was streaming down her right cheek as she looked once more at the red dragon with deep affection and accepted her commission as a Dragon Rider.

Next, The Kumara held the blue crystal skull up into the air signaling her willingness to accept the coveted honor. She bowed to each of the riders, the Commanders, and lastly the dragons, and then placed the crystal skull in the hands of Commander Benoit. They nodded to one another in appreciation.

Arbor stood and announced his gratitude for being among this group, though he expressed confusion as to why he would be considered as it was not he that had actually connected with the red dragon.

Breacher pointed out that he knew that the red dragon did not mean any harm and was prepared to play it music to appease it. Also, Breacher continued, "You are a skilled empath. This is one of the main attributes of a Dragon Rider."

Arbor glanced towards Praeta, who was showing signs of nervous energy, a bit red-faced. He intuited that she had realized that he could feel her emotions. He gave a slight chuckle as her eyes met his, and she glared at him with embarrassment.

Breacher then looked to Alderson for a sign of allegiance. Alderson stood with his feet in a wide stance while holding his wand in his hands behind his back. He then stepped forward and asked if he could show the group his wand.

There were family runes etched into the side of the wand. He then showed what was on the edge of the wand, near the bottom. It was an engraving of a dragon biting its tail. He held it up for all to see and explained that the runes were very significant, but he was never certain of why the carved dragon was placed upon the wand until now.

"I now feel that it is my destiny to serve with each of you as a Dragon Rider." He placed his hand over his heart and did a bow like a court jester, waving his wand in the air as he bowed. Everyone laughed at his theatrical expression.

Only one remained not committed to moving forward. Breacher turned back to the fire, standing opposite to Jinnby now. With a glance her way, he encouraged her to speak from her heart.

Jinnby cleared her throat and spoke, "I have a torn heart in this triumphant moment." Her head looked to her heart as she had tears rolling from her eyes. Breacher looked at her with such compassion as he quizzed her on her spirit's pain.

Jinnby shared, "While within the Quadrivium, I experienced a prophetic vision about my home planet. I saw it explode."

Her tears could not be held back as she fell to the ground, completely overwhelmed with the potential of losing her home and family. "I have to go back. I know this! I am equally aware that it would have been my greatest honor to ride with you all."

Alderson stood by her side and helped Jinnby to her feet. Breacher understood how she felt about her home world and said, "I will relay this information to the other Commanders and see what can be done. I release you now but hope that we will see you again in the future. You are a wise and loving soul, and I wish you all the best." He stepped forward and bowed to her, with his hand on his chest. The other riders offered her hope as they said their goodbyes.

Jinnby left the circle, leaving the others in a solemn state, not wanting to celebrate their achievement just yet.

And the wheel turns...

Chapter 49

The Stone Circle Trail
of Aberdeenshire

Standing in the center of the Loanhead of Daviot Stone Circle, Stella and Bridgit inspected the many rocks that lay upon the Grampian countryside. David and Christopher gave them ample time to feel and absorb the energy from the circle that had stood erect in that very spot for over 4000 years.

The girls both took turns laying upon the recumbent stone that lay horizontal between two tall vertical flanker stones. As they took turns, David began to speak about the potential uses of this circle back in the day, something that he had lectured on at a Geomancy conference in the past.

"It is suspected that this site and many more similar sites like it were built in very specific places to track the cycle of the moon." He stood right next to where Bridgit lay upon the recumbent stone and pointed to the sky as he mesmerized them with his knowledge of ancient history.

"It is presumed that one might have laid here, just where you are

Bridgit, during a ceremony which when the timing was just right, the moon would in effect be shining on this very spot." He pointed towards her belly, enthusiastically.

David began to put his hand upon the flanker stone that exhibited signs of cup markings. As he stood staring at the markings, he continued, "There is also a theory that it could be places like these that one could activate a portal into other realms." He smiled widely and pointed to the hallow marks, cupped shapes, and lines that seemed to portend a message to the observant traveler.

Clearing his throat to get their attention, Christopher walked over to a nearby bench and called them over to take a look at the view from his vantage point.

Bridgit and Stella were taken over by the frequency that the stones emitted and wanted to know more about the cup marks as they took their places on the ground near Christopher's feet, facing the horizon.

Christopher pointed his walking stick upwards and said, "When the moon falls below the horizon, in certain seasons, the lunar energy hits the slab and anyone who might be laid upon it. The ancients believed that this was an entrance into the heavenly realms and therefore made a pilgrimage to these places to be certain to have their loved one meet their maker swiftly." He smiled as the girls took it all in.

Stella quizzed, "Does one need to be already deceased to have access to the heavenly realms through these portals?" she turned to look at his reaction to the question.

"Stella, to give you a simple answer, one could make passage through it but, and there is a but here; one would have to be prepared to walk through the valley of death to move through to the higher realms quickly. It takes much spiritual practice, something that I plan to teach you both." He winked at her as if to portend that they would, in fact, be walking through portals, perhaps in places just like these.

David pointed out another thing of interest. "You will note that beside the stone circle is a lesser circle, and what we know is that, there, underneath all of it, is the cremains of many individuals. There was actually a half-cremated body of a man who held a pendant in his hand." David put his hands in his trousers and turned to look at the ladies as they stared up into his squinting eyes, the sun coming down upon them all.

The trees began to quake with the slightest breeze. The sound of an airplane overhead brought their attention away from the stone man. Christopher mentioned that it would be quite an interesting thing to note that the amount of the deceased buried within the circle numbered just over 30. He began to speculate that there could be a relation energetically between the number of people and the portal.

He quizzed, "Could they be a resonating force that would open a doorway." His bright blue eyes twinkled in the sunlight, and his smile completed the picture of a man enthralled with the world around him.

Bridgit responded to his query. "Are you thinking that these people were all buried here at the same time? Perhaps trying to leave this realm together?"

Christopher noted, "I am speculating that to access the doorways, one needs to be aware of the protocols that would serve as energetic keys to unlock a door."

He pulled his pipe out of his jacket and searched for his bag of tobacco in the other pocket. Stella stood up and looked over the entire area with her third eye. She felt a sudden urge to walk the perimeter of the burial area. Bridgit sat in silent contemplation as David pulled a lighter from his trouser pocket to assist Christopher with lighting his pipe. The scent of cherry and vanilla wafted near Bridgit's nose, bringing her back to the present.

After waiting for Christopher to enjoy his pipe, Bridgit asked, "Christopher, you seem to have an agenda for bringing us here. Would you mind enlightening me on what it is that we are supposed to do or be aware of?" Smiling, Bridgit tried her best to phrase her question politely but felt like he was playing with them far too long and not being forthcoming.

"Miss Bridgit, you are astute." He smiled and took the final few draws from his pipe and knocked the remains on the ground to snuff out the tobacco with the bottom of his shoe.

Tinkering with the pipe, he went on, "This place holds a high magnetic frequency which the stones are in large part responsible. It is one of many hundreds of stone circles all over the world connected to a very ancient, shall we say, mainframe." He looked up as Stella had rejoined them.

"Mainframe? This ancient thing?" Stella blurted and pointed out the ancient relic as if Christopher suggested that it was equivalent to the latest tablet.

He continued, "We are aware that humanity has had numerous periods upon this planet, and these stone circles are from one of those periods, the Bronze age. Even before that age, long ago, there were ancient sites that acted as power plants, if you will, and these power plants were created from rock and, more specifically, minerals such as quartz."

He continued, "Think back to the time of Atlantis, and the control systems that were put into place upon the people of this earth. This is the remnants of a time when off-world beings easily accessed this planet."

Christopher finished kicking the ashes underfoot as David interjected, "We know that the stones have a high vibrational frequency and they actually carry a tune, or a note when struck." He walked over to the large stones and tapped one of the flanker stones with a rock he picked up. He said that though one may not hear the vibration, that it had set off a sound the moment the rock hit the stone.

"Better put, it gave a KEY frequency."

He turned back to the group and said, "It is speculated that these stone circles all over the world might just be connected to a hologram

312

program that has been running to keep humanity in a constant state of frenzy. In other words, the cairns and stones circles could actually be part of an elaborate motherboard of a vast ancient computer that codes our behavior. Change the coding, change the behavior."

"What the heck?" Stella blurted out in anger. "What are you saying? That some ancient race of overlords is programming us?"

"Well, this is speculation coming from various sources. It is people like us that are willing to take off the blindfold and see who is really running the show down here."

David politely countered Stella's outburst to remind her of her origin. "Surely, you couldn't have already forgotten the dark force that has been chasing you, have you, Stella?"

Stella looked at him with dismay, realizing that in truth, the being that had been chasing Bridgit, and now all of them, is, in fact, an off-world Dark Lord. David could see her putting it all together in her mind.

Bridgit then quizzed David. "So, if all the stone circles around the planet, and perhaps the many pyramids too, are connected to some sort of frequency machine, is there another purpose, other than control, as David put it?" Bridgit asked.

"A frequency fence." Christopher blurted out as a matter of fact.

He stood up and spread his feet apart to anchor himself to the ground and said, "There is a frequency barrier around our planet that has us all captive. We will be talking about this more as we gather the other Life Bearers. For now, I wanted you to get a feel for what has been here and for how long it has been going on. This is part of the silent war that has been happening since the beginning of man. I am not saying that it was always this way, but at some point in our history, the darkness advanced and took over what was once a healthy leyline system and is now used against us."

Stella tumbled the words that Christopher and David spoke in her mind trying to see it from all angles. "A frequency war! I see! It is to keep us in a lower vibration so that we won't wake up to who we really are! Enslaving us with chaos, Pop Culture, and heavy work-loads, so that we are too tired or depressed to notice anything else! I assume this frequency fence has a lot to do with the state of people's minds, their mental health? Can it cause depression or anger?" She looked at Christopher for the final word, feeling agitated at that moment.

Christopher shook his head in an affirmative response and motioned for everyone to prepare to leave and gave his hand for Bridgit to stand. "Knowing your own mind is the most important thing you can be aware of right now." He motioned them forward as he used his walking stick for stability.

"Bad weather is coming. Let's get to the car." Christopher pointed towards the formation in the clouds that suddenly appeared.

They walked to the car, knowing that they would have much more to talk about on the way back to the Inn.

And the wheel turns...

Chapter 50

The Last Dragon Rider

With Jinnby taking her leave, Breacher now had to focus on who would replace her. He walked to the dragon's den to bring them their morning meal and prepare them for the introductions to the riders when he found the den empty.

He was alarmed by this as they had never done this before. Placing the food down on the ground, he stood with his eyes closed to scan the area for their imprint. He felt them by the water nearby, so he bilocated over to where he felt them, and there they were, in the presence of a stranger.

He watched for a few moments as this young woman feed them fish from the lake and stroked their necks as she fed them. He could not believe what he was seeing. The dragons were mesmerized by her as if she had a magical hold upon them. This made him uneasy. He felt like the dragons were being tricked into submission. He walked towards the dragons, ready for anything.

His footsteps gave him away as the young woman twirled around in a protective stance. She, too, was ready to defend these creatures by any means necessary.

"Stay back!" She demanded.

"Who are you!? And what are you doing with my dragons?!" Breacher asked as he continued to walk towards the dragons and, in particular, Leto.

The young woman stepped backward as she realized now who stood before her. "Commander Breacher!"

"Yes. That's right. And who might you be?" Breacher asked.

"Oh... I am so sorry! I didn't know." She backed away from the dragons to give Breacher the space closest to the dragons.

"I am Kali, sir."

"Kali? Are you stationed here at the base? A Pegasus rider?"

"Yes, sir. I couldn't sleep. I was having a vivid dream about dragons, and well, as I woke up, I felt like real dragons were communicating with me somehow. It was such a strong dream that I decided to come here, where I was taken in my dream, to see if it was real."

She was desperate to convince him of the truth. "Usually, when I have these kinds of dreams, it actually happens." She shrugged her shoulders, a bit embarrassed, but also happy to know that she was right.

"I arrived just before daylight, but there was nothing here. I sat over there, crying because I truly thought that I would be chosen in the Quadrivium, and when that didn't happen, I have felt so lost." She looked up to see Commander Breacher's expression, and he motioned for her to continue.

She said, "I am an excellent Pegasus rider, but my dream showed me riding a dragon! The connection that I had with the dragon in my dream was so strong my heart connected to it immediately."

She continued as she stood next to Breacher, "When I realized that the dragons weren't here, I just lost it." She wiped her eyes with the palm of her hand as if there were still sleep in her eyes. She cleared the ever-present drops of water floating upon her lid, waiting to drop.

Kali continued, "As I was about to leave, I heard a flapping noise and looked up over the lake. I couldn't believe my eyes! All seven dragons were in flight, coming straight over the lake and landed just there in the clearing." She pointed to the small field near the lake and then looked back at Breacher.

"I didn't call them here. Really, I didn't! I think they called me here... actually." Kali looked down timidly when she said the word "actually" and used her shoe to brush away some twigs in the sand to keep from looking at Breacher.

Breacher looked at the dragons and sent an image to Leto. Leto returned a picture that showed Breacher that she was telling the truth.

"So, let me get this straight. You had a lucid dream of meeting the dragons here this very day?" He quizzed her.

"Yes, sir, Commander. I felt them in my heart, not just in the dream, and even now, I feel them."

"And when you say feel them, explain what you mean by that, please." He stood with his hands in his pockets and feet out like a soldier. His appearance made Kali nervous.

"I am an empath. I see and hear things outside of the normal range. I lucid dream quite frequently as it is a way for me to move about the realms. When I dreamt of the dragons this morning, I was almost certain that they were calling me to this spot. I did not call them, sir. I promise."

"I see. Well, let me ease your mind, Kali. I am very familiar with the ways in which you move about in the other realms, as this is one of the gifts that I look for in a rider. Let me ask you this. Why did you not finish the Quadrivium? You seem to have the skills required."

Kali had a look of embarrassment and said sheepishly, "I had had a dream the night before and saw the trials and could see who made it into the center. I was not one of them. I helped one of the six early on in the trial, a female feline who I had seen in my dream." Kali leaned against a tree and turning away from Breacher for a moment, trying to figure out how to explain to him what it is that she did.

"I have known her before, in another time and place, and I owed her my life in that time. I chose to repay her in this timeline, even though I wanted with all my heart to be a chosen rider." She wiped a tear from her face and turned to the indigo dragon near her and hugged its neck. The dragon licked her face gently as if they had a deep friendship.

She continued to explain her actions, "When you meet up with someone that you owe your life too, it is the law that you make recompense at that time because we never know when or if we will meet again."

She turned to Breacher with such sadness in her words, for she knew it cost her the chance to be a rider.

Breacher felt her energy and knew what her heart spoke. "Kali, I would like you to go back to the barracks and meet me in the conference room in two hours. That will be all."

Breacher dismissed her and gathered the dragons, flying back to the dragon's den as Kali watched from the shore, not knowing if she would be let go from her post for being outside the barracks.

Once back at the barracks, she prepared for her release, placing her possessions in one spot on the edge of her bed, fearing that she had gone against a rule that would see her kicked out of the rider program.

Breacher called all of the Dragon Riders to the conference room for an overview of the mission. Arbor, Praeta, Alderson, The Sage, and The Kumara arrived at the appointed hour and took their seats in the room, talking amongst themselves as Breacher made his way to the desk at the front of the room.

318

"Riders! How are we this fine morning?" He leaned on the desk with his arms folded at his chest.

"Fine, sir!" Arbor yelled out. The others murmured similar sounds but not as confident.

"It seems as if we are all not quite sure how we feel this morning." He had a twinkle in his eye as he stared at each of these riders.

Praeta spoke, "We are just not sure what will happen now that Jinnby could not stay. Will we still be able to complete the mission that you have outlined for us if we are missing a rider?" They all looked at Breacher with anxiousness.

There was a knocking sound at the door. Everyone turned to see Kali standing there in the doorway.

"Come in. Come in." Breacher smiled and waved his hand to allow Kali to enter the room. Everyone, including Kali, had a confused look on their faces.

"Kali, let me introduce you to our team members, the Dragon Riders." Breacher pointed out Arbor first, having him stand so that Kali could have a proper introduction.

"Kali, it is nice to meet you. My name is Arbor. I think I have seen you around?" He smiled, and his kindness gave Kali a warm feeling causing her to feel a bit more at ease.

Then Alderson stood and made his introductions, followed by Praeta, The Sage, and The Kumara.

"Riders, meet Kali, the last Dragon Rider to join the ranks." Breacher smiled towards Kali and took note of her reaction as well as the other riders.

"What? Really?! But, I thought that you were sending me home!" a tear of joy in her eye showed her emotion as she tried to wipe it with her sleeve quickly.

"Kali, you clearly have the gifts required to be a Dragon Rider, and you have something else. You are a visionary with a heart! Plus, the dragons picked you, so who am I to say no?" He grinned and laughed at her surprised expression.

"Ok, riders, fall in." They all stood at attention in the proper stance, waiting for the Commander's orders.

"We will be taking a journey later, one that will open your mind and heart to this particular mission. I will outline the tasks of each of you once we have completed the initiation at Tollan. Are you ready to hear more?"

All the riders had smiles on their faces as they yelled out, "Yes, Sir!"

And the wheel turns...

Chapter 51

The Blue People and the Ringing Stones

In the early hours where dreams bridge with the wakeful state, Stella was dreaming vividly. She had slipped into an alternate world where blue beings were present in the surroundings. She found herself in their village, somewhere in the inner earth realms.

A woman with blue skin and long thick orange hair stood with her as she was being prepared for a celebration. In the dream, Stella walked with the entire clan of blue people towards a hill just outside of their village.

Most of the village people had blue skin and black hair, with a few of them redheaded like her female companion. The companion pointed towards the rock formations for Stella to observe. Stella could see a cave in the distance. Then suddenly she was standing at the formation alone, save for the redheaded companion, who called Stella by her fourth dimension name, Tulina.

"You must jump soon. Etifah!!! Etifah!!" She pointed to the cave, and in the dream, as Stella turned to look at the cave, it was now no longer there. She was now looking at a globe. It marked places where the entry points were on the planet for Stella and her team to enter the void. The word Etifah rang loudly as her companion chanted the name.

Stella looked up at the woman and said, "Yes, I understand. We will make it to these points. Will you help us jump?"

The female companion said, "The Guardians are awaiting your arrival. Look once more at the cave. Etifah!" She pointed to the puck mark that would indicate what to watch for. On the rock, outside of the cave, was markings of concentric triangles. Stella looked up at her companion, understanding that they were to look for that symbol when accessing the portals to jump into the void. Then this part of the dream began to fade.

She now found herself alone, looking at the landscape. She noticed the crimson sky blazing through greyish colored clouds suspended over a violet hillside. The scenery was beautiful beyond description. The beauty of this magnificent creation humbled her.

Buzz.... Stella's alarm began to vibrate her phone. It startled her awake from her dream. She grabbed a piece of paper and drew the concentric triangle puck marks and anything else that she could remember from her dream. The vividness of the dream had her hair standing on end. She felt both excited and wary at the same time.

She dressed quickly and walked down the hall to the bathroom that the ladies shared at the Inn. At that moment, Bridgit came out of the bathroom and bumped into a stranger in the hall, a tall female, wearing a towel wrapped around her head.

She backed away from Bridgit, startled by her appearance. Bridgit apologized, but the quiet woman simply bowed and did not speak a word. The woman moved quickly down the hall, passing Stella, who was walking towards her. The stranger bowed slightly to Stella as well, then made her way to a room on the right side of the hallway.

Stella looked at Bridgit with curiosity and mouthed, "Who was that?"

Bridgit mouthed back, "I don't know."

She shrugged her shoulders with a cautious look on her face as she pulled Stella closer to her in a protective, motherly way. Something about the appearance of this stranger made the hair on her body stand straight up, given that they had already been warned to be vigilant. Bridgit psychically put her shields up immediately.

Still standing in the hallway, Stella changed the subject and asked, "Did you have any weird dreams last night or this morning?" Stella bit her lip to pause while Bridgit answered her question.

"Not that I can recall at the moment? How about you?" She knew that Stella had had one of those dreams. She nudged Stella to move into her room so they could talk.

"Let me go to the lavy. It will only take a sec." Stella finally was able to incorporate a new word into her vocabulary. Of course, she thought it hilarious that it would be something related to the bathroom. Laughingly, she smiled to ease Bridgit's worried mind, then raced to the restroom.

Bridgit went back to her room, noticing that the stranger was peeking at her from her doorway. The stranger quickly shut her door as Bridgit stood there, waiting for Stella.

Moments later, Stella walked back to Bridgit's room, wiping her hands on her pants so as not to waste time with a hand towel. Bridgit held her door open like a sentinel, then pulled Stella into her room quickly.

"Hey, watch it! Why are you acting so weird?" Stella turned to look at Bridgit curiously as she scooted further into the room to get a bit of distance from her crazy relative.

"Something feels weird about that woman. I didn't want you out there alone with her." Bridgit went to her bed and straightened out the blankets so that they could sit next to each other as Stella recalled her dream. Bridgit patted the bed, letting Stella know that she should sit. Stella sat at the far end of the bed silently at first, trying to recall the pertinent information from her dream.

Stella began to share with Bridgit how she was in another world, in the dream, where there were blue people, a whole village of them, and how a redheaded, blue-skinned woman showed her what hallow marks to look for at the jump points.

She continued, "There was a word too! Something like E…ti…fah! Etifah! That's it!"

She said it a few more times then pulled the drawing out of her pocket, "I drew this picture of the markings that I was shown, and it feels like we are supposed to find triangles in the stone or within nature with this special marking when we jump into the void. Does that sound right to you?"

Bridgit examined the picture and handed it back to Stella. "I don't know Stella, but what I do know is that your dreams tend to be foretelling, so let's keep this in mind as we get closer to that time. It is all fascinating, but for now, we need to get our bags downstairs. David will be here any minute, and we don't want to keep him waiting. He needs to arrive at the conference a little early before all the commotion starts."

Stella laughingly agreed. She opened the door to the hallway and stuck her head out to see if there were any strange boogeymen out there, all for Bridgit's benefit. When Stella waited to leave the room, Bridgit asked, "Is it clear?"

Laughing, Stella said, "Yes, Mother! All clear!"

Stella walked to her room, leaving Bridgit's door open as she went to gather her things. Bridgit turned around to grab her jacket and small travel bag, and as she swirled around to grab her purse, she was startled by the stranger standing in the doorway. This time her thick red hair was in a long ponytail hanging over her shoulder to the side. Her face was uniquely unusual, with dark freckles on the bridge of her nose and several on her cheeks. She carried a satchel that crossed over her body.

"Excuse me, Miss. I am sorry to bother you. I am here on important business. Please allow me to execute my orders swiftly."

She reached to open the satchel hanging from her shoulder, and Bridgit yelled, "Stop right there! Who are you?"

Bridgit grabbed her walking stick to quickly arm herself as the stranger put her hands up in the air. "You misunderstand, Miss. I am not here to harm you. I am here to deliver something to you. It is here, in my bag." The stranger pointed to a pouch that was hanging halfway out of her satchel.

Bridgit observed her as she pulled it out slowly. A black velvet bag that was weighted down by whatever was in it.

"Please, allow me." The stranger motioned for her to move towards the dresser as she unveiled what was in the bag.

"I have been given orders to bring this bag here to you. I have been waiting for you for a few days now. I am glad that you returned when you did."

Bridgit detected her accent, and from her presentation, she knew that the woman was not from Scotland. She was about to ask her name when she spoke again.

"I cannot divulge my name Miss, only that I am here on official business and must get back soon. Please, for you." She showed her what was in the bag. Thirteen individual flat gray stone pendants that had the exact markings on it that Stella had shown her just moments ago from her dream.

Bridgit's eyebrows furrowed as she examined the pendants. They each were identical, having the concentric triangles carved into the flat stones which hung from gray colored jute cords. Each pendant was meticulously wrapped around a teardrop-shaped larger stone.

Bridgit looked at the stranger as she counseled, "At the given hour, each of the recipients of these stone pendants will unwrap it from the striking stone. They will need to place the pendant around their neck as they prepare to jump. At this point, they will strike the stone pendant with the attached instrument, the tear-shaped stone, while silently holding in their mind the word Etifah."

The stranger looked at Bridgit to make sure she understood and then repeated the word. Bridgit's mouth was wide open, but she could not find words to say anything. Bridgit was in utter disbelief of what was happening.

The woman repeated the word slowly, "E..ti...fah..." She stared into Bridgit's glazed over eyes, and when she saw that her conscious mind had returned to the present moment, she further explained, "This will create a resonance and pull you into the portal to the correct location."

The stranger looked at her and demonstrated to her exactly how to activate the stone pendants.

Bridgit's eyes were huge and asked, "But how?"

Bridgit was trying to wrap her mind around this interaction, the instructions, and the word Etifah, which was moments ago uttered out of Stella's mouth. Bridgit was dumbfounded and barely had the sense to ask the woman who she was and who sent her.

The stranger looked at her and said, "The time will come upon you quickly. Be ready. You have many watching over you."

She bowed to Bridgit and began to make her way back out of the room when Bridgit yelled out, "Wait! Are you a Guardian?"

"Indeed, Miss Bridgit, I am. I am sorry to have scared you. I do not have much experience interacting with..., shall I say, humans?" The woman smiled and bowed her head.

Her words took Bridgit deeply into thought as the woman left her room swiftly. She stared at the stone pendants for a few moments and then looked back at the door.

This time Stella was standing in the doorway with her overnight bag hanging from her shoulder, "Whatcha looking at? What is that!?"

Stella looked at all of the individual stone pendants, with the gray cords wrapped around teardrop-shaped stones. Her eyes were as huge as Bridgit's, as the two of them stood looking at the puck marked pendants with the concentric triangular image that Stella had spoken about just moments earlier.

Bridgit laid out the pendants on the dresser so that they could examine all of the stones.

"Where did you get these!?" Stella picked up several of the pendants in shock as to how Bridgit had stone pendants with the markings that she had only just described to her minutes earlier.

"The stranger in the hallway gave them to me." Bridgit, still in a state of shock, pointed towards the hall.

"The lady with the towel on her head?" Stella asked with confusion.

"Yes! Didn't you see her just now when you came to my room? She had just left when you showed up. You had to have passed her in the hallway." Stella stood next to Bridgit and just shook her head no, while she just stared at the stones.

Bridgit moved around Stella, towards the door, to look down the hall. The door to her room was open. Bridgit walked down the hall to her room, finding no sign of her. Not only that, there was no evidence that she had slept in the room or used it at all.

Stella placed the pendants down and trailed behind Bridgit after a few moments. She found Bridgit just staring at an empty room. Then the two ladies went back to Bridgit's room. Bridgit went back to the stone pendants on the dresser.

"Stella, the stranger came to my room right after you went to get your things. She told me that she had been waiting for us to return and that she had something urgent to give me. She handed me this bag of pendants and said that when we go to our appointed jump points, we are to wear these around our necks. She showed me how to activate the pendants by using the stone that the pendants are wrapped around as a sort of musical instrument. To make a tone or vibration."

Standing next to Stella, Bridgit took one of the pendants in her hand to demonstrate the activation. "You tap the stone pendant with the teardrop-shaped stone, striking a chord."

Stella asked, "May I?", as she picked one up, gesturing to try it out.

Bridgit nodded and said, "Go ahead."

Stella unwrapped a stone pendant and put it around her neck. The gray pendant was a little more than an inch in diameter and smooth to the touch on one side. The other side was marked with an engraving of three concentric triangles. She then examined the teardrop stone that came with the pendant. It was the same type of gray stone as the pendant, without markings.

Stella took the pointed side of the larger stone and hit it gently on the pendant. A clanky sound happened, but nothing extraordinary. She then flipped the teardrop-shaped stone and hit the wider, rounded part of the stone onto the pendant, and a unique sound reverberated in the room. Stella could feel the energy in her field, as she lay the pendant on her chest to hang.

Bridgit could feel it too.

Bridgit continued, "Stella, the stranger was not ah... how do I say this? Ah... well, here goes... She was not human."

Bridgit looked for Stella's reaction and was pleasantly surprised.

Stella said, "I know."

She looked up at Bridgit and asked, "When I went to my room, I grabbed my bags, and I was studying the picture that I had drawn and was thinking about the blue people, and when I recalled the female being, who was showing me the markings. I, for some reason, flashed to the lady in the hallway. I just put it out of my mind and gathered my things. What color hair did she have? Was it her?"

She looked at Bridgit and continued, "Did she have long red hair? Really thick?" She raised her hands to her head to gesture thick heavy hair.

Bridgit said, "Yes, she did! She could not tell me her name, but she did indicate one thing."

"What was that?" Stella quietly asked.

"You have to sit down for this. I am still reeling from it."

She waited for Stella to sit and then looked directly into her eyes and said, "Remember, moments ago, when you were sharing your dream, and you mentioned the word Etifah?"

Stella stared at her with her nose wrinkled and eyebrows furrowed and said, "Yesssss..."

Bridgit said, "The woman told me an essential part of activating the portal at the jump point is that when we strike the stone, we must silently...in our minds, say the word ETIFAH!!!"

Stella flew her head back on the bed with her hands over her face. She was half laughing and half crying and then popped back upward with her arm sticking straight out with all of her arm hair standing upward. "I cannot believe what I am hearing!! Are you freaking serious with me right now!?"

Bridgit laughed and nodded in udder disbelief as well, but just stated the facts. "She said that it was very important that we hold that word in our minds and only say it inwardly as it will create a connection, so to speak, to where we are going. I guess it is kind of like making a phone call, and the word Etifah is the phone number or a coordinate?"

Bridgit hunched her shoulders and smiled. "Oh yeah... She said one more thing."

Stella wasn't sure that she could take any more surprises.

Bridgit stated, "She said that they were keeping watch over us." Bridgit looked deeply into Stella's eyes and said, "I realized then that she is a Guardian, and I asked her if she was."

Stella's eyes were huge with excitement and asked, "Well! Is she?"

Bridgit smiled at Stella and nodded, yes.

They stared at one another for some time, then reexamined the pendants. Bridgit looked at her watch and realized that David was probably waiting for them downstairs. "We need to go!"

Stella grabbed all the pendants and put them back into the bag while Bridgit grabbed her things. Stella then handed the bag to Bridgit.

Stella asked, "Why did she come to you? I mean, I had an incredible dream about the concentric triangular puck marks and the jump points, and then this woman shows up out of the blue and goes to you?" She formed the sentence into a question as she looked at Bridgit.

"I guess we are both being given key pieces to this gigantic puzzle, one that we can't possibly solve at this point. Clearly, you are the one they communicate with, in the dream time, and now I know to pay even more attention to your dreams." Bridgit motioned to the clock and indicated David was waiting, as they moved quickly down the hall and trotted down the stairs.

Bridgit, still holding the velvet bag of pendants, tucked the bag into her purse, making sure that she knew exactly where they would be. She felt very protective over the pendants as if they were the royal jewels.

David's little chariot, Pearl, was parked outside in the driveway of the

Inn. David sat in the car, reading his texts on his cell phone, waiting patiently for the Ladies' Phare. Stella tapped on the backend of the vehicle so that he could pop open the carriage, and the girls began to pile their bags into the small space.

"Ladies." David jumped out and did a gentleman's bow and then lifted the heavier bags and rearranged what Stella had thrown in haphazardly. He motioned for them to get their seats, as he said, "I've got this."

Stella and Bridgit smiled as Bridgit said, "We have something interesting to share with you."

"Smashing! It will be a long drive, so give me the download! I just ask that we all say a prayer of protection before we get on the road."

The three jumped in the car and buckled up their belts. David led the invocation of the protective prayer, and they left the Inn for yet another adventure.

And the wheel turns...

Chapter 52

The Blueprint Masters and the Builders of Form Meet

The radiation of love and purity filled the room where Archangel Gabriel held the first meeting with the Blueprint Masters and the Builders of Form. The room had living plants growing from the walls, and the light in the room felt as if the meeting place was outdoors. The temperature of the room was warm with a gentle breeze, and butterflies were flitting about from vine to vine.

Archangel Gabriel called the meeting to order after each of the groups had had an ample amount of time to prepare for the moment at hand, the reunification of the three lifestreams that were to be part of God's great plan for the restoration of his Heavenly Kingdom on Earth.

All felt Gabriel's emanations of peace as each member took their seats for the meeting.

"Builders, please come up and introduce yourselves individually and explain to the group what ray you are working within." Gabriel glided swiftly to a seat nearby as he gave a hand gesture for the team of Builders to come forward.

Avery arranged it so that they would take turns in numerical order, by rays. First ray, Second ray, and so on, which meant that he would be first to present himself to the Angelic team.

Avery walked to the front near where Archangel Gabriel sat and commanded the attention of the Blueprint Masters by saying, "I am happy to start with the introductions of the Builder of Form team and say a few words about each of them. It is an honor and a privilege to have this opportunity, for not only ourselves to come together on a project, but, with the added joy of working with humans once more."

Avery gestured towards the Blueprint Masters and continued, "I would ask that we take a moment to align our energies so that we have a harmonious and blessed beginning."

The Blueprint masters radiated love and twinkling sounds, which rang in the room as they each sent their adorations to one another. The elementals indicated that they had caught the frequency and that Avery could begin.

"Let me start with my introductions. I am Avery, the elemental representative of the first ray Builder of Form. The first ray qualities are those of Will and Power. I am an excellent choice, as I am self-assured and purposeful in all that I do." He stood as tall as possible, proud as the Angelic's chuckled to hear his honest assessment of his character.

He smiled with a twinkle in his eye and continued, "As we come together to co-create another of God's great creations, I will be steadfast in my willingness to hold the highest thoughts of purity in all that we do. I will be joining the team working with animals."

After his introduction, Avery could hear various sounds of celestial music coming through the vibrations of the angelic Blueprint Masters. It pleased him deeply.

He continued, "The second ray Builder of Form is Arrea." Arrea floated up to where Avery stood and lit upon his shoulder. Avery gently held his hand out for her as she landed upon it as her platform.

He began to speak of her. "Arrea is a sylph."

Arrea's wings shimmered with the exquisite colors of a beautiful russet sunset, with many oranges and reds. Her bodice was fashioned from the tiniest of leaves, with a flower crown on top of her head. Upon her little neck lay a beautiful pink quartz heart pendant that radiated her energy of pure love to the crowd.

She twirled for her audience as Avery continued. "As a representative of the second ray, she is faithful to her mission and holds deep wisdom of the Earth. She has compassion and love for all things and will be a great addition to the Music of the Spheres team as that team delves into the Air element and the sounds of creation."

Everyone clapped and made other forms of praise as Arrea floated back to where her team sat. Then the third Builder of Form was introduced.

Tabor, the Faun, walked upright to where Avery stood. He wore a yellow vest with a golden chain hanging from the pocket, which held a small key. He played his flute for a few moments to entertain the group. His eyes had a twinkle like Avery's, something that gave away the elemental's mischievous nature. Tabor tucked his flute into his vest as Avery began his introductions.

"This is Tabor, the third ray Builder of Form. Tabor is practical and is a planner. He sees ahead, into the future, and combines his intuition and his intelligence in all he does. He further demonstrates his ability for adaptation, which is a crucial component in the plant kingdom. He will be working with the team who will seed the new plant creations of the New Earth. The flora gives nutrients to others, and Tabor's active mind will inevitably give rise to new expressions of God's creations, with plant life that will assist in nurturing the New Human's growth."

The Angelic's were filled with joy to hear the news as Tabor walked back to the group, and the fourth Builder came up to the front. Something of interest caught everyone's eyes as they saw a beautiful Mermaid walking forward. She had manifested a pair of legs for the occasion; Shapeshifting was something most elementals could do.

"Ah... this... here... is ah...", even Avery was taken by her beauty, as he cleared his throat to start again.

"This is Mersea, the fourth Builder of Form." Chiming and applause came from the audience as the Angelics were happy to see such a beautiful creation, as the Mermaid bowed with grace, placing her hand to her heart.

Mersea's long auburn hair and green eyes were a vision to behold. She wore a short green skirt made of seaweed. Her top was made of a sparkly gold fiber that wrapped her upper body but left her bare belly visible. Her top had a trident emblem on the left side, just over her heart. Mersea was adorned with jewels from the sea from head to toe as she stood in front of the Angelics.

Avery continued, "Mersea's role as a fourth ray Builder is using her gift of creativity. She is an expert at harmonizing with others, especially when there is conflict. She is expressive in all that she does as she works with vibration to bring forth new creations. Mersea will be working with the water element team. Rest assured, all creations from this team will have an element of beauty and order, as is mathematical and per the laws of nature."

Mersea bowed, then took her leave and rejoined the others.

Gordavin, the Gnome, had jumped up and was next to Avery before Mersea had been dismissed. He stood with his legs apart, pulling up his short trousers, and adjusted his belt around the blue tunic that he wore. His unique emblem, a DNA pattern, was stitched onto the left side of his tunic, and upon his right shoulder sat his feathered friend, a blackbird named Weber. Weber was always picking at Gordavin's red, tattered hat, which frequently held bits of seed. Gordavin reached upward to bring Weber onto his hand then looked up at everyone waving their hands in the air to honor him. He smiled and cleared his throat to give the floor to Avery.

"I see that Gordavin needs no introductions!" Laughing with the crowd as the fifth Builder received his accolades from his peers. Gordavin's reputation as an elder Elemental working on many missions of creation had caught the attention of the Blueprint Masters present and from the past.

"Gordavin is the fifth ray Builder of Form and has the most experience as a Builder of Form out of this group here today. He has an uncanny ability to stimulate the mind with his knowledge of science. He carefully analyzes earth compounds and provides mental focus towards the creation of the Earth's minerals."

Weber landed on Avery's shoulder just then, and Avery quipped, "Of course, he is just as handy with the animal kingdom. He seems to have a way the winged ones." Avery chuckled.

"Gordavin will be applying his skills, alongside the others, on the Mineral team. Here, he will be able to assist in the leyline network, using the minerals, plasma, and ether to conduct the forces that will stabilize the new creation. This team will liaison with the Aligners, better known as the Dragon Riders."

The Blueprint Masters stood as Gordavin went back to join the others, in respect of his years of accomplishments and service to Mother Earth.

Avery let the sounds of applause fade out and then brought everyone's attention to the pixie who had floated within a lotus to the front of the room.

Standing only two inches, within the blossom of a lotus, stood the sixth Builder of Form. Padmavati's sleek black hair flowed out from under an indigo-colored headpiece, which was both a hat and a living flower. She wore an indigo blue dress to match her headpiece, which had floral adornments hanging from the trim of the bodice. The neckline of her dress was V-shaped, and upon her neck, she wore a pendant of the beloved Earth, in a Globe form.

"Let me introduce our sixth Builder of Form, Padmavati. Padmavati has worked under the tutelage of the Great Amaryllis, the Goddess of Spring, as well as the Great Director of the Air, Aries. Padmavati's work with the sixth ray energies has brought perfection and attunement to the creations upon Mother Earth. She is devoted to all kingdoms but will focus on the two elements of Earth and Air. Padmavati has earned a place on the team that will be devoted to Whole Systems."

Padmavati floated a few inches above the lotus and then expanded her field, shapeshifting into a large orb that resembled the planet Earth. She then expanded herself once more, and the planet now looked completely different in size and color.

The globe radiated an essence that one could smell that seemed to have a fragrance of a rose. She then morphed back to herself and smiled, holding her hands out in front of her and sending rays of rainbow color light to all those present. Everyone felt the peace that her light emitted and could smell the fragrance of roses as she floated back to her seat.

"And lastly, we have our seventh Builder of Form." Avery pointed to Phyre, who was gliding towards the front of the room. He appeared at first as a flickering, active flame and then jumped out of the fire and stood the same height as Avery, wearing his black hair high upon his head in a twisted bun and dressed in his dark purple ninjutsu attire. A red flame emblem was stitched into the left side of his tunic above his heart.

Avery continued, "As you know, the seventh ray is about ceremonial rhythm and ritual. Phyre will use his abilities to produce new forms within a civilization, once the older form has been purified. Those that work within the seventh ray are Masters of Time and Frequency. They use their energies to bridge time and, in effect, bring spirit into matter. We understand that there are more Time Masters within the Blueprint Masters among us, and therefore, Phyre will be assisting the Time Masters in the fulfillment of the Divine Plan of No Time, the Zero Point, where we will live in harmony through Divine Law and Order."

Phyre bowed to the brethren present and then evaporated into a puff of smoke and reignited back where the other Builders sat.

Gabriel then glided over to where Avery stood and bowed to him. He then instructed Avery to take his place with the others. "Thank you, Avery, for the beautiful presentation of your team."

After Gabriel quickly introduced his team of Blueprint Masters, he then said, " I would like each of the teams to gather in individual groups for a short meeting to get to know one another, and then we will conclude this convocation with a prayer."

Gabriel announced each location for the groups to intermingle. "Time Master Phyre, will you please join Malachi, Platter, and Patina over in this area? Your team will be joined later by one Life Bearer in due time." He pointed to the location, and each of the members began to gather there.

Sitting near the area where Gabriel stood was the sands of time hourglass with a good portion of the sand already sifted to the bottom. Everyone could see that the time was upon them.

Gabriel continued, "The Whole Systems group will be Padmavati and Graeceous for now. There will be several Life Bearers joining your group soon. Please move over to the area near the stream."

Gabriel continued with the next group. "Gordavin, please join our beloved Hiiyup in the blue mineral area for the Minerals team meeting." He pointed to a quiet area where blue minerals had grown in a pattern that was to be used as seats for them.

"Also, Turagus will be assisting your group from time to time, as he will be having a dual role within the two teams. For now, I will ask the two of you to meet."

"Beloved Mersea, please join Jermaine for the meeting of the Water team. I am sure that you will find that Jermaine's vortex and mathematical code work will be an excellent addition to the new vibration of water for the New Earth." Mersea and Jermaine found a cozy spot at the water's edge and immediately immersed themselves within each

338

other's aura.

"You will have two Life Bearers joining your team very soon," Gabriel added as they began their meeting.

"Turagus, please take Tabor into the wooded area, past the harp." A golden harp sat out in an opening to the right of where everyone sat.

"The two of you will be on the Plant team, along with one Life Bearer. We hear she has a deep resonance for the work of nature and has many new ideas that can be focalized. For now, please acquaint your-selves with one another."

The two Plant team members swiftly met within the wooded area just past the harp. They felt an immediate kinship when Turagus pulled out a scroll that held a Divine blueprint of creation for the plant life, giving Tabor a taste of what they might want to create.

It had now become loud with conversations and music. Gabriel called out, "Music of the Sphere's group... Starseed and Arrea?"

He called them up to his side, and he said, "Please know that you will be joined by three Life Bearers, each with unique skills to recreate the Music of the Spheres. As you know, sound is a hidden element that unifies. Please make your way to the golden harp and see what the harp might like to play with the two of you present."

The two musical experts made their way to the harp, and each took turns examining it and stroking the strings. The sounds from this harp and the union of these two beings caused everyone to become silent for a few moments as they absorbed the sounds into their forms.

"Finally, Avery, I saved your group for last. Come sit here with me." Gabriel motioned for Abdonna to join them for a visit.

The Blueprint Master joined them, as Gabriel mentioned that Grae-ceous would be assisting the team from time to time as well. He went on to give a briefing on this team.

"The Animal team will be working on the seeding of new creations, as well as upgrading the existing species as we move up into the higher vibrations." He sat on a chair and folded his leg across the other, then placed his hands upon his left knee, holding it firmly while leaning forward to whisper with the team.

"The animal team will be working with the Guardians and, of course, the Dragons and Riders as well."

He smiled at Avery as he continued. "Your team will consist of the two of you, plus Graeceous, one Life Bearer, and possibly, the Guardian Breacher."

He looked towards Abdonna. "Abdonna, please share the team scroll with Avery. I will leave you to talk amongst yourselves for a little while."

Gabriel patted Avery on his shoulder as he stood and left the group. Gabriel's touch soothed Avery's energy field, calming his mind and allowing the highest vision to be received.

Archangel Gabriel made the rounds to each group giving each team his support and attention. He gave them enough time to develop a rapport, and then signaled them all to reconvene. He spoke to the group about the importance of the mission.

"Over the Eons, the beautiful blue planet has held the Creators many creations and lifeforms, whether it be Human, Elemental, Angelic, or biological forms... the list goes on and on. We have been able to assist Earth and her inhabitants in a unique way, by bridging time and space and upgrading the forms of all living things. Now it is clear that Earth and her inhabitants are ready for the next jump in frequency."

He paused and then elaborated. "That time is now, to move to a higher vibrational frequency where we can all live amongst one another peacefully and joyously, remembering one another within the same frequency band, no longer divided."

He paused once more to connect with each of the members before him. "There is every indication that a new timing frequency is upon us, a new beam, one that fits with the natural world and not the false timing matrix that humanity has been trapped within. The new frequency could be a vibration that will be difficult for most everyone to hold if the mission is not completed successfully," Gabriel cautioned.

He continued, "Each of you, with your teams, will be assisting the Divine Creator of All That Is with a new dimension, or bandwidth, called New Earth. Earth is making her jump to the higher frequency and with her, the entirety of humanity. The third density beings will need to be encased in a new bandwidth, where they will be able to live upon the Earth in harmony. All of the teams here are critical to seeing this new creation brought into fruition."

He cautioned, "This has been done before, numerous times in fact, but each time various outside forces have, shall I say, interfered with the highest creations. We will not allow that this time, so please know that your only task is to do what you do best and what you have been trained to do. Protection is assured."

Gabriel concluded the convocation with gratitude. "Let us say a prayer of gratitude to the Prime Creator, to the Great Central Sun, Alpha and Omega, and the Central Sun, Helios and Vesta. Blessed are we to be in such fine company and protective, sacred light."

They each bowed their heads as Gabriel prayed out loud, and finally, he added, "And a special prayer to all of the Guardians who are protecting God's Divine Creations."

After the prayer, Gabriel said a few more words of wisdom. "It is the science of precipitation that is to be studied by every Man, Woman, Elemental and Angel. The focused attention to precipitate beautiful forms, through their own Will and Power and to protect those creations, is a vital component of the Divine plan. Let us remember the words I AM, when drawing the light to your creations. This is a powerful magnet when manifesting the highest reality."

"Let all intelligent beings remember the requirement of the hour is to recall the power to magnetize energy, secondly to receive it, and finally to distribute the energy. To do these things is what maintains an upward force. You are the storehouse to which an increased electronic substance will fill your beings and be distributed upon the various planes. Guard this life force well. Given that you all represent the seven Rays, the energies that govern all life, I implore you to do the job well."

With those final words, Gabriel held his hands together, bringing them to his heart and bowed to everyone present.

And the wheel turns...

Chapter 53

Geomancers Converge Upon the Salutation Hotel

The drive to the conference in Perth was uneventful. The conversation, on the other hand, was unworldly. Bridgit and Stella shared with David everything that had happened to them that morning, before his arrival at the Inn. Stella gave him the replay of her dream as Bridgit interjected the parts about the stranger in the hall and how she appeared in her doorway.

David's face exhibited a myriad of shocked expressions and exuberance the entire drive to Perth. Bridgit shared how she had met the stranger in the hall back at the Inn right after Stella had come to her room to tell her about her dream. Stella then relayed her dream to David, especially the part about the triangular puck marks and the word Etifah.

Bridgit jumped back in to share that the stranger wanted to deliver a package that seemed urgent. When she told David about the stone pendants and the striking stones, he could barely contain himself.

"Let me get this straight. Some random person just came to your door, and said here you go, lass, the key to the doorway for you and yours? And there are thirteen of these pendants, yeah?" David kept running his hand through his hair, with the other hand on the wheel. A habit that he seemed to do from time to time when he processed these kinds of tremendous happenings.

"Did she have blue skin as well?" he sarcastically asked, as if he did not believe them. In reality, he was afraid to believe them.

"No! She didn't have blue skin." Stella and Bridgit both became a bit agitated at his comment.

Bridgit calmly stated, "She appeared to me as if she was Scottish, but her accent was different. She came and went so fast, and I was startled by her appearance. I was apprehensive about her presence at first, but by the time I realized that she was sent to us, she had left me with the stones and had taken her leave. The only thing she answered was that she was a Guardian."

"This is fantastic! I would love to see the pendants once we get settled at the hotel." David rubbed his face, his hair all disheveled as he contemplated the meaning of this encounter.

"Guardian, huh?" He could sense that he had come off a bit harsh, so he attempted to sound more cheerful. In his mind, he flashed back to the Loanhead of Daviot stone circle and the man holding the pendant. His eyes widened and exploded out loud with his thoughts.

"Say, do you think this has anything to do with the stone pendant at Loanhead? You know, the half-cremated man holding the stone pendant?" as he glanced in the rearview mirror, he could see the look on Stella's face.

"I was thinking about that just now too! Honestly, we just don't know anything for sure at this point. But I hope we don't end up in the same predicament as the man with the pendant at Loanhead!!!!" Stella winked at him.

"If the pendants are the vibrational match to the doorways we are looking for, my best guess is that the fellow at Daviot was a Life Bearer too." Bridgit offered a kind response to David's question.

David said, "This is all so interesting. Hey, do you mind if I show them to one of my mates? I would be very discreet."

"If you show it to your friend, I ask that you not give the person the background story... obviously. We need to be very careful from this point on." Bridgit commented.

David turned to Bridgit, smiled, and said, "You can trust me." He gave her the widest, toothy grin to persuade her further.

The drive to Perth was swift. David shared with Bridgit and Stella that the conference was a yearly event in which he had the honor of being on the organizing team. That is why he needed to get to the hotel a bit early for final preparations.

After two hours of driving, David announced that they were at the location, The Salutation Hotel. He made sure to note that this hotel was the oldest established hotel in Scotland.

The ladies smiled, both silently hoping that they would have wi-fi and a coffee pot in the room, something that in America was standard but in some quaint Scottish towns was a luxury.

David pulled up in the front of the hotel to let the ladies gather their bags, leaving them to sign in as he went to park Pearl. Stella and Bridgit looked around the lobby of the hotel, noting the columns and dark wood accents of a traditional hotel.

"Wow, this is actually quite nice!" Stella blurted while browsing near the fireplace. She touched the fabric of the navy-blue chair positioned near the fireplace and glanced to see what was in the glass display case. All the while, Bridgit took care of the check-in process.

"Isn't this nice, Bridgit?" Stella quizzed her as she walked to the check-in counter.

"Yes. Very nice." Bridgit smiled, handing Stella her room key and pointing to the bouncy Druid coming through the door with his bag and presentation case. Bridgit walked towards him to help grab some of his items and offered to hold them while she placed her hand upon his shoulder to guide him towards the front desk.

David was very grateful for the assistance and could see a few of his colleagues sitting in the open area near the bar, watching him with the ladies. Silently he was happy that they saw him with the ladies. He relished the thought of having people in his life that he considered friends, given that he had very few. Most of his acquaintances were professionals.

He waved to them, and they returned the greeting as David checked himself into the hotel. The woman at the front desk placed him across the hall from his companions. He took his key and the packet of information that had been left for him by the hotel conference manager.

Once he completed his transaction, he turned to the ladies, grabbed his bags from Bridgit, and the three went up to their rooms for a quick respite, agreeing to meet again in no more than an hour.

Stella and Bridgit were still reeling from the morning at the Inn just a few hours earlier and wanted to examine the stone pendants once more.

David went into business mode as he had many outstanding issues to take care of during the girls' rest time. He entered his room quickly while muttering and shut the door behind him before the ladies could even get the key in the door of their room. They laughed at the sight of David changing so quickly from Druid David to professional David. Clearly, he was a multifaceted being and humorous to watch in action.

Stella slid the keycard into the slot and opened the door to their hotel room. She hesitantly walked in, somewhat expecting weird energy to be present since the hotel was approximately four hundred years old. To her surprise, the room's energy was clean. The sun shone through the opened curtains, and their beds looked like they were fit for a

King, with a Tartan swath of cloth laid upon the foot of the bed, over a white down comforter and matching tartan pillows placed in front of four overstuffed feather pillows.

She chose the bed closest to the window and sat on the center edge, then fell back with arms stretched and exclaimed, "I'm in heaven!!"

Bridgit placed her bags down, laughing at Stella's joy of a soft bed, as she made her way to the opposite bed and tried her side out. To her utter shock, she too had the same reaction. The bed felt like it held her in every place that needed support. She laid there for several moments staring at the ceiling in a comforting embrace.

"I could lay here all day. It feels like I am in a nest." She rolled her head over to the right to see Stella, whose head was almost enveloped by the down pillow which she had pulled from the headboard. Bridgit laughed at the scene.

Stella giggled, then breathed deeply and whispered, "It is so comforting."

Bridgit then grabbed a pillow from her bed to prop her head up, and the two ladies allowed their bodies to nestle into the fluff all around them.

After enjoying the comfort of the bed for some time, Bridgit pulled her purse close to her. Not wanting to move her head, she used her hand to feel for the black pouch, which held the stone pendants. She pulled one pendant out for herself and another one for Stella. "Heads up!"

Stella's head popped up, and her hands flew up to guard her face out of reflex as Bridgit watched Stella's cat-like response.

"Now that I have your attention," Bridgit became serious and tossed the stone pendant towards Stella.

Bridgit tried to strike the stone pendant with the accompanying tear-shaped stone, practicing the technique and feeling what the frequency felt like on her body. Stella did the same, and they compared notes.

Bridgit said, "I can feel the frequency vibrating in my body so deeply. It is going deep through my heart."

Bridgit took a deep breath and allowed it to move her into a deep meditative state.

Stella was familiar with the tone emitting from the stones. It woke up a deep memory from her past. She began to hum the song that she sang the first time that she met Bridgit, the song that she played for her Mother.

Stella began to rock back in forth while tuning her body to the frequency of the stone. She felt a deep love at that moment for her life, for her friendship with Bridgit, for her journey that was unfolding, all the while not noticing that Bridgit was utterly silent and staring straight at the wall.

After some time, David knocked on the door as their time of rest was up. The ladies both snapped back to the present, trying to figure out what the sound was. They heard it again. The knocking at the door seemed at first to be more of an echo as if they were in a chamber, but as they came back into the awareness of being in the room, they realized that the stone had taken them deep into meditation. Not having time to discuss what they experienced, they yelled out to David in response. "Coming!"

Bridgit opened the door yawning, looking at the cranky Druid who was not amused at the idea that the girls would rather be sleeping.

Stella moved past Bridgit in the doorway and grabbed David's arm, turning him in the direction of the elevator. "Let's go, David. I didn't realize how hungry I am. Do we have time to grab a bit to eat before the event gets started?" Bridgit followed slowly behind them.

David looked at them with curiosity. He wondered what was going on. One girl was chatty while the other looked as if she hadn't slept in a month. Odd, since they had been fully rested just an hour before, he thought.

"What is going on with you two?" he finally asked.

Bridgit had her hand on her mouth and slightly bumped into the wall as she walked down the hall. Stella swiftly moved towards Bridgit and insisted on holding onto the pendant that Bridgit still was wearing around her neck. Stella wrapped the pendant around the striking stone and put it in her pocket for safekeeping and placed the pendant that she wore tucked away inside her blouse.

"We just had an interesting experience with the pendants as you knocked on the door." Stella apologized and continued.

"Sorry. It feels like I've had a double shot latte, but it has had a more calming effect on Bridgit." The two of them looked at Bridgit, who was still not able to speak, and they decided that coffee was in order. They guided Bridgit the rest of the way.

As they walked into the lobby and towards the lounge, they could see that the conference was well attended. The lobby was swarming with people, some chatting happily with colleagues while a long line of individuals stood waiting to be checked in.

David patted one gentleman on the shoulder and extended his hand, quickly giving directions to him to meet up with him later.

"Ford is one of the presenters," David quipped as he guided the ladies towards the lounge area in the front of the hotel.

As they reached their table, David motioned to the wait staff to bring coffee to the table. He pulled the chairs out for each of the ladies and swirled around to the third seat, which faced the crowd. The lounge was just off to the left of the main entrance, making it an excellent spot for David to be seen should someone need his assistance signing in at the conference desk.

Once Ford and his wife had checked in, they too made their way to the lounge to grab a bite to eat before the conference got underway.

The table next to the trio was empty, and Ford asked if they could join tables for a visit while they ate.

David immediately began to rearrange the chairs and pulled the two round tables together with Ford's help. He smiled, knowing that it was an awkward placement, hoping that the ladies were not too inconvenienced by the intrusion.

The waitress brought several cups over and was already pouring coffee for the ladies. Bridgit took a quick sip to bring her fully back into her body, as Ford and David completed the setup of the chairs around the table.

Everyone made their introductions. David pulled the seat out for Ford's wife and then sat.

Bridgit willed herself to be present, extending her hand and said, "Hi. I'm Bridgit Phare, and this is my cousin, Stella Phare."

Stella stood and extended her hand. "We are new to Geomancy, but David made it sound so fascinating that we both decided to come check out the conference," Bridgit smiled as Stella sat back in her seat. She winked at David and watched him puff up like a proud peacock.

"Well, it is certainly nice to meet the two of you. I am Ford Cassel-man, and this is my bride, Ursula Bevins." Ford's brown eyes remind-ed Bridgit of Sean Connery, and as she listened to him speak, she realized that he did not seem to have as thick of a Scottish accent like most others from the area. When Ursula spoke, it was clear that she was American.

Bridgit said, "It is nice to meet you both. I detect an American accent from you, Ursula. How about you, Ford? Where are the two of you from?"

"Well, I was going to say the same thing of you two," Ford said with a smile, then continued. "I am originally from Scotland, but currently, we live in San Diego, California."

Stella excitedly said, "We are from California too! LA area."

Ford responded, "Oh, cool. It is good to know we have more of the U.S. represented here."

He sipped his coffee then clarified, "I still have relatives in the area and spend a good amount of time in Scotland. I am originally from Paisley, near Glasgow, if you are familiar with the area."

The waitress came to deliver the menu's, and he then continued his background. Stella asked Ford what took him to the United States.

"I left home after attending University and decided to travel to the States. I ended up in California and have been doing geomantic stone landscapes as a business, and I teach geomancy classes at the local community college there." His head bobbed back and forth a bit when he spoke. David jumped in to offer the ladies a bit more background on Ford and Ursula.

"He is the finest landscape artist that I know. He naturally works with the geomantic features of the land to create fantastic landscapes for his clients. Very sought after, this chap here." David was very proud of his friend.

He continued, "And Ursula, here, will be doing a Feng Shui talk on bridging the male and female leyline energies with water features." He winked at her, and the ladies nodded their heads with smiles, acknowledging the importance of her work.

After the waitress came by to take food orders, they continued to make small talk about the conference in general and what colleagues would be attending. The ladies took it all in as the start of yet another new adventure in their lives.

And the wheel turns...

Chapter 54

The Starry Initiation of the Dragon Riders

Breacher instructed the team of Dragon Riders to prepare for the journey to the floating abode of the celestial parents, Tollan. He called the riders into a room where the lighting was dim. Pillows laid upon the floor in a wheel pattern. He asked that they put their heads at the center of the hub of the wheel, their bodies being the spokes.

The rider's heads were almost touching, while Breacher played a tone from a device in the center of the hub, near the rider's heads. He began to speak to them about the process of intentionally leaving their bodies. "This device is designed to assist you in moving out of this dimensional space and into the next." He moved about the room monitoring the team and then spoke once more.

"Where we will be going, we must leave the body behind. We will be taking a journey beyond the stars to the heavenly abode known as Tollan. Here we will meet the Divine Mother and the Weavers for your starry initiation."

Breacher sat on a pillow with his back against the wall near the riders, in preparation for the journey. The riders were now in a relaxed state.

He continued to guide them. "Your body is asleep, but your mind is awake. You hear my voice and know that you are protected. Relax your body deeper and let your mind journey with me to Tollan. Ease out of the body when I count to ten. With the device near you, you will be given the assistance that you need to leave the body behind. You will always be connected to your body by a silver cord, so you need not worry about your safety. Your spirit will easily find its way back to the body when we are ready to return. I will begin the count now. One, two, three, four."

The frequency in the room began to shift, and the device near the rider's head began to make higher and higher pitches with vibrating overtones, which helped to facilitate the rider's ability to leave their bodies from the top of their heads. Breacher watched from his inner vision to see that they all managed to lift out of their bodies and, at the same time, noticing all of the dragon's light bodies swirling around the room.

The Kumara exited her body swiftly, jumping upon the green dragon who was already floating above her in its astral form. She rode around the room, watching for signs of the next rider to pop out of their head. She found The Sage hovering over his body and grabbed his arm. She gently led him to the yellow dragon, where The Sage joyously mounted the dragon's back and waved to Breacher with an indication that he was ready to go.

The orange and red dragons floated above where Praeta and Arbor were laying as if to catch them once they left their bodies behind. Praeta recognized the red dragon immediately as she made her way in her spirit body to her dragon companion.

The orange dragon licked Arbor's face to wake him from a sleepy state, and it worked beautifully. Arbor left his body behind and held his hand out to the orange dragon to scratch its neck, then telepathically sent a message to the dragon that he was ready to ride. Arbor mounted the orange dragon and watched as they waited for the last two riders to find their way out of their bodies.

Alderson's physical body was twitching as if trying to hold onto his spirit. Then suddenly, he popped out of the crown of his head and looked around to find his bearing. The blue dragon that had rescued him from the water in the Quadrivium was hovering over his physical body, waiting for Alderson's spirit to exit.

At that moment, the two beings experienced a mind-meld, and Alderson knew that the soul of his dragon had been with him in another time and place. They were meant to be reunited. The others watched Alderson with reverence as Alderson bowed to the blue dragon and mounted him.

Kali had already exited her body prior to Alderson and was watching as he was reunited with his dragon. Breacher's spirit body floated near hers, as he located the dragon that would be paired with her.

She watched the indigo dragon part from where the violet dragon, Leto, hovered. Kali floated over her physical body as the indigo dragon flew by her several times, weaving a golden stream of energy around her. Soon enough, she realized that with each pass the dragon took, it had wrapped her in a golden cocoon of energy that was lifting her frequency to match its own. Her inner sight began to change. She could see the vast waves of energy pulsating in the room better now.

Breacher watched as Kali and the indigo dragon united, and all riders were ready to move through a glowing portal that had opened nearby. He instructed the team to trust the dragons and to move swiftly, keeping the intention on the destination, Tollan. The riders and dragons moved through the portal, following Breacher and Leto into the unknown.

The jump was swift and painless. Alderson could see the heavenly Tollan floating in a sea of stars, like a deep, dark ocean in space. The rest of the riders came into view, with Breacher making a count of his team.

The Divine Mother stood on the edge of Tollan, with her own dragon swirling in the cosmic ocean nearby. When she saw them approaching, she sent out her blue magnetic dragon to greet the team and escort them to the edge of the floating abode in the heavens. All the riders arrived and dismounted their dragons and stood in awe of where they found themselves.

Breacher made the introductions of his team to the Celestial Divine Mother. The team gave deep respect to the Divine Mother. Then Breacher moved them on towards the area where the Grandmothers worked. Breacher pointed out the fire pit of the Weavers, "This is the area of the Cosmos where light is woven into substance."

Breacher led them to the Grandmother Weavers, who were busy making their starry substances and weaving them into the energy streams carried by the waves. "It is these subtle energies that our dragons drink, so to speak, as a way of helping them disseminate celestial energies."

At that moment, Breacher pointed to where the dragons were corralled, already enjoying the treats from the Grandmothers. The Grandmothers were pleased that Breacher had found this team, and most importantly, that the dragons were in full agreement with the choices. The riders were all a perfect match for the dragons, even if the riders had not yet felt that they were worthy of the honor.

Grandmother Vega looked at Alderson and chose him to begin the starry initiation, as he was the one whose heart seemed to her to be the most fragile. Yet, with that vulnerability, it made Alderson one of the strongest candidates as a rider. Each Grandmother Weaver took a rider to the fire pit area.

Grandmother Vega spoke to Alderson, "To the nimble one with a heart of gold, we ignite you with the starry presence that gives access to the atmospheres of all celestial envelopes."

Vega placed her hands in front of Alderson's chest, over his heart, and imprinted the starry tattoo upon him. "This tattoo holds the frequency of freedom, which allows movement within the realms for service to celestial bodies. A rider, a dragon, and a Weaver will always be bound together in this service."

She stepped backward, removing her hands, and the imprint of a starry tattoo glowed upon his chest through his etheric clothing.

Each of the Grandmother's had likewise offered the riders an initiation, connecting them forever to the service of maintaining the energies of celestial bodies. It was an honor, and the riders knew in their hearts that this was the highest service that they could offer, and what they were born for.

Once the ceremony was complete, the riders were taken inside the floating palace where the Divine Mother and Grandmother Weavers abide. She shared with the riders the mission, the same one that she shared with Breacher on his first visit to Tollan.

The Divine Mother stated, "The net around the third density of Earth has been compromised and will be taken down. Before this, you will work together to create a new net, with new geometries of celestial energies, which the dragons are drinking as we speak." She smiled and pointed towards the window, where they could all see the dragons being fed the new celestial energy.

"There is another creature that is needed in this endeavor and thus will be the first step of this mission. You are to rescue the unicorn." The Divine Mother smiled as she listened to the murmurings of the riders and waited as Breacher settling them down.

Breacher spoke to his team, "Yes, there is still a unicorn alive, and it is being held captive in the Perseus constellation in an area that is known as Algol. This area is a very dangerous region, where monstrous beings are larger and uglier than anything you have ever seen. It is these beings that guard the unicorn."

Breacher looked at the Riders, who all seemed to be stunned. He realized that it was too overwhelming at the moment, so he stopped himself from giving too much detail. "I have been doing some recognizance and will brief you fully once we return to our bodies."

The rider's eyes were all huge, some with their mouths hanging open. No one spoke a word or moved. They were all calculating the risks in their mind and listening intently.

The Mother spoke again, "The unicorn is vital to the activation of the world tree." She moved about and positioned herself to see all the riders.

"You see when Earth's energy was usurped, and the realms were divided, it was the unicorn's mystical horn that pierced the veils and provided the access that kept some of the gates open for all its magical creatures to live upon the 3D Earth plane. When the unicorns were slaughtered, it was a measured attack by the usurpers to enslave humanity. By placing a net of chaos around the planet and killing the creatures who could access the higher realms, no human could exit the 3D realm."

She showed the riders a brief hologram of the moments in time when this occurred and then continued. "There is one unicorn known as the golden unicorn, which is immortal."

She again showed the riders the hologram and pointed to the golden horn. "The unicorn is symbolic of resurrection. It is this unicorn that you must find." She held her hands together in front of her waist and looked into the eyes of the starry initiates. Each clearly understood the mission and were in awe of their part in it.

The Divine Mother then motioned the riders to exit the room as they walked back to where the dragons were being tended.

She continued, "The Grandfathers will be able to open the gates for good, once you have the golden unicorn. Its golden horn will pierce the false veil at the precise location, which you will know when the time comes. Remember, the new net must be in place and active around the false net before it is taken down. This way, the false net cannot reboot itself. At the moment when the veil is pierced, the galactic pulse will commence."

"The galactic pulse?" Kali curiously blurted out.

"Yes. This pulse will be sent out as soon as there is an opening. It is a pulse of pure love that will instantly touch everything in creation. This pulse of love will enter the energetic field around every man, woman, and child, as well as creatures upon the Earth's planes, in all envelopes of existence. It will raise everyone into the highest vibration of light, and their bodies will begin to heal. Their hearts will open as fragments of their souls return to them. This healing will allow them to make amends to all in their lives. Humans will make life changes immediately to honor the body and their spirits."

She looked at each of the riders, "You are ushering in a large facet of the Golden Era of Love, but I want you all to know that you are not alone. You will have help at every turn."

The Divine Mother motioned for Breacher to escort his team to prepare for departure. The dragons were nestled up to their divine parents, the Blue Magnetic Hieros Dragon, and the Red Electric Hieros Dragon.

"Breacher, you have your mission, and your riders now have their starry passports. Be swift, as we have much work to do. The dragons have tasted the Ouroboros energies now. As the offspring of the Hieros dragons, they will be known from this point forward as the Hieros-Ouroboros dragons."

Breacher bowed his head and was about to turn when the Divine Mother gave one admonition. "Beware of the Fox. Alcor is very sly. She goes by alias's."

Breacher knew this to be accurate, having first-hand knowledge of Alcor's treachery. He nodded affirmatively and then smiled as he turned to his riders.

The Dragon Riders thanked the Divine Mother for all that embodies. They then turned to the Grandmother Weavers to offer thanks for their starry initiation. The Grandmothers sang them a song of courage and victory while the Dragon Riders mounted the Hieros-Ouroboros dragons and watched as they flew off into the celestial sea.

And the wheel turns...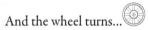

Chapter 55

Back at the Geomancy Conference

Bridgit and Stella had excused themselves from the lunch table to let David, Ford, and Ursula complete their conversation on the final tasks before the conference kicked off. The ladies walked off their lunch meal by taking a stroll down South Street. They followed a square pattern that brought them back to the hotel feeling exhilarated. The girls adored the town, with its rich mixture of colorful doors and window frames that added a freshness to an aged community. The energy felt clean and orderly.

During their walk, they spoke of the energy of the stone pendants and how they affected them differently. Stella held onto both of their pendants in her pocket, for the time being, because they needed to be grounded in their body for David's sake. They also wanted to enjoy the town, so they agreed to discuss the effects of the pendant in detail after the day's events come to an end.

Once back in the hotel, they went up to their room to grab their notebooks and conference paraphernalia. Stella put their pendants back into the black velvet bag that was still laying out on Bridgit's bed.

"We probably should put these in the safe, don't you think?" Stella quizzed Bridgit on the safety of the stones. Bridgit wholeheartedly agreed and put her hand out to take the bag to the safe. Stella, teasingly, made the motion of throwing them at Bridgit, but quickly placed the velvet bag safely in Bridgit's hand. Laughing at Stella, Bridgit looked at the bag, still taken aback by how the pendant affected her energy.

"While you lock up the stones, I will brush my teeth. Be ready in a jiffy." Stella winked at her and was quickly in the loo. Bridgit located the safe in the cabinet between the two beds and placed the velvet bag in the lockbox for safekeeping. She secured the key in her purse. Once the key was in the zippered part of her bag, she grabbed her lip balm to touch up her dry lips.

Still contemplating the happenings earlier at the Inn, she thought of how the energy of the pendant changed once it was hit with the striking stone. The frequency, she thought, was almost as if it opened a portal within her. Like clockwork, her thoughts were once more interrupted by the rhythmic knock upon the door.

Bridgit peeked through the peephole to see David standing outside the door. Opening the door, she said, "We are almost ready." She smiled as David bounded into the room.

"You are not going to believe this!" He exclaimed with heightened exuberance.

Bridgit shut the door to the room as Stella opened the bathroom door with a toothbrush in her mouth, wanting to hear the latest. The two ladies watched as David paced the floor, trying to find the words to tell them what his hunch was. His mannerisms were more pronounced as he turned to them and told them of his conversation with Ford.

"Ford and I began to speak about his presentation after you two excused yourselves for a walk." He pointed at them and used his fingers to gesture walking.

"Ford said that he had something to tell me, and he hoped that I wouldn't be mad since it was a last-minute thing. He goes on to tell me that he changed his entire presentation!" David stood straight as if to stretch his long spine and placed his hands in his pants pockets as he looked around the room, distracted.

"Wow, so sorry, David. That must be stressful for an organizer." Bridgit consoled him thinking he was upset.

"No! That is not a problem at all. It's simple to explain once you hear what his new topic is! The folks that come to these types of events do this kind of thing from time to time when they find more relevant material to share. So, are you ready for this?" He quizzed them but then just jumped into the explanation.

"His topic is finding zero-point within a Landscape with frequency! He even had drawings of the puck marks that are on our pendants! He said that he was inspired by something that a colleague had presented at one of his conferences, and it led him to the zero-point energy and that precise puck marking!" He stood back to gauge the reactions of the ladies but also preoccupied looking around the room for the bag of pendants.

Stella ran back in the bathroom to spit her toothpaste in the sink then quickly came back into the room to listen in.

Bridgit had a look of concern. "What do you mean, David? Did you tell him anything about the pendants?"

"Oh, heavens, no." He threw his hand out, waving the thought away. "I wanted to pull the pendant out straight away, but something told me to wait."

He assured them, "I do know how to keep these things secret."

He winked at the ladies and then pulled on the cord of the pendant and began to fidget with it, trying to examine it once more, now that others were clearly being guided to that specific puck marking.

361

"Where are your pendants?" he asked, noticing the ladies did not have theirs on.

Bridgit spoke in a very relaxed and monotone voice, "They seem to make me feel a bit wonky, and clearly they have the same effect on you."

Stella burst out laughing at the very rare joke that Bridgit delivered so smoothly. David tried not to be offended as he contemplated the word wonky.

Bridgit laughed as she patted David on the back for reassurance that she is hearing what he is saying and that they might be finding more Life Bearers in the process since Ford seemed to be in the know. She could read his mind and knew that he felt it too. Bridgit opened the door for the three to exit.

Stella looked at the two of them and caught the wave too. Bridgit secured the room, and they all walked down the corridor together.

Stella asked, "Why do I feel like this is going to be another family reunion?" Bridgit and David stopped and turned to look at Stella, and the three of them stared at one another with hair standing straight up on their arms.

"It does feel like that, doesn't it?" Bridgit smiled, seeing David beam from ear to ear with joyous pride. "The synchronicities are coming at a steady pace now," Bridgit told David.

David ushered Stella in front of him in a gentlemanly fashion and followed behind the Ladies' Phare as they all entered the elevator. He couldn't remember a time when he was supported in the way that these two women were supporting him. His joy for being part of what felt like a family was overwhelming. He was quite as the elevator opened. He wiped back a tear as they all walked to the conference room. The ladies found their seat while David went up to the podium to make the introductions.

The tear of joy that David experienced was a very cleansing and heart-opening thing for him. As he opened the conference that afternoon, he addressed everyone in such a way that each one of them felt as if he was addressing them personally. His entire demeanor shifted from being somewhat of a loner to a person with full authority. As he spoke about each of the speakers, he highlighted not only their academic achievements, but he spoke about some of their human traits and qualities that had impressed him.

The conference began on a very high note, and everyone noticed it in the room. Bridgit and Stella deduced from his speech that the pendant that the Life Bearers are to wear, and that David was wearing at the time, was designed to amplify each of their gifts and also their heart. The vibration felt during David's speech was a form of pure love mixed with complete admiration for his fellow man. It was a stellar beginning of the conference.

And the wheel turns...

Chapter 56

Return to the Alpheratz Base

Somehow, in the dark ocean of the etheric realms, Breacher maintained contact with the riders. All riders found themselves back in the room where their bodies lay waiting for their souls to return to them. Though the mission was successful, Breacher felt that he was missing a key player, the one known as Jinnby.

The Sage and The Kumara were the first two to snap back into their bodies. They lay there for a moment or two, acclimating to the physical body once more. The Sage had thoughts of the elemental aspect of himself, known as Avery, the elf. He wondered if Avery felt the expansion of their group soul moving through the layers of densities.

The Kumara saw her family in her mind's eye as she traveled the dimensions. It brought her comfort to see them again, even if it was for a fleeting moment. In those brief moments, so much was conveyed. The presence of her parents holding the light for her brought her to tears. The love of her people and for humanity is why she volunteered to train at the Alpheratz Base.

Her training as a Pegasus rider was pivotal to her role as a Galactic Ambassador in the lineage of the Kumaras. Her retrieval of a sacred crystalline skull was a promising portend to her, and now with the gift of the starry tattoo, she had expanded her reach of service. She smiled as she pondered all that had transpired as she waited for the others to return to their forms.

Kali and Praeta entered their biological suits next. Then Alderman and Arbor arrived, having enjoyed the ride through the galaxy and the portal back to the room.

Once the riders had acclimated back into their bodies, Breacher said a few words. He played a musical selection to assist the group to ground their energies as he shut the portal. The team began to sit up and reposition themselves to hear their leader speak.

"You are now officially sanctioned by the Celestial parents, and the Weavers as well. Your dragons have safely returned to their lair for rest. What we have achieved is unprecedented. Seven Dragon Riders with access to all of the dimensions will prove very fruitful for the divine plan. Magical and powerful things can occur when a dragon, a rider, and a Weaver blend their talents on behalf of the Celestial parent's creations."

Kali sheepishly asked, "Can you tell us more about the mission to rescue the unicorn?"

He said, "I am still getting the intel together on this Kali. What I will tell you is that we will have the Alliance working with us on this mission. For now, my goal is to strengthen your connections with the dragons."

Breacher walked over to a table nearby where seven goblets of mead were placed, along with a milky white confection known as divinity. He served each of them their cup of sparkling mead and divinity with deep gratitude. He lifted his goblet and said, "Let us give thanks for one another and the divine plan."

The seven-team members drank in silence and ate their divinity. It nourished them and wove an invisible web of light around them, connecting them forever.

And the wheel turns...

Chapter 57

A Convergence of New Life Bearers

The first day of the Geomancy conference was a great success. Many of the presenters shared new findings in their fields. The evening dinner time was spent getting acquainted with the attendees. Most of the presenters gathered in the bar on the first floor, filling up quickly with attendees grabbing food and drink and enjoying social time.

David and Ford wanted to speak somewhere a bit more private, so Ford suggested a smaller venue where the group could have a conversation without being interrupted by conference attendees. Ford and Ursula invited two other presenters to join the group as well.

Ford said, "Let's go on ahead to get a table. The others will meet us there in 10 minutes or so. Ursula knows where it is."

He maneuvered David towards Bridgit and Stella, who were chatting in the corner of the bar. Ford whispered to the ladies that they were heading over to a pub to have a more intimate visit and invited them to come along.

The four of them slipped out the hotel door and down the walkway. They passed over the South St. bridge, in the direction of Rodney Gardens. Ford knew this town like the back of his hand and directed them to one of his favorite well-kept secrets, a nearby pub called Stalking the Brew.

When they arrived, Ford asked for the long rectangular table in the corner as they entered the pub. The table was near a wide glass window with dark green trim whose paint had seen its days. Bridgit glanced around and observed that one could enter this bar and honestly not know what year it was, as it had a distinct feeling of old-world charm.

Stella drooled over the thickness of the wooden table as she and Bridgit placed their bags down to have a better look. Stella marveled, thinking that it had to be four inches thick in her estimation, and the shellac made the table so shiny that she could almost see her reflection in it.

She looked up at Bridgit with a wide grin and said, "We just don't have this kind of authentically old places in the USA. Everything in here has a story!" She ogled for some time as the others watched.

David was amused. He asked for water glasses to be brought to the table as the ladies continued to look around the pub. Soon enough, the door opened, with Ursula peeking in to see where the group was seated. She brought with her two of their friends from the conference.

As Ursula walked up to the table, Ford jumped up to make room for her. He greeted her with an embrace as if they had been apart for a while. He kissed Ursula on top of her head before guiding her to the seat next to his. She smiled upward at him as if no one else was in the room but him. Stella watched the two interact, and she knew then that this was what it looked like to be deliciously in love.

Ford made the introduction of their companions, Ashneer Sharma, and Freya Franklin, to both Bridgit and Stella. After the initial introductions, everyone perused the drink menu and made small talk until they gave their orders.

Bridgit, facing Ashneer Sharma, asked, "Ashneer, what is it that you are presenting at the conference?"

He grinned and said, "Please, call me Koko. It's short for Kokopelli."

"Ok. Koko, what is it that you do, and why Kokopelli?" Bridgit responded, intrigued by the nickname.

He nodded in appreciation of her interest in him and continued, "I am originally from India, but I live in Vancouver, BC, where I am an Architect. I specialize in Vastu Shastra." He could see the confused looks on their faces and elaborated further.

"Vastu Shastra principles are used in the design and layout of houses, municipalities, gardens, and waterways." There was a momentary pause as they enjoyed a sip of the ale that had arrived. He then explained the similarities of Vastu Shastra and Feng Shui. "These are both systems based on the universal flow of energy."

He continued, "I have also studied the work of Dr. Emoto, which led me to give the presentation tomorrow on the element of water and its response to outside stimuli. My talk will go into the building of sacred spaces with the water element, using the geomantic principles of Vastu Shastra."

"That sounds very interesting, Koko. I look forward to your presentation tomorrow." Bridgit nodded her head and looked at Stella in amazement at being in the company of some very intriguing people.

Then she asked once more, "So why the name Kokopelli?"

Ashneer said sheepishly, "When I studied at university in the United States, my roommate would tell people about his Indian friend. They would always ask American Indian or India Indian?" he chuckled and then said, "We always would say Native American Indian just for kicks, and that is when my roommate started calling me Kokopelli. It just stuck, and from that point on, I was Koko."

Bridgit enjoyed his story and glanced across the table at the fantastic group of people that she had the pleasure of their company. At that moment, she felt a Déjà vu. This scene was familiar. The thought hit her that they all seemed oddly familiar. As Bridgit processed the feelings, she looked at Stella, equally enjoying herself.

Stella had sat next to Freya and asked, "Freya, what is it that you are presenting and also where are you from?"

Freya wiped her mouth with her napkin and said, "Hmm... I am not nearly as interesting as Koko," she chuckled.

"I am from Washington State. I am a nutritionist. I work with clients to encourage eating whole foods, and I teach them about plant-based supplements for optimal health."

Stella said, "Oh! Go green to stay lean?! Right on." Everyone laughed at Stella's bubbly personality and felt it refreshing.

Laughing, Freya commented, "Yes, that too."

She smiled and explained more, "My studies have varied, but what interests me and what led me to Geomancy and the philosophical systems that harmonize one's environment, such as Feng Shui, is its ability to clear energy. Take plants, for instance. I can use plants to clear a space and to provide better air quality. When I work with plants on an intuitive level, I begin to understand the ratios of the nutrients the plant provides within the atmosphere or biome, which is an essential exchange for life support on the planet. Then I translate that information into a nutrition plan."

She realized Stella's eyes were wide, and her mouth was hanging open. "Oh Stella, I'm sorry, I kind of went nerd on you for a moment."

"Please don't apologize, Freya! You had me mesmerized! I could see exactly what you were saying, which helps when I don't necessarily understand your words." Stella indicated that she had second sight by waving her hands in front of her face and continued. "I could see the interchange between the plants and humans, and as you mentioned the nutrients, my body responded electrically, like a charge filling my body!"

Now Freya's eyes were wide. "Wonderful Stella! That is exciting feed-back."

She smiled at Stella for a moment and said, "So I am speaking at the conference as both a nutritionist and as a Feng Shui practitioner. Back in Washington State, I consult with individuals on the importance of plants in their diets and in their homes."

She nodded her head in an honorable way as she completed her background then asked, "What about you two? Do you also have a Geomantic background?", looking at both Bridgit and Stella.

Bridgit answered, "Oh, wow. No. Not Geomancers, though the subject is very intriguing. I am an Arborist. I have been coming to Scotland for a research project. One thing led to another, and I came to know David through a friend." She smiled his way, leaving her relationship with him vague.

David smiled and continued the conversation, "Long lost sister's, so to speak." Grinning at the two of them, he said, "So I invited them along!"

Bridgit said, "David is close to our uncle, and while he is busy else-where this week, we thought it would be interesting to take in the conference and get to know David a bit more." They all were happy to hear what brought them to Scotland and the conference.

Then Ursula said, "And Stella has quite a unique background as well. We have only just met, but I have heard that your harp playing is extraordinary." She leaned in to compliment Stella.

Stella blushed, "Awe, thanks. David must have spilled the beans."

Ford coughed to clear his throat and got the attention of the table. "I know that we want to keep this conversation going, but we should consider getting some rest tonight, as many of us have presentations tomorrow. Might I suggest we take our leave and walk through

Rodney Gardens to have a look at the stars for a bit before we say goodnight?"

Everyone was in complete agreement and took the last few sips of their drinks. As they all began to take their leave, Ford mentioned to David that he wanted to finish their conversation about the puck marks. David looked at Bridgit and then nodded in agreement as they made their way out the door.

And the wheel turns...

Chapter 58

The Ambassador's Gather at Ganymede

Another Council meeting was called. Bewain looked out the window of his craft, viewing the cosmic ocean littered with ships of all sizes headed to a moon in Jupiter's orbit. Ganymede was a stronghold for the light forces and considered to be a major hub where the intelligence-gathering comes in from many star systems to this central location.

Bewain's craft docked as several other crafts were landing as well. Breacher rode in on one of the other ships, to Bewain's surprise.

As they both exited their respective ships with other people in the Lyran-Sirian battalions, they met up with one another just outside the entrance to the station's interior corridor.

"Commander Breacher, it's good to see you here. Let's step over here if you don't mind." Bewain grabbed Breacher out of the line, while others headed inside for the impromptu meeting. Bewain's large paw-sized hand pulled Breacher swiftly without Breacher having a moment to respond.

Bewain leaned in closely to Breacher's ear and, in a quiet voice, said, "There is major activity going on in sector PL93 in the third density of Earth. Have you heard anything?" Bewain quizzed Breacher for some understanding.

Breacher nodded, "All I can tell you is that the area is on full alert. It seems the ancestors are coming out of stasis, and this activity could be related."

The two commanders looked at each other with stressed expressions, as Bewain commented, "This isn't good. Let's hear what the update is and meet back at my craft to go over strategy after the council meeting is adjourned. Come on, let's get in there."

They both walked briskly into the chamber where the elite forces of all of the star systems were gathering. The chamber resembled a courtroom, with a central platform for those leading the meeting. There were long tables to accommodate five members each.

The room had various levels, like an amphitheater, so that everyone could see the speakers with ease. Bewain and Breacher were escorted to a table to the far right in the second tier. This area was where the Lyran-Sirian contingent had always met, when at these gatherings.

They watched as the Mantids entered the chamber and positioned themselves next to the Lyran-Sirian table. Breacher, Bewain and the other commanders gave the universal symbol of peace by the way they stood, their hand movements and their willingness to look all beings in the eyes, or eye, depending on what the case may be.

The energy in the room palpably shifted as everyone at once took notice of who had walked into the room. Commander Benoit of Alpheratz had brought with him several members of the Galactic Confederation Intelligence Alliance (GCIA), who work closely with the Watchers and Judicial Courts. These were the unifiers from many star systems that are brought in when there is a critical junction in the plan for planetary resurrection.

Bewain monitored the group's arrival, scanning the room. He was happy to see a familiar face in the crowd. His beloved Shamalaine was seated with the Andromeda Council, in discussions with the other Strategists. She had not seen Bewain for some time as he had been on active duty for the Lyran-Sirian Council.

She could feel his presence as he stared at her in admiration. She turned and locked her heart and mind with her beloved. She smiled and placed her hand over her heart, nodding, then turned back to her peers with diligence to complete the conversation before the meeting started.

Commander Benoit stood at the podium to open the meeting. He announced the members of the intelligence team, who had arrived to give a briefing on the recent attacks upon humanity in the third-density of Earth. And to discuss a delicate matter that involved all present in the room.

One of the members of the panel was known as Galactic Agent Theta Ebora. Theta wore her black hair in a slanted, asymmetrical cut, turned under below the ear on one side, and completely shaved on the other. Her skin glowed, with a bronze effect. She wore a form-fitted pair of grey slacks detailed with a metallic shiny ribbon stripe down each leg. Her maroon vest fit tightly over a white latex top that covered portions of her neck.

Over her attire, she wore a heavy grey cape with sleeves made from the same metallic fabric as the ribbon on her pant legs. She was the elected speaker for the council meeting as she had seniority within the intelligence group.

"Greetings, Galactic Brethren!" Her voice sounded like a mixture of a melodious tune and an electronic voice modulation. She needed no amplified sound devices as she addressed the gathered members of the GCIA.

"I am here to relay intel that has come to the attention of the GCIA. In a time of great advances for the light, we have expected that there would be some retaliation from our recent maneuvers to keep the chaotics from accomplishing their goals of nuclear destruction of the planetary jewel, Earth. Before I get into that, I will share the good efforts that have been accomplished in the light."

She bowed her head towards crucial members who have been part of the liberation team. "There has been much clearing of the negative forces within the various dimensions of Earth. Up to this point, the chaotic ones had been receiving assistance from a large chaos node near Earth's orbit, which has now been liberated and no longer providing essential energetic support for the dark terrestrial forces."

She continued, "With that said, there had been negotiations taking place between the GCIA and key figures of this rogue group, who, by their actions, have virtually ignored the Treaty of Peace in place to protect those living within the 3D bandwidth of Earth. " She looked around the room as she scanned the reactions of all of the officers and light warriors present.

"Section five of the Treaty, on Retreat, is also null and void. That Treaty section stipulated that the Light forces were obligated to step back and allow the divine will of the people to take place, as part of their eligibility as a species to enter the Galactic Confederation."

Theta looked into the crowd, taking in a breathe, then said, "A key reason why the Light Forces initially allowed this is, as you all know, was the threats to obliterate humanity and Earth if we were to intercede on their behalf. Our Intel confirmed the massive amounts of explosive devices throughout the various bandwidths of Earth, which we took as fair warning that "they" would do what they intended if we should try to intervene. So we all were made to watch, on standby."

She took another deep breath and said, "But now that has all changed. All bets are off, and it is time for action. Since the destruction of the flux tubes, Earth has not been able to maintain its natural orbit and its frequency."

She pulled up a graphic to illustrate. "These things," she pointed to the graph of the orbit of Earth, "have been artificially maintained for some time now."

"Many of our warriors of light have since been called to incarnate into the 3D bandwidth of Earth in the hopes of being able to dismantle the key facilities which have been holding the quarantine on Earth in place. These places are numerous and spread out all over the planetary surface as well as the inner layers and off-world locations as well."

Theta used a projection from a device she held in her hand to throw an image into the air above the heads of all within the room.

"This facility here, located in the third dimension of Earth, in the 3rd density, on Long Island, NY, has been one of the darkest sources of power for the chaotics. A facility there has been maintained with the help of the Reptilian-Draconian elites for a very long time, and now, as of a week ago, the light forces infiltrated their stronghold and were able to liberate untold numbers of humans, who had been incarcerated with the goal of experimentation and mind control. These victims suffered untold torture and have now been taken off-world within the healing crafts, where they are receiving the mind and body healing that our master healers can provide."

She saw the looks on the face of everyone present in the room and continued. "These are some of the worst atrocities to ever happen on any star system, here in this location."

She turned off the hologram and held her head down with her hands crossed and looked at her feet, trying to gather the words to say. "To put it bluntly, this is the proverbial time of the Apocalypse."

Sounds were heard throughout the room. The Galactic Agent walked around the podium and continued, "Apocalypse, as in, the great unveiling of the divine purpose of every man, woman, and child." She smiled, happy that the word caught the audience's attention.

She continued, "The ancients are watching. We are in a time of great myth and legends, coming full circle into the reality of the human beings on Earth, whose veiled forgetfulness will surely be penetrated. We must be vigilant now."

She walked away from the podium towards the audience. "All of the good work of the Light Forces has brought us to this point. Clearing the dark-holds has given us a great advantage, but we must be mindful of what will be unleashed as the chaotics make their final stand to hold humanity captive. They have already made numerous attempts to retaliate and keep the focus away from their operations."

Theta summoned her companions to distribute the glass tablets on which held the briefing of the event. She held a glass tablet in the air, having pulled up the report.

"Take a look at this report. The attacks are mounting all over the world in retaliation for the dark force's stronghold being liberated. These attacks are for no other purpose than to cause fear. The chaotics feed on fear and low-level frequencies, so they can largely be found in areas of deprivation, such as the locale known as Paradise Lost, on the 3rd dimensional plane of Earth."

She continued the explanation, "Fear is the energy required to fuel them energetically when they attempt any large-scale war on humanity. I will give you time to read the report, but one can assume that the recent attack at PL93 is a precursor to something bigger."

She walked around the room as everyone looked through the report. She then called Shamalaine to the podium. Breacher and Bewain both had a sick feeling in their stomachs, as their loved ones, Kaialena and Tulina, were two of those "boots on the ground" light warriors amid the chaos that Theta referred too.

"Many of you know the Priestess of Colorful Strategy, Shamalaine. She comes from the Clan of Phare, one of the highly respected Clans throughout the galaxies. She is among the top Strategists in the Milky Way and Andromeda Galaxy, and we are honored to have her on our team."

"Her title suggests that she is very astute with the implementation of the Seven Rays Frequencies and Law. The color spectrum is not only healing; it also carries information. The use of color to impregnate intel into a symbol, tone, or mandala is her specialty. She will now give the report from the Strategists."

Theta moved aside and bowed her head, whisking her cape behind her back, and pulled her hair from her face. She felt a relief come over her as she had done her best to be clear in her presentation, and her mentor, Shamalaine, was at her side. The powerhouse Strategist, Shamalaine, came to the podium.

"Theta, thank you for your kind words." She bowed her head in honor and then looked to the gathered brethren.

"My love flows to each of you present in this room as we assimilate the energetics of these recent events. As Theta mentioned, we have had a critical success of the light, but with that comes retaliations until we have achieved the final Victory of the Light." She bowed her head slightly as the entire audience applauded the success of the recent event, much to the credit of the Strategists.

She continued, "Take a look at your glass tablets. You will find the design codes for the next layer of the strategies to be implemented. Each layer has a team associated with it and a timing frequency. Each group here will be involved in this next layer of the plan." She looked up to see Bewain and Breacher hovered together, speaking in low tones to one another.

"You will note the symbols that have been created for this strategy will be energetically encoded into the psi bank, the thin sheath surrounding the Earth, with all thoughts contained within it. The Mentalist and Elemental teams will work with the energetics as well as those who have been given access."

She looked at everyone in the room and continued, "The Angelic team has provided the frequency support of love from above, as this is a key emotional element of all Light Force activities. These frequency quotients are imbued in the symbols, then placed within the plasmatic fields and in other strategic locations. It is the antidote to the dark lords and their minions."

Shamalaine was now very serious, "I want you to know that we understand that many of you have loved ones now incarnated in service to Earth and that you are concerned for their well-being. We have called forth a great contingent of Guardians for all of our light warriors in service to the plan. Everyone has an assigned Guardian, and to the best of their ability, the Life Bearers will be protected." She looked directly at Breacher and then to Bewain, and then many of the others in the room who she knew had family members in the 3rd-dimensional bandwidth.

"Please take a look at the strategy and discuss the plan with those in your groups. If you have any need for clarification, we will be here for the remainder of the allotted time to give support." With that, Shamalaine left the podium and greeted her husband in a more heart-filled way.

"Commander Breacher, if you would excuse us for a moment, I need to update Commander Bewain on a few specifics before the two of you proceed to your crafts." She smiled as he knew that she must maintain the official persona as a Strategist in these meetings, and not as family members.

Shamalaine nudged Bewain to follow her to the table where the Strategists and Theta were in conversation.

"Theta, I would like to introduce you to my partner, Commander Bewain, the father of our two daughters, Kaialena and Tulina; two of the Life Bearers serving on 3D Earth at this time."

Bewain's massive hand lifted to his heart. He bowed his head to Theta and said, "It is an honor to meet you."

Theta responded, "Commander, the honor is all mine. I have been keeping up with your daughter's missions with great interest. The Watchers have kept us abreast of their efforts to find the other Life Bearers, and we have great hopes that they will all be united soon. We have only one Life Bearer who has not quite awakened to her mission as of yet, but Shamalaine assures me that this will soon be remedied." Theta looked at Shamalaine with an impressed look upon her face.

Bewain turned to Shamalaine to see her smiling, "That is what I wanted to speak to you about." Shamalaine then bowed to Theta. She excused herself and Bewain so that she could find a private place to speak to him.

They took an elevator up to an observatory room, where they could be alone. Bewain was joyous to have a few moments alone to hold his wife. They held hands as Shamalaine escorted him to a railing where they could view the entire region of the Galaxy.

Bewain held her from behind as they stood staring into the dark sea of space. Shamalaine said, "They will be fine."

She turned to look at Bewain, and he asked, "How can you be so sure? They are going to be prime targets now. The Treaty had put in place the safety of our two beloved daughters, but now that the forces of darkness have negated the Treaty, this means that all protections in place are null and void.

Shamalaine said, "Not when your father is an amazing Guardian." She winked at him as she watched the expression on his face.

"Do you mean…?" he hesitated even to say what he was hoping.

"Yes, you have been given clearance to enter the Earth zone by Commander Ashtar himself. His ship is equipped to handle tactical assignments, and you are being given the assignment of lead Guardian over all of the Life Bearers temporarily. We are finalizing the other Guardians as we speak, but who better to watch over them, for now, than you, my love?"

Bewain grabbed Shamalaine in his arms and held her for a deep embrace. He longed for this war to be over and to have all of his family of light with him. He pulled away slightly from Shamalaine and said, "You are the most unselfish being that I have ever encountered. Your love and wisdom have shone through brilliantly today, and it reminds me of how lucky I am to be your chosen one."

He touched her face, memorizing her shining eyes, her pointed ears, and how her hair fell over her shoulders. "I will miss you, my love."

Shamalaine said, "I will pop in from time to time for the adjustments, but just know that with you being there, with our daughters." Her voice trailed off, and she looked away for a moment to wipe away a tear from her eye, then composed herself and continued, "I'm sorry, I don't have my shell with me." She let out a stressed laugh as Bewain wiped the final tear from her cheek.

She said, "My love, with you there with our daughters, I will be able to rest, knowing that they will be successful. I am working on an issue with one of the Life Bearers now, but hopefully, it will be resolved soon. So please know that we will get through this. The Clan of Phare has survived for eons of time and through many hardships."

She hesitated slightly, then with a determined affirmation, she patted her hands on his massive chest and said, "We survive!"

That was her cue to him to be extremely cautious, and he got it loud and clear.

"Here." She took his jacket lapel into her hand and placed upon it a golden pin that she had made, especially for him.

"What is this?" he asked as he tried to see what she had pinned upon his chest.

Smiling, she said, "They are runes of protection. It is my way of knowing where you are. Here is one for Breacher as well. " She turned once more to look out the observation window as Bewain held her tight from behind.

She then faced Bewain, and with all the will left within her, she said, "Soldier... prepare for the mission." She saluted him, and they hugged one another one last time and walked back to the elevator.

Breacher was looking for Bewain as the two came out of the elevator. "Commander Bewain, may we speak?"

The two Commanders bid Shamalaine goodbye and walked to their table to gather their pads. Breacher had read about the attacks at crucial locations on Earth that had once been vortexes of light held by the divine feminine and had over time been usurped and radically changed into Babylonian chaotic nodes. "This madness has to stop!" Breacher began.

Bewain put his hand upon Breacher's shoulder, placing the lapel pin upon it and said, "That is the plan. Come. Follow me on my craft. I will give you an update."

Breacher's usually calm demeanor was rattled when he learned that the Treaty was now null and void and that his beloved Kaialena and the other Life Bearers would soon be in even more danger than they already had been.

And the wheel turns...

Chapter 59

A Close Call Near Rodney Gardens

Bridgit, Stella, and the others left the pub in the twilight to see Rodney Gardens before dark. Bridgit and Stella were trailing behind the others after Stella stopped to read a flyer in the pub window about a lawn concert featuring a harpist. Smiling with delight, the two girls attempted to cross the street in front of the pub when a black SUV peeled out at the block corner and was heading straight for them.

Suddenly from out of nowhere, a dark red-headed, muscular man called out to the ladies, "Look out!" He had exited his vehicle parked on the other side of the road and saw the SUV coming as he ran to get the ladies off the street. Instinctively he grabbed the two girls, lifting them back to the sidewalk, just moments before the SUV barreled through.

He gently let go of their arms and asked, "Are ya okay there, Lassies?"

"What just happened?" Stella quizzed.

The gentleman said, "My instincts kicked in when I saw that the vehicle wasn't stopping. I am sorry to have caused a scare, Miss. May I escort you both across the street? I would feel better if you would allow me to be your buffer."

Bridgit was shaking her head in disbelief of the episode that just transpired and also as she stared at this man who saved them, feeling a familiarity with his energy. She had a sensation that it was Bewain, but if it was, he had shapeshifted into the form of a Scottish muscle man.

She said, "Thank you so much. I don't even want to think about what might have just happened. The traffic seemed so calm earlier, and all of a sudden, it feels a bit chaotic now. Wouldn't you agree, Stella?" She grabbed Stella's arm as the gentleman grabbed Stella's other arm, escorting the two ladies across the road.

The others in the group ran over to the girls as they had managed to cross safely just moments before. Stella looked at Bridgit and showed her the hair standing on her arms. "Bridgit, from now on, we need to be on red alert."

Bridgit shook it off and internalized the feeling that they were targeted. Their new friends did not realize the extent of what just happened, thinking it was just a freak thing with a drunk driver, but Stella's intuition knew that it was more.

Bridgit looked back to the gentleman who saved them. He made a funny gesture with his hand put behind his back, and his head bowed to her. He jumped back in his car and drove off, leaving Bridgit with the feeling that it was indeed Bewain in disguise. She wondered why on Earth would Bewain be in the third-density watching over them unless they were truly in danger. She was silent as they all walked towards the park.

After a few minutes of fast walking to move the energy, they converged on Rodney Gardens. On the way, Freya spoke of her recent visit to Findhorn, located to the northeast of Inverness, where she studied the influence of the Elementals on the growth of a plant.

Bridgit and Stella knew that this was leading somewhere, with the potential of Freya being one of the people that they had hopes of finding. She was speaking their language.

Freya explained that it was at Findhorn that the Angels and Elementals would communicate with the humans and inspire them in the garden. "They had great success in very unsuitable soil, and this gathered much attention to the small community," she said.

As Freya concluded her inspiring talk, they came upon Benjamin Sky in the park, an attendee of the conference. David greeted him, "Benjamin! I see you found one of the pristine places in Perth."

He put out his hand to shake Benjamin's. He noticed his hand was trembling. His coloring was a bit off as well. "You okay, mate?" David peered into his eyes to see his pupils.

"Yeah, I think so. I just had the strangest thing happen as I left the hotel to walk here. A guy in an SUV almost ran me down as I was heading this way." David looked at Bridgit, and the whole group began pondering the situation.

David asked, "Was it a black SUV?"

Nodding his head, Benjamin said, "Yeah, it was! I just had this feeling like I wasn't safe walking on the street, and at that moment, I jumped onto the brick planter along the sidewalk, and just as I did, the SUV screeched past me, just where I had been walking moments before."

He raised his hand to point in the direction of the pub and said, "It just kept flying by and turned toward the direction you just came from." Bridgit listened intently and picked up that he acted upon his intuition. Everyone gathered around him and explained what had just happened to Bridgit and Stella. They all needed to ground their energy in nature, and thankfully Rodney Gardens was just the place.

Benjamin was grateful for the company and was ready to relax within the confines of the garden. Juel Ryland had the same thought. She was another attendee at the conference and found her way to the garden after the first day's activities. Freya waved to her, as Juel sat nearby with pencils and a notepad, sketching some of the foliage. She waved backed and watched the group enter the gardens.

Juel's dark black hair flowed in ringlets, with a large scarf that wrapped around her head, tied at the nape of her neck. She was a striking and youthful African American woman from Arizona, and was recently in Scotland, studying at Findhorn. She and Freya met there for the first time, and it was Freya who mentioned the conference and helped her get registered with David.

As they entered the garden, Benjamin thought he saw something strange lurking in the tree line. "Did anyone just see that?" He pointed towards the trees straight ahead. No one else saw anything, but they all had a feeling of being watched.

As the group walked further into the area, they gathered next to a large garden that had circular plant beds placed in a geometric pattern. The thick concrete shaped beds created a ledge for them to stand. They decided to each stand on one of the raised beds intending to connect their energy to the Earth and then combine it as one. This was a technique that was discussed earlier in one of the conference presentations, and they all felt the need to gather their energy tightly as one strong presence.

Freya asked if she could invite Juel over, and with everyone's agreement, she went over to see if she wanted to join them for an evening meditation under the stars. Juel gathered her things and thanked Freya for including her. They walked back over to the group, and Freya made the introductions, "Hey everyone, this is Juel! We met at Findhorn. Juel thought the conference sounded like something she would be into, so I encouraged her to come!"

Juel was sweetly shy. She smiled and lifted her hand in a small wave while coming into the crowd of people. "Hello, everyone." Juel looked at them with a childlike grin. She had a natural quality that everyone could feel, which made her a bit mysterious.

David said, "Juel, it is so good to see you here. I haven't had time to check in with you. I do try to get to know the attendees of these programs. Please forgive me if I seemed out of sorts earlier. A lot has been happening." He didn't want to go into it all, so he just nodded awkwardly and let it be.

Juel smiled, "That is totally cool, David. No worries here." David reached down to help her up to the two-foot-tall ledge. She took her place on the edge of the planter wall where David was standing, and he moved to another spot.

It was getting close to dark at this point, and the first stars were seen shining in the sky. Benjamin stood in the middle circle of the garden beds and quietly whispered, "Over there...there it is. It's a faun! I knew I saw something earlier!"

As soon as everyone turned in the direction of the trees, a green superluminal light glowed from behind a tree. Tabor came forward. Bridgit knew exactly who this faun was. She placed her hand over her heart and said, "It's okay. He is a friend." This hushed the group as they watched Tabor advance slightly.

Benjamin smiled, feeling his gentleness. Everyone focused on Tabor with wide eyes so as not to blink and miss it.

Tabor spoke, "This day is a celebration in the realms of the fae. The beginning of a new anthropogenic cycle is upon us. One where humans have a positive effect on nature, rather than the harmful effects of times past."

He pointed upward, "Look up to the heavens for your celestial codes...we have been waiting for you." His superluminal green force shot out into the night sky like cupid's arrow. The energy catapulted into the sky in the direction of URSA, the Great Bear. The light from the luminous arrow lifted their attention to a craft hovering just above their heads.

The group heard one last thing before all went dark, "Please drink from the celestial chalice, our offering to you."

Suddenly the group realized that they were no longer standing on raised garden beds. They were now standing on a round floor balanced on a very long pole. This platform reached into the night sky, with each of their spirit bodies fully connected to their physical bodies back on Earth.

Everyone present couldn't help but notice the great Potina of the Praesepe star cluster, known as the Mistress of the Beehive. She held out her hand to lead them to the humongous golden chalice filled with the nectar of the Gods. She gave each a sip, and at the same time, their foreheads were anointed with honey, each offering was highly potent.

As the honey dripped over their heads, the Potina spoke, "Life Bearers... you are now affiliated with the potent energies of the Beehive. This blessing seals your auras and gives vital protective forces." As she said these words, cosmic honey continued to pour over their etheric body, and the words golden child reverberated in each of the ears and hearts of the brothers and sisters of light.

Very gently, the Life Bearer's spirits returned to their physical bodies. Their bodies were no longer standing on the raised garden beds, but laying in the round, grassy opening connected to the garden beds.

Benjamin raised his head up first and said, "What the heck just happened?!"

Bridgit gently raised her head and said, "It is okay, Benjamin. We all just experienced something amazing. Everyone back?" she checked around as Stella was rolling over on her side with big eyes saying, "WOW! WOW!"

Benjamin asked Bridgit, "Did you just get dipped in honey?"

Bridgit giggled and responded, "Well yes, Benjamin, we were all dipped in honey. You're not allergic, are you?" She patted him on his knee, acting casual, as they both sat up to inspect the rest of the group.

Bridgit then said, "Well, I can see that we are not going to get the early night that we had planned." She was trying to act casual about what just occurred. She knew that something like this could really freak out a person. Looking at her watch, she said, "It is 9:30 now."

Everyone just gasped with the time loss. Many had questions, so Bridgit encouraged them to sit up and make a circle so that she could speak with them about what just occurred.

"Well, I am thrilled to tell you that we just received an amazing gift. For some of you, you will understand what just occurred, but for most of you, this warrants a bit of an explanation."

She looked at David and Stella, smiling because clearly, they had just found a large contingent of Life Bearers.

Bridgit began a dialog with the newly found Life Bearers on what she, Stella, and David had gone through recently. She could have talked for hours, but she decided to give them what she could at that moment, knowing that everyone needed time to process.

She explained the role of a Life Bearer is a person who incarnates into 3D Earth in service, with the ability to activate the codes of creation. She shared that she was tasked to find the remaining twelve Life Bearer's, and once that is accomplished, there would be a time of preparation, which would be led by the oldest Life Bearer, known as Elder Druid Christopher.

Juel asked, "The being mentioned a new anthropogenic cycle. Can anyone explain the meaning of that word?"

David nodded and said, "The original definition of the word is meant to suggest that humans and their miscreation's have largely influenced our current geological epoch. In the sense of the word used this evening, he was commenting on the fact that gathered here are some extraordinary humans who have the intention to work with the Divine plan to assist in the new creation, in a positive and uplifting way.

Each of the men and women in the circle just kept saying, "This is unbelievable!"

Stella responded, "Ever since I met Bridgit, I have been saying those exact words. You should have been there when I first met her! There is really no sane way to explain any of this. You just have to dig down deep and ask yourself one key question, and that is, what am I born to do?" She looked around, and each of them was nodding their heads in somewhat of an understanding way.

Juel and Freya were whispering, and then Freya said, "Stella, I thought that you and Bridgit were cousins? It sounds like you have only just met?"

Stella responded with a bit of trepidation for opening up that point. "Well, Freya, we actually did just meet...recently! That is a long story, but I am sure we can talk about it later." Stella didn't want to completely freak out the group just yet, so she lobbed the conversation back over to Bridgit.

"Okay. We have a lot to talk about, but given the time, let's do this. Why don't we call it a night? Get some sleep, and all of us can reconvene tomorrow night after the conclusion of the conference. We need to have at least a few hours together tomorrow so that I can give you more of the details because it will affect your future plans. Stella and David can help answer your questions as well because now that we have been anointed, it looks as if you all have been chosen for something amazing, and you will have some major decisions to make."

Stella chimed in, "Like lifestyle choices!"

Ashneer had an ah-ha moment, even though he still did not quite know what was happening. He said, "Now I see why I was drawn to let my lease go this last week. Something in me just knew my life was going to change, and it felt drastic enough that I knew not to recommit to a year lease. Wow..., I just can't believe what is happening!"

He was stunned and happy at the same time. "It all makes sense somehow. The dreams that I have been having had been pointing to something otherworldly for some time, but I didn't have any way to understand them until now."

"Wow, Koko! That is amazing! Especially that you went with your intuition, even when there were no outward signs of a change yet! Way to listen!" Ursula patted Ashneer on the back and Stella reached over and gave him a high five, only she called it a Cinco!

Everyone was laughing as Stella shared her need to make slight changes in what is currently hip to say. "Cinco just has a different sound, and I love it!" She teased.

Benjamin laughingly replied, "Why didn't I think of that!? Especially because I am Latino!"

The mood suddenly shifted from happy to serious once more as Bridgit and Stella noticed Freya's demeanor.

Freya, still looking upward, was trying to find a remnant of the green glow and kept chanting words of gratitude. Tears rolled down her face as she kept wiping them away with her sleeve.

She said, "I am forever grateful that I listened to that inner voice too. I chose to do this conference in the middle of so many other things that I should have been doing. I don't understand it all just yet, but like you, Koko, my life is at a crucial point of decision. I want to hear more from you all before I choose, but that really is just a formality now isn't it!"

Freya laughed as her spirit seemed to be in control of her outer world. She liked to think that she had a choice in the matter but knew she had already decided in her heart. She threw her hands over her face and silently chuckled the words, "What is happening!?" The group all had mixed reactions as they continued to ponder the situation.

Bridgit looked at the other two, Ursula and Ford. She watched as they were hugging one another.

She said, "What do the two of you think?" She placed her hand on Ursula's back for support and comfort. Ursula smiled as she felt Bridgit's energy penetrate her body.

Ford spoke first, "Bridgit, I knew the moment I saw you that there was magic afoot. I didn't tell you then, nor you, David," he glanced David's way with a smile and continued.

"I have had many dreams in the last few weeks leading up to this conference. They revolved around a series of adventures to various stone cairns, the ones with the triangular puck marks that I presented at the conference." He looked at David, smiling so that it was clear that there was a deeper reason for him to shift his speech to this topic at the last minute.

"Bridgit, you were in those dreams!" Ford looked at her and then pulled Ursula close to him with such deep love. The two of them stared into one another's eyes, and then Ford looked back to the group. "I had shared with Ursula that since having the dreams, I felt like we were about to have a major change in our lives. We put our home up for sale just before we arrived here."

Bridgit smiled at Ford and then at Stella with such a relief on her face and said, "Every time I think something is without a doubt an impossible task, something like this happens."

She put her hands together like a prayer and said to each one of the Life Bearers, "I am deeply honored to know every one of you. We have been brought together for a mission that is of the utmost importance. Know that I will share the details of the mission as I know them with you all tomorrow, but for now, I feel that so much has already been said, and we are full."

She paused and continued by saying, "We all need deep rest for the next part of this story to unfold. Shall we go back?"

David jumped up and reached to grab Freya's hand as she reluctantly lifted her body off the ground of this sacred garden. Each of them hugged one another.

Benjamin had the largest smile of all, having not felt attached to anything in such a long time, and now, all of his intuition paid off. He reached for Bridgit's arm to say thank you.

She turned, and they bowed to one another and then to Stella, and he said, "My life now makes perfect sense, something that I have never had before. The joy of this evening will sustain me all of my days!"

They each nodded to one another in recognition of the purity of the moment and walked back to the hotel in complete silence.

And the wheel turns...

Chapter 60

The Dreamtime of the Life Bearers

Stella floated out of her body that night. Her energy body still glowing with the golden elixir from the Potina of the Beehive. She located her soul's essence in a dream within a 5th dimensional pocket of time, where she was living another life parallel to this one. She was still in college in a different area of the country, unfamiliar to her.

In the dream, Stella was in the living room of a shared community dorm. She was in the middle of taking a strange device apart when a roommate came into the shared quarters. Stella looked up and took note that the room had two of everything, a mirrored reality, with two sofas, two desks, and so on. The roommate sat down at the desk that butted up to Stella's, watching Stella tinker with the object. She said, "You do know that we have a paper due on Monday, don't you?" She looked at Stella's confused look and continued, "You weren't in class on Friday, were you?"

Stella was lucid in the dream and knew that this was not her timeline, but played it cool and just answered, "Ah, no! I didn't make it to class on Friday. I had something come up. I totally forgot to ask if there was something assigned?"

She put her device down and grabbed a piece of paper so that she could write down the assignment. The roommate held up a newspaper that had a full article above the fold, with a large picture attached and a headline that read, "ETIFAH and THE BLUE PEOPLE."

Stella leaned forward to focus on the newspaper, trying desperately to get more clues as she knew this was important, but the paper went blurry, and the dream suddenly ended.

Stella woke up, back in the hotel room, hearing the alarm going off on her phone. Bridgit was in the shower as Stella recalled how the stranger back at the Inn had told them to say the word Etifah when activating the striking stones at the time of the jump. She reached over to grab her phone and wrote the words Etifah and the blue people in her note's application, then laid there trying to retrieve more of the dream and the significance of name Etifah.

Within another room at the hotel, Benjamin was dreaming the same dream that reoccurred over the past five years. It always started with an SOS call to his starship. In the dream, he always went by the name Captain Skyword, whose role was that of an interpreter of Galactic Languages within the Skyway Patrol. When the SOS calls came in, he would determine the origin and send the communications to the Skyway Patrol in the region, to give support to the light forces.

This dream had a new component. Benjamin, as Captain Skyword, was sent out on a mission to rescue a stranded mining cruiser. Captain Skyword's ability to translate languages was enhanced by a device that held a replica of the eye of Horus. He could locate and communicate with anyone with the simplicity of an intention.

He maneuvered his craft in a range close enough to the stranded ship and beamed the passengers aboard his craft. All five crew members were blue semi-transparent beings with small triangular structures coming out their foreheads at various angles.

They were very tall beings of pure love and joyously accepted Captain Skyword's assistance in contacting their primary craft. Captain Skyword began making the precise coordinates to bring these blue beings to their mother craft when the scene shifted from a rescue mission to a direct communication from his soul group. One of the blue beings spoke, "We depend on your codes to rescue humanity. Your calculations must be precise for the containment field, or else risk the annihilation of the species."

Benjamin's wake-up call from the lobby rang loudly in his room just as the message was being given. Benjamin ignored the ringing phone and grabbed his pad of paper, writing the words down before he lost them in the loudness of the new day.

Each time that Benjamin had this dream, he would wake up sweating and experienced the feeling of foreboding, not understanding the meaning until now. This morning, he finally had insight into the meaning and looked forward to hearing more from the others about what a Life Bearer was.

Across the hall and down the corridor, another Life Bearer awoke from the most vivid of dreams as well, this time it was Freya. She held her eyes shut, trying not to let the dream fade. In the dream, she stood watch over portals and vortexes of light. As a Portal Guardian, her role in the astral realms was to make sure that darkness did not enter the realms of man.

She saw herself holding a golden-hued torch, lighting the keyholes to the doorways. The portal doors were hexagon-shaped and were stacked one on top of another just like a beehive. A golden light surrounded each hexagon, which provided a coating or thin veil that would not let anything pass through it unless it was a vibrational match.

Freya began to stir and tried desperately to recall anything else from the dream while keeping her eyes closed. In her inner voice, she heard the words, "I AM a door for good, only good has access here." This was the mantra that her higher aspect chanted as she stood watch at the intersection of time and space.

397

As Freya laid there thinking, she saw an orb zip by in her mind's eye. She tried to focus but then felt a shift in the room. As she opened her physical eyes, she saw an orb of light exiting the window of her hotel room.

Freya jumped up to see if she could glimpse its ascent into the sky, but she could not find it anywhere. She did see Bridgit walking away from the hotel, so she quickly showered, dressed, and made her way downstairs, excited to see if the others had dreamt as well.

And the wheel turns...

Chapter 61

The Conclusion of the Geomancy Conference

One by one, the anointed group from the night before, began to enter the lobby. Bridgit returned from a walk, which she did to formulate in her mind how she was to proceed. She was contemplating the responsibility that was squarely on her shoulders and the fact that she was not at all sure how these people would react when she presents them with the mission at hand and what it will mean for them. She tried to call Christopher to get some advice, but he was not answering his phone.

Bridgit walked through the front lobby doors to see all of the Life Bearers there waiting for her. Stella had been trying to hold off answering their many questions until Bridgit had arrived.

She walked up to David, who had his head buried in paperwork for the closeout of the conference. He was in business mode and needed to complete this event before he could focus on the mission at hand.

He looked up as Bridgit approached his table in the bar. He smiled and stood up to greet her. "Bridgit, good morning. Might we have a word?" he pulled her towards him. They walked past the attendees who were crowding into the conference hall. They made their way outside through a side door, and David spoke swiftly.

"I really cannot think straight with all of the happenings of last night as I am attempting to formulate even a sentence this morning and I present my subject matter in ten minutes!" He threw his hands up in the air and then combed his fingers through his hair several times. As he flailed his arms about, Bridgit noticed that David was wearing the pendant.

"Hmm... Might I suggest something?" She smiled as she reached for his pendant and began lifting it over his head.

He was clearly not himself and didn't realize that she was removing it. He was computing all of the variables of the talk, the things that had happened at the gardens, the alignment of the stars, and if he had, in fact, remembered to have someone watch over his garden while he was away. All of these thoughts tumbled in his brain without him being able to focus on any of the threads of thought.

Bridgit stood back and watched his demeanor relax once the pendant was off. She watched David pat his chest with relief, and then he realized that she took the pendant from him.

"I think I should hold onto the pendants until mission time, don't you agree?" Smiling, Bridgit patted David's shoulder and asked, "Now, what is it that has you concerned about your talk?"

David placed his hand on his throat. He coughed, then said, "I think after last night's event, it hit home to me that this mission is a huge deal. I was up all night contemplating the consequences of the mission. What happens if we don't make it to the jump points? What happens if a Life Bearer doesn't agree to do it? What happens..."

Bridgit touched his chest and calmed him immediately.

"Listen, I do appreciate your attention to detail, but I feel that it is best to see how things unfold before we begin to fret about something that has not happened. I know that you like to plan, to strategize, but I don't think we can do that at this point. Let's check in with the others and make a plan to gather back at the park after the conference is over."

Bridgit smiled at David, but in her mind, she was as freaked out as David, knowing that it was her role to gather the people and get to the jump points. She knew the details of the jump point locations would be revealed, but time was ticking.

David wiped his brow, and with his lips pursed like a man about to play an instrument, he blew upward. His hair fluttered over his forehead and then fell over to the side of his head.

"Yes...yes, you are right. One worry at a time." He smiled and reached for the door and escorted Bridgit back into the conference hall, where all of the attendees had begun to gather, finding their seats.

Bridgit grinned and nodded, then silently reminded herself to breathe. At that moment, there was a feeling of urgency once more, like a wave delivering a telegram. It said, "Be ready."

Bridgit located Stella and the others within the conference hall. They watched David compose himself and commence speaking on the most astounding topic.

He started his speech by saying, "I contemplate many things in nature, and one of my favorite things to contemplate is stars that throb." David made air quotes after the word throb, with a cheeky grin, and the audience was in an uproar over his dry wit. He spoke about the connection of the celestial bodies to the landscape and its effects in nature.

Stella jabbed Bridgit in the side with her elbow and said, "I am constantly amazed by that guy. Everything okay?" Stella was picking up on Bridgit's freak out vibes by the way she was pulling on her fingers. Bridgit had a nervous habit of working her finger knuckles when she was stressed. Someone had once mentioned to her that it was a quick way to relieve tension, and Bridgit found it to be true most of the time.

Bridgit leaned in and told Stella unconvincingly, "Everything is great. We will all meet at the park after the conference is over, and we will figure out our next step."

Stella knew that it was incredibly hard on Bridgit to be a leader of a mission that was so elusive. She pondered on the personalities that had all come together, which made her shake her head in amazement. All extraordinary people, she thought, and she was so proud of Bridgit and David.

As she listened to David speak about pendulums and elemental forces in nature, Stella thought once more about the blue people. She listened with delight to hear David's perspective on nature, but Etifah and the blue people were ever-present in her thoughts.

The time went swiftly. David informed and entertained the crowd with his intelligence and wit. Soon after, the conference concluded. For David, it was a highlight of his hobby career, even though the conference topics were a side interest, rather than relating to his work as an astrophysicist, he did manage to sneak in a bit about stars.

He realized as he looked out in the audience during his talk, that he had brought together a large contingent of Life Bearers without it being the intention. Even so, he was quite proud of his accomplishments, as was Elder Druid Christopher, when David called him early that morning to share with him the events that had taken place the night before.

The participants gathered their belongings and made their way to the front lobby to say their goodbyes as the presenters gathered their materials and began the arduous task of taking down the equipment.

Bridgit and Stella offered to help David, but as there were already plenty of people on hand, he insisted that they go out for a cuppa and gather their thoughts for the meeting later.

Bridgit was relieved to be excused, and the ladies did go on a search for a cuppa. Bridgit knew just the place. She had found a quaint coffee shop a few blocks away that had cozy, overstuffed chairs and soulful music playing in the background.

"Let's get out of here." Bridgit winked at Stella then bolted towards the door. Stella could barely keep up with her long-legged cousin as they made a swift exit out the side door. The walk was quick, as Bridgit was on a mission.

Once the ladies made it to the café, they ordered lattes and eased into the overstuffed chairs to contemplate what was next. Stella took on the role of hostess and gathered the accouterments while Bridgit stared at her hands, rubbing her knuckles once more.

Stella returned with the lattes and fixings. She sat them down on the coffee table and assisted Bridgit quietly by placing a napkin on her knee and offering her a spoon and sugar without a word spoken.

Bridgit smiled and came out of her inner world to receive the beverage and thanked Stella with a soft word of gratitude and a nodding head. She looked into her cup, mesmerized by the froth puddled over the decadent smell of a dark roast.

Bridgit often would lose herself in these moments of in-between. That place of silence when one prepares their lips for the heat of the first sip of a long sought after cup of coffee. Bridgit stared into her cup a bit longer than usual, as if reading her future, then drank it ever so slowly to remember its exact flavor, scent, and feeling as it went down her throat.

Stella had sat down, quietly drinking her latte and observing Bridgit. Stella reflected on Bridgit being a MOMENT kind of gal. She smiled at the sweetness of Bridgit being so enthralled with her latte, but as time lingered, it bored her. Stella did not know what to say or do, so she blurted, "What would Shamalaine do?", then chuckled at Bridgit's response.

Bridgit's eyelashes batted a few times, trying to compute what Stella had just said. She looked at Stella, who was beaming an angelic smile.

Stella said, "You know... I have been thinking. Shamalaine has seemingly been with you or us this whole time. She sent Breacher to you as an olive branch, and I know she is monitoring us now. I can just feel it!"

She leaned into Bridgit, while putting her cup on the table and asked again, "So, what would Shamalaine do?"

Bridgit was so calm as if her body was coming down from an adrenaline rush. She sipped her drink once more and leaned in towards Stella as she placed her cup down and said, "Thank you! My, my! You know how to get me." She smiled at Stella with gratitude.

"I do?" Stella quizzed with delight.

"Yes, you do." Bridgit rubbed her face, especially her eyes, to wipe away the blinders metaphorically.

"I had forgotten who we are! We are the chosen Life Bearers! We have come back to hold the light on this blessed planet and to provide the pathway for all of humanity to enter the new time, right here on Earth!" Bridgit sat back in her chair, which looked to be swallowing her torso, but her long legs made it out of the mouth of the chair, as Stella watched Bridgit's left leg swing over to land on the knee of her right leg.

Stella chuckled at Bridgit's lack of gracefulness, and at that moment, she noticed the imprint on the bottom of Bridgit's shoe. It was an arrow. Stella had a thing when she saw an arrow as if it was a sign from the Angels. She always looked in the direction of the arrow presented. Stella turned her head away from Bridgit, looking for something unusual.

Bridgit reverted into deep thought again, now about Shamalaine, remembering what she had learned about the mission and, in particular, contemplating that the Builders of Form and the Blueprint Masters were concurrently working towards uniting with them at the jump points. She went to speak but found that Stella had left her seat altogether and was standing in front of a picture hanging on the wall behind them.

"What is it?" Bridgit asked as she came around the left side of Stella only to see for herself what it was. Stella stood in disbelief, and without moving her head away from the picture, she said, "The Triumph of Eternity!" Stella reached out to touch the replica, mounted in a flat, simple wooden frame.

Bridgit could see it meant more to Stella than meets the eye.

Stella turned to look at Bridgit and said, "Did you know that you have an arrow on the bottom of your shoe?"

Bridgit looked down at her feet, confused as to what her shoes had to do with the picture hanging on the wall of the café. Her eyes spoke the question without having to speak it out loud.

Stella placed her hands over her heart in a prayerful manner and said, "Blessed Be." She inhaled at that moment, with her eyes closed, to give a silent prayer of gratitude for being led to the picture on the wall by the arrow-shaped traction on the sole of Bridgit's shoe.

Once she gathered her thoughts, she opened her eyes. Bridgit could see the pooling of tears in Stella's eyes and placed her hand upon Stella's shoulder. "You alright?"

"Hmm. Yes. I am perfect." She wiped her tear and said, "Come on. Let's sit back down. I want to tell you about this picture." The ladies sat back in their seats and had another sip of their lattes. Stella began to share her understanding of the meaning of the picture hanging behind them, especially as they were contemplating the mission.

"This picture is in my Dad's study. Right now, at my home." She pointed to it again, trying to convince Bridgit of this truth, pausing to look at it one more time. She turned back to Bridgit and continued.

"It is the last of six plates in a series known as The Triumphs of Petrarch. This one is the one known as The Triumph of Eternity." She smiled and shared the synchronicity of the moment.

"While I sat here watching you stew over what to do next, I felt Shamalaine strongly. You fell backward into the seat and threw your leg over your knee, and that is when I saw the bottom of your shoe. The arrow caught my attention, and I turned to see what was in the path of the arrow, as I always do, and there it was!"

Bridgit smiled, admiring the ways that Stella interpreted her surroundings.

Stella continued, "This picture is in my father's study because it gave him hope after losing my mom."

Stella thought about the plates and mentioned, "Petrarch tracks the stages of life in each of the six plates. There is a verse in a poem by Petrarch, that speaks about time, among other things, but I remember it because it was one of the passages that my Dad would quote on occasion. It goes something like time not being broken into segments, there will be no more seasons and that all would be one. No more TIME!"

Stella looked at Bridgit intently as she recalled the final line that her Dad would say, "And all the world would transform!" She turned back around to look at the picture once more. "I think we are in that time!" Stella announced.

Bridgit felt the words so strongly that all of the hair on her body stood up, and she, too, was now mesmerized by the picture and the meaning of it in this particular moment. "You constantly amaze me, Stella."

Bridgit gave her a gentle nudge and said, "I can't thank you enough for coming with me. And not just here! I mean, thank you for incarnating with me. Clearly, as you stated earlier, we are being guided, and this picture tells me that we will be victorious. Now, all we need to do is find the stragglers!"

She laughed with the thought of it and continued, "I know that this sounds far-fetched, but so far, the Life Bearers have shown up on time, and at this point, we need to trust that the last three will be arriving soon too."

With that, Bridgit rose from her seat, dusted off her pants legs, and within her heart, had a renewed sense of purpose. She smiled at Stella and asked, "You ready to walk back? Maybe we can look up more information about that picture back in the room? I want to see exactly what these Triumphs are." Bridgit was energized once more and beaming with hope.

Stella sipped her latte down, jumped up and was ready to do more sleuthing, and glad to see Bridgit had returned to her more self-assured demeanor.

And the wheel turns...

Chapter 62

Back at Rodney Gardens

A few hours later, the team reunited at the park. They decided to walk a little further to an area that was private with views of the River Tay. David had stayed behind long enough to complete the checkout process for those that attended the conference. He wanted to personally say goodbye to all the attendees and the other presenters.

Stella had a hunch that David was delayed, so she pulled out her phone to call the hotel. She left a message for David as to where they had decided to meet since the plan had changed.

David completed his goodbyes and had found a small table in the bar to the left of the hotel's lobby entry. He kept watching the door as he filed his papers into an expandable file folder. A hotel registrar walked over to give David the phone message from Stella. He looked at it, happy to know where to find them when Druid Christopher walked into the lobby. Christopher took off his fedora and scanned the room for David. He cleared his throat in David's direction.

David jumped up, and in less than three giant steps, stood next to his mentor in the lobby, extending his hand to greet him.

"Elder, I am happy to see you!" David said with a deep relief now that Christopher had arrived.

"Yes, lad, once you shared that there had been movement, I was keen to come to make introductions. Where are the others?" Christopher looked around the lobby.

David replied with his hand waving towards the door, "Oh, they took a walk towards the Gardens. I just received a message from Stella that they found a private sitting area along the River. Shall we go join them."

"Yes, lets." Christopher placed his fedora back upon his head as they walked out the door.

"I'll fetch Pearl. Won't be a moment." David bounded off across the street and jumped into Pearl. Christopher assessed the energy of the area as he watched David drive down the road and make a U-turn. The white, tiny chariot pulled up in front of the hotel in no time. David jumped out to assist Christopher into the front seat.

Merrily, yet nervously, David drove Christopher to the location of the Life Bearers. From their phone conversation earlier that morning, David had explained the fact that they had found a handful of Life Bearers, and he gave a vague description of the stone pendants that had materialized just before they had left Aberdeen for Perth.

David only had time to give Christopher the bare-bones version of the anointing that took place the last evening when they drove past the area where the Life Bearers sat. David pulled over to the side of the road and assisted Christopher out of the vehicle. Stella ran over to greet them and wrapped her arms around her Great Uncle as they walked to the group.

"I wish we would have known you were coming!" said Stella.

He grinned at her and responded, "I like to be spontaneous." His eyes twinkled with mischief as Stella inwardly thought of how she was starting to really adore this man.

Bridgit stood to greet Christopher, her hands to her heart. She bowed to him in gratitude as his presence relieved her in ways she had not felt in such a long time. The way of a father's presence.

Christopher walked up to Bridgit and kissed her cheek. "Hello Dear. I hear we have a few more members to our team!" The other Life Bearers stood as David jumped in to do the introductions.

Christopher was pleased to make the acquaintance of the handful of people who were now family to one another.

He spoke, "Well, we have some explaining to do it seems, and I couldn't possibly dream of leaving it all to these three and let them have all of the fun, now could I?" Christopher held onto Bridgit in a side hug and motioned for Stella to come to his other side.

"These two lovely ladies are my grand nieces, from separate fathers, which were both my brother's sons." He smiled, enjoying the confused looks on the faces of some of the Life Bearers.

He continued, "The recent chain of events has all the indicators of the reunion of those from the stars. Those who have been called here to this most beautiful planet to help Earth and its people move into the higher frequencies. That which is called the Golden Age, and you, my friends, are those star-seeded ones known as Life Bearers."

He looked for a spot to sit down, with the assistance of Bridgit and Stella. They were both surprised at his swiftness to settle in. He rested his fedora next to him and pulled out his pipe, asking if anyone had objections. He made small talk assuring them that he would continue his story with the first pull of the ol' pipe.

He went on, "We have seen this indicator before, by the way." He let out the smoke, from the first draw, up into rings above the heads of his dear ones. David, Stella, and Bridgit were in anticipation of what

410

he was about to unfold. Christopher began his story centered on the ancestors of the Clan of Phare.

"In the year 1900, in April, to be exact, our dear ancestor Barabell Akira Phare and her three daughters made a courageous attempt to make it to, what is known in today's term, as the jump points," he looked at Bridgit and Stella and indicated to the Life Bearers that Barabell Akira was related to the three of them.

"Barabell had three daughters and four sons, with her beloved husband, Airleas Phare, whose home I reside in to this day." He pointed in the direction of Aberdeen and mentioned that it was not that far from this location.

"Barabell and her daughters were all Life Bearers, carrying the codes of a new creation, known as creation codes of a new era of peace. Just like all of you who sit before me now." He drew another drag of smoke from his pipe and fiddled with the tobacco, punching it down a bit more with a stick lying next to him.

"In those times, innovations were in full swing. Electricity and motorized vehicles came about, to name just two. The politics were volatile, and shifts in world power were happening." He winked at those that caught his eye.

"Well, back to the Ladies Phare...in April of 1900, during the time of the Lyrid meteor showers, Barabell and her daughters received word that the jump points were ready. These jump points were specific places in time, vortices of light. When accessed by the code carriers, these portals opened the exit doors of this current creation and would allow humanity to enter into a new time-space or dimension. But not until the Life Bearers entered the void first and used the light codes of creation that they carried to assist in the creation of the new envelope or dimensional space for which humanity would be allowed to enter and live in peace."

He chuckled and said, "Yes, that about sums it up in a nutshell nicely." He took several drags from the pipe, pushing the smoke upward in a cloud above his head.

"COOL!" Benjamin blurted.

Christopher chuckled, "Yes, it is COOL." Christopher thought for a moment then asked, "Benjamin, is it?"

"Yes, sir. Sorry, I didn't mean to do that. It is just that this is awesome!"

"Ah, yes, it is quite extraordinary. I'll continue now." His eyes twinkled as he scanned the crowd.

"Barabell and her daughters left home on a fine, clear day from their home in Aberdeen, to catch a boat that would take them to the coastal town of Cornwall, where there was to be a gathering of the other Life Bearers in a place known as Merlyn's cave at Tintagel."

Ashneer now could not control himself, "TINTAGEL!!! I love that place!!"

Christopher nodded and continued, "That day became one of the saddest days in our family lineage, but please do not let this scare you. What I am about to say is in the interest of transparency as you will all have decisions to make very shortly, and I only feel it is the proper thing to tell you the whole story before you make the decision. Understood?" He looked to see if there were any concerns.

Freya and Ursula wanted to hear the story of the four women and urged him to go on.

"On that fateful day, the Ladies Phare boarded a ship to carry them to Cornwall. The tides were calm. It should not have been anything other than a delightful sail. Just before they arrived at the outer coastline of Cornwall, a freak storm occurred literally out of nowhere. There were no winds before this, no build-up. The ship captain tried to make it to the coast, but the winds whipped up, and suddenly tornadic energy lifted the boat, twirling it within the vortex, and then it was thrown towards the shoreline, destroying the boat. There were no survivors." He looked at each of the Life Bearers, eye to eye when he said those words.

Ford looked at Ursula, rubbing her leg, trying to get a pulse on her reaction to the story. She looked at him with nothing but love, and a tear running down her face. "I remember this. I feel it in every fiber of my body."

Christopher said, "Yes, the trauma of this event is within us all. It was a terrible moment in history. The Life Bearers of that time were not able to complete their mission to further the light for the cause of advancing the soul. Instead, there was a very dark disturbance that happened, one that took the lives of our ancestors, and now the time has come once more, to move, energetically, into a higher state. You are the chosen ones who are being asked to take part in a deeply profound service for humankind and a hazardous one as well."

David was wiggling a bit when Christopher mentioned the danger.

Christopher looked his way and continued. "These three have recently become acquainted, though it would seem that they have known one another forever. David is my pupil in the study of Druidry, an Ovate, to be exact. He has been training for this moment for some time now, though initially, he did not know. In fact, it was his Druidry skills that helped mitigate a dangerous situation while these three drove to meet me at the Union Terrace Gardens in Aberdeen."

Ashneer looked at David, confused, "Dude, you've been holding out on us?"

David was embarrassed as he tried to explain the situation. "Ah… quite." He laughed then gave some clarity, "We encountered a very unusual creature on our way to meet up with Elder Christopher recently, as he stated, so we know now that we are on the radar of a dark force. More on that later, though." David winced his eyes as he recalled the moment. He did not want to freak out the team completely, so he looked towards Stella for some help.

Stella chimed in, "May I?" she looked at Christopher to see if she could elaborate. She received the affirmative as Christopher was packing more tobacco.

413

"Well, let's see how I can put this. The tornado thingy that our ancestors experienced, that came out of nowhere... is actually a being, and not so much a weather pattern." She laughed as it was the best way she could put it.

Freya had a concerned look and asked her to elaborate more.

"There is a dark entity that lives in the plasma realms, or the astral, for lack of a better word. This being thinks that the Earth and all those in it are his. Period." She looked at Christopher to see if she could continue. Christopher was intrigued by her storytelling and insisted that she continue.

Stella continued with her explanation. "This entity is who caused the shipwreck that killed our Great, Great, Great, Grandmother Barabell, and her daughter's. Had they gotten to the jump points and activated the zones with the creation codes, this world would be much different now." She looked at Christopher for confirmation.

"Excellent Stella," said Christopher. He maneuvered his body and took over from where Stella had stopped. "These ladies were to meet in the area of Tintagel, known as Merlyn's cave, at a precise time. There was a temporal activation underway, which one may see from time to time during meteor showers. At the point, in April of 1900, the Lyrid meteor showers were happening. I estimate that during this meteor shower, the veils grew thinner."

Christopher stopped for a moment and took a deep breath. Then a smile came over his face. He resumed his train of thought, "I shall say it this way... it is a time when the locks to this matrix can be unlocked with the right key codes. You, my friends, are the key codes. Walking codebreakers." He folded his hands in his lap and waited for commentary.

Benjamin said the only logical thing at that moment, "Well, who is the coder, if we are the codebreakers?"

"Interesting question Benjamin," Christopher replied.

Freya jumped in and asked, "So, because we were anointed last night by a Bee Goddess, you think we are truly the ones you say can break a code? I don't understand. Sorry, and quite frankly, I wish you would have opened with something more exciting and not so fear-inducing. I don't mean to be rude, but you have me concerned."

Christopher said, "Well, good. I want you to be concerned."

Freya was taken aback by his frankness.

Christopher remarked, "I would rather tell you all of the scary parts first and save the really good stuff for now. You ready for the really good stuff?" He leaned towards her with a teasing laugh to break up the serious vibe.

Everyone was excited to hear more, so Christopher suggested that Bridgit tell them about how she came to know of the Clan of Phare.

Bridgit's eyes got large, and she swallowed slowly and said, "Sure."

Bridgit began her story, "As I shared with most of you already, I am an Arborist, and was in Aberdeen to study a particular tree for a book that I am writing. I refer to this tree by the name Tuuru. Its name was given to the tree by the community long ago." She smiled at David and continued.

"This is going to be a bizarre story, so bear with me, okay? I am still a bit shy and somewhat uncomfortable regarding what I am about to tell you."

Ford and Ashneer both urged her to continue, and they all agreed that she could take her time.

Bridgit was grateful for their kindness. She looked down and stared at her lap, trying to find the proper starting point. She lifted her left hand towards her face and rested two fingers under her nose, holding pressure under her nostrils as if to ward off a sneeze while she concentrated. She looked up suddenly with a start and began to speak.

"I was staying at an Inn, outside of Aberdeen, within walking distance of the tree in question. I was in my room at night watching the weather out my window become a bit windy, but nothing too severe. I went to bed that night but was awakened by the wind. I heard a voice calling out to me. I don't know how to say this, but I just knew it was the tree. I knew that Tuuru was in distress. It needed me! I grabbed my coat and boots and ran out the door of the Inn to make my way to the tree. As I was walking, the wind picked up around me, and I could feel a shift in the atmosphere, something dark and sinister was near me, yet I was too afraid to turn around and face it."

Freya was wringing her hands, and Stella, the intuitive, knew that this was not making her feel any better hearing that Bridgit came close to this entity. She reached over to grab her harp from her bag and strummed it gently and connected with Bridgit telepathically.

Bridgit could see and feel Freya's concern too. They would have to hold Freya in love and light as they unfolded the story slowly so as not to cause undue stress to her system as she begins to remember her part in the grand plan.

Bridgit said towards Freya, "I am getting to the good part, so bear with me." She made herself smile for Freya's sake.

Freya smiled with relief and urged her to continue. Ford and Ursula leaned on one another to get comfortable, as did the others.

Bridgit continued, "I ran as fast as I could towards Tuuru. I rounded the corner and could feel an electricity in the air just as I made it to the sheltering branches and then it hit." She indicated the dark vortex by swirling her arms overhead and continued, "I fell, hitting my head on the tree root. Unbeknownst to me, Christopher was near the tree and had engaged in an energetic battle with this Plasma being that had entered our dimension and was looking for me!"

She had a tear in her eye and said, "This next part is the part that breaks my heart."

She looked down, her palms were both flat on the Earth, receiving support from Mother Earth to continue the story. "When I awoke, I was no longer here, in this dimension." She patted the Earth that they sat on.

"What???" Ursula asked, sitting up to see Bridgit face to face. "What do you mean?"

"Well", Bridgit scratched the side of her neck nervously and said, "I mean that I had entered the fourth dimension, and more precisely, the realm of myths and legend. I woke up to find an elf watching over me, and soon after, another one came to be with us." She laughed, remembering Avery, and at that moment wishing he was with her.

Benjamin's mind was blown and was waiting to hear more. "What?! Holy Crap! What happened next"? He, too, sat up to see Bridgit's face more closely.

Bridgit continued nervously, "I soon discovered that the world tree that I had been studying had been anchored in three dimensions, and the moment the dark force attacked me, I tripped and fell, hitting my head. When I fell, a powerful force hit Tuuru, the tree, and at that moment, the tree absorbed me into its field, bringing me into the next dimension. I did not know that Christopher was there fighting it. It was Christopher who yelled out an incantation to Tuuru, and that is when I disappeared into the fourth dimension."

The group looked at Christopher with utter amazement, and he smiled and nodded his head in testimony to the truth.

Bridgit continued, "The tree fell that day. No longer alive on this dimensional plane. When I awoke and found that I wasn't in Kansas anymore," she sheepishly laughed and said, "I realized that I had a small gash on my head, which made me consider that perhaps, logically, I was just hallucinating. But no, that was not it. The elves introduced themselves and told me of Tuuru's fate. She had uprooted in this 3D world to protect me from harm. I cried upon hearing this. It is really too much to bear." She turned to wipe her tears as she got through the story.

There was a moment of silence within the group as Bridgit composed herself. Once she wiped her tears with her sleeve, she looked up.

"Freya, I promise it will be okay," Bridgit assured her amid her tears.

Freya now wanted to comfort Bridgit. "I am okay. How 'bout you?"

Bridgit said, "I will be good. This is just the hard part of the story."

She clasped her hands together in her lap and said, "Let me continue. I was now in a place far, far from home. The two elves decided to take me to their leader." She started laughing out loud as she knew that sounded like an alien scenario. Everyone got a chuckle out of her humor.

It was nice to see Bridgit showing her wit, Stella thought, as she continued to add vibrational support to the team with her precious harp.

"I arrived at the Clan of Phare, a fortress within a pocket of the fourth density that is the home of our ancient ancestors. I met the leader of the Clan, a beautiful, intelligent woman who is a mixture of Lyran-Feline and Elven blood. I later came to know her as my mother, Shamalaine."

"What!? Get out of here!!!" Ursula blurted.

Ford laughed at Ursula's response but genuinely needed more understanding. He asked in a gentle voice, "How can this be?"

"Well, I haven't finished. She is also Stella's mother too." Bridgit pointed to Stella, who strummed a few chords for dramatic flair.

Looking at all of their shocked faces, Stella said, "I know, right!?" Stella laughed and continued to play background music to hold the field.

Bridgit told the Life Bearers the rest of the story about meeting her family, remembering the plan with the help of their fourth dimensional mother, who actually birthed her in the third dimension, but had to leave the 3D plane because of Stella.

"So... I grew up here in the 3D world without parents, living with my Grandparents until they passed. I have been without any family in the past few years until recently when I met Stella and her father, Todd, Uncle Christopher, and of course, I am sure that David is connected to the lineage somewhere. To make a long story short, we are all coming together at this time to make it to the jump points, to shift the looping program that is playing out on the planet, and usher in a new world."

She paused for a breath and then quickly added, "The how's are a bit complicated, and I feel like we can talk more about that part later. I did want to bring up one more thing briefly, to give an update to this crazy story." She looked around to see if everyone was okay for her to continue. Everyone gave their thumbs up, so she continued to share the latest.

"Christopher, just before we left the Inn, in Aberdeen, I had a stranger visit me in my room. She was not from this dimension, and she was rushed for time. She came to bring me a bag with thirteen stone pendants for each of the Life Bearers to wear when we make it to the jump points. The woman said that they are a vibrational tool to help us access the jump points." She brought out David's pendant to show everyone.

While she handed it to Christopher, Stella asked if she could share the dream she had. Bridgit encouraged her to do so, so Stella began to tell the group that she had had two dreams now about blue people in another realm, and in one of those dreams, she had been shown the very symbol that was on the pendants.

"In fact, the woman who delivered the pendants could have been who I had dreamt about the night before, except that in my dream she was blue! But besides that, her demeanor was mysterious and otherworldly." She finished her commentary with a few loud strums of the harp and rested the harp next to her on the ground, acting as if the information she just shared was perfectly normal.

Christopher chuckled at Stella's storytelling abilities as he held the pendant in his hand and closed his eyes to feel the energy of the stone.

He looked at Bridgit for more information. "This feels very calm to me. Why is the pendant wrapped around this stone?" He began to unravel the pendant from the teardrop-shaped stone.

Bridgit quickly responded, "Oh... that is the striking stone. I was instructed that we are to strike the pendant with the stone when we are at the jump points. It will reverberate specific energy, I guess?" She shrugged her shoulders, not feeling confident in her explanation.

Christopher wrapped the pendant around the striking stone and handed it back to Bridgit. He thanked her and then continued with his part of the story, "There is so much more to say. We never know when one might find a Life Bearer, or two, and we were not prepared for this conversation just yet, though extremely pleased at the progress of this finding. Let me suggest something. There are many more logistics that need to be addressed. Individual counseling at this point would be helpful as well. When do you all head back to your respective homes?"

The group all gave out their travel plans and found that they each had a few days before they flew back to their homes.

Christopher made a suggestion, "Why don't you come to our family home, just a couple of hours from here, in the morning? We will spend the day going into more detail about the roles that each of you will play if you so choose to participate in this adventure of a lifetime. I am happy to put you up at the Inn so that you may all get acquainted, and we can develop a plan."

The group talked openly for a good ten minutes learning the logistics of the Phare family home, and it was settled. The following day they would be journeying to the Clan of Phare's homestead and learning what it meant to be a Life Bearer.

As they got up to walk back to the hotel, Ashneer and Benjamin walked up to David, wanting to know more about the encounter he had had before coming to the conference. David was assisting Christopher into the front seat of Pearl, and as he shut the door, Christopher heard David's response, "It was my biggest nightmare." They all

420

laughed as David described the encounter while the ladies walked on ahead, chatting with Stella and Bridgit.

Christopher sat alone in the car and looked at his pipe. He turned it sideways to look at the engraving on it. The very same engraving from the pendant was etched into the pipe that had been handed down to him within the Phare family lineage. He just shook his head and chuckled as David opened the car door to whisk him back to the hotel for a nice dinner and a late ride back home to Aberdeen.

And the wheel turns...

Chapter 63

Perseus Constellation-
Operation Unicorn

Breacher held onto the dragon, Leto, as he looked behind him at the other Dragon Riders. They moved through envelopes of space and time, now that they each had the proper energetic symbols tattooed upon their being.

Each rider was fit with a distinctive uniform and mask suitable for breathing in any situation, gifted to them by the Weavers. Their suits and apparatus enabled them to move through space with the cosmic dragons quickly.

They flew with great speed, to make it to the Perseus constellation nearby, and in particular, a dark stronghold on the star known as Algol. In the annals of time, this region was where a notorious and heinous creature of Greek mythology was spawned; the Gorgon, Medusa. The ancients from the blue jewel knew this star, Algol, by another name. It was known as Satan's Head.

Breacher had a bad feeling about this mission. He tapped into the life force of his lineage to strengthen his connection to his spiritual inheritance. He knew it would take more than magic to extract the unicorn and bring it to safety from this hellish pit in the cosmos. Upon their approach of the outer atmosphere, he could see activity ahead. He put his hand up to signal the team to be ready for an ambush, but to his surprise, it was a small ship with alliance markings.

Out of the ship flew a Pegasus with a tall, slender feline woman riding towards them. Jinnby's approach was swift. Her eyes glowed like embers upon her face. Her head was lit by a luminous, stretchy silver headband that covered her ears. She had what looked to be a nose ring hanging from her nostrils, which regulated her airflow.

This brave galactic warrior had her forearms wrapped in a lattice of beaded sinew with her bow hung over her back, as she flew towards them at high speed. She was a welcome sight to all of the Dragon Riders.

Breacher and the other riders floated in space nearby as she approached them. She flew close to Alderson first, to give him a proper greeting.

"Alderson!" Her voice was deep and modulated within the celestial space. She greeted him by placing her muscular arm across her chest, fist closed, and bowed her head. Alderson emulated the same expression, with a tenderness that Jinnby had grown to admire.

She greeted each of the riders with the same heartfelt pound to the chest and lingered near Kali and the Indigo Dragon. She touched the bridge of the dragon's nose to honor their connection and then moved to the end, where Breacher was leaning on Leto, petting the raised ridge on her forehead.

When Jinnby approached, he sat up straight and received their comrade as a Commander would do. Jinnby came close to Leto so that her voice could be heard.

"Commander, I have had much happen in the short time that we were last together. Your team came to my aide, and that of my home planet. The evil plan to destroy my world was averted. Tigris is a very diverse

423

planet, rich in minerals and it was the plan to explode the planet to easily mine the asteroids, once the planet was in manageable pieces. This is why I came to warn you. The situation that you are facing here, on Algol, is where the mined minerals are transferred." Jinnby pointed to Algol in the distance.

She allowed the Pegasus to flap its wings. Once it stabilized, she continued, "I have come here with Commander Bewain."

She pointed to the craft that was now moving out of range. "There is intel that suggests that the evil that had perpetuated harm to my planet is working to do the same on the blue jewel, Earth, and this place is an outpost of the darkest forces at play in our local universe." She pointed once more to the region where the star Algol was positioned.

She pulled back on the Pegasus to hold it steady as the dragons were making waves within the galactic sea.

Breacher confirmed, "Commander Benoit gave me a similar report. But how did you know that we were coming here?"

"The Divine Mother connected me to your Commander. She highly recommended we come here immediately as back up." Jinnby held her head down in a silent prayer of gratitude.

"Ah, Divine Mother. She is always gracious and kind."

Jinnby turned slowly, holding the reins around the Pegasus, and addressed all of the riders. "The minerals that are being taken to Algol are capable of absorbing and emitting light at various wavelengths. We believe they are what is required to run the massive hologram matrix that has kept the Earth and her inhabitants from raising its frequencies."

She said, "A low vibration is targeting the people in the third density of Earth through this means, and the majority are not aware of it. This vibrational fence or grid is keeping their bodies in the lowest possible vibration, and this has been in place for a very long time."

Jinnby looked at the group as the dragons each swirled around her and Breacher and said, "I have returned on the request of the Divine Mother if you will have me now?"

She looked at Breacher for the confirmation to continue with the team. He nodded an affirmative and said, "I will need you to fly with the unicorn, so it is perfect timing that you found your way to us.

Breacher said, "Riders, fall in and keep to the formation. Jinnby, fall in line behind me."

Jinnby flew with her Pegasus into the formation, and the eight riders flew swiftly into the atmosphere of Algol, on alert for an attack.

Breacher called out a command to The Kumara, "Cloak now!"

The Kumara placed the team in an invisible protective field and not a moment too soon. Suddenly, warships were flying through the cosmos from the Algol base, coming straight towards them.

The dragon formation was a strange one in that each of the dragons flew overhead of one another, operating in a straight vertical line. The Kumara threw up the protective shield, like a ladder, that encompassed them all. From the stacked formation, they were able to maneuver quickly by the ships that passed.

The team flew down to an area on Algol that had a dark green sea with jagged cliffs. They located a spot where the team could land and set up a perimeter. Breacher pointed out the area, and they all descended in the same vertical formation. Swiftly averting all scouting ships, the dragons flew quietly to the seashore where the cliffs would provide some cover.

Once landed, Breacher needed time to find the entrance to the underground fortress of the Gorgons. He opened an apparatus on his forearm and scrolled through the intel that Commander Benoit had gathered on his behalf.

"We need to make sure we keep the Pegasus out of sight. There hasn't been a Pegasus in this area for a very long time." He looked around for an area to conceal the dragons and Pegasus. His arm apparatus was scanning the area and located a small entrance into the mountain not far from their location. He sent The Sage to scope it out on foot, ahead of the others. As they waited, Breacher gave the team intel pertinent to the area.

"This is the birthplace of Medusa, the Gorgon, who birthed the Pegasus and its twin, Chrysaor, when Perseus cut off Medusa's head." The Dragon Riders knew that Algol was a dark place and that the Pegasus was born from Medusa, but most of them seemed to forget about Chrysaor.

Praeta spoke up to share what she knew, "Our people have always said that it will be Chrysaor who comes with a legion of demonic souls to claim the world where his mother was slain."

Praeta looked at Breacher and said, "Vengeance begets vengeance."

It shook him to his core. Praeta was right. An eye for an eye was the loop of evil playing out in this entire galaxy. He knew that there had to be a new way to right all wrongs, but at this moment, the mission at hand was to find the KEY. The unicorn was a huge key to unlocking the local galaxies. It was the horn of the golden unicorn that pierces the veil of illusion.

A thought entered Breacher's mind that perhaps the horn of the golden unicorn is a vibrational tuning fork that could interact with the wavelengths created with the minerals. He was contemplating this thought when The Sage returned with his assessment.

"There is a cave just beyond the farthest ridge." The Sage pointed in the general direction of the cave.

Breacher responded as he pulled up the scanning apparatus. "Good. I want all of you to take shelter there for the time being."

He looked around at the riders and said, "I will be checking in with Commander Bewain to determine the timing on the operation now

426

that he has arrived. Stay safe, and I will return soon."

As he turned Leto around, he stopped and turned his head back towards them. "Be ready to act!"

The riders once again moved into the vertical formation for The Kumara to cloak them. They flew over the ridge to the cave by the time Breacher made it to the location rendezvous. He looked up at the atmosphere filled with ships then bilocated himself, with Leto, into the Alliance ship deep below the dark green sea just off of the coastline where Commander Bewain awaited his arrival.

And the wheel turns...

Chapter 64

Underwater Debriefing

In the underwater spacecraft of the Alliance, Breacher prepared a comfortable space for his dragon. He located the replicator to generate food and water for Leto and got her settled quickly. He walked to the common room where many gathered, waiting for his arrival. He placed his hand over a door pad, engaging a green laser scanner.

The door swished open, and there in front of him were several comrades with Commander Bewain sitting around a circular table with a hologram hovering over the center of it.

"Breacher, please, come join us." Bewain stood up to shake Breacher's hand and moved a chair in his direction. "We see that the team made it safely to the cave, and The Sage is on watch duty."

"Thanks, Commander. It is good to see you here, Sir." Breacher leaned forward to grab the back of the chair next to him and pulled it away from the table as everyone took the cue to sit.

Bewain stated, "We have done the diagnostics of this area, and it is odd. There is an operation happening here, but we have not got the intel back to confirm what it is."

Just as he said that the report Bewain had been waiting for popped up on the screen. Bewain read the summary out loud.

"There is an indication that the payload is mainly ore with striations of crystalline matter, that once processed into phosphors, are the base components used to create full-color plasma digital pixels in glass pads and screens." He went on to read the last portion to himself, mumbling with the indications in the briefing.

Bewain added, "It seems to suggest that a quantum computer is functioning out of this base."

Bewain closed the report and asked, "Gentleman, have we just found a programmer base? The minerals that are offloaded here are not only for digital communications for computational devices. They are key components used in conjunction with the plasma blocks used to shield memories in the 3D matrix. If we can take down this operation, it will virtually rid the galaxy of the dark forces hold, and humanity will once again regain their heritage."

The room was in an uproar with the possibilities of this discovery. Bewain had a stern look upon his face. He was utterly taken by surprise with this information.

"Breacher, get back to your team and set up a perimeter. The unicorn is the objective at this point. Once we extract it, we will return with reinforcements and a plan. Collect as much intel as you can, but grab the unicorn and get the hell out of there."

Bewain stood up to escort Breacher out. "One more thing, Commander. I'll walk you out."

Bewain patted Breacher's shoulder and walked with him into the hallway. "I wanted to give you an update on Kaialena and Tulina's mission. They are gathering the Life Bearers and only have a few more to find. We are working day and night to make those connections

429

happen as soon as possible. The ladies are fine and in good hands with Christopher." Bewain smiled at Breacher as he reminisced of his time on Earth, but then the scowl returned to his face.

"I hope Kaialena and Tulina find the Life Bearers soon. We need them in a safe zone, the sooner, the better." Breacher said in a low voice. "Once we get the unicorn, we need to move forward with the grid work."

Breacher stared intently at Bewain, while Bewain processed the information. He was contemplating the vastness of the mission at hand. He thought of the ramification of possibly finding the source of the anomaly that has kept the dimensional envelopes shut off, enslaving humanity for eons. It was both a moment of elation to have discovered the operation and one of great danger, and Breacher's team was right in the middle of it.

Bewain watched Breacher swiftly leave his presence. He walked to the doorway, placed his hand upon the entry pad, and when the door opened, he began a discourse with his team on the potential findings and dispatched each of them to their stations for close monitoring of the situation.

And the wheel turns... ⊛

Chapter 65

The Life Bearers Gather in Aberdeen

The doorbell rang at the home of Christopher Phare. The Druid Christopher listened to the chimes alerting him of the company as he made his way to the entry.

Bridgit and Stella arrived early to assist Christopher in the days unfolding's. As Christopher came into the entryway, his heart was full as he caught sight of his two grandnieces through the glass of the entry door.

Christopher opened the door with a broad smile and ushered the ladies into the house. "My, you two are bonnie lasses." He said it with a twinkle in his eye and in his thickest Scottish brogue in honor of their family's heritage. Having lived in Scotland almost his entire life, his American accent was a mere undertone.

He said, "I could barely sleep last night in anticipation of the day. Come in, come in! Let's go back to the kitchen, shall we."

The ladies each hugged him in the entry and placed kisses upon each cheek. They made their way to the back part of the house where the fire was now embers, and the days early morning chill was subsiding.

"Anyone for tea?" Christopher grabbed the tea kettle and lifted it high in the air for the ladies to decide if he should continue.

"Yes, please," Stella responded.

She rubbed her arms with a bit of a chill, loving the idea of tea by a fire. "Would it be okay if I placed another log on the fire?" Even though it was summertime, the mornings still had a chill in the home that was surrounded by shade trees.

"Quite," Christopher agreed and pointed to the wood and then continued to prepare the tea service. The ladies wanted to have time alone with Christopher before David brought the others from the Inn.

Bridgit sat at the long dining table and looked around the room. She was deep in thought about their ancestors and the loss of so many lives to the mission.

"Bridgit, what is the American saying? Penny for your thoughts? Are you troubled?" Christopher came to sit near her while the kettle was on the stove.

"Hmm. Yes, I guess I am. Now that we have found so many Life Bearers, I realize that we are in a modicum of danger, and I am finding it hard, knowing that I am responsible for this team, and I don't even know what I or we are doing!" Bridgit's face turned red with both frustration and embarrassment.

She burst into tears and sobbed so fully that Christopher stood and pulled her to his chest and held her there, allowing her tears to flow. She was crying the tears of her childhood, of all of her losses, and the potential of losing anyone else was terrifying.

"There, there, child. You mustn't let your fears of loss keep you from feeling the joy of this mission and what it could mean for humanity." He pulled her away and looked into her eyes.

432

"You're not alone. We are all here by your side, and more are going to join us in this adventure. It is people like us who know the risks, and each of us is responsible for our destiny. You are not responsible for anyone but yourself."

He guided Bridgit back to her seat and said, "We are all in this, co-creatively, so let me see a smile, won't you?"

He stared deeply into her eyes, waiting for a response and continued, "We have learned a few things since the turn of the century, and we are well equipped to handle what comes our way. Trust me, dear." Christopher wiped a tear from her eye with his handkerchief and handed it to her to use.

"Thank you, Christopher. Thank you for being here and, well, just being you. You do bring me such comfort." Bridgit wiped her tears and looked at Stella.

Stella was sitting on the edge of the fireplace holding her arms across her chest and asked, "You okay?" Bridgit walked over to her, and the two hugged. They took a deep breath to fill themselves with the feeling of home and then sat at the table while Christopher placed the kettle and teacups out for the ladies.

"Now, let us regroup, and I will tell you what we might want to present to the team. Sound good?" Christopher's smile and the twinkle in his eyes seemed to quite their concerns.

Bridgit pepped up with the idea of a plan. "Shamalaine introduced me to the Builders of Form, so I do know what their gifts are. As far as teams go, it would make sense to pair up Life Bearers, the Blueprint Masters, and the Builders of Form into teams. Perhaps that is what they are doing in preparation?" She looked at Christopher for more guidance.

"Yes, this is the case. When I was back in the realms of the Clan of Phare, this was the plan which Shamalaine laid out. The Angelic realms will meet with the Elementals, and they will be paired together according to the need of the hour. As you have already met the Elemental team members, the Builders of Form, you can easily assess the talents of the Life Bearers as it relates to the Builder's talents."

He continued, "I have received intel on the team categories, which we can use as guidelines."

Christopher took a sip of his tea and walked to the drawer to retrieve pen and paper. "Let's go over the Builders of Form team and their talents. That seems to be as good of a place as any to start this process."

Stella volunteered to be the scribe. Christopher handed the pen and pad of paper to her, as Bridgit dictated the skills of the Builders.

"Let's see. The Builders are a very organized group. They organize themselves by the seven Rays."

She smiled as Christopher quipped, "Splendid. Go on." He pulled his pipe out and fiddled with the tobacco pouch as the girls began to draw up the beginnings of a plan.

Stella drew pictures of the Builders on the sideline of the paper as Bridgit described them.

All seven Builders represented the building blocks of the physical world; water, fire, air, earth, and ether. The list was nearly complete, save for Stella putting the final embellishments on her drawings when the doorbell rang.

"Perfect timing as usual. David is very prompt." Christopher remarked as if he was a proud parent. "Excuse me, won't you?" Christopher exited the kitchen to answer the door while the ladies completed the first task.

They could hear Christopher's greeting from the hallway. "Welcome to the home of the Clan of Phare! Won't you come in?" The team of Life Bearers entered the ancestral home with excitement in their voices, ready to begin a quest.

Bridgit and Stella entered the living room with teacups, kettle, and biscuits and began the morning with updates and then a tour of the home.

Ursula and Ford followed behind Bridgit to assure Bridgit that the team was all in.

Ursula said, "We all talked a bit more last night, and though we don't really know what to expect, we all agree that we came to this planet to be of service and this opportunity, to co-create a world where we are all living in peace... well, that just seems like the best way we can spend our time here. So, relax and know that you don't need to do any more convincing."

"That is such a relief off my mind and heart. Thank you, Ursula. I needed to hear that." She held onto Ursula's arm as everyone got comfortable in the living room. Stella greeted Freya and Juel as she set the tea tray down on the coffee table.

Christopher grabbed Ashneer and Benjamin and asked for assistance. Benjamin held a platter of finger sandwiches while Ashneer brought pastries and fresh-cut fruit. Everyone grabbed small plates and napkins and sipped on their tea and then dived into the current situation.

Bridgit began, "I want to thank you all for making the changes in your schedule to allow for this meeting to take place. As you know, we are a few Life Bearer's short, but I am confident that we will meet up with them soon. In the meantime, I wanted to give you all an overview of the plan and the team members that I have met so far, on the other side of the veil, and share with you their skills and strengths."

"We will formulate a plan and place you each on a development team, determined by your skill sets and by those of the Builders of Form, who provide the mental focus to our thoughts for manifestation. They are, in essence, surrogates for the hierarchy of the Elohim, who implement God's Will."

She took a sip of her tea and continued, "I have yet to meet up with the Blueprint Master's, but I assume that there will be signs of them as we get closer to the time to make the jump. The best way that I can describe to you what we are tasked with is to say that we have been given a grand opportunity to co-create a new world with the assistance of the two other lifestreams, the Builders of Form and the Blueprint Masters. We, the humans, being the middle man who anchors the frequencies on the ground." Everyone nodded in appreciation of the simple and yet complex explanation. They held their questions until Bridgit completed her thoughts.

Bridgit picked up the pad of paper that Stella had written the notes on and stared at the pictures she drew of each of the Builders. "Stella, you amaze me with your talent. These are very good likenesses of the Builders."

Stella was proud of her ability to see into the other worlds and translate what she feels or sees in many ways.

Bridgit continued, "I am going to give an overview of each of the Builders, what ray they represent, and their skills. Sound good?"

David spoke up, "Smashing!" He gave two thumbs up, crossed his legs, then fiddled with his napkin and a biscuit. The group laughed at his ability to add the perfect comic relief, unbeknownst to him.

"Great. Thanks, David. And if anyone has comments while I present this information, don't hesitate to ask," Bridgit assured the group.

Christopher wore a beaming smile on his face, as he watched Bridgit seamlessly take charge.

Bridgit began by defining the qualities of each ray with a brief description of the job of a Builder of Form. "The Builders, or Elementals, give the mental focus required when manifesting anything into form. As an example, an apple resonates at a certain frequency. An elemental of an apple will hold the vibration of the thought-form of an apple until it transduces into matter. That is a laymen's way of describing it. Any questions?" She looked up, and everyone seemed content with the explanation and eager for her to continue.

"The Builders of Form work on one of seven rays of focalized light, under the tutelage of the Elohim of that particular ray. Each ray holds a different quality. I will go over those now." She reached down to the notes that she had laid by her feet.

Bridgit began, "Ray one is will, power and purposefulness. A self-starter might be someone who resonates with the first ray — someone who is self-assured. The Builder connected to the first ray is Avery, the elf. His element is Earth. He is one of the elves that found me when I entered the fourth dimension through Tuuru."

She placed her notes on her lap to speak about Avery freely. "He has many talents, one being an excellent scribe, and another is that he is excellent with animals."

Bridgit had a thought, "Stella, will you make a list of the categories we discussed earlier with Christopher? Animals should be first on the list, then put Avery's name next to it."

"Sure." Stella licked her fingers, then placed her plate down to write the notes. "Okay, I am good to go."

"Great. Thanks, Stella."

She smiled at her cousin and continued, "Now, the qualities of the second ray are love, wisdom, faithfulness, and compassion, to name just a few. The Builder of Form for the second ray is Arrea." Bridgit quickly relayed the story of finding Arrea in the garden, after she was taken into the doorway within the golden-hued room.

"Arrea's element is air. She is a fairy, also known as a sylph."

Bridgit leaned towards Freya to describe Arrea. "She is a tiny creature of love and pure light, and she carries a small harp. The music of the spheres is delivered through the sounds of her harp. She mentally projects the perfection of the spheres to the plants via the sound waves. If she finds that a plant or flower is not performing correctly, she plays it a tune on her harp."

Looking once more towards Stella, "I feel like there should be a music of the spheres category, as sound is part of the creation process. Was music on the list already?"

"Right on! I do believe you had sound covered, but I like Music of the Spheres, as a category, better," Stella said as she put together the chart of categories.

"Clearly, I will be hanging with Arrea!" She laughed, and Bridgit suggested that she put herself on that list.

Continuing with the next ray, Bridgit said, "So, we are now on the third ray."

Bridgit looked at her notes once more. "The qualities of the third ray are practical, active intelligence, mind, and expression. The Builder of Form on the third ray is Tabor. You all met him at Rodney Gardens."

Freya asked, "Oh! He is one of the Builders?"

Bridgit replied, "Yes. Tabor is a Faun who works with the plant kingdom. I would say that one of his traits is adaptation. He is also very stealthy!"

Bridgit shared the story of how she was reintroduced to him while recalling who she was with Shamalaine. "Tabor can move through space and time without a sound and is very light on his feet as he does not want to disturb the foliage. He is a very gentle being." She smiled as she looked at each of the Life Bearer's faces taking in the information.

Bridgit checked her notes once more, then looked up to explain adaptation from the perspective of an arborist. She said, "Adaptation is a key for the longevity of a species."

She placed her hands under her thighs to warm up and said, "Tabor is a planner. He can see ahead, and he too uses music to assist the plants, but for the most part, he focuses his attention on how he can help the plants adapt to various situations."

Freya chimed in as this was a subject that interested her deeply.

"Bridgit, plant life is a large part of our environment. Do we have a plant category? I would love to be on that team!" She rubbed her hands together as if she was going to dive into work that very moment.

"YES! Absolutely! Plant life is invaluable, and it is definitely on the list. So, Freya, you will be working with Tabor and a Blueprint Master. Does that sound good?"

"Sign me up!" Freya acted as if she was writing a contract as she winked in Stella's direction.

Stella was creating the list until she looked over at David, who had quietly pulled out his laptop and created a proper record in a spreadsheet document.

"Dude! You should have told me you were taking this down. You are so much better at this stuff than I am. Is it safe for me to put some hot water on? You got this?" She patted his shoulder without waiting for a response and left the secretarial duties to David.

Bridgit watched their interaction. It was heartwarming to see the two of them so comfortable together.

David motioned for Bridgit to continue, as the team was waiting patiently to hear more.

"Ray four qualities are gifted, sympathetic, someone who is harmonious through conflict. They have cultural creativity, and this I can say is true for the fourth Builder of Form, Mersea. She is a mermaid!" She smiled when sharing that tidbit with the team.

Ursula nearly fell off her seat with excitement. "I LOOOVVVE MERMAIDS!!!" she exclaimed loudly in a deep, raspy voice, especially when she elongated the word love.

She was so excited to hear the description of the fourth ray and said, "You know, the description of Mersea is very much how I would actually describe myself...well, the qualities, not the mermaid part, but man, do I wish I were one!" she squealed a bit in her excitement.

"Tell me more?" Bridgit quizzed, knowing that there was another Life Bearer in the room that had a connection to water. She momentarily looked at Ashneer and smiled.

"Mmm...I am totally a water girl. Any chance I get an opportunity, I like to be in water or around it. I can feel its essence as I attune to it. As part of my Goddess studies, I included the mermaid as the quintessential Goddess of the sea. I even have a tattoo on my shoulder of a Mermaid Goddess."

She looked at Ashneer and asked, "Do you want to team up? There are more Life Bearers than there are Builders."

She then turned to Bridgit and asked, "How many Blueprint Masters are there?"

"Good question. I don't know." Bridgit was honest in her lack of knowledge.

Ursula quizzed Ashneer once more, "What do you think, a male and female human on Team Water? Sound good to you?" Ursula sold herself with great zeal.

Ashneer responded, "I am happy to join you on Team Water." He bowed his head towards her and said, "I look forward to working with you and um, the Mermaid Goddess... Mersea, is it?"

He was a bit intimidated, contemplating working with a mermaid. It was one of the life-long visions that he had had as a child but never shared with anyone. Over time, he would have recurring moments when his mind would daydream, and he would find himself on an expedition of sorts with ethereal beings, which included mermaids. He declined to mention this tidbit to the group as it was too personal. He held it in his heart, protectively.

"Oh, this is going to be fantastic!" Ursula was so happy, and then she had a momentary thought.

She turned to Ford, "Do you mind if we are not on the same team? I am so sorry. I didn't even consult you. I was just so excited. Is this something that we should take a moment to talk about?" Her eyes searched in the deep brown eyes of her beloved.

Ford loved hearing the concern from his partner and placed his hands upon her shoulders to calm her down. "You are correct. The water team is yours to do. I will be fine."

He looked towards Bridgit, "Perhaps there is a landscaping team?" he said with a chuckle, but half-serious, then said, "You know, ley line work. The reason we all came to the conference in the first place?"

Ford explained further, "When I work with the land, it is then that I feel the Divine. I can imbue an entire area with pure consciousness when I go to zero point. I also use the stones themselves to create sacred geometry in the landscape." He watched as David took notes, and Bridgit and Christopher talked amongst themselves for a few moments.

Bridgit responded, "I think that fits in nicely with the qualities of the next ray. The fifth ray qualities are knowledge and science, careful analysis, and intellectual ability." She nodded his way, indicating that she believed that he indeed had the qualities of this ray.

She continued, "The Builder of Form connected to this ray is Gordavin. Gordavin is a Gnome, and as most of you know, gnomes are involved in working with the Earth's energies, the ley lines, and the minerals of the planet. I was lucky enough to have many conversations with Gordavin. He is a very focused Elemental, and I know that you will love working with him on that team." She nodded to Ford with clarity.

She looked at David and said, "Can you place Ford in the category for Minerals and Etheric Forces? That should cover the gamut, wouldn't you think?" looking at Ford.

"That will do nicely." He looked at Ursula and said, "See? All is well."

Ursula smiled and gently touched his hair as he leaned in to kiss her cheek. Everyone could see the purity in their love. The gentleness and care they took with one another in this process were exceptional to watch.

Juel commented as well. "Bridgit, it feels like this category would be a great match for me as well. I have always loved working with crystals and tuning to the Earth's grids. Would it be okay to join Ford on this team?" she shyly asked.

"Oh, that is perfect, Juel. What do you think, Ford?" Bridgit responded.

"I would love to have you on my team, Juel. Welcome aboard!" Ford nodded his head as he saluted her with his teacup as he took a sip.

"Great. Now we will move on to the sixth ray." Bridgit smiled and looked at her notes once more.

"Ray six qualities are knightly qualities such as devotion, idealism, and aspiring to greatness. A being of great reverence. Padmavati is the Builder of Form for ray six. She is the most exquisite Pixie. When I entered the doorway into Padmavati's domain, I was overcome with a sound that lulled me into a trance-like state. Padmavati is unique in that she works with two elements. I am trying to recall more about her because her job is more of an over-lighting presence for all of creation, within the whole system."

Christopher made a suggestion, "Bridgit, let us do this. Let us set up a team of overseers. The two of us will play that role as Life Bearers. Padmavati is clearly suitable for this team as well. Agreed?" He placed his left hand in his vest pocket as he waited for Bridgit's response.

"Yes, that is perfect. It feels like we will be floating a bit from team to team, depending on the needs. Whole systems has a good ring to it." Bridgit looked at the team, and they all seemed to agree. Benjamin was looking a bit on edge as he had yet to find a category that fit him.

Bridgit mentioned to Benjamin, "I think you're next." She winked at him as she began the description of the seventh ray qualities.

"Ray seven qualities are law and order, flowing spirit into matter, and being organized with detailed focus. The Builder of Form on this ray is a Salamander named Phyre. When I met Phyre, he literally jumped out of a torch and stood before me like a ninja. He is a powerful Builder of Form who can invoke great energies and make powerful decrees. His ability to move through time and space is one of his gifts. When I met him, I was taken somewhere off-planet. His mission is about Time. That is as much as I can remember. Therefore, Benjamin, with your dream the other night about calculating codes for the containment field and your studies of the Mayan Time Sciences, I think you would be the perfect Life Bearer to be put on the Time Science team."

Benjamin responded, "Yes, this is perfect. I was starting to sweat for a moment, but as you spoke about Phyre, I could see him in my mind's eye. And your right Bridgit, the recurring dream of me as Captain Skyward is a telling sign. Thank you." Benjamin put his hands together in gratitude for being seen.

Bridgit looked at Christopher and said, "Well now that we have the Life Bearers into teams..."

David interjected before Bridgit finished her sentence.

"I have not been placed on a team." He looked at Bridgit with a cheeky grin.

"Oh, my goodness, David, I am so sorry for the oversight. Do any of the teams that we came up with suit you? Like Ursula mentioned earlier, there are more Life Bearers than there are Builders of Form, so we will have overlap with more than one human on a few of the teams since we have yet to find the last three."

"Yes, I see that. To be honest, I find the Music of the Spheres team to be the most intriguing out of all of them. I do play the piano and have studied music for most of my life."

Stella chimed in, "That is awesome! I think we already make a great team, so I vote for yes!"

David was comforted by Stella's acceptance and awaited Christopher's comments.

Christopher spoke, "David, you are multitalented and therefore could be on any of these teams, but the Music of the Spheres is far more than one might imagine, having to do with vibration waves and you, my friend, will be a perfect fit to co-create in this field with our dear Stella." He looked at Bridgit for the final vote.

"Music of the Spheres it is!" Bridgit yelled out and said, "And with that, I shall take a restroom break!" She hopped up and left the room, while David completed the chart, and the others began to stretch.

Ford asked Christopher if he would give them a tour of his land. They all felt to get some fresh air and move their bodies. Christopher yelled out for them to follow him outside through the mudroom.

The house emptied in moments. Bridgit returned to her spot in the living room and watched out the picture window as Christopher showed the Life Bearers around the grounds of the Clan of Phare homestead. Her heart was full. She glanced back at the list, noting that the first Ray category was not filled as of yet. With three more Life Bearers to find, she hoped that at least one of them would be a champion for animals. She took a deep breath and joined the others.

And the wheel turns...

Chapter 66

Meeting M

It was dark, and a chill ran up Breacher's spine as he made his way through a cavern below the surface of a mining operation that was in full swing. The Sage and Praeta followed closely behind him in complete silence. Breacher sent Jinnby, Arbor, Kali, and Alderson to the other side of the cavern, all looking for clues as to where the Unicorn was being kept.

The Kumara stayed with the dragons and the Pegasus. She sat in meditation, remote viewing what was happening and was able to communicate with Breacher through a communication device that they all wore on their wrists.

Breacher was on full alert as the team went deeper into the underground facility. He came upon a doorway which led into an area where a crew was unloading a payload off of a craft. It was hot, loud, and the smells were a mixture of fertile soil and sulfur. The team swiftly moved passed the area undetected.

They came upon a platform with a small rectangular office with glass windows about 50 yards from the craft. Breacher motioned for Praeta and The Sage to be ready as they climbed up the stairs of the platform to check it out.

Breacher had his weapon set on stun as a precaution. He peaked in the window of the door to see if there was anyone in the room. Sitting at a console was a reptilian being, monitoring the landing craft. Breacher opened the door quickly and jumped forward. The reptilian jumped up towards Breacher, then fell to the floor as Breacher fired his weapon.

The Sage and Praeta immediately went to the console and began searching the system for evidence of where the Unicorn was held. Praeta brought up a floorplan of the facility while The Sage looked through the system for proof of what was in the cargo and who was bringing it. He used a device from his pouch to download the data so that it could be analyzed later.

Praeta downloaded the floorplans while Breacher watched for intruders.

Below, Jinnby and Arbor took samples from some of the cargo that was sitting outside the ship's loading bay, while Alderson and Kali stood watch.

A group of tall, green reptilian beings came into the area, towards their ship. They were laughing and talking to one another loudly as if they were inebriated. One of them carried a large duffle bag over his shoulder as Alderson watched from the shadows. He could hear the muffled sounds of someone calling out for help. The duffle bag was moving. At that moment, Alderson knew what the payment for the minerals was. Human lifeforms. Alderson held Kali to his chest so that she could not see what was taking place.

Jinnby watched as a child was screaming from within the bag, and they could do nothing. She turned away in tears trying not to make a sound.

Alderson watched as the craft began to hover and make its way out of the cavern. Arbor had been watching from another vantage point. He had seen this kind of operation before and knew that there had to be more human life forms present since this was a massive operation. He motioned for the others to follow him to the area where they saw the reptilians enter.

Breacher could see from his vantage point what had transpired and turned to Praeta and The Sage, "Let's get going. We might need the help of the fleet. I think we have another problem here."

Praeta looked up and asked, "What is it?"

Breacher leaned back inside the room, "I think we have a hostage situation. The beings that just left were carrying a child in a large bag. Whoever is running things here are into a lot more than we realized."

Praeta said, "Sir, the floorplan shows what looks like jail cells on level three. I do not see any areas for animals. Should we investigate level three?"

"Got it!" The Sage yelled out once he downloaded the files from the system.

He then saw a group of reptiles heading into the cavern in their direction. "We gotta go, Sir!" He pointed towards the reptilians, and the three made their way out of the door and down the stairs.

They quickly ran down a corridor on the right and found a door that led to a shuttle system. Several shuttle cars were sitting on a track, so the three of them jumped into the first car and rode it to level three. There was no one in sight, or so they thought.

Breacher kept watch and communicated with the team through the wristband, letting the team know that they were heading to level three.

Once the shuttle car arrived at the location, deeper into the underground system, they could hear voices nearby. This area was where the minerals were processed.

Breacher asked The Sage to stay near the shuttle while he and Praeta bilocated around the area to see what they could find out. "We will check out the area ahead." Breacher and Praeta were gone in a flash.

The Sage was not one to stand idle, so he walked in the darkness of the tunnel, looking for an entrance into the main mining operation. He found a communications room, much like the one they were in earlier, which had a viewing screen. He turned off the lights in the room and then activated the viewing screen. What came up was astounding. The screen had several panels to view multiple areas. One showed the mineral processing plant, with untold amounts of human workers, enslaved by reptilian guards.

Another screen showed an area of the operation with large telescopes and what looked like an enormous crystalline chandelier with tubing connecting it to the telescopes.

The screen next to that one showed a small humanoid sitting at a computer module in a room much like the one he was in. He noticed that the child's left wrist was chained to the chair, and armed guards were watching over him.

Just then, The Sage noticed Praeta and Breacher getting close to the room. He used his wrist band to communicate with Breacher.

"Commander Breacher, the room to your right has armed guards. There is a child, a small humanoid boy, no more than twelve years old, cuffed to a chair."

"Copy that." Breacher and Praeta quickly bilocated into the room where The Sage was.

"Let's see what you have." Breacher said. The three riders looked at all of the screens showing women and children being held in cells. The situation was grim. There were torture devices in every area on that level.

Breacher looked up and noticed Praeta's expression on her face. He calmly spoke, "Again, I will remind you that this mission is to find the

Unicorn solely. We are not going to be able to help these people right now." Breacher said with regret.

"But Sir, can we at least rescue the one child? He could possibly lead us to the Unicorn. If we rescued him, we would at least be able to get some information about this place?" Praeta pleaded.

The Sage agreed with Praeta, "We can take those two guards out easily and get the child."

Breacher looked at the screen once more and noticed the crews coming back from their breaks. "Let's go!"

Breacher held onto The Sage, and the three of them bilocated to the hallway outside the door where the humanoid child sat with the guards watching over him. Suddenly an alarm began blaring "Intruders, Level three."

The door to the room opened, and two reptilian guards came into the hallway to look for the intruders. Breacher yelled to Praeta, "Get the kid and take him to the ship immediately!" Praeta moved swiftly.

Breacher and The Sage fought off the reptilian guards. The two put their backs together as the reptilians came towards them. Breacher whispered the plan, and the two bilocated again, this time behind each of the reptiles. Having no other choice, they disarmed the guards and killed them. They pulled the guards into the room and found that Praeta had already released the child from the chain.

Breacher commanded, "Praeta, take this child back to the ship. We will catch up with you in a bit."

Praeta nodded and leaned down at eye level with the child and said, "We are here to help. Don't be afraid." As she said those words, she touched the child's arm, and they disappeared in an instant.

Breacher looked around the hallways and said, "Come on. Let's find the others." They ran down the hall back towards the shuttle car. The area was crawling with an army of reptiles and some human soldiers now. The Sage and Breacher entered a corridor that had no visible doors but had an odor that was so offensive, the signature smell of a reptilian.

The Sage saw movement at the end of the corridor and halted. "Commander, we are going deeper into the lair. We have to turn around." When they stopped to turn around, reptilian soldiers were running towards them.

"We have to get out of here." Breacher grabbed The Sage and hit his communication device. At that moment, all of the Dragon Riders were beamed onto the Alliance Ship, including The Kumara. They all landed on a platform in the command room.

Commander Bewain welcomed the arrivals, as did the other officers. Praeta was sitting at the conference table with the child next to her. She was tending to his wrist and had given him a hot beverage.

Breacher stepped forward, "Sorry, Commander, we had to abort the mission. The place is infested with reptilians."

"Come join us at the table. All is not lost." Bewain said with confidence. He patted down his mane as he escorted the Dragon Riders. The team gathered around the table and looked at the child sitting next to Praeta.

The child looked no more than twelve years of earthly age, white long hair, fair-skinned. He had large almond-shaped brown eyes and an unusual spiral marking on his forehead. His energy field was powerful, and he was not easily scared.

The team sat at the table, looking to make sure everyone was okay. Jinnby looked towards the young boy and spoke a language unknown to the others. She asked if the child was harmed and if his parents were in the mine. The child telepathically spoke to her.

"He tells me that he does not have parents, but that many families are being held there as slaves." Jinnby looked at the team with deep sorrow.

The child spoke again to her, telepathically, "How did you find me?"

Jinnby told the others his questions and responded, "The Divine Mother sent us there on a mission. We did not know what to expect. We did not know that this place is a slave colony."

The child said, "It is much more than that. I owe you a debt of gratitude, but you do not know what you have done."

Jinnby shared the information with the team, and Bewain asked the child to speak to them through a translation device so that they may all communicate.

The child agreed and placed the device around his neck and began to speak.

"You may call me M. Please, won't you tell me the true reason for your arrival? I am happy to give you the intel you require once you tell me why you came to Algol." He placed his hands in his lap and smiled.

Breacher looked at Bewain for approval, and Bewain gave the nod to go ahead.

"My name is Commander Breacher. I am of service to all that is good." He winked at M with a kind smile and continued.

"It is an honor to meet you, Commander Breacher. And these are?" Referring to his team.

"Ah, yes... my team. This is The Kumara. Next to her is The Sage." The Kumara and The Sage both stood and bowed intuitively.

M bowed his head back in a regal manner.

Breacher continued, "Next to The Sage is Jinnby and Alderson. Across from them are Kali and Arbor. And of course, next to you is Praeta." M held his hands outward to radiate a gesture of love to the team. Once he completed his energetic greeting, he motioned for Breacher to continue.

Breacher said, "Our mission was to locate a particular ah... individual, that is crucial to the plan of the GCIA. We were doing recon when we happened upon you. We had to abort the mission once we rescued you, so we will need to go back. They will be expecting us, though." Breacher's face turned from a gentle hello to a deeply disturbed frown.

"This individual you were looking for, perhaps I can help. I know much of the happenings there. I am happy to help as a debt repaid." The team noticed the spiral on M's forehead begin to glow.

Breacher said, "Yes, I would certainly love some help with that, but first, can you tell me how you got there and why you were enslaved? What did they have you doing? You are just a child for Zeus' sake."

"Well, Commander, looks can be deceiving. I am not a youth. I simply have a youthful appearance. I am eons of time in age." He placed his hand upon Praeta's arm to send her a mental picture.

Praeta's eyes were closed as she watched her mental screen open with scenes of various worlds living in harmony. Each culture unique and living in peace. Then, with a sudden burst of bright light, she saw into the multiverse. Stars and planets were swirling out of control. She witnessed two worlds colliding and darkness. Then he showed her a scene where there were unicorns called into action — the true architects of planetary systems.

She was then shown the unicorns in various bodies, not just that of a horse like being with a single horn, but as master shapeshifters who are capable of holding the magnetic frequency of an entire planet. His mental message was that he was a magnetic being from a magnetic universe.

Praeta was speaking out loud everything that she was shown while her eyes were closed. She then saw one final image of a unicorn by a world tree. The unicorn morphed into a humanoid body and walked through the tree. At that moment, she gasped. "IT IS YOU!" Praeta opened her eyes to see M's forehead glowing, and a golden horn spiraled out of his head.

Bewain patted Breacher's back and said, "Well, what do you know!"

M began to speak again, "My full name is Monoceros Eleven. You can call me M. I am the eleventh architect of world systems and was taken by a rogue group of beings from my place of origin. My captures were convinced that they could change the platform on which the planetary bodies are designed and lockout all outside influences, keeping those in this galaxy hostage and disconnecting them from their higher natures."

"These traitors sold me to a group of Gorgon's who run this prison from Algol. They are part of a group that serves the Dark One of Aln. The darkest, most horrendous acts of violence and deceit have been practiced here, and they have used my knowledge of quantum systems to keep the operation going throughout the galaxy." M put his head down in sorrow.

Breacher asked, "Why would you help them all of this time?"

M looked up and simply stated, "Your worlds would not be here if it were not for me. Those people, in the dungeons, their lives would be over. All life as we know it would be over. The Gorgons and their minions are pure evil and do the bidding of the Dark One. They do not care if all life is destroyed. If they cannot have it all, hold power over everyone, then they will blow up the entire operation, and Earth is included in that. I could not let that happen. I knew that the Light Forces would one day come. I have been waiting for you for a very long time."

Breacher immediately thought of the Bird Lord, not surprised that he was connected to this organized darkness.

Commander Bewain commented, "Thank you for this update, M. We have been aware of the quarantine but did not know about this outpost. If we are going to be successful in clearing this outpost and saving the humans, we will need to work together to clear out the roots of this evil."

Monoceros looked into his pocket and pulled out a device that held the intel they would need to make the next mission successful. "I am at your service... but my warning is this; the Gorgons have many minions all over the galaxy. We must be precise in our execution of the removal of each of their programmer bases. We will talk more about this as this is detailed, and it will require Strategists." He handed the device to Breacher.

Breacher received the device and said, "We are grateful that the Divine Mother sent us here. We had no idea what we were looking for, and now I can see that this is a high-level mission to be implemented in many stages. Let's get some rest. We will begin the formulation of the strategy tomorrow. For now, my team needs to tend to the dragons and the Pegasus."

M took note when Breacher mentioned the Pegasus. He shuddered to hear of it. Breacher asked, "Are you okay?"

M whispered, "I just had a chill... That is all."

Breacher looked towards the riders, and with that, everyone rose from their seats, bowed, and left the room.

Monoceros and Bewain continued the dialog. The rest of the crew listened to Monoceros as he laid out the truth of the darkness that had taken over the solar system.

And the wheel turns...

Chapter 67

Bridgit and Stella Return to California

After their whirlwind trip, the Ladies Phare returned to the United States at the end of July, rather than extending their stay in Scotland. Bridgit camped out the rest of the month at Todd and Stella's, as the two ladies planned their next phase, finding the last few Life Bearers.

Stella continued to study the stone pendants to understand just how these pendants would activate. She did not want to let Christopher down as he had asked her to get acquainted with the technology before he arrived for a visit in the coming weeks. Bridgit played catch up with paperwork and emails since they had been gone for an extended period.

The ladies were both in the kitchen where Stella sat painting her nails, babbling about her thoughts on the stone pendants, and how the word Etifah would play into the portal activation. At the same time, Bridgit received an email message from an old friend who lived nearby, inviting her to an evening concert which she was hosting in her home.

"Stella, I would love it if you would accompany me to my friend Traci's home for a house concert. I think you would really love her. I haven't seen her in quite some time."

Bridgit poked at Stella as Stella was putting the final stroke of nail polish on her finger. Stella growled as if she was seriously mad but ended up sounding like a kitty.

Bridgit snapped off a piece of a biscotti that was lying on a plate near Stella and placed it in front of Stella's mouth, saying, "Here kitty, kitty. Come to Traci's with me!"

The two laughed as Bridgit stuffed the biscotti bite into Stella's mouth. Stella moaned in delight, enjoying her favorite treat. It had just the right amount of crunch and softness at the same time. A perfectly baked biscotti was always Stella's weakness.

The two were enjoying having a routine together, and it made Stella happy when she could have a latte and biscotti. Stella paused to gently wipe the crumbs from her mouth with the palm of her hand, keeping her fingernails straight and out of the way. "I tell you what, that was the last biscotti, and I am low on coffee beans. Why don't you come with me to the bakery down the way, where I get the good stuff, and you can fill me in on Traci?"

Stella smiled and walked over to get her keys but hesitated to pick them up for fear of ruining her newly polished nails.

Bridgit walked over and grabbed the keys from off the counter and said, "Come on, I'll drive. Maybe we can get a few treats to bring tonight?" Bridgit smiled as they walked out the door.

They arrived at the bakery and ordered their fair share of biscotti and coffee. They also picked out a few eclairs and pastries to bring as offerings for the concert at Traci's home later.

After picking out a large assortment of items, including two bags of coffee beans and coffee to drink while they waited, Stella asked, "Since we have a while, why don't you tell me about Traci?"

Bridgit smiled, "Sure. When I left home for California, I did not know anyone. Traci was the first person I met when I arrived at college. I went straight to my dorm room, and there she was hanging a poster of a tree with one of my favorite Muir quotes on it."

Bridgit smiled, remembering the moment and continued, "I stood there staring at that poster. Traci smiled at me and introduced herself, then noticed my eyes watering."

"She was the kindest and most sensitive individual, and because of her, I survived my first year of college relatively unscathed. The funny thing was that the only poster that I brought to college was one with a John Muir quote on it too. It was then that we knew that we would be great friends."

Stella was happy to hear that Bridgit had someone that understood her. She asked another question, "So clearly she likes trees and nature. Was she studying to be an arborist also?"

Stella took the coffee and biscotti from the woman at the counter and then looked back to Bridgit for a response.

Bridgit took her coffee in hand as they moved away from the counter.

Stella gave her a biscotti, which Bridgit immediately dunked into her coffee, shaking her head, then answered, "Surprisingly no. She went a different route. In the summer, after our freshman year, she and I traveled down to Brazil with her father. He had a stake in a Tourmaline mine in the Paraiba region, and we were his helpers." Bridgit air quoted the word helpers, with her biscotti stuck between her teeth.

"He paid us really well that summer. It was the best summer job that I ever had." Bridgit snorted with laughter, thinking about how carefree she was back then.

She continued, "We sorted and graded the stones, and we got pretty good at it. Traci was much better at it than I. She had years of working with her Dad in the summers. I just sorted the stones in groups of color and size, and she did the grading."

Stella was fascinated by Bridgit's many hidden talents and asked, "So she went into Geology?"

Bridgit slurped the last of the coffee-soaked biscotti and then answered, "Nope. You would think that she would follow in her father's footsteps, but she is more of a big picture person. She actually went into Ecology. She started a non-profit that brings Ecologists together from all over the world. She is helping to steer policy in the area of Ecological Restoration."

Bridgit nodded her head as she watched Stella's mouth open wide. Stella chomped on her biscotti while hearing about Traci.

"I have to admit she sounds a little intimidating." Stella twisted her face into a contorted position, with her eyes bugging out.

Bridgit laughed, "I assure you, she is not in the least intimidating. She is amazing, and you will love her." Bridgit winked at Stella and watched her face slowly go back to normal.

"Tonight, we will be meeting her boyfriend, Henny. He is the musician doing the concert." Bridgit picked up her phone and pulled up his social media page and pushed the phone towards Stella so that she would have something to read while she drank her coffee and finished her biscotti.

Stella grabbed the phone, thumbing through the photos and came across a pick of Henny with a woman. "Is this her?" Stella tapped the pic to expand it and handed the phone back to Bridgit.

"YES! That's her. She doesn't age. They look so in love in this picture." Bridgit stared at the photo a bit too long, and Stella could feel empathically, where Bridgit had gone.

Stella said, "I have to admit that when you listed all of Traci's qualities, I am embarrassed to say that I sort of expected her to be a little bit more frumpy." Stella covered her eyes with the honest admission.

"Frumpy?! How rude!" Bridgit halfway joked but thought the comment was wild, in this day and age.

Stella said, "I know! I'm sorry. I don't know why I thought that. A pretty woman can be smart, too!"

She wiped her mouth as she heard her name called to pick up her order. "Saved by the bell! Be right back!" She jumped up to grab the goodies and then came back to complete the conversation.

"Well, they are great, and I look forward to meeting them. Let's get the heck out of here. We need to get back and change if we are going to a concert!"

She pulled Bridgit out of a momentary yearning for Breacher, and the ladies were out the door. "You have my keys?" Stella asked as Bridgit pulled them from her pocket and tossed them to Stella with style.

"You're good... my friend!" Stella laughed as they jumped into the car and headed back home.

And the wheel turns...

Chapter 68

A Friendly Home Concert

Bridgit and Stella pulled up to Traci's home, overlooking Topanga Canyon. A gentle breeze caught Bridgit's dress as she exited the car. She stood, staring at the beautiful scenery. Traci lived at the far end of a winding road.

The home was nestled on the edge of a cliff that overlooked the canyon. The house was made with straw bale and covered in a ruddy red shade of limestone mixture. In front of her home was a small garden bed surrounded by a short rustic fence. Plants hung from the eves on both sides of the large wooden door that had forged hinges and a dragon door knocker.

Bridgit noticed someone on the side deck playing the flute. Stella yelled out a greeting, and a tall, casually dressed, handsome man with dark curly hair and bright blue eyes waved them over. The ladies came up the stairway, in front of the house, and onto the right side of the deck, which wrapped around the entire house.

"Hello! I'm Henny. You must be Bridgit." Henny walked towards

Stella with his arms outstretched. He grabbed her with a bear hug, lifting Stella off the ground and wiggled her around without giving her time to respond. Bridgit stopped to watch as Stella's arms were pinned down, and her body was flailing about as Henny hugged her. She giggled out loud, watching Stella's hands flap.

Once Henny put her down, Stella responded, "Ah... it is nice to meet you, Henny, but I am actually Stella, Bridgit's cousin. THAT would be Bridgit." She stepped out of the way, pointing towards Bridgit. Henny shrugged it off, always happy to give hugs to anyone, so it did not bother him in the least that he had just hugged a near stranger.

As Henny approached Bridgit, Bridgit put her hand out to merely shake hands, but Henny did not have it. "Oh, we hug around here!" Henny grabbed her hand and brought Bridgit in for a replica of the hug he doled out to Stella.

He said, "Heart to heart!" as he made sure they matched the left side of their chests, assuring that their heartbeats would somehow match momentarily.

The three of them laughed, and once the bizarre introductions were over, they walked further out onto the deck to see the view. After chatting for a bit, Henny said, "Listen, I will let Traci know that you are here. She is in the bedroom, getting ready. I'll be right back. Take a look around." He winked at the ladies and pointed to the setting sun, as he pulled the sliding door open, leaving Stella and Bridgit in awe of the natural world.

After a few peaceful moments, Stella asked with a chuckle, "Did that just happen?"

"Hum, yes, he is quite the hugger, isn't he?" Bridgit grabbed Stella's arm and walked near the edge of the deck and took in the scene. "This place is gorgeous. Look at this view!"

Stella was calming herself and taking in the beauty, "It sure is. There is something about a setting sun above a canyon that just does it for me!"

Henny pulled the sliding door opened and invited the ladies inside. Another car drove up as the ladies entered the home. "Help yourself to some dip. There is homemade cider on the table there."

The doorbell rang as he was showing them the offerings. "I will be right back."

Henny clapped his hands together to wipe off crumbs from a cracker that he was eating as he turned towards the entry hall.

Stella said, "Oh, wow, I totally forgot to bring in the treats we brought. I will walk out with you, Henny." Henny motioned for her to follow him to the entry hall.

Stella went to the front door and exited after a brief introduction, while Bridgit hung back, listening from the kitchen area to the sweet voices in the hallway. The woman's voice speaking with Henny sounded familiar, Bridgit thought. She had a sudden recognition of whose voice it was. She set down her cup of cider and peeked around the corner. There she saw Alvie Trudchen in the hallway.

"Alvie?" Bridgit stood in the hallway as Alvie pulled away from Henny's bear hug and dropped her purse. She ran towards Bridgit, and the two hugged in a long embrace. Stella walked back in with the baked goods and saw that Bridgit was yet again in the embrace of a stranger, or so she thought.

"How are you!!?" Alvie asked. "I had no idea that you were in town!"

"I'm great! Traci didn't tell me that you would be here!" Bridgit exclaimed.

"Did someone say my name?" Out from the hallway, a gorgeous woman with sun-kissed skin came out to greet her guests. Traci's green eyes matched the emerald green of her dress, and her flowing brown hair was draped around her neck, laying on her right shoulder.

"TRACI!!" Both Bridgit and Alvie yelled her name as they ran towards her. The three college roommates hugged in a triangle, with

462

tears in their eyes.

Stella stood there in shock, holding her biscotti's and pastries and marveling at Bridgit's demeanor in the company of her old friends.

Henny said, "Stella, is it? Let me get you a plate for those. I can almost taste them from here." He winked at her, and the two went into the kitchen to find a platter to plate the goodies.

Stella set the pastries out in an artistic manner and asked Henny about his music. "So, what kind of music are you performing tonight?" She licked her fingers, then went to the sink to wash her hands.

Henny grabbed a hand towel for her and said, "I am a freestyle vocalist. I do a bit of acapella, but I mainly do live looping. My music is meditative, mostly. A lot of yoga studios are playing my sound."

"Right on." Stella folded the towel and followed Henny towards the table. She placed the platter next to the cider. She lingered in the kitchen to give Bridgit time to reconnect with her close friends.

Henny excused himself and went over to where his equipment was near the fireplace. As he was adjusting the equipment, his phone rang. Henny walked back towards the kitchen to take the call while the ladies mingled.

Stella overheard Henny listening to a person over the phone apologizing for not making it to the concert. He was very kind and gentle, giving the person the perfect out by saying that tonight was going to be a trial run on something new and that he was going to record it tonight and could send a demo to him at a later date.

"No worries, man. Okay, catch you soon. Goodnight." Henny hung up the phone and walked over to Traci.

"George is not able to come. He and Grace couldn't get out of town in time, and their manager had to leave town suddenly, so he wasn't going to be able to make it either. So, I guess it is just the five of us."

Traci said, "Oh, Hun, I'm so sorry about that." She placed her hand on his shoulder.

Henny replied, "You know, it's cool. We have some new blood here tonight, and I would love to show you ladies what I have been working on."

He looked towards Bridgit and Alvie and then pointed to Stella as well. "I am just going to finish setting up. Keep eating! You ladies chat while I do this."

Traci turned to see Stella walk up. She extended her hand out to introduce herself, "Stella! Traci Wade. We are so glad that you could join us tonight. I have heard a smidgen about you, but from what Bridgit shared in her email, the two of you have only just found one another? I would love to hear that story!"

She turned and realized that she had not introduced Alvie. "Excuse my manners. Let me introduce you to Alvie Trudchen." Traci stepped aside as Stella leaned forward with her hand out to shake Alvie's hand.

"What's this? A long lost relative?" Alvie's voice went deep and cheerful at the same time. Her grip was as firm as any man's, Stella thought, as Alvie's grip pinched her fingers together.

"Yes, we have not known each other long, but it seems like forever, ya know." Stella smiled, gently releasing her hand from Alvie's grip, then asked, "Alvie, I detect a slight accent. Is it German?"

Alvie responded once more in a low guttural voice at first, with her chest puffed out. The cadence of her voice went from low to high at times as she spoke with her hands to animate her thoughts. "Why, yes! I am from the US originally, but I lived in Germany growing up. I moved back for University, and I have been here ever since."

"Cool! So, you were all three roommates?" Stella looked at the three of them, seeing the joy on their faces.

Traci responded, "Yes! We have known one another since freshman year at UC Davis."

Traci looked at Bridgit and relayed, "I wasn't sure if Alvie, or you for that matter, could make it, so I didn't mention it to either of you. I wanted it to be a surprise for all!" Bridgit and Alvie hugged once more. That is when Stella noticed Alvie's ear.

Alvie had pulled her long blond hair back behind her ear, which was not at all round like a normal ear but pointed like an elf ear. Stella's eyes got huge.

Alvie looked at her and asked, "Is there something wrong?" She put her hands on her head to try to find what Stella was staring at.

Stella pointed, "Your ear! You have the most amazing pointy little elf ear like Bridgit's!"

Alvie looked at Bridgit, surprised that she never noticed Bridgit's ears before. "You have pointed ears too?" Alvie queried Bridgit.

Stella moved closer and asked, "Do you mind?" inspecting the second pair of fairy ears in her lifetime.

"Sure. Go ahead. The other one is the same. It's actually a funny story. My ears are why my mother named me Alvie. My name means an army of elves." She chuckled at the ridiculousness of it as Stella gawked.

Stella quizzed Bridgit, "Did you ever notice her ears?" Stella moved so that Bridgit could see them.

"No, I didn't." Bridgit took a closer look, shocked, and said, "Well, I'll be! You never really wore your hair up much, did you? But then again, neither did I!"

Alvie responded, "No! I was always hiding my ears! I thought for a long time that it was a deformation." They laughed as they discovered something new about one another.

Everyone was still chuckling as Alvie began to pull her hair over her ears, now happy to show them and then inspected Bridgit's. "Wow! I never knew!" said Alvie.

Bridgit said, "Trust me. Mine were always covered. I just felt self-conscious about it then, but I am totally fine with it now."

"I would never wear my hair down if I had pointed ears! I'd totally rock it!" Stella exclaimed.

Bridgit looked at Stella with a broad grin, and all the ladies chuckled as Traci urged them to graze at the table while Henny continued to set up.

Bridgit asked Traci, "Before we tell you how we met," referring to her and Stella, "Can you tell us how you met Henny?"

"Sure. It is a sweet story." The ladies filled their plates with olives, cheese, hummus and crackers, and fruit skewers. Bridgit took note that it was all vegetarian fare.

They each picked out a different kind of pastry, noting how they would pay for it later.

Stella said, "In moderation... or NOT!" Stella patted her bum to indicate that she may not have been moderate in her consumption of delectable treats.

The ladies took their plates to the living room to listen to the story of how Traci picked up Henny at the co-op after his car broke down.

"He is a friend of a friend. We had met once before, but when I saw him at the co-op with a crapped out car, I brought him here to wait the six hours out until the tow service could arrive. It was a scorching day, and so many people had car trouble up and down the canyon that day."

She turned to look over at Henny, "We just hit it off. It has become serious fairly quickly." Traci pulled out her left hand and showed the girls the engagement ring on her finger.

"It is beautiful!!!" Bridgit pulled her hand towards her to examine the stone. She looked back up and said, "Is this a green tourmaline?"

"Yes! You remembered! Tourmaline is my favorite stone, and as you know, I am not into diamonds." Traci admired her engagement ring as Stella and Alvie also pulled her hand towards them.

"Congratulations, guys! This is so exciting!!!" Stella said.

Bridgit was truly happy for her friend. They all chatted a bit longer about the ring and the engagement. It was Alvie's turn for a closer look. After the ladies finished talking about the engagement and the ring, Bridgit set her plate on the coffee table, and that is when she saw the motherlode tourmaline.

"Wow! Isn't this your Dad's prized possession? You have it here?!" Bridgit touched the large pink tourmaline on the table.

Traci shook her head, "Dad is downsizing these days and knew that I would take good care of it, so he passed it to me. It is now my prized possession!"

A jeweler's loop sat in a small saucer for people to use to inspect the piece. She picked it up and offered it to Stella, telling her about the gemstone properties of this unique piece.

Alvie and Bridgit snuggled up next to one another as Stella and Traci discussed the tourmaline.

Alvie said, "So... how are you doing? We haven't talked much since you lost your grandparents. What have you been doing these days? Work keeping you busy?"

Bridgit adjusted herself on the sofa to look at Alvie, eye to eye. "I am doing much better now... now that I have Stella in my life." Stella looked up from the stone, hearing those words. Bridgit smiled her way and continued. Traci reoriented herself to hear Bridgit's story as

467

well.

"I have to admit, losing my grandparents in the same year was intense. Though I thought that I had prepared myself for the eventuality of their leaving the planet, I just couldn't deal with them leaving within months of each other. I quit my job to deal with the estate, and of course, the tree farm business. It took longer than I expected. I spent quite a bit of time in Louisiana dealing with it, and I was exhausted in the end. It was too sad for me to stay there in that empty house, so I sold everything!"

Bridgit got louder as she told that part, as she knew that her friends would think it not like her to get rid of it all. She continued, "Not too long ago, I decided to pull myself up from my bootstraps, and I got deeply involved in a side project of my own."

"Really? Do tell." Alvie was happy to hear that Bridgit was resourceful.

"I began working on a book in my spare time. The book is a study of World Trees, those ancient and beloved trees from cultures all around the world."

She smiled and continued, "What the trees mean to the culture, where they are found, the mythologies around the trees, that sort of thing... and that is when I met Stella! Which is a very wild story! Stella, you are great at storytelling. Want to tell them how we met?" Bridgit glanced at Stella in a pleading gesture.

Stella's eyes were huge at that moment. She coughed to clear her throat then managed to speak slowly while coming up with the story on the fly.

"Sure...sure.... Well, I was in India recently, accompanying my Dad on a business trip. I play the harp and was looking for a place to play on that particular day. I settled on a lovely area where I found an old Banyan tree. One of those ancient World Trees that Bridgit just described." She looked to Bridgit to see how she was doing with the story.

Bridgit smiled and nodded and quickly grabbed a fruit skewer and took it towards her mouth.

"Oh, you play the harp? How lovely!" Traci said it loud enough so that Henny could hear. He looked up and gave two thumbs up and kept tinkering.

Stella nodded yes to Traci and continued, "I was leaning up against the tree, playing a song that I used to play for my mother. She passed away years ago and, at that moment, I was really missing her. I had crocodile tears filling my eyes, so I shut them while I played, and then suddenly, Bridgit just appeared."

The ladies comforted Stella, sorry to hear that she had lost her mother and in resonance with her situation.

Then Alvie gave Bridgit a curious look and asked Bridgit, "What were you doing in India?"

"Well," Bridgit was grabbing at a plausible explanation and said, "I was researching in Aberdeen, Scotland, while simultaneously studying trees from India, which led me to the Banyan tree where Stella and I found one another. As my research in Scotland was slow going, I decide to hit the next place on my list of World Trees and India was it."

Bridgit's eyebrow raised as she looked at Stella for more help.

Stella jumped back in, "Apparently, the tree that I had picked to play my sad songs was the exact tree that Bridgit was studying for her book. We ended up talking that day until late. Bridgit had not even had a chance to make a hotel reservation the day she got there; she literally had jumped off the plane and went directly to the tree!"

Stella chuckled with laughter, and so did Traci. "Yep, that sounds about right."

Alvie said, "REALLY? You traveled to India and didn't make any reservations?" Alvie shook her head, not having the ability or desire to do that kind of spontaneous thing. Alvie was much more of a fixed sign and needed things planned in advance.

Stella saved Bridgit once more, "Normally hotels are a dime a dozen there, but the only ones worth staying at were full, due to a huge convention. So, long story short, I offered to let her stay with me in my suite. My Dad had a day trip that kept him away that night, and she was just too tired at that point to deal, so she agreed to stay the night with me. That is when the bizarre stuff happened."

Stella burst out laughing. "I still can hardly believe what happened next." She looked at Bridgit, who was agreeing with her.

Alvie and Traci were both curious, and Henny had grabbed a plate and joined them at this point. He sat on the edge of the sofa cushion, he too, hanging on Stella's words.

"Well, it was early evening and when Bridgit and I walked into the hotel together. The concierges called out to me very formally by saying, Miss Phare?" Stella tried to say it in his formal accent.

"We both stopped and answered, yes? That is when I turned to Bridgit, and we looked at each other for a moment, not knowing WHAT was happening! I was curious as to why she said yes to the Concierge calling my last name! That night we came to realize that we had the exact last name, same spelling and everything and that we could be related! Eventually, once we got back to the states, we did confirm the fact that we are indeed second cousins. I couldn't make this stuff up. Trust me!"

All three of the people were staring at Stella with their jaws dropped. Henny said, "Are you serious? You met in some random place because of a tree and came to find that you're related? That is the most insane and synchronous event I have ever heard!"

Stella said, "Well, stick with us, and we will bedazzle you with synchronicities! Ever since I met this girl, my life has been one adventure after another. She is the female version of Indiana Jones!" Stella grabbed a cracker and dipped it into the hummus and began to ooh and ah. Everyone just shook their heads in amazement and took bites of the delicious food.

Stella then looked at Alvie and asked, "I'm sorry, Alvie. I didn't ask what it is that you do." Trying to change the subject and yet genuinely interested.

Alvie grabbed her card out from her cell phone case and handed it to Stella. I am a wildlife rehabilitator. I run a non-profit nature sanctuary where I rehabilitate mostly birds and small woodland creatures. I live reasonably close by, so if you want to come check it out, let me know. I hardly ever leave there, so this is a huge treat for me tonight."

"Alvie's parents were both major contributors to the Audubon Society, and so she grew up with all kinds of animals." Bridgit winked at Stella, proud of her collection of friends.

"Yes. Sometimes I wish that I would have been born a deer or a bird! Humans are not my favorite species." Alvie jabbed at Traci, and they both laughed.

"Alvie, are you seeing anyone these days?" Bridgit pried.

"Nah. It is too much effort. I don't have the kind of time it takes to develop a relationship. Besides, I'm pretty hard to live with. My animals take up all the space in my house!" She laughed as she pulled the phone out to show pictures of her birds. She also showed them pictures of the raccoons and the fox that are her regular guests.

"Wow. You are amazing!" said Stella. "I would love to see a fox that close up!"

"Well, you are more than welcome to come for a visit. I have a guest room. You should come!"

She looked at Bridgit too. Alvie had such a warm nature about her, and Bridgit admired how she walked the planet. Bridgit always thought highly of Alvie and knew that her presence on this Earth made the Earth a better place to live.

"We will have to do that!" Bridgit nodded. She stared into Alvie's eyes and felt at that moment a deeper connection, something that needed further inspection.

Henny jumped up, looking at the clock on his cell phone and exclaimed, "It's showtime!"

The ladies were all genuinely excited to hear the music man do his thing. They refilled their drinks and snuggled up on the sofa, with Stella opting for the large floor pillow next to the coffee table.

Once the ladies were seated, Henny began a short intro into his style of music and what inspires him.

"Thank you all for coming at such short notice. Clearly, it was divine synchronicity that you are all here at this moment, and the other guests were sadly not able to join us...so consider this concert to be a consecration of our friendships, old and new." He smiled at the ladies, looking at Traci with deep love. She blew him a kiss, and he began.

"I have long loved whales and dolphins, so this first song is inspired by the sounds of the sea and, in particular, my whale brothers." Henny bowed in reverence and took his place behind his equipment.

His musical instruments were a microphone and a looping pedal on the floor. Henny took a long breath and began a deep guttural sound with his hands wrapped around his mouth. He began to create the sounds of the whales, using the floor pedal to capture the music, which played in a constant loop.

He then made a different sound, somehow mimicking the sounds of water ebbing and flowing. He laid one track over the other. He continued to do this several times until he had a melody of sounds that created a feeling of comfort in the room, intending to give them all the sensation of floating in the ocean.

At this point, he encouraged the ladies to close their eyes as he added the sounds of the crystal bowls and a very particular tuning fork. The room was in full array of both celestial and oceanic sounds as the women surrendered to the journey that Henny was taking them on.

Stella felt to lay down, and Bridgit slipped down to the ground to stretch her legs out around the side of the coffee table, leaning up against the front of the sofa. Both ladies telepathically connected, feeling something special was about to happen.

Alvie and Traci were both leaning back on the sofa with their eyes shut as Henny began to guide them all on a fantastic underwater journey. His voice carried the vibration of love, as it was sent out into the ocean. He gently rocked back and forth while making whale sounds.

Everyone was connecting to the whales within their hearts and hearing the ocean sounds as if they were truly transported deep into the ocean.

Alvie and Traci sunk deeper into the sofa, as if magnetically being pulled into the depths of the ocean floor. After some time, a light began to emanate from within the tourmaline on the coffee table that was between Stella and Bridgit.

The sounds and frequencies in the room were steadily rising, and the two women on the sofa were completely gone. Stella and Bridgit could see the light emitting from the stone within their mind's eye, and they both opened their eyes to investigate.

Henny was blissed out, listening to the sounds that he had created with the looping machine. Suddenly, Stella sat up, startled by a being standing in the corner of the room. She observed the being come more into form within an etheric substance, like a cloud surrounding it.

Bridgit was facing the other way, and Stella did not want to lose the connection with this being, so she opted to stay silent and observe.

The being was tall with pearlescent white, shiny skin. He wore a white robe with a sash across his chest. The being's hair was long and white, and its bright blue eyes were as blue as the ocean. She attempted to communicate with the being telepathically. What she heard next was a high-pitched sound. She asked that the being modulate its frequency so that she could understand it, and within a few seconds, the person spoke within her mind.

"Your team is now assembled. You must explain to them what the mission is, and gently guide them to understand why they came together this night, and how the two of you really found one another. Time is of the essence. The divine plan is soon to be active, and all of your presence is required."

The being lifted his arms, sending a ray of light into the top of Alvie's head.

He sent another telepathic message to Stella as she watched Alvie's activation. "Alvie's deepest fear is trust. It is why she does not engage well with other human life forms. She has always known that she would need to be alone to accomplish something, yet she knows not what it is."

The being continued to send energy. The energy was now sent to Traci's head. The being relayed information about Traci this time. "Her heart and mind are balanced with love and wisdom. She has great intellect and will be able to see and know how to work with the higher forces. She won't think she is good enough, but she has had many lifetimes to prepare. She is ready."

Stella continued to hold her gaze on the white-haired being, all the while still tuned into the sounds that Henny was creating intuitively.

The being looked at Henny and said, "He is a Master, here to provide sound and vibrational healing. He is a vibrational specialist from another universe and incarnated to bring a new kind of sound. He will be a great addition to your team."

At that moment, Henny stopped singing and looked straight at the being in the corner. His eyes widened as a flash of light zipped by him and entered the tourmaline that sat on the coffee table. The flash was so bright that all of the women opened their eyes with a start.

"What just happened?" Traci asked. "Did you see that flash?!" She turned to Stella as Stella nodded her head.

Henny looked at Stella as she was the only one in the room who could have possibly seen what he did, yet he didn't want to say what he saw, in case it was too weird for her. He just pointed to the corner and asked, "Did you see anything over there?"

Stella looked at Bridgit and said, "Here goes!"

She turned to Henny and said, "Dear man, that was a true visitation, and I would like to share with all of you what it was all about. But first, I need to speak to Bridgit."

She turned back to Bridgit and said, "Can I speak to you outside?" Stella jumped up and made apologies to Henny for the interruption.

Bridgit was in shock. She knew that something significant just happened. She followed Stella outside on the back porch through the sliding door.

"What is happening?" Bridgit looked into Stella's eyes, hoping it wasn't what she thought it could be...for all kinds of reasons.

Stella said, "Okay. Here is what happened." Stella spoke fast to get it all out before Bridgit could interrupt.

"A white-haired being came out of the tourmaline on the coffee table and was watching us all from the corner of the room. All of our energy fields had expanded as Henny masterfully raised us into a heightened state. I sensed something at a certain point, and that is when I noticed the being hovering in the corner. I began to speak to it telepathically, and at first, it was just a high pitch sound. I asked it to modulate its energy so that we could communicate. It did so, and then it began to give me messages about each of the three people in the room, as LIFE BEARERS!!"

She grabbed Bridgit's shoulders to shake her so that she did not miss that part and gasped for air.

"Life Bearers!!? These three? REALLY????" Bridgit moved her hair back behind her neck and asked Stella to continue.

"Well, I would like to share this with the group so that I don't have to repeat it, but trust me, they are the final three Life Bearers. The being gave me messages about each of them, and I think it is time to be a little more forthcoming about how we really met? You okay with that? The being told me to tell them the whole truth, but it is your call, as they are your friends."

Stella bit down on her lips, her front teeth showing while she wrinkled her nose in anticipation of Bridgit's response. She shrugged her shoulders as if she wasn't sure which way to go, and trying to relay to Bridgit the seriousness of the situation said, "It was real... trust me!"

"Well, I guess if these three are Life Bearers, then we need to tell them. It would be nice to have a normal night with you one of these days!" Bridgit laughed at Stella's facial expressions.

Stella retorted, "This kind of thing started happening the moment I met you so PA-LEASE GIRLFRIEND!" Stella made a gesture with her hand in the air, and they laughed with anxiousness and excitement.

Bridgit said, "Let me start it off, and then I will hand over the floor to you. They are going to have a lot of questions. It's going to be a late night."

And the wheel turns...

476

Chapter 69

Breacher and the Dragon Riders Spin the Merkabah

Once more, the Dragon Riders were in the training room with Breacher as their teacher. He had brought them all together that day to demonstrate how one works with the energies of the planetary grid network. He felt he had to keep them busy while the Alliance worked on a plan to clear Algol.

He lectured for hours on the topic of grid work, and at the end of the class, he led them outside, where the dragons were grazing. He noted that since they all had their starry tattoos, this would be an excellent time to take a journey into the galactic ocean to do some toroidal spinning.

Praeta had heard of this concept once before, the idea of tweaking the node points of the galactic net. Everyone jumped on their dragons and followed Breacher into the cosmic sea.

Once they were in position, Breacher explained, "We are going to nose dive into the active regions of the key nodes within the planetary body. The dragons will provide an influx of energy into these key points, expanding these nodes to allow for energetic upgrades. In other words, we will open the nodes up so more galactic energy can flow through. Think of it like stretching a rubber band."

Breacher led the team into the Cosmic Ocean. It was effortless and took only moments to ride into the cosmic waves where the dragons swam quickly in a magical display.

All of the dragons swirled around Breacher, and the Dragon Riders held on tightly in preparation for their first assignment.

Breacher continued his instruction, "The plan is that you each will go to a particular node, and at the same time, in a synchronized way, you will dive into the energy field with your dragons spinning as fast as they can."

Breacher used his hands to show the procedure. "Dip and spin. Then pop back out again and see what happens. I will forewarn you...this is not for the faint-hearted. You most probably will get a little queasy."

Breacher laughed and said a final word, "Leto and I will be hovering above so that I can monitor the points and calibrations. Once you feel that you have the spinning down, then you can meet me up there." He pointed to a location, and then the team dispersed.

Breacher flew upwards, and through their intercom system on their wristbands, each of them waited to hear Breacher's command. "On your marks, get set... GO!"

The Kumara jetted downward in a green flash as her dragon flew swiftly to the appointed node. The rest of the dragons followed suit. Swirls of green, yellow, blue, and red crisscrossed around the planetary grid until they each found the appropriate nodes.

The dragons began the dance of dipping into the nodes, spinning the Merkabah of the planetary body of Earth. A sacred geometry began to appear where the nodes of two or more lines intersected. The dragons nosedived into the connecting points, then spun as quickly as they could to create a vortex.

The Sage and Alderson jumped out of the nosedive quickly. Breacher watched as they pulled out and flew swiftly to his side. The three Dragon Riders observed the planetary light body change shapes numerous times. The energy of the planet expanded.

Soon, the others joined them. They all viewed the spectacular event that was occurring. At each node, the vortexes were pulling in light from above. The highly charged solar light began to flood the planet through these vortexes. The planet's body morphed into an elongated tube, rather than a sphere, and the vortexes continued to swirl around the planetary body, with one swirling first at the bottom, clockwise, then one swirling at the top, counterclockwise, holding the planetary axis in perfect order.

Soon another swirling energy built up in the center at the equator of the planet. The dragons wanted more. Breacher yelled out to the team to dive back in and hold it, but no more spinning.

"The light has pierced the regions now. We must be gentle with this influx of light. Too much can be detrimental," Breacher explained.

All of the dragons and their riders flew in a rainbow of colored thread. As they entered the vortexes of light, the dragons each drew in the breath of the cosmic energies, holding it in their bellies. They slowly did a counter spin while letting out just enough of the breath to stabilize the flows. The Earth's Merkabah slowed back down, and the planetary body resembled a sphere once more.

Kali and Arbor stayed in the longest, holding the expansion of the node as long as possible, then at the last possible moment, they both jetted upward on their dragons, just in time to see a flash of solar light extinguish. The beauty that the Dragon Riders witnessed was likened to a double rainbow lighting up a pitch-black sky. They observed stars blinking in response and rainbow-colored light explosions, and then calmness.

Breacher monitored the expansion and then motioned for the team to follow him back to the base. The dragons flew swiftly. Exhilaration was the mood of each team member. Nausea was the feeling, as it somehow rearranged something within their beings. Breacher was very proud.

And the wheel turns...

Chapter 70

The Remembrance

Bridgit and Stella made their way back into the living room where the last of the Life Bearers sat waiting to hear what had happened just moments ago.

Alvie and Traci were still reasonably relaxed, but Henny knew that something huge had just happened. All of the hairs on his arms were standing straight up.

Bridgit sat next to Stella on the floor, facing the women and had a view of Henny to the left of them.

Bridgit fidgeted with her knuckles then began, "Well, there are some things that we need to tell you, and I ask that you bear with us as both. Stella and I want to give you the details of what just happened. You will have questions, but I ask that you let us get through this as best as possible."

She turned to Henny and said, "Henny, I do apologize for the interruption of your concert. Truly I do."

Henny was beaming with a gigantic grin and said, "Bridgit, it is quite alright. I know something just went down, so let's hear it." He rubbed his arms as he came closer to the sofa. Alvie scooted over so that he could sit next to Traci, allowing him the middle spot on the couch.

Bridgit started with the tourmaline. She touched it, using it as a focal point to gather her thoughts. "This tourmaline is an extraordinary example of the precious gifts that come from nature. I remember how delighted we were when we found this one at your dad's mine." She looked at Traci with a smile, then continued.

"Minerals each have their own frequencies, and they can assist our bodies and minds in ways that have not yet been examined. With that said, it seems that this particular tourmaline was used as a portal for an ancient light being to come forth, who gave Stella some information about our group, or better put, the three of you." She watched their reactions and then raised her hands to indicate that she was not finished.

"Before we tell you what the message is, it is important that we share more about ourselves and what we have been through in the last three months or so. Is this alright with you all?" She smiled and watched as they all prepared for the story.

"I will start the story by telling you that this is going to be the wildest thing that you have ever heard. I would like for you to contemplate who I am, as the two of you have known me a very long time, and you know that I do not tell stories." She used her fingers in the air to embellish the word stories.

She continued, "What I am about to tell you will take a while to sink in, and it is long, but you are all three a part of the story."

Alvie got cozy, and in her deep voice, with a bit of her German accent accentuated, she said, "Oh goodie, I love a good story. Go on!" She smiled in support of the idea.

Henny was still feeling the energy in his body, and his arm hair was still standing. "Please continue."

Traci rubbed Henny's back and reiterated that the ladies continue with the story.

Bridgit began, "I need to give you more context on how Stella and I met. We kind of left out a few key things." She looked at Stella and then turned back to speak to the group.

Bridgit spoke about how she had entered the fourth dimension through a tree, where she spent time with the Clan of Phare. She then went into how she met her mother in that dimensional space, who was also Stella's fourth dimensional mother.

Bridgit then told them how Shamalaine had helped her to regain some of her memories of who she really was and what her souls' mission was. She shared that, though she was not in the 4th dimension for very long, it felt like a lifetime.

"I was shown that I am what is called a Life Bearer, someone who carries the codes of creation. Shamalaine introduced me to seven elementals, who are on a team known as Builders of Form." She looked at Stella for help here.

Stella chimed in and said, "Elements have a consciousness or a spirit that embodies it. Any living thing has consciousness. The elementals of fire, or rather, the spirit within the fire, are known as a salamander, and the elemental of air is a sylph or fairy. They give deep, mental concentration on their creation to bring it into form."

Stella continued, "Most people are familiar with the idea of angels, as formless helpers in another vibration. Well, elementals, like the angels, are also helpers in the unseen realms."

The trio on the sofa nodded to indicate that they understood well enough for Bridgit to continue.

"I was shown that I am to gather twelve other Life Bearers for an extraordinary mission, and I was told that I needed to find them ASAP!"

She watched their excited faces, wanting to ask questions. "We will get to that in a minute. I want to tell you what happened when I returned to this realm before we speak about what happened here tonight. Okay?" She smiled and received the okays from all of them.

Bridgit pushed her hair out of her face and said, "When it was time for me to come back to the 3D Earth, I made my way back through a world tree in India." The trio all started to ask her questions when she mentioned the tree in India.

Henny couldn't refrain from asking a question. "How did you manage to get all the way to India?!"

"I had entered the fourth dimension through a tree in Scotland, but that tree fell in the process, so for me to return, we had to find the nearest world tree, which happened to be in the third dimension in India!"

The trio all said, "WHAT?!"

"Yes! India!! That is where I found Miss Stella sitting by the tree." She patted Stella's leg, and Stella grinned wide with joy as the trio on the couch shook their heads, looking at one another to see if they were buying it.

Bridgit continued, "I had made my way through the dimensions with the help from the Clan of Phare and the Elementals. As the vibration of the tree activated to release me back into the third dimension, Stella happened to be sitting there playing her harp while her father was in a business meeting."

Traci, Alvie, and Henny just looked at Stella and Bridgit with their eyebrows raised, almost coming out of their skin with anticipation as to how this story includes them.

"Long story short, Stella and I began a dialog that went into the night and the next day, and it was then that we realized how fate had brought us together in such bizarre circumstances. To find out that we were related was almost beyond what either of us could comprehend,

484

but it is true."

Bridgit and Stella shared a momentary glance, still marveling over the events that led to their uniting. After a brief pause, Bridgit said, "Soooooo many more weird things continued to happen."

She looked at the tourmaline once more then said, "We have come to understand that we are to gather the thirteen Life Bearers for the mission of a lifetime. This mission is critical to the plan for humanity and the New Earth at this time. The time that we are living in really is the dawning of the Age of Aquarius. Have any of you heard of the idea of a New Earth or the Aquarian Age?"

Henny chimed in, "Yes! Of course!"

He busted out in song, "This is the dawning of the Age of Aquarius," he stopped himself from singing the whole tune and said, "It is what I think of and meditate on all of the time!" He turned to Traci to give confirmation.

Traci said, "Well, yes, he is right. We have talked about what it would look like to have peace on a renewed earth, where we live extraordinary lives in deep respect with nature. That is what I have dreamt of since I was a small child. It is what drew me to Henny as it is within his heart as well."

She smiled, and they quickly gave one another a peck on the lips. She looked at Bridgit and said, "It is also why we are ecologically minded and advocates of the Earth in our own ways."

On the other end of the sofa, Alvie held back tears and remarked that she had always wondered why she incarnated into such a harsh place where the animals are in danger due to humanity's barbaric ways.

She wiped her tears and said, "I have worked all of my life to provide sanctuary to the animals. In a perfect world, we live side by side in harmony, which is the visualization I use every night when I go to bed."

Bridgit felt her sorrow and then said, "Well, to date, Stella and I have had some extraordinary adventures which led us to find all of the Life Bearers, save three." She put three fingers up for a visual effect.

"We have been waiting, not so patiently, to find the last three. I will let her tell you what occurred tonight." She sat back on her pillow as Stella lifted upward on her knees to begin the explanation.

"Henny, let me start by saying that I am impressed with your ability to bring us all into a cohesive rhythm, as it spiraled us higher and higher until we blended our energies as a group. It was at that point that a flash of light occurred. I opened my eyes to investigate and witnessed the flash of light lift up out of the tourmaline and hovered over in the corner of the room."

Stella used her hands to elaborate, "It soon took shape within a cloudy substance, and I could then see a tall being with shiny white skin and long white hair. Its eyes were large and deep blue like the ocean. It took me a bit to connect with it telepathically because it sounded like a high-pitched noise at first. I asked it to modulate the sounds so that I could commune with it, and it did so."

The group had the same facial expressions. All of their eyebrows were raised once more, with a shocked look upon their faces.

Stella smiled and said, "This is not my first rodeo!" She laughed and repositioned herself as the trio realized that Stella was Clairsentient.

"The being had come to give us a message. He said that our wait was over and that we were in the presence of the final three Life Bearers."

"REALLY!?" Henny shouted out the question and then shook his head and burst out crying with this confirmation. He put his hand to his face and hid his face in his lap as Traci rubbed his back in support.

Alvie rubbed his arm from the other side of the sofa, hoping to give him support as well. Everyone paused while Henny gathered himself. He lifted his head and used his sleeve to wipe his tears of joy.

"I am so happy! I don't even know what this means, but I am just so happy!! Please continue."

Stella smiled as she told each of them what the messenger had shared. The room was filled with an orange hue as if a flame was lit around them. They talked into the night about the roles that they would play. They discussed their hopes for the Earth and their fears. The night was spent giving the trio as much information as they could withstand so that they could make a crucial decision about what was to come next.

Stella and Bridgit gave them the pros and cons of the mission. The con being that they would be away for a while, and that would mean that everything in their lives would be on hold.

They made sure to tell them that there would be a gathering where all of the Life Bearers would come together for guidance and training before the mission could proceed. This meant that they would have only a short amount of time to decide if they were able to heed the call of their mission.

The five talked through the questions that came up until it was clear that they were saturated with information and needed to sleep. Alvie was spent and decided to stay the night. Stella and Bridgit left Traci's home with the three new Life Bearer's minds blown.

Once Bridgit got into the car, she began to cry. "I can't believe how amazing this life is! I am in constant amazement at the miracle of life. Every time we follow synchronicity, it leads to yet another amazing discovery. It is also amazing how large of a world this is, and yet so small."

She wiped her eyes as Stella kept an eye on the road. Bridgit remarked, "I am not sure that I would have been able to communicate so eloquently with that being as you did. You were meant to be here tonight!"

Stella could see that and said, "Now the real work begins!" She drove into the night, relieved that their team was assembled.

Bridgit was not quite relieved. She knew how hard it was to say yes to her mission, and three individuals were now affected by this, and each of them would have to summon the courage to say yes. As she contemplated this thought, Stella yelled, "Brace yourself!!!!"

Stella grazed a deer that jumped out of nowhere. The car screeched to a halt, halfway in the ditch. The car was upright with no airbags deployed.

"You okay?" Stella quickly assessed if Bridgit was harmed.

"What just happened?" Bridgit was foggy as she was not paying attention to the road at all.

"A deer just ran out in front of me and grazed the front side of the Jeep. Let me check it out. Just stay here."

Stella was able to back the car up, out of the ditch and onto the road again. "Thank God for 4-wheel drive!"

She jumped out to inspect the vehicle for damage. Fortunately, the only damage was to the fog light below the main headlight and a small dent in the front end of the bumper near the headlights.

She went back to the driver's side door and jumped back into her seat. "We will be alright. There is a small amount of damage, but we lucked out, girl! Thank you, ANGELS!!! It could have been a lot worse!" She looked at Bridgit with a stern look, as this was yet another attempt to get them off track.

Bridgit said, "I hope the deer is okay."

Stella said, "It just kept running so I think it will be okay. Keep an eye out for any more animals. I will take it slow."

And the wheel turns...

Chapter 71

The Choosing of One's Destiny

It was now two weeks after the last three Life Bearers were found. Over those two weeks, Bridgit and Stella guided and nurtured Traci, Henny, and Alvie as they came to terms with the understanding that they were the last three Life Bearers.

This time was incredibly stressful for all involved, as it meant a complete change in all of their lives. No one knew what the future held, and leaving their current status in life for an unknown amount of time seemed too daunting for Alvie in particular.

Traci and Henny knew deep in their souls that this life event was what they had subconsciously been searching for. To be of service to humanity is all that they had ever wanted. After deep contemplation, they agreed to put off their marriage until this mission was completed.

Bridgit was grateful that Henny and Traci were on board. Still, she was having trouble finding a way into Alvie's mind on the subject. Initially, Alvie was happy to be a part of the team until reality set in.

All Alvie could think about was leaving her sanctuary and the animals behind.

Bridgit spoke with Christopher on the phone the day after they found the three Life Bearers. With the news, he told her that he planned on arriving in California in the coming weeks with the other Life Bearers for the final preparations before they entered the next phase of the mission.

Christopher stressed to Bridgit to find a way to get through to Alvie. Bridgit decided that an impromptu visit with Alvie at her nature sanctuary was in order, which was one and a half hours west of Stella's home, near Santa Barbara.

Stella stayed to prepare for the onslaught of visitors. Todd was traveling again, which allowed Stella to make the arrangements as laid out by Christopher. There were many details to attend to, and David was expected to arrive early to help Stella as well. Bridgit's only job was to convince Alvie that she must join the team.

On the drive to Alvie's place, Bridgit had a knot at the pit of her stomach, contemplating how to get through to Alvie. She only had days to get her on board. She pulled up to an open gate with a sign next to it that read: Trudchen Wildlife Rehabilitation and Nature Sanctuary. Bridgit continued slowly down a gravel road with live oaks on both sides of the driveway.

She pulled the car into a parking area just off to the right of a large white lime-washed home with rustic windows and a large wooden door. To the left of the home were two other large buildings used to house the small rescue animals and hold equipment and feed. Behind the building was a large fenced pasture.

As Bridgit took in the beauty of the place, she walked behind the animal facilities and around the fenced pasture. She noticed someone nearby and walked the fence line to ask where she might find Alvie Trudchen. The lady pointed Bridgit in the direction of the pond.

Large live oak trees shaded the area, and there was a multitude of birds enjoying the flowers and water from the small pond just beyond the pasture.

As Bridgit got closer, she recognized Alvie, who was wearing a floppy hat and sitting on a bench near the pond. Alvie sat in silence, staring towards the pond. She did not notice that Bridgit was present.

Bridgit watched as Alvie laid her hand on her lap with her index finger out, and a hummingbird immediately landed upon her finger. Alvie spoke to it softly and lifted a small glass feeder towards the hummingbird. She assisted it to the feeder, allowing it to drink from her hands.

After a few moments, the bird flew off. Alvie hung the hummingbird feeder on a large hook that was near the birdseed feeder. At that moment, another hummingbird flew up and landed on Alvie's hat.

Bridgit could see how much Alvie loved to care for the birds and small creatures. She also knew that it was the only thing that sourced her.

Alvie turned around and found Bridgit standing there with a grin on her face.

"Oh my! You scared me!" Alvie said in a flustered voice.

"I'm sorry. I didn't want to disturb you while you were in deep thought. You clearly have a way with the birds." Bridgit smiled and walked towards Alvie.

"Nice place! Do you mind if I join you for a bit? I have something that I need to share with you?" She waited for Alvie to respond.

"Sorry that I didn't call. I just jumped in the car, and here I am." Bridgit pleaded.

Alvie motioned to her to take a seat on the bench. The two old friends had an awkward pause as they sat down.

"Alvie, I know what I have laid on you is incredible, and I wish that I could take it all back, and we could all just live out our lives according to how we thought we wanted to live them, but this situation is bigger than any of us. It is about remembering who we really are and why we incarnated here on this planet."

Alvie had a nervousness about her. She asked, "How did you think I would feel? I haven't seen you in years, and suddenly I am supposed to believe that your cousin Stella received information from a being in the room that night that would change all of our lives, and I am supposed to drop everything that I am doing here and go with you to who knows where and do what exactly?" Alvie's voice began to tremble.

"I am so angry at you!" Alvie blurted.

She continued her emotional purge. "Don't you see that this is everything to me? I don't have a family. The animals are my family...they are my life!"

Tears were pouring down Alvie's face. Bridgit pulled a tissue from her purse and handed it to her and just sat there helpless to give Alvie comfort. Bridgit could not muster words of encouragement, because, in truth, she completely understood.

Bridgit retorted, "Alvie, I am as alone as you are, and it scares the shit out of me most days! When Shamalaine laid all of this on me, I, like you, was angry. But, once I saw who I was for myself, who I really am, and who and what I left behind to come here to help Earth and its people ascend.... once I realized what I gave up coming here..."

She pointed to the Earth, "I could not say no, for in saying no to this mission, would wipe out all reasoning as to why I am here in the first place and nothing that I experience on this Earth is worth that to me!" She jumped up, now agitated with Alvie for being selfish, and not wanting to make matters worse, Bridgit turned to look away from Alvie.

She said one final thing while looking at the birds in the trees. "There is so much that each of us is giving up and have already given up for this mission."

Bridgit then turned to look at Alvie once more, "We could use someone like you on our team, but I understand if you can't see your way through this."

After what seemed like a minute of silence, Bridgit started to walk away then turned back to Alvie to end it on a pleasant note. "I have always known that you would do great things." She smiled at her dear friend.

Alvie managed a smile back while wiping her tears.

"You have my number if you change your mind." Bridgit turned and walked away, leaving Alvie sitting in her sanctuary.

And the wheel turns...

Chapter 72

Shamalaine's Special Request

Shamalaine had been cautiously monitoring all of the facets of the plan and knew that the Life Bearer's time had come. She had many ways of watching over the key players and knew of Bridgit's failure to secure Alvie's participation in the plan. It was time to send in the Guardians to Alvie's aid.

As Shamalaine stood in the Great Hall of the Clan of Phare, a gentle breeze fluttered her skirt. She turned to see Breacher standing there in the pose of a soldier at attention.

Shamalaine said, "Breacher, so glad that you could join me so soon."

She motioned for him to join her at the long table for some tea. As they walked, she asked, "How was your journey?"

Breacher smiled and said, "Swift and unexpected." His response was quick due to his interest in knowing what could be so important that she would take him away from his duties. He was hoping that it would include another visit to his beloved.

Shamalaine gestured for him to join her.

Breacher said, "Ladies first," as he put his hand out for Shamalaine to lead. He made himself comfortable as Shamalaine poured the tea, then she made her request.

"I have a favor to ask of you, but first, I will give you an update on Kaialena, as I am sure that you are aching to hear the news." She winked at him and watched his face relax as a sparkle in his eye showed his eagerness to hear more.

"By all means, please share what you can of Kaialena and Tulina's efforts." Breacher took the teacup and sipped the tea.

"The ladies are doing well with their hunt for the Life Bearers. In fact, they have found all of them, but there is a slight problem. There is one known as Alvie, who is a tremendous empath and is deeply connected with the earth and, most especially, the animal kingdom. Kaialena has not been able to persuade Alvie to leave her home to fulfill her destiny."

Breacher was glad to hear that the ladies were so close, but the problem with Alvie disturbed him. "Shamalaine, I do understand that Kaialena has a major issue here, but as you know, I am in the midst of my own issues and timings, now that we have located the Unicorn, Monoceros. I don't have much time to be away from the team but will do what I can. What is it that you want me to do?"

Shamalaine stated, "Breacher, I almost didn't call for you, but I think it is essential that you show up for Alvie's sake. Tell her who you are. Tell her of the mission that you are undertaking, and the loss that you have endured by being separated from Kaialena. Let her see that this mission is real and that it is larger than her, larger than any of us. Perhaps by you "popping" in, it will help her understand that it is not a figment of Kaialena and Tulina's imagination. I think she is afraid to believe that the mission is real, and who could blame her. She needs proof."

She smiled and took a sip of her tea, then continued. "I would like for you to take Butler and pay Alvie a visit. Butler is willing to stay on there in her stead and care for the animals. Make sure she understands that her sanctuary will be watched over by highly specialized beings, seen and unseen."

"I can do that. Is there any chance of my seeing Kaialena while I am there?" His eyes squinted, bracing himself for her response.

"I am sorry, Breacher, but Kaialena cannot be distracted now. All of the Life Bearers are about to descend on her, and Christopher will be keeping her busy from this point on. Besides, I know Bewain needs you back with him as soon as possible. Can you be swift with this mission?"

Breacher laughed at the question. "When do you want me to go?"

"Butler is waiting for you in the garden." She smiled and pointed towards the door as she stood to say her goodbyes. He was swift, indeed, as he vanished in thin air. Shamalaine walked to the window to look out upon the garden. Butler and Breacher had already taken their leave.

"Good...very good." Shamalaine was hopeful that Breacher and Butler would be able to make a difference in Alvie's mind and heart.

And the wheel turns...

Chapter 73

Back at the Wildlife Sanctuary

It was early morning at the sanctuary. The rooster crowing was the loudest of nature's many sounds to be heard. The peacocks were pecking around, while a few sheep gathered in the pasture grazing.

Alvie was in the kitchen of her home, preparing a cup of coffee. As she stood at the sink, filling up the coffee pot, she caught a glimpse of a white horse beyond the pasture. "What in the world?!"

Alvie put the coffee pot down and ran to the back door, where her boots stood waiting for her. She quickly shoved her feet into them, grabbing her hat and a long sleeve shirt to put over her pajama top.

With the brim of her hat in between her teeth, she twisted her hair into a ponytail as she passed the barn near the sheep, who were waiting impatiently for food on the other side of the fence. She tussled her hair back and put the hat on her head.

Making a quick pace, she rounded the end of the fenced pasture and could see the white horse just beyond the pond and bench. She stopped for a moment then ran back to the barn to grab some hay and a few pellets of grain. She knew that for her to get close, she would need an offering.

She quickly grabbed fresh hay and threw some grain into her button-down shirt pocket then once again made her way to where the horse was. She rounded the end of the fence line and walked quickly towards the pond. She did not see the horse anywhere. "That's funny! Where did it go?" she said out loud.

A voice came from behind, "I think it found its way back to its rider."

Alvie let out a scream and held her hand to her heart as if to keep it contained in her chest. The hay was now all over her chest and a bit in her face as she peeked through it to see who was speaking.

"Geez, you scared me! Where did you come from?" Alvie's heart was racing as she watched the gentleman take off his cowboy hat and address her.

"Please forgive me, ma'am. I do apologize for frightening you." Breacher bowed his head with his hat in hand and stepped backward slightly, trying to emulate a cowboy with his words and mannerisms, thinking it would comfort Alvie.

She calmed herself by breathing a few deep breaths then asked, "Can I help you?"

"Well, actually, I am hoping to help you, ma'am. My name is Breacher." He motioned behind her and said, "Ah, here she comes."

At that moment, a very tall, large man walked up with the white horse on a lead.

"Is she yours? I saw her through the window from way over there!" Alvie pointed to the distance of her home.

"Good Morning Miss. My name is Butler, and this here is Pretty Girl. My apologies for letting her get away from me. She made a beeline for this place as I was walking her."

"It is quite alright. She is beautiful." Alvie came closer to offer some hay.

"Do you live around here?" Alvie quizzed as she stroked Pretty Girl's side while the horse ate the grain that Alvie pulled from her pocket.

"No, ma'am. We are just visiting. Checking out the area." Butler smiled and called to Pretty Girl to follow him.

"Thanks for the grain, Miss." Butler bowed his head as he walked Pretty Girl away from Breacher and Alvie.

Breacher asked, "Do you mind if we speak privately for a few moments? We have someone in common, and I need to be forthright with you."

Alvie looked away from the horse and at him. The sun was coming through the trees, shining in her eyes. She secured her hat closer to her eyes to look at the newcomer. "We have someone in common? Who might that be?"

Breacher said, "That would be Bridgit Phare."

Alvie looked down at her feet, "I see. Sure, let's sit here."

Alvie turned towards the bench and murmured, "You must be one of them."

Breacher joined her at the bench and said, "One of them? Oh, you mean a Life Bearer? No... ma'am, I am definitely not a Life Bearer." Breacher continued to use the mannerisms and vernacular of a cowboy, while he kicked at the ground. Hearing this somehow settled Alvie's nerves as she allowed the stranger to present his reason for being there.

"First of all, Bridgit does not have a clue that I am here. I haven't seen her in some time, but I am here on her behalf and yours."

499

"Mine?" Alvie was confused.

Breacher continued, "I will try to make this as simple and quick as possible. And when I tell you about Butler and myself, please bear with me, won't you?" Breacher patted her knee quickly and winked at her.

Alvie's eyes got big and asked, "Do I need to take a pill for this?" Alvie was half-joking and half not, hoping that these two men were there to propose possibly boarding of the horse; at least she had high hopes that it was a simple reason, but she knew better.

"I think you will be okay." He smiled and then took a deep breath and said, "When you were four years old, your family took a camping trip into the Black Forest. There you were held in a zone of nature that nurtured you more deeply than your own mother's caress. Each year your family trekked there almost as a pilgrimage." He looked at Alvie, whose jaw was now wide open.

He continued to read her aura as Alvie responded, "How do you know this?" Alvie asked, dumbfounded by this stranger's information. She began to feel a chill in the air and an uncomfortable feeling of being intruded upon.

"I know a lot more than that, and though I don't have a lot of time, I have to dispense with the pleasantries of getting to know you first. Just know that I have information to share with you today if I may continue?" Breacher politely asked with a smile.

"Okay, I guess." Alvie's deep voice and German accent were more pronounced as she stepped back into the memory of her childhood. She knew that if Breacher was here on Bridgit's behalf, that she should let him speak out of courtesy, besides her curiosity was equal to her discomfort.

"As a child, your body responded to the environment of nature, while being in a home or a school environment taxed your very being. You began to spend almost all of your waking time outside whenever you could, and you found a kindred connection to all of nature's creations.

Not just animals but the plant life as well." He pointed to the beauty around them. The flowers, shrubs, and a menagerie of animals.

"As you grew, your intuition developed. You could read people. What they were thinking and even stronger, you could feel what they were feeling, but you took this for granted and never spoke of it to others."

He was staring into the distance as he was reading her Akashic records, and then he turned to look at her. "You feel more love and more concern for the planet and all creatures more than almost any human that you have ever met." He stared into her eyes with deep compassion.

Alvie did not say a word. Breacher could feel her pain, anxiety, and love. She wiped a tear from her eye and then said, "Now you know why I can't leave this. I think I would die!"

She began to sob uncontrollably. A force from within her unlocked and all of the fears came flowing out in torrents of saline. Breacher put his hand on her shoulder for support and waited it out. Butler came back into the clearing with Pretty Girl. They were still at a distance, when Breacher said, "This man, Butler... he is no ordinary man."

Alvie looked up and wiped her face, then said, "What? What do you mean?"

"You know how Bridgit explained what a Life Bearer is?" Breacher waited for Alvie to acknowledge his question.

"Yes?" Alvie looked confused.

"Well, Butler... he is not from here." He pointed to the ground and looked at Alvie.

"What do you mean, not from here?" Alvie's forehead furrowed.

"What I mean to say is that WE are not from here. The two of us, like you, are members of a team, but we are not Life Bearers, nor do we live in this particular bandwidth, known as 3D Earth." He let out a slight chuckle as he said that.

"What are you talking about? What do you mean by bandwidth? Where are you from anyway?" Alvie was concerned and curious.

"This is where it gets weird." He let out more chuckles and wiped the rough stubble on his face then said, "I was called here by a very special ally. Her name is Shamalaine, and she is the Leader of the Clan of Phare."

"Phare!? That is Bridgit and Stella's last name! Bridgit told us about Shamalaine!" Alvie blurted out as she remembered the story that Bridgit told about her time with the Clan of Phare.

"Yes. She is related to Bridgit and Stella." Breacher paused his words to think. "The thing is, Alvie, there are multiple dimensions within this planet. Each bandwidth holds a particular frequency, and as you know, when one resides in a certain frequency, there are still higher levels of frequencies one may not be able to see, but that does not mean that there isn't life there. It is just vibrating at a different rate of speed. Does any of this make sense to you?" He pierced her eyes to probe her psyche deeply.

Alvie responded yes to his question. "Bridgit told us about her time in the fourth dimension. To be honest, it sounded too good to be true, but I know Bridgit. She would never make something like that up, but it is just so confusing and too much."

Alvie then looked deeply into Breacher's eyes and then asked, "So, if you are from there, what is your mission, and why are you here with me?"

"Ah, that is a loaded question." He smiled and bobbed his head up and down while looking at his feet, to gather his words carefully.

"Well, I will share a bit more about Bridgit and me and our mission." He leaned in towards Alvie and bumped shoulders with her.

"I have known Bridgit for a very long time. In fact, before Bridgit incarnated into the third dimension, she resided in the fourth dimension, with me...as...my wife, Kaialena."

He heard a gasp coming from Alvie and nodded an affirmative as he looked her way. "Yes, we are married. And we miss one another terribly." He puffed up a bit and put his hands in his pockets, acting as if he had a chill, but in reality, speaking of his separation from his beloved is all that was required to run a chill down his spine.

"Wait, let me get this straight! You and Bridgit are married!?" Alvie was beside herself with interest.

"Alvie, this is where it gets more complicated. Let me try to explain." He rubbed his stubble once more and then turned to her, putting his knee on the bench so that he could look at her straight in the face.

"Before Bridgit incarnating here, she resided in the fourth dimension, and she was and is still known as Kaialena. She is the daughter of Shamalaine, the one who sent me here to speak with you." He raised his hand to ask that Alvie not ask questions just yet, as she had her mouth open with multiple questioned lined up in the queue. Alvie closed her mouth and motioned with her hand to continue.

"Kaialena and I fell deeply in love, and I knew at the beginning that at some point she would be called to fulfill her divine mission, as would I, and we would be separated for some time. I was training for my role as a Guardian, but neither of us thought that it would come so soon. We barely had time for our sacred sacraments to one another, when she was called to stand before the Elders. She was informed that she would incarnate into the world of 3D form on Earth, and there, she would live in relative solitude until it was time to implement her mission." He looked at Alvie, and once again, she had tears.

"May I speak?" She politely asked.

"Yes, please do." Breacher stopped his story to honor Alvie.

"When I first met Bridgit, our first year at University, I had a feeling that she held the weight on her shoulders. That is something that we share in common."

"Yes, that is a trait of a Life Bearer. Always in the back of your mind, you are searching for something hidden, that could make a difference to the world if only you could find it. So you search and search." Breacher explained.

"YES! Constant searching, for what, I don't know!!!" Alvie reiterated his thoughts.

"It is the inner knowing that you are to do something grand for this world and the people, but until now, neither of you remembered what that was." He looked at Alvie and placed his hand on her knee and said, "I was sent here to guide you. To provide some insight to help you remember, just like Shamalaine did for Bridgit. If that is okay with you?"

Alvie nodded in agreement, "I would appreciate that very much. But first, what is the deal with him?" She pointed to Butler. "Who is he in all of this? My husband?" she half-laughed, scared to hear the answer.

Breacher let out a giggle and said, "No, he is not your husband. He is a Guardian. He protects sacred space, watches over portals, and in his spare time, he is a Guardian of animals and nature, much like you. It is his greatest joy to watch over the woodland creatures. He is here to serve you." He pointed to him to show Alvie how gentle he is with the animals. Butler had braided Pretty Girl's mane and was brushing her while they spoke.

"To serve me?" She quizzed.

"Yes. Shamalaine asked Butler to be here should you agree to participate in the mission as a Life Bearer. Butler will be happy to stay here during your time away to keep watch on all that happens here. He has many talents."

Breacher paused and said, "So just think about that as I complete my story. Bear with me."

Breacher continued to share, "When Kaialena was called to perform her mission, she and I knew that our love for one another would get us through it. Her mission required that she incarnate into the 3D world as a sort of boots on the ground beam of light, a lighthouse. My mission would be working on the Galactic side, with multiple roles, working within the various dimensions."

"Galactic?!" Alvie's eyes were wide once more.

"Yes. Galactic. Bridgit's fourth dimensional parents and I are part of an Inter-Galactic Confederation of Star Systems working towards bringing the third dimensional Earth into the Galactic family and lifting the veil that has shrouded this dimension, which includes working to help people here remember who they are. This part is very detailed, so I will leave it at that, but my job has many facets."

Breacher laughed, thinking about what he is juggling at the moment then said, "I have been trained in the Melchezidek order and have Alliance training as well, which is like the military here in your realm."

Alvie shook her head, "Amazing!"

"Yes, well, the missions that Kaialena and I have activated is ONE big mission. We just have different tasks, which means that we don't get to see one another during this transition time, except on a rare occasion." He scratched his shoulder, then put his hand on his knee and turned to look at her seriously.

"I work with the ley lines of the planet, which is something that you once did as well before your incarnating here. Did you ever wonder how you know where to place things, what feels good when you place the contents of your home in a certain place or how you knew to put this pond here in this exact spot?"

Alvie responded, "I just have always naturally known where things should go, and you are right, I do feel it. If my home is not in proper order, I get agitated."

"Yes, I imagine you would. It is because prior to this incarnation, you

505

worked on many world systems designing habitats under the direct influence of the great Elohim, Vista. You have always been under the influence of the great Builders of Form while embodied in the physical, as you can see here, with this beautiful sanctuary." He turned to her more seriously now.

"Alvie, with all of this that you have created here, do you still have a feeling like something is missing? Like you are searching for something to fill a hole that has yet to be filled?" He browsed over her body to read the etheric, as she pondered the question.

"Every day! Every single day of my life, I have been waiting for something unknown. I want to do more. I just feel like there is so much more that I could be doing!" Again, she wiped a teardrop from her eye.

Breacher responded, "Bridgit has not chosen you for this mission. It was you that chose this mission, and I have come to remind you of that choice. There are things that every one of us must give up, sacrifice, to be of service to the divine plan."

"And just what is that again?" Alvie wiped her nose on her sleeve.

"During this time, a great shift of light is coming in waves. This light is pure love. We are grounding that light now into the 3rd dimension through our balanced heart chakra and connecting it into the 5th dimension. Many of us who work with Light and Energy help to diffuse it so that it is not overwhelming to the human body. If the human heart is out of balance, this wave of love could cause it to wobble. The more we can do to help humanity work through their pain and suffering and bring their hearts back into balance, the easier of a transition it will be for humanity when the consecutive waves arrive."

Alvie listened to every word that Breacher spoke and could see in her mind's eye what he said was true.

He continued, "The Life Bearers are Starborn souls who carry the codes of creation. They work in conjunction with the Builders of Form and the Angelics to bring forth a New Earth that is being prepared in the higher bandwidths, like an overlay to the present Earth. As part of my mission, I have trained six others to work with the ley lines of the Earth in preparation for the shifting of the energies from 3D to 5D. We work with the cosmic forces and direct the energies to key focal points on the Earth via the dragon lines."

He chuckled briefly and said, "I will let you in on a secret. We actually do ride dragons." He smiled with that little tidbit.

"WHAT DID YOU JUST SAY? DRAGONS!?" Alvie's atoms almost came unglued, hearing of the dragons.

"Yes. I am a Dragon Rider, and there are six others. Each of the Dragon Riders come from various star systems, and the Divine Mother herself has ordained us. She wants Gaia, Earth, to ascend, and the work that we do with the ley lines is vital."

Breacher made a suggestion. "Would you allow me to guide you in a short visualization, which will most likely help you see or feel what I have been telling you?"

"Sure, if you think it will help." Alvie kindly accepted Breacher's offer, and she prepared herself to relax. She was slowly coming to the understanding that he was who he claimed to be.

Breacher instructed, "With your eyes closed, I want you to count backward from ten to one, three times. Then count from three to one, once."

He watched her count out loud the first sequence. Then she began to mouth the second sequence, as the sounds took too much energy to push out. Alvie had begun her inner journey. As she finished the last sequence of ten to one, she was already having a vision in her mind's eye. She heard Breacher say the final count down, "Three-two-one."

Alvie sat there on the bench, mesmerized by visions that his voice eased her into. Alvie watched in her mind's eye the work of the dragons and remembering how the ley lines enter into each dimension. She recalled the work she did on a different star system.

Breacher sat holding space for her as she saw herself working with the teams to create habitats on other worlds. Breacher began to raise the vibration around her to assist her in seeing and knowing more, similar to the chair of remembrance.

Alvie began to shake as if she was shivering in the cold. Her cellular memory was activating her DNA, which caused her bodily reaction.

Breacher lowered the frequency and rubbed her arms to give warmth back into her body. He very quietly explained, "When one has a cellular memory, it is usually followed by uncontrollable chills. This is a good thing as your body is always the best barometer of what you are experiencing. It tells you if your experience is real. What are you seeing?"

Alvie responded through her chattering teeth. "I am surrounded by Elder Beings. They are wearing white robes with what looks like a rose emblem on their chests. I am sitting there, in a chair, with a book in front of me. They are speaking to me of my desire to incarnate to Earth."

"Good. Stay with it. See if you can hear the conversation as the Akashic is open for you to hear or read from the book." Breacher held the force field for her to continue.

Alvie whispered, "I am the one pleading to join the mission! They are telling me of all of the things that could keep me from it. They are reminding me of the spiritual traps or consequences of entering into the 3D matrix. They are saying matrix." Alvie shook her head quickly, then her body followed suit.

She continued, "I hear them telling me that the love of my creations could be my downfall. I am pleading with them that I can overcome whatever I may encounter in the 3D realm because I know that my particular gifts are required. I tell them that I know that I would never say no to an opportunity to serve the divine plan for humanity's ascension." Her body convulsed again.

Breacher lowered the energy field around her once more, to calm her mind and body. He began to bring her back by guiding her upward with the numbers from one to ten. Alvie opened her eyes, tears flooding her face now.

Butler walked up at that moment. In his hand was a small cup of warm liquid. He offered it to Alvie, not saying a word, and walked back to where Pretty Girl was grazing.

Alvie drank from the cup. It was an unusual elixir of light, heavier than water, having a sweetness and perfume that she found familiar. The warmth and the frequency calmed her entire being.

Once her body settled, she looked at Breacher with gratitude. He smiled and nodded in the silence.

After Alvie drank all of the beverage, she put the cup to her side and asked, "So how does this work? If I am to join the team, how long will it take, and will Butler be able to stay here for that extended time?"

Breacher responded with a positive attitude, "You merely have to say yes to your destiny. Bridgit is gathering all of the Life Bearers at the home of her cousin, Stella, tomorrow."

Breacher then gave a little background on Stella. "In the fourth Dimension, Stella is known as Tulina and is Kaialena's sister. Both are from the Clan of Phare, and both have left so much behind to act as a lighthouse during the coming wave. Stella has experienced profound loss in this lifetime, and when Bridgit came across her, all of her unconscious questionings began to come into clarity, as I hope it will be for you as well."

"For now, you will learn more about your particular part of the plan when you join them at this location. He handed her the address of the location on a small piece of flax paper. If you are willing, you should arrange to travel there tomorrow. I will leave Butler here with you for as long as you need him."

Alvie stood up and hugged Breacher. "Thank you, Breacher. For everything. Please give my love and thanks to Shamalaine. I hope to

509

meet her one day."

She thought about it for a moment then asked, "Have I met her already?" Alvie laughed, confused as to how this multidimensional living worked.

"Shamalaine knows you well, and in time you will remember her too. For now, you will have glimpses of memories returning. When they come, be gentle with yourself. Parts of you are returning to yourself with every memory reclaimed. In those moments, your DNA is changing, and this is why your body shakes."

He winked at her and said, "It is time for me to go. I leave you in the great care of Butler, one of the greatest Guardians of our realm. This is our gift to you for saying yes." He looked deep into Alvie's eyes to verify that she would indeed say yes to her mission.

She nodded and said out loud, "Yes... Okay, I'm in." He turned to Butler, who brought Pretty Girl closer. As Breacher made his leave, Butler handed Pretty Girl's leads over to Alvie.

Alvie kissed Pretty Girl on the nose and looked up to say thank you to Breacher once more, but he was gone. She had a terrified look that relayed to Butler her need for comfort.

Butler spoke, "Breacher is needed in many realms and had to go, Miss."

He changed the subject swiftly, "I promise you, that in your stead, I will honor all of the creatures here, and if you don't mind, I will bring a little magic of my own to the sanctuary. For now, I think it best if you could show me how you would like me to go about caring for these creatures." He walked with Alvie to the outbuildings for a tour.

The two of them spent the morning getting Butler familiar with the staff, the protocols, and animals. They worked out that he would carry out specific tasks and stay in the small apartment over the building closest to the pasture.

Alvie had no idea what to expect, but her heart was full for the first time in all of the time that she had been on the planet. Never had saying yes to something unknown to her, feel so good. Yet it frightened her all the same.

And the wheel turns...

Chapter 74

The Life Bearers Reunion

Stella and Bridgit sat outside on the back porch of Stella and Todd's home, having coffee in the early morning hours. David picked up Ford and Ursula, who had arrived the night before, and went straight to their hotel. David and Ford agreed to take the early shift at the airport the next morning to pick up Ashneer and Freya.

Christopher was due in around noon, and the Ladies Phare would personally go to the airport to receive him. Juel and Benjamin were both driving in separately and were expected in the early afternoon.

Bridgit said, "I love the early morning. It is the calm before the storm." She lifted her shoulders as she took a deep breath in preparation for the day. She was thinking of Alvie.

Stella asked, "Do you think she will change her mind? You sent her the invite, so she knows we are meeting today, right?" Stella just had to ask.

"Yes. I sent everyone the same invite, and all responded except for her.

Traci said that she hasn't heard from her, either." Bridgit scratched her arm while staring down at her feet.

"I don't know what to do about this, Stella. She has not returned my phone calls." Bridgit was trying to keep calm, especially since all of the rest of the Life Bearers were coming in that day.

Stella brilliantly remarked, "It seems to me that every time we have had something happen out of our control, it takes care of itself. My prayer is that all will be taken care of with swiftness, and with grace and ease!"

Stella said those words with such force that when she said the word ease, Bridgit jolted.

"YES!! Grace and EASE! A-ho!" The two ladies concluded the prayer as the birds were greeting one another. The wind picked up, providing a slight chill to the morning air. Bridgit pushed her windblown hair away from her cheeks and reached for the itinerary.

Stella got up to move closer to Bridgit. "So how are we going to do this?" she asked. Stella watched Bridgit go over the itinerary with a fine-toothed comb. As Bridgit looked closer at Stella, she tried to make out what was on Stella's t-shirt.

"What does your shirt say?" Bridgit's eyes were trying to focus in on the t-shirt as Stella stretched it out in front of her, reading it upside down.

"It is a great one. It says, what is a MOM... But the sunshine of our days and the North Star of our nights! I gave it to my mother just before she passed. I wear it on occasion when I want to have her close by. It also seems appropriate in light of Shamalaine's constant vigilance on our behalf." Stella grinned and indicated how cozy it was by rubbing the material and cooing for a few seconds.

Bridgit sat with it for a moment, unexpectedly moved. It seemed to be the theme, Bridgit thought. Mom's guiding like a compass.

After a few moments of silence in honor of Evie Phare and Shamalaine, Bridgit asked delicately, "Shall we get a move on? We should probably get out of here soon if we are going to meet up with the first group."

Bridgit gathered the itinerary and coffee cup as Stella picked up her cup and opened the door to the kitchen. Stella was in a slow and mellow state, still connecting her energy to her mother's.

"I'll get a quick shower and be down in 20." Bridgit quickly moved towards the stairs as Stella arrived at the kitchen sink to linger, finishing the last sips of her coffee.

Stella yelled out, "You go, girl!"

Thirty minutes later, the Ladies Phare was on the road headed to a nearby hotel, where they would check in with the Life Bearers who were arriving.

Ashneer and Freya's planes both arrived within 20 minutes of one another. David and Ford were waiting for them in the passenger pick up lane. Ursula was back at the hotel catching up on her rest as she was not a morning person.

After Ashneer and Freya joined David and Ford, the four Life Bearers enjoyed having time alone together. They were all friends for some time who were gathering together for an adventure of a lifetime. It was all they had thought about since the conference in Scotland.

David spoke, "Just an itinerary update," he smiled then continued to share the schedule. "We will go to the hotel to get you two checked in and get settled. We arranged for early check-in. Bridgit and Stella will swing by for a quick visit before they head out to pick up Elder Christopher."

Ashneer and Freya both indicated how excited they were to see Bridgit and Stella again.

David and Ford both added to their excitement, and then David continued with the schedule. "This evening we will be dining together in an extraordinary venue. We are really excited about it too because it is the perfect place for all of us Life Bearers to reconvene. Stella has been working very hard to find just the perfect spot, and by the sound of the name, I think she has hit the mark! It is called Inn of the Seventh Ray!" He winked at Freya as he spoke to them from the front seat of the vehicle.

Freya responded, "Oh, wow! I have heard of that place! I am so excited! My friends have told me if I am ever in the LA area that the Inn of the Seventh Ray is a magical place, and the food is all organic. The chef even gives a blessing over the food!"

Ashneer's neck turned suddenly, "Really!? That sounds amazing! I look forward to this conscious culinary experience." Ashneer put his hands in a prayer position and took them upwards towards his head as he nodded with joy. He was so happy to be among his colleagues once more.

He had been anticipating this day ever since they all left Scotland. These were his people, the kind of people who truly understood him. He came out of thought then asked, "So, David, catch us up. What have we missed?"

David pulled his seat belt loose so that he could turn sideways in his seat to speak to the trio from the front seat, as Ford drove.

"Ah, well, I spoke with Stella earlier on the mobile." He wiggled his cell phone in front of them and continued, "There has been so much that has happened since we last saw one another. As you know, when we left each other last, we were all told to tidy up loose ends in preparation for an extended journey. On that note, Ford here just shared before you two got into the car that he and Ursula sold their house and put all of their belongings in storage." He smiled and paused.

"That is great, Ford!" Freya and Ashneer both congratulated him.

Ford nodded and said, "Thank you," as he watched the map on his phone for his exit.

David asked, "Before I share more, how have you two been getting along in that area?"

Ashneer said, "Well, when we were in Scotland, I mentioned that I had let go of my lease, and after the conference and the activation, I decided to sell pretty much everything that I own. It felt so good just to let it all go."

Freya gasped. "Everything?"

Ashneer said, "Yes. Everything. What do I need it for? I don't know how long we will be gone, and it just feels like we will be completely changed when we arrive back to this world... if that is what happens?" He said that in a question for David to provide some follow-up.

David nodded and said, "Yes, well, at this point, we don't know what it will look like, but it is a great idea to lighten the load chap. Good on you." He looked to Freya for any updates, but Freya didn't have much to share in that area. He winked at her and drank a sip of water, then continued.

"So, the latest update from Bridgit and Stella is that they have found the last three Life Bearers, but there has been a slight Snafu. Well, really, it is quite a large Snafu, actually." He drew out the first part of the word large with his Scottish accent, to give the trio a heads up that all was not well.

David continued, "Bridgit found out that two of her dear friends from her University days are Life Bearers. In fact, these two ladies were her roommates!"

Ashneer said, "That is crazy!"

David continued, "From what Stella has told me, the male Life Bearer is a musician and is one of the ladies Fiancé." David was animated in his delivery of the latest dish.

"Sooo, the SNAFU surrounds one of the ladies. She is super sensitive, from what Stella has shared. She runs a wildlife rehabilitation sanctuary and can't seem to say yes to this mission because she is not at all sure that, one, this mission is real and two, that she could overcome her quilt in leaving the animals to serve as a Life Bearer." He took a breath and noticed Ford turning into the drive of the hotel.

Freya said some comforting words, "I certainly can relate...to all of it, and if we get a chance to meet her, perhaps we can persuade her, hmm?"

David thanked Freya for her kind words and agreed. "We are here! Welcome to our home away from home." The four Life Bearers exited the vehicle and retrieved the bags.

At that moment, Stella drove into the nearest parking spot in front of the hotel, honking her horn in excitement. They had timed their rendezvous perfectly.

David noticed the dent on the driver's side of Stella's Jeep immediately. As he walked over to Stella's vehicle, the two ladies jumped out of the car.

David, being much taller than Stella, reached down to hug her, and picked up Stella in a bear hug.

For Stella, It brought back the memory of Henny's bear hug, and she let out a burst of laughter that became contagious. David wiggled her around and snuggled her for a few moments as the others cheered him on and laughed at the silly antics that David performed on Stella's behalf.

"Are you well, Stella?" he asked as he put her down. He looked towards her dent near the front of the car. "I heard through the grapevine that you had a close call." David was genuinely concerned for Stella.

"David..., brother... I am just fine. It was scary at the moment, but it is just what happens when you live in these parts." She smiled at him and gave him one more hug for being sincerely concerned. They turned to see Bridgit engaged with Freya and Ashneer.

Stella asked, "Who is here?"

David responded, "So far, it is just us early birds. I expect Benjamin and Juel to arrive this afternoon. They are both driving separately, so I don't know when to expect them precisely. They know that dinner is promptly at 5:30 on the spot." He winked to assure the ladies that all was fine.

Bridgit waved them on and said, "Let's go inside, and once you are all checked in, maybe we can grab some coffee in the lobby and have a chat." Bridgit was graceful in her approach and was hoping for the EASE part of their prayer earlier to show up soon.

Once Ashneer and Freya got checked into their rooms, they quickly took their bags to their rooms and then came back down to the lobby. Ford had now retrieved Ursula as they were all reconvening in the hotel lobby.

Stella somehow had procured a pot of coffee and cups from the Concierge.

Bridgit waited for everyone to get comfortable and watched as Stella played hostess. Everyone had coffee and were commenting on how lovely it was to be together.

At that moment, a dark-haired young man entered the hotel lobby with a suitcase in one hand and sunglasses in his other hand. He stood in the doorway, wearing a t-shirt that read-WHAT HAVE YOU GOT TO LOSE?

"Benjamin! Over here!" Stella set down the coffee and raised her hand upward as he approached her. "CINCO!" she blurted awkwardly, still trying to make the phrase stick.

Benjamin shook his head and said, "Man... I was going to say that!! CINCO!"

They slapped hands while laughing and then hugged as if they were siblings.

Ursula turned around in her seat and yelled out to Benjamin, "Great shirt, Brother!" She got up and walked over to offer Benjamin a hug as well, and soon they all gathered back at the sofas.

Bridgit gave Benjamin a warm greeting, holding him in a hug longer than usual for her.

David said, "Great timing, mate. We weren't sure when to expect you, but you must have a good tracking system because we all just sat down to have a cuppa and a check-in of sorts."

"Awesome! It's so good to see you guys again! I got into the area a few days ago and have been visiting some friends. I wanted to get here early. I didn't want to miss a thing!" He laid his sunglasses on the table and asked, "So how is everyone? How long have you all been here?"

Bridgit responded after everyone said good, in their various ways. "A few got in last night, and Koko and Freya arrived this morning, We are still waiting on Juel and Christopher."

Bridgit then realized that she should explain why the newer Life Bearers were not joining in just yet. "The other Life Bearers live in the area and said that they would meet us at the restaurant later this evening. They are still in a major push to tidy up a few outstanding engagements so that they can be with us this weekend."

Benjamin said, "Great." He looked at each of the faces before him and said, "It feels like it was just yesterday that we were sitting together at Rodney Gardens! I am so stoked to be here with you guys!"

Everyone repeated his sentiments and savored the moment of the reunion.

Bridgit added, "Yes, I am grateful to have you all here. You don't know how much this means to Stella and me to have you all here with us." She smiled at Stella, as Stella was pouring Benjamin a cup of coffee.

"Let me give you just a few highlights, as we will need to be heading to the airport here in just a few minutes. Basically, we are shy by one

Life Bearer. We found the last three, which is why you are all gathered here now, but we just can't seem to get through to one of them to commit to joining us. This, as you all know, is the most difficult decision that we are asked to make, and all of you are amazing individuals because here you are. All of you made the decision, and I thank you from the bottom of my heart. Well, my whole heart actually... if I am being honest!"

Everyone cheered as Bridgit revealed her heart.

Bridgit smiled again at Benjamin and commented on his shirt. "Benjamin, your t-shirt is so fitting. That saying is what we need to contemplate. The planet is ascending, and we need to help it. If we don't, I can't even imagine what we could lose."

"True. Very true." Benjamin said.

Freya sheepishly asked, "You know... I am a bit embarrassed to ask this, but what do you think we could lose?"

Bridgit's facial expression went solemn. She anchored her energy before she responded. "Shamalaine gave me an overview of a scenario that could happen. I have yet to share this because it is too painful to think of, but I will give you my understanding of it."

She shifted in her seat and started. "Our planet is connected to many other planets in the solar system as we know. At certain intervals in time, the planetary bodies are allowed the opportunity to advance into higher frequencies, and this is usually done as a group. From what I understood from Shamalaine, she expressed that the Earth is in a precarious situation due to the darkness that overtook this planet some time ago. Earth is now under quarantine, so we, as a species, cannot receive the higher celestial frequencies, which brings purifying energies that help us continue our journey into the higher states."

Bridgit looked at her hands to formulate more and continued, "We have to break the quarantine, for the Earth and its inhabitants to receive the higher frequencies. This part is of the plan is the role of the Dragon Riders and Guardians. More on that part later. But in essence, from what Shamalaine said, if we can't assist the planet during this interval of time, we won't get to make the planetary jump, and it will be a very long time before the next opportunity comes around again. Does that make sense? I am not good at repeating things second hand."

Benjamin stated that he was familiar with the topic and chimed in, "It makes perfect sense, Bridgit. From what I can tell, the planet was cut off from the galactic community, and ever since the Harmonic Convergence back in 1987, humanity has a certain amount of time to get on the bandwagon with our ascension, or we join the ranks of what is known as the laggards."

Bridgit commented, "What Shamalaine shared was that those of us making strides to remember who we are and to hold the light are the lighthouses during this time, to help others remember their part. At the time of the great event, when the planetary bodies make their jump up the frequency ladder, so to speak, those of us on Earth who have made an effort won't be left behind."

She continued, "Shamalaine showed me a hologram of this situation, and in that hologram, there was another, secondary planet earth. In essence, the 3rd dimensional Earth would separate from the higher dimensions, and those of us who advance go into the higher dimension, and the rest will continue their incarnation in the 3rd dimension, until the next round, or what Shamalaine called the next In-Breath of God."

She paused and said one final thing. "Our goal as Life Bearers is to enter the void, the center of creation within Earth, and plant the seeds of our vision for humanity. When we use our minds and hearts for a cause such as this, the law of precipitation will manifest it. We literally can affect this situation as Life Bearers. We are called to bridge Heaven and Earth, and not allow the split of Gaia's being. She deserves to advance fully into the higher realms..., and so does all of humanity."

Ashneer shook his head in confirmation and said, "I feel this in all of my being. I am holding the intention that every man, woman, and child on Earth receives what they need to move into the higher states.

I hold this vision in my heart."

Stella commented, "That is the idea. That we take everyone with us!" All of the Life Bearers took a moment of silence, and then David winked at Bridgit as he looked at his watch.

Bridgit continued, "We will talk more about this at dinner tonight, but for now, Stella and I must take our leave. Ford and David will give you all the details on the dinner venue. I can't wait to introduce all of you to the other two Life Bearers, and fingers crossed, maybe the last one will show up too! Love you guys!" She got up and gave hugs out to everyone. Stella did the same. The Life Bearers stayed on in the lobby to catch up as they watched Stella and Bridgit take their leave.

And the wheel turns...

Chapter 75

Christopher's Arrival in LA

Stella and Bridgit waited for Christopher to enter the baggage claim area. They were chatting about how good it felt to be back with the team. Stella noticed a friend in the baggage claim area and went to say hello, leaving Bridgit to wait for Christopher.

Bridgit watched Stella chatting with her friend and pondered how small the world is in moments like those. She contemplated the population of LA, being over 4 million people, and it boggled her mind to see Stella bump into someone she knew. With all of the people in LA, it seemed the odds for that would be extremely low. Bridgit then realized that synchronicity was about the power of magnetic attraction and fate.

Bridgit sat in silence, contemplating the synchronicities that she had experienced related to the mission. They were too many to count. She then thought of Alvie and wondered what more she could do to get her on board with the mission. She did a silent prayer that if Alvie was to be a part of the team that some synchronicity would present itself to her and make it clear to Alvie that she belonged with the group.

While deep in thought of her predicament, Christopher nudged her from behind and said hello.

"Christopher! You scared me!" She put her hand on her heart and took a deep breath.

"I did? I do apologize, Miss Bridgit. I was under the impression that you were expecting me." He chuckled at the idea of scaring the young lass, as she was the one waiting on him to arrive.

"Where is Miss Stella?" He looked around and spotted her chatting nearby with a few people. "Well, she sure is popular." He watched as Stella began to conclude her visit when she noticed him waving at her.

Stella ran over to where Christopher was waiting and nearly knocked him over when she threw her arms around him. Bridgit grabbed his arm, the one with the walking stick, and held him steady as he responded to Stella's exuberance.

"Uncle Christopher!!! You made it!" Stella loved saying uncle, so she decided to try it out to see his reaction.

"My, my, Miss Stella. I guess I have grown on you. Aren't I just the luckiest old man?" He laughed as he grabbed her for a good squeeze.

He looked at Bridgit and said, "I had hoped to have a similar greeting from you, my dear. I see you are in a state of complex analysis."

Christopher reached over to Bridgit for a slight hug and placed a gentle kiss on her forehead.

Bridgit apologized and kissed Christopher's cheek in response to his loving gesture. "Thank you for your observations, my dear man. I can't get Alvie out my mind; that's all." She rolled her eyes and attempted a half-smile.

Christopher responded, "Alvie has a tough decision, but if she is truly the Life Bearer that you say she is, then I suspect that she will come around. We can't worry about it now. Let us move along. We have much to think about. We need to gather the troops, and as a team, we will come up with a plan."

He plucked his bag from the baggage carousel and smiled in anticipation of the day. "Shall we get to it then? It has been decades since I have stepped foot on this soil, and I am keen on seeing how much it has changed."

Stella replied, "That's right! You have been gone for a long time!" She grabbed his bag from his hand.

Christopher thanked Stella for her assistance and noted, "I never thought that I would step foot in the United States again, but what a delightful turn of events this has all been, and to be with you two on my return is more than I could have hoped for."

The Phare trio left the airport for Calabasas. Stella was the perfect hostess as she pointed out things of interest on their drive to her home.

And the wheel turns...

Chapter 76

Two Life Bearers Converge at a Co-Op

The morning that all of the Life Bearers were arriving into town, Traci and Henny were also making preparations. Henny took off to run errands before the weekend's events were underway while Traci made salsa from the produce in her front yard garden beds. It was her specialty, and she wanted to share the salsa with Bridgit and the others, but she ran out of mason jars. Traci decided to drive to the nearby co-op to get supplies and pick up a few extra things for welcome bags.

After a fifteen minute drive, Traci pulled into a parking space at the co-op, parked the car and jumped out, with her recycled grocery bags and her list of the few things she needed. Upon entering the store, Traci looked to her left, contemplating getting a juice from the organic juice bar when she noticed Alvie waiting in line.

"Alvie! What are you doing here!?" Traci was confused as it wasn't exactly her area of town.

"Wow! Traci! I can't believe it! I was actually coming to see you!"

Alvie reached over to hug her.

Traci grabbed her, holding her tightly, not wanting to let go. Traci pulled away from the embrace and asked, "Have you changed your mind?"

"That is what I wanted to talk about with you. I had a fascinating interaction with a friend of Bridgit's, and I wanted to share it with you. Want to get a juice and go sit outside by the tree out there?" Alvie pointed to the beautiful shade tree in the corner of the parking lot.

"Sure. I tell you what, if you order the juices, I will go grab a few things. I'll meet you outside in a bit." She reached in her purse to grab some cash to give to Alvie, which Alvie refused. Alvie told Traci to get her things and meet her outside.

Soon enough, Traci came out of the co-op with her bag of goods. She stowed the jars in the back seat of her car, then strolled towards Alvie. She sat down on a fluffy patch of grass next to where Alvie was sitting and beamed a grin at her old friend.

Alvie handed Traci a juice and smiled. "Here ya go, friend."

Traci squealed with excitement, "Thanks so much! I am so happy to see you!!!" She asked Alvie to give her the update.

Alvie began, "Well... what I am going to tell you is as wild as our last conversation with Bridgit." She paused for Traci's reaction.

"I didn't think that there could be anything that could match our last visit with Bridgit, but try me." Traci laughed as she sucked the juice from her straw.

Alvie chuckled, "Well, there is. I meet Bridgit's husband!"

Traci choked on the juice she was sipping and took a few minutes to cough up what went down the wrong pipe. As she gained her composure, she said, "What did you say? Bridgit has a husband?"

Alvie squinted her eyes as if she was telling a little white lie, and responded, "Yes... kind of. Sort of...yes...it is her husband...from the fourth dimension!"

Alvie knew it sounded crazy and just started laughing so loud that her laugh infected Traci too. The two of them could not stop laughing. After a few minutes, Alvie was able to compose herself and said, "Oh man, that felt good. I haven't laughed like that in I don't know how long!"

Traci snorted as she was still trying to compose herself. "Well, you better start talking, sister... I need to know the deets."

Alvie laughed and said, "I get ya.... Okay, here goes. The other day I had a visitation by two strangers. Their horse was loose, and it made a beeline for my property. I went out to investigate, and a man approached me who said that he was a friend of my friend, Bridgit." Alvie looked at Traci to see if she was with her.

Traci nodded, anxious to hear who he was.

"Well, when he told me it was Bridgit, I had this sinking feeling in my stomach, but he told me that he was there on her behalf and mine, but that she did not know that he was there at all. He told me that he and the other man, who was now with the horse, were not from here. I asked what he meant by that, and he went into a bit of a story about who sent him. Are you ready for this?"

Alvie had Traci glued to every word. "Yes! Go on!" Traci smacked Alvie on the arm playfully.

Alvie's juice spilled out from the straw onto her hand, which made the two ladies start laughing once more.

"Geez Trac...let me get the juice in my mouth!!" Alvie enjoyed sparring with Traci as she put her hand out, indicating for Traci to give her a moment as she drank her juice and wiped her hands.

"Sorry... you just have me so excited!" Traci put her juice down so that

528

she could concentrate on every word that Alvie said.

Once Alvie had a few sips of her juice and cleaned up the spill, she too sat her drink aside and continued the story.

"He said that his name was Breacher and that the leader of the Clan of Phare had sent him to me to assist me in deciding if I was going to commit to being a Life Bearer. At first, I felt that he was wasting his time, but he was persuasive." She smiled at Traci, indicating that she had decided to be on the team.

"That is great, Alvie!! I am so relieved to hear this as I am sure that Bridgit was when you told her!"

"Oh, I haven't told her yet!" Alvie declared.

"What?!" Traci's joy turned to concern.

"I took some time to think about it, and well, I am getting ahead of myself. Let me keep going." Alvie shifted her bottom away from the root of the tree and positioned herself to see Traci face to face.

She continued, "Breacher shared with me the deeper story of Bridgit's life, and honestly, it is heartbreaking. I knew that she grew up without her parents. Still, the saddest thing is that before Bridgit incarnated into the 3D world, she and Breacher had recently married in the higher dimensions and had just started their lives together as man and wife when they were both called into active duty with this mission. He relayed how much they loved one another and that when Bridgit recently reentered the 4th dimension, at the home of the Clan of Phare, Shamalaine insisted on not telling her that Breacher was her husband, for fear of Bridgit not fulfilling her destiny!"

Alvie and Traci were equally sad to know the loss that Bridgit has endured.

Traci responded, "So Bridgit had this amazing love in her life, and she had to leave it behind? For the mission?"

Alvie nodded, "She was called into duty, as was he. He is... , get this... a Dragon Rider! He is also what is called a Guardian. He has many other duties in the Galactic Alliance...or something like that, and his mission took him somewhere else within that dimensional space!?" She said it as a question, not sure if that was precisely how to describe it.

"Wow! How sad. And also, it shows that Bridgit had made the decision to be a Life Bearer before she incarnated." Traci said while contemplating what Alvie was sharing. "I guess we all did..."

"Yes, that is what I am trying to get at here. Breacher said that he wanted to give me a glimpse into who I was, so he led me into a meditative space where he somehow helped me raise my vibration enough for me to see for myself what I had chosen before my incarnation."

She put her hand on Traci's lap and said, "Traci, I saw that I was pleading with a council, begging them to let me come and be a part of this mission. They kept warning me about all of the traps that could keep me from accomplishing my mission. They said that my love for my creations could hold me back!"

"What? Your creations?" Traci quizzed.

"Yes! Apparently, I have been on these kinds of missions in many star systems and have worked with the creation codes helping to create various habitats that would be of the highest benefit for the plants and animals. It resonated with me as Breacher began to quiz me about how I knew where to put the man-made pond on my property, or how I knew intuitively what the plants or animals needed. As I watched the vision of me pleading with the elders, my body responded by convulsing, and my DNA seemed to be activated. Breacher commented that it was my body responding to the truth that I was witnessing as a remembrance."

"That is amazing. So, do you feel that you preplanned this to happen then? This whole Life Bearer thing? That maybe we all had this in the plan before we even arrived here?" Traci quizzed.

"Well, it seems so." Alvie moved her hair away from her face and pushed it back behind her ear, leaving her point exposed. Traci loved seeing it in the sunlight and smiled at Alvie.

"Alvie, you are an amazing human being, and I suspect, more than a human being!" Traci put her hand on Alvie's knee and looked into her eyes. "Anything else happen?"

Alvie thanked Traci for the kind words and then continued with her story.

"Yes! There is more! The other male that was with Breacher...he is this amazing "man" who has many roles, and as a gift to me, from Shamalaine, she sent him to stay at the nature sanctuary while I am away fulfilling my role as a Life Bearer. When I heard that, I was deeply relieved beyond words. I honestly don't know the last time I felt this calm and peaceful."

Alvie wiped a tear from her face and said, "Don't get me wrong, it will take everything in me to leave it behind, but when I saw myself pleading, trying to convince the elders that I could do this, I knew that they were right. If I am not careful, I could fail my mission because of my love for the animals. I realized that I had to trust this man, Butler, to help watch over the place while I am away. Sooo... I agreed to do it!"

Alvie and Traci cheered and hugged one another, and then Traci said, "Should we call Bridgit and put her out of her misery?"

Alvie's pixie came out and said, "Nah. I think I will just show up tonight at the restaurant and see her face when I walk in. Are you okay with that? She did put me through some misery, so fair is fair. Right?"

Traci said, "Fair is Phare!", reluctantly agreeing to Alvie's plan.

Alvie continued, "Can I come back with you to your place? I thought we could ride together to the restaurant later."

"You sure can! Let's do it! Maybe you can help me jar the salsa? I bought some healthy chips to go with it. I thought it would be nice to put together gift bags for all of the Life Bearers, you know, to have something made with love, as a snack, while they are at the hotel."

"That is so thoughtful. Sure, I would love to help put together the bags with you."

"Okay, then, let's do it. Just follow me back. I can't wait for Henny to see you!"

The two ladies jumped up and got into their cars and made their way back to Traci's home.

And the wheel turns...

Chapter 77

Dinner at
The Inn of the Seventh Ray

Bridgit, Stella, and Christopher spent the late afternoon back at Stella's home, discussing various matters pertaining to the evening gathering of the Life Bearers. They were putting all of the final arrangements together for the meal that evening, when Christopher asked Stella to give him more details on her choice of restaurant and if they would have enough privacy.

Stella replied, "The name of the restaurant is Inn of the Seventh Ray, though it is not an Inn, but rather a dining experience to feed the soul and body, in a setting like a secret garden. Also, there is a spiritual bookstore attached to the building called the Spiral Staircase. The venue has a magical ambiance!"

Stella smiled and continued, "I have reserved a table on the patio, under a curtained glass-topped Gazebo. It is considered to be one of the most romantic spots in the entire LA area because it is situated in nature, with a creek running alongside the outdoor seating area."

She looked at Christopher, who was nodding his head in delight, and she said, "Trust me when I say that this is THE place for a reunion of Life Bearers! The food is lovingly prepared. They actually charge the food with the Violet Flame." She saw Bridgit nodding her head, with her eyes closed, feeling the description of the place as Stella shared more.

"They offer fresh vegetarian fare as well as meat dishes. Its all organic and locally sourced too!" Stella was so proud of herself for organizing such a lovely venue. She excused herself to call the restaurant to give them the final headcount, as they were leaving it open in case they heard from Alvie.

She made her way into the kitchen with her cell phone in hand, leaving Bridgit and Christopher outside on the back porch. Christopher pulled his pipe from his tweed jacket and set it on the table, while he fiddled in his other pockets for the tobacco. The pipe fell off the table, and with Bridgit's quick reflexes, she caught it just before it dropped. She lifted it up and looked at it as Christopher thanked her for the save.

He had his pouch out and his lighter handy. As he reached for the pipe, he noticed Bridgit examining the side of the pipe with great interest.

She felt the etching with her fingers, wanting to be sure it was what she thought it was. She looked at Christopher with a studied look on her face, trying to piece together how he had a pipe with the same etching on it as the stone pendants.

Christopher reached for the pipe and said, "See something that strikes your fancy?" he chuckled as he used the word strike to bring it all into her mind.

"Where did you come by this pipe, Christopher?" Bridgit handed it back to him.

All the while, Stella watched the interaction from the kitchen until someone picked up the call at the Inn of the Seventh Ray. "Hi... yes. My name is Stella Phare, and I have a reservation for thirteen people

534

at 5:30 this evening."

The woman that answered the call said, "Yes, I just spoke to someone about this reservation. Was that you?"

Stella said, "Ah... no, I made the reservation last week, but I was not sure if everyone in our party was going to make it. I was hoping to have a total of thirteen people for the reservation, but it looks like we will only need settings for twelve."

"Oh... Well, the woman that I just spoke to said that she was not sure if she was able to come at first but had worked it out so that she could join the group and confirmed to me, thirteen people. Do you want me to just leave it at thirteen, and if we need to remove a place setting, we can certainly do that without a problem?"

Stella still watched Bridgit and Christopher from the window as she processed what the woman was telling her. "Yes. That would be great. Please just leave the settings for thirteen. It was a woman, you say?"

"Yes. Probably no more than thirty minutes ago." The lady responded.

"Great. This has been very helpful. Thank you so much. I really appreciate this news!" Stella hung up the phone smiling from ear to ear. Bridgit saw her in the window and motioned for her to come outside to see what she had discovered, both ladies having big grins and secrets to share.

Stella walked out onto the porch to see Bridgit pointing to Christopher's pipe. Christopher asked Stella if all went well with the phone call. "Yep. Everything is ready! It will be an amazing night!"

Stella, at that moment, chose not to tell them about what she had just learned. She did not want to get Bridgit's hopes up, in case she was wrong about Alvie.

Bridgit said, "Thanks for doing that. I just am not that good at reservations and making plans like you are. I really appreciate your taking the time to find us the perfect venue and dealing with the details too."

She hugged Stella while still holding Christopher's pipe. "Look at what I discovered! Christopher has been holding out on us!"

"It has been my pleasure!" Stella was happy that Bridgit honored her skills. She looked at the pipe in Bridgit's hand and quizzed, "How has Christopher been holding out on us?"

Bridgit hands her the pipe, pointing to the side, showing her the triple triangle etching on the side of the bowl.

Stella studied the engraving for a few moments. "Seriously, Christopher?! What is the story on this pipe!" Stella blurted, intrigued by this mystery as she handed the pipe to Christopher.

"Well, it has been in the family for at least one hundred years. It was in great condition when I found it, and with a little cleanup, it became my favorite pipe. I also was keen on the etching, and as you now see, it is more significant than I had realized." He chuckled and began to pack it with the tobacco.

As Christopher packed his pipe, he changed the subject quickly, and addressed Stella, "My dear, I would like to take the team somewhere out in nature, perhaps tomorrow morning, for a bit of instruction. Then perhaps, we can all come back here for deeper communication. Do you have any suggestions as to where we can go for a leisurely hike? Somewhere that we can do some visualizations without being disturbed?"

"Hmm...let me think about that. There are a lot of places near here that fit that description, but the place that comes to mind, actually, it is near Traci's place." Stella looked at Bridgit to see if she agreed.

Stella said while looking at Bridgit, "We passed it on the way there. I commented on the park's location."

Bridgit agreed that it was a good location as far as she could tell from the road.

Stella said, "There would be privacy for sure, and it is not far. It has easy access and some caves too."

They went back inside to look into the location of the hike. Stella pulled up the website, and they all agreed that it looked like a relatively easy walk on the trail, so they decided upon the location.

The afternoon went by quickly, and It was soon time for them to leave for the restaurant. They each had taken time to change clothes and freshen up.

Stella was waiting in the living room when Christopher came into the foyer and asked, "Stella dear, I wonder if you have a bag in which I can place this selection of teas? I brought each of the Life Bearers proper tea from Scotland." Christopher had his arms full of small gift boxes.

"Sure, I do! That was so sweet of you to bring a gift for everyone." She quickly retrieved a bag and then helped Christopher stuff the teas into it. She set aside Bridgit's and her tea. "I can't wait to try it! I loved having tea at the Phare homestead!"

He commented, "It pleases me that you enjoyed our family home."

Stella smiled and winked at Christopher as she grabbed her purse and keys. She walked into the foyer and yelled up the stairs to Bridgit.

Bridgit came down the stairs wearing a royal blue dress with a silver shell pendant around her neck. Stella was stunned with Bridgit's beauty and felt a bit under-dressed in a cotton skirt and lace top. Christopher complemented Bridgit and kissed her on her cheek then turned to Stella.

He whispered in her ear, "You're equally beautiful tonight and always."

Stella kissed Christopher's old hand and ushered them out of the house towards the driveway.

Bridgit eased into the back seat of the car and texted David that they were heading over to the restaurant and that if the group wanted to come early, they could take a walk around the property of the restaurant and adjacent bookstore.

She inquired about Juel, which David sent an affirmative message that she had arrived no sooner than when she and Stella left for the airport. "You literally just missed her!"

Bridgit texted back, "Dang! I wanted to see her! Let her know that we are looking forward to seeing her soon! Thanks, David!" She completed her messaging and put her phone away, with a little bit more joy hearing that Juel had arrived. She was struggling to stay in a positive mode with the Alvie situation hanging over her head.

Stella and Christopher chatted during the drive to the restaurant. Old Topanga Canyon Rd was the same road that she and Bridgit had been traveling on when they left Traci's house and hit the deer, she explained to Christopher.

Bridgit sat in the back seat, listening and commenting from time to time. In her mind, she mulled over her conversation with Alvie, still wondering if there was anything else she could have done to make her change her mind. Bridgit knew that what she was asking of her was the most difficult thing in the world.

Christopher turned slightly in his seat to see her from his peripheral view. "Bridgit... are you thinking positive thoughts?"

"Well, to be perfectly honest, I am feeling like a failure. A huge failure!" Bridgit just had to lay her cards out on the proverbial table.

Stella chimed in, "Bridgit! Failure is not even in your vocabulary, so take that back!" Stella was peeved to hear her sulking in the back seat, especially because she was pretty sure it was all going to work out.

Christopher laughed, "It really will be fine, my dears. There are many forces at play than any of us know. We haven't come this far to let this slight bump in the road keep us from our destiny." Christopher's demeanor was always on the positive.

"Speaking of bumps in the road, sorry about that!" Stella said as she made a bumpy turn into the parking area of the Inn of the Seventh Ray. The valet was out front. She pulled up, and the three exited the car. Stella handed the valet her keys and pointed out the bookstore to Christopher and Bridgit.

"This is magnificent, Stella! Just perfect!" Bridgit said as she shifted her internal process and, on a more positive note, took a look around. There were trees everywhere. The environment settled her soul down in quick measure.

They were a few minutes early for their reservation, so they peaked into the window of the bookstore and then walked around the back, down by the creek, enjoying the sounds of the water and birds. Then the hostess gladly showed them to the reserved table.

David's crew drove up next and were unloading in the parking lot. Freya and Juel wanted to take a peek in the bookstore. Juel could see stones and incense listed as items on a sign out front. The group quickly looked around and then looked at the time. "Let's see where the others are, shall we?"

As they walked out of the bookstore, another car was pulling into the parking area. David had already walked quickly to the entrance of the restaurant, anxious to see Elder Christopher and the Ladies Phare.

Everyone followed behind him, to the back of the restaurant, and found Stella, Christopher, and Bridgit sitting under a glass-topped gazebo with curtains down the sides and twinkle lights decorating the ceiling. The outdoor patio was close to the stream, and because they had had a late seasonal rain, the water was flowing just enough to provide a calming sound.

Inside the gazebo was a long table with place settings for thirteen. The table had twinkle light candles and wildflowers in small vases, and several cheese plates already set out for everyone to enjoy.

David took several long strides to get to the table, greeting the ladies with a hug and Christopher with a firm handshake.

Christopher said, "Good to see you, lad! Who do you have with you?"

David moved to the side as the group of Life Bearers came around the table. "I brought Ford, Miss Ursula, over there...Benjamin, Miss Freya, and Ashneer. Trailing behind them is the lovely Miss Juel." David awkwardly presented his troupe and then stood tall, backing away so that others could proceed to their seats.

"Hello! Hello! It is so good to see you all once again and in this magnificent setting!" Christopher exclaimed. Each of the group members came up to shake his hand and give hugs.

Stella kept eyeing the door and saw what she was waiting for. Traci and Henny came through the doorway and walked up to the table, but hiding in the doorway of the interior of the restaurant, was a shy Alvie, peaking around the door, checking out the scene.

Stella tapped Bridgit's shoulder and said, "Looks like you might have to coax that little pixie over here." She pointed to Alvie and then waved.

Alvie shyly lifted her hand in response and sheepishly started to walk towards them.

"Introduce Traci and Henny, won't you? I'll be back in a bit." Bridgit wanted to meet Alvie halfway. As she passed Traci, Bridgit put her hand on her dear friend's arm and said, "Thank you."

Traci nodded and sent her an air kiss and nodded for her to go retrieve Alvie.

Stella gladly greeted Traci and Henny and took them to the table where the other Life Bearers awaited them. Stella was in hostess mode once more, making sure to introduce the newest members of the team and ensuring that everyone ordered a drink and appetizer.

"Sweet Alvie! You came!" Bridgit let her guard down, and tears rolled down her face.

"Shhh... It's okay. I am so sorry for putting you through the waiting. I see now that I should have called you. I just wanted to surprise you, and honestly, I only just decided to come yesterday!"

Alvie rubbed Bridgit's shoulder and said, "Can we talk privately for a few minutes? Before we join the others?"

"Of course. Let's go sit over on the stone bench." The two ladies stole away and found a secluded spot on the other side of the patio.

"Bridgit... I feel bad about my behavior, and I ask that you forgive me. I thought that I was angry at you, and then I realized that I was really angry with myself. I was not able to hear the call and let go of my entanglements." She looked into Bridgit's eyes and said, "It wasn't until your beloved came to see me, that I was shown the truth."

Bridgit's eyebrow furrowed and said, "My BELOVED!?? What are you talking about!?" Bridgit had not shared anything with her about Breacher, and now her deepest secret had been exposed. "Please...tell me what you mean by that?"

Alvie said, "I had a visitation by none other than Breacher and the Guardian, Butler, who, by the way shared with me how he and a few others helped you get back to the 3D world through the tree!"

"What!!??? My mind is failing me, Alvie. Details...Please!" Bridgit couldn't believe what she was hearing.

"Sure...sorry!" Alvie faced Bridgit with the sincerest look upon her face and said gently, "Breacher and Butler came to see me on the request of Shamalaine."

"So, you believe me!?" Bridgit asked in relief as she grabbed Alvie's shoulders.

"Oh, yes! I believe you...now!" She laughed and continued her story as she patted Bridgit's arm for comfort.

"Shamalaine astutely knew that for me to understand the seriousness of the plan, that I would need proof, so she sent in the troops! Breacher showed up at my home with Butler and a lovely horse, out in my pasture, and he claimed to be your friend and wanted to speak to me on your behalf. He assured me that you knew nothing of the visit, and to make a very long story short, he helped guide me in meditation so that I could see for myself what choices I had made for my life here."

Alvie looked deeply into Bridgit's eyes, trying to communicate as clearly as possible. "When I say meditation, it was really more like hypnosis. He is really good at that!" She smiled, and once more, Bridgit was tearing up.

"Yes. He is really good at a lot of things." She wiped her eye and smiled warmly at the thought of her beloved.

"Bridgit, he did tell me something that I know you had not shared for obvious reasons, but I am glad he told me of your... marriage." Alvie looked at her dear friend as she quietly spoke the word marriage, and then said, "I know now what you have given up. Beyond the price of a family in this world, you gave up the man of your dreams to be here!"

Alvie wiped a tear from her eye, and the two just looked at one another with amazement. They held each other's hands so tightly as Alvie continued.

"There is so much more, but I will save it. Suffice it to say, I learned that I did plan this life, and I knew of all the risks involved. I was even shown that I would come to be too close to my animal companions, which I was warned could cause me to not go ahead with my mission. This is where your mother is quite clever! She offered the Guardian, Butler, to be of service at the Sanctuary until our return! Can you believe that?!"

"Oh, my dear mother! Thank you, SHAMALAINE!!!" Bridgit yelled out her gratitude so that somehow Shamalaine might hear her and lifted Alvie's arm. "Let's go introduce you to the others. They are all anxious to meet you, our final Life Bearer!" They linked arms, wiping away their tears, and walked towards the table where the others watched with excitement.

Alvie saw him immediately. The Elder in her vision who had told of her potential failures sat before her at the head of the table.

Christopher stood up, and with a smile on his face, he said, "Miss Alvie!"

He introduced her to the others, "It is with great honor that we have amongst us one of the greatest habitat specialists this dimension is so fortunate to know. We have been expecting you. Do come and sit here next to me. We have some catching up to do, don't we?" His eyes twinkled as he knew that she would not fail him.

Bridgit and Stella stood there in amazement with their jaws equally dropped, then finally took their seats. "This is going to be an interesting evening", Stella whispered to Bridgit.

The waitress arrived with the menus and took the orders. The Life Bearers were told that they could order anything off the menu and to please splurge as this was a one-off celebration. Christopher, in jest, said, "This could possibly be your last meal!"

Everyone laughed and then talked amongst the table as they took in the view. Bridgit could now relax as she watched Christopher speaking in whispers to Alvie as if they had already met.

The menu was decadent with things like Miso Glazed Black Cod, Poached Loch Duart Salmon, Creamy Truffle Risotto, and Linguine with Sunflower Pesto. Literally something for every palate. Fresh sourdough bread was brought to the table with lightly salted fennel-infused butter. The salad selections were many, with the kale and sesame salad being the favorite option at the table.

The Life Bearers were in absolute heaven, knowing that their meal was an authentic farm to table experience, in nature, amongst dear souls. Once the entrees arrived, Christopher stood up with his glass of scotch and offered an invocation. He spoke of the trials that each of them had made in their personal journey to be sitting at that very table. He gave thanks and honored each Life Bearer personally. It was a sacred moment in each Life Bearer's life.

As he sat down, he said, "Now comes the fun part! I have been saving this information for the team until the last few Life Bearers came forward. Henny, Traci... Alvie. We are so delighted that you heard the call! I can't tell you how this moment in time has been in my heart for years! I have seen this moment..., right here..., right now..., in my mind's eye for decades. Truly before most of you were even born!"

Everyone felt Christopher's word within their hearts. Several of them shook, with the hair on their arms erect. Freya and Traci sat across from one another and smiled. Traci had tears of recognition for these people that she had just met, already feeling so familiar.

Ashneer and Benjamin sat across from one another. David and Stella were seated next to them, respectively. Ford, Ursula, and Bridgit sat at the end of the table, with Henny to Bridgit's right. They all looked at one another and just remarked constantly as to the Déjà vu feelings that they were each having.

Bridgit stood briefly to share with the group how she found the last few Life Bearers. Stella chimed in from time to time to give full details of the Being that came out of the tourmaline. The group was amazed that Traci, Alvie, and Bridgit had known each other since college but had been living separate lives and had no idea of the spiritual nature that they each carried.

After the dessert tray arrived with the most decadent selections, the Life Bearers sampled one another's desserts while each person gave a little bit more background on themselves, since there were three new Life Bearers in the group.

Benjamin told the ladies that it was a bit overwhelming for him to have been introduced to all of this through a Bee Goddess who dipped them all in Honey! The waitress came by while he was speaking. She smiled as if it was a perfectly normal conversation they were having.

Alvie laughed out loud hearing Benjamin, describe the honey dipping ceremony but was intrigued to hear more about Tabor. "Oh, we will give you great details on those other team members tomorrow," said

544

Bridgit.

"Speaking of tomorrow..." Stella chimed in. She looked at Christopher and asked, "May I?"

"Please do." Christopher enjoyed seeing Stella take charge.

She stood up and said, "Tomorrow morning, we will be going out in nature for an opportunity to ground our energy as a group and do a tune in."

Benjamin jumped in, "As long as it doesn't involve Bees!" Everyone laughed at his sense of humor.

Stella laughed and remarked, "I cannot make any promises!"

She continued, "There is a great hiking trail in the Red Rock Canyon, with caves and rock outcroppings. I think that would be a great place to do a little tune in. Plan on wearing hiking gear, bring plenty of water and some munchies, oh..., and some note pads too." Stella looked at Christopher to see if he liked the sound of her pitch.

"Thank you, Stella, that sounds splendid. Let us say we shall meet at the park entrance in the morning at 8 am. Oh! By the way..."

He leaned down to grab his bag of teas. "Please select one of these boxes of teas that I have brought all the way from Scotland. My gift to you. It might help you wake up and be bright-eyed for tomorrow's endeavors." He chuckled as he sent his bag of tea around the table.

Traci jumped up and said, "That reminds me! I also brought a little something for each of you. Henny moved his seat so that Traci could hand out small bags, walking around the table to personally hand one to each of the Life Bearers.

She commented, "I prepared the salsa from the produce in my garden and added some organic chips, so you have something to snack on at the hotel. Alvie and I also put into each of your bags a small tourmaline from my father's mine. It seemed only fitting that you each have one of these precious stones, as it was a tourmaline that got the ball rolling for the three of us!" She looked at Henny and Alvie, and everyone was already oohing and aahing.

"This is an amazing specimen, Traci! Thank you so much!" Freya was touched to receive such a lovely stone.

Benjamin and Ashneer were eyeing the chips and salsa as they put their tea box in with their other gifts.

The waitress came to deliver the bill, handing it to Christopher. It was Christopher's pleasure to treat them to such a lovely evening. He thanked the Ladies Phare for doing their part to get them all there and, in particular, to Stella for finding the perfect place to celebrate their reunion.

Everyone left the restaurant with peace in their hearts that they had not felt in a very long time. The kind of peace that a child would have, with not a care in the world.

Bridgit felt it too, and not wanting to play into anxiety or fear, she pushed away the nagging feeling that this was a temporary bliss, one that would soon be replaced with every kind of attempt to stop the Life Bearers from reaching the jump points. She knew that it was a time to be ever more vigilant, as she had been the one to be knocked into another realm after being attacked by a dark being.

She shook the thoughts out of her mind and smiled, saying goodnight to all as everyone got into the cars.

She watched as the other two cars began to drive off. Bridgit rolled her window down to wave and yelled out, "Be very careful on these winding roads!!!" Giving one last warning was all she could do.

And the wheel turns...

Part Three

The Journey

Chapter 78

Strategists Meeting with St. Germain

Shamalaine sat at the table with the articulated eye, viewing the many potentials of the plan to date. The Ascended Master, St. Germain, summoned her and several other Strategists to his private retreat within the higher bandwidths of no time. It was, in fact, the very same meeting place where Bridgit first remembered Gordavin the Gnome, and where the Life Bearers gathered in their dream bodies.

As St. Germain entered the room, the Strategists stood to greet him. The room was immediately infused with the violet fire, clearing all thoughts of those present, and adjusting the very flow of energy in the room to accommodate the highest ideas. This was a meeting to bring forth the highest potentials for Earth and Humanity.

The meeting began once the alignment was complete. Shamalaine represented the group of Strategists and started her presentation. St. Germain listened and applauded the group's evident knowledge of the laws of precipitation.

After Shamalaine presented the plan, she asked St. Germain for a special prayer to bless all of the Life Bearers, the Dragon Riders, the Builders of Form, the Blueprint Masters, and the Guardians.

St. Germain graciously offered a benediction on behalf of each team member. He also included the Galactic's, whose starry family members were involved in the liberation of Humanity. The Clan of Phare, in particular, received his immediate protection, which brought a tear to Shamalaine's eyes.

The brief meeting closed with trumpeting by a group of cherubim. Each participant bilocated back to their reality, to continue to support the Alliance teams, as well as the boots on the ground in the third dimension. Shamalaine returned to the Clan at the Great Hall, having a renewed sense of confidence in the plan. Knowing that victory was assured, she was lifted into a higher vibration. In this state, she was able to perceive the pitfalls and create the highest strategic plan for the light forces.

And the wheel turns...

Chapter 79

Early Morning Hike with the Life Bearers

Christopher awoke in the early morning hours with what can only be described as a zip file uploading into his consciousness from Shamalaine. He sat in the guest room of Stella's home, interacting with a communications medium, similar to a laser beam loaded with data delivering it directly into the brain.

The information download took only seconds to receive and acted as a video playing in his mind. It took an hour for him to digest the contents. The information contained new intel from the Strategist about the mission. He saw in his mind's eye how they would enter into the void once all the Life Bearers made it through the portals.

It was the Life Bearer's task to move on their intuition and the guidance given from the other side to make it to those places where the magnetic fields of the Earth interact with the magnetic fields of the 5th dimension. This is where they would find the jump points.

He was shown how to guide the Life Bearers that day, to help them access their codes of creation. He was to deliver crucial information that would give them confidence on their journey.

He concluded his meditative download with a pull from his pipe. He opened the window of the guest room to blow the smoke out and gazed into the night sky as it began to fade, and the morning sun began to peek out to greet the day.

Christopher made his way down to the kitchen and put water in the kettle that sat on the stove. The kettle was well worn. Christopher surmised that it must have been Evie's and that Stella and Todd kept it for sentimental reasons. Stella set out a teapot for Christopher the night before.

To give Christopher more options, she grabbed a tea mug with a filter in case he decided to use a cup. She left a note that read, "Feel free to use the teapot, or if you rather, you can simply use this teacup with the strainer. There is cream in the fridge. Help yourself to anything you'd like. See you in the morning! Stella." She ended her note with X's and O's.

Christopher found his way around the kitchen with efficiency. He prepared his tea to his liking and sat on the back porch with his pipe in hand when Bridgit and Stella came down for coffee. Bridgit chatted with Christopher while Stella got the coffee going.

Christopher said, "My dear, we will be having a significant event today. I have learned a few things overnight that came in loud and clear, and it is good that we can all gather together now as the time draws near." He drew from his pipe a few times then blew the smoke upward.

Bridgit responded, "Have I told you what a comfort it is that you are here with me? Well, with us." She smiled as Stella walked outside.

"Ah, it is you two that bring comfort to this very old man." He leaned towards Bridgit and patted her knee and gave her his classic twinkle in the eye smile that could melt anyone's heart.

Stella handed Bridgit her coffee as she listened to Christopher going over the morning's itinerary. They spoke about the home that Stella shared with her father Todd, who always seemed to be away on business, Christopher silently took note. He said, "I was looking forward to meeting Todd. Will he arrive before I depart?"

Stella said, "My Dad is a mystery to me. He has a lot going on, but I hope that he will make it back before you leave. I will call him later today to see if we can arrange something." She smiled and sipped her coffee. They had more small talk until Christopher looked at his watch.

"Shall we get ourselves ready?" As Christopher stood, the ladies realized that he was not wearing the tweed jacket that they had always seen him in. This time he was wearing a shirt with multiple pockets.

Stella pondered his choice in attire. He had a pocket for his pipe, a pocket for his tobacco, and a pocket for his lighter. She thought it was something that a photographer or a person on Safari would wear. He wore a pair of khaki slacks and hiking boots as well. Stella let out a little chuckle as he and Bridgit stood on the porch, wondering what was so funny.

"Oh, nothing...it is just so sweet to be with you both. Let's get going!" she said.

A half-hour later, the three made their way to the Red Rock Canyon hiking site. The conversations in the car were so interesting that it felt as if no time had passed at all when Stella pulled into a parking lot.

Stella jumped out to pay for their parking as Christopher questioned the reasoning for paying to have the benefit of enjoying nature. "Nature should be free!" he roared, with only Bridgit in the car.

Bridgit gave him her perspective on the importance of gathering funds, "It contributes significantly to the upkeep of the land and the roads to access the parks.

"I see." Christopher took in the information as he maneuvered out of the car.

They got out to stretch their legs and watched the sun making its appearance overhead. They could hear the sounds of vehicles coming closer. They waited in anticipation for the team to enter the parking lot.

The first car that arrived was Benjamin. He brought Juel and Freya with him. The next vehicle to come was Ford and Ursula in the front seat and Ashneer and David in the back. As the Life Bearers unloaded the cars, they began their prepping with water bottles being pulled out, and protein bars doled out to whoever needed one.

Finally, Henny drove up with Traci and Alvie. These three looked like real hikers. Stella felt a little self-conscious as she had never bothered to buy official hiking gear and always used her purring kitty backpack to carry her gear. She grabbed her backpack from the back of the car and gently put her lap harp into it. She placed her water bottle in the side pouch and put a few bags of trail mix into the zippered pouch in the front of her pack.

Bridgit greeted everyone and played the hostess this time, asking the natives if any of them would like to lead the hike. Henny was a seasoned hiker and volunteered to be the guide for the day.

"I am not sure what you are all up too regarding how long of a hike you are up for, and if I am correct, from what I gathered from you, Christopher, you would like to find a place off the path to have a quiet tune in." Henny looked to Christopher for some guidance on how to proceed.

"Thank you, Henny. I feel that a nice walk will do us all some good, and then once we have got the circulation going, we can find a comfortable spot suitable for a tune in. Please, lead on."

He put his hand out to suggest that they all get going and said, "As I am the oldest in the group, I shall take up the rear and go at a slower pace."

David bounded over towards Christopher's side, as a reflex. "I will join you, sir." David bowed and grinned at his mentor.

David was feeling particularly happy and anxious to see what the day would hold. He watched as the team began chatting as soon as the hike started.

The ladies all gravitated towards one another as Henny, Benjamin and Ford lead the group, with Ashneer taking photographs close behind. Henny had a backpack in which he carried all kinds of accessories that they may need while hiking. The group began to pace themselves rhythmically, and at times went silent to take in the beauty around them.

After a twenty five minute hike, they soon came to a shaded archway that was the perfect place for the group to have a rest and do a little tune in.

Henny dropped his pack and reached inside for the one small collapsible stool that he set up and offered to Christopher. He then pulled out two lightweight, woven blankets to set up a space for the ladies to sit. Stella pulled out a circular blanket as well, and soon the group all had places to sit on the earthen floor with the archway above them, which gave them ample shade.

Christopher sat on the stool with his feet planted three feet apart. He leaned his forearms on his lap, looking towards the ground, gathering his thoughts as the group got comfortable.

He began his lecture, "My dear Life Bearers, it is truly an honor for me to be present with you up to this point. There were moments when I was not sure that I would see the day."

He chuckled and said, "I am now in my seventy fourth year, and my body has aged, but in truth, I am in pretty good shape for an old guy!"

Everyone laughed with him as Christopher opened his heart to them.

"My dears, you have all heard the call of a lifetime, and it is an extraordinary thing to see this many of you say YES to this path. I knew that you would, though there were a few moments that did make me question it." He looked at Alvie and smiled.

"Alvie, my dear, again, I thank you for your presence." She nodded her head several times, feeling ashamed for putting them through the uncertainty of her decision.

He continued, "Each of us has faced deep personal trauma's in our lives, losses that most have no understanding. Yet, the losses are what has prepared us for this moment in our lives. Giving us compassion for our fellow humans and the desire to keep another human being from ever having to experience the pain of losing a loved one. This is the moment when we become once more, the lighthouses for the souls of Humanity."

"Each of you carries a key. A coded frequency... a skill set that you may very well not even know that you possess. This is where my skill-set comes in handy." His eyes twinkled as he smiled with a large grin on his face.

"I am going to take a few moments inward so that I may access each of your original divine templates. This is something like a book that one would find in a library. One in which is solely about you." He positioned himself and said, "If there are no questions, I will begin."

He looked to see if the group was ready to hear their messages. "These messages will deliver to each of you, the awakening of dormant thoughts, memories, or skills that you once had in other times and places." With that, he began.

Christopher closed his eyes as a butterfly flew over his head. Juel was sitting closest to him, and so he began with her. Christopher asked if she permitted him to access her book of life. Juel granted it with a loving nod.

With his eyes closed, Christopher began. "Juel, my dear, your codes suggest that you are a species specialist. In times past, your research was in cellular regeneration. DNA repairs. You also have a deep connection with the wisdom keepers of the inner earth kingdoms. This will be a great memory to tap for you in this now moment. An inner earth wisdom keeper trained you in the knowledge of symbols and runes. You learned the power that comes from these symbols and the mystery around them. All is frequency, and symbols carry frequencies. Let us unlock this memory within you now. Do you agree to recall the memories of the knowledge of the runes and symbols?" With his eyes closed, he paused to hear a response.

Juel was staring into the air, seeing what he was presenting to her, in her mind's eye. She replied, "Yes. I do."

Christopher spoke words that were not of this world, a kind of light language that seemed to arrange a package of information to flow directly into Juel's mind's eye. As she listened to the light language spoken, it translated into her mind's eye as words, formulas, and knowing's. She sat there saturated in the energy field of her past, catching up to her.

Juel saw the ancient one, the wisdom teacher of the inner Earth, speaking to her, and then her mind went blank. She could not hold onto the vision, though she tried with all of her inner strength. She opened her eyes and held her hands to her chest when she felt complete.

Christopher moved on to the next Life Bearer. Stella sat straight up with her legs crossed as Christopher asked for her permission to access her book of life. Stella nodded her head and prepared to receive the download.

Christopher began to access her codes within the Akashic. "My dear Stella, you have wisdom beyond your years, which comes to you from eons of time with the Arcturus Council. You have Pleiadian, Arcturian, and Sirian energies. All of these energies combined packs a wallop!" He smiled and listened to her giggle for a few moments, then continued.

"Your codes reveal that your specialty is, of course, through sound, vibration, and healing. Music is one avenue in which you use your hidden talents. Another is your humor." He waited for her to comment and true to form, Stella cracked a joke, all the while keeping her eyes closed and intent on listening.

"Humor is a useful tool to ease people down from serious situations. Sometimes people are so deeply wounded that they do not see the humor in anything. To say that the Creator, GOD, likes a good joke is an understatement. Humor transmutes emotions that could otherwise stay stuck in one's body. Humor, in your case, Miss Stella, is your Ally. It has been a way for you to transmute your pain, and you have held this tool for many of your incarnations. Your music is sometimes used in awkward situations to dispel tension, and it is also used when you want to make someone laugh. This is your medicine. Laughter!" He opened his eyes to look at the natural born comedian who was enchanted by his report.

His final words for Stella was this, "You have always been a healer Stella, and your work in the realms of the Music of the Spheres in times past will now be upgraded from your life as a human on this third-dimensional plane. Does this make sense to you?"

Stella wiped away a teardrop that was about to fall and said, "Yes. It makes perfect sense. Music and laughter are my two main comforts, you know, aside from my lattes, biscotti's, and Mani-Pedi's!" Everyone started laughing as she entertained them with her wit.

Christopher said, "I will take a moment to pronounce a few things in the language of light, which is our original language, and if you will Stella, please take these words into your heart space and your minds' eye to see and feel the knowledge that you possess."

Christopher began to speak in the language of light and flowed the knowledge that Stella was to remember back to her heart and mind. She unlocked it as soon as it touched her essence. She could feel a vibrational shift, like the sound of her harps string strumming. Her body was in complete surrender to the vibrational unlocking of her codes. As they both completed this exchange, the others sat in anxious anticipation for their gifts to return to them.

Stella indicated that she was complete, and Christopher moved on.

David was next. Christopher grinned and asked David if he gave permission for him to reach into his history. David nodded with the full trust of his mentor.

Christopher tuned into David's energetic makeup. It was winding and long and took him to other worlds. He saw David's soul's essence as a planetary body. A true celestial being.

He shared, "It is no wonder that you contemplate stars that throb for a living," Christopher chuckled, "As you are one of the most delightful, throbbing, starry bodies!"

David was wide-eyed with fascination when hearing this hidden detail of who he was. The other Life Bearers were chuckling as Christopher described David as somewhat of a heavenly body. David was very amused too.

"David, your codes reveal that you have an innate understanding of energy and planetary systems. The actual knowledge of the order of the universe is within you. You are very orderly in the way you conduct yourself. This comes from your higher presence, and your musical abilities also come from your knowledge of geometry and ratio. These, my dear boy, are your hidden talents, not to mention the talents that you have been able to unlock in this lifetime already. You were fully loaded my son, and it is my pleasure to give you these insights about yourself."

David bowed his head in gratitude.

"As I begin the transmission of the light language, please soak it all in and allow it to unlock your highest potentials." Christopher was beaming like a proud father. David was perfectly still with a straight back, bracing himself as if the energy would potentially knock him over.

Christopher began the language of light invocation for David. The sounds flowed directly to David's heart. David breathed deeply several times, and then tears rolled down his face as he began to see a scene play out on his mental screen. The scene was one of the planetary bodies sending out loving frequencies through the cosmos. The music of the spheres was a divine gift of love to the entire universe and beyond.

He suddenly recalled what happened in the cosmic sea, when the planetary wars began, and many planetary bodies were destroyed. Those events changed the musical symphony that once played. The harmonics of love were brought down to lower vibrations, and it was he and others like him who were dispatched to locales in distant star systems to repair the music of the spheres.

The repairs entailed raising the planetary bodies back to their original divine essence, from the blueprint, through sound, geometry, and vibration and piecing the planets back together, energetically, to form a new physical world in certain instances...but not all. The harmonics of the universe had been permanently altered, and David shuddered with the memories.

Christopher completed the transmission and waited as everyone held space for David to complete his download. He was holding back an ancient bereavement of times past when actual beings, which were planetary bodies just like Earth, had been blown up in planetary wars. His pain and sorrow came to the surface, and he began to howl like a dog.

His sorrow was coming out full force, and both Stella and Bridgit latched onto his arms from either side of him and held him tightly as if he would run off into the woods on a full moon night.

David grabbed them and brought them into his chest. Bridgit kissed his cheek as Stella naturally put her healing hands upon his chest and allowed him to feel the healing that would come soon. She reminded him through her own energy body that this is what they had come for; the complete healing of all. Everything was to be made right once more. The Music of the Spheres would sound the fifth chord, and all would be right. She telepathically told him that they would see to it. She stared into his eyes, and he heard every word she spoke to him.

After the intensity of the moment had passed, David nodded to Christopher to proceed. He went limp in Stella's arms. Christopher, knowing that Stella would look after him, looked on to see Bridgit

559

on the other side of David. She managed to smile in anticipation, but after what she just witnessed with David, she was hoping for a gentler reading.

"Well, this all began when you showed up in Scotland, my dear. So, shall we take a peek at what instigated your awakening if you give your permission?" Bridgit settled in as Stella and David continued to hold onto one another. Bridgit nodded for him to begin.

Christopher went internal for a more in-depth look and took his time accessing her file. Bridgit breathed in deeply and awaited her codes to be delivered.

"I will begin with the fact that within each of us is the Divinity spark of our Creator God, within our heart. Throughout the cosmos, there are those who guard the divine sparks of life. There are many sparks within creation, such as the Three-Fold Flame, the Flame of the Immaculate Concept, and the Flame of Liberty, just to name a few. These flames are guarded over by Keepers of the Flame, and you, my dear Bridgit, have been and still are, one of those keepers."

Bridgit smiled and nodded.

Christopher continued, "There are also those who guard over the bridge of time. The places where the veils are the thinnest. Places where one might accidentally find oneself in an unfamiliar environment. This is what happened to Miss Bridgit, and is why we are all gathered here today." There were murmurs of appreciation from the group, then Christopher continued.

"This explains some of the stories over the past centuries of people finding hidden treasures in areas that are deep in the jungle only to not ever be able to find it again. They had momentarily ingressed into a time-space that was not their own, and thus, there became a need for Guardians of sacred spots, places, and energies."

"Bridgit, you come from a long line of Keepers and Guardians. It is your birthright to guard and protect the sacred treasures of this planet in all of her layers until such time that it is safe to create an opening into a new layer." He winked at her as Bridgit intently listened and took in the information.

"That new layer is the New Earth vibrational zone that all of Humanity will have the ability to live within, once the frequencies and creations are complete. It is within your job description, dear Bridgit, to be the open door or the bridge when the time comes, where you will assist Humanity in this massive migration, much like the Mayans, Incas and Aztec's of old had done before us. All of you will play a part in this great assistance during the time of the shift of the ages."

Christopher looked at all of the Life Bearers and said, "I have waited a long time to find her, and to my pleasant surprise, it was in my own backyard."

He looked once more to Bridgit, "I would like to give you the blessing of your codes, which will unlock as they are transmitted to your heart. Are you ready, my dear?" He checked in with Bridgit to see if he could begin the transmission of light language.

Bridgit prepared herself to receive the transmission. Christopher began the deliverance of her codes to be brought upon her mental screen and within her heart space.

Bridgit listened to the most unusual sounds coming from Christopher. The sounds were more like clicks of the tongue and chattering as if he was emulating a tribal song. He got louder and louder and then stood up, with his feet firmly planted and continued to sing out the light language codes with rhythmic slaps on his thighs, as if he was playing drums. Finally, the transmission calmed down to a gentle rhythm.

Bridgit was taken into a deep place of remembering. She held fire within the palms of her hands, the eternal flame that was her birthright and all life everywhere. She sat in a circle with elders, who were the original keepers of the flame, and she listened to their stories that spanned eons of time.

Christopher was now quiet, having completed the transmission.

561

Bridgit waited until she absorbed all of the memory and details and then nodded with gratitude. She was moved to tears but wanted to stay inward, so she motioned for him to continue. She put her hands to her chest to show her gratitude.

Christopher looked at the next person. Sitting in the semi-circle next to Bridgit was Benjamin.

Christopher waited as Benjamin prepared himself to receive the codes. Benjamin looked up and gave two thumbs up, giving Christopher access to his book of life. Christopher looked deeply into the ancient archives of Benjamin Skye.

Christopher began, "The eye of Horus is a seal within your energy field. It is used to look through all things to see the truth and stamp out all that is other than perfection. The pyramids were created using a technology like this. It was to assist this planet in bringing about an artificial vibration, as the planetary bodies within this solar system had been severely out of harmony due to the effects of the planetary wars."

Christopher looked deeper and took a breath, then continued, "You were an etheric engineer whose job it was to come up with solutions in the interim when there was damage to bodies in our solar system, much in line with David's skill set." Christopher took another deep breath and gave a slight yawn as the energies made him feel unusually sleepy.

He continued, "Your codes reveal that you are a true visionary and that you are a master codebreaker who unravels the mystery. This particular skill set could definitely come in handy, my boy. Finally, I see that your latest exploits within the local star cluster, before your most recent incarnation, was that you were something like, for lack of a better word, a sky patroller. It seems that you would be about rescue missions, like a planetary search and rescue operation, and I see you using the eye of Horus device on these planetary missions as well. Very intriguing, my boy."

Christopher was delighted to see such talent organized in front of him.

Benjamin was beside himself with this confirming information. Christopher asked if he was ready to receive the information package and suggested that he breathe deeply and enter his heart space.

Benjamin calmed his body, which was surging with adrenaline. Christopher began to speak yet another kind of star language that had a hint of Egyptian flavor. The message was quick paced, just like Benjamin. The energy rose and then came to an abrupt halt as if it was an order. Benjamin rocked back and forth while the others held space for him to unlock his package within his heart.

As Benjamin slowly began to speak, he said, "Thank you for that wonderful delivery. That was by far the best gift that I have ever received. What it did for me was to confirm the memories that have been popping up in my mind and dreams, those that I shared with you, Bridgit... and Stella. The dream about Captain Skyward and the Horus device, all of this is truly fantastic, and something else that amazes me and makes me wonder who my parents are is that they named me Benjamin HORUS Skye. I am mind blown that they somehow knew me! They knew to call me by that name."

He shook his head and said, "That is amazing, and it was a lot to download and process, so please, feel free to go ahead with the next person. I will contemplate all of this, and thank you so much!!"

Christopher nodded and smiled as Benjamin was uncharacteristically calm and composed.

Ford was at Benjamin's left-hand side. Christopher nodded to him to see if he was ready. Ford sat straight up and latched onto Ursula's hand. For a moment, he was slightly intimidated by the crowd of amazing people whom he had the pleasure of being in their company.

He felt like he didn't belong. Not good enough to be called a Life Bearer, though he wanted it to be true. Ford recognized the dark force creeping into his mind and, in that moment, declared that he was ready to remember who he truly is and defeat the nagging thought that he was never going to amount to anything. It took deep surrender.

Once prepared, he nodded for Christopher to begin. Christopher asked him for his full name. Ford gave him his name and once more held onto Ursula.

Christopher inhaled slowly and deeply. He felt the torment in Ford's mind as he opened the archives of Ford Lucius Casselman. He saw the name Lucius, which was given to him from his father's side of the family. A family rife with struggle and egregious ways. Christopher could see it all. The dark forces that had swirled on the periphery of Ford's conscious mind.

He began, "The Solar Lords called forth the Kings of the Kingdoms to bring forth their finest warriors for the Sun Dance. The one who carried the most burden on behalf of the people would be chosen to have great knowledge and light bestowed upon him on behalf of the planet and people. He would become the Luminous One, and this is the meaning of your secondary name, Lucius. The Light. It also is why there are forces that you push away yet are always near your field. It is those who possess the brightest of light that attracts the darkness. We will speak more of this at a later time, but for you, dear Ford, I see that you are carrying the male energy of the Christed Light. You can imbue any creation with the Christ light. Entire regions are affected by your intentions to hold the light."

Christopher smiled as he continued, "You understand the sacred in nature, and your elemental lives have been what has prepared you in this life as a Human. I would venture to say that your DNA is more Elemental than human. Your work in the third dimensional plane of Earth has been to clear frantic energies by the use of stones. Your talent for landscaping is one that you brought in with you, and it is why you will be working with the mineral kingdom once more. Your codes show that the etheric forces are at your command. This is a talent that you have honed over many lifetimes, and you have now brought this into form at this time. Let us make the transfer of your codes now as you will be downloading even more than I have been able to transmit out loud."

Ford smiled with deep relief, as he always had wondered about so much of what Christopher had just revealed. Especially the part about the dark forces being so close to his field all of his life.

Christopher began the light language transfer. Ford held his breath in anticipation of the delivery. It eased gently, first into his mind's eye as a brilliant flash of solar light. Then it became a bright blue star that traveled into his heart — the energy released into his chest as Christopher sent rhythmic sounds from Ford's starry origins.

Ford could see the light aura around his body and saw information streaming in the form of pictures of times long ago. He was seeing himself in various lives, but not all were on planet Earth. It was remarkable to see how a being of light interacts on multiple planes and different worlds. Ford was calm and steady as he held in his heart the codes that were downloading. He did not want to come out just yet, wanting to explore more, so he tipped his head and lifted Ursula's hand to indicate that Christopher could move on.

Christopher smiled at Ursula, who had been holding onto Ford as his gentle rock. She beamed with such love for her soul mate and was honored to be his partner. Christopher asked for her full name, and if she permitted him to access her codes. She gently gave her name and consent in a whisper.

"Ursula Rene Bevins, I am activating your ancient archives. I am honored, my dear, to be sitting with one of the Mary's of ancient days. The name MARY is indicative of the females who worked the MER lines or the Mary lines, which, as you all know, are the geomantic vortices connected to Mother energy."

He continued, "Similar to your partner, to whom you are well suited, you carry the Mother energy of creation. Your codes suggest that you are a portal specialist, much like Miss Bridgit. The portal technology is truly ancient Stargate technology from other star systems. You have spent ample lifetimes training in the operations of stargates as well as training in the Ambassador program to be a liaison for the Pleiadian Council."

"Let us go back to the Mary or Mer lines. Aquatic beings such as the merfolk supervise the Mer lines, and you, my dear, have a direct lineage with these elemental beings, so it is no wonder that you were thrilled to work on the water team." He smiled at Ursula, who had now buried her head into her lap and was sobbing as he shared these words.

"Ursula? Do you want me to continue?" He very kindly asked as he watched her bob her head up and down to indicate a yes response. He could hear her say yes in a little voice as she hid her face.

"Ok, my dear. Prepare your heart and mind to see and feel the lineage and light codes through this transmission of light language." Christopher belted out a piercing sound which he sent in the form of waves. It felt like a slap on the face energetically, like a wave of water lapping in the ocean and then hitting the sandy beach.

Ursula saw in her mind's eye the water and oceans on the planet. She then was taken under the water, where there were worlds hidden deep within the ocean. The energy ley lines known as the Mer lines, or Merlin(s), were magically producing vibratory action within the water.

As the females, Mer beings maintained the lines, she could see how it shifted slightly as the energy came to the physical surface and would gather in a vortex of energy, which when appropriately maintained, would hold a vibration of perfect health and wholeness, as well as pure loving vibration and peace. Her lineage was responsible for a genuine Goddess vortex.

Christopher completed his transmission and watched her rocking as if the water was taking her body into the sea. Her mind was wading in the ocean, contemplating the Goddesses that all had something to do with maintaining the plumbing of the lines. She heard Galactic Plumber, and that is when she started laughing out loud, uncontrollably.

Everyone watched as Ursula processed her codes with an unexpected reaction of absolute joy and laughter. As she laughed, the others laughed with her, feeling her joy. Ford began to come out of his inner realms and was in such peace that he too began to giggle.

Christopher sat back in the seat and took a sip of water as if this was perfectly normal behavior. A hiker walked by during this moment and laughed as well as he made his way around the group. He, too, felt the high energy while he kept on his path. Once the laughter began to subside, and the smiling faces looked to Christopher, he said, "Life should always be this delicious!"

He sat down his bottle and smiled at Ursula. She nodded in his direction with gratitude.

Christopher looked to see who was next on the Life Bearer list. It was Freya Franklin. "My dear, are you ready for me to access your Codes?"

Freya was so happy to be in his presence and said, "Please. I can't wait to hear what is hidden within me." She rubbed her hands together and then placed each hand upon her knees as she sat with her legs crossed and back erect as the others had done.

Christopher dove in. He breathed deeply and said, "Freya Franklin, the power of Thor is within you as your name is intimately connected to the Norse myth. The Norse mythology is also intimately connected to the inner earth beings from which you come. In particular, the awareness of how to activate the Rainbow Bridge is in your repertoire."

"The next thing that is unfolding is your knowledge of plant life, and in particular your skills at understanding the ratios of nutrients and air required for a plant to maintain its vitality in a habitat suggests that you are a Galactic Atmospheric Specialist. I see your many lives as this Atmospheric Specialist working on many moons, both in this solar system and beyond. You're mainly connected to plant life but have served on spacecraft where you emulated natural environments, all from your training and lifetimes with this planet's inner realms."

"You also have created many tinctures for the health and well-being of creatures and galactic citizens far and wide. To further your skills over time, you were active on many treks where you were acting as a Life Bearer, in the same way, that you are now acting as a Life Bearer for Earth. You have many advanced skills, but your passion is for the plants of each planetary body that you have worked upon. The knowledge of nutrients in the soil and working with the elemental kingdom, the Builders of Form, has been one of your highest honors and is why you incarnated once more into this plane because we needed a specialist, and that is what we have." He opened his eyes and smiled at Freya, so pleased to see her among the group.

"Are you ready for the light language transmission?" He asked.

"Yesssss." She licked her lips with anticipation of the transmission.

Christopher spoke yet another version of the light language, that was more low tones and whispers. He breathed deeply and continued another round, again and again. It was as if he was reciting a poem in another language, cosmic poetry, akin to the Norse Prose Edda.

Freya suddenly began to do sign language, and yet this was not the signing for those who were deaf, but a signing that was another version of light language.

She and Christopher communicated back and forth in this way until Christopher stopped speaking. Freya made one last flowing gesture with her arms and hands and shut her eyes to absorb the conversation that just took place. Her Pleiadian heritage had just anchored.

Memories were now in place for her to access in the coming days. She bowed her head and acknowledged her fullness, and Christopher moved on.

Ashneer "Kokopelli" Sharma was next on the list. He permitted Christopher to access his book of life before Christopher even asked.

Christopher shifted his position in the camp stool and put his head down to tune into the history of Ashneer's soul essence. Ashneer sat in reverence, awaiting the codes to be revealed.

Christopher began, "My boy, you are for lack of a better term, a Water Bearer. Your codes reveal that on other planetary systems, outside of this one, you worked with the element of water to imbue intelligence into all substances that it interacted with. Knowledge is held in every formation of a snowflake, in water wells and large bodies like lakes and oceans. The element of water is cyclic, malleable, and formless. It is connected to emotion. Emotions flow like water." Christopher breathed in deeply, looking for more.

"Your work in Vastu Shastra is in line with your particular skill set, as Vastu Shastra is an ancient system based on the knowledge of the flow of universal energy. The water component set within the garden and plot of land where a home is placed, is vital, as it assists in the natural flow of chi. I am seeing many lifetimes where you were a master builder in some lives, a gardener in other lives, and always the element of water was the common thread for you."

"To conclude, Koko, the aspect of you in this life, that goes by Kokopelli is also indicative of your traits. He was known to be a mischievous sort, who played his flute and was and still is a symbol of fertility and replenishment. This is his gift, and it seems to be in line with yours." He chuckled. He opened his eyes and winked at Ashneer as the others whispered about Koko's fertility gifts.

Ashneer beamed with joy and took it all into his heart. Christopher said, "I will begin my transmission, but, do you by chance, carry a flute with you similar to the one Kokopelli played?"

Ashneer turned red and said, "Noooo. I wish I knew how to play the flute."

Christopher said, "No worries my boy, I know that someone here has a flute." He looked over at Stella, as she pulled a wooden pipe out of her bag and twirled it in her fingers.

Christopher laughed, "Ah, there it is. Would you mind playing a soft tune while I bring through his codes?"

Stella said, "I've got ya."

Ashneer leaned backward to stretch his body, giving his torso more room to hold the energy that was about to download into his aura. He then placed his hands into a mudra position and nodded to Christopher to begin the transmission.

Christopher began humming the Om sound as Stella played a soft tune on the wooden flute. He centered his being and then started the light language dialog. This was a deep and emotional vibrational sound, mixed with words from another star lineage. Christopher would stop for moments, almost too overwhelmed with emotion to continue the transmission. He then translated what was happening in English.

"There is a star council present who are delivering this message to you, dear boy. These are your ancestors from the star system of Vega. There is much that was relayed in the urgency of our mission. The light codes that were imbued within this transmission is the key codes to unlock the LOVE frequency that was emitted in the Lyran constellations that have since been destroyed. Your ancestors are giving you this frequency, and you now hold it in your cellular DNA blueprint, and this will be activated within the template for the New Earth. It is part of the repair work happening with the Galaxies."

Christopher stopped momentarily. He looked to the sky and pointed upwards. "They are presenting themselves to us now so that you know that they are here with you and will be providing assistance. Take a look."

Everyone looked upward and saw a spade-shaped craft hovering just below a cloud overhead. The sunlight hit the craft, and the outer shell looked multicolored. It had an umbra effect that went from dark purple to gray to light blue. Everyone could see it clearly. The craft then blended into the clouds for a few minutes and then zipped away from sight.

Ashneer held his hands to his heart while tears of emotions streamed from his eyes. He had just witnessed his family of light give him the sign that he had been asking for. Everyone was providing their insights until Christopher quieted down the group.

"Koko, you are blessed, and we are so happy to have you as a team member. It is quite an extraordinary thing to have family members follow you around." Christopher winked at him and pointed upward.

"This has been a great unfolding, but I must say that my body is in need of movement and some nourishment. I propose that we reconvene this soiree at Miss Stella's home. She has kindly offered to host us there for the rest of the day, and food is also provided. Once we get some food and tea in us, then I will complete the last three Life Bearers codes, and then we can get onto more revelations. Any objections?" Christopher looked for responses, and everyone was pleased to be able to move their bodies.

David stood up and said, "I am always happy to eat! Thank you, Elder Christopher, for your fine words and your keen ability to read our codes. This has been a very enlightening session. Difficult...but enlightening."

He walked over to Christopher and offered his hand to assist ridding Christopher of the small chair that was sticking to the back of his jacket as he stood up. "There we go... I've got it."

He folded the chair and handed it to Henny and held onto Christopher as support. "Let's go over to this lovely tree just there, and perhaps take a moment to fill up? Hmm..."

Christopher wobbled slowly, stiff from sitting in such a low seat and exhausted from the energy it took to read the Life Bearers codes.

David knew that tree energy would work wonders for Christopher. He couldn't have been more correct. Christopher stood under the sycamore tree for a few moments in silence. The Life Bearers helped dust off the sandy blankets and put their water bottles away. Henny gathered the group a little further down the path to show them the view.

After a short respite, Christopher had a pull from his pipe and was good to move onward. "Let us get back to the house, and we shall see what more comes forward. Are we ready?"

571

Everyone cheered for the idea of food and more information as they happily walked back the way they came and left the Red Rock Canyon park a little brighter and more magical than it was the day before.

And the wheel turns...

Chapter 80

In the Etheric Realms

Avery was wandering in a meadow, contemplating his upcoming jump into the place of no time, the Cave of Creation. He considered his role in the plan and was deeply concerned that he had no schedule for when the jump would happen. He instinctually knew it was any time, and it made him feel a bit uneasy.

He lifted his head to the sky when his thoughts went to the last time the Elemental and Human kingdoms interacted consciously in a co-creative endeavor. It ended poorly, with the elves, and all of the fairy kingdom, retreating from direct interaction with Humans. He knew that he needed to shift his awareness quickly onto something positive and uplifting.

He went into prayer, honoring the sky, in gratitude, for the beautiful day. He caught a glimpse of a golden ray high above him. As it got closer, Avery could see a large golden eagle flying towards him. The sound of the eagle screeching a greeting was music to Avery's ears. It was the sign he was anticipating.

Avery stood still in the meadow as the golden eagle lowered just enough to swoop Avery up in its talons.

The blessing of the golden eagle lifting Avery was that he could see the whole of creation in the realm of the fae. The eagle soared to such great heights, taking him over the very mountaintop that Avery hiked when he met with the Watchers.

The eagle soared through the valleys and mountains and finally brought Avery to the final destination. Between two mountain peaks, a portal opened into the Angelic realms. This was a special occasion for all of the Builders of Form as they were each delivered by a Golden Eagle into the Retreat of Archangel Gabriel.

Waterfalls and foliage were interspersed between Grecian buildings. The trees were 40 feet tall with vines hanging to the ground covered in magenta-colored flowers. The landscape was unique in that instead of the land being flat, it sloped as if they were inside of a large tube.

The air was crisp, and the birds were singing. Clouds hovered over the buildings to give ample shade from the bright light coming from above. A glow emitted from within each building and the most exquisite aroma filled the air.

Trumpeting could be heard coming from a large white temple, where the eagles delivered the Builders of Form. Each member of the Builders team was greeted and shown into the great hall of the temple. Glorious music played in the background, and the Consecration flame burned brightly in the center of the platform at the far end of the room.

Archangel Gabriel walked into the room from a side entrance, and behind him flowed the nine Blueprint Masters. Gabriel announced that it was time to begin the great works of the triad of Humans, Angels, and Elementals working together to affect the freedom of Gaia.

To this end, he said, "I will be escorting all of you to a Midway Station, where you will be brought into resonance with the frequency of the Cave of Creation. There you will hold the field until the Life

Bearers arrive. At that time, you will begin the New Earth co-creation project."

Cheers erupted, and the music once more filled the room. The light in the room exponentially grew. A cloud filled the space, and then it went silent. Time seemed to stand still as if everything in the world was on pause, and then a whirring sound began to hum louder and louder.

They were no longer in the temple. Gabriel and the team members were in a flux tube shuttle system. Within the flux tube was a burnt orange colored light, and as the shuttle zoomed through it, on occasion, the ribbing of the tubing could be seen.

Gabriel stood while each of the members of the team was seated on benches. He delivered a final speech and, in the end, a blackbird that accompanied Gordavin began to crow.

The shuttle came to a stop, and the team offloaded. They stood within a large round chamber on top of a platform. The room was white with windows along the center of the wall, with a 360-degree view of pitch-black space.

From there, Gabriel left the teams with the Sentinels, blue-skinned beings who operated the flux tubes. He raised his hand in a farewell gesture, and he was gone.

The Builders of Form and Blueprint Masters were shown to the center of the room where there was a shuttle system that took them to their final destination.

A petite woman with long black hair greeted them. Her face was veiled except for her eyes, which were glowing an electric blue.

She spoke in a gentle manner, choosing her words meticulously. As the members of the teams walked with her to their respective caves, they passed through wavy distortions within the landscape. They were in a place where the veils were not fixed, where one flowed with less density.

The host offered the teams time to acclimate and showed them to the libraries within the caves so they could dive deep into the history of the planet Earth, something that even Elementals and Angels had not been privy to know, until now.

And the wheel turns...

Chapter 81

Round Two
Revealing the Codes

The Life Bearers were well fed after a very heartwarming adventure at the Red Rock Canyon. Stella provided salads and juices from the local health food store and had various chocolates sitting out on the coffee table in the living room.

The men brought chairs from the kitchen table into the living room and situated them around the sides of the sofas to provide everyone with a spot to sit as they prepared for the second round of codes to be revealed.

Stella and Bridgit asked that everyone prepare their beverages in the kitchen and then find a spot to relax while they waited for Christopher, who was out on the back porch with David having a discussion.

Benjamin looked around the kitchen and asked Stella random questions about her home. Stella was trying to answer while cleaning up the coffee grounds that Bridgit had somehow managed to drop on the floor. Stella was aware that Bridgit was not fully present, so she suggested that she check out what was going on outside on the patio.

Instead of fixing his beverage, Benjamin grabbed the broom from Stella and began cleaning the grounds. He threw them into the trash and noticed that the can was full. He instinctively lifted out the bag and found another bag hidden inside the can. He pulled it out and replaced the bag and pointed to the filled trash bag with a look on his face as to where he might take it.

Stella smiled, happy to have a helping hand. She pointed him towards the back door and instructed him to find the large trash receptacle on the side of the house off of the patio. Within moments, the deed was done. As he was coming back towards the kitchen door, Christopher motioned for Benjamin to join them. He was sharing with David and Bridgit something that was on his mind.

Christopher waved Benjamin over, "Come join us, Benjamin."

Benjamin wiped his hands on his backside and grabbed a chair, honored to be included in what felt like a private conversation. "What's up?"

"Well, as I have been within Miss Stella's lovely home, I have had the feeling that I was missing something... concerning her father, Todd, who is my Nephew. I have not had the privilege of meeting him." He paused for a moment trying to best word what he was about to relay.

He looked at the trio of Life Bearers before him. He said, "When I received the intel package earlier, I also had a message that was surprising and yet not. It was about Stella's father."

Christopher looked at Bridgit and said, "Todd Phare is more than meets the eye. He is an advanced being here on Earth. He is part of a program that interacts with many different galactic races, as an Ambassador of sorts. Thus, his constant travel and secrecy. I am in a quandary as to what to do about this intel as Stella is not aware of his involvement. Todd's mission is on the Alliance side of things, and I feel we may end up meeting him very soon, in his formal capacity."

Bridgit said, "The Alliance?! You mean, he could be involved in the part of the mission that Breacher and our parents are involved in?"

She leaned in to try not to speak too loudly. "I mean Bewain and Shamalaine, of course."

"Yes, exactly, my dear. Todd is a Phare, and within this lineage, we carry multiple responsibilities, due to our many ABILITIES. I am not sure what Todd's abilities are at this point. Still, I received clear intel this morning on the subject, and now I am not sure if I should speak of it just yet, as Todd has gone through great lengths to keep it a secret from Stella...most likely just to keep her from worrying."

He scratched his head as Stella popped her head out of the kitchen door and said, "We are all ready, and the tea is steeped!" Stella winked at Christopher. He took it as a cue to move on inside and table the conversation for later.

Benjamin, Bridgit, and David just stood and grinned then walked behind Christopher back inside. Christopher stopped at the kitchen island to prepare his tea. David stood by his side, waiting for him to complete the task, then took Christopher's cup over to the side table, next to the Queen Anne chair. Everyone else was seated, waiting for the rest of the group to sit.

Henny, Traci, and Alvie were the last Life Bearers to receive their code activations. Christopher took a sip of tea, grinned with delight as the warmth of the tea slid down his throat. He placed the teacup on the side table and looked at the three Life Bearers who were waiting to be activated. He decided to start with the ladies first.

"Miss Traci, it is my pleasure to read your Akashic record, if you would allow me access?"

Traci said, "Please! I give you my permission", as she nodded to him to begin. Traci asked if it would be okay to record what he was about to say, and he agreed. She had Henny activate the recorder on her phone, and then Christopher began.

"Traci, dear...you are overshadowed by a great eagle with an eye on all currents. What I mean by this is that everything makes a ripple. Every movement, word, and sound creates a vibrational wave. Each of these currents effects the other and the whole of creation. You have been part of a team that monitors the currents of planetary systems. The Eagle is a being of great vision and can see the whole patterns. This is your gift, as well. You could say that you carry Eagle medicine. Your mind works on these higher levels, more concerned with the whole, rather than the parts."

He looked at Traci and asked, "As I recall, you are steering ecological policy?"

Traci answered yes. Christopher continued.

"This is a perfect example of how you find the highest places to use your skills. What I see within your codes is that you are great at manifestation. You also are something of a wordsmith. These are all qualities of a universal delegate, who sits on Overseeing Councils."

Christopher came out of his in-depth analysis and offered a comment. "I would suggest that you be placed on the Whole Systems team as we progress. We can talk about the teams later, to bring you up to speed, but, with your talents of organization, this would be the perfect team for you. Shall I begin the transmission?" He looked to see if she felt complete with his reading, and she agreed to begin the transmission, knowing that more insights would come.

Christopher pulled himself to the edge of his seat and opened his chest, breathing deeply. He let out an OM sound, then an overtone followed within his throat. It was an ancient throat sound that com-municated a package of data from the Galactic Center. Solar flashes were seen in Traci's mind's eye that activated her latent clairvoyant gift. She saw herself on various councils over time as scenes played out like a movie in her mind as Christopher continued the wave of OM sounds.

Traci heard a particular frequency of light that pierced her heart and opened her to visions of the New Earth. She could see the many layers of the plan, each one connected to a particular element. She knew how to pull all of these elements together in a cohesive format. Her heart was happy to regain the knowledge that she had worked for eons to attain. A tear of joy ran down her face, and then she fell backward against the sofa. She lost consciousness for a few moments as Henny grabbed her.

Christopher said, "Just hold her steady. She will be just fine. The frequencies were almost too much for me to bring through, and now that she has let the body go, she is most likely retrieving the final codes. Just give her a moment."

Traci began to come back into consciousness within ten seconds, and in that ten seconds, the download was complete. She opened her eyes and saw Henny's smile. "All good?" he asked.

"Oh yeah... did I lose consciousness?" Traci looked around to see that she was now leaning against Henny and not where she positioned herself initially.

"Yeah, babe... you kind of went zooming there for a little while." Henny tried to make light of it.

"Wow. I feel so light." She looked at Christopher. "That energy was powerful. Thank you. I have gained so much insight into my past. I will contemplate this and would love to be on the Whole Systems team."

Christopher smiled at Alvie, then spoke to the whole team. "For those who do not know, Alvie and I are already familiar with one another, but not from this lifetime. As I have been sharing your multidimensional lives with you, I must interject a bit about myself, as it relates to Alvie here."

The group all looked at one another, puzzled, but also with excitement and Alvie in particular.

"You see, in my other form, in the higher planes of existence, I have been on a council that chooses who, out of all of the possible candidates in the Cosmos, would be needed for particular missions such as these. In this particular case, I have actually interviewed all of you in your higher forms."

581

He let that sink in for a moment or two and chuckled. "Alvie recognized me from her recent vision, but in truth, we have all been together in many capacities over the eons of time. My role as a Life Bearer this time around is as an overseer, jointly prepared for this mission with Miss Bridgit as the other lead." He smiled her way.

Bridgit and Stella just shook their heads with wonder. David's mouth was wide open.

Alvie said, "I did recognize you at dinner last night!" She nodded her head in amazement, and he looked at Alvie, not surprised.

"Yes, Miss Alvie, and you have been the wild card! It was you that I recommended, and I am going to choose my words carefully here... it was you that I recommended not to be put on the list as a Life Bearer."

Everyone started to murmur, and he hushed them quickly. "Let me explain."

He looked at Alvie and said, "Dear, you have a passion for all life, which is a cellular gift from the ancients. Your passion for souls not embodying a human vehicle has been your primary concern and, in particular, those beings who cannot fend for themselves. The delicate creations such as the woodland creatures, the birds, and other species other than Humans."

Christopher took a deep breath and continued, "This mission is twofold; to access our divine codes of creation to prepare the way for the New Earth and to activate humanity in preparation for the ascension. When looking at your future, the codes revealed that you had a great potential to alienate yourself from humanity. We had many sessions where you pleaded with the council to let you have a chance at being a Life Bearer for Gaia's ascension. We showed you the many pitfalls, and yet you pleaded with us that you would do everything in your power to heed the call when the time came."

He looked around the room and then back to Alvie. She had tears in her eyes and nodded in agreement.

Christopher said, "You convinced me that you had what it takes to be a co-creator and for all creatures, including humanity. And so..., we as a collective, said yes. You were prepared for the mission, and now, with all of that being said, let me tell you how proud I am of you."

He reached his hand out towards her, and she reached out her's. They held hands for a few moments, looking deeply into one another's eyes. She wiped her tears and smiled.

"Now then, let us see what your codes might further reveal."

Bridgit placed her hand upon Alvie's shoulder. Alvie patted it and held her hand on Bridgit's.

Christopher began toning, and then the light language flowed smoothly. The sounds danced off of his tongue with fluidness, and it was as if one could taste the sounds. Synesthesia occurred within Alvie. Within her sensory body, the sounds were activating all of her senses of taste, sight, and feeling.

Christopher began to translate what had just occurred as Alvie stayed with the awakening.

"This is part of the reawakening of her electric and etheric forces and is vital in dealing with the balancing of the male and female energy within the heart. The gifts that she carries come from her lineage. She is from the bird tribes known as Alteans. The Altean DNA is much like the Albigensians, or Elven beings. She has this in common with Miss Bridgit. The Clan of Phare is an extension of the Clan in which Alvie comes...that of the Dragon Clan."

He smiled at the two college friends and went on. He waited for the clamoring to quiet down then completed his transmission.

"She has been trained as a habitat specialist. Her empathy for all living things is what drives her. Alvie, you will be placed on the Animal team. You will be working with Avery, the Builder of Form from the first Ray. We have yet to meet the other team members, but at this point, you are the lone wolf on the Animal team, but I think that you will be just fine." He winked at her and then cleared his throat. Alvie thanked him quietly and nodded that she was complete.

He wiggled a bit to move energy and took a sip of tea. After a few moments of integration, Christopher said, "Who is next?"

Henny waited patiently for all of the other Life Bearers to be given their codes, and he was chomping at the bit to see what his codes revealed. He raised his hand and said, "That would be me, kind sir."

"Ah, yes... Master Henny!" he smiled, and everyone did too. Master Henny suited him.

"What is your full name, son?" Christopher inquired.

"Henderson John White, but my friends just call me Henny." He rubbed his outstretched legs and then brought them closer in by folding them pretzel style with his feet underneath him.

"Excellent. I am now accessing your records.... yes... hmmm. Master Henny, your codes reveal that you are a frequency specialist. In your many lifetimes as a Sound Engineer, for lack of better words, your job was to modulate vibrations to uplift, move, or to clear energy within an environment. This was and still is how one cleans up an environment, so in reality, you could just as easily be called an Environmental Engineer."

In Henny's mind's eye, he could see a scene of him clearing energy, and then suddenly, a garbage truck flashed in his mind. He started laughing so hard he fell over to his side. As he sat up, Henny's southern accent heightened when he asked Christopher, "Are you telling me that I am a galactic garbage man!?" Traci pushed him back over, wanting him to be more serious.

Christopher laughed out loud too, and said, "Well, I guess in some ways I am, my boy!"

"Great.... Great... Story of my life, man!" Henny's sense of humor had the whole group laughing.

While everyone was laughing with Henny, Christopher glanced at the entryway, where Todd stood staring into the living room with an odd look on his face. He set down his luggage and moved his sunglasses onto his head.

"Oh my, I didn't realize that we were having a party. Please excuse my barging in like this." Todd said while looking at Stella.

"Oh, Dad! Your home!!!" She jumped up and excused herself and led her father into his study. "Christopher, please...Carry on!" she yelled out from the foyer.

Christopher said, "Very good, then. Let's see, where were we? Oh yes...the galactic garbage man, as you so cleverly put it!" he chuckled once more, as did all of the team members, and then he said, "I tease you, Henny. Truly, you have led a noble mission of vibrational healing, clearings, and creations of many sorts." He rolled his hands in the air to explain.

"An environment is the first step of creating a habitat, and this is what we are all called to assist with now. You will be placed on the team called the Music of the Spheres. This team, as we have stated before, is not just about music; it is about the essence and environment of complete balance and harmony. Your fellow Life Bearers, Miss Stella and David, join you on this team. It will be well represented."

Stella walked back into the room and gave the thumbs up that all was well. She was excited to overhear that Henny was joining her and David.

Christopher positioned himself to send the transmission through the Language of Light. "I am sensing a color that I would like for you to concentrate on while I give the code activation. It is golden yellow."

He looked at Stella and David. "And now, I will ask that Miss Stella and David assist us. Stella, dear, can you give me a pitch in the A note?"

As Stella toned in the note of A, he looked to David. "Can you hold the tone of C, and then Henny, you carry the note of G. Just tone a sound in those pitches as I unlock the codes." The sounds at first were disjointed, but soon they blended beautifully.

Christopher began his melodic delivery of the Language of Light codes from Henny's archive.

The sounds vibrated Henny's throat area, and he began to feel the music rearranging his mind. The golden yellow enveloped him as if he was in a golden brazier. Soon, a vision opened onto his mental screen. It showed him sitting in the darkness of the void, where he was using his thoughts to run programs that would create new environments.

He realized at the moment that everything starts with a thought, then the thought is made manifest. It was a powerful visualization, and though he had heard of the premise of manifestation beginning as a thought, he did not fully understand it until that very moment. It made him go deep.

The sounds stopped, as he could no longer hold thought and sound in balance. Everyone was quiet, waiting for him to return. Moments later, Henny moved his head from side to side, keeping eyes closed just a bit longer.

He said, "I want to remember this space and feel it so deeply that I will never possibly forget what it is like to be in such a deep and pure space where the perfection of creation is made manifest."

"Very well put my boy," Christopher spoke softly.

Henny smiled and finally opened his eyes. "Wow! My mind is blown!"

He looked around the room, and, in his heart, he genuinely felt feelings for these people. He said, "I LOVE YOU GAIA'S!!!"

Bridgit laughed at his clever wit, and how genuine of a man he is, and she knew why Traci had picked him.

Stella then said, "Now that we have completed this part of the agenda, let's stretch a bit and maybe get some fresh air outside. Help yourself to more refreshments in the kitchen." Playing the hostess role was Stella's utter joy. She loved making sure that everyone had what they needed.

Christopher interjected. "Stella, dear, I think what would be best is if the group goes back to the hotel to have some integration time. There has been much shared today. We are all a bit tired from the hike earlier, and I know that I would like some time to chat with my Nephew." He grinned, and the group agreed that they could all use a few hours break.

"Sure... that sounds like a great idea." Stella was happy with the alternative, and everyone agreed as well. They all began to hug Christopher for his loving assistance in opening their minds and hearts with insights into all of their unique gifts.

Christopher said, "We will reconvene for dinner later. Stella insists on making an Italian meal for us this evening," he proudly announced.

David chimed in, "Pasta!? YES!"

He approached Stella, " If you need any help with the food prep, I would be happy to come back early to help."

"Sure! That would be great. Give me about 2 ½ hours. I will run by the hotel to pick you up. We can stop by the store to get the salad stuff." She winked at her newly found brother from another mother.

David lifted his hand to give Stella a Cinco, then lowered it considerably so that Stella could reach it. The two were in stitches at that moment, giddy with joy.

"Very good. We will see you all back here a bit later this evening." Christopher stood and watched as all of the Life Bearers gathered their things and made their way to the cars.

Bridgit held the door open and waved to them all as Stella began to pick up water glasses and move chairs back into the kitchen.

Christopher excused himself and left the room.

And the wheel turns...

Chapter 82

Christopher and Todd Meet

Todd was in his study, putting away the briefings from an Alliance meeting into the wall safe that was behind the painting called The Triumph of Eternity. A knock at the door startled him. He shut the vault door, quickly moving the picture back into place as Christopher pushed open the door and peaked in.

"Hello!" Todd smiled, and joyfully greeted his Uncle.

"Am I disturbing you, son?" Christopher wanted to be discreet and moved into the study without being invited.

"No! Not at all. Please come in. Sit! I am so happy to meet you after all of this time!" Todd came around to the front side of his desk and shook Christopher's hand.

"I really can't believe it is you. When Stella told me that she had found you while on her trip to Scotland, I was bowled over." Todd scratched his chin as if he had a beard.

He continued, "I am sorry I haven't been in touch as of yet, but work has been excruciatingly busy, but I am happy that you are here. Can I pour you a drink?" he pointed to the small bar set up in the corner of the room.

"Yes. I could use a good scotch about now. Neat is fine." He took a seat and looked around the room as Todd went about preparing the drinks. He, too, took his scotch neat.

Todd turned to Christopher, handing him the glass. He leaned up against his desk and crossed his foot over the left leg, and raised his glass. "To family!"

"To family!" Christopher cheered. He sipped the scotch and grinned from ear to ear.

Seeing the bottle on the side table, "Fine choice, lad! Old Particular Craigellachie is an upstanding scotch. Glad to see that you honor your lineage by drinking a brand that is run by a multi-generation family. Speaking of multi-generation families, can we speak candidly?"

Todd sat his glass down and pulled up the other chair nearby and said, "Of course."

Christopher finished his scotch and thanked Todd once more. Todd reached over to take the glass and set it on the desk.

Christopher stared at his knees, dusting off some dirt from his earlier escapades and turned to Todd directly. "I know that Miss Stella and Miss Bridgit have been very open with you about what happened to them while in Scotland."

Todd nodded and said, "Yes. They are both extraordinary individuals, and we have certainly enjoyed studying our family history. The Life Bearer thing was a bit of a large pill to swallow, but I am keeping an open mind." Todd winked at Christopher, waiting to hear more. He was playing his cards close to his chest.

"Yes, well. I do imagine that it could be surprising to just about anyone, but you somehow took it all in, as if it didn't actually surprise you, and this is what I wish to speak to you about." He leaned in and smiled, his eyes glistening as he single-pointedly focused on Todd's reaction.

Todd folded his leg over the other, with a grin on his face, enjoying the interaction.

Christopher pulled his pipe out, "Do you mind?"

"Please do." Todd waved him on.

Christopher gathered his thoughts as he packed the tobacco into the pipe and lit it. After pulling the first draw from the pipe, he released the smoke and, for a moment, concentrated on the aroma, then said, "Todd, I am well aware of your affiliation with the Alliance. I would like us to drop all pretenses due to time restraints and let us get to the nuts and bolts of this situation, because clearly, you have not shared with Stella your involvement in the plan, and I am well aware of how sticky of a situation this is for you."

Todd leaned forward, putting both feet on the ground and shook his head. "How much do you know?"

"I know very little actually, only what I need to know as we go along. It wasn't until I came here and was in your vibration, that I received an Intel package and within that, I gained knowledge that you were involved, but I would like to hear from you just what aspect of the plan you are about doing my boy."

Todd stood up and walked towards the window. He looked out it for a few moments and then turned back towards Christopher.

He grabbed his chair and sat at his desk and said, "It all started after I lost Evie, Stella's mom. I was in so much pain; her loss was almost more than I could bear. I had been working as a software designer on a project for a government contractor. Top secret stuff. Things that I really can't speak much about, even now. The technology that I began working on was dealing with time travel and bilocation. I was having great success, and what drove me was to somehow find a way to go back in time," his voice began to trail off as he recalled his motivating force.

He continued, "I wanted to find a way to be with Evie again. Nothing was going to stop me until one day, and I don't know why I didn't think of her before this, but one day, I realized that I would never be able to utilize the technology because of Stella." He wiped a large tear that had not yet dropped, with the palm of his hand, and jumped up to pour himself another scotch.

Christopher had his cane in front of him, with both hands resting upon it. He said, "So, how is this technology being used now? And by whom?"

Todd made a sound as the scotch burned down his throat. "Let me finish the story, and I will get to that." This time, Todd's eye had a twinkle.

Todd continued the story, "While in India, I had a visitation by a Commander of a Galactic Alliance. He is a friend of a friend, who helped me flush out the bilocation technology, and now I provide support on this side of the veil for certain ground operations."

He looked at Christopher, seriously wanting him to understand. "There are two parts of the Alliance groups. Those who are from this side of the veil and those that are Intergalactic. Meaning they have access here but are not from this dimension. They look like you or me, but they are not from here."

He smiled and continued, "For some time now, I have been acting as an Ambassador when these "people" give support to the ground operations. Are you with me so far?"

"Oh, yes. Most assuredly." Christopher winked at him, glad to hear that Todd was candid.

"Once I realized that there was no way for me to be with Evie again, like we were, that is, I focused my attention on the projects that would help Humanity and, of course, Stella's needs. She is a pretty self-contained little unit, and bless her, she loves to take care of her old pops, but she needs me more than I realized and vice versa."

"She is a dear girl. A very unique individual with unique talents." Christopher stopped Todd's story to add a bit of back story of his own.

"That brings us to the role that she plays, along with myself and Miss Bridgit. Shall I go into a bit of that now, and then we can continue where you left off momentarily?" Christopher asked.

"Yes, the more information you can share, the better. I was not aware of Stella's involvement in the plan until after Bridgit came into the picture, and Stella eventually shared what was happening." Todd waved him on to proceed.

"I see. Well, I, too, will start at the beginning." He put his cane to the side of the chair and repositioned himself to see Todd. He drew the smoke in from his barely lit pipe and puffed it swiftly to bring life back into the embers. Once he blew out the smoke, he continued.

"The Phare family lineage is an ancient lineage from off-planet. Lyra constellation to be exact. From time to time, we incarnate at pivotal points, like now, as we assist in the shift of the Ages."

He nodded to Todd and then continued his story. "I know that the ladies shared the back story of our forefathers, and mothers...that of Airleas and Barabell Phare. These two individuals came at a time when the planet was about to find everlasting peace. Then somehow, something or someone interfered with the timelines. An evil presence invaded the surface world of the 3rd dimension, and the Life Bearers of that time were..." He put his head down and closed his eyes.

"They were tragically lost in a battle for the resources and souls of planet Earth. The being, a dark ethereal presence, hovers between the worlds, feeding on the darkness that has invaded this bandwidth. We are now at the most crucial time in our planetary history. What happens here in the coming years will determine how Humanity evolves spiritually, and where we evolve too, dimensionally."

Christopher searched Todd's eyes for a reaction or an understanding as he was choosing his words carefully.

Todd said, "Now that I have had time within the programs, I am fully aware of the "energetic" forces at play. I have to tell you that my heart sinks, knowing that Stella could be in danger, but the Alliance has assured me that she and all of you are being monitored. So that is something I can bring you up to date on. Do you want to hear more?"

"Yes, of course. Please share what you can, my boy."

Todd got up and went around the other side of his desk to the wall. He pulled the picture frame away from the wall and opened his safe to retrieve the documents that he stored earlier.

"I have just returned from the GCIA outpost. Have you heard of it?" Todd leaned over the desk to show the documents to Christopher.

"Oh, yes. I am familiar! Though I have not personally been there, I know of some individuals who frequent those meetings. Have you met up with Commander Bewain or Commander Breacher there?"

"Not yet, I am sorry to say. I have had briefings with their names mentioned, and of course, the girls have spoken of them, but I am hoping that in the future, our paths will cross." Todd sincerely answered Christopher's question as best he could.

Christopher continued as he held Todd's documents. "Well, let me give you some family intel while I can. I don't think that Bridgit nor Stella have communicated this little fact. Commander Bewain is both Bridgit and Stella's fourth dimensional father." Christopher waited for Todd's response.

Todd coughed when he heard those words. "What? What do you mean? I am going to need more information to swallow that pill!"

Christopher chuckled, seeing Todd's protective nature of Stella come out.

"Indeed. In this realm, you are Stella's father, and she loves you dearly, but in the multi-dimensions, we all have various parents in those realms. In the realm where the Clan of Phare abides, Commander Bewain and his wife, Shamalaine, are the parents of our precious ones known to them as Kaialena and Tulina."

Before Todd could speak, Christopher put his hand up and continued.

"Bewain incarnated in this realm briefly, along with Shamalaine, as Thomas and Prudence Phare." He let that sink into Todd's psyche for a few moments.

"My cousin Tom is Commander Bewain!?" Todd wanted to reach for the scotch bottle but knew better than to skew his thinking at this crucial point in the family disclosure.

"Yes. Your cousin Tom is part of the Alliance, like yourself, and also plays the role of a Guardian. He is presently working with Miss Bridgit's love, Commander Breacher, on the part of the plan that involves the clearing of certain dark forces and their minions within the lower orbit of Earth and in the local star cluster. From time to time, Shamalaine sends them on 3D Earth missions when it has to do with the Ladies Phare or the Life Bearers."

Todd rubbed his face extremely hard until it was red and blotchy. When he finally finished rubbing his face, he just shook his head. "And I thought my intel would be hard to swallow. I had no idea that our entire family had such a tremendous role in all of this. I thought I was in this alone for so long. When Stella met Bridgit in India, I somehow knew that something strange was happening...it was too synchronous to believe it was all out of the blue."

Christopher said, "Hmmm. Indeed."

Christopher shifted the conversation and said, "We don't have any intel on the other Phare men, but it is my opinion that your father is involved in this as well. He was one of the finest Air Force pilots of his time, and so it wouldn't surprise me in the least to hear of his presence in this operation at some point."

"What about Evie? Is there any way that she, too, is somehow involved?" He looked for hope in Christopher's eyes.

"Ah... I cannot give you any false hope as I have no information on your Evie. The only thing I do know is that one of our Life Bearers seems to have her surname, Truce. This one little thing gives me hope that there is a connection. One day, Todd, you will be reunited with your beloved, I just don't know what that will look like. Our world is changing."

A knock at the door brought them out of the intense moment. Stella popped her head in to check on them.

"Hey, guys...I am going to run some errands and then go to the hotel to pick up David. We are making a run to the store, and then we will come back here to prepare dinner. Do you need anything?" Her bright eyes brought them both back into a happier space as they both declined her offer.

"Do you have money, sweetie?" Todd asked.

"I have my card!" She winked at him and then shut the door behind her. They could hear Stella saying one last thing from the hallway. "Bridgit will be upstairs if you need anything!"

Christopher smiled at Todd. "Miss Stella...she has stolen my heart. You can be very proud of her, Todd."

Todd wiped a tear. "I am incredibly lucky that she got most of Evie's traits."

Christopher said, "So let's get back to the original question. Where is the time-traveling technology, and who is using it now?"

596

"A well-hidden organization; white hats who are well aware of the galactic mess that is happening. They have borrowed the technology to help with certain crucial rescue missions here on Earth. I provide upgrades to the software and help to configure the coordinates when there is a need for an extraction. They contact me when they need my help, and I travel to specified locations to assist them. That is what I was doing in India when the girls found one another."

Christopher replied, "This is all very fascinating. I wonder if your technology can be of assistance in helping us locate and triangulate the jump points? I now know approximately where to look for the places in which we will make the jump into the void, but I will need frequency readings in the locales to narrow down where the exact spots will be. Can you help us with this task?"

Todd said, "Sure, I can. My technology will be able to pick up any anomaly in the area of the jump points, detecting the veil."

He stared at Christopher with intense eyes. "Just where are you going? When you say the void...what do you mean by that?" his concern was evident.

"The void is an in-between place. It is where all thought is placed prior to creation. We will only be there a short while, but I have no idea how long it will be in Earth time. We must enter the void to activate the codes of creation there. Each team member will be working with the Builders of Form and Blueprint Masters to activate the various aspects of creation. Once this is done, we will make our way back here to the third dimension and wait for the signs, since manifestation into physical reality can take time. At some point, the doorways will open, and we will have access to this new creation, where every man woman and child will be welcomed into the New Earth."

"Oh!!! Is that all!" Todd laughed at the simplicity of Christopher's explanation.

Christopher laughed at Todd's humor as he attempted to stand. "Let's see if we can get a kettle going. It is time for tea, don't you think? Then we can dig in a bit more before the entourage shows up. I think we can give the team a state of the union address if you are willing to come clean with Miss Stella??"

Todd looked like his heart sank a little bit, thinking of Stella's reaction.

Christopher said, "You need to give her the benefit of the doubt. I think it would please her to no end to know that you were not only fully accepting of her mission, but that you will be a guiding force for us all as we navigate the jump points. What do you think?"

"I guess there is no time like the present to tell her what I have been up too." He half smiled, hoping that it would all be okay. He couldn't bear to have Stella upset with him, and he knew how relieved he would feel about telling her the truth.

"Let's go put the kettle on and see if we can drum up some biscuits!" Christopher slapped Todd's shoulders and led him out of the study. Todd knew exactly where he had stashed the molasses cookies. The two gentlemen made haste to prepare their treats and get down to business.

Christopher went back over the intel from earlier in the morning, "Perhaps we can take our tea on the patio, and we can jump right in!"

Todd laughed at this play on words and was somehow comforted with his Uncle's presence. He had so many more questions about all of it, but time was of the essence, and they needed to prepare.

And the wheel turns...

Chapter 83

Clearing Algol

The pitch-black sea of the galactic frontier was calm in the moments leading up to the greatest rescue mission of an eon. The Alliance ships were parked, cloaked just on the perimeter of the Perseus Constellation. Bewain and Benoit stood at the helm on each of their respective ships, in command stance.

More ships were cloaking into position for the beginning of Operation Aphesis. Breacher's heart began to race as he wondered what atrocities they would find there. Algol was a place of an ancient evil. With all ships in place, he listened as he heard Commander Bewain give the command to shatter the barrier. Suddenly a large beam hit the loading dock, at the base on Algol, blasting open the massive cargo door where the payload ships docked.

Bewain waited for signs of crafts leaving the airspace. Several dozen ships attempted to escape, only to be hit by a beam from the ship. Bewain opened the communications system to relay a message to those who might be in the airspace, and on the base, to surrender.

There was no response. Bewain waited for a team to secure the entry then he made the command for the forces to enter and locate the prisoners.

Breacher sat down at his podium, monitoring the action, with a bad feeling in his gut. He pushed the intercom button and asked Bewain, "What do you think? It seems way too easy."

Bewain responded, "My thoughts exactly. I will send in the sweepers." Bewain pushed the control panel to send in the sweepers. Small drones flew out into the atmosphere, scanning for hidden passageways, heat signatures, and any anomalies.

After the drones cleared the area and the teams were sent in, Commander Benoit sent an update, being the lead Commander on the ground. "No signs of the captors, but Sir, this is bad... Commander ... You are going to need to call in Celeste-108. This is one of the worst atrocities that I have ever witnessed."

As Benoit walked within the interior corridors, deep under the Algol base, the stench of urine and feces made his stomach turn, causing him to pause. Bewain could hear Benoit choking up the contents of his stomach.

Benoit wiped his mouth and then came back on the com. "Sorry, Sir. It is literally gut-wrenching. Celeste's team will need to be notified, ASAP, Sir."

"Understood. Commander out." Bewain reached for the communications manual, looking in the directory for the healing craft command center.

Flustered, he pushed a button and said, "Get me 108!"

Everyone knew who 108 was. Celeste 108 was a notorious healer known throughout the galaxy. Her reputation proceeded her. It was Celeste's ship that would take the fallen, the tortured, and those left for dead. She and her team had developed healing platforms for regenerating tissues, limbs, and organs. They could put a soldier back together and get them back to their positions in record time. Her motto was if there was but one drop of blood or plasma left, she could save them. But, when it came to torture, it was a much more delicate thing.

She once told Benoit that when the mind is splintered, the healing procedures were much more detailed and time-consuming. It was never a guarantee that the soul could or would stay connected to a body that held the memory of the gruesome crimes that had been perpetrated upon it.

"Commander. Celeste and her team are on their way. She will beam aboard in twenty" Bewain thanked the person on the communication monitor and held his breath. He waited.

Breacher's crew were still hovering nearby. Overhearing the conversation on the communications device, he knew that there was nothing he could do but wait for an order. Bewain beamed on board his craft and entered the Command station.

Everyone stood up as the stately lion, Commander Bewain, entered the room. "At ease!" Bewain looked for Breacher and saw him at his post.

"Commander Breacher... a word!" Bewain walked over to the observation deck and waited for Breacher to join him.

"108 will be here shortly. We have more intel that has just come in. Algol is one of the most heinous and elaborate human trafficking outposts that we have ever encountered. This is multi-layered, and it is big. We have entered a hornet's nest. I will fill you in on the details, but at the moment, we have the operation under control. For now, get back to the Dragon riders, as your team will need to be ready."

"Understood." Breacher nodded his head and turned away.

Bewain said, "Check in with Shamalaine, won't you?"

Breacher stopped and turned to Bewain. "Will do."

601

Breacher made a note of the look of sheer horror on Bewain's face. "I will be watching for Benoit's report!" Breacher said, as he walked out of the room and made the gesture to his crew to be at ease.

And the wheel turns...

Chapter 84

Life Bearer's Dinner
Take Two

Stella and David came back from the store, immediately getting to work in the kitchen, whipping up a pasta extravaganza. Stella learned that David's other little known talent was for baking.

While Stella got the sauces going, David took it upon himself to create two kinds of Crème Brulee, vanilla bean, and chocolate orange.

Bridgit assisted with the salad making, creating her own delicious citrus Italian dressing. The trio was busy in the kitchen creating their individual masterpieces, at separate stations within the kitchen. Stella remarked at how quiet it was in the house, as they worked to create the perfect meal to present that evening.

"How do you think it is going with Dad and Christopher?" She quizzed both Bridgit and David.

David shrugged his shoulders, not wanting to take his attention from the most crucial moments in his creation. The steaming of the custards.

Bridgit smiled while watching David. She pointed to him so that Stella could take in the sweet moment of David's concentration while he put the ramekin's on a baking tray. He said out loud, "And with just enough water to give them a good bath... into the oven they go!"

Then Bridgit responded to Stella's previous question, "I feel a tremor in the force. What about you?" Bridgit was thinking of what Christopher had mentioned earlier while she, David and Benjamin, were on the porch. She knew that sometime soon, something had to be brought forward about Todd's role. She waited to hear what Stella thought was going on.

Stella stood watch over the sauce and pondered Bridgit's words, then said, "I haven't seen my Dad much, as you know, so I haven't been able to relay some of the things that we have found out about Bewain and Shamalaine."

She licked her finger then wiped it on a cloth, continuing her thoughts out loud. "You know... how they are our parents in another realm? I couldn't figure out how to tell him something like that!"

She put a lid on the sauce and lowered the temp so that she could take a break, and as she turned around to face Bridgit, Todd and Christopher were standing in the living room, having heard her concerns.

"Dad!" Stella blurted.

"Yeah, I think you can relax now, Stella. Christopher has brought me up to date on that little detail, and so much more."

Stella ran over to Todd and hugged her father tightly. He rubbed her back and said, "It's okay pumpkin. We are good. You and I, we are a team. It doesn't matter who we are in other realms. In this one, you are my daughter!"

"Oh, Dad! I love you so much!" Stella squeezed him and then kept her arm around his right side as she turned to the group.

Christopher announced, "We have more intel to share, but we will leave that for when the rest of the team arrives. For now, I will excuse myself and get cleaned up for dinner." He had a skip to his step and a joyful look on his face as he exited the living room.

Todd made a similar excuse so that he would not have to answer any prying questions before the others arrived. "I will be back in a bit as well."

He patted David on his back and said, "Hey, thanks, man. I don't think I have said that to you yet, but I want you to know that it comforts me that the ladies have you as a friend and colleague. A man that has talent like yours and can cook! Well, that is the whole package!"

He winked at David and then sauntered off down the hall and left the trio to complete the meal prep.

David was left in shock. He had never had such a high compliment from another male before.

Twenty minutes later, the doorbell rang, and the group from the hotel and the other three Life Bearers had all converged at once. Henny, Traci, and Alvie had gone to hang out at the hotel with the others, and they all arrived well-rested and ready for more unfolding.

Bridgit opened the door and greeted the guests. The women put their bags down in the entry, slipping off their shoes and immediately offered to help with anything that was needed.

Stella gave out the duties. Wine needed to be opened, and glasses set out. She instructed them to gather the table cloth and place settings from the hutch. Stella gleamed with pride as she orchestrated the group.

Freya brought flowers in a beautiful green vase that she set out on the table after the men had pulled the table leaf out to elongate the setting for fourteen places.

Stella made room in the fridge for David's crème brulee to chill while she handed Bridgit the salad.

Christopher and Todd entered the kitchen and greeted the crowd, and everyone began to gather around the table, still standing.

After Stella introduced her father formally, Christopher said, "Let us take a moment to give thanks for another fine moment together, where we are fortunate to share a meal in the home of yet another Phare Family."

Everyone nodded in agreement as they all held hands and listened to Christopher give a blessing.

The candles were lit. The table was dressed, and all that was required now was food on the plates. "Let's dig in!" Stella announced.

Everyone took their plate to the kitchen island, where the pasta was beautifully displayed in Evie's bone china serving dishes. A wooden platter held baguettes, with herbed olive oil in several small bowls nearby for dipping. The salad sat within a hammered copper bowl with toppings in individual smaller copper bowls to the side, with the homemade dressing in an old fashioned clear milk bottle.

Juel commented, "This looks amazing! I feel like we are about to eat art!" Everyone laughed as they agreed that the food was beautifully presented and that it did feel that they would be ingesting art. It was the topic of conversation, how art is defined, and what art meant to each of the Life Bearers. Everyone had a different take on the subject.

Todd was overwhelmed with the large contingent of Life Bearers that had so quickly become some of Stella's closest friends. His heart was full, and so was his belly. The hour-long conversation was stimulating. He was impressed with Stella, Bridgit, and David's ability to create such a lovely meal and atmosphere.

He thought about them being Life Bearers and how this was possibly one of many talents that a Life Bearer possessed. He contemplated the creation of an ambiance as being an art form. In his mind, he defined the word ambiance as a "feeling" that paired well with the physical creation of food, with music, and with great company. He shared his thoughts with the group.

Stella was happy to hear her father's thoughts on the subject and interjected her addition to the subject. "I suppose that ambiance, in this case, can be likened to the pairing of cheese to wine. It takes thought and your sensory body to know what pairs well together." Everyone nodded their heads in agreement.

Ashneer wiped his mouth and looked to David. He leaned in with a grin on his face and said, "So, what's for dessert?!" His eyes ogled David.

"Ah! One moment!" David laid his napkin down and jumped up with that cue and went to the refrigerator. He pulled out two baking trays that held ramekins full of Crème Brulee.

Ashneer's eyes widened as David announced his creation to the group.

Ursula looked at Ford and said, "Damn. There goes my diet!" She then covered her mouth, forgetting for a moment who she was with. She, like Stella, said a few words that she wanted to delete from her vocabulary, but would spontaneously pop out of her mouth from time to time. She apologized for her lack of a better word choice.

Ford rubbed her leg and said, "No one here will throw a stone. We are here to break that pattern!" He leaned in and kissed her on the head. Nothing she said would ever diminish his feelings for her. To Ford, Ursula was perfection.

Stella and Bridgit watched the sweet interaction, both not having partners to love at that moment.

David put the final touches on his creation by using a small blow torch to crystallize the sugar topping. He presented the table with their choice of either vanilla bean or chocolate orange crème brulee. From the moment that all of the women ate their dessert, they all made sounds that mimicked utter delight.

Juel was stuffed and wanted to wait for her food to digest, so she declined the dish and watched as the guys were then presented with their dessert.

Ashneer, like the ladies, melted in his chair. He looked at Juel, offering her a pinky dip. "You have to taste it!"

Juel reluctantly accepted and reached over to dip her pinky into the ramekin. The moment that the silky custard touched her taste buds, Juel started laughing and said, "Damn... there goes my diet too! I will take the chocolate one!"

Laughter ensued. David was pleased to serve her a dish of his artful creation.

Benjamin and Christopher were sitting next to one another. Christopher mentioned that this was one of his favorite desserts that David would make for him on special occasions. As Benjamin received his dish, Christopher told him, "Expect to be wowed!" His eyes twinkled as he watched Benjamin take his first bite of the vanilla bean Brulee.

Benjamin, like the ladies, was in a moment of rapture. "This flavor palette is incredible! The vanilla bean reminds me of the old days when my Grandfather made real vanilla ice cream!" Benjamin wiped his mouth as the others nodded.

Henny said, "Flavor palette!? Dude! You must be a foodie too!"

Henny chuckled and then said, "All kidding aside, this flavor palette is epic!" Henny and Benjamin ribbed each other and ate the Brulee in record time.

David stood. Placed his hands to his sides and bowed. "Thank you. Thank you very much." His attempt at imitating Elvis Presley was not the best. Everyone laughed, seeing this tall, lanky Scot try to do an impression of a Southern icon.

David turned red then said, "But with all seriousness, I must say that my desserts do not hold a candle to the dinner that Miss Stella prepared. Furthermore, I do not think I have ever had a more delicious salad than that prepared by Miss Bridgit. Let's give these ladies a hand, shall we?" He led the clapping, and the entire table applauded the meal and the efforts made.

Stella said, "Well, it isn't The Inn of the Seventh Ray quality, but hey, it was darn close! I even did a little prayer of my own when I prepared it!"

Bridgit said, "I did too!" The ladies smiled and kept eating their Crème Brulee.

Soon everyone had completed their dessert. Several of the Life Bearers offered to do the dishes and let the cooks rest. Christopher and Todd went out on the porch one last time before the next phase of the evening began.

Stella set out the glass storage bowls for the food and then sat down where she kept her floor harp. David asked if she would mind if he tickled the ivory of her Grand piano that stood between the kitchen and living room, in the open space that Stella called her Conservatory.

Stella gladly agreed, and the two began an impromptu concert for all who were in the kitchen, cleaning dishes and putting the food away. The sounds were very Celtic.

Once they completed the first piece, David spoke softly to Stella, giving her guidance on what tune he wanted to play next. "Do you know Ten Penny Bit?" She nodded and intuited her part of the ensemble.

Henny wanted to jump in and found her violin on a stand in the corner of the room and pointed to it as Stella watched him join them in the Conservatory. She nodded approval for him to use it. Henny grabbed it and, with no effort at all, began to play it in tune. Ashneer saw that Stella had a dulcimer and he too joined in the music concert.

David grinned as he was thrilled to have Ashneer and Henny collaborate on a song with them. The blending of the musical instruments was a beautiful sound, especially as these four Life Bearers had never played music together.

The music started soft and then flowed louder, and soon, the entire home was filled with the music of their Scottish ancestors. Bridgit stood in the kitchen with her hands to her heart with utter joy on her face.

Christopher and Todd could hear the concert going on from outside. They finalized their brief meeting and entered through the back door to see the Life Bearers honoring the old ways of Celtic Life, by performing music after a shared meal with friends and family.

Christopher made his way to the Queen Anne chair in the living room to soak in the scene. From his vantage point, he could see all of the dear ones whom he had been waiting for over a half-century. He teared up and pulled his handkerchief out.

Bridgit made her way around the musical group to bring Christopher a small sampling of Schnapps. He gratefully accepted it and held her hand as the music began to wind down.

Todd was standing off to the side, leaning on the wall where the spoon pictures hung. He glanced at them and thought of Evie and of how much she was missing. Their daughter had grown up and was an accomplished person in her own right. Musically talented, with two college degrees. She could whip up a meal for fourteen people like it was no effort at all.

He marveled at her talent and the loving way that she carried herself. As he watched her sing a song in a language that was not her own, it moved him to tears. He turned from the group and looked for a napkin to wipe his eyes.

Juel was standing nearby and instinctually reached over to hand him a napkin. She smiled and said, "She is quite extraordinary."

"She truly is. Thank you." Todd accepted the napkin and held it to his eyes.

Stella completed her song, and everyone silently put away the instruments. She stood and placed her harp back on its stand. Stella walked into the kitchen where her Dad stood with a glint in his eye and a proud look on his face. She hugged him tightly, and then the two gathered the chairs to take into the living room.

Todd, all the while, was thinking of Stella and what her reaction would be when she found out that he had been involved in things that he had yet to reveal to her. Would she forgive him? He was about to find out. He could barely breathe thinking about it, but he knew his time had come.

Christopher spoke, "Come. Let us quickly get situated because we have much to speak about. I want to thank you all for that lovely, impromptu musical selection. If I didn't know any better, I would say that the four of you had played together on many occasions. It was delightful!" He clapped his hands and rose from his seat to give them a standing ovation.

He continued, "It is music like this that evokes emotional responses and, in some instances, can change time itself. It was lovely, and so was dinner. Thank you again." He sat down in his chair, as did the rest of the group.

Todd pulled a rolling desk chair in from his office and positioned it near the entry. The others had the kitchen chairs circling the room.

Christopher looked at Ford and Ursula, who was already cozied up to one another on the sofa. Henny and Traci were petite enough to share the overstuffed chair at the far side of the couch. He observed these two lovely couples, thinking how fortunate they were for coming into this life together.

He then looked at all of the other Life Bearers. Though they were not in relationships, they were all balanced and loving and fortunate to have found one another at this stage of their life plan.

Then he looked at Todd. It was earlier in the day that Todd had shared his sorrow over his loss of the love of his life. Now he sat across from his daughter, with anxiety, but brave enough to give the nod to Christopher to begin.

Stella noticed her father's demeanor and blew him a kiss. Todd caught it in his hand and put it towards his heart then blew one back at her.

Everyone settled into their spots with joy in their hearts. Love was in the air, but with Christopher's first words, the mood changed suddenly.

"My dears, I have a bit of a dilemma. As we have all been thrust together for a mission that is unfolding at our feet, each moment revealing new information, I am at odds with how to proceed in a delicate matter. It was not my intention to do this publicly, before having spoken to you, Miss Stella, about the topic that will be presented tonight, but we did not want to disturb you while in the delicate matter of infusing love into the lovely meal."

Christopher's typical glistening eyes and sweet smile was now replaced with a solemn look.

Stella's mood shifted, and she prepared herself. Full shield's up. The hair on her head and arms went straight out. She looked gravely at Christopher, having no idea what he was about to say, but her joyful nature turned quickly into a mild panic attack, even before he said a word. She could read his energy, and what she was receiving scared her.

"Miss Stella, this concerns you and your father, Todd." He pointed over to Todd's direction, and Stella looked at her Dad, confused.

Christopher began, "Let me start by saying this, earlier this morning, before our hike, I received an Intel package that took me a bit to sort out. Within it, I was given the general vicinity of the jump points. I also learned that we would have help in locating these places." He looked in Todd's direction and continued.

"It occurred to me that Todd, being a Phare family male, had more to do with our particular mission than just hosting us here, or guiding you, Miss Stella. He, in fact, has shared some pertinent information today, and I will let him tell everyone what he shared with me earlier today."

"Again, Miss Stella, this is all unfolding now, and therefore neither of us were able to bring you up to date on this intel, so please keep this in mind as your father shares some revelations."

Stella looked at Bridgit, who was sitting next to her. Bridgit grabbed her hand as she knew that it would be hard for Stella to take.

Todd looked at everyone in the room and said, "I am at a loss for words as I sit here trying to figure out the best way to give you all a bit of my background and somewhat of a soft disclosure." He put his hand on his chin, with three fingers upward, letting it rest there for a few moments as he accessed the best way to go about the disclosure.

When Stella heard his words, her eyebrows furrowed.

Todd looked at her and then the rest of the group and said, "I have led an extraordinary life, both as a husband and father and as someone who has been involved in high-level special operations having to do with Galactic and Intergalactic missions."

"What!!?" Stella blurted out. "What did you just say?" She couldn't believe her ears.

Henny and Traci sat in the chair near Stella, wide-eyed and shocked at Stella's outburst. Henny said, "Stella...breathe...it will be okay."

Stella tried to smile at Henny and took a deep breath. She held her composure and asked her Dad to continue in a calm voice.

"Stella, pumpkin, bear with me as I unfold this and forgive me for not coming forward with this information before now. It has been difficult keeping these things from you, but there was a very good reason for it. Let me finish?" He asked.

Stella said, "Dad, I am just shocked...completely shocked and embarrassed!"

Freya gave her a sympathizing look as they turned back to Todd.

Firmly, Todd said, "Just let me finish." Todd gave her a look that assured her that it would be okay.

He addressed the Life Bearers. "My professional background is in software design. I was married to Stella's mom at a young age, and we had an incredible love. The kind that so few are lucky to find. When she got sick, I scoured the internet for healing modalities, but to no avail. She succumbed to breast cancer and left us too soon. Our hearts were completely broken." He shook his head as he brought it all back into his mind, and his heart still hurt.

"The way I handled it was to throw myself into work. I had been approached by a friend of a friend to work on a software project that was top secret, and for some reason, I was recommended for the job."

He looked around the room and continued, "I was brought into a secret program, where I was given access to new technologies. This technology was brought to us by higher vibrational beings, beings not from this 3D Earth."

The group was all intent on listening as Stella wondered just who her father was. She was scrolling back her memories, recalling all the times he missed her recitals, school events, even college functions. She knew he worked hard, but she had no idea that he was in some secret organization. She continued to listen, trying her best to stay calm.

Todd was saying, "I began to have great success with a new technology that I helped develop for time travel and bilocation, and have used it numerous times to get our guys out of sticky situations when they were captured in the field."

He saw Stella's face, then clarified his statements. "NO.... I wasn't involved in the actual extractions but was a support member on the team. I upgrade the software for the technology. Soon they had me working in other capacities as a liaison or ambassador when these Extra or Intra terrestrials showed up. That is all I can say about these beings."

He rubbed his hands together and then said, "Christopher and I got to talking, and we realized that I could be an asset to your team as a sort of IT support, helping to do the calculations for the jump points." He looked at Christopher for help as Stella was steaming from the other side of the room.

Christopher said, "Let's take a fifteen minute break and go outside to check on the position of the stars."

He started to get up from his seat and motioned to David. "David, my boy, why don't you point out the Big Dipper to the team while Stella and Todd take a moment to have a few words?"

Everyone jumped up and single-filed out the back door, leaving Stella sitting there staring at her Dad.

"Stella, please say something."

"Dad, I am at a frickin loss for words! And that rarely happens! I'm angry, and I'm concerned!" Stella had tears in her eyes as Todd came to her side.

"Pumpkin, I wish I could have told you about what I was doing, but you were too young, and we were both still processing your mother's death. I did not want to add to your burden or cause you any undue stress worrying about me. After a while, it just seemed too late, and there never seemed to be the right time to tell you...., but what I want you to know is that I was trying to find a way to find..."

Todd's words trailed off. A huge lump in his throat kept him from speaking. He was overwhelmed with emotion and started to break down.

"Find???" Stella was looking for more from him.

"Find your mom... I was looking for a way to bring her back to us!" He grabbed Stella and held her so tight that she could barely breathe as her father dropped tears on her shoulder. His body shook as he finally let go of the years of sorrow.

Stella held him for a moment, then pushed him away, looking into his eyes. "DAD! You were trying to bring back mom? How? What made you think that was an option?" Stella cried with him as she looked for his sanity.

Todd did his best to explain. "She was the very fiber that kept my body erect! Stella, without your mother, I was lost. She guided me in everything I did, and when she was gone, it left me with a hole that I could not fill, and I had you to raise. I was one hundred percent NOT in my right mind. At that point, I would do anything to get her back. So, when the opportunity came along for me to work on this bilocation and time travel technology, my mind immediately thought of Evie. I worked long hours, perfecting the technology. The galactic beings guided me. I should tell you that I was taken to several off-planet meetings. It is hard to describe. I wouldn't blame you if you didn't believe me."

Stella laughed. "Now that is funny! With all of the crazy stuff that I have shared with you, and you're worried that I wouldn't believe you?! That is what I am mad about! OF COURSE, I would freakin believe you! I wish you would have told me! I was horrified to hear this in front of all of these people!"

Benjamin, David, and Bridgit stood outside. David pointed to a few constellations, but no one was interested in stars knowing that Stella and Todd were having a meeting of the heart, and they felt for them both.

"I can totally see why Todd wouldn't have told this kind of thing to Stella. It sounds like it started when she was still a kid, and she would have had no reference for it until now." Benjamin mulled it over in his mind.

Bridgit said, "I see your point, but Stella is proud, and it's her Dad. She thought they told one another everything, so it is a bit of a bruise to her ego." She understood it from both sides, but she had Stella's back first and foremost.

David glanced in the window and saw Stella and Todd embracing. "Guys, I think it's okay. They are hugging." He squealed a bit in relief.

Christopher looked at his watch and knew that time was short. "Shall we all go back inside?"

Everyone went back inside as Stella was wiping her eyes and forced a smile. Todd stood there, a true host, greeting them back into the living room. "Please, everyone, take a seat. I know that we still have much to talk about."

Christopher sat back in his assigned seat and was happy to see Stella calmed down. She looked in his direction and caught a wink from her Great Uncle. It somehow calmed her even more. She was ready to move on.

That night, the Life Bearers talked about the plan to determine where the jump points were, based on Christopher's intel, and to utilize Todd's technology to determine where the veil was the thinnest. They still had to find the triple triangles within the landscape, which was the very first thing they found out about the jump points; that there would be a sign, in the form of three triangles at each site.

Christopher and Todd still had to map out the details further and promised that by morning, that all would be discussed in detail.

And the wheel turns...

Chapter 85

Preparations for a Trial Jump

The next morning the Life Bearers gathered at Todd and Stella's home once more. Christopher gathered the team in the living room after refreshments were served. "Let us go back over what we have learned."

Stella placed the coffee carafe on the coffee table and set out coasters for the cups. Everyone pulled out their journals and situated themselves to hear what Christopher and Todd had worked on after they all had gone back to the hotel.

The room smelled of rose incense, and the instrumental music in the background, The Sirius Odyssey, was explicitly picked to assist with their mental focus and tranquility, as this musical selection was designed to keep the energy of the room in perfect harmony.

Christopher pulled out his note pad while Todd opened his laptop. "Todd and I have gone through all of the intel that I have received. The Strategists have been clear that we will need to do some recon to find where the triangular inscriptions are located."

Bridgit asked, "The Strategists? Do you mean Shamalaine?"

"Yes, dear. She and many others are gathering the intel from the inner earth beings." He looked at Stella and defined his words.

"Those beings that have been communicating with you in your dream time. They have been beneficial in providing energetic support to find and open the doorways. They remind us to utilize the striking stones, as well as the word Etifah. It is that word that we need to focus on as an intention for where we are going. Which reminds me..."

Christopher looked back at Bridgit, "Be sure to bring those stones out before our departure. From this point on, we are to be ready. Everyone should have their stone pendants."

Bridgit said, "I will go get them now." She excused herself momentarily to retrieve the pouch from her room. On her return, she sat the velvet pouch on the table and continued to listen to Todd and Christopher. She went to sit down on the sofa, looking at Freya as she sat. Freya had an excruciating look on her face, and Bridgit noted that her coloring was off.

Bridgit patted her knee and asked in a whisper, "Are you okay?"

Freya nodded with her hand waving back and forth and said, "So, so."

Benjamin and Ashneer were uncharacteristically quiet, and both found themselves needing to lay down. Christopher looked up as he took a scan of the room and said, "Ah, I need to stop for a moment and address something here. My apologies for not addressing this sooner. It is about your bodies."

He put his note pad down and moved up towards the edge of his chair with his back erect. "Yesterday, during the reading of your Akashic records, we activated your core being. Who you really are. When doing this kind of cellular work, the body responds to the information that streams into and out of the cells."

Freya asked, "Why does it always seem to be so painful to remember ourselves?" She winced as her body became achier at that moment.

Christopher explained, "It has more to do with the light or frequency that is pushing out the lower vibrational thought forms and feelings that have been stuck in the cells. Many of you might be experiencing things such as chills, perhaps a low-grade fever, aches, and pains, or sudden memories that are somewhat traumatic. It is important to work with your body to clear these things out as quickly as possible because where we will be going, you will need to be as clear as possible. The jump can be difficult on the physical body."

Juel nodded her head, having had numerous cellular upgrades to her body in the past. She asked, "Once we enter the jump points, where exactly are we going? I have heard the void so far, but that seems vague."

Christopher responded, "In essence, we are going to the center of the earth. When I say the center of the earth, I mean the dimensional space that is known as the void or the center of creation, whence all things come. All creations are seeded there. To some, it is called the Seven Caves of Tollan, and to others, it is known as Agartha. I would venture to say that Etifah is either a way station or a being. I really can't say as of yet."

He listened to all of the sounds in the room and smiled. "We have been given the opportunity to go into the realms of higher vibration where each team will be taken into the appropriate "Cave" to work with the plan of creation for the New Earth. That bandwidth that will be opening for all of humanity in a very short while." He smiled as the Life Bearers were all trying to stay with him, all the while some could barely keep their eyes open.

"Your bodies need rest now. I am sure it would be fine if you all took a nap or rested on lounge chairs outside on the porch. The fresh air will do you some good. In the meantime, Todd and I will map out the spots and give you all of the information a little bit later on this afternoon."

Stella and Bridgit offered their rooms to anyone who needed to sleep.

Several of the Life Bearers chose to go outside to lay on the lawn under the shade of the trees. David and Ashneer made some clove tea and joined the others outside. They shared the tea, as Ashneer explained that it was a powerful immune builder and eased inflammation.

Christopher and Todd continued the work. "Todd, take a look at these areas and see if you can input them into your program, won't you?"

Todd took the information and began plotting the coordinates of each of the jump spots. The first coordinate that he entered was for an area nearby. He looked up at Christopher and asked, "This coordinate is for the Santa Barbara area?"

Christopher nodded his head, "Indeed. Apparently, our Miss Alvie has been sitting on a portal vortex all of this time at her Nature Sanctuary. The team has had communication with Butler, and he has found the first jump point site. That is the only one we know the exact location of."

Todd was shocked. "She doesn't have a clue that it is there?" Dumbfounded with the news, Todd shook his head as Christopher reiterated that she did not know of it.

The second set of coordinates that Christopher gave Todd indicated that the jump point was somewhere in Haifa, Israel.

He said, "Of course, once I take the coordinates and enter them into the software at work, I will be able to tell you more precisely where the anomalies are... within a quarter-mile radius, at least. It should be a piece of cake to locate the triangles."

He smiled at Christopher, who was very relieved to hear it and asked, "Maybe you can steal away for an hour or two while the group is resting? We need to get this information to the team as soon as possible."

Todd looked up from the computer and nodded. "Sure, I can do that, no problem. Just give me the rest of the coordinates, and I will get going."

Christopher handed the coordinates to him. Todd threw on his shoes and was out the door. Christopher stood to stretch his legs then went outside to have a pull from his pipe and see how the others were doing.

Stella had loaned Alvie a swimsuit, and Christopher chuckled when he discovered Miss Alvie sitting in the hot tub, to the right of the porch, upon a high wooden platform. She gave him a thumbs-up and said, "I hope you don't mind, I needed to warm my body."

He laughed and said, "My dear, a soak in a hot tub seems perfectly reasonable to me." He let out a chuckle and found a spot to sit. He pulled up a chair at the round glass table then pulled out his pipe.

Ford and Ursula decided that a nap was required and utilized the upstairs bedroom offered up earlier. The rest of the Life Bearers rested on the lawn, under the trees, rejuvenating their bodies with the help of mother nature.

After about an hour and a half, the Life Bearers started to stir. Alvie had gone inside to change while Benjamin and Ashneer were in the kitchen looking for some fruit to munch on.

Todd entered the kitchen with a spreadsheet and his laptop, having returned from his office with the data. "Where is Christopher?"

Benjamin pointed to the sofa. Christopher had laid down on the couch to take a short nap while they waited for Todd to return.

Todd turned to see the old gentleman snoring and did not want to wake him, so he looked for Stella and Bridgit. He found them upstairs in Bridgit's room. "Come in!" Stella yelled out when she heard the knock at the door.

"You girls rested?" Todd smiled as he walked by Bridgit's room and peeked inside the open door. Freya was lying on the floor under the light of the window. Stella had put her on a far-infrared heating mat and explained to Freya that the warmth of the mat would penetrate her body and assist her body's natural healing process.

Stella smiled as Todd asked if they had rested. She left Freya's side and sat on the edge of the bed as Todd came further into the room.

"Kind of. We all have been feeling a bit off, but nothing to be concerned about. Where did you go?" Stella asked.

"Ah, I went to the office to input the coordinates into the system. I have everything we need." He winked at her as she jumped up and threw her arms around her Dad. Stella always thought of her Dad as her hero, and in this case, he most certainly was proving helpful like one.

Bridgit got up and looked at her phone. "The time is getting away from us. Let's gather everyone up and see if we can get a bit further before dinner is upon us."

Todd assisted Freya as she attempted to get up on her own. She monitored how she was feeling after about 20 minutes being on the mat.

"I am amazed, Stella! I feel much better!" Stella grinned ear to ear as the four walked downstairs and entered the living room. Christopher was sitting up as David and Ashneer meet the group in the living room.

Todd said, "I have the data. Shall we gather the troops?" David looked to Christopher to give the okay and then bounded towards the back-porch door to gather the others.

Stella went back upstairs to knock on her door, where Ford and Ursula had taken respite for a short nap. Once everyone was gathered, Christopher made his announcements.

"Finally, the time has come," Christopher said as he looked over the work that Todd had delivered.

"This looks promising, Todd. I am very pleased." He smiled and gave a wink in Todd's direction.

"Okay, my friends. Let us start." He looked around at the room filled with the most amazing individuals.

They all were ready to hear the details of their mission. Stella and Bridgit took a seat last, after handing out water bottles. Like a mother, Stella repeated a mantra to the group, "Hydration, hydration, hydration!"

Once they were seated, Christopher began. "Here is how it is laid out. There are seven jump points. I will list the jump point region and the team that is related to it. I do have a list of the Blueprint Masters now, but just their names. Nothing more."

He paused to look at his intel sheet and then said, "But first, I want to inform everyone that we will be preparing our bodies from this point on so that we can sustain this kind of energetic jump. We will do a preliminary jump on October 31st, when the veils are thinnest. It is a perfect time for our practice run." He winked at Bridgit, and she smiled back, nodding her head in agreement.

David liked the idea of doing the practice run at that specific time as Druids knew it as one of the four solar festivals, which was considered sacred.

Christopher continued, "Todd suggested the practice run so that we can monitor our bodies' reactions to a jump. We will work out the bugs so that we can be physically ready for the real jump. Make sense to you all?"

Everyone was nodding in approval, and so he continued.

Christopher said, "My intel suggests that we will be jumping during the Leonid Meteor shower, which peaks November 17th and 18th. Once we work out the kinks of the practice jump, we will all need to travel to our locations and start the process of looking for the anomalies."

Everyone understood that it was becoming real and that the jump would be just around the corner. Ford and Ursula held each other tight, feeling the truth that they would soon be parted.

Henny and Traci also sat together in a solidified manner. They had talked about this moment extensively and had prepared.

"Here we go. This first one needs some explaining." Christopher looked towards Alvie, who was looking quite refreshed at that moment.

Christopher said, "The first jump point is connected to the Animal team. Alvie, you are the only Life Bearer on this team, but you will be joined on the other side by Avery, who is a Builder of Form on the first Ray. Joining you both will be a Blueprint Master named Abdonna."

He studied his intel sheet and then said, "I must admit that I am a bit dumbfounded to discover that your jump point is actually located somewhere on your property at the Trunchen Wildlife Sanctuary."

He smiled as she lifted her body towards him with a questioning look.

"Yes. It is true. The Guardian, Butler, has confirmed the location. He found a series of triangular puck marks on a cave near a large downed tree. He called it the alligator tree. Do you know which one he references?" He looked at her for confirmation.

Alvie said, "The alligator tree? Yes! It is a huge tree that fell a couple of years ago! It has a gnarled looking trunk that is divided in two, like the mouth of an alligator. It was so large that I decided to leave it there so that the creatures could use it as shelter."

"Well apparently, near this spot is a cave that has been covered by shrubbery and vines. Butler knew that there was an anomaly on the property, and he traced it there. He reported that there was poison oak all over the area, which is what had been hiding the cave this whole time."

Alvie shook her head. "I know exactly where he is talking about, though I have never seen a cave there! I stupidly dug around that area looking for an animal that was hurt and ended up breaking out in hives from the poison oak. I have not bothered cleaning up that area. I just let it go wild."

Alvie scratched her arm as she recalled the ordeal.

"Well, Butler is working on the clean up because you will need access to the area."

"Great! So that is easy!" Alvie smiled, knowing that the others would most likely be traveling far distances, but it brought her much comfort knowing that she would be on her own land when it came time to jump. It also verified in her heart that she was meant to be a Life Bearer.

"Yes, it is good for you." Christopher winked at her knowing full well that it was the best possible outcome for Alvie. He then looked at his sheet for the next jump point.

"The second jump point is in the area of Haifa, Israel. It is the jump point for the Music of the Spheres team. Stella, David, and Henny, you three will travel there together. Once you locate the exact spot and jump, the other two team members will meet you on the other side. That will be the Blueprint Master, Starseed, and the Builder of Form of the second Ray, Arrea."

Stella, David, and Henny were wide-eyed. "Israel? WOW!" Stella looked to be in shock, hearing of the location.

Henny just smiled and said to Stella, "So much has started in Israel. We will be together, so it will be fine."

He attempted to reassure her, but Stella was not worried as he thought. She was shocked. Once she heard the words Haifa, Israel, she already had a clue as to where the jump point could be. She decided to hold that hunch to herself until later. David just took in the information, listening, and feeling into it.

Christopher announced the third jump point. "The next jump point is in the Moray region of Scotland, near Findhorn Bay."

He smiled and looked up from his list. "Glad to know that Scotland is connected to the Inner Earth entrances."

He cleared his throat of the pride he carried and continued, "This trip will be for a singular Life Bearer, Miss Freya, who is the lead for the Plant team. Your team members, who will meet you on the other side, are Tabor, who is a Builder of Form on the third Ray and TurAgus, the Blueprint Master."

Freya was happy to hear that she would be traveling somewhere familiar as she would, in essence, be alone.

Christopher read her thoughts and announced, "If I haven't mentioned this before, you will be watched over and guided by the Guardians assigned to you, so please do not worry about being alone. Several of you will be on singular missions, presumably, but this is not the reality. The Guardians will be near you at all times. I just wanted to remind you that you are never to be alone."

Everyone was relieved to hear this reminder.

Christopher continued. "The next jump point location is for the Water team, located on the Big Island of Hawaii."

Christopher looked at Ursula and Ashneer and said, "This will be where the two of you jump. We will get you the precise coordinates, but it is somewhere near the Kilauea caldera. Jermaine is the Blueprint Master assigned to the Water team, and Mersea, the Builder of Form for the fourth Ray, is also on this team."

Ursula looked at Ashneer with a smile and then turned to look at Ford. She was both excited and saddened at that moment. "I am usually game for any adventure, but it usually involves Ford. Sorry babe, I guess I will have to go to Hawaii without you this time." She smiled and reached over to pat his back.

Ford squeezed her leg in jest. "How dare you!" he cackled. They all laughed, seeing the two become feisty with one another.

Christopher said, "Oh, not to worry, Ford. You will have an equally delicious place to travel. The next jump point involves you and Juel, and the rest of the Mineral and Etheric forces team. Your jump point is in Visoko, Bosnia. The precise location is somewhere near the newly discovered pyramid of the Sun, and in particular, it's Ravne underground tunnel system. Gordavin, the Builder of Form of the fifth Ray, will be joining you on the other side, as well as the Blueprint Master, Hiiyup."

Ford and Juel stared at each other speechless, but Juel couldn't hold her excitement. She finally squealed out, "I've heard about this discovery from a friend of mine who has been there! It sounds so amazing! There is so much mystery surrounding this particular pyramid system because it has healing tunnels, called..."

She paused for a moment to try to recall the name of the underground system that Christopher had mentioned moments earlier.

Christopher decided to help her out. "The underground tunnel system is called Ravne."

"YES! The Ravne tunnels! Thank you! My friend told me that she experienced an absolute healing of her body while she was there." Juel realized that now was not the time to go further with her excitement, so she winked at Ford and said one final thing. "I will tell you more about that area when we finish here." She had an enormous smile and was so animated in her excitement that Christopher set his paper on his lap and offered her more time to speak.

"Are you sure?" Juel did not want to interfere with his presentation.

"Yes, please, share what you know. I am sure that we would all be delighted to hear more."

She took a sip of water then carefully placed it on the carpet next to her as she then calmly stated, "Well, in the underground tunnels, just below the Pyramid of the Sun, the area is considered to be a healing chamber. There are also man-made rocks that have been placed in strategic locations to counteract the negative vortex's where certain ley lines cross. You know the ones, the Hartman lines." She looked to Christopher and then Ford for acknowledgment. They nodded their heads.

She then continued, "Well apparently, whoever created the tunnels, and they are old, like close to thirty thousand years old... but, whoever created the tunnels placed the ceramic rocks, with crystals inside them, over those harmful Hartman lines, subduing the negative energy. And because there is no radiation in the tunnels and almost one hundred percent negative ions happening down there, it is the perfect healing chamber!!"

Juel was so excited that she knocked her water over with her hand as she spoke. Ford grabbed it swiftly. He took a napkin from the table to pat down the water while Stella ran to the kitchen to grab a hand towel.

"Sorry about that! I forgot that it was there." Juel went quiet as she watched Stella hand Ford the towel to cleaned up the water spill. Everyone else just sat silently in respect and waited for her to continue.

"Thanks, Ford." She patted his shoulder as Ford came back to her side after discarding the wet napkins and towel.

"Well, the last part that my friend shared with me is that one of those man-made ceramic stones has rune inscriptions on it, which was translated by an expert. The translation means something like..., The Stargate is closed..., We will have to fight or hold our ground or something like that...until such time as the Stargate opens again!"

Christopher remarked, "Well, there you are, my dear...a Stargate location." He was so pleased that a friend had already given her a download, and it confirmed to him, yet again, that these jump points were accurate.

"Thank you, Juel, for that informed update. If you can find out more from your friend, that would be wise. Preparation is the key."

With that, he took his paper from his lap and said, "Let us move on to the next jump point, shall we?"

Christopher looked towards Traci and then to Bridgit. "This jump point is for the three of us."

He smiled as he looked at his notes and began. "Our jump point is located at the exact spot that our ancestor Barabell Phare and her three daughters were journeying to that fateful day. Ladies, we will be jumping in Cornwall, at Merlyn's Cave in Tintagel."

When Bridgit heard those words, her entire body broke out in shivers. A DNA response occurred. The hair on Traci's arms stood straight up, but it was Bridgit that was genuinely having a cellular release hearing those words. She tried to use her hands to warm her arms as her body suddenly went cold.

Christopher said, "It will be okay, my dear. We are going to make it this time! No Fear! Just absolute conviction." His words trailed off as he watched Stella calm her with soft, whispered words.

He then said some final words on this team's partnership. "We will be joined by the sixth Ray Builder of Form named Padmavati. We will also have the Blueprint Master named Graeceous joining our team.

Christopher thought it best to move on. He read out loud, "The final jump point is once again a singular adventure for Benjamin."

Benjamin was very excited to hear where he would be traveling too. He had his pad of paper ready to transcribe notes.

Christopher spoke. "Benjamin, my dear boy, you will travel to an area within the Transylvania region of Romania. The coordinates suggest that the location is in or near Cioclovina Cave, which has much folklore around it. This cave holds secrets of time travel, from what my intel suggests. Somewhere in this area is the anomaly. You should research this area at once."

Benjamin asked Christopher to spell the name of the cave, then said, "Romania? Right?"

"Yes, my boy. Romania. Romania holds many Inner Earth secrets, so I am not surprised that one of us would be traveling there. The veils are very thin in this region, particularly for portal travel into the inner space of Gaia known as Agartha."

Christopher leaned towards David and had him pass the notes that held the name of the cave system so that Benjamin could write down the exact spelling.

Benjamin wrote the word Cioclovina down and then handed the paper back to Christopher.

Christopher looked to his notes once more and said, "The other Time Science team members will join you once you jump. Those team members are Phyre, who is the Builder of Form on the seventh Ray, as well as the Blueprint Masters named Malachi and twin angels, Platter and Patina."

He set his paper down and smiled. "You will be well attended, my boy."

Everyone began to chat in whispers, and then Christopher opened the discussion so that he could answer any questions. Todd was also helpful in answering questions as the subject of the practice jump began.

That day was spent finalizing the next phase of the plan. The Life Bearers would be traveling back to their homes for one final closure.

Christopher relayed that he would send packages with travel itinerary and more specific details as they came. He reminded them that all of their needs would be met; all they needed to do was show up.

He made one final declaration. Christopher told all of the Life Bearers that they were to each begin to phase out meat and alcohol from their diet and move towards a plant-based diet as soon as possible. He explained that in order for them to keep their bodies in a higher vibrational state, it would require a strict health regime from this point on. He handed each of them a list of dos and don'ts in this regard.

The team left California the next day for their respective homes to prepare for the eventual practice jump.

And the wheel turns...

Chapter 86

The Guardians Gather at the Great Hall

Before the Life Bearer's practice jump, Bewain arranged for the Guardians to meet at the Great Hall before being sent out to the regions where the Life Bearer's would jump.

Due to the ongoing healing protocols required after the rescue of thousands of tortured victims on Algol, the plan had changed. With the discovery on Algol, Bewain's role as Commander of an Alliance fleet took precedence over his role as a Guardian.

Breacher had not been further briefed on the Algol mission due to his need to focus on the Dragon Riders training and other side missions that Shamalaine requested from time to time.

It was Benoit now holding the position of second in command under Bewain so that Breacher could be at the ready when the Life Bearers made the jumps. This was Shamalaine's promise to Breacher, and he was holding her to it.

Eldorman entered the Great Hall before the others, being the Guardian designated to gather the team. He was dressed differently than his usual attire. He wore a tufted silver vest with a hood. Under the vest, he wore a black and copper wrap-around tunic with two knotted buttons and a sash to hold it closed. His pants were made from the same material as the tunic, and were loose-fitting. He wore a thin copper band around his forehead, which acclimated his ethereal body to a more solid form, due to the need to travel into the denser bandwidth of Earth.

Eldorman saw to the assembly, under the guidance of Bewain and Shamalaine. As the other Guardians arrived and were all accounted for, Eldorman guided them to the long table in the Great Hall, where Shamalaine was waiting.

The size of the Guardians varied, many being too large for the regular seating in the Hall. Giant, wooden throne chairs with wide girth and length were set up while extra bench seats were placed around the long table for those of elven stature.

Shamalaine encouraged everyone to sit, signaling Eldorman to begin the introductions. Breacher suddenly popped in, having caught wind of the meeting and slid into a chair next to Shamalaine. She looked at him with surprise. He nodded to her, wondering what game she was playing.

Eldorman took note of the exchange and started the meeting, explaining that fourteen Guardians were the requirement, two for each Life Bearer grouping.

Breacher, being astute in mathematics, could see, with himself included, that there were fifteen Guardians present. His posture stiffened, and Shamalaine whispered, "Don't make a scene. I will explain it afterward."

Breacher knew that she was pulling him from his role as Guardian of Bridgit. He could barely sit still. Thinking about it made him furious.

Eldorman presented the first team of Guardians, assigned to Alvie. Butler and a female named Saso proudly stood as he presented them to Shamalaine.

Saso was not tall, but her demeanor was that of power. She had long blond hair with a woven headband around her forehead. She wore battle regalia from the ancient Dacian era. Her arms were muscular, with golden cuffs over her tattooed biceps. Saso had spiral tattoos over her forehead as well.

Her turquoise cape hid her battle war hammers, which were crossed and held in a back brace. Her presence was comforting to Shamalaine. She picked up on the Mother energy, which Saso exuded. The kind of mother that would die protecting her loved ones.

Shamalaine spoke kind words to the Guardians as she inspected their appearance. Butler needed no introductions as she was already intimately familiar with him and regarded him as family. She was grateful that Eldorman was able to pull Butler back from his duties at the nature sanctuary, even for just a brief interlude.

Shamalaine felt that Butler and Saso made perfect Guardians for Alvie. She nodded her approval as Butler and Saso retreated to their seats.

Eldorman introduced the next two Guardians assigned to protect David, Stella, and Henny. Osman and PharaEtti stood up and approached Shamalaine's side of the table, as they had been seated at the furthest end, due to their size.

Osman wore his long, strawberry blonde hair teased with bits of his hair in braids near his ears, which matched his straggly, long beard that held two small beads dangling from the two braids that adorned both sides of his face.

He wore a large brown leather frock with chainmail woven in the upper portion of his sleeves. The frock material continued below the elbow, with tightly wrapped leather strings latticed around his forearms, where he held small knives in place.

His belt held an assortment of battle weapons, making it difficult for him to sit. Therefore he stood for the entirety of the meeting.

PharaEtti stood closest to Shamalaine now. Her bright red hair had flecks of gold streaking through it. The only thing that out shined her blue skin was the fact that PharaEtti had four arms, an indication that she was an Inner Earth being from Agartha. Shamalaine took note that her name was similar to Phare.

PharaEtti had a wild look in her eyes and wore very little in the way of garments. She wore a tube-like band over her chest and a short brown skirt with a chain hanging around her waist, which held thin metal discs, that were extremely sharp.

Her bare abdomen was hard to the touch, and her thighs were as chiseled as her abs. A shield hung from her neck, resting on her back. The shields crest displayed a Lions Head. The inside of her shield held two battle axes for easy access.

She did not speak as Shamalaine inspected her energetically, but bowed to her when Shamalaine was complete, then backed up to sit without turning her back to Shamalaine.

Shamalaine felt that PharaEtti was most assuredly from the same Lyran race of long ago. She was pleased with these two Guardians.

Shamalaine nodded for Eldorman to present the next pair of Guardians. Eldorman called Randelf and Hotaru to Shamalaine's side. He noted that these two would be guarding over Freya in the Scotland region of Moray.

Hotaru was an Elven Samurai whose name meant Firefly. Her wings, when fluttered, sparked flames around her. She held her sword at her side, as she presented herself to Shamalaine.

Shamalaine took note of Hotaru's beautiful and delicate features. Her black hair was held in a high ponytail, which featured Hotaru's delicate elven ears. She wore a white headband on her forehead with her feathery bangs flowing over the headband at an angle.

Hotaru bowed with her hands to her side and stepped aside to allow Randelf to be introduced. Shamalaine was speechless, feeling the caliber of warriors that Eldorman gathered.

Randelf came forward.

He looked like a 3D human with incredibly vibrant blue eyes. He wore a forest green linen shirt with four large wooden buttons.

He had no weapons with him, and Shamalaine began to wonder about this candidate until she saw his ring. He wore a stone Shen Ring with a turquoise patina, a protective amulet that could cast rings of protection with a spoken incantation.

She knew that appearances could be deceiving and that this Guardian could easily be one of the mightiest, not in stature, but skill. Randelf bowed in quiet reverence and returned to his seat.

Eldorman called forth the next two Guardians, who would be protecting Ashneer and Ursula.

Ali'Ioka and Eferhild came forward. Ali'Ioka was a strong tribesman of Polynesian descent, who had been trained as a Guardian of the in-between realms since he was a young boy. He had three large dark circles painted on his face. His bare chest shimmered, and he wore a long colorful sarong that hung over his bare feet. Tribal tattoos were displayed down his backside.

He gave Shamalaine a long stare before providing a formal greeting from his tribe. Shamalaine was pleased with her interaction with Ali'Ioka. He bowed and moved away to bring Eferhild forward.

Eferhild took three giant steps and stood in a warrior maiden stance, with one foot forward, with her body at an angle to Shamalaine. In her custom, until the Clan leader addressed her, one never stood shoulder to shoulder with one of higher stature.

Eferhild wore a massive bear fur garment. She wore the claws of the bear around her neck, and she held a bow and arrow upon her body.

Her hair was long, with shades of red and blonde highlights.

Shamalaine asked her to come forward.

Eferhild approached Shamalaine and bowed.

Shamalaine asked about her bear garment. Eferhild said, "The bear is my ally. My people have guarded over the mantle of Mother Bear for eons of time. This bear fur represents the strength and the tenderness of the mother.

Shamalaine felt the fur and saw an image in her mind's eye of the great mother attending to the souls of children who had been split from their bodies by trauma. The vision faded. Eferhild saw the vision as well.

She made a final comment, "The bear mother holds the souls of many Clan's children in her cave until the souls are called back to their body. She is great in her compassion. It is due to the Great Bear's healing nature that my people are honored to watch over the Bear tribe."

Shamalaine could see why she would be chosen to guard over Ursula, as Ursula took her name from the Great Bear, as a sign of her soul's heritage.

In the vision, Shamalaine could see that the tortured souls from Algol had been delivered into the den of the Great Mother Bear. It was an essential piece of intel that would be passed on to Celeste 108, during the soul retrieval portion of the healing process for every man, woman, and child who were found in the dark prisons in the recent purge on Algol.

Shamalaine bowed to Ali'Ioka and Eferhild. She pleasingly nodded to Eldorman and then sat down once more, waiting to be presented with the next set of Guardians.

While the Guardian went back to their seats, Eldorman came forward with the next Guardian. He said to Shamalaine, "I would like to introduce to you my counterpart, Aife, who will join me in guarding over Ford and Juel when they journey to the Bosnian Pyramid region of Visoko.

Aife, a slender Elven Warrioress, held a bow in one hand and a sword in another. Her hair was both black and green, depending on how the light hit it. She wore brown clothing resembling fall colored leaves stitched together as a garment. Her cape looked like both wings and leaves, leaving it to the imagination if she was a flying elf or perhaps a rogue protective dryad. The bone clasp on her cape had a symbol of a Celtic Tree Cross carved into it. That was the only symbolism she carried.

Aife flung her long hair behind her back as she presented herself to Shamalaine.

Shamalaine could see exactly who Aife was. An ancient protector of World Trees, like the Great Oak, Tuuru.

Shamalaine stood up at this moment and reached for an item within the pouch that she kept at her side. The item was a small wooden cube made from the trunk of Tuuru. Shamalaine placed it in Aife's hand, holding it tightly in Aife's clasped fingers, and stared into Aife's eyes. Tears welled up in both of their eyes as an unspoken sorrow passed between them.

Shamalaine touched her forehead to Aife's, sending a telepathic message, and then Shamalaine turned and found her seat. Aife bowed, holding the cube tightly as she, too, found her seat.

Shamalaine bowed her head to Aife and Eldorman. It brought her comfort that they would be monitoring Ford and Juel. She peacefully waited to be presented with the next set of Guardians.

As Amazonia stood, Shamalaine looked upwards to see the face of the giant before them. Amazonia's height was 6' 5". Her physique was muscular, her skin chestnut brown with tribal tattoos prominent upon her body.

On her chest was a Hunab Ku symbol, burned into a piece of wood that hung from her neck. The symbol indicated the great mystery, the one giver of movement and measure. Amazonia wore this symbol as an acknowledgment of duality united in the one.

She stood tall as Shamalaine inspected her aura. Amazonia's straight black hair fell to her hips. Her weaponry was simply a shield and spear. Her corset was made from the hide of a jaguar, tied with leather straps in the back. She wore colorful feathers as a belt, which wrapped around her waist, over a skirt made from the same hide as her top. Much of her skin was revealed.

As Shamalaine came back around to the front of Amazonia. Amazonia knelt to come closer to Shamalaine's level. Shamalaine stared into her eyes, which were the most profound black pools that Shamalaine had ever seen. She could feel Amazonia's essence within her eyes.

The tattoo upon her face, between her eyes and around her nose, was a stylized spider that covered most of her forehead and darkened the lids of her eyes completely.

Shamalaine completed her inspection and knew that Amazonia was a mighty warrior and Guardian. She nodded and returned to her seat, while Eldorman brought forth Esmond.

Esmond stood up and walked towards Shamalaine, bowing to Amazonia as she made her way back to the large chair near where Butler was seated, proudly watching the presentation. He knew most of the Guardians, and it pleased him to be in such excellent company.

Esmond wore a black and dark blue tunic with a leather belt at his waist. The back of his tunic had gathered pleats across the shoulders. On his arms, he wore black shiny, leather guards that covered his forearms from his wrist to just under his elbows. He wore black, straight-legged pants, tucked into a pair of black laced boots.

He had his long blonde hair platted in three sets of braids on the side of his head. On the top part of his head, he wore in a ponytail, with the bottom portion of his hair completely shaven. His dark brown eyebrows highlighted his ice-blue eye.

Shamalaine was fascinated with one particular addition to his face, a ring that hung between his nostrils. She thought that his piercing would blend into the 3D Earth environment, allowing him to fit in as a human. She smiled at Esmond and listened to Eldorman explain his background.

Eldorman relayed that Esmond was a Middle Earth being who studied off-planet for his role as a Guardian. He relayed that these two Guardians would be present in Romania, guarding over Benjamin.

Shamalaine picked up his connection to the Cetaceans, as Esmond stood in front of her. Once she mentioned this connection, Esmond demonstrated his special gift. He closed his eyes and morphed his being into a much taller version of himself, shapeshifting into part humanoid, part dolphin.

Esmond's face was surrounded by the formation of a dolphin head, with his dolphin eyes much higher up on his forehead. His fin was now popping out of his tunic, which was designed to open at the pleats when Esmond morphed. Shamalaine realized he wore oversized clothing to accommodate his transformation.

His weaponry was ultrasonic sound waves, and his combat style was hand to hand combat known as Glima. He trained in this style of martial arts as it was specific to combat without weapons. Esmond's upper body strength was highly developed, as he was used to throwing large objects or bodies.

Shamalaine took all of this information in as she watched Esmond reconstitute his original body. She nodded in high approval of his strengths and heritage. Esmond placed his arm over his chest to salute Shamalaine and then swiftly took his seat.

Shamalaine was anxious to see who Eldorman presented as the final Guardians, as the Guardians so far exceeded her expectations.

Eldorman called on Leka and Zigrid to present themselves. Leka insisted that his counterpart go first.

Zigrid smiled and delicately presented herself to Shamalaine. She spoke in a hushed and stately manner as she greeted Shamalaine on behalf of her clan.

Zigrid's skin was sun-kissed and supple, with a sheen to it. She wore a white linen tunic over a long beige skirt. She carried a wooden shield in one hand, that was painted with a red and black stylized dragon upon it. In her other hand, she held a spear.

Shamalaine stood as Zigrid bowed.

Zigrid announced herself, "I am Zigrid, your highness. I am honored to be in your presence and in the company of the most honored Guardians of our time." She bowed to Shamalaine as Shamalaine lifted her emerald green dress and walked towards her.

Shamalaine circled Zigrid, feeling into her energy field. Shamalaine could see the fierceness behind the gentlewoman standing before her. The kind of woman that was full of surprises. She noted the small scar just at the edge of Zigrid's right jaw bone.

Shamalaine welcomed Zigrid with a handshake. Zigrid felt the strength of Shamalaine's grip. At that moment, the two women transmitted to one another on another level entirely. Zigrid's power was her gentleness.

Shamalaine SAW her.

Zigrid had a tear in her eyes as she too could see Shamalaine, and it pleased her greatly. Zigrid bowed her head in honor of the connection and receded to allow Leka to come forth.

Eldorman presented him and said, "Leka and Zigrid will be guarding over Christopher, Bridgit, and Traci at Merlyn's Cave."

Leka took a few steps forward. The heaviness of his boots thudded on the floor as he walked, and with each step, the boots made a soft squeaking sound. He wore a fur cape over a beige linen tunic. His dark brown locks flowed to his shoulders. He was a handsome man with golden eyes, and facial hair covering his pale skin. He had a broad chest and physically was appealing to most females that he encountered. He held a shield of power with the runes of protection upon it.

Shamalaine watched Leka kneel before her. He held his head to his knee as she passed by him. She asked him to rise as she felt his strength within his gentleness, just like Zigrid. Energetically the two Guardians could be twins in that respect. Leka was a reverent soul devoted to the protection of Gaia, and now he was devoting himself to the protection of Christopher, Bridgit, and Traci.

He said, "It is my deepest honor to be guarding your precious one, Kaialena. We met in our formative days, as we trained for our missions."

He looked to Breacher at that moment and said, "We all know what is at stake Commander Breacher. We also know that Kaialena is your betrothed, and in your stead, I vow to bring her home to you."

Leka placed his closed fist over his chest as Breacher stood, having put his fist across his heart and walked over to his brother in arms. He helped Leka stand, and the two hugged like old friends, as Shamalaine stood back in gratitude for Eldorman's conscious choice of such a Guardian for Kaialena. It assisted her greatly as she would need Breacher's attention elsewhere.

Breacher said, "If the time comes and I cannot be with her, I am pleased, Leka, that you have been chosen to guard her, and Zigrid. You are my trusted and loyal friend." He patted Leka on the shoulder as Shamalaine smiled and sat in her seat.

Eldorman then spoke to Shamalaine. "If it pleases you, we will join together in a ceremonial toast, and then I would like to give each team their orders."

Shamalaine nodded as glasses of elderberry wine were served in small cone-shaped flutes. Once Eldorman officiated the ceremonial blessings, Shamalaine pulled Breacher aside, and the two walked to

Bewain's study.

Shamalaine shut the door behind them and showed Breacher to the two chairs in front of the roaring fire. "Let me bring you up to date." She put her hand out for Breacher to sit. He did as she asked.

"Bewain has been working with Monoceros to understand what has taken place on Algol, but it has been slow going. During the presentation of the Guardians, I received insight into where the souls of the tortured are being held. I need to get that information to the team immediately."

She looked at Breacher, pausing to read his aura. "I need you to do me a favor."

Breacher moved to the edge of the chair, wanting to leave before she could get the request out, knowing that the favor would take him away from his duty as a Guardian of Bridgit.

She smiled and winced her eyes at him. "I want you to deliver Monoceros to Christopher, Bridgit, and Traci at the time of the jump. The Strategist and I have determined that Monoceros, being an Architect, should be with the team in the cave of creation." She looked into Breacher's eyes. She saw a glimmer of hope.

Breacher stood, "You mean I can see her? Touch her?" he then pressed his feet to the floor, standing straight, as he wiped his face and then said, "I mean, I am happy to take M to the team, but is it okay if I speak with her before she jumps?"

"Yes, dear, you may speak with her. You may even kiss her goodbye." She smiled and held her hands clasped together.

Breacher asked, "When do they jump?"

Shamalaine responded, "Soon. Let's join the others. Eldorman is giving the details about their practice jump now."

They walked back into the Great Hall overhearing Eldorman discussing the Life Bearer's practice jump. He was preparing the team for an imminent departure. They were each discussing their strategies for not being seen in the world of form. Some of the Guardians could easily shapeshift and blend in as a human, and some, not so much.

Shamalaine said to Breacher, "You are welcome to join them in guarding the team during their practice jump, but soon, I will send word to you of the real jump when the Leonid meteor showers are peaking. I will need you to pick up Monoceros and deliver him to Merlyn's Cave at Tintagel. The other two Guardians will be there also, just out of sight."

Breacher went to hug Shamalaine, not as the Clan leader, but that of a mother. She fixed his lapel pin as he approached her, then reciprocated a hug. Breacher was gone in a flash.

Shamalaine watched the others in the Great Hall, preoccupied with the plan. So much was shifting from moment to moment.

And the wheel turns...

Chapter 87

Halloween - The Day of the Practice Jump

Late August quickly flew by, and before they knew it, it was the end of October and time for the Life Bearers to come back together one last time as a team for their practice jump. Christopher had sent all documentation to each team member with the latest updates, including itineraries for travel.

Christopher had stayed on at Stella and Todd's home, working diligently with Todd to further develop the plan. Todd had traveled several times during this period to meet with the boots on the ground Alliance members on a few missions, during which time he was able to solidify his plans to utilize the technology on behalf of the Life Bearers.

David stayed with Bridgit at her home during the interim period as well. They both did their share of research on the regions where they were to jump. Bridgit was comforted by David's presence, while she finalized things at her home. He was a great help doing the physical work in the yard, while she took care of the footwork in finding some-one to sublet her place.

During the downtime, each of the Life Bearers concentrated on maintaining a high vibration that included daily meditation, little to no media, and maintaining a plant-based diet that would provide their cells with more light. Christopher explained that they would benefit from the Chlorophyll within the plants, as it would purify the blood, which was the carrier of their own unique sine wave.

He, too, would be giving up the 3D things that he had grown fond of in his earthly suit. He vowed to omit alcohol and his beloved pipe. Everyone thought that if Christopher could do that, then surely, they too, could eliminate things from their diet for the cause.

Stella stood at the refrigerator door, looking at the offerings. Kombucha, raw sauerkraut, mixed greens, and fruits that she had already cut and placed in glass bowls. She looked at Christopher and Todd sitting at the dining table and asked, "What will it be, boys? I can make a kale salad, or we can juice our meals today."

Todd and Christopher had no preference, and rather than make noise with the juicer, Stella pulled the greens out and began prepping for a large salad full of vitamins, protein, and light. She placed her hands over the salad to bless it with codes of awakening, and in her heart, she spoke to her body, telling it that all good things were coming its way.

She secretly wished that coffee and biscotti were plant-based. She then asked, "Since coffee is a bean that comes from a plant, can I...."

"Nope," was Christopher's response before she could finish her question. They all laughed at her attempt, as she poured hot water into the teapot filled with green tea, moringa leaf, and lemons.

She said, "Green tea, it is!" The men laughed at her need for something familiar.

Stella joined them at the table, bringing with her the bowls of greenery. She slid the cutlery and napkins to Todd as she went back to gather the glasses filled with tart cherry kombucha.

"To our health!" Stella cheered as the trio lifted their glasses in gratitude.

Christopher enjoyed the salad very much and told Stella how much he appreciated her talents in the kitchen.

"You are very gifted in the kitchen, Miss Stella. This is a vibrant meal. Thank you." He nodded his head in gratitude, and the three ate their meal and spoke of the mission.

Todd looked at his watch and asked, "Do I have time to hit the gym before the team arrives?"

Christopher said, "If it is quick. They should be arriving within the hour. Wouldn't you say, Stella?"

Stella confirmed, "Yeah, Dad. Maybe you can do a quick run here on the treadmill?"

Todd had not eaten much of his meal and got up to put his salad in the fridge. "I think I will do that. I think better when I run. I will do a quick jog and shower, and then I should be good to go."

Todd walked off, leaving Stella and Christopher at the table. Christopher's eyebrows arched then said, "He is nervous."

Stella looked at him with a strained look on her face, "Yes. Apparently, it is going to be quite the ride when we all go to the practice location. I think he needs to make sure in his mind that he has covered all the bases."

"Yes, well, it will be fine. It will be over before we know it." He raised his napkin to his mouth and sipped his beverage. "What do you call this drink?" He held the drink up in front of him to see what it was.

Stella laughed, "It is called Kombucha. It is a fermented drink. This one has cherries in it. It acts as a probiotic, and it is supposed to aid our digestion. If you don't like it, I have the green tea ready; say the word, and I will switch it out." Stella winked.

"It is lovely," Christopher responded. After a few minutes, they completed their meal. Stella began to clean up the kitchen, while Christopher went into the living room with a teacup in hand to meditate on the upcoming event.

Soon, the group began to show up at Stella's home. Todd came downstairs, freshly showered. Exercise cleared his head, and he was ready for the adventure that he was sure was about to ensue.

Bridgit and David arrived first. Bridgit and Stella were already chatting in the kitchen as Todd joined David and Christopher in the living room.

Todd said, "I have it all figured out. I need to run to the office to gather the wrist bands for the team. I will be back in a jiffy."

"We shall hold the fort!" Christopher said in his Scottish brogue.

As Todd pulled his car out of the garage, the entourage of Life Bearers was driving into the driveway. He rolled his window down and waved to the group. He yelled out from the window, "I will be right back!"

The Life Bearers began to file into the Phare home a little at a time. They passed a witch and pumpkins strategically placed on the front porch. The sounds of screams were activated as they rang the doorbell. When Stella opened the front door, Ursula and Freya yelled out, "Trick or Treat!!"

Stella responded, "TRICK!!!!"

They all hugged and put their things away, excited for Halloween, the night of their big experiment.

Alvie arrived last. She rang the doorbell, and when Stella answered it, she broke out in laughter.

Alvie entered the home, and as she came into view, everyone could see why Stella was laughing. In an uncharacteristic move, Alvie had dressed up as a contemporary witch. She was wearing a pair of tight black jeans, Dingo boots, and a black pleather jacket.

Stella looked outside then back to Alvie. "Did you just ride in on a motorcycle or a broom?!"

Alvie laughed and held up her broom! Her head was the object of laughter. Covering her face was a witch's mask attached to a wiry black wig. Her hands were covered in a pair of gloves that looked like green witch's hands, with warts and all. Alvie put on a show for the team as she pretended to fly with the broom between her legs and then parked the broom back in the entryway.

Once the team had time to greet one another, Christopher opened up the discussion. "You all look so vibrant! Including you, Miss Alvie!" He watched her remove her mask and clapped his hands to give them all a round of applause for honoring his request to eat clean in the past two months.

Ursula responded to Christopher, "Thank you! You look great too! How are you feeling these days?"

Christopher responded, "Excellent, my dear! Never better!" He demonstrated that his leg had healed quite well, and he did not require his cane any longer.

He then mentioned, "Miss Stella kept a good eye on me, and by the grace of God, we survived our cleanse with flying colors."

Freya said, "That is great! I typically eat a plant-based diet anyway, but I did cut out three things, oil, coffee, and chocolate. It was almost too much to bear, but I did lose 5 pounds in that time! So I'll take it!!!" She slapped her knees with delight as she sat on the sofa.

"Wow! I was going to say that you look amazing, but honestly, everyone does!" Bridgit responded kindly with a pat on Freya's shoulder as she made her way to the seat next to her.

The room was filled with a new brightness as the thirteen Life Bearers enjoyed a joy-filled reunion. Todd walked in and went to take off his sunglasses to greet everyone when he suddenly put them back on and said, "Wow, guys! It is so bright in here!!!"

Stella said, "Right?!! We were totally just talking about that!" her heart was full, seeing Todd acknowledge the team's energy field.

Todd bounded into the center of the room and placed a bag out on the coffee table. He greeted everyone individually, then got to it.

"I have a wrist band for each of you to wear for tonight's main event. This device has been thoroughly tested, and it is the same one that is being used by various Alliance team members. It is a tracking and communications device, and it can also be used to teleport the team members when needed."

Benjamin and David leaned forward to take a better look at them.

Todd continued, "Of course you will also want to wear your striking stone pendants for this practice round, as it will be the pendants that will activate the jump points when we do this for the real mission. I want to monitor the effects the pendants have on each of you since the girls reported unusual experiences when they tried them on. Tonight is a simulation to work out the potential physical kinks when jumping."

Todd passed the wrist bands to each member and demonstrated how to turn them on and use them. He then said, "Tonight, we will be going to the Overland Park Observatory for our practice run."

Stella said, "Oh, really?! So that is why you insisted that we go to see the Light of the Pleiades?!"

She turned to the group and told them that the Observatory put on the program, and Todd seemed suddenly interested in seeing the show, "Though he managed to excuse himself for most of it!"

Todd winked at her and said, "It was a twofer. I thought you would enjoy the program, and I could iron out some last-minute details."

David was very curious at this point, "Why the Overland Park Observatory? Or do I need to ask?" David hinted that he thought he knew, as he was aware that the Observatory housed a Tesla Coil that was demonstrated during tours.

Todd smiled a silly grin and replied, "You will most likely know this, but for the sake of the team, I will say this. The Overland Park Observatory is a solar observatory, which houses several interesting items. For one, there is a Tesla Coil inside the building, and on the outside, in the front of the building, stands an Obelisk that I will say has the qualities required to safely move an object through space and time, with the assistance of my technology. It is the closest place that I could find, and it should work fine. When you jump for real, you will not have to be concerned about this, as the portals will open to you, and as long as you focus your mind on the given word, you will be taken to where you need to go."

Juel and Freya both said at the same time, "Should?" The ladies were focusing on the immediate need to understand Todd's meaning of the technology possibly working or not.

Todd said, "Will. It WILL work fine."

The team members listened as Todd discussed the entire plan for the evening. They also talked about how everyone processed the information of their Akashic records, how their bodies responded, and what memories were recollected.

The day went by quickly, and it soon was into the early evening. The team went out for juice at a local juice bar and returned to Stella and Todd's home to prepare. Everyone gathered their stone pendant, then put their wristbands on. They piled into three cars and made their way to the Observatory that night, after 10 pm, when the building was closed to visitors.

Todd had requested that the Alliance provide a security team for the evening. Waiting in the periphery, Breacher and the Guardians set a perimeter around the entire facility. They watched as the team of Life Bearers drove up and parked.

Bridgit stood in the night air. She inhaled deeply and released any anxiety as she held a focus on her mission. Her arm hair rose, suddenly sensing Breacher at that moment.

Breacher stood nearby, watching with binoculars, from behind a tall tree with a large hole directly in the middle of it. He guarded the tree, in particular, as he knew this tree was the In-Tree, or entry, for their jump. It was triangulated to the area specifically for this event.

Breacher watched Bridgit turn around, looking in all directions for something. As he watched her in the binoculars, he could tell that she sensed his presence. She made a slight motion with her hand, a quick wave, to whoever was watching her, then she walked with the team towards the Observatory.

The Guardians watched each team member make their way to the outdoor passageway where an astrological instrument calculated the sun and the moons daily activities.

Todd situated each team member within the hallway in a sine wave pattern on both sides of the instrument and then swiftly made his way inside the building. "Stay here. I will be back in just a minute."

He had been given exclusive access to the facility so that he could turn on the Tesla Coil.

A few minutes later, he quickly made his way back outside and asked the Life Bearers, "Everyone ready?"

Some of the team members moaned while others were epically hyped to experience bilocation. Benjamin yelled out, "Hells, yea! I'm ready! Let's do this!"

Stella said, "Let's rock n roll!"

Ashneer and David stood close by and shook one another's hands in a moment of appreciation. Everyone was in place as Todd looked at each one and gave some final words of encouragement.

"Remember, this is a programmed jump. You will be sent eleven miles away, and then within sixty seconds, you will return here to this spot. There are circular orifices in the area through which your energy will be pulled. You will then be brought through the circular orifices on the other side as well. I don't have time to explain the particulars, but this place has all of the energetics naturally set within the environment for a perfect jump experience."

He looked at his watch and said, "Everyone ready?"

The team members were positioned three feet apart as Todd hit the switch and watched all thirteen Life Bearers disappear in a flash of light. Breacher monitored the energy of the Life Bearers being pulled through the tree, and then all of the Guardians immediately teleported to The Cosmo, a building eleven miles away from the Observatory.

There, the Guardians observed the team reappearing within the outdoor passageway, through the circular water features and spiral art installations situated in various patterns.

As Christopher reappeared, Breacher swiftly grabbed him as he wobbled upon entry. He stabilized Christopher and dashed back to his vantage point without anyone being the wiser. Christopher was not even sure what had happened, as he looked around to take note of everyone's entry.

Christopher observed the stone benches crafted into the side of the stone walls were in a sine wave pattern. He also noted the various orifices that Todd referred too around the patio of the outdoor space at The Cosmo.

"Mother Trucker!!!" Stella yelled. She and Ursula were cursing like sailors, exhilarated, and freaked out all at the same time.

Juel bent down, thinking she was going to throw up as Benjamin yelled out, "Aw... man!" Everyone turned to see if he was okay.

Benjamin was the only one who was standing within the circular water feature, where his feet were completely soaked. At this point, most everyone was laughing hysterically, giddy from the ride.

Ford helped Benjamin out of the water feature as Freya checked on Juel.

Bridgit and David monitored the rest of the team. Henny and Traci were standing near Alvie, and all of them nodded that they were okay.

As quickly as they arrived, everyone was pulled back through the conical art installation to the other side, where Todd stood waiting.

The Guardians were on alert and back at their posts at the Observatory.

Todd verified that everyone was okay, and all were accounted for. He asked Ford to get everyone back to the cars, asap, while he ran back inside to turn off the Tesla Coil and lock up the facility. "We need to get out of here as quickly as we can. There will likely be helicopters swarming here soon."

Traci asked, "Is there a chance that there is satellite surveillance of what just happened?" She watched just enough television to know that there were ways to detect and track down people.

Todd responded, "The organization that I work for handled all of that for us. Remember, we have a lot of special friends right now." Todd left her with that and quickly ran back into the building.

Ford and David facilitated all of the Life Bearers getting back to the cars. Christopher was going slower, tired from the energy exchange, but they managed to get him to the car by the time Todd arrived. Everyone rendezvoused back at the Phare home.

The Guardians stood watch over the entire team that night, without the Life Bearers knowing of their presence. Todd, however, briefly excused himself to make a phone call to verify that all went well with the mission on the other end. He was pleased to hear that the event didn't cause too much of a stir.

Todd shared with the team that the Observatory was searched, and they found that a janitor had accidentally turned on the Tesla Coil while cleaning the area. "That was the official story anyway," Todd said with a coy expression on his face.

He was able to give the team the good news, then set out his computer to link each of the Life Bearer's wristbands to it. He downloaded each of their biometrics. He wanted to see if they had any adverse reactions so that he could provide them with the exact frequencies and nutrients needed after their body experienced the jump.

Stella marveled at her father in his element. She said, "Wow, Dad, I guess I have never seen what you do before. It is all so complex." She was incredibly proud of her father.

Todd looked up and said, "I am glad that I can finally be forthcoming with the work that I do, but Stella, please realize that if anyone asks what I do, you still need to say that I am a software engineer." He winked at her and then continued to download the data.

"Yeah! I got that!" Stella patted her dad on the shoulder and laughed.

The doorbell rang at that moment. The witch screams went off, outside on the porch. Everyone stood still with fear on their faces. Todd jumped up and strolled to the door peeking through the glass side panels. Standing on the porch was a group of high school kids yelling trick or treat.

Todd opened the door and said, "Sorry, kids. We are completely out of candy." He turned off the front porch light and watched them leave the driveway.

The entire room of people breathed in a sigh of relief. They all slept there that night on air mattresses, spare beds, and outdoor loungers, as Todd ran the diagnostics.

He set each Life Bearer up on a machine that would energetically feed back to them the energetic nutrients and frequencies required to bring them into balance. Todd shared that this technology offered them insights into their physical imbalances so that they would be ready for the BIG jump that was coming.

And the wheel turns...

Chapter 88

Conclusion of Operation Aphesis

Back on an Alliance ship, Breacher held a glass pad in his hand. He opened the latest mission dossier by activating the passcode that the Strategists put into place. He read the key points of the mission. The first words in the briefing were: Galactic Mission- Clear Algol Base. Rescue Lifeforms. Disrupt Quantum computing at programmer bases. Deliver M to Life Bearers. Dragon riders set a new net.

He put the glass pad down and looked out the window of the Alliance ship. His heart began to pound, thinking of the depths of horror that was happening on Algol. The dossier was filled with Intel detailing the most disturbing scenes of human atrocities.

The operation had the same energetic signature of a similar base on Long Island, in the 3rd density of Earth, which made him think that Algol was most likely the origin of what played out on Long Island many decades ago.

After his team of Dragon Riders infiltrated the base on Algol, the Alliance sent in a larger team to clear the base. The dossier described in detail what was found.

It described a massive operation of not only human trafficking but of the elite tracking system that virtually effects every man, woman, and child upon the 3rd density of Earth, with the use of particular blocks embedded into the plasma fields of human bodies.

Within the document, Breacher and all of the Alliance members within Operation Aphesis became aware of the programmer bases that had been strategically placed and controlled by various satellites orbiting Earth.

These bases were the insurance of a very dark force, used to hold Humanity in a virtual world, of ever-increasing darkness. He read about the horrific activities of the dark forces, which were satanic at its core.

It included murder, blood sacrifices, and trauma programs running in all areas of existence on the 3D plane, from religious groups to media, as well as many corporate giants.

Breacher was well aware of the game plan, which included producing trauma as a way to induce fear as energy.

The dossier went on to detail the end game — the Harvest. The food of a cosmic predator was held within the hormones produced in a traumatized victim.

Breacher thought back to the words of Theta Ebora, the Galactic Agent, at the Alliance meeting. He recalled how Theta relayed that it is the time of the greatest battle on all realms of Gaia. The battle of good vs. evil.

Breacher stood in thought after reading the dossier. The reptilian race had infiltrated all of the areas of human life and had struck a deal with power-hungry participants who wanted wealth and notoriety above all else.

This Harvest would be on a massive scale, and it sickened Breacher to see how Humanity was being taken over by the evil that had penetrated the world of man. It went deep.

Breacher contemplated his mission and that of his beloved. It was the lightworkers and warriors who incarnated into the 3D matrix who would be the only hope for Humanity now. Those beings who remembered the mission. The boots on the ground Lighthouses, the Life Bearers.

Breacher prayed at that moment that the thirteen Life Bearers had the support of the Heavenly Host and that all teams would make it safely to the cave of creation. He was relying on the Guardians to see to it that the Life Bearers did their job. He knew he needed to focus on his job.

The Alliance was the key to ridding Earth of the darkness. It was time to implement the plan while the Life Bearers prepared the way for the Reunification of the realms.

He gazed at the incoming ships docking as the teams were arriving to get their orders for the expanded mission. Pleiadian ships, Andromedan ships, Lyran and Sirian ships, and countless others, were all entering the atmosphere around the station. It would be the largest Galactic and Intergalactic meeting with forces gathered from all around the local star systems. All hands were on deck, and from the looks of it, everyone answered the call.

And the wheel turns...

Chapter 89

The Jump

Christopher delivered on his promise to fund each of the Life Bearer's expenses for travel to their respective locations. The Guardians were dispatched to follow the Life Bearers from the start of their journey to the moment of jumping.

Each jumper was instructed to synchronize their wrist bands to jump at the peak of the Leonid Meteor shower between November 17th-18th. The Life Bearers would be traveling all over the planet to their designated jump points, which meant that they would be jumping at different times, depending on their location.

The Guardians would do their best to stay out of sight and blend into their environment. Those who could not blend in would utilize cloaking devices to move about without being seen, but the Guardians who could pass for humans, or could shapeshift, were able to be close to the Life Bearers as warranted.

Each Life Bearer team spent time in their assigned location looking for an anomaly with a triple triangle symbol somewhere within the environment. Todd relayed that in his experience, the triple triangle could be on a cave wall, a tree, or somewhere in the middle of a city.

The technology that Todd gave the team assisted greatly in narrowing down the possibilities. Everything was going according to plan, though there were several moments of distraction and threats.

Shamalaine sent word to Breacher to gather Monoceros and deliver him directly to Christopher, as his team was soon to arrive at Merlyn's Cave in Tintagel, Cornwall.

Breacher bilocated to Bewain's craft to find Monoceros. While Bewain was in a meeting, Breacher approached Monoceros and told him that it was time. Monoceros had been waiting for him and was prepared to accompany Breacher to the human world.

Back in the 3D realm of Earth, the Life Bearers on the Whole Systems team made their way to Cornwall utilizing the night train, after traveling from Los Angeles to London's Heathrow Airport. They made their accommodations at a hotel steeped in Arthurian legend.

The next day Christopher delighted in sharing historical legends of King Arthur with Bridgit and Traci as they strolled within the labyrinth on the backside of the hotel premises.

Christopher explained that the labyrinth was an excellent tool to focus their minds in preparation for the jump.

Each day they spent studying the tides and taking walks down to the cave at low tide to search for the triangles within the landscape. Their wristbands went off only when they were inside the cave, so they now knew for sure that the portal was somewhere inside the cave.

On the day before their jump, the team was back at the cave, exploring. Bridgit remembered the Bee Goddess of Praesepe, recalling her out of body experience where she activated the Praesepe portal and anchored it somewhere, etherically, within the cave. Then it hit her. She recalled the sound of the bees, and intuitively felt called to the deepest part of the cave.

Christopher and Traci explored the cave that day, as well. Bridgit motioned for them to follow her. "I have a memory of using the sound of the bees when interacting with portals." She pointed towards a wall and began to feel for triangular puck marks carved into the wall, but the cave walls were cold and sharp, and it was too dark to make out any signs.

Christopher made a suggestion. "Why don't you sit over there on that dry rock and concentrate on the sound of the bees. Remember what it was like to be in that space where you saw the portal activate. Perhaps you need to invoke the energies? In the meantime, Traci and I will use the wristbands to try to hone in on the anomaly."

The team went about discovering what was hidden to the average person combing through the caves each day.

Bridgit began to make the sound of the bees, and soon, the cave reverberated with a buzzing sound. Suddenly, an amber glow appeared on the wall where Bridgit instinctually assumed it to be. Three distinct concentric triangles appeared on the wall, deep within the cave.

"There it is!!! Do you see it?" Bridgit yelled out to the others.

Christopher watched as Traci started to pull out her striking stone. "Don't do that just yet, Miss Traci!" Christopher rushed to her side and touched her arm to halt her striking the pendant.

Traci looked confused. "Why not?"

Christopher said, "It is not time yet. Let's hold off on using the pendants until the moment we jump. Sound good?"

Bridgit and Traci understood his reasoning and agreed. The three Life Bearers watched as the energy faded as quickly as it appeared, once Bridgit stopped humming.

With the knowledge of the location, the team went back to the hotel for a hearty meal. They were anxious knowing that the meteor shower would be peaking the following evening.

Bridgit commented to Christopher, "We were really cutting it close, weren't we?"

"Yes, we were, but I had full faith in you!" He smiled as they sat down to share a meal back at the hotel.

Traci smiled as she took a sip of water while looking around the restaurant. She had noticed a handsome man watching her earlier, and now he was in the dining room with a woman. The two seemed to be preoccupied with something happening in the front part of the dining room. Traci turned around and saw two men in dark clothing, and wearing sunglasses enter the dining room.

The handsome male passed by Christopher, dropping a card with a symbol of concentric triangles on the table. It was Leka's way of identifying himself without speaking.

Christopher grabbed it and turned to see the female, Zigrid, standing nearby, twisting her head to indicate that they should follow her. Leka made some noise to distract the men, as Christopher said to Bridgit, "We need to move quickly. Don't ask questions. Get up and follow me."

Traci was watching the whole thing and grabbed Bridgit's arm to assist her in moving towards Zigrid. They followed Zigrid out the back door and around the side of the hotel, where a car was parked outside the door.

After Leka distracted the dark-suited men, he walked out the front of the hotel and met the team at the car. Christopher had jumped into the front passenger seat, opposite Zigrid, who was now jumping out to make room for Leka. Zigrid then moved swiftly to the backseat where Traci and Bridgit sat wide-eyed.

Leka drove down the road to find a secluded area, while Traci was trying to explain to Bridgit what was happening since she was reading the menu when the men came into the restaurant.

Zigrid made introductions, "My name is Zigrid. We are your Guardians."

Traci smiled and said, "Oh my gosh! Hello!"

Zigrid said, "I apologize if I made you feel uncomfortable earlier. We did not have time to speak with you."

Traci said, "I sensed something was out of sorts. It is nice to know that you are here with us. Where do you come from?"

Zigrid explained that she comes from a region in the inner realms closest to the 3D area of Earth, known as Sweden.

As Leka drove the vehicle, he spoke to the team as well. "It is my pleasure to serve you, my lady." He looked in the rearview mirror at Bridgit. All she could see was his eyes. Her mind flashed back in time to those eyes as she recalled her friend. "LEKA!!"

Leka laughed, "Yes! It is I, Leka!" His accent was similar to Zigrid.

Bridgit leaned forward, over the seat to hug him from behind. He patted her shoulder and said, "I bring greetings from your Beloved! And Shamalaine as well!"

"Really? You have seen Breacher?" She quizzed, not even remotely concerned about the men who were looking for them at the hotel.

Leka found a secluded spot to park the vehicle. The group sat in the car with the windows down, discussing what just went down.

Leka said, "Those men, they are plastic in nature, not human."

Christopher responded, "Do you mean programmed life forms?"

Leka said, "Yes, that is a better word. Pardon my language skill."

Christopher responded, "Your skills are fine, Leka."

Christopher turned to the ladies and said, "We have been noticed. We will need to make a plan to get back down to the cave between 10 pm and midnight tomorrow evening."

He turned to Leka and said, "We will need you both to be stationed outside of our rooms and the cave when we go in. We don't want any intruders tonight. We will need to be stealthy and keep watch this evening."

Zigrid commented, "We will provide you with the support you need. No one or thing will get by us."

Bridgit was waiting patiently for the others to come up with a plan so that she could ask Leka more questions about Breacher.

Leka said, "He should be here soon."

Bridgit was stunned, "Here? Really?"

Leka and Zigrid both nodded their heads. Zigrid said, "He is bringing the Unicorn."

Christopher looked at her, concerned, and asked, "The Unicorn? There was no mention of a Unicorn in the mission. What has changed?"

Leka said, "This is all sudden, we know. The Divine Mother asked Breacher to go to Algol, where he was to retrieve a Unicorn. What he and his team found on Algol was horrific. They rescued a child there and thought that the mission was a failure, but the child was, in fact, the Unicorn. He is an architect of world systems. Shamalaine feels that he will be helpful to you and the Life Bearer's mission."

Christopher sped up the conversation as it was getting late, "Yes, well, let's get going. It is getting late." Christopher was agitated hearing about the Unicorn, as it was not in the mission plans, though he knew the plan could change at any moment.

Traci and Bridgit whispered in the back seat while Leka drove to the hotel.

Once they arrived back at the hotel, Zigrid got out to inspect the area. The ladies watched her walk away, and Christopher fiddled with his pipe, setting it down in the console between the seat to adjust his wristband. He was restless and ready to get out of the car. It was moments like this that he would take a pull from his pipe or have something stronger. "I would love a stiff drink about now!"

Bridgit's eyebrows furrowed, thinking that Christopher was concerned about the men in dark suits. He kept his thoughts inward, trying to smile as the situation was becoming foggy with the intruders and the addition of another team member.

Zigrid motioned to Leka that all was well. The trio was escorted to their rooms that night. The Guardians watched over the two rooms that were next door to one another. The next day they received room service for all of their meals, waiting until the cloak of the night before leaving the protection of their rooms.

Finally, the time had come.

Leka walked in the front of the group as the Life Bearers walked straight down the path from the hotel towards Merlyn's Cave. Zigrid followed from behind, monitoring all directions.

The Life Bearers were quiet the whole way down to the cave.

The weather was dry earlier in the day but had become chilly in the clear night air. Traci detected the first of the Leonid meteors flashing across the sky.

Christopher looked down to see his wristband light up, sounding an alarm. Traci and Bridgit's wristbands went off as well.

Christopher, Bridgit, and Traci entered Merlyn's Cave at the appointed hour. It was dark inside the cave, but Traci had flashlights in her bag. She handed them out as they walked deeper into the cave. Zigrid and Leka monitored the cave from the entrance, after verifying that it was clear.

The Life Bearers suddenly felt a shift in the air, and a light began to flash. Standing a few feet away from them stood Breacher and a small child, Monoceros.

Bridgit ran forward, "Breacher!"

Traci shined her flashlight on Breacher so that he could see Bridgit coming. The lovers embraced and gently kissed, only for a few seconds.

Christopher remarked, "Well, you have great timing, my boy. Introductions would be appropriate", motioning to who Breacher had in his care.

Breacher said, "This is Monoceros, the Unicorn. He is an Architect of Worlds."

"An Architect? How did you find him?!" Christopher quizzed Breacher for the sake of clarity.

Christopher noticed that the Unicorn was wearing a striking stone as well, though it was not exactly like the ones that the Life Bearers had.

"It is a long story, which we don't have time for now. I can't stay long. I need to get back to the ship. Shamalaine asked me to deliver Monoceros to the three of you, as she felt it was wise to have counsel with the Architect while in the Cave of Creation."

Christopher said, "I see." He subconsciously held tightly to the striking stone in his hand, as he contemplated having an extra jumper. He assumed that Shamalaine knew what was best, but he was alarmed at the change in the plan, having not been notified of this in an intel package.

Monoceros smiled and reached his hand towards Christopher to shake it as was the proper form of introduction in the 3D world.

As Christopher reached towards him, he began to slip on the wet surface. Breacher grabbed him, supporting his arm, and helped him to a more stable footing.

Breacher moved towards Bridgit and said, "I have to go, but I am happy to see that you made it to your designated spot. It is time to be about your work. See you at home later?" He grinned, and the two laughed as he touched her cheek.

He pulled her close, and she said, "I will see you at home later." The two kissed once more and then Breacher stepped a few feet back and was gone in a flash.

Traci was watching Bridgit as she interacted with Breacher and had so much compassion for her dear friend. Bridgit never complained about her life to her, though she would have every reason too.

Christopher encouraged Bridgit to begin the bee sounds.

"It is time, my dear," Christopher reoriented himself to the new plan, observing the Architect in his periphery.

Bridgit walked over to the area that she had lit up earlier and began the humming of the bee sound. The sound vibrated her tongue as she held the notes, keeping her front teeth closed.

The cave brightened as the concentric triangles began to glow in an amber hue, becoming brighter as Bridgit generated the electrical frequency to activate the portal.

Traci and Bridgit moved closer to the energy field of the portal as the wavy lines became noticeable.

Monoceros encouraged the ladies to go first. "I will jump with Master Christopher." Monoceros gently held his hand out to escort Traci further into the range of the portal, then bowed his head and stepped backward.

Traci held her striking stone in one hand, with the pendant in the other, and kept the word Etifah in her mind as she hit the stone against the pendant. Immediately the portal fully opened. Bridgit hit her stone pendant as well. They both looked back at Christopher and M, and then the two walked into the portal together. The energy pulled them in like a vacuum.

Christopher began to inch his way closer to the portal, allowing Monoceros to hold onto his arm as he sounded the vibration with his striking stone against his pendant. At that moment, Monoceros yanked the pendant from Christopher's hand and pushed him backward, to the ground. Monoceros shapeshifted as he entered the portal laughing.

Christopher caught a glimpse of Monoceros's transformation as his body entered the portal. All he could see was the backside of a much larger warrior who carried a golden sword on his right side. The portal began to shrink as the vibration of the striking stones faded.

Christopher was unable to get up in time before the portal closed. He screamed out for the Guardians. Just as the portal narrowed to a close, the warrior tossed something through the portal. It rolled into the cave and made a noise as it slowed down and came to a stop on the floor near where Christopher was trying in vain to stand. He reached for the item. In his hand, he held an ancient golden coin with an emblem of a Fox.

Christopher yelled out in the darkness as the light of the portal faded.

Leka and Zigrid came running in. "What has happened?" Zigrid got to Christopher first.

"Breacher brought the Architect here, on Shamalaine's request."

Christopher accepted Leka's help to stand, then said, "I don't think that was the Architect!"

Leka helped Christopher out of the cave as Zigrid looked for clues.

Christopher handed the coin to Zigrid, and as she looked it over, it gave her chills. She looked at Leka and said, "Electra!"

Leka and Zigrid accompanied Christopher back to his room that night, after retrieving his cellphone from the hotel safe.

The Guardians kept watch outside his door as Christopher made a call to Todd. Christopher could see that Todd had already tried to call twice.

While waiting for Todd to pick up the phone, Christopher reached in his pocket for his pipe, but it was not there. He was usually calm under pressure, but the situation was bad, and not having his pipe now made it worse. He walked over to the side table where a minibar was set up and poured himself a drink while leaving a message for Todd to return the call.

In the meantime, Breacher had made it back to his ship and continued monitoring the Algol mission. He was in his quarters with his glass pad, reading the mission report when he came upon a video of the people that were rescued.

As he scrolled through the video, something caught his eye. He paused it and rewound the video to the spot, then zoomed in. There on the video, he saw Monoceros among the other victims. He was walking in a manner of a trauma victim, almost in a zombie state.

Breacher threw the pad across the room and bilocated to the healing ship. He burst into Celeste 108's office, where she was reading case files. "We have a problem!"

Celeste looked up from her files and stood. "Commander Breacher, what seems to be the issue?"

Breacher pointed to her glass pad and asked her to open her files and, in particular, the video of the rescued people on Algol. He had her stop the video at the point where he did earlier, and asked, "Where is this one? Where was he taken?"

Celeste didn't have the exact answer but said that they were all taken to the healing rooms where they will receive the reprogramming and healing protocols.

Breacher was pacing back and forth, trying to understand what had happened. His communication device buzzed his arm. "Breacher!" He responded.

"Commander Breacher. We have a problem." Benoit reported.

"Todd Phare sounded the alarms. His communication device is sending a red alert signal to the Alliance." Benoit said. "Apparently, the child, Monoceros, is a shapeshifter, and not the true Unicorn."

Breacher looked at Celeste and said, "Find him! Start the reprogramming on him now. We need to know who he is, or who the other one is!"

Breacher flashed in the blink of an eye back to Cornwall, in Christopher's room. His presence startled Christopher, causing him to drop his phone.

Leka heard the noise and opened the hotel room door, seeing Breacher standing there. He entered the room, leaving Zigrid on duty in the hall.

Christopher picked up the phone and resumed his call with Todd, explaining that Breacher had arrived and that he would call him back.

Leka said, "A thousand apologies, Commander! All was in perfect order until the Architect infiltrated the field. I am confused, my brother!" Leka was mad, and yet he knew his place. He was waiting to hear how this disaster happened.

Breacher apologized. "I am well aware that we have a problem. I was asked to bring him to the team, but I did not know that this being, Monoceros, is not who he says he is. We are trying to get through to Shamalaine and the Strategist now. What I can tell you is that after I dropped him off with you, I was back on the ship and came across a video clip of the people who had been rescued on Algol. They had been abused to the point that most of their soul essence left their bodies, and what is left is zombie-like shells, barely animating the flesh."

Breacher looked at Christopher sitting in the chair near the window with a glass of scotch. Breacher watched him push back the drink before asking, "Are you okay?"

"Yes. My ego is not, but physically, I am fine." He placed his empty glass on the desk and said, "I had a feeling in my stomach the minute you brought him to us!" He looked at Breacher for more understanding.

"I don't have any answers! All I know is that the real Monoceros is on the healing ship, and until we get him through the reprogramming, we have no idea of who or what we are dealing with."

Christopher pulled out the coin from his pocket and handed it to Breacher. He said, "Zigrid tells me that this is the fox emblem of Electra. Whoever went through that portal left it as a calling card."

And the wheel turns...

Chapter 90

The Midway Station

A whizzing sound, not unlike the sound of bees swarming, was the sound that Bridgit and Traci heard as they moved through the portal into a space between worlds.

They exited the portal in a weigh station in the middle of the cosmos. It was a large white room that resembled the deck on a spacecraft. There were windows around the perimeter of the room. Nothing but darkness was seen through the windows, save for a few twinkling stars in the distance.

Two blue-skinned beings stood at a podium, waiting for the ladies to join them. They bowed their heads as the ladies approached.

Traci and Bridgit walked towards them and stood to wait for one of the beings to speak. Instead, they monitored the podium for the next incoming transfer. A light began to flash, and a horrible sound radiated from the area of the portal. One of the blue beings flipped a switch on the podium, and the ladies turned to see what was happening.

The blue beings swiftly ran to the portal area. Bridgit and Traci watched as a mirrored, three-dimensional triangular-shaped enclosure completely encapsulated the area from which they came. A jail system to capture intruders had suddenly appeared as the being impersonating Monoceros came through the portal. He screamed out in anger, trying to break his way through with his sword. He was shocked in the process and fell to the ground.

Bridgit and Traci were stunned to see that instead of Monoceros or Christopher, it was this being who entered through the portal behind them. They could see he was a tall warrior with a thirst for vengeance.

Bridgit was terrified. "Where is Christopher!? Who is he!?" She looked at Traci, who was equally concerned. They were somewhere in an in-between place, alone without Christopher, and now they could see that their plan to get the Life Bearers to the cave of creation had been infiltrated.

One of the blue beings went back to the monitor where Bridgit and Traci stood. He pushed a button on the panel, which sent the captured being away. Whoever he was, he was not allowed access, and they dealt with him swiftly.

The sounds of the portal began to buzz once more, and this time Bridgit stood, staring at the portal, hoping that it was all a fluke and that Christopher and Monoceros were next in line to come through. She watched as the vibration of the portal presented Shamalaine.

"Shamalaine!" Bridgit ran to Shamalaine's side. Traci followed.

"Shhh... It's alright. You are fine." Shamalaine held onto Bridgit as Bridgit wept in her arms.

Bridgit looked up at her mother and asked, "What just happened?"

Shamalaine walked the girls back to the podium, where the blue beings stood waiting. She held out her hand to Traci to comfort her as well. "Are you okay?" She asked.

Traci responded, "I am as okay as I can be. Where are we? What just happened?"

Shamalaine brought up a report by the Strategist. She began to tell the ladies that the Strategists had detected a nefarious plan instituted by a being known as Chrysaor. She relayed the story of his mother, Medusa, being killed ages ago and that one of her sons, Chrysaor, was part of an evil plan to bring pain and destruction to the 3D world of Earth for many reasons, one of which, for him personally, was retribution for his mother's killing.

"Their plan is multifaceted and involves many beings that are even more devious than he. We received a report that he was impersonating the Unicorn, who is the Architect of this world. Apparently, the real Monoceros was captured and tortured and is now in the good hands of our healing crew, thanks to the Alliance, and your father..." Shamalaine looked at Bridgit when she shared the last part.

"What?" Bridgit was so confused.

Shamalaine continued, "Breacher's team found the Unicorn at a base on Algol. They found that there was a massive operation happening there that involved human trafficking and many other heinous activities. Breacher was able to alert the Alliance."

Shamalaine grabbed Bridgit's hand and held it momentarily, looking into her eyes. "The Alliance went about clearing the base and rescuing the people there. We did not know at the time that the real Monoceros was somewhere in the lower levels. Breacher and his crew rescued who they thought was a young child that could help them with intel. He turned out to be Chrysaor, disguised as Monoceros, the Unicorn."

Shamalaine paused momentarily to put the next words into context delicately. "Though Breacher did not know M was Chrysaor when he brought him to the three of you, the Strategists and I had received intel of the truth of his identity, and we were prepared to intercept him. This was the only way to capture him." She was honest in her part of the plan, knowing that Bridgit would be outraged.

Par for the course, Bridgit grew angry with her mother. "You lead him straight to us?! How could you do that? What if he killed us? In fact, where is Christopher? Is he alright?!" Traci patted Bridgit's shoulder to calm her down.

Shamalaine tried to quite her and said, "We knew the odds of him wanting to jump was higher than him bringing harm to you. His goal was to reach the Cave of Creation, where he could stop you all and capture you there forever."

Traci pleaded. "What? What are you saying? I had no idea that we would be hunted down by mythological beings! Help me understand this." It was Bridgit's turn to comfort Traci, but she did not have it in her. Both ladies felt utterly betrayed by Shamalaine.

Shamalaine kept her cool and continued, "Chrysaor and the Pegasus were born from Medusa when Perseus killed her. This is a long battle of good and evil and of many of the old Gods who feel that this planet is theirs. Chrysaor is a pebble in a large pond of dark ones. He is working with a very sinister female, known as Electra Fox."

Bridgit shook her head. "Where is Christopher?"

Shamalaine said, "He will be along once he finds his pipe. He is the least of my concerns right now. Trust me, he is fine. A little bruised ego is all. Breacher is with him now."

Bridgit looked at her mother and said, "Breacher is going to be furious with you!"

Shamalaine turned off the monitor, keeping her cool, and motioned for the blue beings to take the girls to a rest area while they wait for the others to arrive.

She turned to Bridgit and said, "You must trust me. I have always put your safety first. You are safe and can be about your work in a very short amount of time. Breacher will need my help now, so I must go. The others will be here shortly. Once you are all together, you will leave from here and enter the Cave of Creation."

677

Shamalaine quickly went back to the portal as the blue beings activated it once more. She looked back at Bridgit, "I am sorry for this inconvenience. I did what had to be done. The others will be here soon. Good luck!" She then turned and vanished in the portal.

And the wheel turns...

Chapter 91

Back at Tintagel

Shamalaine greeted Zigrid in the hall of the hotel in Tintagel. She softly knocked on the door, overhearing Breacher and Christopher discussing what has happened. Shamalaine opened the door in a crack and then turned to Zigrid, "Could you please retrieve Christopher's pipe? I believe he left it in the motor vehicle." She smiled at Zigrid and watched her walk away. Shamalaine entered the room with two men looking bewildered.

"Gentleman. I am sure that you were expecting me." She smiled and found her way to the window, watching Zigrid open the vehicle and retrieve Christopher's pipe.

Christopher stood from his chair, greeting his old friend with civility and kindness, patiently awaiting an explanation, but Breacher was not quite that patient.

"What the hell has happened!?" Breacher walked close to the window to see what Shamalaine found so fascinating. He caught sight of Zigrid then looked to the door, aware that Leka was making the rounds about the perimeter, and Zigrid was supposed to be guarding the hallway.

"Don't worry. The threat has been eliminated. Zigrid will be back to her station shortly."

She turned to Christopher and asked, "Are you hurt?"

Christopher responded, "Only my ego, my dear. I wish that we were meeting under different circumstances. Do tell us, who was that being that went through the portal, and furthermore, are the girls okay?"

Zigrid knocked at the door and peeked her head inside. She held Christopher's pipe in her hands, which Breacher walked over to the door to retrieve. Zigrid smiled and nodded her head, then shut the door.

Breacher walked over to Christopher and questioned, "I am sure you have been looking for this?"

Christopher said, "Thank you! YES... I have been searching for it. I can't tell you how important this pipe is to me." He pulled out his tobacco pouch and looked at Shamalaine, who was holding her thoughts until he was ready to hear more.

"Do you mind?" he quizzed Shamalaine.

"Please. Go right ahead. I will wait." She bowed her head in honor of this dear old man.

Christopher packed his pipe and took several draws from it, filling the room with a cherry-scented smoke billowing around his head. He nodded to Shamalaine to continue as his body began to release the anxiety.

Breacher sat on the edge of the bed, staring at his boots as she began.

"First of all, let me tell you that Bridgit and Traci made it to the Midway Station just fine. They are a little worse for wear, but under the circumstances, anyone would be. They were extremely concerned for Christopher, knowing that the being that went through the portal was not Monoceros. He is none other than Chrysaor, the son of Medusa."

Shamalaine watched as the two men reacted in very different ways.

Christopher was more relaxed, and level headed, taking in the information. Breacher, on the other hand, was furious.

"When did you know?" He looked at her with disgust. "When did you figure it out?"

Shamalaine came over to sit near him and placed her hand on his knee. "Calm down, Breacher. She is okay."

Shamalaine started with the primary concern, which was Bridgit. "Bridgit and Traci made it through the portal just fine. The blue beings at the Midway Station were notified that it was likely that a being would attempt to enter the portal without proper authority, and we set the trap. If I had warned you of this, you would never have gone along with the plan, and it was the only viable one we had."

Breacher bit his tongue to keep from saying what was on his mind, as she was the leader of the Clan of Phare, Kaialena's mother, and the lead Strategist.

Shamalaine turned to Christopher. "I am truly sorry that you were not included in the plan, Christopher. The Strategist and I came up with a foolproof plan and felt that the fewer people that knew about it, the better."

She then turned back to Breacher, "Chrysaor has been captured and dealt with, but he is one of many involved in a massive plan of control over the Earth and its inhabitants."

She looked back to Christopher, "I understand he left a coin?"

Christopher reached for the coin that lay on the table. He handed it to Shamalaine.

"Yes. This emblem is the sign of Electra. This is getting sticky." She looked at Breacher and said, "Electra is the mother of one of your Dragon Riders. Kali."

Breacher took in a deep breath and let it out, deflating his chest and shook his head in disbelief.

"What does this mean for my team now? Is Kali involved in this evil?" He searched for hope in Shamalaine's eyes.

Shamalaine smiled. "She has distanced herself from her mother, knowing of her treachery. Her father, on the other hand, is caught in the middle."

Breacher looked up at her, remembering his encounter with Dardan, the ship captain with the Draco emblem on his jacket. "Dardan?"

Shamalaine continued, "Electra's team is monitoring Dardan. He is essentially her prisoner. Dardan is one of our... family members. We know his heart and his allegiance, and he won't let anything happen to Kali, even if it means being under Electra's control for now."

Breacher was even more agitated now, having not been given this intel, which could jeopardize his mission. "When you say he is a family member, are you referring to the Clan?"

Shamalaine said, "Dardan incarnated into the 3D Earth as August Phare." She turned to look at Christopher, choking on his pipe smoke.

Christopher looked at Shamalaine, "August, you say?"

Shamalaine smiled and replied, "Yes. Dardan is none other than August Todd Phare, your brother, and Todd's father." She looked back to Breacher and continued, "And Stella's Grandfather."

Christopher had a tear forming in his right eye. He swiped it away quickly and then asked, "Is he in mortal danger? And his daughter, Kali, how will we proceed with this knowledge?"

Shamalaine said softly, "Kali has chosen the side of Light. She has a love for her mother but does not condone the choices that her mother has made. She hates that her mother is controlling her father because of her, and there is nothing she can do about it. Kali is trapped."

Breacher responded, "It is too late to replace her. She is quite gifted as a rider, and the dragons chose her. I guess we have no choice but to see where this goes."

Shamalaine said, "There is more. This is about Chrysaor and Monoceros." She looked at both Christopher and Breacher, who seemed to both have a winced look upon their faces, as if they knew she saved the worse for last.

She continued, "Chrysaor infiltrated this realm long ago. He assisted Monoceros in the creation of the security programming for this matrix. He is a shapeshifter, as you know, and is highly intelligent."

Shamalaine read Breacher's mind and continued. The real Monoceros is a pure being. He had no understanding of Chrysaor's treachery."

"Let me get this straight. Chrysaor has access to the programming codes?" Breacher wiped his forehead as he stood up.

"Yes, well, he did. We have him in custody, so he shouldn't be a problem now, but yes, he installed the program for the net that surrounds the planet. The very one that you and the Dragon Riders will be upgrading. We too have the codes, and it is your job to clean up this mess. It is what you have been training for Breacher."

Shamalaine was almost complete with her communication. As she made her way to the door, she said, "Dardan is an ally. He was once responsible for the portal into Agartha, but because of his love for Kali, he locked the gate and left his post. He is now, as you know Breacher, a ship captain, with Electra's Draco minions watching over him. He does what he is told so that they won't harm Kali."

Shamalaine breathed deeply, this time, letting her guard down and allowing Breacher to see her tender side. "Keep Kali safe. She and all of the riders are integral to the success of the overall plan."

Christopher put his pipe in a bowl on the table and got up from his seat to say goodbye to Shamalaine. She reached over to pat his shoulder and whispered, "Don't lose that pipe; it is your ticket to reuniting with the team."

"Understood." Christopher was a bit embarrassed to have misplaced something of such value.

She looked at Christopher as she opened the door, "When the tide is low, Leka and Zigrid will escort you to the portal in Merlyn's cave. The portal is still active, just strike the pipe on the cave wall near the portal. When the portal opens, mentally think of Etifah before entering."

With those last words, Shamalaine exited the door and was gone.

And the wheel turns...

Chapter 92

In the Meantime
Around the World

Benjamin flew from Los Angeles to Bucharest, Romania. He caught a train to a small town on the outskirts of Gradistea Muncelului-Cioclovina Nature Reserve. There, he met up with a guide, who would act as his translator as well. The guide, Silviu, spent time in the United States as a child of a Romanian diplomat in his childhood. His English was perfect, and Benjamin was relieved to have the company.

The plan was to stay at a lodge within 6 miles of the Cioclovina cave, giving Benjamin access to the entire nature reserve. Silviu knew the area like the back of his hand, as this region was his Ancestor's homeland. His family settled there on their return to Romania when he was a teenager. Silviu was anxious to share his knowledge of Dacian folklore and, in particular, his experience of the cave that Benjamin was interested in investigating.

All the while, Esmond and Amazonia, were presenting themselves as a tourist and booked Silviu for the same tour with Benjamin. This way, they could blend in as humans and keep watch over Benjamin. The

Guardians had already checked into the lodge and were waiting in the lounge when Benjamin and Silviu entered the lobby.

Silviu guided Benjamin to the reception desk and set the bags down near the stairway. He noticed the two individuals waiting in the lounge and assumed them to be his other clients. He introduced himself immediately.

Amazonia stood and said, "Hello! I am Amazonia, and this is my partner, Esmond." She stood towering over Silviu, who was not a short person in his own right, but next to her, he was dwarfed.

Silviu grinned from ear to ear, seeing such a lovely and fit woman interested in his homeland. "It is nice to meet you," Silviu bowed his head towards her. They shook hands quickly.

He reached out to shake Esmond's hand as well. Esmond jumped up from his seat and planted his feet in a stance. Silviu took note of Esmond's attire. His biceps nearly ripped the seam of his short-sleeve button-down shirt that had very little give due to his muscular upper body.

Silviu went swiftly to his knees, as Esmond, not realizing the power of his handshake, grabbed Silviu's hand like an opponent, rather than a friend. Silviu shrieked modestly, trying to take it like a man. Esmond laughed it off and slapped Silviu's back as he released his grip and helped him to his feet.

"Sorry about that! Let me help you up." Esmond looked at Amazonia with wide eyes as she mentally sent a message to tone it down. He nodded her way, telepathically saying that he understood.

Benjamin walked up to the trio with a key in hand. He was told ahead of time that his Guardians would be physically present with him. He was gobsmacked when he laid eyes upon the duo in the lounge. "Hello! I am Benjamin. Are you...?"

Amazonia jumped in quickly with her announcement before Benjamin could finish his question, "Yes! I am Amazonia, and this is

Esmond, my partner."

She moved towards Benjamin to give the traditional warm, human greeting. Her awkward hug gave Benjamin an inner chuckle. He reached his hand out to shake Esmond's hand, and Silviu involuntarily chirped, "Watch it there! He has a ferocious grip!" He laughed as he rubbed his hands to get the feeling back.

Benjamin nodded towards Silviu and shook Esmond's hand. It was a firm grip, Benjamin took note, but nothing overpowering as Silviu had suggested.

Silviu laughed and looked at Esmond, "I see what you did there."

They all started laughing as Esmond grabbed Silviu by the arm to lead him towards the door and asked where he could get a meal.

They spent the evening getting to know one another and planning the coming day's adventure. Benjamin wanted to speak alone with the Guardians, but Silviu was at his side the entire evening.

Some nine hundred miles away, Stella, David, and Henny arrived in Aberdeen, Scotland. The stopover was due to David's need to attend to a few loose ends before they traveled onward to Haifa, Israel. It also helped divide the flight time, which relieved Stella. She could barely do the ten hour flight as it was, much less another five or six hours longer.

She was grateful to have a bit of time between the next flight to Tel Aviv. She immediately wanted a cuppa upon her return to her Ancestor's homeland. She smiled, remembering when she first laid eyes on David and their quirky interaction getting Americanos. Sadly, she had to settle for tea this time around.

Stella grabbed the guys for tea and chatted with Henny about how anxious she was to show him the Phare family home since he was not in Aberdeen when the others met at Christopher's home, after the Geomancy conference.

Christopher gave Stella a key and full reign over the house. He told Stella that it was her's and Bridgit's home as much as it was his.

Time went by quickly in Aberdeen as David completed the list of things that Christopher had asked of him, and soon the team was ready to head back to the airport for the final leg of the trip.

David had arranged for a private sedan to be waiting upon their arrival in Israel. Once they landed, they gathered their bags and were met by a man with a placard with the name Phare. Stella was weary from travel and happy to have the comfort of someone familiar with the area to take them to their hotel.

The trio followed the driver to the car, and off they went into the evening nightlife of Tel Aviv. They had arranged to stay overnight the first evening there and then have the driver take them to Haifa the next day.

Haifa in November was surprisingly comfortable weather, considering David was used to a more chilly and wet autumn season.

Stella remarked that it was in the low 60's when they left LA, so she was happy that she packed well for the trip.

Henny liked all kinds of weather and came prepared with a fleece-lined jean jacket and a black beanie. He wore thick socks with his high top sneakers and carried a backpack with him, with a scarf hanging from it that Traci sent with him to keep his throat warm.

The first morning in Haifa, the trio found a café near their hotel to map out where they would begin their search for the triangular-shaped puck marks. Stella ordered the group herbal tea, a fruit medley, and broccoli-cheddar quiches, while the boys found a comfortable table outside under the covered patio. They pulled out the map and coordinates and were synchronizing their wrist bands when Stella approached the table with their tea.

David stood quickly to help Stella with the tea tray. "Thank you, Stella. This looks great. A good cup of tea in the morning should help

688

us get the day started. Any milk for the tea?"

Stella smiled and said with a moan, "Don't get too excited, it's herbal tea. They will bring almond milk with the meal. It won't be long."

"Dandy!" David grinned, but inwardly he too was miserable without his strong black tea in the morning. He pulled a seat out for Stella and waited for her to sit, then tried to enjoy the herb tea.

Henny asked Stella, "Do you mind letting me sync your wrist band? Todd instructed that we should do that as soon as we get into the area. Once we get close to the anomaly, we should get a ping. Then from there, we can start looking for the triangles."

"Sure! Go for it!" Stella removed her wrist band and handed it to Henny. The waitress came to the table with the milk and mentioned that it would be a few more minutes for the food to arrive.

Stella took her teacup and walked towards the edge of the patio, looking at the view. Her body was acclimating to the energy of Haifa. A chill ran down her back, not from cold air, but rather from an energetic shift. She turned around to look at the guys to see if they had felt it too, but they were busy with their map and wristbands. She came back to the table to set her teacup down and said, "I'll be right back."

Stella walked to the outskirts of the café towards the street to see if she could zero in on what was coming through. She knew this feeling. It usually was foretelling of something significant.

Stella walked behind the café towards an alley. She noticed graffiti on the back wall of the café, near the trash bins. The graffiti looked fresh and colorful. As she approached it, she realized that it was a peace wall with quotes and sayings in various languages. Her eyes were brought upward, to the right, where a peace sign was painted with the only words in English. The words read- We want a TRUCE! Peace begins now! The word Truce was in capital letters, and Stella felt that shiver down her back again. She thought it was a message from her mother, Evie. She pulled out her phone to take a photo then went back to the table to show David and Henny.

As she entered the café, she noticed two individuals sitting at a table near the door, a male and a female, who were dressed strangely and speaking to one another in a strange dialect. For a moment, she thought it was perhaps their Guardians, then she thought twice about it and said, "Nah!", laughing at the thought as she joined the guys.

David was concentrating on the map as Stella approached the table.

"Where is Henny?"

David pointed across the courtyard. Henny was on his phone.

David said in a low tone, "It's a music exec."

Stella looked towards Henny and could read his body language. Henny hung up the phone and came back to join them at the table. Stella asked, "Is everything okay?"

Henny sat down and put his hands over his face and just let his head be held in his cupped hands for a few moments, then came out of it. "That was a record producer that I have been sort of courting for some time now, and wouldn't you know it, now that I am going to be out of pocket for a while, he calls to tell me that he wants to record with me."

Henny's face turned red. He looked up to the sky in anguish. "It is everything that I have been working towards, and he calls now!! In this freaking moment!" He let out the deepest sigh as if he had held his breath for months in anticipation.

David said, "This is what one would call a fork in one's road."

Henny said, "Details would be nice, man." He tried to smile but needed David to be less cryptic.

"In moments of great acceleration on one's spiritual journey, a random carrot is thrown out in front of us to entice us to another path; thus, you stand at the fork and ponder, which way should I go? On the one hand, each path offers great pleasure, but only one path can one take.

690

You must decide if your calling is to be a co-creator of the Musical Spheres or if your musical career in the third dimension is what truly calls you." David had professionally delivered a whopper, without emotion, and with absolute clarity. The choice was now up to Henny.

David stood up and asked, "What did you tell him?"

"I said that I was out of the country and that when I get back, I will give him a call." Henny shrugged his shoulders and stood up, wiping his hands on his legs to pull his pant legs down.

"I am full in on the Life Bearer thing. I really am. I just think it is odd that he calls me now. It's a huge carrot, man!" Henny laughed as they walked away from the table, saying one last thing. "I'm good... I just ate! Who needs a carrot anyway?!"

David and Stella hugged him tightly. The triangular Life Bearer hug lasted for a few moments, and then they were off. Stella shared her findings of the peace wall as they went out on their adventure.

On this same day, in Forres, Scotland, Freya was alone, but well equipped with everything she needed to find the triple triangles. She had checked into her hotel in Forres the night before and had already synced her wristband.

Todd was in contact with her for moral support. He suggested that she start somewhere near the Findhorn Community and methodically work her way outward for a quarter mile in each direction until she felt a ping on the wristband.

Her Guardians, Randelf, and Hotaru, were near her every step of the way, though they did not make contact with her. They used the cloaking device to stay nearby, without her or anyone else taking note of their presence.

Freya filled her backpack with nuts, water, and a veggie sandwich and was on the move. After a short ride from the hotel, she entered the Findhorn Ecovillage and went directly to where one of the staff members was waiting for her. Freya had made many friends while there earlier in the year when she and Juel shared community duties during their last visit.

Freya and her friend Marva chatted over a cup of tea. Freya wanted to be as casual as possible during this time while she was trying to locate the anomaly. She asked Marva if there was a particular spot on the property that people had strange experiences. Marva shared that there were so many people that came through the community each month. She relayed that they were always mesmerized by the gardens, and it was there that most people attempted communication with the nature spirits.

Marva smiled, sipped her tea , then said, "Oh, well, of course, many people report having incredible spiritual communion in the nature sanctuary. Didn't you enjoy the energy of the sanctuary when you were last here?"

Freya smiled and nodded with the last sip of tea in her mouth. She swallowed and then replied, "Absolutely! It was amazing!"

After a few more minutes of small talk, Freya stood to say her good-byes. She wanted to get out on the land before sundown, so she told Marva that she would meet her at the nature sanctuary later that evening. The two women hugged, and Freya was out the door.

She walked around for a while and came to a stop sign. She laughed as she always loved that stop sign. Underneath the word STOP was another word in smaller letters. It read: STOP worrying. Freya thought how appropriate that message was.

Juel texted Freya at that moment. Freya grabbed the phone from her bag and found a quiet spot to sit as she read Juel's texts. Juel wrote, "We arrived in Sarajevo, after a few hours of flight delays. Exhausted, but good. Heading to the hotel soon."

Freya texted, "Made it to Findhorn!! I wish you were here with me!!! I just had tea with Marva, and am about to do some exploring. Meditation tonight at the Nature Sanctuary. Hugs and Kisses! Hang in there!"

Juel sent back a reply, "I wish I could be there too, but I am equally excited to experience the Bosnian pyramids!! Good luck, and see you soon!"

She sent another text behind the first one that said, "That sounded so weird to say. I still don't understand why we all had to travel to strange places to access the jump points! Why couldn't we have just jumped altogether?"

Freya responded with a voice recording, "Exactly!! I asked Todd and Christopher that very question, and they indicated that it has to do with a vibrational match. The Strategist worked with the Inner Earth beings to find the doorways into the inner realms, for each of our energetic signatures. It sounds weird to me too, but hey, we get a free trip out of it, so we can't complain! See you in a few! Fingers crossed that we all find the triangles and meet in the inner realm! Love you, Juel!! Bye for now!"

Juel sent a thumbs up, and vibrating heart emoji in response. They brought one another comfort even when they were miles apart.

Juel looked for Ford in the sea of people waiting in the restroom line at the airport. She saw him exit the bathroom and head her way. She stood up and grabbed the bags and handed Ford his backpack as he approached her.

"Okay... let's go find our driver!" Ford winked at Juel, and the two strolled towards the airport exit. They located their driver by the sign he was holding up. It read, Casselman and Ryland, in large bold print.

Ford and Juel were swiftly escorted to their hotel. That night the two enjoyed a meal in the rotating restaurant at the top of the hotel. Juel looked out the window as they waited to be seated and said, "I have never had dinner in a restaurant with a 360-degree view of the city. This is so exciting!!"

She then turned to him, completely changing the subject, "I can't wait to go to the pyramids tomorrow!!! Ford chuckled and was enjoying Juel's love of simple pleasures.

The wait staff showed them to their table, and as Juel pulled her seat in, she remembered her conversation with Freya. "Oh!!! By the way, I heard from Freya. She made it to Scotland just fine and was already at the Findhorn Ecovillage." Juel grabbed a piece of bread and buttered it quickly as Ford was checking his phone for messages.

Ford said, "That is good to hear!" He then looked at his phone again to recheck messages. "Hmmm. Ursula has not texted. I sent her a text when we landed." He took a deep breath and exhaled, then laid the phone on the table.

Juel said, "I am sure that she is fine. Did you try Koko?"

"No. I will wait a little bit longer then try him after dinner." Ford smiled then grabbed a roll.

Juel said, "Remember those Guardians we are supposed to have? I am sure that they are watching over Ursula and Koko right now. She is probably still in transit anyway." She took another bite of her bread and started to look around the room.

Ford said, "What are you looking at?"

Juel's eyes were childlike, and with a mischievous grin, she said, "I guess we should be on the lookout for our Guardians too?" She shrugged her shoulders and pointed to a slender man that was seated two tables away.

"He could be one for all we know!" She pointed in the man's direction again as Ford casually turned his head to see who Juel was referring too.

The man looked his way and nodded. A few moments later, a waiter walked by the gentleman's table, thinking he nodded for assistance. The gentleman spoke with the waiter, pointing to the piano that sat in the corner of the room. As the waiter walked away, he went over to lift the lid of the keyboard, exposing the keys. The waiter wiped down the seat and the keys and then motioned for the gentleman to enjoy the use of the piano.

Ford and Juel were served their soup and salad and ate their evening meal listening to the musical selection of the stranger. The music in the dining room and the view of the city made their first night in Sarajevo unforgettable. At the end of the meal, they shared a small piece of sugar-free pie, their first dessert in months.

After dinner, they synced their wristbands before they went to their rooms that night and made plans to meet in the lobby at eight a.m.

As Ford walked to his room, he could feel the pyramid's energy pulsing. He was as anxious as Juel to explore the pyramids, but he was distracted by Ursula's radio silence.

As Ford was settling into his room, his phone rang. It was Ashneer calling. Ford said, "Hello? Koko?

Ashneer responded, "Ford! Yes! How are you???"

Ford quickly relayed that he was well and asked, "How is Ursula? I haven't heard from her."

"Hmm. She is having a migraine. So she is not so good at the moment. She asked me to call you to tell you that she will be fine. She felt that the energy here is off the wall intense, her words, not mine!"

Ashneer laughed and then continued with the message. "She took some migraine medicine and went to bed. She also said that she was sorry that she was not able to wait for you to arrive in Bosnia, but she just couldn't stay up."

Ford moaned in disappointment. He missed his wife already, and he hated not being with her while she was having a migraine. "That's okay. I wish I could be there to help her. Her migraines can last for days. Make sure she has plenty of water, will ya?"

Ashneer replied, "Sure thing. I will leave some water bottles by her door. No problem, man. And if she is not well tomorrow, I will go out on my own and do some looking around."

Ford thanked Ashneer for the call and climbed into bed. He texted Ursula one more time, "I know you are sleeping but know that I am in Bosnia and thinking of you. Hopefully, we will be reunited soon, but in the meantime, sweet dreams, my love."

Ford knew Ursula well. She was nervous. Anytime Ursula had anxiety about something, it would typically manifest as a migraine, to shut down her system while she came to terms with whatever was causing her stress. Usually, it was a major life decision. Ford knew that she was struggling.

He set the alarm on his phone for seven am and placed the phone on the nightstand. He immediately went into a vivid dream state. There he found Ursula in a closet, screaming for help. It was locked, and she was having a hard time breathing. Ford opened the closet door, picking her up from the floor. He dried her tears and held her and said, "Shhh, I am here. You are okay. We are going to do this together."

Ford woke up, startled by the dream. He sat in the dark, trying to clear his energy. He looked at his phone and saw that he had missed a call from Ursula. She sent her love and said that her migraine was easing up, but she was going to try to get more sleep. Ford texted her a heart emoji and said that he would check on her in the morning. He placed his phone on the nightstand and drifted back to sleep.

Back in California, Alvie was preparing for her jump in a few days. Butler had left temporarily to attend the Guardian meeting. When he returned, he had Saso with him unbeknownst to Alvie. Saso stayed out of sight to keep Alvie calm. Alvie spoke with Butler of her fears. Butler assured her that he would not only guard over her but that there were many unseen helpers to make sure that her animals would be safe while she was away.

Saso read Alvie's energy field as she moved around the room and could see that she was not concerned about the animals. It was something deeper. She was not confident in her abilities and was wondering if it was all too much. Alvie was not sure if she could commit to something she may not be able to fulfill.

The days were long. Each Life Bearer would be tested, stretched to their limits, as they not only looked for the jump points but let go of all of their attachments to the life that they each had lived up to this point.

The following days were spent reevaluating each of their commitments, as well as their talents. They called one another to check in from time to time for moral support, and in the end, they were all still present and accounted for.

And the wheel turns...

Chapter 93

Jump Day for the Rest of the Life Bearers

The Leonid meteor showers were on full display. Shamalaine received intel on each of the Life Bearers, as well as monitoring the capture of Chrysaor. He was held in a secure cell at the midway station until someone from the Alliance could intercept him.

Shamalaine sent word to Bewain to meet her at the Great Hall. The plan was now fully activated. Electra Fox was being monitored now, and from all reports, she and her cohorts were furious when they found out that Chrysaor's plan to stop the Life Bearers had not succeeded.

Shamalaine, in her wisdom, knew that this was just the beginning, and now more than ever, it was vital for the Guardians to stay alert.

In Romania, Benjamin and his team had already set out to explore Cioclovina cave. The plan was to camp out over night, at least that is what Silviu thought. They walked quickly up the trail alongside the creek. At one point, they crossed the creek bed by jumping onto logs that were lying in the stream.

Once across, the team again moved quickly, being careful in the steep areas where the brown fall leaves littered the forest floor, making the terrain slippery. It was a strenuous hike but exhilarating, knowing that they were close.

Finally, the cave came into view. The team climbed more rocks to get up to the entrance. They stopped outside of the cave for a few minutes for a break. Everyone drank water and took in the beauty of the environment. The waterfall and the sounds of nature were captivating.

Silviu put on his helmet and instructed the others to do the same. He told them that he would enter the cave first to check it out for safety precautions and would be back to get them in five minutes. He quickly entered the cave and was out of sight when Benjamin turned to Amazonia and Esmond and lifted his wrist upwards. "My band is pinging already!" he said with a wild-eyed smile.

Esmond responded, "Yes. I can feel the energy here is strong. Energetically, the power source seems to be coming from deep inside the cave, but that does not mean that the portal will be there. We must look around the perimeter as well. I will stand watch and look around here."

Benjamin nodded then asked, "Won't Silviu be suspicious if you don't go inside the cave? You have hiked all of this way."

Esmond replied, "I will tell him that I feel light-headed and not up to the exploration. I will tell him that I need to eat something. That should convince him."

Amazonia agreed and began to look around. She added, "This entire region has great power. Many untold secrets lay below our feet."

At that moment, a sound came from the area just beyond where they had climbed. Esmond's keen hearing could make out footsteps of many people coming their way.

Amazonia grabbed Benjamin and yelled out to Esmond, "Intruders!" She could see them coming up the creek bed. She literally picked up Benjamin and, in three large bounds, entered the cave, where Silviu was coming to retrieve them. Amazonia put Benjamin down as Silviu was coming towards them.

Silviu smiled, "Ah, I was just coming to get you. Where is Esmond?"

Amazonia pushed both of them away from the entrance and said, "He needs to sit this one out. Let us make haste as the day is getting away from us."

Silviu nodded his head, "Yes. It is quite strenuous just to make it to the cave much less explore it. I will take you in for a little while, as it will be dark soon, and then we can come back again in the morning after a good breakfast. He motioned for them to put on their helmets and follow him, as he began the tour of the cave, happy to see Amazonia's positive attitude and can-do spirit.

Benjamin kept looking behind his shoulder at Amazonia, trying to detect if anyone was following them through the entrance. That is when he heard a strange sound. Suddenly bats by the hundreds began flying overhead towards the exit of the cave. Esmond had used his sonar abilities to call them forth, creating a distraction.

Amazonia grabbed Benjamin and Silviu and pulled them to the ground, covering them with her body. It took at least a minute for all of the bats to vacate the cave. When Silviu stood up, he was shocked by what just took place. Amazonia and Benjamin could both see from their vantage point that a portal was beginning to activate right behind Silviu.

He was leaning down dusting himself off, thanking Amazonia for her assistance when she reached over as if to help Silviu dust off his shoulder, but rather, she pinched his neck, Vulcan style, and grabbed him as he passed out.

The walls of the cave began to disappear. Standing within a portal was an extremely tall male being. It appeared to be a Wizard, staring at Benjamin through the veil.

Amazonia said to Benjamin, "He is a Solomonari. A magical being of great power."

The Solomonari was wearing a light grey robe with three concentric triangles glowing upon his chest. He stood, waiting for Benjamin.

"Quickly! You must go now. I will deal with Silviu. He will be fine and won't remember this. I will make sure of it. Go now!!"

At that moment, Esmond caught up with them. "All is secure!" He noticed the Solomonari standing on the other side of the veil. He said, "Better not keep him waiting! Safe journey, Master Benjamin. It has been an honor to be at your service!"

Benjamin thanked them while he pulled out his striking stone and pendant from his pocket. He unwrapped the pendant, and with the word Etifah clearly in his mind, he struck the pendant and stepped into the wavy area of the cave. The Solomonari took his hand, and they were gone.

Ford and Juel had spent the last few days gearing up for the main event. They had already explored the Ravne tunnels in the days leading up to the jump, and both of their wristbands pinged when in a specific area of the underground tunnel.

With their things now stored in the safe at the hotel, Ford and Juel were now prepared, with their striking stones in their pocket, to make their way to the Ravne tunnels. Outside of the hotel, they caught the tour bus and headed back to the nature park, where the Pyramid of the Sun stood tall atop the underground tunnel system.

Eldorman and Aife, being cloaked, were able to enter the tour bus, sitting in the back to monitor all of the humans on board. They were on full alert after hearing the news of Chrysaor's capture.

They were close enough to Ford and Juel to hear them talking about the Leonid meteor showers and acknowledging that they realized that the last time Life Bearers attempted this, it did not end well.

Juel said a prayer right then, to honor the past Life Bearers and to ask for divine guidance and protection. Once she completed the prayer, she felt something shift.

"Hmm. Did you feel that?" She looked at Ford as she showed him her arm. "My arm hair is standing up."

"What is it? What do you feel?" Ford had a concerned look on his face.

"I feel like we are being watched!" Juel twisted her head backward in a quick motion, in the hopes of catching whoever was watching them before they could disappear.

Eldorman smiled as he and Aife sat perfectly still, watching the humorous humans. He was already quite taken with Miss Bridgit, and now he was pleased to watch over another lovely young lady and her male counterpart.

After a thirty-minute ride, the bus turned off the main street onto a very narrow and bumpy road. It passed by an area of parked cars and continued toward the parking lot closer to the base of the pyramid.

Ford turned to Juel, "Did you see those men!?" He pointed behind them. Juel looked back to see who he was referring too. Several men wearing dark glasses and black gloves had been leaning against their cars and were now running towards the bus.

At that moment, Aife and Eldorman jumped up, still cloaked, and ran to the front of the bus. As the bus stopped, the door opened for people to get off. Aife did an enchantment to daze the people, keeping them frozen in their seats, while Eldorman created an invisible force field around it, hiding them from view.

The men turned around, looking in all directions, dumbfounded by what just occurred. Eldorman did another incantation to suggest that the men leave the location. He exited the bus and watched them shake their heads, get into their cars, and go.

Eldorman gave the signal that it was clear. Aife released the humans from her enchantment.

Still looking out the window, Ford said, "That's funny! They are gone! Where did they go?"

He grabbed his backpack and said, "Let's stay close. Something isn't right."

As he exited the bus, he turned back to Juel and said, "I just hope that our Guardians are here already." As he stepped off the bus, he walked right by Aife and Eldorman.

Juel walked by the Guardians as well, looking back behind her as she passed them, almost as if she could see them. She knew they were there but couldn't prove it, so she just nodded and followed Ford to the entrance of the Ravne Tunnel.

They bought a ticket for the tunnel tour and picked out their head-gear, a large, yellow helmet to keep their heads safe in the tunnels. As they prepared to enter the tunnel, the guide shared that the ceilings were somewhat low in some places, but in due time, they would be able to stand up straight and walk at a normal pace.

Soon enough, the tour guide brought them into an area that had seating around a large ceramic stone with etchings.

Juel said to Ford, "This is the kind of stone that I was telling the group about!"

The tour guide then shared that these stones were made of a kind of concrete, encasing crystals within them. They were intentionally placed on the ley line areas that were generating negative energy.

He went on to say that these ceramic stones transformed the energy into positive healing energy, due to crystals inside the rock. The guide spoke about how the organic materials used in the rocks were over thirty thousand years old, and that the underground tunnel system was proof of the oldest underground engineering complex in the Balkans, as referenced in the pamphlet that he had handed out to each of the people in the tour party.

After the group had ample time to feel the healing energy, the tour guide suggested that they move on. This was the area where their wristbands had pinged the day before, but they had yet to find the triple triangles. Ford acknowledged to Juel that their wristbands were once more pinging. It was time to make a move.

Ford told the tour guide that they were very familiar with the tunnel system and that they wanted to stay behind to meditate in the area and that they would catch the next tour group. The guide was familiar with the two of them as they had been there the last several days, so he nodded but told them that it would be the last tour so be sure to leave..

They had at least fifteen minutes before the next group was to come through there, which wasn't much time to find the triangles. Their wristbands were beeping at a faster pace, so they knew they were close.

While they explored the area, they were still unaware of Aife and Eldorman's presence. The Guardians could not risk being seen with so many humans around, so they stayed cloaked. Eldorman knew the triangular puck marks location, as he could clearly see its vibrational imprint, but he had to bring it to the Life Bearer's attention somehow. He picked up a rock and began tapping on the wall next to the triangular puck marks, which were on an inner wall of a small alcove nearby.

Juel turned to Ford, "Did you hear that?"

Ford responded by walking close to the area where Eldorman was tapping the rock. Eldorman then said an incantation, to light up the triangular carving that was now beginning to glow.

Ford said, "JUEL!!! Over here! Look!" A vibrant blue color emanated from the alcove with the triple triangles clearly seen.

"That's it!" screamed Juel, excited, and equally surprised.

Ford looked at his watch and said, "Quick! Grab your pendant! The window for the meteors just started!"

The two had their pendants in hand when they heard the sounds of the next group coming towards them. It sounded like someone was running in their direction. They struck their pendants at the same time and silently spoke the word Etifah in their minds as the resonance of the stone pendant activated the alcove, and a doorway appeared. At that moment, Juel grabbed Ford's hand and said, "Here we go!"

They walked hand in hand through the doorway. As the portal was closing, a hand reached in, attempting to grab the Life Bearers back into the tunnel, but it was yanked away immediately, as Eldorman and Aife pulled the perpetrator away from the portal.

Juel and Ford could hear a scream echoing as the portal closed. Together, Aife and Eldorman bilocated with the intruder, back to the fourth dimension, where they would hand over the intruder to the Alliance.

Ursula was thinking of Ford around the same time of his entry into the void. He felt far away to her, and by her time table, she knew that he could very well have already made it through the portal, as he was not answering his phone. She was relieved that he did not respond. Had he answered, it would mean that something had gone wrong.

She grabbed her jacket and bags and met Ashneer downstairs in the hotel lobby. The plan was to take their things to a storage unit just a few blocks from their hotel. They arranged with the manager of the storage facility to hold onto their key, as they would be traveling and did not want to lose it during their journey. The manager was happy to do that for a small fee, which Ashneer happily paid.

They left the storage unit and headed to the Kilauea Caldera, by way of a hired car. Ursula was carrying with her a small jar and asked the driver to make a stop by the water's edge. She wanted to gather water as an offering to Pele, the Goddess of Fire, as she and Ashneer were the Life Bearers representing the water element. Ashneer thought that it was a great idea and wanted to offer a blessing over it before they offered it to Pele.

The day before, Ashneer scouted out Kilauea, while Ursula was recovering from her migraine. He had already walked the entire trail, and as he was midway into the hike, his wristband pinged. He searched the area until he found a small alcove that was well hidden from the trail. He scoured the area, and on a rock wall, he found it. Three stacked triangles carved into the stone of a rock wall.

Now that Ashneer and Ursula were together at the trailhead of Kilauea Iki crater, Ashneer was anxious to bring Ursula to the location of the triple triangles, but he could feel Ursula was not present, at the moment.

As they walked through a lush grove, he tried to engage her in conversation, but she was in a trance, it seemed. Then out of nowhere, they came upon a Hawaiian gentleman wearing a colorful shirt. He had noticeably unusual circular tattoos upon his face.

Ursula stopped in her tracks. She had been in deep meditation since they started the walk. She snapped out of the trance when she saw the man standing in the grove of trees. She had seen him in her mind's eye, about five minutes before they came upon him on the trail.

The man stepped out onto the path and said, "I am Ali' Ikoa. I am your Guardian. Eferhild is waiting further down the path." The Guardian pointed in the direction towards the caldera.

Ashneer and Ursula greeted him with a respectful bow. Ursula said, "I felt you moments before I saw you. We bring a gift to Pele as representatives of water." She held the jar of water in her hand, which had sand and a shell floating at the bottom of the jar.

Ali' Ikoa said, "Very good. It is important to give gratitude to Pele. The gift of water is a great blessing. Let us take a moment to silently set our intentions for a peaceful and blessed walk to your journey's end. Let us ask for the protection of Pele as we walk the path."

After a few moments, Ali' Ikoa said, "We must walk in silence from this point on. Be alert and respectful."

They walked one by one until they reached the area that Ashneer had found the day before. Eferhild stood on alert. She picked up on some movement with her keen eyesight and told the Life Bearers to hide behind a rock outcropping until they could check out the energy signatures that were coming their way.

Eferhild spoke in unusual terms. She stood in a power stance as Ursula took in her appearance from behind the rock. Eferhild carried bear medicine, Ursula surmised. Ursula guessed that she had heightened vision and sense of smell and could tell when an intruder was in the midst. She watched as Eferhild monitored the landscape and moved methodically.

Suddenly a horn was sounded, and Ali' Ikoa ran towards Ursula and Ashneer, chanting an invocation. The rock outcropping next to the Life Bearers morphed and a multitude of Menehune, little gnome-like beings, appeared and created a dome of protection around Ashneer and Ursula. The dome was like an invisible rock, one that they could see out of, but no one on the outside could see in.

As Ashneer and Ursula sat huddled together in each other's arms, Ursula watched as the Menehune held the force field around them. Outside of the domed rock, strange beings, not of Earth origin, were scouring the area for signs of the Life Bearers.

Eferhild and Ali' Ikoa threw a net over the intruders. A net of such strength that the intruders could not move. Eferhild secured the net and told Ali' Ikoa to take the Life Bearers on to the portal. "It is time." She looked up to the sky as the day was turning into dusk.

The Menehune released their magic and scampered back into the rock formation, as quickly as they had arrived.

Ali' Ikoa asked, "Are you okay?"

Ashneer looked at Ursula, who was shaking her head, yes, and he replied, "I think we're okay." He laughed a nervous laugh as he helped Ursula to her feet dumbfound by the experience.

They followed Ali' Ikoa to the appointed place where Ashneer had located the triangular puck marks. By the time they reached it, they saw the first shooting star in the sky.

They waited at the site until the appointed time, and then they heard the whirling sounds. Ashneer and Ursula opened the jar of water and poured it in front of them. They placed the sand and shell on a small rock shelf to the left of their feet and handed the jar to Ali' Ikoa.

He held it upward and spoke in his native tongue as the Life Bearers watched the portal vibrating. The two Life Bearers lifted their pendants from their neck and struck them with their striking stones, all the while staring into one another's eyes with the word Etifah in their mind. Wavy energy appeared, and they entered the portal with grace and ease.

Ali' Ikoa said words of praise and gratitude as he watched the doorway close. He then joined Eferhild. "We must take these clones to Commander Bewain." With that, they bilocated with the apprehended intruders for the Alliance to handle.

Around the same time, Alvie was watching the meteor shower, still hesitant to jump. Saso and Butler were with her, though Saso had continued to stay out of Alvie's view. Saso was intuitive, and knew that Alvie was deeply sensitive. It was good that Alvie had time to acclimate to Butler and felt somewhat of a kindred spirit with him.

Alvie asked about the other Guardian, and Butler commented that she checked in from time to time, giving her a wink.

They walked towards the Alligator tree that evening in reverence. Alvie would ask a question of Butler, like how it would feel going through a portal, or did he feel that she had given him enough instructions to care for the animals. Butler laughed and told her that all was very well understood, and portal jumping was as easy as walking through her own front door. This eased Alvie's mind considerably.

They soon came upon the very tree that had laid there on the property for some time. The one that gave her the poison oak months ago, but now had been cleaned up and made into a small oasis thanks to Butler.

Butler had built a stone bench near the tree and planted flowers that had already bloomed.

Alvie sat on the bench, then burst into tears. "This is it! The moment that I came to Earth for and the very moment that I have been dreading since I said yes to this mission!" She buried her face in her hands and sobbed uncontrollably.

Saso appeared from behind the tree and said, "Dry your eyes, my Lady. It is the time of the great awakening. Let your tears drain the last of your sorrow and stand tall. You are a Shining One. Everyone who knows you from the inner realms knows that you are one who keeps your word, and your skills are unmatched." Saso bowed her head temporarily, giving Alvie a moment to process that she had arrived. She then introduced herself, "I am Saso, at your service."

Alvie wiped her eyes. In between where Saso stood and where she sat, a viewing screen appeared, hovering over the alligator tree. In the scenes that played out, it showed Alvie on many planetary systems where she acted as a Life Bearer, always focused on the animals. She was shown many successes and some failures, but still, victories came after each defeat.

Then Saso said, "You see, your inner fear is that you will fail. We are here to tell you that you have learned from your mishaps, and you are a unique being in that your soul's presence will not let you fail any longer. You have passed all the tests. It was your failures that led to your highest achievements. You have graduated from every level. This, what you are being asked to do, is like, as they say in this realm, kindergarten. Be happy this day to be of service, my lady. We have been waiting for you."

As she said those words slowly and rhythmically, the screen closed, and the portal began to activate. At that same time, horses could be heard coming in their direction. It was a full herd, and from the feel of it, the timing was just too coincidental.

Butler stood tall and put his fingers to his mouth to call Pretty Girl. Pretty Girl galloped up immediately. He jumped on her back and looked back towards Saso and said, "Get her through the gate now!"

Alvie ran towards Saso as Saso lifted her arm and made a particular movement with her hand, telekinetically lifting the mouth of the tree open. Saso blew powder into the tree, making the invisible visible. There, inside the mouth of the tree were three carved triangles stacked one upon another. The energetic frequency of the triangles activated.

The triangles began to glow. Alvie instinctually grabbed her stone pendant and striking stone, hitting one upon the other. At that moment, wavy energy came into view. A doorway opened. Saso escorted Alvie closer to the Portal.

"Be brave, Miss Alvie. You have achieved miracle after miracle. Why should you do any less than what you have already done in the past?"

She smiled and guided Alvie further towards the doorway.

Alvie asked, "Is Butler going to be okay? What about my staff and the animals?" Alvie was torn but knew that the Guardians could handle it.

Saso bowed her head and said, "We will do our job, please... do yours."

Alvie turned around, held her head up high, and in her mind, she spoke the word Etifah over and over. She walked through the portal as easy as walking through the door of her home.

Todd was monitoring the wristbands of each Life Bearer that had made it through the portals. So far, he had Bridgit, Traci, Benjamin, Ashneer, Ursula, Ford, Juel, and Alvie's wristbands now off the grid. All that was left was Freya, Christopher, David, Henny, and his daughter, Stella.

Freya was sleeping in the early morning of November 17th. She was having a dream about the portal. In the dream, a deer was walking in the Findhorn village and then began to walk down the road past the stop sign that read STOP worrying.

In the dream, she watched as an observer and knew that all was well. Suddenly, the deer came to a magical tree on the property where her friend Marva lived. Marva shared a home with two other staff workers with a beautiful shared garden between several neighboring houses.

In the dream, the deer entered the garden and was grazing near a magical tree. Freya could see that at the base of the tree, on its roots, was a triple triangle symbol that was vibrationally humming in a whispered tone. The triangles lit up in a vibrant green color, and when the deer looked up, it had vibrant green grass in its mouth. The deer had somehow eaten from the other side of the veil.

Suddenly, Freya woke with a start. She jumped up and wrote in her journal the details of the deer in the garden and of the magical tree. She showered and walked downstairs to eat breakfast. She sat in the hotel dining room, having some tea with a small breakfast plate of fruit and avocado toast, digesting the meal along with the dream.

She watched the clock on her phone and then paid her final bill and checked out of the hotel.

Freya grabbed a ride to the Findhorn Village, where she was to meet Marva at her home. She had made arrangements with Marva to store her things while she was allegedly away on a retreat.

The taxi dropped her off directly in front of Marva's home. Freya was anxious with anticipation to see Marva and, more importantly, to check out her back garden. Hearing the door chime, Marva opened the door with a piece of toast in her mouth and curlers in her hair. "Come in! Come in! Quickly now! Nice to see you, dear."

She scooted Freya inside the door before her beloved cat could escape.

"Mrs. Triangles cannot go outside. She is a little Houdini! She comes up missing all too often, so I'd rather her not go out this morning if there is no one to watch her. If you go out in the garden, she can go out with you as long as you keep an eye on her. Otherwise, the little minx will disappear on me again!" Marva walked into the kitchen and threw her toast on a plate. Freya followed.

"Excuse me but, what is your cat's name? I couldn't quite make it out with the toast in your mouth. Did you call her Mrs. Triangles?" Freya inquired desperately.

Marva shook her head, yes. "Sorry about that! I do apologize for speaking with food in my mouth. Forgive me. I am running late for a meeting. Yes. Her name is Mrs. Triangles. She is a Tonkinese. A few neighbors and my household share her. A true lady she is, but one that likes to stay out for days at a time without any warning."

Marva leaned down towards Mrs. Triangles, pointing at her with her finger.

"A few moons back, an elderly man in our community had to relinquish her, as he was showing signs of Alzheimer's. He kept going on about triangles and portals and his magical cat!! Of course, he is the one who named her Mrs. Triangles!"

She laughed and continued as Freya just shook her head in amazement of what she was hearing, especially in light of her dream.

Marva spoke in riddles, "Do I believe in portals? You bet I do! But some of the things that the man went on about made his family and doctors think that he was an absolute loon! Poor chap."

Marva leaned down to get a few kisses from Mrs. Triangles and then said, "The man left her with our group to look after her, as his family took him to live with them in Edinburgh, and they couldn't accommodate the cat. It does take a village to keep up with her, though!"

Marva began removing her hair curlers in the powder room nearby and yelled out, "Do make yourself comfortable. When I get back, later this afternoon, we can share a meal with a few of the neighbors. I want to give you a good send-off before you leave on your retreat!" She yelled out as she threw her jacket on over her sweater and fluffed her hair once more.

Puffs of hairspray formed a cloud over her head as Marva put the finishing touches on her hairdo.

She came back into the kitchen, whirling around. "How do I look? Presentable? I will be recording a video today. That is why I did my hair in curls." She winked and hugged Freya.

The smell of amber mixed with hairspray wafted near Freya's nose as she hugged Marva. It reminded her of the first day they met. The scent of amber drew her into conversation with Marva, and that was how their friendship grew. Nature provides so much. She contemplated their relationship as she watched Marva's whirlwind parade around the home.

Marva grabbed some food from the fridge and was out the door. She poked her head back through the doorway and said one last thing, "Food is in the fridge! Help yourself and do keep an eye on Mrs. Triangles. If you take her outside, make sure to use those treats on the kitchen table to entice her back inside."

Freya was still in the kitchen and shook the bag of organic cat treats and said, "Got it! See you later. Have a great meeting."

Marva was out the door once more.

Freya stood at the kitchen sink, looking out the window to catch her breath. She then moved her bags from the foyer to the backroom, off of the kitchen. Marva had said that she would find the appropriate place to store her things later once she returned that evening from work.

Freya then found a piece of paper and wrote a note to Marva to explain her absence, which read:

"Dear Marva,

Thank you for allowing me to hang out at your home for the day. Unfortunately, I misread my itinerary, and my car is coming to pick me up much earlier than I had originally told you. I will most likely be gone by the time you arrive back home. I will be out of touch for a little while, but when I return, I look forward to catching up with you and Mrs. Triangles! She sure is magic! See you soon! Freya"

Freya placed the note on the table near Marva's plate of half-eaten toast. She picked up the other piece and slathered jam on it. She thought in her mind, just a little bit of jam couldn't hurt. She ate it with delight, then washed her hands.

She turned off her phone and placed it in her purse. She then put her purse inside her luggage. Now, all that was left was to find that magical tree. She kept repeating the mantra "Stop Worrying" over and over as she had yet to find the triple triangles, being that she was just one Life Bearer and had no help, save for a call from Todd on occasion for moral support.

Freya absentmindedly opened the back door from the kitchen, with the tree on her mind. As soon as she opened the door, Mrs. Triangles zipped past her legs in a mad dash.

Freya yelled out for her, but the cat did not stop. Freya shut the door behind her and ran towards the cat. The cat went straight to a large tree in the back garden. Just as Freya got close to the tree, her wristband began to ping.

Mrs. Triangles flopped down at the base of a tree that resembled the magical tree where the deer in Freya's dream was eating the grass.

Freya came up to Mrs. Triangles and sat down on the ground, at the base of the tree, to pet the cat and search for clues. She felt the roots for signs of puck marks, and suddenly the cat transfigured into an Elven Warrior with a battle sword and armor.

Freya jumped up quickly in absolute panic as the warrior made a purring sound while touching the tree. The tree shook as triangles began to light up, superimposed over the tree, like an etheric blanket. The warrior stood up and unfurled her green cloak that was hanging from her neck, on her back. The print on her cape had triangle shapes all over it, and in particular, the concentric triple triangles.

The Elven Warrior said, "I am sorry to have scared you, Miss Freya. I am your Guardian, Hotaru. I have been waiting for you for some time now. The portal window has opened." Her black hair was now flowing over her shoulders, and her sheer wings pointed out from her cloak.

Hotaru pointed to something above Freya's head. Sitting, perched in the tree, high up on a sturdy branch was the other Guardian, Randelf. He stood on the branch, as if he were a professional gymnast. He dismounted the tree, landing on the ground in front of Freya.

"Randelf, at your service, my Lady." He took Freya's hand and kissed it, but Freya could not feel much of a kiss. It felt to her like a tickle as Randelf was more etheric than physical. Freya stood there in absolute delight.

She finally realized that she was gawking and had not said a word. "Oh, forgive me! It is nice to meet you. Finally!!! I am so glad to be in your presence."

Hotaru's wings began to glow, and she looked at the tree. The triangles were now solidifying, and the activation of the portal was occurring.

Randelf watched as Hotaru took Freya's hand and guided her towards the tree. "Miss, the time has come to send you through the portal. Do you have your stone necklace?"

Freya yelled out loud, "My necklace! Damn it! Oh Gosh! I am so sorry. I didn't mean to say that! Darn it!!!! I left it in my purse inside the house! I will have to run get it."

Randelf bowed to her and said, "Let me escort you. We must be swift now." He linked arms with Freya, and they were off in a flash. She was at the kitchen door in seconds, a little out of breath, but exhilarated.

"I won't be a minute. It is just in my bags over there." She pointed to the area where she had set her bags. Freya looked at her luggage and realized that they had been opened, and the contents were strewn about the floor. "Oh, no!"

Randelf immediately launched into the front room and out the front door.

Hotaru came into the kitchen with her sword drawn. Freya couldn't find her striking stone and pendant anywhere. "Who could have taken it so quickly?!"

Hotaru told her to stay put as she looked in the front for signs of an intruder with Randelf. As Hotaru stood at the front door, she heard a noise in the room upstairs. Hotaru was gone in a flash, leaving traces of light like a firefly in her wake.

Freya hid in the closet under the stairway as soon as she heard Hotaru's sword striking another sword. Randelf reappeared and came to Hotaru's aid, just as she finished tying up the assailant, a half-pig half-man, but was a youth sent to do a warrior's job. He was no match for Hotaru.

As Hotaru escorted the assailant downstairs, she looked at Randelf and said, "Take him to the Alliance. I will see to it that Freya enters the portal. Take him now!" She pushed the assailant the rest of the way down the stairs. As soon as Randelf touched him, they were gone.

Freya stood quivering in the closet holding her breathe, saying every prayer she knew. The closet door flew open, and Hotaru stood there holding Freya's stone pendant.

"Now, where were we? Ready to meet your destiny?" Hotaru held the closet door open for Freya to emerge. Freya was shaking and needed comfort.

Hotaru offered her hand and said, "Your prayers were answered. Let us go now to the tree of everlasting potential. It is waiting for you to enter the portal."

Freya wiped her eyes and breathed in deeply. "Well, when you say it like that who can resist a tree of everlasting potential?"

She half laughed to calm herself down as her nerves were shot. She rubbed her hands on her thighs to get the feeling back in them as she had held her hands so tightly in prayer that the lack of circulation made them numb. It also helped her move energy into her legs. She slowly ventured away from the closet and followed Hotaru.

As they were walking to the tree, Freya asked, "I don't mean to be unappreciative of what you did for me, but could I ask a favor of you when I leave?" She looked at Hotaru with a look of shame.

Hotaru nodded and said," Of course, I am at your service, my Lady."

Freya said, "It is a bit embarrassing to ask this of you, as you are a highly respected Guardian, but, since you have been living with Marva for some time now, I was hoping that you could tidy up whatever crashed upstairs and make sure my luggage is put back together in an orderly fashion. I would hate for her to think that I trashed her home before leaving on my retreat. Marva is a good friend." Freya was embarrassed for asking, but it was a last-minute 3D thing that needed attention before she left.

Hotaru smiled and said, "Consider it done. Miss Marva has been very good to me while I prepared for you. I shall see to it that everything is repaired and put right again."

They were now coming near the tree, and standing next to it was a large dog with a green collar. Dangling from the collar was a round, golden disk with three triple triangles upon it.

Hotaru said, "When you strike your pendant, let the vibration activate the portal further. In your mind, remember to say the word

Etifah."

The wavy energy activated, indicating the portal was open. The dog stood near the threshold of the portal as Freya struck the pendant with the striking stone. Freya thought the words Etifah in her mind as she entered the void.

Back in Haifa, Stella, David, and Henny had searched the immediate areas around the Stella Maris Lighthouse, the Carmelite Monastery, as well as the area around the Cave of Elijah. None of their wristbands pinged, which meant that they were not in the vicinity of the anomaly.

Stella called her father, Todd, to get some suggestions. "I don't get it! We walked all over the grounds of the monastery and the lighthouse, and nothing happened." She was frustrated as they were running out of time. "We went to Elijah's cave... and nothing!"

Todd said, "Look, pumpkin, you are close. Don't get anxious now. What I suggest is that the three of you separate to cover more ground. Extend the search 2 miles out, then reconvene when one of you gets a ping."

"Okay, I guess we can do that. Thanks for the advice. I will keep in touch." Stella put her phone away and looked at David and Henny, who had been sitting next to her on a bench with a view of the port.

"Dad says to split up to cover more ground. I guess I will head out that way, towards the Maritime Museum, and you guys spread out from here. Keep your phones on, and let me know as soon as you find something."

David stood up, looking at the map on his phone for clues. He informed the group that he would head to the left for a mile or two, and motioned for Henny to take the other direction, away from the port. David and Henny said goodbye and began their investigations on foot.

Stella used her rideshare app to have a car take her the few miles down the road to the National Maritime Museum. It was not that far as the crow flies, but to get there, one had to backtrack a mile or two.

She had an intuitive feeling about the place when she read an article about the museum's permanent anchor exhibit. Her car arrived, and she set off to see if her hunch was correct. Anchors, Sea Fearers, it was too obvious, she thought.

When the car pulled up at the Museum, she stepped out onto the sidewalk and looked back towards the Stella Maris Lighthouse. When the car drove off, she heard a beeping sound. "What is that noise?" She looked down at her phone and then suddenly realized that her wristband was pinging. "I knew it!!"

She called David's phone first, but no answer. She left him a voice-mail to meet her at the National Maritime Museum. Then she called Henny.

He answered, "Hello! Did you find it?" Henny was out of breath as he was hiking up a hill, hoping that his hunch would pay off, and the anomaly would be in some obscure place that was off the beaten path.

"Well, no, not yet, but my wristband is pinging, so that means we are closer! Get down here as fast as you can. I left David a message, and hopefully, he will arrive soon. In the meantime, I will take a look around."

Henny reminded her to be safe. "Watch your surroundings, Stella. I will be there in a jiffy!"

"Okay. Thanks, Henny." Stella's call-waiting was beeping. It was Todd.

"Hey, Dad! I guess you saw my wristband go off?" She was proud of herself for going on her hunch.

"Yes, Pumpkin! Great job. From what I can tell, you are actually in close range. When the band beeps quicker, you will know where it is. Are the guys on their way?" Todd quizzed.

"I left a message for David, and Henny is on his way." She looked around as she was speaking, trying to stay aware of her surroundings. "Okay, Dad. I will call you back when we find it. Love you!"

"Listen... it's late here, and I need to get some shut-eye. Leave me a text when you find it. I will set my alarm for four hours from now. I just need to get enough sleep to function. Be safe, Stella... and Pumpkin... I am really proud of you. Love you, honey."

Todd hung up the phone after Stella agreed to be safe, wishing he could be there with her. He knew that the others had issues before their jump but didn't want to alarm her and make her nervous. It was all in the hands of Osman and PharaEtti now. They were the ones charged with keeping them safe. He had some comfort in knowing that they were present with her, and so far, the other Guardians did their job perfectly.

David looked at his phone and saw that Stella had tried to call. He checked his messages and was excited to hear that her wristband was pinging. He hailed a cab and jumped in. To his surprise, the cab driver was a burly, strawberry blonde male with hair that looked like he had walked out of the pages of a Viking history book.

David said, "Umm, to the National Maritime Museum, please."

Osman turned around in the seat and said some words in an ancient tongue then spoke in English, "My name is Osman. Buckle up, it might get bumpy!"

David nodded with wide eyes, "Okay, will do!" As he reached for the seat belt, Osman threw the car into gear and screeched off down the road. David flew back in his seat, still searching for the seat buckle to click the belt into its slot. He watched Osman looking in his rearview mirror, and suddenly he realized that they were being followed. He now had an inkling of who Osman was.

"What is going on?!" David turned to look out the back window of the cab.

Osman made a sharp turn at the corner and entered a parking garage, putting the car in park. "Stay here!" Osman commanded as he jumped out of the vehicle and morphed into his battle regalia.

David slid down in the floorboard of the seat to hide and dialed Stella's phone.

"Hello? David!? Where are you?!" Stella blurted with excitement.

"Don't freak out Stella, but I am currently hiding in the back seat of a taxi. It would seem that my taxi driver is one of our Guardians. We were being followed, and now, a car is pulling up."

David peeked out of the window. "O mo Chreach!! Three huge men are attacking Osman!!"

David started to pull at the door handle to do what he could to help him, but as he tried to open the door, a body leaned up against the window. A blue-skinned woman with four arms and red hair yelled in a deep throaty voice, "Stay inside, Life Bearer!"

PharaEtti ran towards the attackers, doing several front flips before she landed by her target. She stood in a warrior's stance, yelled a battle cry, then grabbed the maces from her back and attacked.

Osman and PharaEtti attacked with a vengeance. David kept Stella on the phone so that she could verify that he was okay. He gave Stella a blow by blow play, at odds with the fact that their Guardians were wild, fierce animals, shedding blood with every blow.

David said, "Stella, the Guardians have managed to clean house with this crew, but you must call and warn Henny! I will try to get there as soon as possible!"

She replied, "Henny just pulled up and is walking towards me now. We will go inside the museum and stay in a crowded area until you get here. And David, I can't believe this is happening! I am so glad the Guardians were watching over you! I know that it was gory, but they were doing their job to protect you at all costs!"

David agreed with her. "Hey, they are coming towards the car. I've got to go!"

Stella said, "See you in a bit."

Stella hung up the phone and grabbed Henny in a big bear hug as he approached. "You are not going to believe what just happened! I was just now on the phone with David. He is with the Guardians! David said that he was being followed, and the Guardians showed up to help him fend off some attackers who followed them into a parking garage! They handled it and are on their way here now!" Stella wanted to wait outside a bit more but knew that it was dangerous to be out in the open.

Henny grabbed Stella's arm as both of their wristbands were pinging in unison, "Let's get inside where there is a crowd. For all we know, we are sitting targets!"

Stella said, "My thought's exactly!"

At the moment, Stella looked up to the sky, with her arm protecting her eyes from the sun as she watched a large plane fly overhead. The sound of the plane's engine was so loud that they couldn't carry on a conversation. They ran towards the entry, not hearing the faster beeping on their wristbands due to the noise from the plane.

They entered the building, looking for the anomaly. Further inside the exhibit hall, they found somewhere to gather their thoughts. Stella rechecked her wristband. She noted that it was beeping at the same pace that it was earlier.

She and Henny looked around, trying to see if there were any distinct triangles in the immediate vicinity.

Stella said, "Let's do this. I will look for the triangles while you watch for intruders, and then we can switch. We need to find the anomaly! When David arrives, we can all search while the Guardians are watching us."

"Sure, Stella. Go ahead and look around. I will keep an eye out for David and any suspicious people. Just stay close, okay?" Henny was nervous but couldn't say no to Stella.

Stella began combing through the Museum. She spent ten minutes looking around while waiting for David to arrive. Henny watched the front entrance and tapped Stella's shoulder when David walked through the front entry. "He is here!"

Following behind David were two tall people, wearing regular street clothes but looked anything but ordinary. The two Guardians had transformed their appearance to blend in as it would be a major news event if a four-armed blue person walked into a museum.

Stella recognized the female as the one who delivered the striking stones back at the Inn, in Scotland. Henny waved at them from a distance. As David approached them, he said, "Did you guys see that Fresnel lighthouse lens out front? My wristband went wild when we walked by it!"

"No! We didn't! Where was it!?" Stella blurted out, embarrassed as she was now being towered over by two very intimidating Guardians.

She looked upward and said to the female Guardian, "By the way, I am Stella, we didn't properly meet the last time we were together, and this is Henny." She patted Henny's shoulder then pulled him closer to her.

PharaEtti nodded her head and said, "I am happy to be in your presence once more. We are at your service!" Osman bowed his head slightly but was monitoring their environment, so did not exchange pleasantries.

PharaEtti then said, "It is an honor to serve the Clan of Phare and most especially you three Life Bearers." She looked around distractedly and held onto Stella's arm. "Time is of the essence, though. We should go now."

Stella looked at her with wide eyes, taking in every nuance of PharaEtti's facial expressions. She desperately wanted to talk to her about the family of beings that she visited in her dream. She was confused because, in the dream, she was shown a cave and given the words Etifah, but she checked Elijah's cave, and it was not the entry point. All of these things were rolling around in her head, as David repeatedly called her name.

"Stella... Stella... STELLA!! Snap out of it! We've got to go!" David waved his hand before her eyes to bring her back to the present.

"Oh, sorry!" Stella turned red in the face and said, "I was just trying to resolve some things now that we are in the presence of our Guardians. The cave wasn't the jump point, so none of this makes any sense to me."

Osman rumbled under his breath, "Where you are going, it is a cave... a womb... where creation is made."

Stella's face winced when she heard Osman speak. "Of course! The dream was symbolism for where we are going, not how we are getting there! Got it! Thanks, Osman."

Osman and PharaEtti escorted the trio out the front door, looking for intruders. None were seen. They walked outside on the sidewalk where a Fresnel lens sat in the landscape in front of the building.

Stella stopped while on the sidewalk to tie her shoe. She was still in thought as the others went over to investigate the lens. She set her phone down on the sidewalk while she tied her shoestring and there, on the pavement of the sidewalk, was a one inch set of triangles inlaid into the concrete, stacked upon one another. The triangles were inlaid with three different colored ground quartz. She reached over to rub the etching to verify that it was three concentric triangles, and as she looked up to tell the others, the lens began to flash.

"Found it!" Stella blurted out from behind David and Henny.

David turned back around to Stella and said, "That was weird! Did you see that flash?!"

Henny was mesmerized by the old lighthouse lens and started babbling about how this type of lens was able to project light further, helping to guide people to safety from well over 20 miles away. He speculated how the lighthouse in Cornwall probably had a lens just like the one in front of them.

Stella said, "Come, look over here! Look what I found!" She grinned with relief. "The triangles!"

"Really?! Well Done, Stella!" David bounded over to the spot and leaned down to investigate the triangles. As he touched them, the lens flashed again.

Osman said, "You have found the anomaly! We must come back at dark fall. Let us go now!"

PharaEtti led them towards the car, and Osman followed up in the rear. The Life Bearers were now prepared. All they had to do was wait.

Stella suggested that they return to the hotel to put all of their things in storage and check out. Then she asked the Guardians a strange question, "Do you guys eat?"

Osman laughed. "We eat what nature provides, and as you can see, nature is plentiful." He was quite serious, but the Life Bearers all laughed at this strange character.

That evening, after checking out of their hotel, they shared a final meal with the Guardians and waited for the appointed time. Stella called Todd to say her goodbyes since it was evening now, and he would be waiting to hear from her.

Todd gave her a pep talk and reminded her that she will be back and that he will be waiting for her. He again relayed how proud he was of her. He held back tears of joy and sorrow, hoping in his heart that she would return to him.

The Life Bearers returned to the Museum that night with the Guardians on full alert. There were people nearby on the street, so PharaEtti began an enchantment to give them cover as they activated the portal.

Henny was given the honor of touching the triple triangle on the sidewalk and watched as the lens flashed three times. He joined Stella and David next to the lens, and the three of them took their pendant with striking stones out of their pockets. They placed the necklaces around their necks, and Stella reminded them to say the word Etifah.

David said, "On the count of three. One... Two...Three." The three Life Bearers struck their pendants, mentally saying Etifah.

The lens transformed into a blinding light. The wavy lines of a doorway appeared, and the three took two steps forward and disappeared into the void.

Todd saw that all three of their wristbands went silent, and he knew that they made the jump. Tears flowed again. Letting Stella go was the second hardest thing that he ever had to do. The first was letting go of Evie.

Osman and PharaEtti returned to where they had left the attackers tied up in a storage room. They gathered them and bilocated to the Alliance facility to bring them in for questioning. The last Life Bearer was now prepared to make his jump alone. Christopher was in touch with Todd and had heard that all of the Life Bearers had already made the jump.

After Chrysaor took Christopher's striking stone pendant, Shamalaine inspired him to use his pipe with the triangular inscription as the portal activator. It was time to make it back down to Merlyn's cave to try activating the portal before the window of opportunity closed.

Leka and Zigrid were on high alert. Zigrid cloaked all three of them as they made their way down to Merlyn's cave that second evening. "No signs of intruders," Leka announced as he ventured out first to see if the coast was clear.

They waited for low tide and then slipped down to the cave at the earliest possible time. The water was still receding, so Leka carried Christopher on his back part of the way. Once inside the cave, Christopher pulled out his pipe.

As he stood staring at the pipe that had been handcrafted by his ancestor, Airleas Phare, he rubbed it with a cloth. The wood became shiny as if it was newly made. The pipe began to put off a sound and a smell. Christopher looked toward the area of the portal where Bridgit and Traci had entered. He could see an image appearing on the cave wall. The triple triangles were glowing once more, and the portal was beginning to activate.

Christopher looked at Leka and Zigrid and said, "Well, that was easy!" He chuckled and thanked the Guardians for their service and walked with a slight limp towards the portal. He held his pipe out in front of him and silently repeated the word Etifah, and then he walked through the wavy field of energy and was gone.

And the wheel turns...

Chapter 94

Meeting Etifah and
the Blue People

Each Life Bearer had come to enter the Midway Station by various portals throughout the third dimension of Earth. The blue beings governed over the portal system, capturing the devious warrior, Chrysaor, who was impersonating the real architect, Monoceros.

The Life Bearers reunited in a place outside of their world. At the Midway Station, the Life Bearers stood in a room together, waiting to be shown to their final destination. The portal from which they had arrived began to activate once more. An iridescent shimmer hovered over the portal area as Breacher walked through.

Breacher looked towards Bridgit. His heart was thumping wildly, seeing her beauty. He was relieved to know that she and the others were safe. "I come with an apology from the Alliance and most especially from the Guardians." He moved closer towards the group.

"Unbeknownst to me, the being that I thought was Monoceros was, in fact, Chrysaor, the immortal son of the Gorgon Medusa."

Breacher looked at Bridgit as he continued, "The Strategists had discovered his plan to thwart all of you here at the Midway Station. Shamalaine prepared the defense, knowing that they could contain him as he entered the portal. I promise you. I had no knowledge of this. I would never have allowed it."

He looked to Christopher and said, "I am truly sorry for the chaos and pain that you have been put through. I wish that Shamalaine could have found another way to contain Chrysaor."

Christopher said, "Without a doubt, I know that Shamalaine had a good reason for doing what she did. I am fine." He wiggled his leg outward with a grin.

Breacher said, "The real Monoceros is with Celeste 108 now. She is part of a healing team that specializes in trauma victims. She is making it a priority to run him through the deprogramming. Unfortunately, he was badly traumatized. 108 will help him clear out the negative programming, but it will take some time. Once he is cleared, I will bring him to you. Shamalaine tells me that M is a vital participant in the creation of the New Earth."

Breacher bowed his head as he heard the portal start to activate once more. It was his cue that his time there was over.

Bridgit called to Breacher. He looked towards her and stared into her soul as she said her final goodbye, "See you at home later?"

She wiped a tear from her face and watched him as he disappeared into the portal.

Stella held onto Bridgit as the blue beings directed them into an area where thirteen pods were lined up on a rail system. The pods were white with a transparent shell top, that opened like a hatch door.

Each Life Bearer was told to sit in the pod. It felt to Stella as if they were going to drive a race car, one that was self-driving and presumably much faster. A helmet was placed on each of their heads, which had a breathing apparatus connected to it, and a mouthpiece in which they were instructed to bite down upon.

Once their heads were secured and their breathing apparatus was in place, the blue beings shut the hatch door, telling them to watch the count on the screen in front of them as it counted from 1 to 441, a co-ordinate connected to Etifah, which would take them to the occulted location.

The sounds of the rail system hummed as the pods shot into the tunnel system one at a time at high speed. All that the Life Bearers could see was the counter and outside of the pod, a muted neon orange color within the tunnel system which looked as if it was ribbed or had circular connections, like that of a hamsters tube system.

Bridgit breathed deeply, and with her eyes closed, she counted in her mind. As she lay there, speeding through the inner realm, she had a recollection of this moment, a Deja Vu. She felt a shift in the energy just as she was at the end of her count. She opened her eyes, and with her teeth gripped on the mouthpiece, she hummed the last few numbers "438...439...440...441..."

The pod came to a slow stop. The orange light faded. It was dark, with muted light in the distance. As the hatch door opened, another blue being stood there ready to assist. It reached down to help Bridgit with her helmet. Bridgit took the breathing apparatus out of her mouth and handed the helmet to her helper.

The blue being emitted a quality of peace that she had not felt with the other beings at the Midway Station. These beings were almost angelic, she thought.

Stella was already out of her pod and walked towards Bridgit. The rest of the team were now all standing up and getting their bearings. Looking around their environment, they could see that they were in a very large space. Looking upward, Bridgit and Stella could see how the room was four-sided, reaching upward to a point. They realized that they were standing inside a large pyramid.

The sound of the pod system got their attention as the pods began to reverse backward, disappearing in moments.

David escorted Christopher closer to where Stella and Bridgit were standing. The others were marveling at the location, wondering where they were. A few moments later, the entire team of Life Bearers watched as a light descended from the top of the pyramid. It was a powder blue cloud, expanding into the room as it lowered to their level. A woman appeared within it and flowed effortlessly towards them.

Benjamin and Ford stood closest to her. They moved back to allow her to come closer into the circle that the group had made. She touched their faces as she floated by them, stopping to look into each Life Bearer's eyes.

Who was she? Benjamin thought, stunned at the appearance of the deity.

Etifah grounded her energy onto the floor, dissipating the cloud.

The Life Bearers were at a loss for words. Her appearance was like nothing they could have anticipated. She was beautiful and unique in her features, and her presence captivated their souls.

Etifah stood silent for some time as they all studied her appearance and she theirs. She was small in stature, her skin, highly melanated. At the bottom of her face, where a chin would be on a human being, was a clairiphant, a dangling sixth sense apparatus, which resembled the trunk of an elephant. It hung approximately twelve inches from her chin, laying upon her chest.

Etifah said her first words, "I am Etifah. My name means the arrival of a beam, a tone, which shifts something, or someone, from one state of being to the next higher state. To be with you in this place of no time, the Inner Tollan, is a cause for a grand celebration among our people and augers a shift of your humanness into a New Human. She lifted her arms upward, and the darkness lifted.

The Life Bearers were standing with Etifah in the lower level of a pyramid, where a race of blue beings were watching the proceedings from the higher levels.

Freya and Juel shivered as a warmth flooded their bodies. It was a sacred greeting from the original ones.

Etifah then said, "These are the people of OMA, the original matrix attained. They are the original ones who have maintained their presence within the Earth for eons of time. They have held Gaia's frequency until you, the Life Bearers of this time, join us to raise the frequency of Gaia to her next level."

Etifah's clairiphant lifted from her chest. She began ceremoniously touching each Life Bearer on their foreheads with her sixth sense apparatus. It suctioned onto their heads and triggered an in-depth memory retrieval process. They remembered her in a time long ago when this very moment was planned in their distant past.

Her appearance unlocked a memory, the final memories, of what they needed to recall. The memories flooded their minds, like a computer program downloading directly into their corpus callosum.

Etifah stood in front of Juel for a few moments, monitoring her process then lifted Juel's arm. Etifah felt her pulse quickening and guided her to one of the blue beings who would escort her into the Cave of Creation at the proper time.

Each Life Bearer was downloaded with a life review of all of the lessons they had gained in their past lives on various world systems. As they came back into the present moment, Etifah said, "You have come to seed the Noosphere of Earth with the Solar Codes that you embody, with the ultimate intention of demonstrating how to become a new human, living in a higher vibration of Earth."

She walked up to Christopher and placed her Clairiphant upon his chest as if to listen to his heart.

She continued, "The new human, Homo Noosphericus, has the capacity to activate it's innate psi capabilities by the use of the holomind perceiver, it's sixth sense organ held within the balanced brain."

She smiled and flipped her clairiphant upwards and then said, "You will not need one of these, as you already have the technology built inside of you. You only need to remember how to use it. You will learn how to reconnect your mind's circuitry to the circuitry of the planetary mind, activating your sensory bodies, and unlocking your true potential as the New Human."

Stella's eyes were huge. She recalled her many dreams where she was in a classroom setting, learning all about the activation of the sixth senses. She remembered seeing the others there too. She turned to Ursula and Ford and said, "I remember this! We have been practicing telekinesis in our dreams!"

Ford smiled with tears in his eyes. He hugged her, nodding in remembrance of all of it.

At that moment, a trumpet sounded as Archangel Gabriel floated into the lower gallery via a rainbow of light coming from above.

Following him were the Blueprint Masters and the Builders of Form. The trumpeting concluded as Archangel Gabriel stepped on the lower level near Etifah. He generated serenity and grace as he too stared into the eyes of each Life Bearer.

Gabriel started his welcome speech with these words, "I come in remembrance of a pact between Humans, Angels, and Elemental beings. This is a day of great honor." He motioned to the Angels and Builders to introduce themselves to their counterparts, the Life Bearers.

Henny and Traci stared as Platter and Patina approached them. The light and love that emanated from these angels were intoxicating.

Henny asked if he could hug them, and the angels nodded in acceptance of his love.

All of the Life Bearers interacted with the Builders of Form and Blueprint Masters for some time. It was an opportunity for three lifestreams to weave their light together for the upliftment of humankind, knowing that they had significant work to do, and they were the chosen ones who had all of the skills required to usher in a new age of peace. They were the way-showers for the whole of humanity.

As they each had ample time to commune with one another, Etifah and Gabriel called the groups together for their final consultation.

Etifah spoke, "Within Inner Tollan, there are seven caves of creation, which you are all soon to be indwelling therein. The caves are like wombs, where the creation of new world systems are birthed. Each team will have their own cave to create the highest blessings."

She looked around the room at all of the humans present. "The time is now. All is prepared. Go with your team to your cave, and with every fiber of your being, charge the creations with the purity of love."

Etifah and Gabriel stood in the center of the gallery as they watched the teams of Humans, Angels, and Elementals, be escorted into the caves of creation. Time would tell how these extraordinary beings would affect the lives of many in the age of enlightenment. The lights faded within the gallery as Etifah and Gabriel made their ascent. Soon the creation of the New Earth would come into physical manifestation, and the Life Bearers would need to return to be a part of the great awakening.

And the wheel turns...

Biography

First time author, Deborah Haight, lives in Las Vegas, Nevada with her husband of 35 years, Brian. They share four children and two grandchildren.

The Hierophant – Book One: The Return of Memory is her first offering in The Hierophant Series exploring the nature of reality, through the imaginative worlds that she has created.

CPSIA information can be obtained
at www.ICGtesting.com
Printed in the USA
JSHW030207281220
10548JS00003B/17